Praise for the series

'A richly imagined world and vibrant characters . . . an exhilarating adventure'
Elspeth Cooper

'A vividly imagined story of conspiracy and empire'
Col Buchanan

'A complex and fast-moving fantasy set in a world where treachery and intrigue are everywhere, accomplished through ferocious brutality, subtle intrigues, and everything in between'
L. E. Modesitt, Jr

'Following in the footsteps of George R. R. Martin, Joe Abercrombie and the like . . . Brutal, intriguing and continuing to head toward exciting events and places unknown'
Kirkus Reviews

'A thrilling fantasy adventure that blends together politics, action and magic . . . Each of the disparate storylines contribute to a much greater whole, and the end result is a wonderfully machined novel that simultaneously plays out a more immediate storyline and its place in a much larger story . . . I was reminded of the sense of history displayed in J. R. R. Tolkien and George R. R. Martin's fantasy epics'
Io9

'I loved every second of it . . . As more and more people discover what a talent Staveley has for creating a full, immersive, magical and exciting world, with characters to match, his popularity will soar. Go and find a first edition of *The Emperor's Blades* while you still can'
Fantasy-Faction

D0415454

THE LAST
MORTAL BOND

After more than a decade teaching history, religion, and philosophy, Brian decided to write epic fantasy. He now lives on a steep dirt road in the hills of southern Vermont, where he divides his time between fathering, writing, husbanding, splitting wood, skiing, and adventuring – not necessarily in that order.

His blog, *On the Writing of Epic Fantasy*, can be found at bstaveley.wordpress.com and you can see his other social media haunts below.

Twitter: @Brianstaveley
Facebook: facebook.com/Brianstaveley
Google+: Brian Staveley

By Brian Staveley

The Emperor's Blades
The Providence of Fire
The Last Mortal Bond

THE LAST MORTAL BOND

Chronicle of the Unhewn Throne,
Book Three

BRIAN STAVELEY

TOR

First published 2016 by Tom Doherty Associates, LLC

First published in the UK 2016 by Tor

This paperback edition published 2016 by Tor
an imprint of Pan Macmillan
The Smithson, 6 Briset Street, London EC1M 5NR
EU representative: Macmillan Publishers Ireland Ltd, 1st Floor,
The Liffey Trust Centre, 117-126 Sheriff Street, Upper
Dublin 1, D01 YC43
Associated companies throughout the world
www.panmacmillan.com

ISBN 978-1-4472-3583-5

Copyright © Brian Staveley, 2016

The right of Brian Staveley to be identified as the
author of this work has been asserted by him in accordance
with the Copyright, Designs and Patents Act 1988.

Pan Macmillan does not have any control over, or any responsibility for,
any author or third party websites referred to in or on this book.

5 7 9 8 6

A CIP catalogue record for this book is available from the British Library.

Map artwork by Isaac Stewart
Typeset by Palimpsest Book Production Ltd, Falkirk, Stirlingshire
Printed and bound by CPI Group (UK) Ltd, Croydon, CR0 4YY

Visit **www.panmacmillan.com** to read more about all our books
and to buy them. You will also find features, author interviews and
news of any author events, and you can sign up for e-newsletters
so that you're always first to hear about our new releases.

For my friends:
slower than the Kettral, louder than the Shin,
sloppier than the Csestriim, and yet still, somehow,
the inspiration for all of it

ACKNOWLEDGEMENTS

Without the faith and hard work of my agent, Hannah Bowman, and my editor, Marco Palmieri, this story would never have seen the light of day. I am forever grateful to both of them for giving me the chance to write these books and for all their support along the way.

I'm grateful, also, to every reader who has picked up this tale. Whenever I reach a tough spot with the writing, a place where I feel I can't go on, I imagine you, all of you—snuggled under blankets or listening in the car on the way to work, reading in the hallway while your kids are falling asleep or perched atop some rock in the backcountry—then I plant my ass back in the chair and keep going.

Finally, my wife, Jo. It may not look like it, but this is a love story, and I wouldn't understand the first thing about love stories—not how to write them, not how to live them—without her.

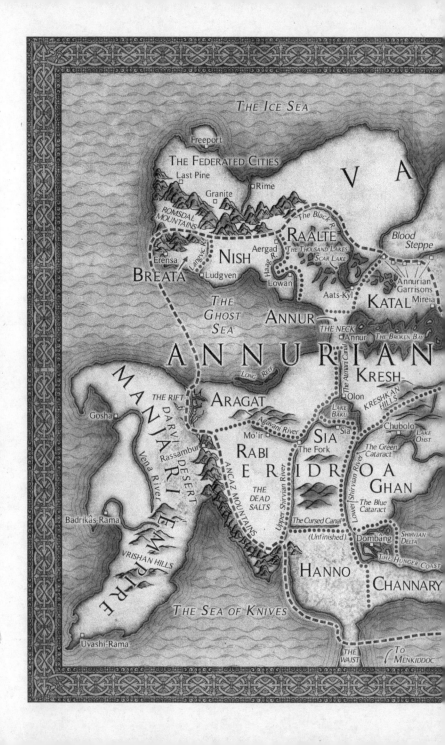

S H

Far
Steppe

Golden
Steppe

Ashk'lan

Dry Steppe

BONE MOUNTAINS

KINGDOM
OF
ANTHERA

Cold River

The White River

SEGHIR DESERT

Annurian
Garrisons

The Lexa

The
Bend

Bright River

Anthera

Bashkimi

Loshk   Haskovo

THE BLOOD CITIES
(Independent Poleis)
Vratsa   Vritsa

Kava

Simi

Dark River

EMPIRE

Banner R.

SELLAS   Alphi

SELLAS

THE   IRON   SEA

LANDS CLAIMED BY ANTHERA
(Some disputed with
the Blood Cities)

THE
SKULL

Sarai Pol

THE
QIRIN
ISLANDS

THE
TWINS

JAKARIAN

Ganaboa

BASC

BASC

BALIIN

Keoh-Kang

Red Beach

2013

THE LAST
MORTAL BOND

PROLOGUE

The dogs were closer.

Axta closed her eyes, unbraided the tightening knot of sound into the individual threads of canine baying: three dozen beasts a quarter mile off. She ran the angles—half a hundred of them—mapping the memorized terrain against long-established patterns for the propagation of sound.

"They have taken the bait," she said. "Four groups." She pointed back the way they had come, through the shattered boulders, thigh-high ferns, and the mossy trunks of the great, rotting pines. "There and there. There and there."

Sos didn't look. His eyes were fixed on a break in the trees, where the gleaming tower bisected the sky. If Axta had set her snare correctly, there would be fewer than forty humans left to guard the base of that tower, forty mortal women and men, and behind them, somewhere inside that inexplicable artifact, their gods, trapped in their mortal skins.

In the branches above, a jay notched four strident notes on the sky, then fell silent.

Axta unlimbered her bow, her few remaining arrows.

If she had known earlier what was happening here, if she had known that the gods of the humans would converge on this one point at this one time, she could have built a better, surer trap. But, of course, she had not known. She and Sos—on a different mission altogether—had stumbled across the convoy purely by accident. There was no time to go back, to try to bring to bear the feeble force of Csestriim that remained. There wasn't even time to make more arrows.

"I will cover your attack," she said. "But they have bows of their own."

Sos nodded. "I will go where the arrows are not."

The claim seemed implausible, but Axta had watched him do it before. She was the better tracker, the better general, the better stones player, but no one navigated battle's labyrinth more readily than Sos. Alone, he had slaughtered the human garrison at Palian Quar. In the dark woods of the winter-long battle at First Pines, he held together the whole western flank of the Csestriim force, ranging through the trunks and shadows, carving apart his human foes day after day, week after week, until they crumpled, fled. Sos fought like a cartographer following his own perfect maps through a world of the blind, baffled, and lost.

He slid his twin swords from their scabbards.

Axta studied the moon-bright arcs.

Alone among the Csestriim, Sos had named his weapons: Clarity, he called one sword; the other, Doubt. She had watched him stand against three Nevariim once, thousands of years earlier, bearing those same blades.

"How do you tell them apart?" she asked. The weapons looked identical.

"One is heavier, one sharper."

A few feet away, a butterfly landed on a fern's serrated leaf, flexed indigo wings. Axta had spent a century, thousands of years earlier, in the study of butterflies. This species had escaped her catalogue.

"Which blade is which?" she asked, turning her attention back to the warrior.

"I have not decided."

"Strange, to let the names come so untethered from the world."

Sos shrugged. "It is what language does."

Axta calved off a portion of her mind to consider that claim. Had there been more time, she would have pressed Sos on the point, but there was no more time. Behind the dogs' baying she could hear the men with their blades. She turned back toward the tower.

"If we kill the gods today, we win. This is what Tan'is believes. If we carve them from this world, we carve away the rot that blights our children."

Sos nodded.

The butterfly twitched into flight.

"What will you do," she asked, "if there is no more war?"

In all his long years, the swordsman had kept no catalogue of butterflies.

"Prepare."

"For what?"

"The next war."

Axta cocked her head to the side, wondering how he could miss such a simple point. "If we defeat them here, today, the humans will be gone."

Sos considered his own ancient blades as though they were strange in his hands, artifacts of unknown provenance, farming implements, perhaps, or instruments.

"There is always another war."

He cut through the shocked human guards in moments, stepping from safety to safety as though he had studied the whole battle in advance, as though he'd spent a week charting his course through the bloody scrawl. Axta followed him—slit a woman's throat, a bearded man's hamstring—and then they were inside.

The Csestriim had studied the tower, of course. In the long years before the war, it had been empty, a gleaming, indestructible shell from some age antedating all recorded thought. It was empty no longer. The humans had built a massive wooden scaffold inside the space, huge pines notched and pegged one to the next, framework for a rough staircase spiraling up and up into the light.

Behind Axta, soldiers poured through the doorway bellowing, screaming. Sos, like a careful craftsman about his masterpiece, killed them. Axta started climbing. Somewhere up there, in the dazzling light, were the gods—Heqet and Kaveraa, Eira and Maat, Orella and Orilon—whose touch had polluted her people, whose corruption had turned the Csestriim into beasts like those broken creatures below, hurling themselves into Sos's defense, parting their soft necks on his blades.

Axta climbed like an insect trapped in the sun's amber, her constant movement a form of stillness. Why the gods had come here, she had no idea, nor why the humans had spent so much time building the scaffolding and the winding stair. As her hot heart shoveled blood through her veins, she tried to parse the probabilities. Reason bucked, buckled. Inference and deduction failed. At root, all knowledge required witness, and so she kept climbing.

When Axta reached the tower's top, stepping from light into light, Sos was a pace behind her. Clouds scoured the sky's blue bronze, polishing it smooth. On the tower's wide summit, the gods—all six of them: Heqet, bull-shouldered and carved with scar; hiss-thin Maat; Orella and Orilon, one bone white, the other dark as storm; Kaveraa with her long fingernails; Eira, huge-haired, who might have been a girl—lay closed-eyed and still.

Wind fileted its invisible flesh on Sos's naked blades.

Axta didn't move.

Finally, the swordsman slipped one of the weapons into its sheath and knelt, pressing his fingers to Heqet's neck, then to each of the others in turn.

"Dead," he said finally, straightening from the corpses.

Dead. Axta revolved the notion in her mind, tested it as though it were late-winter ice. For decades and more these gods had walked the world inside their chosen human shells. Tan'is had managed to take two, to kill them, but the others had survived, had eluded all attempt at capture. The ongoing existence of the humans was predicated on that survival.

"No," she said.

Sos arched an eyebrow.

"These are human bodies," Axta continued, "but the gods that lived inside them are gone."

The swordsman sheathed his other blade.

"Where?"

"Wherever it is they came from." She studied the flawed, lifeless flesh. "Strange. Just when they were winning."

Sos shook his head. "Not winning."

Axta turned to him. "They've taken every important fortress, seized every road. There can't be more than a few hundred of us left. Some of the humans have even learned to use the *kenta*."

"They are not winning," Sos said again. "They have won. This is why their gods have departed."

They have won.

Axta studied the proposition for flaws, found none.

At her feet, the broken bodies that had carried those broken gods—just so much meat—were already turning to rot in the afternoon sun.

1

Men the size of mountains plowed waist-deep through the world's oceans. Polished blades—each one long enough to level cities—flashed sunlight. Boots crushed delicate coastlines to rubble, obliterated fishing towns, gouged craters in the soft, green fields of Sia and Kresh.

This is the way the world ends. This was Kaden's first thought, staring down on the destruction from above.

A city, after all, was only stone; a forest, no more than sap-wet wood. What was a river's course, but a slash carved through the land? Apply enough force—the world itself would deform. The shapes of ridge and valley meant nothing. Bring enough power to bear, and you could split cliffs, tear down mountains, rend the very bedrock and see it scattered across the waves. Bring fire, and the world would burn. Bring water, and it would sink beneath the deluge. The old forms of sea and stone could be remade in flood and deflagration, and those other shapes, the desperate, petty lines that men and women dreamed across the dirt to indicate their kingdoms, their little empires, those, too, would be annihilated with all the rest in a heartbeat's armageddon.

No. This was Kaden's second thought. *It is not the world. It is just a map.*

A vast map, true, the size of a small parade ground, the most expensive map in all the world, commissioned by a vain

Annurian Republic for their council chamber, but still just a map. Legions of craftsmen had labored day and night for months to complete the project; masons to carve the mountains and seaside cliffs, gardeners to cultivate the myriad grasses and perfect stunted trees, hydraulic engineers to guide the rivers in their courses, jewelers to cut the sapphires for the mountain tarns, the glaciers of glass and diamond.

It stretched the full length of the hall, some two hundred feet from end to end. The granite of the Bone Mountains came from the Bone Mountains, the red stone of the Ancaz from the Ancaz. Pumps hidden beneath the surface fed the great rivers of Vash and Eridroa—the Shirvian, the Vena, the Agavani, and the Black—along with dozens of streams whose names Kaden didn't know, those flowing between high banks and around oxbows, over miniature cataracts and through wet swamps built up from soft green moss, emptying finally into the small world's seas and oceans, oceans that, by some clever contrivance, rose and fell with the orbit of the moon.

One could stroll the catwalks above, staring down at astonishing replicas of the great cities: Olon and Sia, Dombâng and the Bend. Annur itself sprawled over a space the length of Kaden's arm. He could make out the sparkling facets of the Temple of Intarra; the great avenue of the Godsway, complete with diminutive statuary; the tiny canalboats swinging at anchor in the Basin; the stark red walls of the Dawn Palace; and, stabbing like a lance up past the catwalk, so high that you could reach out and touch the tower's top without stooping, Intarra's Spear.

Like the men and women who sat day after day bickering above it, the massive map was both magnificent and petty. Until that moment, it had served a single function: to make those seated above it feel like gods. To that end, it had showed nothing more than a dream world, one unmarred by all their failures.

No fires raged unchecked in the northern forests. No towns burned in the south. No one had churned the grass fields of

Ghan to mud or blockaded the desperate port of Keoh-Kâng. Small, painted soldiers indicated the location of field armies. Tiny men representing Adare's treacherous legions and the council's own more numerous Republican Guard dotted the terrain, swords raised in motionless postures of challenge or triumph. They were always standing, those false men. They never bled. Of war's ravages and destruction, the map bore no trace. Evidently Annur lacked the craftsmen to sculpt starvation, or terror, or death.

We didn't need craftsmen, Kaden thought. *We needed soldiers with heavy boots to remind us what we've done, to grind this little world of ours to mud.*

The sudden, unexpected, undeniable violence made the map more accurate, more true, but these men with their steel had not come to bring truth to the world's most elaborate map. Kaden shifted his gaze from the destruction playing out below to another knot of armed men surging across the catwalk. Aedolians. The men charged with guarding the rulers of Annur.

Despite his own training, Kaden felt his stomach lurch. Something had obviously gone awry. Maut Amut—the First Shield of the Guard—would not have ordered his men into a sealed meeting of the council otherwise. This was no exercise. Each soldier wore half his weight in gleaming armor, and all had broadblades drawn as they spread out through the hall shouting orders, taking up positions at the perimeter, guarding the doors to keep someone out . . . or in.

Half the members of the council were trying to stumble to their feet, tripping on their long robes, spilling wine over carefully cut silk, bellowing questions or crying out in dismay. The rest sat rooted in their chairs, eyes wide, jaws agape, as they tried to make some sense of the unfolding madness. Kaden ignored them, kept his own gaze trained on the Aedolians.

Behind these men in steel, the memory of other soldiers filled Kaden's mind, Aedolians hacking their vicious way through Ashk'lan, murdering the monks, hounding Kaden himself through the mountains. He had spent months after his return to the Dawn Palace reviewing the records of the remaining guardsmen, scouring their personal histories for any hint of treachery, of allegiance to Adare or to Ran il Tornja. The entire guard was placed on parole while hundreds of scribes investigated thousands of stories, and in the end, the council had dismissed more than a hundred before reinstating the rest. Kaden reminded himself of those measures, but he could feel the tension in his shoulders all the same.

See the world, he told himself, taking a long breath then letting it out, *not your dream of the world.*

Two dozen Aedolians charged over the suspended catwalk, then surrounded the council table.

Kaden rose to his feet, discarding his own fear as he did so.

"What is happening?" Despite his misgivings, his voice was steady.

Maut Amut stepped forward. The furious motion of the Aedolian entrance was finished. Waves lapped at the shore of the map, tiny tsunami. Sun streamed through the skylights overhead, warm and silent, playing over the armor of the soldiers, glinting off their naked blades. The members of the council went suddenly silent, frozen, like statues littering the catwalks, caught in the various postures of their own unreadiness.

"An attack, First Speaker," Amut replied grimly, eyes scanning the walls, the doors, "inside the palace itself."

Kaden glanced around the room.

"When?"

Amut shook his head. "We are not certain."

"Who?"

The First Shield grimaced. "Someone fast. Dangerous."

"How dangerous?"

"Dangerous enough to enter the palace, to get inside Intarra's Spear unnoticed, to subdue three of my men, three Aedolians, and then to disappear."

2

Night was a foreign nation.

It had always felt that way to Adare hui'Malkeenian, as though the world changed after the setting of the sun. Shadow elided hard edges, hid form, rendered sunlight's familiar chambers strange. Darkness leached color from the brightest silk. Moonlight silvered water and glass, made lambent and cold the day's basic substances. Even lamps, like the two that sat on the desk before her now, caused the world to shift and twitch with the motion of the captured flame. Night could work this unsettling transformation on the most familiar spaces, and these cold rooms high in the stony keep at the edge of Aergad were hardly familiar. Adare had lived inside them almost a year without ever feeling welcome or safe, even in the daytime. Night transported her even further, to a place that was hard, and alien, and barbarous.

The sounds of night, too, required translation. Morning footsteps in the hallway were normal—servants and castle staff going about their work. Past midnight, however, those same footsteps sounded furtive. A shout at noontime was just a shout; a night cry might herald danger, disaster. The courtyard outside and below Adare's window was a chaos of activity during the day, but this late, with the gates long locked, it was usually silent, and so, when she heard the clatter of hooves on the cobbles, the terse commands snatched away by the wind, she set down her seal of office abruptly, careful to keep the ink from puddling on the pages, then, with her heart hammering inside her, crossed to the closed window.

A messenger at midnight was not the same thing as a messenger at noon.

She throttled her fear as she nudged open the shutters and the northern air slid cold over her sweaty skin. A rider at this hour could mean anything—Urghul crossing the Black River, Urghul already *across* the Black, Long Fist's savages burning another border town, or his mad leach, Balendin, twisting the fear of Adare's people into some new, foul kenning. A rider could mean she was losing. Could mean she'd already lost.

Reflexively, she looked to the river first, the Haag, carving its way south just beneath the high walls of the city. She could make out the stone arches of the single bridge spanning the flow, but night hid from her any sign of the sentries posted there. She took a deep breath, relaxed her hands on the casement. She'd half expected to find the Urghul, she realized, barely a quarter mile distant and storming the bridge, ready to lay siege to the city.

Because you're a fool, she told herself grimly. If Balendin and the Urghul had broken through Ran il Tornja's legions, she would have heard more than a few horses on the cobbles. She shifted her attention to the courtyard below.

Aergad was an old city, as old as Annur itself, and the castle she had taken for her own had been the ancestral seat of the kings who ruled the southern Romsdals long before the rise of her empire. Both the castle and the city walls looked their age. Though the builders had known their work, there had been no need to defend Aergad in more than a century, and Adare could see gaps in the tops of the ramparts, gaping spaces where ice had eaten away at the mortar, sending huge blocks of stone tumbling into the river below. She had ordered the walls repaired, but masons were scarce, and il Tornja needed them to the east, where he was fighting his months-long holding action against the Urghul.

Moonlight threw the jagged shapes of the southern wall onto the rough stones of the courtyard. The messenger was dismounting in the shadow; Adare could see his shape, and the shape of his horse, but no face, no uniform. She tried to read something in the posture, in the set of those shoulders, anything that would warn her of the message that he carried.

A whimper broke the night's quiet, an infant's cry from the room behind her. Grimacing, Adare turned away from the courtyard, to where Sanlitun hui'Malkeenian, the second of that name, twisted uneasily in his small wooden crib, disturbed by the hooves on the cobbles or by the cold northern air from the open window. Adare crossed to him quickly, hoping that he hadn't truly awoken, that she could soothe him with a soft hand and a few words, that he would slide back into his slumber before she had to confront whatever news was coming.

"Shhh," she whispered. "It's all right, my little boy. Shh . . ."

Sometimes it was easy to soothe him. On the better nights, whispering meaningless comfort to her squirming child, Adare felt as though someone else was speaking, a woman who was older, slower, more certain, some other mother who understood nothing of politics or finance, who would fumble even simple figures, but who knew in her bones the soothing of a colicky child. Most times, however, she felt lost, baffled by her motherhood, desperate with her love for the tiny child and terrified by her inability to calm him. She would hold him close, whisper over and over into his ear, and his body would shudder itself still for a while. Then, when she thought the grief had passed, when she pulled back to study his face, his chest would heave, the sobs would force his small mouth wide, and the tears would well up all over again.

He had her eyes. Looking into them when he cried was like staring into a mountain pool and finding red-gold embers glowing unquenched beneath the water's surface. Adare wondered if her own eyes looked the same behind tears. It seemed a long time since she had cried.

"Shh, my little boy," she whispered, running the back of her fingers softly over his cheek. "It's all right."

Sanlitun screwed up his small face, strained against the swaddling, cried out once more, then subsided.

"It's all right," she whispered again.

Only when she returned to the window, when she looked out once more and saw the rider had moved into the moonlight, did she realize she was wrong. It was not all right. Maybe the child had known before she did who had come. Maybe it wasn't the cold or the wind that had woken him at all, but some infant's knowledge that his father was near, his father, the Csestriim, the *kenarang*, general of Adare's shrinking empire, murderer of her own father, possibly a mortal foe, and one of her only allies. Ran il Tornja was here, striding across the courtyard, leaving a groom to lead away a horse that looked half dead. He glanced up toward her window, met her eyes, and saluted, a casual motion, almost dismissive.

This sudden arrival would have been odd enough in the daytime, but it was not daytime. It was well past midnight. Adare pulled the window closed, tried to still her sudden shivering, straightened her back, and turned to face the doors to her chamber, arranging her face before he entered.

"You should have the men on the gate flogged," il Tornja said as soon as he'd closed the door behind him. "Or killed. They checked to make certain it was me, but let my guardsmen pass without a second glance."

He dropped into one wooden chair, shoved out another with the heel of a boot, put his feet up on it, and leaned back. The nighttime ride that had half killed his horse didn't seem to have wearied the *kenarang* in the least. A little mud speckled his boots. The wind had been at his dark hair, but his green riding cloak and tailored uniform were immaculate. His polished sword belt gleamed. The gems laid into the hilt of his sword glittered with all the brightness of lies. Adare met his eyes.

"Are we so spoiled for soldiers that we can start knocking them off for minor infractions?"

Il Tornja raised his brows. "I'd hardly rate a lapse in the Emperor's security a minor infraction." He shook his head. "You should have my soldiers at the gate, not the Sons of Flame."

"You need your men to fight the Urghul," Adare pointed out, "unless you plan to prosecute this war all by yourself. The Sons are capable guardians. They let your men pass because they recognized you. They trust you."

"Sanlitun trusted me," he pointed out. "I put a knife in his back."

Adare's breath caught like a hook in her throat. Her skin blazed.

My father, she reminded herself. *He's talking about my father, not my boy.* Il Tornja had murdered the Emperor, but he had no reason to harm the child, his own child. Still, the urge to turn in her chair, to see the infant sleeping safely behind her, settled on Adare as strongly as a pair of clutching hands. She forced it away.

"Your leash is shorter than it was when you killed my father," she replied, meeting his eyes.

He smiled, raised a hand to his collarbone as though testing for the invisible cord of flame that Nira had set around his neck. Adare would have been a good deal more comforted if she could still *see* the 'Kent-kissing thing, but a writhing noose of fire would draw more than a few eyes, and she had enough problems without admitting her Mizran Councillor was a leach and her *kenarang* an untrusted murderer and a Csestriim on top of that. Nira insisted that the kenning was still in place, and that would have to be good enough.

"Such a light collar," il Tornja said. "Sometimes I forget that it's even there."

"You don't forget anything. Why are you here?"

"Aside from the chance to see my Emperor, my son, and the mother of my child?"

"Yes. Aside from that."

"You're less sentimental than I remember."

"When sentiment feeds my troops, I'll look into it. Why are you here?"

Behind her, Sanlitun stirred uneasily, whimpering at the sound of her raised voice. Il Tornja glanced over her shoulder, studying the child with something that might have been interest or amusement.

"He is healthy?"

Adare nodded. "He had a cough two weeks ago—that 'Shael-spawned wind off the Romsdals—but it's mostly over now."

"And you still keep him with you, even when you work?"

She nodded again. Prepared to defend herself. Again. Nine months since she first arrived in Aergad, an exile in her own empire. Six months since Sanlitun's birth. Only six months, and yet it felt she hadn't slept in a year, in a lifetime. Despite his name, Sanlitun had none of his grandfather's calm, none of his stillness. Either he was hungry or he was wet, puking or fretful, clutching at her when awake, or kicking her as he slept.

"A wet nurse—" il Tornja began.

"I do not need a wet nurse."

"Driving yourself into the dirt does no one any good," he said slowly. "Not you, not our child, and certainly not our empire."

"*My* empire."

He nodded, his smile barbed. "Your empire."

"Women raise their own children all the time. Six children. Ten. I think I can manage a single baby boy."

"Shepherds raise six children. Fishermen's wives raise children. Women whose cares don't extend beyond keeping the hearth lit and the sheep fed. You are the Emperor of Annur, Adare. You are a prophet. We are at war on two fronts, and we are losing. Fishermen's wives have the luxury of caring for their own children. You do not." He did a thing with his voice then, a shift in tone or register that, coming from anyone else, might have indicated a softening. "He is my child, too. . . ."

"Don't speak to me," she growled, sitting back in her chair, putting more air between them, "of your children. I know too well how you have gone about rearing them in the past."

If she'd hoped to dent his armor, to knock his mask askew, she would have been disappointed. Il Tornja assembled the planes of his face into a regretful smile and shook his head again.

"That was a long time ago, Adare. Many thousands of years. It was a mistake, and one I have labored long to correct." He gestured to Sanlitun, an unfolding of the palm at once paternal and impersonal. "He will not grow stronger or wiser from your coddling. He may not grow at *all* if you neglect everything else."

"I am *not* neglecting everything else," she snapped. "Do you see me sleeping? Nattering endless nonsense? I'm at my desk each morning before dawn and, as you can see, I'm still here." She gestured to the papers. "When I put my seal on these treaties, our men will eat for another season. And when I'm done with these, there's a stack of petitions from Raalte to address. I live in this room, and when I'm not here, I'm with Lehav reviewing our southern strategy, or reviewing the troops, or drafting letters."

"And fortunately for us all," il Tornja added smoothly, "you have your father's brain. Even sleep-addled, even clutching a child to your breast, you think better than most Annurian emperors I have known."

She ignored the compliment. Il Tornja's praise seemed as genuine as the rest of him, and like the rest of him, it was false, weighed to the last hair, measured and parsed, distributed only where he thought it was needed, where it would be useful. The point, the heft of the statement, remained: she was doing her job.

"There you have it. I will raise Sanlitun *and*—"

The *kenarang* cut her off.

"We don't need you to be better than most of your ancestors, Adare." He paused, fixed her with his general's stare. Not his real stare, thank Intarra, not the fathomless black gaze of Csestriim contemplation she had seen just the once above the battlefield of Andt-Kyl, but the other one, the one he had no doubt studied for generations—a hard look, but human. "We need you to be better than *all* of them. For that, you require rest. You must give up the child, at least occasionally."

"I will do what needs doing," she growled, doubt's sick flower blossoming inside her even as she spoke.

The truth was, the past six months had been the most brutal of her life, days filled with impossible decisions, the nights an unending torment of Sanlitun's screaming, her own fumbling with the blankets, drawing the child into her bed, murmuring to him, praying to Intarra and Bedisa that he would fall asleep once more. Most times he would take the nipple, suck greedily for a few heartbeats, then shove it away and begin bawling.

She had servants, of course, a dozen women seated just outside her chamber who would come darting in the moment Adare called, arms piled high with dry swaddling or new bedding. That much help she would accept, but sending the child away, training him to suck at another woman's breast . . . that she could not ask of him. Or of herself. Even when she wanted to weep from exhaustion, from the flood of sleep-addled confusion brimming in her blood, she would look down at her child, at his fat cheek pressed against her swollen breast, and she would know as she knew any great truth about the world that she could not give him up.

She had watched her mother die, coughing her shredded lungs onto the softest silk. Adare had stood beside her father as he was laid into his tomb, imperial robes hiding his wounds. She had killed one brother herself, and was locked in a desperate, vicious war with the other. Her family had been whittled down to this one child. She glanced over to the crib where he slept, watched his small chest rise and fall, then turned back to il Tornja.

"Why are you here?" she asked for the third time, voice ripe to bursting with weariness. "I doubt you left the front, the fight, to discuss the finer points of my parenting."

Il Tornja nodded, steepled his fingers, studied her for a moment, then nodded again.

"We have an opportunity," he said finally.

Adare spread her hands. "If I don't have time to raise my son, I certainly don't have time for your fucking riddles."

"The republic has offered to treat with you."

Adare stared.

"My men intercepted the messenger—the man is waiting below. I wanted to talk to you before you saw him."

Slowly, Adare told herself. *Slowly.* She studied il Tornja's face, but could read nothing there.

"A messenger sent to *whom*?"

"To you."

"And yet *your* men intercepted him. Hardly a model of trusting cooperation."

Il Tornja waved a dismissive hand. "Intercepted. Tripped over. Escorted. They found him—"

"And they brought him to you," Adare said, trying to keep a clamp on her anger, "instead of me. What are your men even *doing* in the south? The Sons have that front secured."

"Staring fixedly in one direction is a good way to get dead, Adare. While I don't doubt the devotion of the Sons to both their goddess and their prophet," he inclined his head toward her slightly, "I learned long ago not to rely on units outside of my command. My men found the messenger, they came to me, and when I learned his message, I came directly to you." He shook his head. "Everything is not a conspiracy, Adare."

"You'll pardon me if that doesn't ring true." She leaned back in her chair, ran her hands through her hair, forced herself to focus on the heart of the matter. "Fine. A messenger. From the republic."

"An offer to negotiate. To make peace. From the sound of it, they're starting to understand that their government of the people isn't working out."

"How perspicacious of them. It only took nine months, the loss of two atrepies, the deaths of tens of thousands, and the specter of widespread starvation to bring the failure to their attention."

"They want you back. An emperor on the Unhewn Throne again. They want to heal the rift."

Adare narrowed her eyes, forced herself to breathe evenly, to think through the situation before speaking. It was tempting, so tempting. It was also impossible.

"There's no way," she said, shaking her head. "No way that forty-five of Annur's most rich and vicious aristocrats are going to give up their newfound power. Even if the city were burning down around them, even if the palace was on fire, they wouldn't change course. They hate me too much."

"Well . . ." Il Tornja drew out the word with an apologetic shrug. "They don't want to give up their power. Not exactly. They want you back as a sort of figurehead, but they want to keep making the laws, deciding the policy. They say bark, you woof obligingly—that sort of thing. . . ."

Adare slammed a palm down on the table, more violently than she'd intended.

Sanlitun squirmed in his crib, and she paused, waiting for his slow, shallow breathing to resume before speaking.

"Their fucking *policies,*" she hissed, "are destroying Annur, gutting the empire from the inside out. Their policies are *killing* people. And now they want me to be complicit in their shit?"

"As far as I understand it, they want you to be more than complicit. They want you to perch atop the pile and grin."

"I won't do it," she said, shaking her head.

He raised an eyebrow. "There was a time, not so many months

ago, when you thought there might be room to negotiate with the council, when *you* were sending the messengers to *them*."

"Messengers that they imprisoned. Good men who might be *dead* now for all I know. I used to think the rift could be healed. Not anymore. It's too late."

Il Tornja frowned, as though tasting food gone slightly bad. "*Too late* is not a phrase that should ever pass an emperor's lips."

"I would think an emperor is served by facing the truth rather than running from it."

"By all means! Confront the hard truths! Just do it in private. You don't want to plant fear in the hearts of those who follow you."

"I couldn't plant fear in your heart if I was sowing it with a shovel."

"I'm not talking about me."

"You're the only one here."

"You have to practice your face, Adare," he said. "All the time."

She opened her mouth to object, but he raised his hands, forestalling her. "I didn't come here to quarrel. I came here because this is an opportunity."

"An opportunity for *what*? To give up everything we've been fighting for the past nine months? To let the idiots destroy what's left of Annur?"

"It is Annur that I'm trying to save," il Tornja said, suddenly grave. "I need you to go back. To heal the rift between the empire and the republic. I would not ask if it were not necessary."

Adare frowned. "You're losing," she said finally.

The *kenarang* nodded, then shrugged. "Even genius has limits. My armies are stretched thin as yesterday's smoke. The Urghul outnumber us, they fight beside an emotion leach, and are led by a god."

"You still believe Long Fist is Meshkent," Adare said, trying for the hundredth time to wrap her mind around the notion. Failing for the hundredth time.

"I'm more convinced than ever."

"How do you know? Explain it."

"You wouldn't understand."

Adare bridled at the remark. "Try."

The *kenarang* spread his hands. "The . . . shape of his attacks. The rhythm of them." He rose, crossing to the map. "He hit us here and here at exactly the same time. Then, half a day later, here, here, and here. All that time, another group was sweeping west, to arrive at Irfeth's Ford just when the first group had retreated."

Adare glanced at the map, the scattering of positions il Tornja had indicated. The events were clear enough, but the pattern— if there *was* even a pattern—meant nothing. He waved a conciliatory hand. "The human mind was not built for this."

She stared at the rivers and mountains, the forests, the small lines indicating armies and positions, willing herself to find some shape in the attacks. "He did something smart?" she asked finally.

The general shrugged. "Not particularly."

Adare suppressed a growl. "Then *what*?"

"He did something . . . inhuman."

"Humans are all different," Adare said, shaking her head. "There's no such thing as a 'human' line of attack. A hundred generals would make a hundred different decisions."

"No. They would not." He smiled, a wide, bright smile. "Sometimes you forget, Adare, that I have fought against thousands of human generals. Two thousand and eight, if you care for the precise figure. You like to think you are unique, that each man and woman is different from the one before, but you are wrong. In all those battles, all those wars, I saw the same things, over and over, the same handful of little tricks, the same set of clumsy gambits and tactics played over and over again with tiny, irrelevant variation. I know the lineaments of a human attack, and this is not that. Long Fist is Meshkent. You can take my word for it. He wants to spread his bloody worship through Vash and Eridroa, and, much though it galls me to admit it, he is winning."

"I thought you said he wasn't brilliant."

"He doesn't need to be, when his army outnumbers mine twenty to one. I need more men, Adare. I need the Sons of Flame. And I need a secure southern front. At least until the war is over." He smiled wolfishly.

Adare studied her general. The *kenarang* looked hungry. His eyes were fixed on her, lips parted just enough to show the shadow of teeth. He looked ready to smile or snarl, ready to bite. Of all his carefully cultivated human expressions, this one was easiest to believe. Beneath all the casual banter and bright buckles, Ran il Tornja was a predator, a killer, the greatest general Annur had ever known, and this killer's face stretched across his features seemed right, true.

Nothing he shows you is true, she reminded herself.

He had peeled away one mask, that was all. This hunger and savagery was just one more face beneath all the other faces, a better, subtler act, one she wanted to believe. She could understand the brutal slashing and biting for power. She could control it. The truth of il Tornja, however, was no simple animal snarl. It was something else, something older and worse waiting beneath all the faces, something awful and inhuman, unfathomable as the space between the light of the stars.

Fear crept over her skin, raising the fine hairs on her arm. With an effort, she suppressed a shudder, forced herself to meet his eyes.

"And when it's over?" she asked.

"Once Meshkent is defeated and the Urghul are driven back . . ." He smiled wider, pushed back until his chair was balancing on two legs, poised between falling and falling. "Well, then we can look into—how should we say it? The long-term viability of the republican experiment . . ."

"And by *look into,*" Adare said flatly, "you mean kill everyone who doesn't want me back."

"Well . . ." He spread his hands. "We could kill a few at a time until the others recall the golden glory of Malkeenian rule."

Adare shook her head. "It feels wrong. The great emperors of Annur, the ones who presided over a peaceful empire, punished treachery and rewarded those who stayed loyal. I've read the Chronicles. Now you want me to turn a blind eye to the treason and idiocy of this 'Kent-kissing council?"

The *kenarang* smiled. "I'm *in* the Chronicles, Adare. I wrote two of them. The great emperors of Annur were great because they did what they needed to do. *Whatever* they needed to do. Of course, you'll be putting your own life on the line. . . ."

Adare waved a dismissive hand. He was right enough about the risks. It would be easy to arrive in Annur, present herself to the council, then be hauled off promptly to her own execution. The thought made her palms sweat, but there was no point dwelling on it. She'd visited the front, traveled to villages just after Urghul raids, seen the bodies carved open; the corpses spitted on stakes; the charred remains of men, and women, and children, some still sprawled over makeshift altars, others tossed into haphazard piles—the horrifying remnants of what the Urghul called worship.

Annur—imperial, republican, it hardly mattered—all of Annur was teetering at the edge of a bloody abyss, and she was the Emperor. She had taken that title, had demanded it, not so she could primp atop an uncomfortable throne to the flattery of courtiers, but because she'd believed she could do a good job, a better job, certainly, than the man who had murdered her father. She'd taken the title because she thought she could make life better for the millions inside the empire, protect them, bring peace and prosperity.

And so far, she'd failed.

It didn't matter that Kaden had made an even worse hash of things. It didn't matter that she was the first emperor in centuries to face a barbarian invasion. It didn't matter that even her father had failed to predict the chaos that enveloped them all. She had taken the title; it was her job to set things right, to mend the rents dividing Annur. Kaden's council might have her torn limb from limb if she returned, but they might not. If she returned, there was a chance—and the chance to save Annur, to save the *people* of Annur, to push back the barbarians and restore some measure of peace, of order, was worth the possibility of her own bloodless head decorating a stake.

"There is something else," il Tornja added. "Something you will discover when you reach the city." He paused. "Your brother has made a friend."

"We do that," Adare replied. "Humans. We form attachments, develop feelings for people, that sort of thing."

"If he had befriended a human, I wouldn't be concerned. The third Annurian representative to the council, the man who goes by the name of Kiel—he is not a man. He is one of my kind."

Adare stared stupidly. "Kaden has a Csestriim?"

Il Tornja chuckled. "Kiel is not a horse or a hunting dog, Adare. I have known him for millennia, and I can assure you, if anyone *has* anyone, it is Kiel who has your brother, who has possessed his mind and poisoned his will."

"Why didn't you *tell* me?" Adare demanded.

"I only just realized the truth myself. When I didn't recognize the name of the third Annurian delegate, I asked for a painting and description. Unfortunately, the fool responsible sent back a gorgeously inked parchment depicting the wrong person—one of the Kreshkan delegation, evidently. I discovered the error only recently."

Adare scrambled to make sense of the revelation. Il Tornja was a weapon, an instrument of destruction. She had him collared and brought to heel, and still she worried that she'd overlooked something, that one day she would give a tug on his leash only to find it gone terribly slack. Learning that there was *another*

Csestriim in the world, one allied with her brother, one over whom she had no control whatsoever . . . it made her stomach churn.

"Kiel was the one who drafted the republican constitution," she observed.

Il Tornja nodded. "He has never been a lover of your empire. In fact, for hundreds of years he has labored to destroy it. Every important coup, every plot against Malkeenian rule—he was behind it."

"Except for yours, of course. Except for the coup when you killed my father."

He smiled. "Yes. Except for that."

Adare studied him, hoping again to read something in those unreadable eyes, to see the gleam of a lie or the hard light of truth. As usual, there was plenty to see. As usual, she couldn't trust any of it.

"You're worried that Kaden knows who you are," she said.

"I am certain that Kaden knows who I am. Kiel has told him."

Behind her, Sanlitun twisted in his crib and cried out. For a moment, Adare had a horrible vision of the Urghul pouring over the bridge, the pale-skinned horsemen shattering the castle walls, smashing into her room, seizing the child. . . .

She stood abruptly, turned so that il Tornja couldn't see her face, and crossed the room to the crib. She watched her son a moment, watched him breathe, then lifted him gently into her arms. When she was certain she'd mastered her expression, she turned back to the *kenarang*.

"I'll go," she said wearily. "I'll try to mend the breach. I can't promise more than that."

Il Tornja smiled, teeth bright in the lamplight. "Mending first. Later, perhaps, we can see to more . . . permanent solutions."

3

"They wanted you," Maut Amut said. "The attackers wanted you."

Kaden paused in his climb, leaned against the banister as he caught his breath, then shook his head. "You can't be sure of that."

Amut continued on, taking the stairs two at a time, indifferent to the gleaming weight of his Aedolian steel. He reached the next landing before realizing that Kaden had fallen behind.

"My apologies, First Speaker," he said, bowing his head. "My shame makes me impatient."

The guardsman fixed his eyes on the stairs, settled a hand on the pommel of his broadblade, and waited. Even at his most animated, the First Shield of the Aedolian Guard was a stiff man, marmoreal, all right angles and propriety. Standing there motionless, waiting for Kaden to regain his strength, he looked like something carved, or hammered out on an anvil.

Kaden shook his head again. "You don't need to apologize for the fact that I've gone soft."

Amut didn't move. "Intarra's Spear is a daunting climb, even for hard men."

"It's only thirty floors to my study," Kaden replied, forcing his legs into motion once more. He made the climb almost every day, but always at a leisurely pace. More and more leisurely, he now realized, as the months had passed. Amut, on the other hand, had pushed hard since they left the council chamber, and Kaden's legs had begun to burn by the tenth floor. He put from his mind for the moment the grim fact that he planned to climb well beyond the Spear's thirtieth floor.

"When I lived with the monks," he said, pausing again when he reached Amut's landing, "a climb like this would have been a rest, a respite."

"You are the First Speaker of the republic. You have more important things to do than tire yourself on the stairs."

"You're the First Shield of the Aedolian Guard," Kaden countered, "and you find the time to run these stairs every morning." He'd seen the man training a few times, always well before dawn, always in full armor with a bag of sand across his shoulders, hammering up the steps, his face a mask of determination.

"I run them every morning," Amut replied grimly, "and still I failed in my duty."

Kaden turned away from the stairs above to face the guardsman. He made his voice hard.

"Enough of your shame. I am alive. The council is safe. This self-reproach is an indulgence, one that will shed no light on what happened here."

Amut glanced up at him, ground his teeth, then nodded. "As you say, First Speaker."

"Talk while we climb," Kaden said. There were still fifteen more floors before they reached the study. "More slowly, this time. What happened up here?"

Hand still on his sword, Amut started up again. He spoke without turning his head, as though addressing the empty staircase before him.

"Someone infiltrated the palace."

"Not hard," Kaden observed. "There must be a thousand people who come through the gates every day—servants, messengers, merchants, carters. . . ."

"Then they gained access to the Spear."

Kaden tried to puzzle that through. There was only one entrance to Intarra's Spear, a high, arched doorway burned or carved or quarried from the unscratchable ironglass of the tower walls. Aedolians guarded it day and night.

"Your men below . . ."

"The Spear is hardly a sealed fortress. Imperial . . ." Amut shook his head, then corrected himself. "*Republican* business is conducted here. People come and go. My men at the door are tasked with stopping obvious threats, but they cannot stop everyone, not without causing untold disruption."

Kaden nodded, seeing the outlines of the problem.

Intarra's Spear was ancient, older than human memory, even older than the most venerable Csestriim records. The architects of the Dawn Palace had constructed their fortress around it without knowing who had built the tower itself, or how, or why. Kaden had dim childhood memories of his sister reading tome after tome exploring the mystery, codex after codex, each one with a theory, an argument, something that seemed like evidence. *Sometimes, Adare,* Sanlitun had finally told her, *you must accept that there are limits to knowledge. It is possible that we will never know the true story of the Spear.*

And all the time, of course, he *had* known.

"I told your father the Spear's purpose," Kiel had said to Kaden months earlier, only days after they reclaimed the Dawn Palace, "just as I will tell you now."

The two of them—the First Speaker of the fledgling Annurian Republic and the deathless Csestriim historian—had been sitting cross-legged in the shadow of a bleeding willow, at the edge of a small pond in the Dowager's Garden. A breeze rucked the green-brown water; light winked from the tiny waves. The willow's trailing branches splattered shadows. Kaden waited.

"The tower is," the historian continued, "at its very top, an altar, a sacred space, a place where this world touches that of the gods."

Kaden shook his head. "I have stood on the tower's top a dozen times. There is air, cloud, nothing more."

Kiel gestured to a narrow insect striding the water's surface. The pond's water dimpled beneath the creature's meager weight. It twitched long, eyelash-thin legs, skimming from darkness to light, then back into darkness.

"To the strider," he said, "that water is unbreakable. She will never puncture the surface. She will never know the truth."

"Truth?"

"That there is another world—dark, vast, incomprehensible— sliding beneath the skin of the world she knows. Her mind is not built to understand this truth. *Depth* means nothing to her. *Wet* means nothing. Most of the time, when she looks at the water, she sees the trees reflected back, or the sun, or the sky. She knows nothing of the pond's weight, the way it presses on whatever slips beneath that surface."

The insect moved across the reflection of Intarra's Spear.

"The reflection of the tower is not the tower," Kiel continued, then turned away from the pond and the water strider both. Kaden followed his gaze. For a long time, the two of them studied the gleaming mystery at the heart of the Dawn Palace. "This tower, too," Kiel said at last, gesturing to the sun-bright lance dividing the sky above them, "is only a reflection."

Kaden shook his head. "A reflection of what?"

"The world beneath our world. Or above it. Beside it. Prepositions were not built to carry this truth. Language is a tool, like a hammer or an ax. There are tasks for which it is ill suited."

Kaden turned back to the water. The water strider was gone. "And the gods can pass beneath the surface inside the tower?"

Kiel nodded. "We learned this too late in the long war against your people. Two of our warriors stumbled across the ritual, but by the time they had climbed to the tower's top, the gods were gone. Only the human carcasses remained."

"The human vessels of the young gods," Kaden said after a moment's thought.

Kiel nodded.

"How?"

"The *obviate*. The ritual Ciena demanded when Triste put the knife to her own chest."

Kaden frowned. "How does it work?"

"This," the historian replied, "my people were unable to learn. The tower is a gate, this much we know, but it seems that only the gods hold the keys."

A gate for the gods, Kaden thought grimly as he climbed the stairs behind Maut Amut, his own breath hot and snarled in his chest. There was nothing to say that whoever had broken into the Spear earlier in the day understood that truth. Then again, there was nothing to say they didn't.

Carefully, deliberately, he stepped clear of that avenue of thought. He could hear Scial Nin speaking, the old abbot's voice calm and quiet: *Consider the task at hand, Kaden. The more you try to see, the less you will notice.*

"The attackers could have posed as slaves or ministers," Amut was saying. "Visiting diplomats, almost anything . . ."

It made sense. Most of the Spear was empty—an unbreakable gleaming shell—but the earliest Annurian emperors had built inside that shell, constructing thirty wooden floors—thirty floors inside a tower that could have accommodated ten times that number—before giving up, leaving the thousands of feet above them vacant and echoing. The lowest of those human levels were given over to pedestrian concerns: ministerial offices and audience chambers, a great circular dining room affording views over the entire palace. Three whole floors were devoted to suites for visiting dignitaries, men and women who would return home to boast of their nights spent in the tallest structure in the world, a tower surely built by the gods. And then, of course, there was all the necessary service apparatus and the cooks, slaves, and servants such service entailed.

If anything, Amut had understated the case—there was constant traffic in and out of the Spear, and no way for the

Aedolians to search everyone on every floor. The attackers, however, hadn't been skulking around in the kitchens. Somehow, they had gained the thirtieth floor, a place that was supposed to be secure.

"What happened at my study?" Kaden asked.

Amut's voice was tight when he responded. "They took down the three men I had posted there."

Kaden looked over at the First Shield. "Killed them?"

Amut shook his head curtly. "Incapacitated. They were knocked unconscious, but otherwise unharmed."

"Who," Kaden wondered, slowing on the stairs, "could get past three Aedolians at their post?"

"I don't know," Amut replied, his jaw rigid, as though trying to hold back the words. "That is what I intend to find out."

"I'm starting to see," Kaden said, glancing down the stairs behind them, "why you think they're dangerous."

When they finally reached the study, it was aswarm with Aedolians. Kaden glanced through the doorway. The guardsmen seemed to be cleaning up, mostly, putting codices back on the shelves, furling maps, rolling out the massive Si'ite rug.

"It's clear?" Kaden asked.

His shoulders were tight, he realized, and his back, as though he were expecting some assassin's knife at the base of the neck, some snare to cinch closed around his ankles. He took a moment to ease the tension.

See the fact, not the fear.

The study was the same as it always had been—a huge, semi-circular room filling half the floor. The curving ironglass wall offered an unparalleled view of Annur, and for the most part Sanlitun had done nothing to obscure that view. Bookshelves lined the interior wall, and massive tables stood in the center of the space, but along the smooth arc of that unbreakable wall there was almost nothing: just a table with two chairs and an antique *ko* board, a simple plinth holding a fossil, a dwarf blackpine in a pot, trunk withered and twisted.

"I've had my men go over it a dozen times," Amut said, following him inside as the Aedolians filed silently out. "I checked for every trap I know how to set, then had the dogs here all afternoon sniffing for poisons. We went through every drawer, scroll, and codex looking for munitions." He shook his head. "There's nothing. It's clear."

"Too clear."

Kaden turned at the voice to find Kiel standing by a far bookshelf, running a finger over the wooden frame.

"In your search for traps, you have obliterated any sign of the intruders."

Amut's fingers tightened on the pommel of his sword. "There *was* no sign. They were good. Better than good."

Kiel considered the Aedolian a moment, then nodded. There was no concern on his face, only curiosity. It had been that way even in the Dead Heart, when the historian was still caged deep in the bedrock of a forgotten fortress by madmen bent on exterminating the last members of his kind. Kiel had learned to feign emotion well enough, but most of the time he didn't bother. People considered him an eccentric genius, but then, Annur was filled with eccentrics and geniuses.

Kaden watched the historian as he crossed the room, his stride marred by a slight hitch, where something broken inside him had mended imperfectly. Kiel had walked the world for millennia, but his face, sober and barely lined, might have belonged to a man in his fourth or fifth decade. Eventually, he would need to leave the council and the palace, probably need to leave Annur altogether before someone noticed that he never changed, never aged.

Provided we're not all dead before that happens, Kaden amended silently.

"So why did they come?" the historian asked.

"Theft," Amut replied. "It has to be."

Kaden raised his eyebrows. "Is anything missing?"

"I wouldn't know, First Speaker. Aedolians are guards. We

stand outside the door. Now that we are sure the study is clear, I hoped you might shed some light on what was *inside*. Something missing?"

"All right," Kaden replied. He crossed to the middle of the room, turned in a slow circle. "Seems safe enough. Nothing's killed me yet."

"It is the safest room in the Dawn Palace right now," Amut said. "I would stake my life on it."

Kaden shook his head. "And just how safe," he asked quietly, "is the Dawn Palace?"

Only when Maut Amut left the room did Kaden turn to Kiel once more.

"What do you think?"

The Csestriim considered the closed bloodwood door. "It was by observing men like that Aedolian that I learned the meaning of your human word *pride*."

"I meant about the study. You think Amut was right? That it was all some sort of elaborate theft?"

The historian shook his head. "It is impossible to say. The guardsmen moved everything."

Kaden nodded. He visited the study nearly every day, could, with a moment of thought, call up a reasonable image of the half-round room, but he'd never bothered with a formal *saama'an*. The spines on the codices in his memory were hazy, the arrangement of the scrolls imperfect. Still, it would have been a decent place to start if the Aedolians hadn't been at the chamber for the better part of the morning. Kaden considered the mental image for a few heartbeats, then let it go, focusing on the room itself.

The sun was setting, sagging down the western sky until it hung just above Annur's rooftops. No one had yet bothered to light the room's lamps, but enough daylight remained for a cursory inspection. Instead of turning to the tables or the shelves, however, Kaden crossed to the wall overlooking the city, to a small section of the bloodwood floor that was polished to higher shine than the rest. It wasn't hard to imagine Sanlitun sitting there, the last true emperor of Annur, cross-legged in the way of the monks who had trained him. Kaden let his own thoughts go, trying to slide into the mind of his murdered father.

Annur was the largest city in the world's largest empire, home to more than two million men, women, and children; their homes and shops, temples and taverns all built shoulder to shoulder. People ate and fought there, loved, lied, and died—all within a few paces of their neighbors, no more than a cracked teak wall between the pain of a laboring mother and the lovers locked in a hot embrace. After the emptiness of Ashk'lan, the space and the silence, it was all . . . too much, even inside the Dawn Palace. Kaden could inhabit his father's desire to climb out of the wash of humanity, above it, could imagine Sanlitun ignoring the heavy wooden chairs to sit on the bare floor, eyes closed, blind to the city that surged and hummed beyond those clear, unbreakable walls. . . .

He let the *beshra'an* go.

Maybe that wasn't it at all. Maybe that particular patch of floor had been worn smooth by something else, something irrelevant—one of the silver smoke cats that prowled the palace, or a small table shifted a thousand times in cleaning. Kaden could see his father sitting there still and silent as a Shin monk perched on a granite ledge above Ashk'lan. He could see it, but he'd never actually *seen* it. Sanlitun was a shadow, a dim shape cast on the present by the things he'd left behind.

Kaden turned from the memories of his father and the sight of the sprawling city he had ruled to consider the room once more. The Aedolians had been neat in their search, stacking the loose papers in piles on the tables, returning the codices to the shelves with the spines perfectly aligned. The soldiers did not, however, have Kiel's memory or Kaden's. He sighed as he crossed to the nearest table, flipped through a few pages, then let them fall.

"I'm not sure I kept anything here worth stealing," he said.

"There were pages detailing troop movements," Kiel replied. "Supply lists."

Kaden shook his head. "There are easier places to find those papers. No need to infiltrate the Spear itself. No need to subdue three Aedolians." He paused, trying to make sense of it. "This was something different. Something . . . more." He glanced at the heavy door—three inches of banded bloodwood with Aedolian guardsmen just beyond it. Only a madman would try to get past that. A madman, or someone very, very determined. "It was il Tornja, wasn't it?"

"We have reliable reports of your sister's *kenarang* in the north, but his reach is long."

Kaden nodded slowly. "He knew this study. He's been here. If he needed something, he would know where to look, and he knows the kind of people who could manage something like this." Kaden hesitated before saying the rest. "And, like you, he knows the truth about the Spear. What it is for."

Kiel inclined his head slowly. "He does."

A cold weight settled in Kaden's chest. He glanced up, as though he could see through the ceiling, through thousands of feet of empty air that waited in the tower above, through the steel floor of the cage dangling there, to where a young woman with black hair and violet eyes, a woman of impossible beauty, a priestess and a murderer, a human with a goddess trapped inside her flesh, waited in chains to meet her fate.

"We have to get Triste out," he said finally. "We have to find a way to do it now and do it safely. If il Tornja can get into this study, he can get into the prison."

"And yet it is only atop this tower that the girl can do what must be done," Kiel replied.

"She doesn't know how. And even if she did, she wouldn't do it." He had explained to her the truth. They'd been over it

a dozen times, to no avail. "There's no point keeping her in the
Spear if she can't perform the *obviate,* if she won't. Everyone
knows she's in the prison, and even if no one has attacked her·
yet, they will."

"All of this is true," Kiel replied, his eyes going distant. After
a long pause, the Csestriim turned away, crossed to the small
table that still held Sanlitun's *ko* board. He seated himself in
one of the two chairs facing it. Kaden watched. He had spent
enough time around Kiel since their flight from the Dead Heart
to have grown used to these lapses. Even after thousands of
years lived among humans, generations chronicling their lives,
habits, and histories, beneath his unremarkable manner, behind
that human façade, Kiel's rhythms of speech and thought
remained alien, unknowable. Kaden schooled himself to patience,
watching as the Csestriim removed the lids from the twin boxes
and began playing, one side against the other, the only sound
the quiet click of the stones against the board: white, then black,
then white, over and over.

A stranger would have imagined Kiel preoccupied. Kaden
knew better. The man played *ko* easily as breathing. He could
go through entire games without looking at the board, and he
never, ever lost. Whatever private war he was waging against
himself, it had nothing to do with the game itself.

After forty moves, he paused, studied the stones a moment,
then looked over at Kaden, picking up the thread of the conversation as though he had never dropped it.

"It is possible that il Tornja wants you to move her. That this
entire episode was engineered to *force* you to move her."

Kaden frowned at the board, as though there were some sort
of answer in the sprawling patterns. "To strike at her when she's
outside the prison."

Kiel nodded. "Right now, Triste is the most securely guarded
person in this republic. Someone who wants to attack her, even
someone who manages to get inside the Dawn Palace, still has

to go through five locked doors and twenty guardsmen. It is not an inconsiderable obstacle."

"They got in here."

"One door," Kiel pointed out. "Three guards. Today's attack could be no more than a feint, an attempt to make you panic. He will come for Triste eventually, but he will not have to come for her if you give her up."

"And if we keep her here," Kaden said, "when he finishes with Long Fist in the north, he can come for her at his leisure."

Kiel nodded.

Frustration gnawed at the edge of Kaden's calm. "So if we move her, we lose. If we keep her, we lose."

"It all returns to the *obviate*. You must convince her. She may not know the way, but the goddess inside her knows."

"The ritual will kill her," Kaden said. "That's what your warriors found all those millennia ago, right?"

Kiel didn't blink. "She is Ciena's prison."

"She is a person, not a prison. She didn't ask for Ciena to inhabit her flesh, and she certainly hasn't volunteered to undergo a slaughter intended to set the goddess free. It is murder."

"It is sacrifice," Kiel corrected him. "To the goddess. For the goddess."

"And how do we know," Kaden asked, "that killing Triste won't annihilate Ciena's touch on our world anyway? That's what il Tornja wants to do, right?"

"Method matters. The *obviate* is not a murder, it is a ritual, one in which Triste consents to let go of her goddess. This is not a knife in the dark. It gives Ciena the time to depart the human flesh whole and unbroken. The *obviate* lays down the safe path she will take out of this world."

"At least that's what you believe," Kaden said, staring at the Csestriim.

Kiel nodded fractionally. "It is what I believe. It is what happened with the young gods."

"And if you're wrong?"

"Then I am wrong. We act on the information we have."

Kaden watched the historian a moment, then looked away, out over the darkened rooftops of Annur. Without a word, he slipped outside his own emotion and into the unending emptiness of the *vaniate*. He could do it at will now, could manage it walking, even talking. Scial Nin's words came back to him, spoken directly across the space of the intervening year: *You would have made a good monk.*

Inside the trance, all pressure fell away. There was no urgency, no worry—only fact. Il Tornja would find a way to murder Triste, or he would not. She would agree to perform the *obviate,* or she would not. They would find a way to rescue the trapped goddess, or they would not. And if they failed, if all pleasure vanished from the world, how would that be any different from the vast peace of the *vaniate*?

"Come out of that, Kaden," Kiel said. "You should not spend so much time so fully severed from yourself."

Kaden hesitated inside the stillness. The *vaniate* had frightened him at first, the hugeness of it, the indifference, the cool, absolute smoothness. That fear was, he thought now, the way that one of the Annurians below, a man raised his whole life inside the hum and throb of the city, might feel were he to wake one clear morning on a glacier in the Bone Mountains: a terror of too much space, of too much nothing, of not enough self to fill the gap between snow and sky. Only, Kaden felt at home on the glacier now. He found, when the world grew too loud, too close, that he was unwilling to leave that infinite blank.

"Kaden." Kiel's voice again, sharper this time. "Let it go."

Reluctantly, Kaden stepped out of the emptiness and into the cloister of his own irritation.

"You live inside it all the time," he pointed out, careful to keep the emotion from his voice.

Kiel nodded. "Our minds were built for it. Yours is not."

"Meaning what?"

The Csestriim didn't reply at once. Instead, he rose, lit a

lamp, then another. Light filled the room, warm as water, pressing out against the ironglass of the Spear. Only when the room was fully lit did he return to his chair, studying the *ko* board intently before he sat. After a pause, he placed a white stone, then a black, then another white. Kaden couldn't make sense of any of the moves. It seemed as though Kiel had forgotten his question, or ignored it, but finally the historian looked up.

"You saw what happened to the Ishien," he said quietly. "To some of them."

Kaden nodded slowly. His weeks as a prisoner in their damp stone cells were not the sort of thing a person forgot, even one better equipped for forgetting than Kaden himself. He could still see Trant's wide, agitated eyes, could still watch Ekhard Matol screaming spittle one moment, smiling that wide, awful smile the next. They were insane, all of them. They had tried to kill Kaden twice, once in the labyrinthine tunnels of the Dead Heart, and once on a sun-bright island ringed with *kenta,* awash in a wide sea. For all he knew, they were still trying to find a way to get at him. And yet . . .

"The Ishien aren't the Shin," Kaden replied. "Their methods . . ." He hesitated, remembering the scars, the descriptions of self-inflicted torment. "Those methods would break anyone."

"Yes," Kiel said, nudging another stone into place, "and no. The Shin discipline provides a gentler, subtler path, but the destination is the same. The *vaniate* is like . . . the deep sea. You can dive deeper and deeper, but the ocean is not your home. Stay down too long and it will crush you. Surely you heard of this happening among the monks?"

For months, Kaden had tried to put all thought of Ashk'lan from his mind. The memories of sky and silence were tangled up too tightly with the killing that came later. The truth that he could have done nothing to save the monks, to save Pater, or Akiil, or Scial Nin, sat too closely to that other, harder truth, that he *had* done nothing. It was easier to dwell on his failures here in Annur.

"Did none of the Shin let go when you were among them?" Kiel asked.

Kaden stared at the board, unwilling to meet the other man's gaze. "Let go?"

"My people had a phrase for it: *Ix acma.* It means 'Without self. Without center.'"

"I thought that was the whole point," Kaden protested. "I must have recited the mantra a hundred thousand times: *The mind is a flame. Blow it out.*"

"It is a vivid figure of speech, but it lacks precision. The flame, if we keep to the figure, dims, it wavers, but it continues to burn. You need your emotions. They keep you . . . tethered to this world."

"The walking away," Kaden said quietly.

Kiel nodded. "That was what they called it when last I visited Ashk'lan."

One of the Shin had walked away just a few months after Kaden first arrived in the mountains. Little was made of the event. The monk—Kaden was still too young, too untrained to recall his name—had simply stood up in the meditation hall one afternoon, nodded to the others seated there, then walked into the mountains. Akiil, always the curious one, had demanded to know what would happen to him, when he would come back. Scial Nin just shook his head. "He will not come back." It was not a cause for sorrow nor for celebration. A man, one of their own, was gone, absent, his stone cell in the dormitory suddenly empty. But then, the Shin had lived with emptiness a long time.

"I always thought that the ones who walked away were the failures," Kaden said. "That they were the ones who couldn't take it. You're telling me they were the only ones to really master the *vaniate*? To enter it fully?"

"Success or failure," Kiel said, eyeing the board, "depend very much on one's goals. A cold death in the mountains would not be accounted a success by many of your kind, but those who walked away found what they sought. They blew out the flame."

"And the rest? Rampuri Tan and Scial Nin and all the others?"

Kiel looked up. "They did not. You do not live long, any of you, severed from your emotions."

"Which is why il Tornja wants to cut that cord. Why he's so intent on killing Ciena and Meshkent."

The historian nodded.

Kaden blew out a long, slow breath. "I'll go talk to Triste."

"What will you say?"

It was a good question. A crucial question. Kaden could only shake his head, mute.

4

Nira's stare might have been hammered out on an anvil.

"Just tell me," the old woman demanded, "what's the point a' havin' a fuckin' councillor if ya're not plannin' ta listen ta any of her counsel?"

"I listen to your counsel," Adare replied, trying to keep her voice low, reasonable, patient. She was reminded, suddenly, of her childhood visits to her father's hunting estate northeast of Annur. While Sanlitun had never been a hunter, he kept a kennel of dogs—some gifts from foreign dignitaries, others whelped on the estate—and Adare liked to visit the dogs in the early morning, before most of the servants and slaves were up and about their business. There was an old red-coat hound bitch, blind in one eye, half lame and wholly vicious, to whom Adare took a perverse liking. She'd bring the aging beast a bone from the kitchen, toss it into the pen, then stand back while the bitch gnawed with the good side of her mouth, eyeing Adare balefully the whole time.

The hound had died more than a decade earlier, but talking to Nira brought back all the old instincts. Like the hound, the woman refused to let something go once she got it in her teeth. Like the hound, she'd snap at any hand that got too close, even the hand that fed her. Like the hound, she'd survived her share of fights, fights that had killed off all her peers.

And unlike the hound, Adare reminded herself grimly,

Rishinira is more than a thousand years old, and once helped to destroy half the world.

"I would like to have you in Annur," Adare said slowly, trying to pry this particular bone from Nira's mouth without getting bitten, "but I need you here more." She glanced toward the door of her study. It was closed and latched, but even so, she pitched her voice lower. "I have allies, Nira, but no friends aside from you."

"Friends, is it?" the woman barked. *"Friends!"*

Adare ignored the interruption. "Right now you are the only person I really trust, Intarra help me."

"Which is why, ya dumb cow, ya want me by your side when you trot off to this fool fucking meeting you're so keen on."

"No. It's why I need you *here,* to keep an eye on il Tornja."

Nira's face hardened at the mention of the name. "Eyes are for fools. If all I kept on him was an eye, he'd a' been gone long months back, disappeared, slipped outta your weak little paws completely."

"I don't think so," Adare said slowly, considering for the hundredth time the events of the past year. "He's not fighting this war for *me,* but he's also not fighting it because you put some invisible leash around his neck. He was here, in the north, weeks before we came. He has his own reasons for going after the Urghul, for going after Long Fist."

"Oh, I'll grant him his reasons. Every creature's got reasons, even a miserable, manipulating bastard like your general. *Especially* someone like him." She shook her head. "Sticky thing about his reasons though, is just that: they're *his* fucking reasons." Adare caught a glimpse of brown teeth as the woman smiled. "That's where the leash comes in."

"But if you travel with me, if you go farther away, you won't be able to . . ."

"Won't be able ta *what?*" Nira raised an eyebrow. "You become a leach all of a sudden? Added that ta your long list of shiny titles?"

Adare shook her head, trying to keep her rising anger in check.

"Of course I am not a leach," she said quietly.

Nira hooted, screwed her wrinkled face into a parody of surprise. "Not a leach? You're *not* a *leach*? Ya mean ya *can't* actually twist this shitty world to your will with a half second's thought?" Before Adare could respond, the woman leaned forward, poked her in the chest with a bony finger. Nira's levity had vanished. "Then quit tellin' me what I can and can't do with my kennings."

She pulled the finger back, then stabbed it toward the northern bank of windows. "I know where he is, right now. That's one a' the things the leash does, ya tit-headed excuse for an emperor. If he decides to ride west tomorrow morning, I'll know it. If he doubles back, I'll know it. I'll know it if I'm here, in this miserable hovel you call a palace, and I'll know it if I'm hip-deep in the newly smeared shit of some Raaltan farmer's field.

"And here's another piece a' wisdom I could be sellin' that I'll just give ta you for free: I can pull that leash tight from wherever I want, too. I could be sunnin' myself on a slow boat just off the coast of Dombâng, some pretty, naked boy workin' a nice oil into my aching feet, and if I wanted your general dead I could snap my fingers, feel him die, then roll over to let the oil boy go to work kneading my withered buttocks.

"So when ya say ya need me here to watch il Tornja, you're either dumber than a poleaxed ox, or you're lyin', and I'd be hard-pressed to say which I like less."

Adare forced herself to count to three after the woman finally fell silent. Then to five. Then to ten.

"Are you quite finished?" she asked finally.

"I am not," Nira snapped. "There's Oshi ta consider, too. Even if ya didn't trust the leash, my brother's right there with the bastard, doggin' his every step."

Adare shook her head. "Oshi's not there to watch over il

Tornja. He's there in the hope that the *kenarang* might find a way to *cure* him, to fix his memory, his madness. He doesn't even know who il Tornja *is* anymore."

Nira snorted. "And the Csestriim bastard best keep it that way. Oshi'd burn him ta ash if he remembered the truth."

They locked gazes. Adare could remember a time, not so many months earlier, when a tirade like that, delivered with all the woman's bony conviction, would have shamed and dismayed her. Not anymore. Months spent wrangling with Lehav about the southern force and il Tornja about the northern; months of negotiating with the local merchants' guilds over grain prices, with aristocrats over taxes, with the endless string of impotent ambassadors from Kaden's 'Shael-spawned republic, hard-talking idiots who made dozens of promises and twice as many demands without delivering any actual change; months of knowing that a single mistake, a single piece of bad luck, and she would have failed all the people she had sworn to protect; months of listening to her son scream himself to sleep night after night after night—after all those months, she wasn't as easy to cow as the terrified princess who fled the Dawn Palace a year earlier. And yet, there was nothing to be gained by locking horns with her own Mizran Councillor, especially when the woman was right.

"I did lie," Adare said. "I want you close to il Tornja, but more than that, I need you here to watch over Sanlitun. To take care of him while I'm gone."

"Ah," Nira said, nodding slowly. "So that's the heart of it. You've finally agreed ta part from the child."

"There's no other choice," Adare said, hoping even as she spoke that she might still be wrong. "I have to go to Annur. The legions are undermanned, undersupplied, and exhausted. If I can't save them, they can't save Annur, can't defend the *people* of Annur, and then what fucking good am I? What's the point in being Emperor if you let a horde of savages tear apart the people you're supposed to be protecting?" She shook her head grimly. "That 'Kent-kissing council might just want me there so they have an easier time planting a knife between my ribs, but it's a risk I have to take. *I* have to take it. My son does not. It's safer for him here."

She shivered as she said that word. *Safer.* As if any place was really safe with an Urghul army pressing down from the northeast, a false council of incompetent, power-grabbing whores holding Annur, the near-utter collapse of the legions in the south, an utter abdication of all peacekeeping within Annur itself, thieves and bandits prowling the land, and pirates pillaging the seas. There was every possibility that in leaving Sanlitun behind, Adare could be leaving him to die far from her arms. . . .

She forced the thought from her mind.

Aergad's walls were battered, but they stood. The Haag flowed deep and fast to the east, a final barrier between the city and the Urghul. Beyond the Haag, il Tornja's legions still fought their desperate battle. There was danger everywhere, but Aergad was still safer than the dubious welcome that awaited her in Annur.

"Look, Adare," Nira said. For once, the woman kept her mockery and her anger in check. Her voice, too, seemed to have shifted, leaving behind the gutter slang of which she was so fond for something simpler, older, more sober. "You're smart to leave your boy—for a dozen reasons—but not with me."

"Yes, with you. You're my Mizran Councillor."

"Your councillor, yes. Not your wet nurse. These tits wore out a thousand years ago."

"I don't need you to nurse him," Adare said. "Or to change him or clean him or swaddle him. I have a dozen women who can do that. I just need you to watch over him. To keep him safe."

Nira opened her mouth as though to reply, then shut it abruptly. To Adare's shock, tears stood in the old woman's eyes, glimmering in the lamplight.

She had a child. The realization hit Adare like a fist to the face. In all the time since she first met Nira on the Annurian Godsway, she'd never thought to ask. For half a heartbeat she checked her memory of the histories of the Atmani, but the histories, for all their macabre detail when it came to the decades of war, were silent on the subject of children. As far as Adare knew, Nira had never married, not that that was any impediment to the bearing of children.

"I'm not the one, girl," the old woman said, the whole weight of the centuries pressing down on her shoulders, voice rough as unsanded wood. "I'm not the one ta be watchin' over children."

Adare stared. She had learned to stand up to the woman's curses and hectoring, but this sudden, quiet honesty left her dumb. "What happened?" she managed finally.

Nira shook her head. Her gnarled hands clutched each other on the table before her. Adare watched, trying to make sense of that awful, mute grief.

"I can't do it, girl," the old woman said finally. "Not again. I won't."

In just a few words, Adare heard the full scope of her own midnight horror. Since Sanlitun was born she had tried to tell herself that her nightmares and waking terrors, the endless litany of fears for her child, were nothing but the product of an exhausted, overworked mind. *He's healthy,* she would remind herself, studying the child's plump brown cheeks, his strong fingers wrapped around hers. *He's safe,* she would whisper, glancing out her window toward the walls of the city. *There's no reason to be afraid.*

Over the months since Sanlitun's birth, Adare had built these feeble walls between herself and the wilderness of awful possibility that lay beyond. She had half convinced herself that through love, and care, and unending vigilance, she could keep all harm from the fat, fretful child, this tiny, inarticulate being that meant more to her than her own heart. The tears in Nira's eyes, the twist of her hands, her few quiet words—*I can't do it, girl*—tore through those walls like a knife through wet paper. A sudden desperation took Adare by the throat, and for several heartbeats she could barely drag the air into her lungs.

"I don't . . . ," she began. Her voice cracked, and she took a deep breath, fixing Nira with her eyes, trying to make the woman see, to understand. "I know it's not perfect. I know you can't protect him from everything. But I don't have anyone else."

Nira shook her head mutely, and Adare reached across the table, taking the woman's hands in her own.

"You're smart," she said quietly. "You're strong. And I trust you."

"They trusted me to rule a whole continent once, girl, and I let it burn. I *burned* it."

"We're not talking about a continent."

"I know what we're talking about," Nira snapped, something like the old querulousness creeping back into her voice. "I had a boy, too. My own boy. I couldn't save him."

Adare nodded. She could imagine the horror. She tried not to. "I'm begging you, Nira."

The woman glared at her through the tears, then pulled her hands away to scrub her eyes. "An emperor doesn't beg. An emperor commands."

Adare shook her head. "Not about this."

Nira turned back to her. "About everything, ya silly slut. That's what it is to be an emperor."

"Then you'll do it?"

"Is it an order?"

Adare nodded silently.

"Then I'll do it," Nira said. She blew out a long, ragged breath. "I'll watch over the sobbing little shit while you're gone."

Something inside Adare, some awful tension, went suddenly slack. She felt like she, too, might start weeping.

"Thank you, Nira."

"An emperor doesn't thank her subject for following her orders."

"Well, I'm thanking you anyway."

Nira shook her head grimly. "Thank me when I put the brat back in your arms and he's still breathing."

5

With burning lungs and cramping thighs, Kaden forced himself to keep climbing the spiraling wooden stairs. Maut Amut had assured him that the attack on the Spear went no higher than Kaden's own study, the thirtieth and last of the human floors built into the base of the ancient tower, and yet, after a restless night during which sleep eluded him, he realized he needed to see her, Triste, needed to look at her with his own eyes, to know that she was alive, safe; or safe as he had been able to make her.

It took only a dozen steps from the landing outside his study to climb free of the last of the lower floors, out of the human rooms and corridors and into the impossible, godlike space looming above. The stairs continued, of course, the only human construction in the echoing emptiness of the Spear, a tight wooden spiral at the tower's center, supported by their own carefully engineered scaffolding, by the wrist-thick steel cables hanging down from the unimaginable heights above. Everything else was air, emptiness, and light, and far, far above, the highest dungeon in the world.

When Kaden was five years old and Valyn six, one of them had discovered *The Design of Dungeons*. He couldn't remember how they had stumbled across the old codex, or where, or why they had even bothered to pick it up, but the book itself he remembered almost perfectly, every page, every meticulous diagram, every horrifying story of imprisonment, madness, and torture related in a dry, indifferent, scholarly tone. Yuala the Basc, the author of the treatise, had spent ten years visiting no fewer than eighty-four prisons and dungeons scattered over all fifteen Annurian atrepies and beyond. He had seen the Stone Pit of Uvashi-Rama, the Hot Cells of Freeport, and the infamous Thousand and One Rooms where Antheran kings and queens left their enemies to die. The diversity of the dungeons was nearly endless, but they shared a few common traits—they were underground, dark, and built of stone. On all three counts, the dungeon of the Dawn Palace defied expectation.

Though there were a handful of holding cells beneath the Hall of Justice—small, secure rooms for prisoners awaiting trial or processing—the greatest dungeon of Annur was not some crude, brutal hole hacked out of the bedrock. It was not a hole at all. You could mine a hole, after all, even one of stone. With enough time and the right tools, you could dig your way in or carve your way out. No one, however, in the whole history of the Annurian Empire or, indeed, earlier, had found a way to make the slightest scratch in the ironglass of Intarra's Spear, and so the builders of the palace prison had chosen Intarra's Spear for their work.

They didn't use the entire tower, of course. The whole Spear could have housed a hundred thousand prisoners, an entire nation of spies, traitors, and conquered kings. One floor was sufficient, one floor hundreds and hundreds of feet above the ground, accessible only by this staircase spiraling up through light and silence, suspended from a dizzying apparatus of steel bars and chains.

From a distance, Intarra's Spear looked impossibly slender, the tower's girth insufficient to support its height. It seemed that a light breeze would snap the brilliant needle in half, that the clouds scudding against its sides would shatter it. From the inside, however, after climbing free of those first human floors, it was possible to judge the true diameter of the thing. A man with a decent arm might throw a stone from the staircase at the center to one of those clear walls, but it wouldn't be easy. After the human dimensions of the rooms below, emerging into the huge empty column was intimidating. The staircase spiraling up inside looked fragile, futile, a bold, doomed effort to climb something that was never meant to be climbed.

Kaden counted a thousand steps, then paused on a landing, gathering his breath. The climb was no more brutal than some of the ascents in the Bone Mountains, no harder than running the Circuit of Ravens two or three times after the year's first snow, but, as Amut had pointed out, he was no longer a Shin acolyte. After nearly a year inside the Dawn Palace, his legs had softened, and the flesh had thickened over his ribs. When he worked hard, as now, his heart labored in his chest, stubborn, baffled at its own inadequacy.

Leaning on the wooden railing, he looked down. Swallows had invaded the space, hundreds of them, roosting in the scaffolding, soaring through the empty tower, their sleek, dark forms darting and twisting in the rich light. Kaden glanced up. A few hundred feet above him, another man-made floor cut across the Spear's girth, a floor of solid steel supported by great arches of iron and wood that spanned the enormous space. There was no way to carve the glass walls of the tower, no way to drill into them, but the Spear, like the stone cliffs Kaden had spent his years climbing, had its own natural features: shallow cracks and ledges, inexplicable gouges both small and large that might have been worn away by wind and weather. Only there was no weather inside the Spear, no wind.

Whatever the cause of those irregular features, the builders of the dungeon had used them to anchor their structure high inside the tower, nearly two-thirds of the way to the very top, a single floor set atop those arches. Kaden was close enough now to see the blocky forms dangling listlessly beneath—the steel cages of the condemned like ugly pendants hung from heavy chain. He slowed his heart, pushed more blood out into his quivering limbs, and kept climbing.

After a hundred more steps, the staircase wound its way into a metal sheath, like a corkscrew into the neck of a steel bottle. Fruin the First, the dungeon's architect, had bolted huge plates of steel—each one larger than the bed of a wagon—onto the wooden beams of the stairs, blocking out the light and ruining any possibility of a would-be rescuer throwing a rope—or a vial of poison—to one of the prisoners.

Kaden paused inside the sudden darkness, his robe soaked with sweat, his lungs heaving inside him, to allow his eyes to adjust. Then, with trembling legs, he climbed on, forcing himself to grind out the last three hundred feet in one brutal push. There was no way to know, inside the near-blackness of the stairwell, when he was approaching the level of the dungeon itself. There were stairs beneath his feet, a railing in his hand, and then, abruptly, a landing lit by a lamp. The stairs continued on, twisting up and up, straight through the dungeon into another immeasurably large space and finally to the Spear's top. Kaden ignored them, turning instead to the two armored guards—jailors rather than Aedolians—flanking a steel door hung from heavy hinges in a steel wall.

"First Speaker," said the nearer of the two with a low bow.

Kaden nodded in return, glancing past the man at the closed door. It seemed Amut was right—the attackers, whoever they were, hadn't made an attempt on the dungeon.

"Be welcome," the guard said, turning from Kaden to the door. It swung silently open on well-oiled hinges.

For all the steps that Kaden had climbed, the admittance chamber to the dungeon of the Dawn Palace might as well have been underground after all, some windowless room in the base of a squat stone fortress. Skylights would have admitted ample light, but Fruin hadn't allowed skylights into the design of his prison. That left hanging lamps as the only light. Kaden paused as the door thudded shut behind him, considering the room, studying the space for anything different, anything strange. Below the lamps, half a dozen clerks sat at a row of desks, bent over their papers, the scratch of their pens interrupted by a light chime when they dipped those pens into the ink, then tapped the excess free against the glass rims of their inkwells. Kaden took a deep breath, relaxed his shoulders. Here, too, all was calm.

In fact, only the unrelieved steel—the walls, the ceiling, the roughened floor, the three doors leading out of the room— suggested anything other than an ordinary ministerial office. The steel, and the fact that the man sitting beside the far door, sitting at a desk just the same as all the rest, wore full armor.

At the sight of Kaden, he rose quickly to his feet, then bowed.

"You honor us, First Speaker. Your second visit this month, if I am not mistaken."

"Captain Simit," Kaden replied slowly, studying the man.

He made a point of carving a *saama'an* of every guard each time he ascended to the prison, comparing them week to week, searching for some change in the angle of the mouth, the tightness around the eyes, anything that might tell of a betrayal before it came. He had come to trust Captain Haram Simit—one of the three chief jailors—more than most of them. The man looked more like a scholar than a guard—thin-fingered and stooped, a haze of uncut gray hair gathered in a kerchief beneath his helm—but there was a steadiness to him, a deliberation in his actions and his gaze that reminded Kaden of the Shin. Kaden considered his face, comparing it to the various *saama'an* he had compiled over the previous months. If there was a change, he couldn't find it.

"You have come to see the young woman?" Simit asked.

He was careful like that—never *the leach,* or *the whore,* or even *the prisoner*—always *the young woman*.

Kaden nodded. He kept his face still, composed. "Have the Aedolians been up here? Have you been notified of the attack below?"

Simit nodded soberly. "Shortly after the third bell yesterday."
The jailor hesitated. "Perhaps it's not my place to ask, First
Speaker, but what happened?"

"Someone attacked three of Amut's men. They broke into
my study, then disappeared."

Simit's face darkened. "Not just inside the Red Walls, but in
the Spear itself . . ." He trailed off, shaking his head grimly. "You
should be careful, First Speaker. Annur is not what it was. You
should be very careful."

Despite the warning, relief seeped into Kaden like a cool rain
into cloth. *She's still alive,* he told himself. *Unharmed.* Suddenly,
standing had become an effort. His legs were slack, whether
with that same relief or simple exhaustion, he couldn't say.

Simit frowned. "I hope you didn't feel the need to climb all
the way up here just to check. I can assure you, First Speaker,
that this prison is secure."

"I believe it," Kaden said, wiping the sweat from his brow.

Simit watched him for a moment, then gestured to a chair.
"Would you care to rest for a moment? The climb is taxing,
even for those of us who make it often."

"You're the second person who's told me that in two days."
He shook his head. "If I start sitting I don't think I'll get up."

"Wise," the jailor said, smiling. "I'll let the cage-men know
that you're here to see the young woman."

"Thank you," Kaden replied.

Simit crossed to a discreet bellpull set into the wall beside
the steel door, gave it a dozen tugs, some short, some long, then
waited for the cord to twitch in response.

"Different code," Kaden observed.

The guard smiled. "Most people don't notice."

"How often do you change it?"

"Daily."

"And what would happen if I tried to go through that door
without it?"

Simit frowned. "I could not permit that."

"And what would they do below, at the cages? Let's say the attackers from my study had come here instead. Let's say they'd forced their way past you."

"We have measures in place."

"Measures?"

The jailor spread his hands helplessly. "I'm not at liberty to say, First Speaker."

"Even to me?"

"Even to you."

Kaden nodded. "Good."

The main door opened onto a long, dim hall—steel ceiling and floors, steel walls punctuated by steel doors on heavy steel hinges. Kaden's light slippers were nearly silent on the rough metal, but the guard who had come to escort him—Ulli, a younger man with a blotchy face and lopsided ears—wore heavy boots that rang out at every step, as though the whole floor of the prison were one great gong. Answering clangs and clankings came from deeper inside: other boots, other doors slamming open or shut, chains dragging over rough edges. They had to pause twice for Ulli to unlock heavy gates. The prison was built in different zones, of which Triste occupied the most remote and inaccessible.

"How is she?" Kaden asked as they approached her cell door at last. A small number "1" was etched into the steel.

Ulli shrugged. He was never talkative. Unlike Simit, who understood the formalities of life inside the Dawn Palace, Ulli had all the formality of a sullen innkeeper serving late-night ale to drunkards. Most of the other council members would have bristled at the treatment, but then, most of the others weren't ever going to climb thousands of stairs to the prison. Kaden found the young man's indifference a relief.

"Is she still eating?" he pressed.

"If she stopped eating," Ulli replied, swinging open the door, "then she'd be dead, wouldn't she?"

"Does she still have the nightmares? Is she still screaming?"

Ulli put his shrug to use once more. "Everyone screams. That's what happens when you put people in cages."

Kaden nodded, and stepped into the cell. The first time he had visited, nearly a year earlier, he'd been momentarily shocked to find it empty—no sign of Triste inside the narrow steel box. That, of course, was because Triste wasn't kept inside her cell. A leach and a murderer warranted an even higher level of security.

Ulli swung the door shut behind them, locked it, then gestured to an hourglass standing on the floor in the corner.

"Gave her the dose of adamanth at the start of the shift. She looked healthy enough then."

"Healthy enough?"

"No point in me telling you when you're about to see for yourself."

Ulli gestured to a chain suspended from the ceiling. A steel bar the length of Kaden's forearm hung horizontally from the final link in that chain. It looked like a crude swing and served much the same purpose. Kaden crossed to it, took the chain in both hands, seated himself on the bar, then turned to the guard.

"Ready," he said.

"You want the harness?"

Kaden shook his head. It was foolish, perhaps, always refusing the harness. Sitting on the wide bar wasn't difficult. No doubt, thousands of children all over the empire gamboled on something similar every day. Those children, however, would be hanging from tree limbs or barn rafters a few feet off the ground. Unlike Kaden, if they slipped, they wouldn't fall thousands of feet to their deaths.

There was no practical reason to take the risk, but month after month, Kaden insisted on it. Back in the mountains there had been a thousand ways to die—slipping from icy ledges, getting caught out in an early fall blizzard, stumbling across a hungry crag cat. In the council chamber far below, however, *danger* was something distant and abstract. Kaden worried he was forgetting what it actually meant. Sitting on the slender bar alone, with no harness, was a way of remembering.

The metal doors dropped open. Kaden looked down. He could see the edge of Triste's cage hanging from its own, much heavier chain, a few dozen feet below and to the right. A hundred feet below that, a pair of swallows turned in a lazy gyre. Below them—just air. Kaden looked back up in time to see Ulli throw the catch on an elaborately geared winch at the corner of the cell. The bar lurched, dropped half a foot, then steadied. Kaden slowed his heartbeat, smoothed out his breathing, forced himself to relax his grip on the chain. And then, with a clanking that sounded like some massive, mechanical thunder, he was lowered out of the prison and into the dazzling bright emptiness of the Spear.

Triste's cage was not the only one. There were at least two dozen, hanging from their chains like huge, angular, rusting fruit—reserved for the most vile, the most deadly. Each had three solid walls and a fourth of thick steel bars. The cages were staggered, some closer to the floor of the prison above, some hanging much lower, all facing the walls of the Spear. The prisoners could see Annur spread out below—a different portion of the city depending on the orientation of the individual cage—but none could see each other. A few had a clear view of Kaden as he descended. Some cried out or cursed, some stretched imploring hands through the bars, a few just watched with baffled eyes, as though he were some unknown creature lowered down from the skies.

One poor soul had no cage at all. Instead, he sat wide-eyed and gibbering on a narrow platform barely one pace square, a platform supported at each corner by a chain. Simit called it, simply, the Seat. As punishment for defiance, or aggression, or violence, a prisoner was put on it for a week. The men subjected to it fell, went mad, or learned to behave. To Kaden it was a vivid reminder: while the Urghul openly worshipped Meshkent,

Annurians had their own ways of paying homage to the god of all suffering.

He shifted his gaze to the cage below him, Triste's cage, watching it approach as Ulli lowered him. The whole thing—the wrist-thick chains, the heavy steel plates, the bars—looked built to hold some monster out of legend, some unimaginable horror. When Kaden's seat finally jerked to a halt, however, when he looked across the narrow space separating him from the hanging cell, when his eyes adjusted well enough to see inside, there was only Triste: small, bound, half broken, and even here, in this awful place, almost impossibly beautiful.

For the first month of her imprisonment, she had cowered all the way in the back of the steel box, as far from the bars as she could crawl. During Kaden's earliest visits, she kept her face turned away, as though the light burned her eyes, flinched each time he spoke, and offered only the same unvarying words: *You put me here. You put me here. You put me here.*

Had Kaden allowed it, those words would have cut. Despite the massacre in the Jasmine Court, despite the terrible truth of the goddess buried inside her, Kaden couldn't help thinking of the young woman as an ally, even a friend. Which was one of the reasons he had insisted on this cell. Whatever toll it would take, it kept her safe. Safe from the vicious members of the council, and safe from outside attackers, like whoever had raided his study earlier. He had tried to explain that, but Triste was beyond hearing explanations, so far gone that for months he worried she might die inside the cell despite his precautions, hollowed out by her own despair.

Recently, however, she had stopped huddling. Instead of cringing against the steel floor, she sat cross-legged in the very center of her cage, hands folded in her lap, eyes fixed on the bars before her. Kaden recognized the pose from his years of meditation among the Shin, but where Triste had learned it, or why she had decided to adopt it, he had no idea. She didn't look like a prisoner; she looked like a queen.

And like a queen, she seemed barely to notice him during his most recent visits. An effect of the adamanth, according to Simit, of so much adamanth administered over so many months. Necessary, if they were to block all access to her well. Today, however, Triste raised her eyes slowly, as though considering Kaden's dangling, slippered feet, then his chest, and only after a very long time, his face. He tried to read that gaze, to translate the planes and surfaces of the flesh into thought and emotion. As usual, he failed. The Shin were great ones for observing nature, but a life among the monks had given him scant opportunity for the study of humanity.

"I counted ten thousand lights last night," she said, her voice low and rough, like something almost worn out. "Out there." She inclined her chin ever so slightly, the gesture intended to encompass, he supposed, the whole of the world beyond the grim ambit of her cage, beyond the clear walls of the Spear. "There were lanterns hung from bamboo poles. Cook fires burning in the kitchens of the rich, in the fish stalls of the markets, on the streets of the Perfumed Quarter. There were fires of sacrifice on the rooftops of a thousand temples, and above those fires there were the stars."

Kaden shook his head. "Why are you counting lights?"

Triste looked down at her hands, then over at the steel walls of her cage. "It gets harder and harder to believe," she said quietly.

"What does?"

"That it's a real world. That each of those fires has someone tending it, cooking or chanting or just warming her hands." She glanced up toward the sky. "Not the stars, of course. Or maybe the stars. Do you think the stars are on fire?"

"I wouldn't want to speculate."

Triste laughed, a limp, helpless sound. "Of course you wouldn't."

Though Kaden had come to expect the rambling, disjointed thoughts, Triste's incoherence still left him struggling to keep up with the conversation. It was like seeing a mind in the slow process of disintegration. As though she were a woman of packed sand thrown into a great, invisible river.

"How are you, Triste?" he asked softly.

She laughed again. "Why ask the question when you don't care about the answer?"

"I care about the answer."

For a moment she seemed to look at him, to actually *see* him. For just a fraction of a heartbeat, her eyes went wide. She started to smile. Then it was gone.

"No," she said, shaking her head slowly. The exaggerated movement, back and forth, back and forth, reminded him of some half-tamed creature testing the range of a collar and leash. "No, no. No. What you care about is *her*. Your precious goddess."

The other cells were dozens of paces away, well out of earshot, but Kaden glanced over his shoulder reflexively. The other prisoners, even if they *could* hear, weren't likely to understand the conversation, and if they understood it, weren't likely to believe that a goddess was trapped inside the young woman imprisoned in a nearby cage. The price of discovery, on the other hand, was disaster. Kaden lowered his voice.

"Ciena is your goddess, Triste. Not mine. That is why she chose you."

The girl stared at him. "Is that why you keep coming up here? Are you having little chats with her while I'm drugged into oblivion?"

Kaden shook his head. "She hasn't spoken. Hasn't . . . emerged since that time in the Crane, when you put the knife to your stomach."

For the first time Triste raised a hand, the movement slow, groping, like the searching of some blind creature as she probed the flesh beneath her shift, searching out the old wound.

"I should have finished it then," she said finally, voice low but hard.

Kaden watched her in silence. It seemed a lifetime ago that Tarik Adiv had arrived on the ledges of Ashk'lan with a hundred Aedolians at his back, with the death of an emperor on his tongue, with Triste. She had been a girl then. She was a girl no longer.

He'd known her barely a year, and in that year there hadn't been a single day in which she wasn't running or fighting, lying in a cell or screaming beneath an Ishien knife. Not one day. Kaden's own struggle had worn him, hardened him, and yet his own struggle had been nothing beside hers. A year of pain and terror could change a person, change her forever. Triste was no longer the wide-eyed daughter of a *leina* caught up in currents she could neither swim nor escape. That much was obvious. What she had become, however, what the pain and fear had made of her, what she had made of herself . . . Kaden had no idea.

"If you had continued driving the knife, you would have killed more than yourself and your goddess. You would have severed her touch from this world. You would have killed our capacity for pleasure, for joy."

"At least, that's the story your Csestriim tells you," Triste spat. "The story he tells me."

Kaden shook his head. "I've gone beyond Kiel's account. Well beyond. The Dawn Palace has the most complete chronicles in the world—both human and Csestriim. I've been down in the libraries almost every moment I haven't been struggling with the council. Kiel's account fits with what I've read, with the histories of the gods and the Csestriim wars."

"I thought he *wanted* to kill me," she said. "It's the only way to set his goddess free, right?"

"She is your goddess," Kaden said again.

"Not anymore, she's not. She stopped being my goddess when she forced her way into my head."

"She chose you," Kaden countered, "because of your devotion."

"That *can't* be true. There are scores of *leinas* in the temple, all of them more adept in Ciena's arts than I'll ever be, all of them utterly committed to the service of their goddess." She grimaced. "I was . . . a mischance. Some minister's by-blow."

"Tarik Adiv had the burning eyes," Kaden pointed out. "Your father was related, however distantly, to my own. Which means that you, too, are descended from Intarra."

The notion still surprised him. For hundreds of years the Malkeenians had staked their imperial claim on that lineage, on those eyes, on the claim that there was only *one* divine family. Forking branches of the tree could lead to civil war, to the ruin of Annur.

Triste shook her head. "It doesn't make sense."

"It makes perfect sense," Kaden replied. "It is the only thing that makes sense. According to the legend, Intarra bore the first Malkeenian millennia ago. The family would have ramified. My branch cannot be the only one."

"I don't have the eyes," she countered.

"Neither does Valyn."

Triste bared her teeth. "Even if it's true, what does it mean? What is it *worth*? What does it have to do with this bitch lodged inside my skull?"

Kaden could only shake his head. Even Kiel's insights extended only so far. Even the Csestriim, it seemed, could not peer into the minds of the gods.

"We don't know everything," he said quietly. "I don't know everything."

"But you still want to kill me."

The words weren't angry, not anymore. Something had snuffed her anger, quick and sure as a fist clamped over a candle's flame. She sounded exhausted. Kaden himself felt exhausted, exhausted from the long climb and from the fear that someone had broken into the dungeon, found Triste, hurt her.

"No," he said quietly, searching for another word, some phrase adequate to convey his worry. The Shin had taught him nothing, unfortunately, of human consolation. If he could have, he would have put a silent hand on her shoulder, but he could not reach through the bars. There was only that single syllable, and so he said it again, helplessly, "No."

"I'm sorry," she replied. "I misspoke. You want me to kill *myself*."

"The *obviate* isn't suicide. There is a ceremony to be observed. A ritual. Without it, the goddess can't escape. She cannot ascend." He paused. "And this is not something I *want*."

"Cannot ascend," Triste said, ignoring his last comment. "Cannot *ascend*." Her laugh was sudden and bright as a bell. Then gone.

"Why is that funny?"

Triste shook her head, then gestured to the bars of her cage. "It's a good problem to have. That's all. Forget about ascending—I'd be happy to get out of this cage for the night."

For a while they were both silent.

"Has she . . . spoken to you?" Kaden asked finally.

"How would I know? I never remember the times when she's in control." She fixed him with that bright, undeniable gaze. "For all I know, you're making the whole thing up, everything about the goddess. Maybe I'm just insane."

"You saw what happened in the Jasmine Court," Kaden said gravely. "What you did. What Ciena did through you."

Triste drew a long, shuddering breath, opened her mouth to respond, then shut it and turned away. The memory of the slaughter sat between them—the ravaged bodies, shattered skulls—invisible, immovable.

"I won't do it," she said finally. "Your ritual."

"It isn't my ritual, and I didn't come here to ask you to take part in it."

"But you want me to." She still didn't look at him. "You're hoping—or whatever monks do that's like hoping—that I'll accept it, that I'll embrace it. Well, I won't. You'll have to carve her out of me."

Kaden shook his head. "It doesn't work like that, as I've explained before. The *obviate,* were we to attempt it, seems to require your consent, your active participation."

"Well, you can't *have* it," she snarled, turning on him in a sudden fury. "You can't fucking *have it*! My mother gave me up to my father, my father gave me up to you. This 'Shael-spawned *goddess* is inside my skull, she forced her way in without ever even *asking* me, and now *you* want to sacrifice me. And you *can.* Obviously. All of you can give me up, can trade me from one person to the next, pass me along as long as you want.

"You can hit me, and you have. You can hurt me, and you have. You can lock me in one prison or the next"—she waved a hand around her—"and you have. You can give me to Rampuri fucking Tan or to the Ishien or to your council." She glared at him, the late sun's light reflected in her eyes. "I'm used to being given up by now. I *expect* it. But I'll tell you what I won't do—I won't *accept* it. I won't play along. For a while, a tiny little while, I thought you were different, Kaden. I thought we might actually . . ." She broke off, tears in her eyes, shaking her head angrily. When she spoke again, her voice was low, furious. "Everyone trades me away like a stone on the board, but I will not trade away myself."

Kaden nodded. "I know."

She stared at him, teeth slightly bared, breath rasping in her throat. "Then why are you here?"

He hesitated, but could think of no reason to skirt the truth. "To check on you. There was an attack."

She stared. "Here? In the Dawn Palace?"

"In Intarra's Spear." He pointed down through the dizzying emptiness toward the human floors thousands of feet below.

"And you needed to tell me?"

"I needed," Kaden replied carefully, "to see that you were all right."

Triste looked moved for half a heartbeat, then the expression melted off her face. "To be sure *she* is all right," she said again. "You think it was il Tornja, trying to get at the goddess."

Kaden nodded. "I think it is a possibility."

She glared at him. "Well, since you asked, I am *not* all right, Kaden. I haven't been all right in a very long time." Her eyes had gone wide, vacant. She wasn't focusing on him anymore. "I don't even know what *all right* would be anymore. We're all going to die, right? Probably horribly, most of us. Maybe all you can do is die where you want to die, end things on your own terms."

"Few of us have the luxury to act only on our own terms." Kaden shook his head. "I do not."

"But you're not in *here, are* you?" Triste said, raising her hands to seize the bars for the first time. "You're free."

Kaden watched her silently for a moment. "And what would you do, Triste, if you were free?"

She held his eyes, then seemed to slump, as though collapsing beneath the weight of the very notion of freedom. When she responded, her voice was thin, far away: "I'd go somewhere. Somewhere as far from your 'Kent-kissing palace as possible. There's a place my mother used to talk about, a little village by an oasis in the shadow of the Ancaz Mountains, just at the edge of the Dead Salts. *As far from the rest of the world as you can get,* she used to say. I'd go there. That village. That's where I'd go. . . ."

It was hard to know how seriously to take the words. Triste's eyes were unfocused, her speech slightly slurred with the adamanth. She had fixed her gaze over Kaden's shoulder, as though on something unseen in the distance.

"If I could get you out," he began slowly, "if I could get you clear of the prison and the palace for a while, somewhere else, would you be willing to consider—"

All at once her attention was there, concentrated furiously on him. "I already told you," she snarled. "No. Whoever comes to kill me—il Tornja, or Kiel, or you—he's going to have to do it himself."

"And the goddess . . ."

"I hope she fucking feels it when the knife bites."

The descent from the prison took Kaden almost as long as the climb. By the time he neared his father's study, his legs wobbled beneath him and his hands felt twisted into claws from so much clutching of the railing. The simple fact that Triste was alive should have come as a relief, but despite her survival, there was no comfort in the larger picture.

Every visible future was grim. Triste killing herself without performing the *obviate,* or being killed. Il Tornja's assassins hacking off her head, or the council throwing her alive onto a pyre with a few self-righteous words about law and justice. In some futures, it was Kaden himself killing her, holding the knife when there was no one else left to hold it. He could feel the girl's blood hot on his hands, could see her angry, helpless eyes locked on him as he tried to carve the goddess free of her flesh.

He wanted nothing more, when he finally stepped from the luminous emptiness of the Spear into human floors below, than to lock himself inside his study, set aside all emotion, and drift in the *vaniate.*

Kiel, however, was still in the huge chamber, sitting motionless in the half darkness, pondering the *ko* board before him, setting the stones on the board slowly—white, then black, white, then black—working through the moves of an ancient contest first played by men or Csestriim centuries dead. Kaden watched in silence for a while, but could make no sense of it.

After a dozen moves, he shook his head, turning away from the incomprehensible game on the *ko* board, from Kiel's un-wavering gaze. For a moment, he looked at Annur; the city was even more baffling than the game of stones, the very sight of it a reproach. Kaden had survived the attack on Ashk'lan, had survived the *kenta* and the Dead Heart, had managed to over-throw Tarik Adiv, seize the Dawn Palace, establish the republic, and thwart Adare and il Tornja, and for what? Annur was in shambles, and il Tornja, according to Kiel, had managed to outmaneuver him at every juncture from hundreds of miles away. Kaden blew out a long breath, crossed to the wide wooden table, and flipped idly through the loose parchment stacked there.

Intarra knew that he tried to keep track of it all. To make sense of it. Orders for conscription, new laws intended to curb banditry and piracy, new taxes intended to fund all manner of ill-founded projects in the faltering republic. He read it all, but what did he know about any of it? What did it all—

He paused, finger on a sheet he hadn't seen before. Just a few lines of inked text. A simple signature. No seal. He shook his head in disbelief.

"What?" Kiel asked.

Kaden stared, reading the words again, and then again.

"What?" Kiel asked again.

"It wasn't a theft," he managed finally. "They didn't break in to take anything."

The Csestriim raised his brows. "Oh?"

"They broke into my study," Kaden said, raising the sheet of parchment, "to leave this."

6

At first, the steady *thock, thock, thock* of arrows striking wood was comforting. It was familiar, at least, from a thousand memories, long days training on the Islands, pulling bowstrings over and over until your shoulders ached and your fingers bled. The long warehouse in which they waited, however, was not the Islands. The air was hot and close, so dusty that breathing was difficult. Gwenna had chosen it for tactical reasons—long sight lines and redundant exits, proximity to the water if everything went to shit—but the place was beginning to feel like a trap. A fucking boring trap, but a trap all the same, and the relentless thrumming of the bowstring and thudding of arrows wasn't helping. Not anymore.

"Annick," Gwenna growled. "You think you've had enough target practice for the day?" She pointed to the arrows lodged in the timber post. "I think it's dead."

The sniper drew the bowstring, held it, then looked over. "Is there another way you think we should be spending our time while we wait?"

"What about resting? Maybe even sleeping. We *did* just break into the Dawn Palace. You're allowed to take a break, you know."

Annick watched her a moment more, then let the arrow fly. Before it struck the beam, she had another notched and drawn, and then *it* was flying. Then another.

Thock, thock, thock.

Like a woodpecker—only woodpeckers weren't that persistent. And woodpeckers didn't kill you.

Annick cocked her head to the side, studying her work. The shafts were clustered together, packed into a space the size of an eyeball. A small eyeball. If the performance gave the sniper any pleasure, she didn't show it.

"Not tired," she said, then started across the warped floorboards to reclaim her shafts.

Gwenna opened her mouth to respond, then clamped it shut. There was no point arguing with Annick. If she wasn't tired, she wasn't tired. Gwenna herself was exhausted. She felt like she'd been exhausted forever, since fleeing the Qirins, at least. The last nine months should have been a rest, of sorts. After the battle of Andt-Kyl, all three of them had been busted up, and bad. One of the Urghul had put half a lance through Annick's leg. Talal had three broken fingers, three broken ribs, and a fractured scapula—all, presumably, from the final blast that had crippled Balendin. That same blast had sent a chunk of stone into the side of Gwenna's skull, and another into her leg, fracturing it just above the knee.

They should have been dead, all of them. Those wounds would have killed anyone else. Talal had some theory, though, about how the slarn egg protected them, made them more resilient and faster healing. Gwenna didn't feel fucking resilient. None of them, in the immediate wake of the battle, could walk more than a quarter mile at a stretch, and Gwenna kept passing out when she moved too quickly. They searched slowly and futilely for Valyn. After a month, there was nothing left to search, not if they didn't intend to scour every bit of forest south of the Romsdals.

The three of them had found an abandoned cabin southeast of Andt-Kyl, some hunter's shack or outlaw's hovel already gone half to seed. They had hunkered down and worked really hard for the next few months on just not dying. That task had proven a good sight harder than any of them expected, and by the end of it—after months trying to lie still in between hacking up blood, of washing and dressing wounds, of living off the mushrooms they could gather within a few paces of the cabin and whatever birds Annick could bring down with her flatbow—the three of them looked more like corpses than warriors.

It meant months of convalescence, the rest of the summer and fall—walking before she could run, floating before she could swim, lifting the fucking swords before there was any point in trying to swing them—before Gwenna felt even half qualified to call herself a Kettral once more. An entire summer and fall gone before they could even contemplate going anywhere or killing anyone. Gwenna had no idea where to go or who to kill, but it seemed like they were going to need to do plenty of both. When they were finally whole enough to travel, the snow was already piled up to the eaves. Covering half a mile took half a day. And so, for *another* season, they were forced to hunker down, live off of venison stew, and try not to kill one another.

The extra winter months up north weren't all bad. It meant they were all fully healed before heading south, at least as strong and quick as they had been back on the Islands, wounds that should not have closed at all finally knitted. The disadvantage was that the rest of the world hadn't been convalescing inside a snowbound cottage for nine months, and when Gwenna, Talal, and Annick finally emerged, they had no idea what the fuck was going on.

Nothing good—that much was clear as soon as they broke free of the northern forests. The Urghul were everywhere, burning shit, killing people, erecting altars to their suffering and their god, generally getting blood on everything. Worse, Balendin was still alive. Gwenna had hoped that somehow, in the chaos and carnage of Andt-Kyl, the traitorous Kettral leach would have taken a blade to the brain. It seemed plausible, at least, given the twin Annurian armies that had swept up the coasts of Scar Lake.

Hope, as usual, proved to be a miserable bitch.

They weren't even out of the woods before they started hearing reports of an Urghul commander who was not Urghul, a man with dark skin and dark hair, a leach with black eagles perched on either shoulder, a warrior whose thirst for blood outstripped even that of the Urghul. The horsemen called him the Anvil, but it was obviously Balendin. He couldn't be fought, people whispered. Couldn't be defeated. He could light whole forests ablaze with a wave of his hand, could snap his fingers and watch the heads of his foes explode.

"We could kill him," Annick had suggested.

Gwenna had mulled it over. It was tempting, but following your temptations was a good way to get dead.

"No," she said finally, "we can't."

"Why not?"

"Because we don't have a bird and we don't have a full Wing."

"You don't need a bird or a full Wing to kill a man."

Talal had shaken his head at that. "He's not just a man, Annick. His power—it's self-fulfilling. Everyone across the north is terrified of him, and all that terror just makes him stronger." His face was sober. "The things he could do back on the Islands, or even in Andt-Kyl . . . those were nothing."

"He should be punished," Annick insisted.

"He will be punished," Gwenna said, "but since it looks like we're the ones who are going to have to do the punishing, let's try to get it right the first time, eh? We need a bird, we need more people, and we need to know what in Hull's name is going on."

"Where are we going to get all that?" Annick asked.

"We're going to start by finding Valyn's brother and beating some answers out of him," Gwenna replied. "Which means we're going to Annur."

She had steeled herself for an argument, for Annick to demand an attack on Balendin, or for Talal to insist on an immediate return to the Qirins.

Instead, Talal nodded. "All right," he said quietly. "Annur."
Annick just shrugged.

It was disconcerting, this deference, unsettling. Gwenna
wasn't the Wing's commander—with Valyn and Laith dead, there
was barely even a Wing left to command—but the other two,
for reasons she couldn't begin to fathom, had started accepting
her decisions as though they were orders, as though she weren't
just making it all up as she went along, as though she had some
larger, more coherent vision in mind beyond just keeping them
alive from one day to the next. Which she most certainly did
not.

It didn't make any sense. Talal and Annick were both better
soldiers than Gwenna. Annick was already a legend among the
Kettral snipers, and Talal—though he lacked Annick's obvious,
ostentatious skill—had a good military mind and was cool
enough to use it, even when the world was burning down around
him. Either one of them could have commanded their truncated
abortion of a Wing better than Gwenna herself . . . and yet they
didn't.

Annick might argue some small tactical issue, but mostly she
seemed to want to oil her bow and take target practice. Talal
would actually say more than two or three words on a given
topic, but he seemed to prefer advising to leading. And so
Gwenna ended up making the choices, despite the fact that she
had no fucking idea what she was doing. The whole situation
made her itchy, twitchy, irritable, but what could you do?
Someone had to make the 'Kent-kissing decisions.

And so they came to Annur, set up shop inside the warehouse,
cased the Dawn Palace, broke into it, then into the Spear,
knocked out the Aedolians guarding what was supposed to be
Kaden's personal study, planted the note, and slipped out. The
whole thing, as it turned out, was ludicrously, stupidly easy. The
problem with having the largest fortress in the world was just
that: it was fucking *large*. There were thousands of men and
women inside, maybe ten thousand: bureaucrats to push the

papers, masons to fix the walls, gardeners to keep the plants in line, petitioners dumb enough to think anyone in charge actually gave a pickled shit about their fishing rights or rice supplies or guild licenses or whatever. With a minimal amount of planning and improvisation, you could pretty much go anywhere you wanted. With a little more effort, Gwenna felt pretty sure they could have killed Kaden or any of the other members of the council, but she didn't want to kill him. At least not yet. Not until she had a better sense of what in Hull's name was going on.

"You think he found the note?" she asked of no one in particular, scanning the dim space of the warehouse as though the answer might be hidden between the dusty crates.

Annick ignored her, probably because Gwenna had asked the question a dozen times already.

"If he hasn't yet," Talal replied, "I think he will soon. That monastic training . . ." He shook his head. "Evidently they can remember everything, remember it perfectly."

"But do you think he'll know what it *means*?"

"I think," Annick broke in, tugging her arrows from the wooden post, checking the shafts and the fletching one by one, "that there's nothing we can do about Kaden now. What's important is focusing on our own readiness in case he does come."

Gwenna blew out an exasperated breath. "Fuck, Annick. How much more ready do you want to be? I've got every door and window rigged, that post you're shooting at is ready to blow, we've packed enough steel into those crates," she gestured toward the wall, "that Talal should be able to . . ." She squinted at the leach. "What can you do with that much steel, exactly?"

Talal crossed to one of the wooden crates, set a hand on it as though it were a woodstove he was testing for heat. After a moment he turned, hand still on the crate, narrowed his eyes, and then Annick's arrows, gathered in her fist like a deadly bouquet, leapt free, aligned themselves into a hovering phalanx, then hung quivering in the air.

The sniper didn't flinch. "Don't break them," she said.

Talal flicked a finger, and the arrows flew the length of the warehouse, burying themselves in the far wooden wall. It was enough to see him burned alive in almost any part of Annur outside the Qirins; enough to see him burned alive, but hardly an overwhelming display of military force.

Gwenna frowned. "Is that it?"

"It's not as easy as it looks."

"I'm sure it's not. But we already have Annick to shoot the arrows. I was hoping you could, I don't know . . ."

"Raze entire towns?" Talal suggested. "Build bridges on thin air?"

"Both might come in handy, yes."

He shook his head. "I'm not Balendin, Gwenna. With a few crates of steel here, I can help, but my well is never going to be the crucial factor in a fight. I'd rather trust to these," he said, reaching over his shoulder to touch one of his twin blades, then shrugged. "Hopefully we won't need any of it. There's no reason for Kaden to distrust us."

Gwenna snorted. "I'm starting to think that people don't need reasons. The thing is—"

A low, metallic chime brought her up short. It wasn't loud, but it didn't have to be. Ever since she'd rigged the belled line the day before, she'd been waiting for it to ring, listening with one ear even when she was asleep. The fact that it was ringing now meant someone had finally come. She hoped to Hull it was Kaden. She hoped she wouldn't have to kill him.

She turned toward the other two Kettral, but before she could even start to give the orders, Annick and Talal had flanked the door, slipping silently back between the piled crates to either side, the sniper with her bow half drawn, the leach with one of his short blades naked in his hand. A few steps took Gwenna herself to the wooden post where she had tacked up the ends of the wicks leading to her various munitions. She lit one, a slow-burner, measured the distance to the charges strung up around the doorway—two dozen paces—then walked that same distance, easily outdistancing the hissing fuse.

The bells rang again softly just as she reached the doors. She slid the belt knife from the sheath at her waist, glanced over her shoulder to check on Talal and Annick, flipped open the long iron latch holding the twin doors shut, then stepped back. With an aggrieved shriek, the doors swung ponderously open. A moment later, a hooded figure stepped inside, paused when he saw Gwenna standing just a pace away, smoke steel at the ready, then turned to push the doors shut, latching them in place behind him.

Give it to the fucker, Gwenna thought. *He knows how to keep cool.*

"Hello, Gwenna," the figure said, turning back to her, then pushing the hood clear of his face.

It was Kaden. She remembered him well enough from the Bone Mountains, and even if she hadn't, there was no mistaking those burning eyes. It was Kaden, but the intervening months had changed him. His cheeks were less lean than they had been, his whole frame fuller. It made sense—governing a republic didn't shave the fat from the bones in the same way as running up and down mountains in the middle of winter. Anyone would get soft after a few months living in Annur.

But he's not soft, she thought, careful to keep still as she studied him.

Regardless of the extra flesh, there was something about Kaden that looked . . . pared down. Hardened. Gwenna had known plenty of hard women and men over the years, killers willing and more than willing to lay waste to whole villages if it meant finishing out the mission. Kaden didn't stand like a fighter, didn't carry himself with the poise of the Kettral or the Skullsworn, but for all the flame in those Malkeenian eyes, they made her shiver. Not that she could show him that.

"Hello, Kaden."

"You caused quite a stir in the palace."

"I thought we were admirably restrained."

"The Aedolian Guard was convinced that il Tornja had finally sent a legion of assassins." He shrugged. "So was I."

"Assassins would have done more killing," Gwenna said. "Your Aedolian Guard is worse than useless, by the way. You should have them replaced."

"With whom? Almost every soldier in Annur is in the field already, fighting Adare's troops, or the Urghul, or the Waist tribes, or trying to keep order in what's left of the empire. Trying and failing. We don't have the numbers to spare."

"You don't need numbers. One Wing of Kettral would be more useful than all those hundreds of clanking idiots."

Kaden hesitated. For the first time since stepping into the warehouse, he appeared unsure what to say.

"What?" Gwenna demanded.

"Where's Valyn?" Kaden turned slowly in place, looking up into the rafters, scanning the haphazardly stacked goods. Gwenna gritted her teeth. She'd known this conversation was coming, but she didn't have to like it.

"He's dead." The words came out wrong, all hard and indifferent, but Kaden was a grown fucking man. He didn't need the truth spooned out with a helping of honey. "He died trying to kill Ran il Tornja."

For a few heartbeats, she thought he hadn't heard her. He kept studying those barrels and crates as though he expected his brother to step out from between them. Or maybe he had heard what she said, but thought the whole thing was some kind of fucked-up trick or test. Gwenna was still trying to come up with something else to say, ideally something that might convince and comfort him at the same time, when he turned back to her, those cold eyes bright as a fire's heart.

"You're sure?"

"As sure as you can be with these things. We never found the body, but all of Andt-Kyl was bloody as a butcher's floor."

"Then there's a chance—"

"That's what I thought," Gwenna replied, cutting him off roughly. "Until now."

Kaden watched her in silence. "You think he would have come here," he said finally.

"I'm certain of it. The only thing I can't figure is how il Tornja beat him. I understand that the bastard's a great general, but tactical smarts aren't the same thing as skill with a sword."

"He's not just a general," Kaden replied.

"What does that mean?"

Kaden exhaled slowly. "There's a lot that we need to discuss."

Gwenna glanced at the closed door behind him.

"Are you alone?"

"More or less."

"I was hoping for *yes*."

"But you weren't expecting it."

"I've learned not to get my hopes up."

"They have orders to stay outside. To stay out of sight."

"Orders are wonderful things," Gwenna replied, stepping past Kaden to throw down the heavy bar over the two doors. "But you'll forgive me if I back them up with a little bit of steel."

She studied his reaction as the bar slammed into place. Or rather, she studied his lack of reaction. Most people, even Kettral, would be edgy walking alone into a closed, locked space controlled by trained soldiers of questionable allegiance. It was starting to seem, however, that *edgy* was a little beyond the scope of Kaden's emotional register.

He nodded toward the doors. "That bar doesn't seem like much. Are you sure it's safe in here?"

Gwenna watched him a moment longer, then turned, sending her knife spinning across the room in an easy overhand toss. It severed the thin, dark fuse that she had laid atop the baseboard of the warehouse.

"Now it is."

Kaden raised his brows. "What was that about?"

Gwenna just pointed at the fuse. A few heartbeats later, the flame emerged from behind a line of crates, bright as a tiny star, hissing quietly, snaking its way along the cable until it reached the knife, the break. It sputtered for a moment, then went out.

"Munitions," Kaden observed.

Gwenna just nodded.

"What would have happened if you let it burn?"

"Less talking," she replied grimly. "More screaming."

Kaden studied the knife for a moment, then followed the dark line of the fuse to the charges tacked up on the posts to both sides of the door.

"Seems risky."

Gwenna barked a laugh. "Risky would be *not* rigging the place. Last time we met everybody got along all right, but that was last time. You've made some . . . unexpected political decisions. I've got no way to be sure you don't have another Kettral Wing getting ready to smash through that door while we chat, do I?"

Kaden turned back to her, face grave. "Where have you been, these past nine months?"

"Around," Gwenna replied, waving a hand airily.

He stared at her. "You don't know, do you?"

"Don't know what?"

"There *are* no more Kettral, Gwenna. The Eyrie's wiped out."

The words were like a brick to the face.

"That's ludicrous. No one would ever go after the Eyrie. Who could destroy an island packed with Kettral?"

Kaden met her stare. "Other Kettral," he replied grimly. "Your order destroyed itself."

"Half the Kettral backed the empire," Kaden said, spreading his hands. "Half backed the new republic. The whole thing was over in three days."

The low stone basement of the warehouse in which they had

gathered suddenly seemed cramped and stifling, the still air almost too thick to breathe. Annick and Talal stood at the two entrances, both with weapons drawn, but for the moment they both appeared to have forgotten their posts, turning in to stare at Kaden.

Gwenna shook her head. "I don't believe it. If the Kettral are really gone, then who *told* you this 'Kent-kissing story in the first place?"

"A few made it out," Kaden said. "A woman named Daveen Shaleel flew in on a bird a few days after the fight. The creature died a day later, along with one of her Wingmates. Weeks after *that,* one more soldier showed up. Someone named Gent, all alone in a rowboat. He claimed to have rowed it all the way from the Qirins."

"Where are they now? Shaleel and Gent?"

"Daveen Shaleel is down in the Waist. We put her in charge of the legions there. According to the reports, she's about the only thing keeping the entire front from collapsing. Last I heard of Gent, he was on a ship charged with finding and sinking pirates."

"They were the only two?" Gwenna asked, her voice little more than a whisper.

Kaden met her gaze. "Shaleel said a few others got away. Maybe a bird or two. Scattered. No one knows where they went."

Gwenna could feel herself staring. The whole Eyrie— destroyed. It seemed impossible. The Islands were the safest place in the world, the only chunk of land that no kingdom or empire would ever dream of attacking. But then, Kaden's story wasn't one of kingdoms and empires.

"It makes sense," Talal said quietly.

Gwenna turned on him.

"It may turn out to be true, but what about this insane story makes *sense*?"

"Think it through, Gwenna. Put yourself in the shoes of the

Wings back on the Islands: you know your foe has the same training as you. You know that, just like you, she has birds. You know that, just like you, she's got enough weapons and munitions to storm a small city."

"And she'll do it," Annick said, voice flat. "That's the important point."

Talal nodded. "You know that she'll attack you, because it's exactly what you would do."

"Would," Gwenna pointed out, "is not the same as *will.* These are men and women who've lived on the same island, fought on the same side their entire *lives.* If they'd bothered to talk it through for half an afternoon, they could have found a way around it."

"Talking's a risk," Annick said. "If you come to talk, and they come to fight, you lose."

"I'll tell you when you *lose,"* Gwenna spat. "You lose when the entire 'Kent-kissing Eyrie destroys itself."

"That's true," Talal said. "But to talk, you need to trust." He shook his head. "The Eyrie taught us plenty, but trust wasn't a big part of the curriculum."

"Fuck," Gwenna said, shaking her head, turning her attention back to Kaden. "Fuck."

If he was bothered by the fate of the Eyrie, it didn't show.

"Actually," he said after a moment, "it's lucky for us."

"Lucky?" Gwenna growled. "How is it lucky, you son of a bitch?"

"I'm sorry for your friends," Kaden replied, "for the loss of the people you knew, but if il Tornja had the Kettral, if he had them intact and loyal, we'd be finished, dead. There'd be no standing against him."

"Maybe that wouldn't be such a bad thing," Gwenna retorted. "I've got no love for the *kenarang,* but everything we've heard on the march south suggests this republic of yours is even more useless than Adare's rump of an empire. At least she and il Tornja are holding back the 'Kent-kissing Urghul."

Kaden frowned. "The Urghul aren't the only threat. Nor are they the greatest."

"Spoken by someone who's never been an Urghul prisoner." Gwenna stabbed a finger at him across the table. "We all spent weeks in their camp. Long Fist, may Ananshael fuck him bloody, forced Annick and me to take part in their sick little rituals." She shook her head, unable to speak for a moment, faced with the full folly of Kaden's idiocy. "Maybe you don't know this," she managed finally, "because you've been perched atop your throne—"

"The Unhewn Throne is no longer in use," he said, cutting her off. "And I am not the Emperor any longer."

"How convenient for you. If you were the Emperor, you'd probably already know that Balendin is with them." She cocked an eyebrow. "Remember Balendin?"

Kaden nodded. "The emotion leach. The Kettral."

"Yeah, except he's not Kettral any longer. The bastard has gone over entirely to the Urghul."

"We heard something about one of Long Fist's deputies. A leach. There was no reliable information."

"Well, here's some information: Long Fist is a sick, dangerous bastard, and Balendin is at *least* as bad. He's only getting more powerful as his legend spreads. . . ." She waved a hand at Talal. "You explain it."

Talal studied Kaden a moment. "You know that Balendin is an emotion leach. That he draws his power from the feelings of others, especially feelings directed at him by those physically close to him."

Kaden nodded again. "I remember our fight in the Bone Mountains."

"Except in the Bone Mountains there were only a few of us to give him strength," Talal said grimly. "Now he has hundreds, thousands. His legend grows every day and with that legend grows his strength. If he breaks through the northern front, it will only get worse. By the time he reaches Annur, he will be as powerful as Arim Hua, as powerful as the greatest of the Atmani. Maybe more so."

"And *this*," Gwenna cut in, "is the threat that you think might not be so bad as Ran il Tornja, who, as far as I can fucking tell, is the only one holding these bastards back."

"I didn't realize . . . ," Kaden began, then fell silent.

There was something new behind those burning eyes, some imperceptible change in the way he held himself. Gwenna tried to pinpoint what she was seeing. Anger? Fear? Before she could put a name to the expression, it was gone.

"So why is it," she pressed, "that you think your sister and her general are so dangerous?"

"Perhaps they are not," he admitted quietly. "Not compared to the threat you've described."

Gwenna watched him warily. She was asking him to see past his hatred of the man who had killed his father, past his jealousy of the sister who had stolen his throne. It was no small demand. At best, she had thought, it would take hours to convince him, if such convincing were even possible. Instead, he seemed to have absorbed the new facts in a matter of moments.

"But you're still determined to carry on this war against Adare," she said, shaking her head.

"No, in fact."

"Meaning what?"

"Meaning that the council has offered her a truce. More than a truce—a treaty. An offer to end all hostilities. She will be reinstalled on the Unhewn Throne with all her titles and honors while the council will retain legislative authority."

"Meaning you make the laws and she enforces them?"

Kaden nodded.

"It won't work," Annick said from the doorway, not bothering to look over her shoulder.

Kaden turned to her. "Why not?"

"Whoever has the power will destroy whoever doesn't."

"The treaty divides power between us."

"Divided power," Gwenna snorted. "That sounds promising."

"A moment ago," Kaden replied, "you were urging me to make peace with Adare and Ran il Tornja."

"I was hoping for an arrangement that might last more than a week."

Kaden didn't respond. Instead, he watched her over the table for what felt like a very long time. Gwenna held his gaze, resisted the impulse to fill the empty space with words. If he could sit with the silence, then so could she.

"Why did you come back here?" he asked finally. "To Annur?"

"To learn what was really happening." She hesitated, then told him the rest. "And to be sure that Valyn wasn't here, wasn't still alive somehow."

"And now that you know what's happening," Kaden asked quietly, "now that you know that Valyn's dead, what will you do?"

There was no sign that Valyn's death bothered him.

Gwenna glanced over her shoulder at Annick, met Talal's gaze for a moment, then turned back to Kaden. "I'll need to discuss it with the Wing."

"What if I could furnish you with a ship back to the Islands?"

"The fight's coming here," Annick broke in from the doorway. "Not to the Eyrie."

Kaden nodded. "And it would help us to win that fight if we had birds. Even two or three could make an enormous difference. We could have accurate reports of troop movements, could convey orders from army to army more quickly, could even attempt to get at . . . Long Fist, or Balendin, without going through the entire Urghul army."

Gwenna studied his impassive face, then turned away, staring at the swirling dust motes, trying to sift her emotions from her reasoning.

"It makes sense," Talal said at last. "Any birds that survived the battle will stay on the Islands. They won't leave their roosts."

"I could get you a ship," Kaden added. "Ready to sail on the morning tide."

Gwenna shook her head angrily. "A ship will take forever, and Annick's right. The fight is coming *here,* it is coming *now.* Why didn't you send someone nine months ago?"

"We did," Kaden said, meeting her gaze. "We've sent half a dozen expeditions."

"And?"

"And none of them returned."

"What happened to them?" Talal asked.

Kaden shook his head. "We have no idea."

"Let me get this straight," Gwenna said. "You sent *Daveen Shaleel* back to the Islands to recover birds and she just fucking *disappeared?*"

"No. Shaleel wanted to go, but the council refused. She was the highest-ranking Kettral to survive, to return to Annur. Even without a bird or a full Wing, she's too valuable to risk."

"But we're expendable," Gwenna said.

Kaden met her gaze. "Yes. You're expendable." He raised his brows. "Will you go?"

"Well, shit." She turned to her Wing. "Talal? Annick?"

"I don't see that we have any other choice," the leach replied gravely.

Annick just nodded.

Gwenna studied them both a moment. Once again, it was up to her to make the final 'Kent-kissing choice.

"Fine," she said finally. "Whatever's waiting there, it can't kill us unless we fuck up."

7

"Twenty paces," Lehav insisted grimly. "With weapons ready to hand."

Adare shook her head. "Fifty paces. No swords visible."

"That's insane. A mob could kill you a dozen times over before my men got close enough to help."

"It would have to be a very efficient mob, Lehav. Either that, or you brought a hundred of your slowest men."

The soldier had pointed out half a dozen times that his new name, the name given to him by the goddess Intarra in a dream, was Vestan Ameredad—the Shield of the Faithful. She continued to use the name he had given her when they first met, both of them in mud up to the ankles, down in Annur's Perfumed Quarter.

Shielding the faithful was all well and good, but Adare was surrounded by people with new names, new identities, surrounded by lies and lives meticulously tailored to cover the truth and obscure the past. Lehav, at least, she could call by the name his mother had given him when he was still bloody and squirming, before he ever heard of Annur, or Intarra, or Adare herself. A given name was a strange thing to insist on, but it struck Adare as a sort of honesty, and there weren't so many truths lying around that she could afford to give them up.

He was young, this commander of the Sons of Flame—maybe half a dozen years older than Adare herself—but he had a soldier's hands and a zealot's eyes. Adare had watched him whip his men for laxity and blasphemy, had seen him kneeling in prayer in the Aergad snow during the dawn hour and at dusk, had glimpsed him from her tower running his circuits of the walls, breath steaming in the icy air. She remembered their meeting in Olon almost a year earlier, when he had threatened to feed her to the flames. He might be young, but he was harder than most men she had met, and he approached his duty as her guardian with the same cold fervor he brought to the rest of his life.

Now, staring at her, he shook his head. "The five score men you allowed me are my most reliable, but they are five score against the population of an entire city. Your Radiance."

The honorific still came slowly to the commander of the Sons of Flame. There was no disrespect in the words, but most of the time, as now, they sounded like an afterthought, a title to which he remained more or less indifferent.

It was a good reminder, if Adare needed a reminder, of the complexity of her situation. Il Tornja and the legions fought for her because she was a Malkeenian, the only Malkeenian left who seemed willing to sit the Unhewn Throne. Lehav, however, and all the Sons of Flame, retained their old distrust of the empire. They followed Adare because of what had happened at the Everburning Well, because of the tracery of shining scar laid into her flesh, for the flames in her eyes. It was Intarra's touch upon her that they trusted. The empire she was working so hard to preserve was incidental at best, disposable.

"Whatever we've been doing in Aergad for the past nine months," Adare went on, "Annur is my city, my capital. I grew up here."

"So did I," he replied, "and I learned early not to trust it. Not Annur. Not Annurians."

"Good," Adare said, eyes on the city sprawled out to the south. "Your job isn't to trust people—it's to keep me safe."

That, too, was a change. There was a score of Aedolian

guardsmen in Aergad, men Fulton had swept up when passing through Annur almost a year earlier. Adare had no cause to fault their devotion or their service, but after Aats-Kyl, they worried her.

According to Valyn, a contingent of Aedolians had come for Kaden, had murdered close to two hundred monks in a failed effort to kill him. Fulton, the Aedolian who had watched over her since childhood, had proven his loyalty a dozen times over, proven it with his death. The others, however, were just so many vaguely familiar faces, a lot of big men in bright armor. Aedolians swore to guard the imperial family, but Adare had not forgotten that it was Ran il Tornja, hundreds of years earlier and wearing a different name, who had founded the Aedolian Guard.

The Sons of Flame, on the other hand, were *hers;* she had risked everything to make peace with them in Olon, and they had followed her north, first to fight il Tornja, then in a desperate scramble to stop the Urghul. For nearly a year now they had marched beneath her banner, sung their hymns and offered their prayers as they guarded her in camp and castle, bled and died for their goddess of light and for Adare, the woman they believed to be Intarra's prophet. And so the Sons of Flame had come south, to Annur, while the Aedolians were conscripted into their own unit to fight the Urghul.

The march to Annur had been exhausting, and not just physically. The long miles between Aergad and the capital offered a catalogue of the ways in which Adare had failed her empire. Though it was spring, half the fields they had passed lay fallow—the farmers fled, whether from the Urghul or the threat of banditry, Adare couldn't say. Three towns they passed had been burned to the ground, and nearly every day they passed bodies, some rotting silently in ditches, some hung from the limbs of blackpines. In most cases, it was impossible to say whether the killings had been crimes or rough justice.

Not that it mattered. Annur was collapsing; and though Adare dreaded her arrival in the capital, dreaded the fate she might face there, with each mile she grew more convinced of the necessity of her return, of the need to try, at least, to heal the horrible rift cleaving her nation. Every body they passed was a spur in her side, every burned farm a reproach urging her to hurry, hurry. Now that they had arrived, it was time to see if she would survive her precipitous return.

· "You have a hundred men, Lehav," Adare said quietly. "Enough to protect me on the road, but not here."

"If we are closer," he said, "we can set up a viable cordon—"

She cut him off, laying a hand on his shoulder. "Lehav. If a mob of ten thousand is waiting on those city streets to rend me limb from limb, you can't stop them. It doesn't matter how close your men are walking."

The words were light, but they belied the cramp in her stomach. She had almost forgotten, after nine months' exile in Aergad, just how *big* the empire's capital really was, a sprawl of temples and towers, homes and hovels that spread across half the Neck. You could enter the city in Westgate and walk east along the Godsway for the better part of a morning before reaching the Dawn Palace, red walls sloping down into the lapping waters of the Broken Bay; the north-south avenues were nearly as long.

Of course, it hadn't always been Annur, not all of it. From where Adare stood in the middle of the Imperial Road she could still make out the older clusters of buildings folded into the hollows. They had been towns of their own once—Hundred Bloom, Jade, Old Cranes and New Crane—each with its own market square and cluster of squat temples, independent, each ruled by a lord or merchant council or mayor before the city of Annur, gorged on its own success, swallowed them up.

Now the land between those old hamlets, land that had been used for crop and pasturage a hundred years earlier, housed a new wave of settlement—rough shacks and taverns tacked up in haphazard neighborhoods that had, over the course of decades, settled into their own illogic, new homes built on the foundations of the old, the roofs of covered markets spanning the space between until all the land south of her and east to the sea's faint haze was an unbroken façade of human habitation: Annur's northern face.

Adare could study that face all day long. The trouble was, she couldn't see anything *past* it. The flat cropland in which she stood afforded no vantage to look down on the city, to see past the homes of these most recent immigrants, to spy on the heart of the capital. She could see the meager houses shoved one against the next, the flash from the distant towers, the slant and pitch of palace roofs on the slopes of the Graves, copper gone green with verdigris, and then, above it all, stuck like a bright knife in the sky's wide belly—Intarra's Spear.

Ruddy afternoon light gleamed on the tower's glassy walls, reflected and refracted until the entire Spear glowed yellow-orange as though lit from within. Adare craned her neck. The tower's top, so often lost in cloud or fog off the Broken Bay, was visible today, whittled thin as a needle's tip by the impossible distance between it and the city sprawled below. Adare had stood atop that needle dozens of times, had stood there to see the ceremonial fires lit for the solstice twice each year, and once, as a small girl, to watch as her father ordered the city burned. It seemed unreal now, as though the tower were not her home but someplace foreign, unimaginably distant, a relic from another land, another life.

Adare turned away from the Spear to confront Lehav once more.

"I trust you," she said quietly. "I trust your men, and above all I trust in the will of the goddess."

It wasn't true, not really, but it was the sort of statement Lehav would usually accept. This time, though, he shook his head.

"There should be no comparison between the trust you place in the goddess and that you have invested in me." He gestured to the city. "If I stood at your shoulder throughout the entire negotiation I could not guarantee your safety. There are too many variables, too many lines of attack, too many—"

Adare cut him off. "That is exactly the point I am making."

The words brought him up short.

She tried to soften her voice before continuing. "I don't need a guarantee, Lehav. We will do, both of us, what we can do, but it is Intarra who will see fit to preserve us, or she will not. I need you to keep the Sons back, mostly out of sight, because when I ride into the city I need the people of Annur to witness an emperor, confident and sure, returning to her home."

"Emperors have guards. Your father did not ride down the center of the Godsway unattended."

"My father had the luxury of a stable reign. He was secure on his throne. He could afford to be careless with his image."

Careless, in truth, was not the best word to ascribe to her father. Sanlitun had been a deliberate, contemplative ruler, even a cautious one. Adare, however, could not afford caution. She'd been out of the city for nearly a year, and not a day of her absence had gone by without the 'Shael-spawned council spreading some sort of vicious rumor about her. Her spies had been reluctant to tell her most of it at first, worrying, not without reason, that even to speak such slanders openly before an emperor might cost them their posts, their lives. Adare, however, had insisted on the unvarnished truth. If she was to serve the people, to rule them, she needed to understand what they thought—and so she heard it all:

She was il Tornja's whore, the sex-mad puppet of a shrewd general. She was a leach who had used her power to kill Uinian and then, later, to fake a miracle at the Everburning Well. She had murdered Sanlitun herself, luring her father into the Temple of Light to stab him while he prayed. She was bankrolled by Anthera, or the Manjari, or the Federated Cities—the specifics changed with each speaker—bent on the overthrow of Annur, determined to see the empire delivered into the hands of her ancient foes.

The endless lies were exhausting, infuriating. To hear, after nine months defending Annur from the Urghul, that she was an agent bent on Annur's destruction made her want to scream, to seize someone by the throat and start shaking, to bring half a dozen of the 'Kent-kissing horsemen back to the capital and let them loose in the streets just so the bastards could *see* the horror that she was working day and night to hold at bay.

Her knuckles ached, and she looked down to find her hands strangling the reins, twisting them until the leather dug into her skin. Slowly, she relaxed her grip. The fault lay with the council, not with the people of Annur. You could hardly blame the city's shopkeepers and washermen, artisans and builders, for being taken in by the lies of their leaders. They hadn't been to the north, after all. They didn't know Adare, couldn't observe the workings of her mind. Most of them, if they'd ever caught a glimpse of a Malkeenian at all, had seen her in some imperial procession, glimpsed for a moment from behind a writhing mob, through a cordon of guards and soldiers.

She was riding alone now to fix that. To show herself.

She took a long breath, then looked over at Lehav, wondering how much of her agitation he'd noticed. If the man had been watching her, he was looking at the city now. "I don't want to die," she said finally. "But we are at war, Lehav. I don't know the first thing about swords and formations, but I know you cannot win a battle without taking risks. Listen to me when I tell you this, and listen well: we will not survive this battle—not you, not me, not any of the men—if the people of this city do not look at me and see a woman who believes in herself, in her empire, and in them."

"They are fools," the man replied. "They have no idea what to believe."

Adare shook her head bleakly. "My father told me something once. I haven't forgotten it: *If the people are foolish,* he said, *it is because their leader has failed them.*"

*

For a long time no one said a word to her. She rode down the center of the bustling street in a shifting eddy of calm. Every person she passed—shopkeeps and carters, street sweepers and grocers—refused to meet her gaze. In a way, it was nothing new. Adare had lived a whole life in which people were uncomfortable around her eyes. Even high ministers and atreps preferred to drift past her without looking, fixing their own eyes elsewhere, moving just a little faster as she approached.

For a long time, this was like that—an entire city refusing to meet her gaze. They followed, though, gathering like birds at a scattering of crumbs, holding back at what seemed a safe distance, whispering, hissing, arguing almost inaudibly, dozens then scores drawn from their day's affairs by the possibility of celebration or bloodshed.

Let it be celebration, Adare prayed.

It was not.

By the time she reached the Godsway—riding out toward the massive marble statue of Anlatun before turning east—word of her arrival had spread, the cluster trailing her swollen to a crowd. More and more people flooded in from side streets and alleys, skidding to a halt when they finally spotted her, pulling back, falling suddenly silent. Everyone seemed to experience the same shock, as though they hadn't believed the words of their neighbors—*The last Malkeenian. Alone in the city. Riding south.* That shock, however, was fading, and the mob was drawing closer.

As she angled down the Godsway, Adare's heart throbbed behind her ribs. She'd lost sight of Lehav and his Sons. They were out there somewhere, lost in the tide of humanity, close enough to hear her if she screamed, probably, but too far away to do any good. She was starting to question her wisdom in keeping them back, but there was no time for questions. She had returned to Annur. A thousand eyes were upon her. Two thousand. Five. There was no counting them. The voices were getting louder, too, so loud she could barely hear her gelding's hooves clopping over the enormous flagstones. She fought down the urge to wipe her sweaty palms against her robes, kept her eyes forward, fixed on Intarra's Spear in the distance.

At least I didn't bring Sanlitun. The thought calmed her. Whatever happened next, whatever came of the growing mob, her son was hundreds of miles away in Aergad, tucked behind the castle walls with Nira watching over him. *He is safe,* Adare reminded herself.

Then the first stone struck.

It hit her just above the eye—a hot, white explosion that knocked her halfway off her horse. For a moment, it was all Adare could do to stay upright, to see anything beyond the pain's brilliant blaze. She managed to keep her saddle either by good luck, divine favor, or sheer force of will. Blood ran down the side of her face in a hot sheet. Her stomach clenched, heaved; she thought she would vomit. Then, when she had fought that down, she realized they were chanting, shouting again and again the same terrible word: *Tyrant. Tyrant. Tyrant.*

Her horse tried to bolt, but she pulled the reins back tight. If the mob thought she was trying to flee, they would tear her apart. She wanted to cringe, to curl into herself, to cover her bloody face with her arms before someone threw the next stone. Instead, when she'd managed to bring the horse back under control, she let go of the reins and spread her hands slowly, her unarmored body an offering to the crowd. They quieted a moment, and she spoke into that quiet.

"You call me a tyrant. Does a tyrant return alone and unarmed to a city that hates her?"

The words couldn't have reached more than a dozen paces, but Adare could see the effect on those closest. They looked confused, hesitant, as though suddenly wishing they were farther back, away from the center of whatever storm was about to break. The mob pressed them forward all the same, forcing them, with its sheer weight, to step closer.

Never speak to a crowd. Her father's words, measured and

steady. *Especially not a crowd of thousands. Always speak to a single person.*

Pain hazing her vision, Adare picked one at random, a gaunt, middle-aged woman carrying a basket on her hip, just one of Annur's millions dragged along by her own curiosity. Adare clung to that woman's stare when she spoke again as though it were a post holding her up, a spear to lean on.

"My generals told me to bring an army, but I did not bring an army. My guardsmen urged me to ring myself with their steel; I refused. My councillors implored me to return to Annur in disguise, or in the middle of the night, sneaking through the streets with my eyes hidden, my face obscured." She raised her chin a fraction. The blood was hot on her face. Her head throbbed. She wondered if she was going to fall out of the saddle after all. "I did not. I will not."

The next rock grazed her chin. A third stone, smaller than the first two but sharp as a knife, sliced her cheek just below the eye. Her face was awash in blood now. It dripped onto the sleeves of her robe, onto the leather of her saddle. The horse, sensing the rage of the crowd, was starting to shy beneath her once more, snorting heavily and tossing his head, searching for a way out.

The poor beast didn't understand the truth, *couldn't* understand, in the dim workings of his animal mind, that there *was* no way out. There never had been. Not since Adare fled the Dawn Palace a year earlier. Not since Ran il Tornja put a knife in her father.

And now they'll kill me, Adare thought. *This is where I die, here, on the streets of the city where I was born.*

The packed savagery of the mob had grown too heavy. Any moment now, all those bodies would surge forward to collapse the fragile space in which she rode. Another stone would fly, and another, and another, until the blow that finally knocked her from the saddle. Her horse snorted again, on the edge of panic. Adare urged the beast on with her heels—better to die moving forward than standing still. One step. Then another. And to her surprise, the ring of space around her held.

She tried to read some expression in the nearest faces. There was anger, and surprise, and disbelief, twisted lips, narrowed eyes, leveled fingers. A few tried to keep up the chant of *tyrant,* but most had let it go. They didn't love her, but their curiosity had overwhelmed, at least for the moment, their fury. It was an opportunity, and Adare seized it.

"I have come," she said, raising her voice, "to heal the wound in Annur's heart, to see the damage undone, even if it means my death."

"Or because the Urghul drove you from the north," jeered a man a few paces away. Huge, lopsided face. Scraggly beard. Adare met his gaze.

"My armies still hold the northern front—"

Cries of pain and surprise cut her off, the bellowing of soldiers and the pounding of hooves on stone. People turned, baffled, fear's awful flower blooming within them, and Adare turned with them, searching for the source of the sound. Horror struck through her at the sight of the men on horseback, horror that Lehav had disobeyed his orders, that he had somehow collected the Sons for a desperate charge into the sea of bodies.

As the riders drew closer, however, Adare could see that they were not the Sons of Flame after all. She stared as the mounted men drove into the mob, laying about with clubs and the flats of swords. The armor was wrong for the Sons—all steel, no bronze ornament—and there were too many of them: three hundred, maybe four, more pouring out of the side streets, battering the men and women of Annur, cursing as they worked.

They weren't trying to kill, that much was clear, but a few pounds of hard-swung steel—even the flat of a blade—could finish a man. Adare stared, aghast, as a massive charger reared back, steel-shod hooves flashing in the light, shattering a woman's skull. The man beside her screamed, a piercing wail of grief and rage as he tried to wrap the woman in his arms, to protect what was obviously past all protection. A cudgel took him in the back of the head, and he fell, still clutching the woman, both bodies disappearing under the trampling boots and the grinding hooves of the horses.

"Stop!" Adare screamed. *"Stop this!"* Nausea churned in her gut, horror obliterating all pain. *"Stop!"*

It was pointless. The mob, on the edge of murder only moments before, had crumbled, forgetting Adare entirely. All they wanted was escape. Panicked men and women stumbled into her horse, clutched at her legs, scrabbled at her bridle or saddle, tried to lift themselves clear of the violence. One man seized her by the knee, cursing as someone behind him, a boy not much older than ten, tried to shove him aside. Clinging desperately to her saddle's cantle, Adare thrashed with her trapped leg, flinging the man free, then kicking him in the face with her boot. He screamed, nose smashed, then went down beneath the feet of his fellows. Not dead, but doomed.

People dove into the small streets off the Godsway, cowered in doorways and storefronts, scrambled onto the plinths of the statues to get above the mad, killing press, and all the time the soldiers drove on, sun flashing off arms and polished armor, weapons rising and falling in the day's late light, over and over and over.

Finally, one soldier, smaller than the others, but closest to Adare, raised his cudgel, pointing at her.

"Here!" he bellowed over his shoulder. "The Malkeenian! We have her!"

It was hardly necessary to shout. It was over, Adare realized, just like that. The Godsway, ablaze with noise only moments before, had gone horribly, utterly quiet. The soldiers were closing in, but Adare barely noticed them. She stared, instead, at the dead.

Dozens of crumpled bodies littered the ground. Some moved, groaning or sobbing with the effort. Most lay still. Here was a dead boy with his arm twisted awfully awry, like a bird's broken wing. There was a broken woman, her shattered ribs thrusting white and obscene through flesh and cloth alike. Blood pooled everywhere on the wide flagstones.

The short soldier kicked his horse forward through a knot of corpses, men and women who had died holding on to each other, then reined in next to Adare. She thought briefly of running, but there was nowhere to run. Instead, she turned to face the man.

When he pulled off his helm, she saw that he was panting, sweating. Something had opened a gash just at the edge of his scalp, but he paid it no mind. His eyes, bright with the setting sun, were fixed on her.

"Were you so eager to see me dead," Adare demanded, surprised that her voice did not shake, "that you cut a path through your own people?"

The soldier hesitated, cudgel sagging in his grip. He glanced down at the bodies, then back at Adare.

"See you dead?"

"Or captured," she replied coolly. "Clapped in irons."

The man was shaking his head, slowly at first, then more vigorously, bowing in his saddle even as he protested. "No, Your Radiance. You misunderstand. The council sent us."

"I *know* the council sent you," Adare said, a sick horror sloshing in her gut. It was the only explanation.

"As soon as they heard, they sent us, scrambled up as quick as they could. You took a horrible risk, Your Radiance, arriving in the city unannounced. The moment they heard, they sent us."

Adare stared at him.

I am a fool, Adare thought bleakly, the truth a lash across the face. She was covered in blood, her face hot with it, sticky. She scrubbed a hand over her brow. It came away soaked.

"How badly are you harmed, Your Radiance?" the man asked. He was worried now, on the edge of fear.

Adare studied the blood, bright against her darker palm. She watched it a moment, then looked down at the flagstones, at the bodies strewn there, dozens of them, crushed to death, eyes bulging, limbs twisted in the awful poses of their panic.

I am a fool, and people have died for my folly.

They'd been ready to kill her, of course. Probably would have, if the soldiers hadn't arrived. It didn't matter. They were her people. Annurians. Men and women that she had sworn both privately and publicly to protect, and they were dead because she had thought, idiotically, that she could return in triumph to the city of her birth. She had thought she risked only her own life.

So very, very stupid.

"You're safe now, Your Radiance," the soldier was saying. He had slung the cudgel from his belt, was bowing low in his saddle once more. The others had arranged themselves in a cordon around her, ten men deep. What foe they expected to hold back, Adare had no idea. "You're safe with us," the soldier said again.

Adare shook her head, staring at one corpse splayed out on the ground. It was the woman, the one person in the crowd to whom she had spoken, brown eyes fixed blankly on the sky.

"Safe," Adare said. She wanted to cry, to puke, to scream, but it would not do for the Emperor of Annur to cry or scream. "Safe," she said again, more quietly this time, that single syllable rancid on her tongue.

8

Gwenna stood in the bow of the *Widow's Wish,* squinting toward the horizon. Though it was clear overhead, storm and the coming of night had bruised the eastern sky a livid purple darker than the sea itself. She couldn't make out any land above the low, shifting swells, but the seabirds perched in the rigging meant they were close.

"We'll take the smallboat from here," Gwenna said, turning to the ship's captain.

Quen Rouan raised his bushy brows. "I wouldn't recommend it."

"I wasn't asking for your recommendation."

Gwenna had nothing against Rouan. Twelve days on the ship, and he'd treated her Wing with respect, even deference. He'd handled his vessel well through the squall that kicked up east of the Broken Bay, kept his men firmly in line, and didn't ask questions. Gwenna had watched him, one calm afternoon, dive into the water with a rope around his waist to retrieve an albatross feather floating on the waves. *For my daughter,* he'd said after the men had hauled him back aboard. *She's never seen one.* Rouan was a good sailor. A good captain. Maybe even a good man. Which was all the more reason to try to keep him from getting killed.

"I don't know how much you were told about this particular run . . . " Gwenna began.

Rouan held up a hand to forestall her. "I go where I'm told. That's it. This time I was told to deliver you to the Qirins, and the Qirins are still at least thirty or forty miles east, depending on how much time we made up today. I'll know as soon as the sun drops and the stars come out. Whatever the distance, it's too much to cover in a smallboat."

Gwenna snorted. "Gent and I rowed a dory a hundred miles once, and that was before I turned thirteen. The distance is the whole point, Captain. Ships that get too close to those islands haven't been coming back."

"I understand there is risk," Rouan replied, stiffening, glancing east as though he expected to see topsails cresting the waves.

"Well, there doesn't have to be. Not for you. Get the boat in the water, and we'll be out of your hair."

Rouan hesitated. Gwenna could read the pride in that hesitation, the reluctance to leave an honest job unfinished, the unwillingness to run from an unseen threat. He was brave, but he wasn't trained for this.

She made her voice hard. "I'm not asking, Captain."

He met her eyes a moment, then nodded brusquely, turning to bark orders at the half-dozen men on the deck. It was a good crew, and before the sun had slipped much farther down the western sky, the boat was bobbing in place, small hull bumping up against the larger vessel like a duckling against her mother. Two barrels of gear—food, mostly, and water, and extra weapons—had been packed a week earlier, and it took no time at all for Talal to secure them beneath the thwarts of the boat.

"You'll want the sail," Rouan said. "At least partway."

Gwenna shook her head. "No, we won't."

She started to turn, but the captain brought her up short with a hand on her arm. Gwenna went for her knife, had the 'Kent-kissing thing half drawn before her mind could calm the reflexes of her flesh. Rouan looked at the steel, pursed his lips, and withdrew his hand.

"The world's all upside down," he said quietly. "I'll grant you that. But not everyone's trying to kill you."

Gwenna forced herself to shrug. "That hasn't been my experience."

He watched her for a long time.

"How old are you?" he asked finally.

Gwenna met the gaze. "Does it matter?"

The man shook his head slowly. "I suppose it doesn't." He turned east, toward where the Islands lay over the horizon. "What do you think you'll find?"

"After two weeks, you want to start asking questions now?" Gwenna asked. "Questions get people killed, same as blades."

He didn't shy away. "I just want to know what the chances are."

"Depends on whose chances you're talking about."

"Ours," he said gravely.

"Yours and mine?"

"Annur's."

Gwenna started to make a crack, then stopped herself. It was an honest question and it deserved a real answer. She glanced down into the boat. Talal and Annick were already aboard, the leach at one of the oars, the sniper in the bow, her shortbow held loosely in one hand. Daylight was fading fast, and the low sun lit the chop to the east, making the small wave crests look like scratches on the dark surface of the sea. Somewhere beyond that darkness, the Islands waited, an upthrust atoll barely large enough to support human settlement, and then, beyond that, the open plain of the indifferent ocean. She looked back at Rouan.

"Our chances suck."

He shook his head. "You don't sound worried."

"Me?" Gwenna asked. "I'm always worried."

"A hard way to live," Rouan murmured.

Gwenna glanced over at him, this man who collected feathers for his distant daughter, who feared his world might be collapsing around him. She clapped him roughly on the shoulder. "I didn't know there was an easy way."

Annick noted the incoming kettral in the same voice Gwenna might have used to discuss the blister that the oar was raising on the flat of her palm. In fact, Annick sounded considerably less concerned about the bird than Gwenna was about the blister, despite the fact that one was a minor inconvenience and the other had probably come to kill them all.

Still holding the oar, Gwenna twisted in her seat, searching for movement against the dark cloud piled up in the east.

"There," Talal said, pointing upward, higher than she'd been looking. "Looks like a patrol. Call it five miles out."

"Well, shit," Gwenna said.

She looked back to the west. They weren't far from the *Widow's Wish*—maybe a mile or so—and the sun had only dipped fully beneath the horizon in the last few hundred strokes. She could still make out the dark lines of the ship's masts, the sail full of the evening's breeze and the last red light of the lost sun. In the growing darkness, the billowing canvas might have been ablaze.

"Shit," Gwenna said again.

It was good luck for her Wing, actually. The ship was impossible to miss. Whoever was flying the bird would almost certainly be focused on it, hopefully so focused that they missed Gwenna's own boat with its sails down, nosing forward silently through the waves. The conversation with Rouan came back to her suddenly; her flippant remark, *It all depends on whose chances you're talking about.*

"Barrels out," she said, eyes still on the ship. Rouan had swung west just after dropping them, aiming his bow away from the Islands. It didn't matter. No ship could outrun a bird in flight. "Bodies over. Talal, is there enough steel about to scuttle this bitch?"

"They haven't made us yet," he observed quietly. "And forty miles is a long swim."

"Good thing we like swimming," Gwenna snapped. "Can you scuttle the boat, or should I start prodding at the caulking with my knife?"

Talal met her eyes, then nodded. A moment later, a section of planking ripped free with a groan. The boat jerked as though they'd struck a reef, but there was no reef here. Gwenna had anticipated the motion, had demanded it, in fact, and she still felt a twist in her gut as water started pouring into the breach. They'd trained for this very event hundreds of times, but there was still something unsettling about seeing your boat slip beneath the waves in the middle of the open ocean, beneath the roiling arc of the blackening sky.

Gwenna flipped both oars out of the oarlocks, tossed them free of the sinking boat, rolled over the gunwale, kicked her way clear, then turned. Treading water, she watched the small boat vanish beneath the waves. For a few heartbeats she imagined it sinking, settling down through the water, washing back and forth like a leaf, nosed at by curious fish as it drifted deeper and deeper into the gloom. She waited for it to hit the bottom, but it just kept sinking through her mind's dark depths.

"Incoming," Annick said.

Gwenna pulled her eyes from the spot where the boat had disappeared and looked up.

The bird was much closer—almost directly overhead. It looked as though she'd dropped a little bit of elevation— *Scanning the waves,* Gwenna thought grimly—but it was hard enough to see a swimmer's head above the waves in daylight, let alone after sunset. She let herself sink deep in the water, just her nose and eyes above the low chop, and watched, half holding her breath, as the bird cut across the clouds, so silent it might have been no more than the shape of the night wind.

"Whoever it is," Talal observed quietly, "they're headed for the *Wish.*"

"Might just be taking a look," Annick said.

Gwenna stared at the sniper. "You really think that?"

Annick shook her head. "No."

They watched in silence as the ship heeled over, fleeing help-lessly west toward the setting sun. Gwenna was breathing hard, and not with the effort of treading water.

"You want to go back?" Talal asked. "Can't be more than a couple of miles."

"And do what?" Annick asked. She'd already tied one of the barrels to her waist with a short leash of rope, tossed her arm over one of the discarded oars. It was a cumbersome technique, sluggish but easy. With that much floatation, they could go for days. Annick had already started, ignoring the ship as she set out east in a slow sidestroke calibrated to cover the distance ahead.

Gwenna watched the bird as it glided in on a low approach to the ship.

"It's not even a navy vessel . . . ," she breathed.

The flash cut her off, a bright, incandescent burst, then another, then another. It took longer for the sound to come, and at the distance, with the ocean's waves slapping at her ears, it might have been no more than far-off thunder. It might have been, but it wasn't. Gwenna had spent her whole life around Kettral munitions, studying them, designing them, deploying them. Faint or not, distant or not, she recognized the vicious growl of starshatters, the shape of their explosion against the sky. When she turned her head, the afterimage followed her, and when she turned back, she could see that the real fires had already begun, the deflagration of decking, and masts, and sail-cloth.

Rouan's men would try to put the fires out. They would, even now, be desperately hurling buckets of water on the blaze, hoping to keep their ship afloat. They would fail. Gwenna thought she could hear them screaming, but the wind was blowing the wrong way for that. Even after the slarn egg, her ears were not so sensitive.

"Go back?" Talal asked again.

Gwenna watched as the fire lapped at the sky. She'd lost sight of the bird behind the blaze, but whoever was on it would be circling back to finish the work if it wasn't already finished. She imagined Rouan watching, his hand clutching the rail, teeth gritted. Stupidly, pointlessly, Gwenna wondered if the albatross feather had already burned.

For the first time in her life, she saw the Kettral—the birds and the soldiers that rode them—not as warriors, but as agents of an unstoppable, almost unspeakable horror. For all his competence and pride, Rouan could do nothing against explosives shot from a soaring bird. It wasn't a fight, sinking a boat from the air like that; it was a slaughter.

Gwenna watched the ship burn a moment more, then turned away, waves cool against her burning face.

"Annick's right. We can't help. Let's do what we came here to do."

She started swimming east, faster than was really wise, cutting through the waves, not bothering to look back to see if Talal and Annick were keeping pace.

9

Blood still wept from the gashes to her face and scalp as Adare slammed open the doors to the council chamber. At least, she had intended to slam them open. The great bloodwood slabs—each one twice her height and thick as her arm—proved heavy as oxen, and though she threw her whole weight against them, grunting with the effort, they swung only grudgingly on their huge oiled hinges, gliding silently through their arcs, coming so gently to rest that most of the men and women assembled in the chamber failed to notice their opening.

For a moment, Adare just stared. She had heard about the council's famous map chamber, of course. While their republic disintegrated at every border, while the citizens of Annur fought and starved and died, the newly appointed rulers of Annur had embarked on their construction project, diverting funds that could have fed tens of thousands into their glittering hall. Adare had heard more than her fill of the fucking map, but hearing was not the same as seeing. Standing inside the huge doors, perched on the edge of this wooden walkway suspended above the world, watching the oceans slosh in their basins, the rivers tumble through their carefully crafted courses, she found herself hesitating.

It wasn't the council, not the aristocrats seated around the circular catwalk at the hall's center, that gave her pause. She'd been handling aristocrats since she was a child, and judging from the idiocy of the past months, this lot was even less capable than most. No, it was the sight of Annur itself that brought her up short. She had her own maps, of course, dozens of maps, scores of them. Maps of Vash and Eridroa, of every city on the two continents, of strategic passes and likely battlegrounds. Her maps were the best available, meticulously inked records of coastlines and tax zones, watersheds and disputed boundaries. She had thought that those maps captured all that needed knowing about her crumbling empire. In this, as in so many things, she erred.

It was the scope of the empire that had escaped her. She stared at it. Some recent violence had marred the work, but it hardly mattered. The cities were miniature marvels of glass, and stone, and jewel, every palace, every house, the work of a hundred hours for a master craftsman. Forests of dwarf pine skirted the base of the Romsdals while tangled vines snaked across the choked terrain of the Waist. She looked north, to Aergad. There was the ancient castle that had served as her imperial seat these past nine months, standing proudly on the stone promontory overlooking the Haag. Her son was there in that squat, north-eastern tower, probably crying for his dinner, crying for her. She forced the thought from her mind.

It was too much. The whole thing was too much.

She had thought she knew the magnitude of her task when she returned to Annur the first time, when she decided to take on the imperial mantle of her father. She had thought she'd seen the scope of the land after her forced march from Olon to Andt-Kyl. She'd thought she understood the responsibility after watching the battered men and women fleeing south, refugees from the Urghul assault. She'd thought she had plumbed the depths of the sacrifices required after witnessing the battle at the northern end of Scar Lake, after seeing Fulton cut down, after burying the knife in her own brother's ribs.

A map, after all that, even a huge map, should not have come as a shock. And yet there was something about seeing the land spread out before her, the whole huge ambit of her rule in a single room, the unbroken extent of the territory she had taken it upon herself to guard and protect, that made her stop, hands balled in fists at her sides, blood hot and wet on her face, dumb heart pumping more and quickly, horrified at how much depended on her, at how fully she could fail.

". . . if she is harmed, the treaty is *lost* . . ."

She had stumbled, still unseen, into some ongoing argument at the center of the room.

"Some of us did not want this treaty in the first place."

"Then you were a fool. We need unity."

"And if the mob kills her, we have it. Let us not forget that it was Adare who decided to enter the city unannounced, unescorted, without warning the council or asking our permission. Her death can hardly be laid at our feet."

"We don't know she is dead." A quieter voice, this one. Vaguely familiar. "We ordered the soldiers out as soon as we had word of her arrival. They could have reached her in time. We don't know anything."

Adare gritted her teeth, tore her gaze from the great map spread out beneath her, and advanced down the catwalk, a graceful curve of cedar and steel suspended by thick cables from the ceiling far above. She passed over the crescent of the Manjari Empire, over the Vena, then the gold-red sand of the Darvi Desert, passed beneath the lamps, glass blown into great globes meant, evidently, to echo the moon and stars. Most were unlit, wide cloth wicks floating silently in the clear oil. The council continued to bicker.

"The patrol said she was alone."

"Precisely, which means the idiotic woman is probably dead. Which means—"

Adare cut through the words with her own.

"She is not. Idiotic, I'll grant you, but not dead."

She ignored the exclamations of confusion and surprise, the scraping of chairs hastily shoved back, the arms and hands

thrown about in postures of shock and alarm. A dozen more
steps took her over the peaks of the Ancaz, bloodred sandstone
thrusting up as high as the catwalk. Her face burned. That, too,
she ignored.

"I'm sure my survival is a disappointment," she went on,
pausing just to the west of the earthen walls and low domes of
Mo'ir, "but life is filled with disappointments. I would imagine,
given the miserable state of your so-called republic, that you've
grown accustomed to them by now. I certainly have. The relevant
question is what we intend to do about them."

She raised an eyebrow, studying the men and women of the
council for the first time. She had learned all forty-five names,
of course, had studied their families and histories, tried to ferret
out, wherever possible, their reasons for joining Kaden's doomed
cause. Most just wanted power; they would have leapt at any
chance to see the Malkeenians brought low. Bouraa Bouree was
one of these—she picked him out easily, all sweat and silk and
sullen anger—as were Ziav Moss and Onu An. There were a
handful of idealists in the mix, most notably Gabril the Red.
He sat almost directly across from her, his dark eyes hawklike,
sharp and predatory. In the past, the kenneled intensity of his
gaze had made her look away. Not anymore. She met his eyes,
nodded once, then turned her attention to the Annurian delegation.

If Sweet Kegellen was surprised at Adare's sudden entrance,
she didn't show it. Annur's most dangerous criminal raised a fat
hand, waggling her fingers in an incongruously girlish greeting,
then smiled from behind her paper fan. Adare nodded, the same
nod she had given Gabril. Kegellen hadn't earned her various
names—The Queen of the Streets, That Unkillable Bitch—by
sitting demurely behind her fan. The woman was at least as
deadly as anyone else in the room, fans and waggling fingers or
no.

Another time, Adare might have studied her further, or the
lean figure seated beside her who could only be Kiel. Now,

however, her gaze slid past them to the third member of the Annurian delegation, Kaden, her brother. The one she hadn't killed.

"Your Radiance," he said quietly, rising as she met his eyes, then bowing low.

There was no meekness in the movement, no submission.

"I understand," she replied grimly, "that you've acquired a title of your own. First Speaker." She inclined her head a fraction of an inch.

He didn't look like a holder of titles. His robe was simpler in both cut and cloth than those of the other council members. In a room full of flashing gems, he had scorned all ornament. He was taller than she had expected, taller than Valyn, and leaner. His shaved scalp reminded her of the legions she commanded, and there was something, too, of a soldier's discipline in the way he held himself. Unlike those men she had seen at the front, however, there was no bluster to Kaden, no swagger. His strength was in his stillness, his silence. And in those burning eyes.

My brother, she thought, staring at those fires with unexpected wonder. Then, remembering their surroundings, she erased all expression from her face.

After the confusion and consternation caused by her entrance, the assembly had fallen abruptly quiet. It was a quiet that Adare remembered well, a quiet she had first heard when she stood in the palace infirmary with her dying mother. A team of useless surgeons and physicians had attended the Emperor's wife through the final days of her illness, bickering in scholarly whispers as she coughed blood into meticulously boiled cloths. When Adare stepped into that bright, white room, however, the greatest medical minds of the empire had fallen suddenly silent, as though she might forget they were there, might believe she had been given a moment of privacy with her mother.

It hadn't worked then, and it didn't work now. Whatever exchange she was about to have with Kaden, it would be public, political. The angles of this particular silence afforded no space for intimacy. Not that she had any intimacy to offer.

"So this is the heart of your republic," she said, not bothering to keep the scorn from her voice, letting her anger boil through the words. It wouldn't hurt for him to see her anger, for them all to see it.

He shook his head. "Not mine. Ours."

Adare could hear her father in that response, in the cool deliberation of it. There was no shock in his eyes, no dismay, only the steady burning of those twin fires, cold, and bright, and distant. In this, too, he was like her father. Adare couldn't remember ever seeing Sanlitun surprised.

"How inclusive," she replied grimly.

Kaden spread his hands. "If you had warned us of your approach, we could have given you safe passage through the city. I will call a surgeon to see to your wounds."

She shook her head curtly. The motion sent pain up her neck. She ignored it.

"There's no need for a surgeon, and no time for one either. What were you *thinking* ordering armed men into the streets, ordering them to raise weapons against your own people?"

Kaden blinked. That, at least, was something new. Sanlitun would not have blinked.

"We heard that a mob was forming. An angry mob."

"And so you sent out a few hundred brick-brained fools to *murder* them?"

"Murder?" Gabril demanded sharply.

"Yes," Adare said, rounding on the man. "Murder. People trampled by horses, their skulls shattered by the flats of swords, their bodies scattered across the Godsway like offal. I think I'd call that murder."

"The guards were ordered to protect you," Kaden said. "At all costs."

"At the cost of dead Annurians?"

This time he did not flinch. "If necessary, yes. Without you, we would have nothing. No alliance. No peace. None of the unity necessary to hold Annur together."

"And how much unity do you think you're going to have with a few dozen bodies sprawled out on the stones of the Godsway? How much 'Kent-kissing peace?"

Her anger, so useful just moments before, was getting the better of her now. She could hear it; she was too loud. Nira had counseled her again and again on the importance of holding her tongue and her peace. Ironic, given the source, but good advice all the same. Adare could hardly rule an empire if she let herself be goaded into fury by one insane decision by the council. An emperor listened, waited, judged men and women in the silent chambers of her mind, and only spoke when it was necessary, when she was ready to wed the words to action. Adare knew it all well enough, but there was no holding her rage in check. In fact, the more rein she gave it, the greater it grew.

"I understood the risks," she said, turning to confront the other members of the council, "when I rode my horse into the city alone."

"Evidently not," Ziav Moss cut in. The Kreshkan touched his cheek with a fingertip as though to remind her of her wounds. The gesture was gentle, understated. From another man it might even have been deferential, but Moss was not built for deference. The man came from one of the oldest families in the empire; he was all dark, oiled hair and urbanity. His words were soft, but pillows were soft, too, and Adare had read of rulers being suffocated in their sleep with them.

"I *accepted* the risk," she said. "After all your slander, it was necessary for the people to see me alone and unarmed, coming back to this city not as a conqueror with a hundred guardsmen at my back, but as an emperor walking among her people."

"Looks like they didn't like what they saw."

Adare rounded on the newest speaker, a salt-haired, sun-browned woman well into her sixth decade.

Randi Helti. Of course. The boat lady. Aside from Kegellen,

Helti had the only self-made fortune in the room, and no reverence for royalty.

"The crucial thing, Captain Helti, is not the liking, but the fucking *seeing*." Adare gestured to the ceiling high above their heads, huge windows set into it like gems, glass gold with the afternoon light. She swept a hand over the catwalks, the chairs, the grand, ridiculous map, all the way to the huge bloodwood doors through which she had entered. Those had swung shut again as silently as they had opened. "You think you can do all your work from this room?" She turned to confront the others. "You think you can sit in your impeccably crafted chairs and rule an *empire*?"

"You dare . . . ," Bouree sputtered, leaning forward in his seat until Moss waved him down.

"We have ruled this *republic*," the Kreshkan said mildly, "for nearly a year now. And we will continue to do so. The only question is whether or not your . . . theatrics will prove useful to the task." He frowned, as though genuinely disappointed. "I suspect not. You've been out there, scuttling all over the north, rubbing elbows with your precious people, and what has it gained you? Hmm?"

Adare stared. "What has it gained me?" Her pulse pounded in her temple. Blood was running down her face again. "What has it fucking *gained* me?"

"Do you intend to answer the question," Moss asked, brows raised, "or would you prefer to simply repeat it with foul language added for flavor?"

"What it has gained," Adare snarled, "is our survival. Mine. Yours. All Annur's."

"While we all appreciate your enthusiasm, surely that is overstating the case. While the common soldier may respond to this type of hyperbole, it is not necessary here. The men and women of this council are learned and worldly. You need not rant, nor throw your hands about in this ludicrous manner, nor overstate the situation to the north."

Adare clenched her hands into fists at her sides. "I am not overstating it," she hissed. "The situation to the north is nothing short of desperate. Long Fist is killing people. He is cooking them. He is taking them apart piece by piece and making sculptures from those pieces. And then there's Balendin, a Kettral-trained leach. He grows more powerful every day, and he's every bit as vicious as the man he obeys."

Most of the faces around the table had closed—tight lips, narrowed eyes, clenched jaws. They didn't like hearing the truth, and they certainly didn't like being lectured about it. Kaden was watching her intently, hands flat and still on the table before him. She couldn't read his face, but he looked as though he wanted to tell her something, to warn her, but it was too late for that. The moment for conciliation, if it had existed at all, was past.

Another emperor would have found a way to avoid this situation. Her father would never have screamed at the council, would never have shoved their faces so directly in their failures. Kaden seemed cut from the same cloth—calm, deliberative, measured. Another emperor would have seen a way to make peace with the council, but then again, there *were* no other fucking emperors. Sanlitun was dead, and Kaden was . . . whatever he was—cowardly, or complacent, or gelded. She wasn't doing the greatest job, but at least she was trying to *do* her 'Kent-kissing job.

"We have received the reports," Bouree was saying. He seized a long pole from the table before him, gesturing with it toward the north of the map, toward the hundreds of small lakes obscured between the tiny pines. "You need not lecture us about your . . . difficulties."

"My difficulties?" Adare spat. "*My* difficulties? If you plan to rule all Annur, if you plan to pass laws and enact policy as our treaty stipulates, you might want to start thinking about events beyond the walls of this very beautiful chamber as *your* problems, too."

Moss raised a hand, calling for calm as though he were the only adult in a room of petulant toddlers.

"A semantic slip, young lady."

"Your Radiance," she growled.

He pursed his lips, as though the very thought of the words was sour.

"If you intend to heal the breach," she went on, "as you claim. If you intend to abide by the treaty we have both signed, then I am the Emperor, Annur's Emperor, and *your* Emperor, and you will address me properly."

"I've always found that those most insistent on their titles," Moss replied, "are those least deserving of them." He shook his head, an understated performance of urbane regret.

A few seats away, Kegellen smiled. "I couldn't agree more," she said brightly. "I suggest we all relinquish our titles, emperors and aristocrats alike. At once, if possible." She raised a hand, fluttering it in the air. "I make the motion."

People shifted uncomfortably. This was a group, after all, who relied on their names and titles for life and livelihood, for the privileges and prerogatives they had enjoyed from childhood, from birth. It was one thing to challenge Adare's imperial claim; another to see the foundation of their own positions suddenly vulnerable to assault.

Moss frowned. "We will, of course, adhere to the forms of the treaty. Your Radiance. But to return to the matter at hand, I believe my Channarian colleague was simply observing that all these dire tidings that you present with such . . . shrillness are already known to us."

"We have read the reports," Bouree bellowed again. "Every day."

Adare stared at them, looking from face to face. Many were nodding. One man with a square head and a crooked nose was gesturing to a sheaf of papers spread out before him, as though the mere existence of those papers would prove his commitment to Annur. Moss had steepled his fingers before his face, watching from behind them. Kaden's blazing eyes never left Adare. She considered going toward him, for a moment, then turned the other way, circling the table slowly.

"Perhaps the reports have failed to convey the necessary gravity," she said, managing to lower her voice for the first time. She kept walking. People twisted in their chairs as she passed behind them, trying to keep her in view. *As though they think I'm going to stab them one by one, when they're not looking,* she thought grimly. And they didn't even know about Valyn.

"Perhaps," she went on, "the elegant phrases of your reports lack the *urgency* required by the situation." The gashes to her face burned. The scar laid into her skin by the lightning burned. The blood covering her face scalded. "Perhaps you are confused about the nature of your nation, about the scope of your commitment. Perhaps you don't understand the price of failure."

She was approaching Bouraa Bouree now. His face was screwed into a scowl.

"You presume too much," he snapped. "We convene here every day, all day, in the governance of the republic." He waved his long pole at the map below. Even that pole was a work of fine craftsmanship, rings of precious metal laid into the polished shaft. The length of wood with its inlaid gold and silver was worth a farmstead, worth what a large, hardworking family might earn in ten years. All to point out places on a map. Bouree gestured with it vaguely to the borders of the empire. "While you've been pleasuring your general up in the north, we have been *ruling* Annur."

Adare ignored the gibe. "How can you rule Annur," she asked quietly, "when you don't even understand it?"

"And what," asked Ziav Moss from across the width of the table, voice languid, almost bored, "would you have us understand? Your Radiance?"

She glanced over at him, then turned back to Bouree, seized the long pole in both hands, then wrenched it from the Channarian's grasp. He shouted, tried to rise to his feet, to take it back, but she was already twisting away, swinging it in a broad, vicious arc overhead.

"This."

The wood connected with one of the huge globes overhead, shattering the glass. She didn't wince as the shards crashed down around her. A few more slices to her face would hardly make anything worse. Lamp oil spilled over the catwalk, acrid and glistening, slicking the planks and pouring over onto the land below. She took two steps forward and shattered another globe.

"This," she said again. "And this . . ." *Smash.* "And this . . ." *Smash, smash, smash.*

People were on their feet, shouting their objections, waving their hands or wringing them pointlessly. Probably no different from what they did when their precious reports rolled in. A scarred, bearded man tried to take the pole from her. Adare broke it over his head, knocking him half over the railing. She continued swinging the jagged end, breaking the glass lamps over and over and over until she came to one, finally, that was lit.

"What I want you to understand . . ." She was screaming now. She didn't care. "What I want you to fucking understand, you 'Kent-kissing assholes, is that this . . ." She stabbed the shattered pole at the perfect landscape laid out below. You almost couldn't even see the oil slicking the rivers, dousing the trees. "This is not Annur. It has nothing to do with what is going on out there. Nothing to do with what is happening in your republic right fucking now."

"All right." Kaden's voice. Still calm, but carrying. "All right, Adare."

She extended the pole out toward the lamp, almost gently this time. It took only a moment for the oil-soaked wood to catch. She held it before her like a torch, watching the fire twist, writhe.

"No," she said, turning to face her brother, speaking more

quietly now, channeling his calm. "It is not all right. That is what I'm trying to tell you."

She threw the burning brand over the catwalk railing.

There was a great whoosh of wind, like the last, terrible breath of the earth, then the flame.

Everywhere, the flame.

10

A full night, and a day, and part of another night had passed by the time Gwenna finally hauled herself out of the surf onto the slick stones. When she tried to stand, her legs wobbled beneath her, dropping her back into lapping waves where she sat for a moment before reaching out to grab Talal's wrist, dragging him up onto the rock.

"That was . . . harder than I expected," the leach groaned, sinking to his knees.

Gwenna could only nod.

Hook and Qarsh had crept above the horizon sometime around noon. Gwenna's Wing, however, slowed by the barrels of supplies and their own weariness, didn't make land until almost midnight. Gwenna had inwardly debated going for Qarsh, but Hook was closer, and besides, they needed a little time to get their feet back under them before going toe-to-toe with whoever was flying the birds. The west coast of Hook provided as safe a landing place as any, and so she'd aimed for a miserable little stretch of rocky shingle wedged between high cliffs. If she remembered the spot correctly, no one was likely to be there in the middle of the night.

"We need a perimeter," Annick said.

The sniper shook her head to clear the water from her short hair, then stood unsteadily, managed half a dozen steps, then collapsed onto the stones. It was a good reminder that, despite appearances, Annick wasn't invincible. She needed food and rest just the same as anyone else—she just refused to admit it.

"Forget the perimeter," Gwenna said.

"We're vulnerable without a proper perimeter."

Gwenna snorted, then lay back on the uneven rocks. "You can't even stand, Annick. None of us can. Let's just concentrate on getting the barrels up the beach while not drowning. It would be a shame to swim all this way just to pass out in the surf."

Overhead, the clouds had finally cleared. Gwenna could pick out constellations—the Jade Peaks, the Smith, the Serpent—stars so bright they might have been on fire. She shouldn't have been glad for the starlight. The Kettral worshipped Hull for a reason—his dark cloak covered their approaches and retreats—but after two nights swimming, floating between the bottomless dark of the ocean and the endless overturned hull of the cloudy sky above, it was a relief to lie on the hard rocks, to look up at the hard stars.

The water lapping around her legs was warm enough that she could have fallen asleep right there, halfway between the land and the sea. There was, however, that whole drowning thing to worry about, and Annick was already trying to drag the barrels up out of the surf by herself. Each one weighed almost as much as the sniper, and she was struggling, rope over her shoulder, straining forward as though leaning into the wind. Gwenna groaned, hauled herself to her feet, staggered over to the barrel, put her shoulder to the wood, and shoved. The small stones shifted beneath her feet, but she refused to stop until the thing was clear of the waves, up the shingle, then tucked beneath the overhanging limestone cliffs. The second barrel was even heavier, but the work put a little life back into Gwenna's legs, and by the time they had all the gear stowed beneath the cliff, she was starting to think she might actually survive the night after all.

"Water," she said, prying off one of the lids, then handing a full skin to Talal. "And food. Then sleep."

Talal took a long draft from the skin, bit into a strap of cured beef, and chewed thoughtfully.

"You think we're safe here for the night?"

Gwenna coughed out a laugh. "I don't think we've been safe since before Hull's Trial, but this spot . . ." She glanced out at the narrow strip of broken stone once more, at the greedy sea. "I'd say it's as good as any. We're out of sight from the air. It's too rocky to land a boat. They can't patrol everything on foot." She shrugged.

"They," the leach said, leaning hard on the word, the obvious question left unspoken.

"Kettral," Annick said flatly. Instead of eating, she'd been tending to her bows, unrolling dry string from the barrels, checking the mechanical action on the flatbow to see that it hadn't been damaged. It occurred to Gwenna suddenly that they were all moving about as though the stars shed as much light as the sun. It was hard to remember what it had been like before Hull's Hole, before drinking from the eggs of the slarn, but she was pretty sure it would have been tough to see her hand in front of her face. Did the bastards who destroyed the *Widow's Wish* share the same advantage?

"We don't know they're Kettral," Talal said. "Not for certain."

Gwenna raised her brows. "Soldiers flying on a bird? Lobbing Kettral munitions?"

The leach frowned. "Could be civilians. Someone who found the birds and the bombs after the Eyrie tore itself apart."

"Unlikely," Annick said.

Gwenna stared up into the night sky, trying to reason it through. Whoever carried out the attack on the *Wish* had managed not only to wrangle a bird, but to fly one; fly it effectively. And then there were the munitions to consider. You didn't need to be a genius to set off a starshatter, but to hit a ship from any height, to calculate the ordnance necessary to sink a vessel of that size . . .

"The good news," she said finally, "is that the birds are here. One bird, at least. As for the rest of it—we always knew there might be Kettral left on the Islands, a Wing or two gone rogue."

"I was hoping for pirates," Talal replied. "Drunken pirates."

Gwenna half smiled. It was the sort of crack that Laith might have made. Then she thought back to what had happened to Laith. Her smile withered.

"And what have we all learned," she asked grimly, "about hoping for shit?"

It was still dark when Gwenna woke to the smell of smoke.

Annick was curled in a bony ball just a few feet away, while Talal sat up outside the cave, keeping watch. Over his shoulder she could see the bright stars of the Smith's hammer dipping into the waves. A couple of hours until dawn, then. An odd time for someone to be lighting fires. Large fires.

Gwenna sat slowly, suppressing a groan. A few hours of sleep on the stones and the muscles of her back and shoulders were twisted into knots. She stretched her neck one way, then the next, buckled her blades across her back, and moved out to the front of the cave.

"You smell that?" she asked.

Talal nodded. "I noticed it not too long ago. Thought about waking you, but it's pretty far off. Nothing urgent, and I figured you could use another hour of rest after that swim."

"After that swim I could sleep for a week." She twisted at the waist, cringing as the muscles seized, then relaxed. She knuckled them for a moment, then took a deep breath through her nose, sorting the before-dawn scents of the island.

There was salt, and beneath the salt, sand. The warm green reek of vegetation farther up the cliff, hanging vines and twisting shoots, languid and sinuous. It still amazed her, whenever she paused to think about it, how much, how well she could smell. It was like she had lived her whole life blind, and then woken one day to a riot of shape and color. There were a few fish rotting down the beach. She could make out the shit of the seabirds dried by the sun, crusted on the rocks above. And she could smell the smoke.

"Could just be someone up early," Talal suggested. "Kitchen fires over on Buzzard's Bay."

Gwenna closed her eyes, dragged the air over her tongue, testing it, tasting it. Someone was burning wood and dung, but not just that. There were other smells twisted into the scent, stranger and less wholesome. Even after a year away, the training came back to her easily. Paint was burning. And hair. And flesh.

She exhaled heavily, suddenly eager to have the air out of her lungs.

"It's not just kitchen fires."

Talal studied her for a moment, then nodded.

"Are we going?" Annick asked.

The sniper had risen silently to join them while Gwenna was still puzzling over the smoke. Annick hadn't slept much longer than Gwenna herself, but if she felt worn out or sore from the swim, she didn't show it. Her smoke steel blades were already buckled, and she had her shortbow in one hand, the quiver strapped across her back.

"We're in no shape for a fight," Talal observed. "Whatever's going on here, it's been going on for months. Another day won't change it."

"You're probably right," Gwenna agreed. The smoke was stronger now. Thicker. It reminded her of Andt-Kyl, of the burning of an entire town. "On the other hand, some days are more important than others."

"You think this is one of them?"

"Only one way to find out," she replied.

The trail up to the ridgeline was rocky and steep, so steep in places that Gwenna found herself searching for toeholds in the pocketed limestone, balancing on precarious buttresses, hauling herself over tiered ledges using whatever purchase she could find.

At least it's not more fucking swimming, she reminded herself.

By the time she reached the crenellated ridge, however, swimming sounded like a relief. You might drown in the water, but the waves wouldn't cut you to pieces one nasty slice at a time. Her palms were bleeding, and her knees. She could smell her own blood on the stones, and Talal's, and Annick's.

"I remembered this being easier," she muttered, straightening up. "There was one time . . ."

The remaining words died in her mouth. From atop the ridge she could see almost the entire island of Hook, the dark waters of the sound beyond, and still farther to the north, the low-slung bulk of Qarsh. That is, she could have seen Qarsh if she'd thought to look at it. Instead, her gaze was glued to the conflagration raging below, a massive fire roaring through the streets of the island's only settlement. Hook had been a shitty little town even in the best of times, a haven for pirates and smugglers, criminals whose luck had run out on the mainland, whores, drug peddlers, and fishermen, both the enterprising and the insane. It was an amusing irony of the Islands that Hook was allowed to persist just across the water from the empire's most powerful military force, but the Eyrie had decided there were uses to a civilian settlement on the island, regardless how corrupt, and so the small town had survived, even prospered in its twisted way.

It wasn't prospering anymore.

"Someone's burning down the whole west end of the town," Gwenna observed quietly. "I guess they got tired of the smell."

"The fire was set on purpose?" Talal asked. "You're sure?"

"Look at the flames," Gwenna said, gesturing. "They started in three places at the same time. There. There. There."

Talal glanced at Annick. The sniper just shrugged.

"How long ago?" the leach asked.

"Not long. None of the buildings have collapsed yet."

They hadn't collapsed, but they were getting ready to. Half a dozen roofs had already fallen in. Flames lapped from windows and gaping doors. Timber framing groaned as the sudden strain torqued it out of place and crucial beams gave way. Buzzard's

Bay itself was bright with borrowed fire, slick waves reflecting back the shifting red and yellow, as though the water itself were burning.

"Someone's pissed off," Gwenna said. "I think we can be pretty sure of that."

"It's Hook," Annick replied. "Someone's always pissed off."

"And the Kettral aren't there anymore," Talal said. "To keep them in line."

Gwenna nodded slowly. The Eyrie had never really bothered to police the southern island, and it wasn't unusual to find bloated bodies floating facedown in Buzzard's Bay, to hear screaming from inside the garish taverns built out over the water on rotting stilts. The Kettral didn't care about the private vendettas of pirates and profiteers. Open conflict, however, was destabilizing, and whenever some overzealous captain took it upon himself to turn the Island into his private kingdom, the Eyrie's response was invariably quick and conclusive, the message clear: *Kill each other if you want, but do it quietly.*

Obviously, no one was sending that message any longer.

"Not our problem," Annick concluded. "We're here for the birds, not to bring Hook back into the Annurian Empire."

"Republic," Gwenna said absently.

Talal was still studying the town. "We could take a look," he said.

Gwenna watched the fire rage a moment. Probably Annick was right. Probably the hot, smoldering violence that had always plagued Hook had finally exploded. On the other hand, whoever started that fire had taken some care to see it done right. It wasn't a stretch to think it might have something to do with the assholes on the birds, the ones who had sunk the *Wish*.

"We go down," Gwenna said finally, "find a few poor bastards who aren't throwing water on the blaze, and figure out what the fuck's going on."

*

It was worse up close.

Up close, Gwenna could hear the crackling of the blaze, the cries of anger, and terror, and pain. The townsfolk of Hook raced back and forth in a chaotic effort to extinguish the fire, but they were doing a piss-poor job of it, screaming recriminations and bellowing threats instead of working together. When she emerged from the cover of a narrow alley on the unburning edge of the town, Gwenna could feel the heat on her face, hotter than the noonday sun, even at a distance.

No one so much as glanced at her. Not at her, or Annick, or Talal. It made sense—a few unfamiliar faces didn't mean much when half the town was burning down. Skulking, if you didn't do it right, tended to draw attention, and so rather than skulk, Gwenna and her Wing moved through the streets quickly, purposefully, as though, like everyone else, they were going somewhere. The important thing was to keep moving. To keep moving and keep listening, trying to pull the useful information from the noise.

Unfortunately, while there was a great deal of noise, the inhabitants of Hook proved short on useful information. It seemed common knowledge that someone had set the town ablaze intentionally. People understood that the western end was burning while the eastern half was relatively safe. A few opportunistic fools, arms piled with dubious treasure, were trying to organize raids into the burning streets. It was idiotic. Gwenna could tell just from the sound—a greedy, growing roar—that no one going in now was likely to come out alive, but she hadn't crossed the Iron Sea, swimming the last few dozen miles, just to wag her finger at looters.

There was an abrupt surge of noise a few blocks to the north—shouting, screaming, chanting, then a vicious explosion, then relative silence.

"That was a flickwick," Gwenna said.

Annick pointed. "North. By the docks." She switched to Kettral hand sign, hooking a finger. *Move out?*

Gwenna glanced at Talal, then nodded.

"Docks. Three approaches. Annick, west. Talal, east. Rally point is the ridge above the beach."

It wasn't far—maybe a hundred paces—to where the buildings gave way before a broad open square fronting the docks. From the head of the street, Gwenna could see the whole harborside, the western shore ablaze, the east lit only by a few lanterns and lamps flickering in the windows. What looked like most of the population of Hook had gathered in that square—maybe two thousand men and women crammed together, faces smudged with smoke and soot, streaked with sweat, fitfully illuminated by the fire raging through the town. Despite the fire to the west, they were all looking north, toward the harbor.

Well back on the center dock, high as a house, talons lodged in the rotting planks, perched a kettral; huge, silent, black eyes glittering and gelid. Gwenna hadn't seen a bird up close for nearly a year, and for a moment she, like the townsfolk before her, could only stare. In the stories told across Annur, the kettral were cast as glorious flying mounts, huge horses with beaks and wings. *So wrong,* Gwenna thought, gazing up at the bird. The kettral had been trained to accept human riders, but that training did nothing to obscure the more ancient, enduring truth: they were not mounts, they were predators.

With an effort, Gwenna shifted her eyes from the bird to the five men who stood on the dock just in front of it. Despite their Kettral blacks, the Kettral swords buckled over their backs, the Kettral bows held ready in their hands, Gwenna recognized none of them. They'd formed up in a standard diamond wedge, and it was clear why: twenty feet in front of them lay a dozen bodies. A few were still feebly convulsing, twitching, trying to drag themselves clear. Most were perfectly still, the flesh slack, mangled, tossed aside.

The situation was as obvious as it was ugly: the mob came for the men with the bird, tried to attack, then ended up flattened by a few flickwicks. The five Kettral—if they *were* Kettral—had a good position. Any halfway decent sniper could take them down, but it didn't look like there were many snipers in the disoriented mass. Most people, clearly rousted from their beds by the growing fire, were barely clothed. Aside from the Kettral, only one man that Gwenna could see carried a weapon—a sailor, judging from his gait. The man lugged a bare saber, but was otherwise naked, his cock swinging in the wind; interrupted while pissing, or fucking, or sleeping off his drunk. He didn't look like much of a threat, especially not to a Wing of Kettral.

Gwenna shifted her eyes back to the men on the dock. The one in front, a tall, wide son of a bitch with a shaved head and skin almost as pale as hers, was raising a hand. He smiled smugly, as though he were a popular atrep preparing to address a gathering of his most fervent supporters.

If he expects to make a speech, Gwenna thought, *he's going to be disappointed.*

Between the fire and the mob she could barely make out voices a few feet away. When the Kettral opened his mouth, however, the words emerged hard-edged and clear, as though he were speaking directly into her ear.

Which meant that one of them was a leach. Gwenna hadn't expected a milk run when Kaden asked her to go back to the Islands. It had been obvious, even from Annur, that there would be blood on a lot of blades before the whole thing was over. This, however, was looking worse and worse. She gritted her teeth.

"Your town is a shithole," the man began, smiling all the time as though offering the most fulsome praise. "It is a shithole, but we didn't want to burn it down."

The mob surged forward at that, men and women bellowing their rage and shame. They'd almost reached the dock when one of the soldiers raised a starshatter above his head. The fuse was already burning—a hot, bright point of light against the darkness beyond. The crowd trembled, hesitated, then recoiled, as though the whole mass were a single creature, one that had learned through hard discipline to avoid that horrible, brilliant light.

The speaker smiled even more widely, white teeth bright in the fire.

"So, as a gesture of good faith . . ." He extended one hand, palm up, slowly and dramatically toward the western portion of the town. ". . . we have only burned half of it. At least for now."

There were shouted protests. Accusations. Screamed curses.

"No one here did nothing ta you!"

"My husband's dead. He's dead! He's dead!"

"If you didn't want to burn the town, then why did you burn it, you bastards?"

The speaker put a cupped hand behind his ear at this last question.

"Why?" He cocked his head, as though to hear better. "Did someone ask *why?*" He waited a moment, through a few more curses and questions, then nodded vigorously. "Ah, I think I understand the difficulty. Elsewhere in the world, this would not be a problem. Elsewhere people have a notion of law, crime, and consequence. Here on Hook, however, you have been . . . deprived of such notions."

He leaned back on his heels, tucked his thumbs into his leather belt, and smiled even more widely. He wasn't much to look at—a wide, heavy face, lips that twisted up cruelly whenever he wasn't talking—but the son of a bitch had the voice of a trained orator—rich, and strong, and supple. He had the voice, and obviously he liked to use it.

"It's not your fault, of course," he went on. "No people can be expected to circumscribe their own . . . baser impulses without the outside imposition of law, of order. Formerly, the Eyrie let you all run amok because it suited their purposes to have you disordered, fragmented. A grievous lapse," he said, shaking his head. "A lamentable lapse. Fortunately, we are here to introduce you to these notions. This," he went on, leveling a steady finger at the flames, "is *justice.*"

For a few moments, the mob just stared, first at the man in Kettral blacks, then at the flames consuming their miserable homes. To Gwenna's ear it was all a lot of horseshit, long on talk and short on explanation. On the other hand, no one was trying to kill the bastard anymore, so he had to be doing something right. In fact, when Gwenna turned to scrutinize the faces around her, she found them filled with fear and resentment, but no confusion. Protest they might, but they understood why the men in black were burning their homes. She shifted her attention back to the dock.

"When you harbor dissidents," the leader said, allowing himself a flourish of rhetorical anger, "*this* is what happens. When you take rebels into your miserable cellars and hovels, *we will burn them down.*" He spat onto the dock. The gesture looked fake, somehow, like a performance he'd rehearsed back in the barracks. "You should be grateful. The shacks we burned weren't fit for the rats you shared them with. Try to do better when you rebuild. And when those creeping vermin come to you again begging for help and hiding, remember that I'll pay a gold Annurian sun for every head. On the other hand, the next time a field of our yellowbloom is burned, I'll be back to torch a dozen more houses." He shrugged. "Your choice."

The mob started to growl once more, but another voice cut through the rumbling discontent.

"You want a head, you bastard?"

Gwenna spun to find a woman standing on a flight of low stone steps almost directly behind her. She was tall, taller than Gwenna herself, long limbed and dark skinned, hair shaved down to the scalp. She was fine-featured, almost aristocratic in her face and bearing, but though she spoke with chin raised and her dark eyes flashing, Gwenna could smell the fear on her, a bone-deep fear held just barely in check. At first glance, in the night and fickle firelight, she appeared unarmed. As the mob stared, however, she pulled a blade from over her right shoulder. A short weapon, smoke steel and carried in the Kettral style.

Despite the blade, however, the woman wasn't dressed like the men on the docks.

Instead of blacks, she wore a sleeveless tunic and dark breeches, practical enough in the hot island weather, but a little too loose for good fighting attire. She knew how to hold the sword, which was more than you could say for most of the idiots swaggering around Hook, and had chosen her position well—high ground, back to a building, double escape routes—except for an open right flank, where a long alley offered a perfect angle of attack. It took less than a heartbeat to see it, but seeing was the easy part. What did it *mean*? The woman defying the Kettral on the dock was almost Kettral herself, but imperfect, like someone who'd been spying on the Eyrie for years without taking part in any of the actual training.

"If you want a head," she shouted again, voice fraying on the sharp edge of her growing panic, "then why don't you come and take mine? I'm not hiding in a cellar, you murdering bastards. I'm right *here*. You want my head? Come and take it."

She had the attention of the men on the dock—that was pretty fucking obvious. Her sudden appearance had scraped the condescending smile off their leader's face, and two of the soldiers behind him had half raised their bows. It was a pointless gesture; the woman could step back into the open doorway the moment they put an arrow in the air. The men on the dock seemed to understand this, and neither bothered trying to get off a shot.

People shifted, moving clear of the coming violence, opening a straight path from the Kettral to the lone woman on the stairs, an empty avenue, as though for some emperor's procession. The frightened woman held her ground. Which meant she was either very stupid, or had an end beyond simple taunting in mind.

"I hope you're pleased, Qora," said the Kettral leader, drawling the long first syllable of her name. "People died here because of you." The tone was casual, almost lazy, but Gwenna saw the man shift. She caught a whiff, below all the smoke and sweat, of the sudden eagerness pouring off him.

Qora shook her head grimly. "I don't remember setting any fires."

"You should have realized when you chose to use civilians as shields that shields get battered. They get broken."

Qora's face tightened. "No one's fooled, Henk. They see who's doing the breaking, and for what. People know a tyrant when they see one."

"And do they also know a coward who hides behind children?"

She spread her hands. "I'm not hiding now. If you want me, here I am."

So—a trap. Obviously.

Gwenna glanced over the square again, evaluating the angles and approaches. The woman—Qora—was trying to draw the Kettral south, off their dock. *Into what?* There were a few good spots to plant charges, but charges wouldn't discriminate between attackers and civilians. Not necessarily a problem, but this woman seemed keen on the distinction.

A sniper then.

Qora knew that the men on the dock would have someone covering them, maybe several someones. She was clearly hoping that her appearance on the steps would lure those someones out, that the hidden Kettral with the bows—wherever they were—would get into position to take a shot at her. There was one obvious choice. Gwenna looked back down that street to the east, the open flank on Qora's right. If there were Kettral hidden in the alleys, that's where they'd move to take their shot. Which meant that if *Qora* was setting a trap, she'd have someone waiting down that very alley, someone ready to hamstring the sniper right . . . *there.*

Qora's companion was tucked back into a shadowy doorway, but his blade was drawn. A smoke steel blade. As traps went, it was clumsy, obvious—Gwenna had run through the whole thing in a few heartbeats—but you had to admire the woman on the steps for playing bait, facing down five Kettral and a bird in the hope of flushing one or two of her foes into the alley. You had to admire her, and you had to do it fast, because she was about to get all kinds of killed.

Two bowmen—the Kettral snipers Gwenna had known would be there—stepped into the long alley forty paces back. Gwenna waited for the man with the sword, Qora's hidden companion, to spring the trap. He didn't. Instead of leaping from the shadows, he froze in place. The snipers, advancing down the alley with their bows half drawn, didn't notice him, and as they approached, stalking forward, eager for their prey, the lone man melted back into the shadows, disappeared.

" 'Shael's shit on a stick," Gwenna muttered, turning to signal to Annick.

Before she'd dropped her hand, Annick's arrows were in the air. A moment later, the snipers in the alley collapsed. Of Qora's cowardly companion, there was no sign. Gwenna scanned the crowd slowly, loosening her focus, ignoring the individual faces, searching for unexpected movement in the mass of people. Where there were two snipers, there could well be another.

It only took a few heartbeats to find what she was looking for. A dozen paces back, emerging from a side street—two men moving against the drift of the larger current, pressing *toward* the woman on the steps when everyone else was trying to get clear. A third was coming in from yet another angle, all of them moving slowly, but with more purpose than the situation seemed to require. None carried bows, but you didn't need a bow to kill a woman, not if you got close enough—and they were definitely closing.

"Well, fuck," Gwenna said, more loudly than she'd intended.

She eased her belt knife in its sheath, eyes still roving over the scene.

The Kettral on the dock didn't move, but they had more than three accomplices seeded through the crowd, she realized. Four, five, six . . . Gwenna had figured on one extra Wing scattered about the square, but there were at least two, both of them clearly intended to cover the main act out on the dock, both now converging on the woman on the steps. Qora didn't seem to notice. Instead, she was stealing glances up the side street toward where her companion had disappeared, slipping away while their shitty plan tore apart at the seams.

Briefly, Gwenna considered letting the woman die. It hardly made sense to start putting knives in people until she'd sorted out who, exactly, was who, who needed killing and who just needed a swift kick in the ass. On the other hand, the basic contours were clear enough—the men with the birds were burning buildings to try to get at the others, the rebels. Qora was a rebel. Hull only knew how many more rebels there were, or where they were hiding; both pieces of information seemed useful.

"Well, fuck," Gwenna said again, sliding her knife between the ribs of the first Kettral as he passed.

The man's eyes widened, but pain stole his breath. He reached briefly, weakly, for the blade, fingers dumb and fumbling. Gwenna wrapped an arm around his waist, as though he were a friend with too much to drink—she'd learned that trick from a Skullsworn assassin a whole continent away in what seemed like another life—then lowered him gently to the stones. She hadn't given Annick another signal, or Talal, but how much of a 'Kent-kissing signal did you need? It ought to be pretty clear that it was time to start killing people.

When she straightened up, she saw they'd followed her play. One of the other Kettral was folding slowly over, grasping at an arrow in his chest. Then a second stumbled, coughing up blood. More were coming, though, and Annick didn't have angles on all of them.

"Qora," Gwenna called, trying to get the attention of the woman on the steps without alerting the entire square. *"Qora."*

Qora looked down. Her eyes were wide and baffled, ablaze with the still-burning fire to the west, hot with her own fear and rage. Gwenna motioned her toward the nearest street.

"Time to go."

The woman's only move was to lower her sword at Gwenna,

an unfortunate gesture that drew every eye in the crowd. Another Kettral, just a few feet away and closing, turned to stare at Gwenna. When he saw the bloody knife in her hand, he drew a sword from beneath his cloak.

Gwenna shook her head. "I'm on *your* side, you asshole," she hissed to the man.

He hesitated, glanced back up at Qora, who was staring down at both of them. Gwenna stepped in and cut his throat. People were starting to shout, to scream. Behind her, on the docks, the men with the bird were moving. Things were ugly and about to get a whole lot uglier.

"I wasn't really on his side," Gwenna growled, meeting Qora's eye. "And it really is time to go. Now. The crowd's seeded with them."

Qora shook her head, took half a step back toward the doorway behind her. "Who are you?"

"Look, bitch," Gwenna snapped, losing her patience. Off to her right, a man began to charge. Annick's arrow took him in the eye. "You're spunky, but you're stupid. Now get off the fucking stairs and let's go." She stabbed a finger down the nearest street. *"That way."*

Just behind Gwenna a woman started screaming, pain mingled with panic. She was just one of the baffled folks who had stumbled outside in the middle of the night to see half her town burn. She had nothing to do with the unfolding fight, but the sound seemed to jolt Qora from her confusion, and she vaulted off the stone steps, finally showing a touch of the competence Gwenna had hoped for.

Instead of following, however, Qora paused, staring up that alley to the east. "There's someone else," she hissed. "Jak—"

"Forget him," Gwenna said. "He's gone."

"He was supposed to—"

"I know what he was supposed to do. He didn't do it."

Qora hesitated, jaw clenched in an agony of indecision, then let herself be led. Together, they raced down the muddy street.

Within a dozen steps, Gwenna could hear the clatter of their pursuers. She grabbed the woman by the elbow, dragging her down a side street as more arrows thunked into the wooden walls. Talal was there, his own blades bare, one wet with blood.

He pointed to a low wall between buildings, just high enough to scramble over.

"There," he whispered. "Straight shot out of town on the other side."

Gwenna shoved the other woman toward the short wall, but she yanked away, twisting back toward the square. *"Jak!"* she whispered desperately. "My partner. Where *is* he?"

"How the fuck do I know?" Gwenna snapped. "East somewhere."

"I have to find him. Go back for him."

"No," Gwenna said, taking the woman by the arm once more, sizing her up. Qora was an inch or two taller than Gwenna herself, but slender, light enough to knock out and carry if she kept up with the idiotic heroics. Gwenna shifted, wrapping an arm around her neck, but Talal stepped forward.

"Describe him," he said. "Jak."

Qora's eyes were huge as moons. She twisted her head to look at Gwenna, then turned back to Talal.

"Short. Strong. Pale. Shaved head. Twin kettral inked on his shoulders . . ."

It wasn't much of a description, but Talal nodded, then darted off down the alley before she could finish.

Gwenna hissed her irritation, started to call the leach back, then muzzled her objection. Talal could take care of himself, his assurance had calmed Qora, and they'd be more likely to confuse the pursuit if they split up.

"Get to the rally," she growled after him. "And don't fucking die."

11

Adare sat at the end of the dock, bare feet rising and falling in the water as the low waves slapped against the pilings. It was hardly an imperial posture, but she'd been trying to look imperial all morning, sitting spear-straight in her chair above the smoldering ruins of the great map of Annur, trying not to choke on the day-old smoke and ash as she signed into law the treaty intended to heal the rift between her empire and the republic. It felt good to recline on her elbows at the end of the palace docks, to watch the great ships out in the bay lean with the breeze, to forget for just a moment how close she'd come to destroying it all.

It would have been *nice* to forget about it, but her brother refused to let her.

"How did you know," Kaden asked quietly, "that the entire hall wouldn't catch fire?"

"I didn't."

"How did you know someone on the council wouldn't attack you? Kill you?"

"I didn't."

"How did you know they'd agree to ratify the treaty after all that?"

"I didn't, Kaden. I was fucking terrified, if you want to know the truth, but I didn't see any other way." She blew out a long, frustrated sigh, then turned to face him.

Kaden sat cross-legged, hands folded in his lap, his posture, like the rest of him, contained, closed. Adare had no idea how he could sit like that with the burns. The fire in the council chamber had turned the air instantly, if only momentarily, to flame. Adare's own skin was tender to the point of agony, a hint of sullen red spreading beneath the brown. The cold water felt so good on her feet and legs that she was tempted to jump in, to float on her back in the cool shade under the dock itself.

She used to love to swim beneath the docks as a child, maybe because it drove her Aedolians to distraction. But Birch and Fulton were gone now—one quit, the other dead—and she was not a child but a woman grown, the Emperor, since the morning's signing, of all Annur. There could be no more floating beneath docks.

"You have no idea," Kaden said slowly, "how difficult it was convincing the council to agree to this treaty. They did not want you back."

"And you *did*?" Adare asked, studying him warily.

The man who sat before her on the rough planks of the dock bore little resemblance to the boy she remembered from her childhood. At eight, Kaden had been thin and bony, all elbows and knees, dark, unruly hair flopping into his eyes whenever he ran, which seemed to be all the time. He and Valyn had been raised in the same palace as Adare, disciplined by the same parents and guards, schooled by the same tutors, and yet the two brothers had managed to find a freedom inside the red walls that Adare had never truly felt.

It wasn't that she had resented the Dawn Palace as a child. Far from it. Every time she walked the long colonnades, or prayed inside the scented stillness of the ancient temples, or stood in the cool shadow of the Unhewn Throne, she felt the pride brimming within her, pride of her family, of her name, of her palace, and of the history it represented. Every time she strolled through the immaculately kept gardens, sprays of jasmine and gardenia winding above her, or paused to look up at the graceful angles of the Floating Hall, suspended a hundred feet above the courtyards, every time she stood at the top of Intarra's Spear, gazing out over an empire that stretched away over ocean, and forest, and tilled ground, stretched away toward every horizon, every time she thought of the scope and breadth and majesty of it all, she felt her own good fortune.

That fortune, however, had weight. Like the golden robes her father wore during celebrations of solstice and equinox, Adare's own glittering, gorgeous position lay heavily on her slender shoulders. For as long as she could remember, she had felt it, that weight. To be a Malkeenian was to acknowledge the full heft of history, to feel present events, like some priceless silk, slide between her small hands. The high red walls of the Dawn Palace, instead of keeping the world back, instead of blocking it out, held *in* the whole elaborate apparatus of state; it was the hub around which the spokes of that great world spun. Adare felt that spinning, felt it every day, almost from the moment she woke . . . even though she knew she would never be the Emperor, that the unfathomable weight of her father's responsibility would never be hers, but Kaden's.

Kaden, for his part, had always seemed blissfully ignorant.

The boy she had known was always at his older brother's side, sneaking away from lessons, trying to elude his own guardsmen, racing around the ramparts or delving down into the deepest cellars. He shared the burning eyes with Sanlitun and Adare, but he seemed to have no idea of or interest in what they *meant*, in what he would have to do. Most times, Adare could imagine Krim, the kennel master sitting on the Unhewn Throne before Kaden; the kennel master, at least, approached his work with a serious, sober regard.

The only times Adare had ever seen Kaden go still were when he thought he was alone, when he thought no one was watching. Once, frustrated with her failure to understand some mathematical proof, Adare had climbed up to the seaward wall after her lessons, determined to sit there, regardless of the hard salt wind, working through the problem until she unlocked it. To her surprise, she had stumbled across Kaden. His Aedolians were a hundred paces off, blocking all approach to the high wall, and he was leaning against the stone, staring east between the ramparts. Adare started to approach, then paused, suddenly, almost preternaturally aware that this was a part of her brother she had not seen before, or had seen but not noticed. She couldn't say what he was looking at—Ships in the harbor? Gulls overhead? The jagged limestone karsts of the Broken Bay? She could only see his stillness, an absence of action so perfect, so absolute, that it seemed impossible he should ever move again. Then, after a very long time, he turned. When he saw her watching him, his burning eyes widened, the boyish grin slipped back onto his face, and he raced away, his Aedolians hollering protests as they gave chase.

It seemed, now, that that boy, the one who had raced and grinned, was gone. Almost a decade among the Shin had sanded the easy smile from his face. The dark hair was gone, shaved. Though his eyes still burned, the fire was distant now, cold, as the fire in her father's eyes had been. Adare might not even have recognized him, were it not for that one day on the seaward wall a decade earlier. What she saw, when she looked at him now, was that stillness, that silence, that utterly unfathomable gaze.

"Your return to the city was not a matter of desire," Kaden said finally. "It was a matter of necessity."

She shook her head, weary and confused. "If we were going to be on the same side anyway, you could have decided to join forces a little earlier. Right when you got back to Annur, for instance. Instead of tearing each other apart, we could have been allies all this time, a united Malkeenian front."

"A united Malkeenian front," Kaden repeated, studying her. Adare felt like some rare bug beneath that gaze, a specimen carried in from the northern forests. "We'd need Valyn for that," he went on after a moment. "Do you have any idea where he is?"

Adare's heart lurched inside her. She forced her face to stay still. She kept her eyes on the waves, kept lazily kicking her feet in the water as the awful scene played out inside her mind all over again: Valyn appearing from nowhere on the roof of the tower in Andt-Kyl; Valyn stabbing Fulton, her last Aedolian; the hot blood pumping from beneath Fulton's armor; the guardsman's body so horribly heavy as Adare tried to lift him; the way the steel refused to come free; Valyn threatening il Tornja, threatening to kill the only general who could save Annur; the knife light in Adare's hand, then buried in her brother's side; her own screaming like a spike in her skull. . . .

Maybe there had been another choice, but she hadn't seen it at the time. Without il Tornja, they would have been lost; the Urghul would have crushed all of Annur beneath the hooves of their horses months ago. Valyn had gone wild, had become half insane, judging from the look in his eyes. He'd been nothing at all like the boy Adare remembered; all the play was gone, all the joy and mischief, replaced by hate, and horror, and black, obliterating rage. And so she'd done what she needed to do to save the empire. Adare had been over her own reasoning scores of times, hundreds, since watching his limp body tumble from the tower's top into the waves below. She could find no other choice—not then, not in the long months since. That knowledge did nothing to stop the nightmares.

"The last time I saw Valyn," she replied, careful to meet Kaden's eyes, to keep her voice level, not too loud, skirting the border of indifference, "he was a kid getting on a ship for the Qirin Islands."

She forced herself to breathe in once, then out slowly. A lie, like a midwinter fire, was not a thing to rush.

Instead of responding, Kaden just watched her with those burning eyes. No emotion played over his face. He might have been looking at a blank wall, or a patch of ragged grass, but he *kept* looking, on and on, until Adare felt a sweat break out on the back of her neck.

He can't know, she reminded herself. *There's no way he could know.*

Those eyes continued to burn. She felt like a hare, some small, hot-blooded creature caught in a hunter's snare.

What if someone saw? The voice inside her head sounded like Nira. *Thousands of poor bastards in the battle just below—one of them might'a seen you put that knife between Valyn's ribs.*

For months, Adare had worried about just that. After all, a body falling from a tower wasn't tremendously hard to miss. On the other hand, when Valyn stumbled from the tower, bleeding and reeling, his own knife stuck in his side, he'd fallen south, toward the lake, away from anyone watching. More importantly, the whole thing had played out while the battle was still raging in the streets below. All those close enough to see would have been fighting desperately, each man swinging a sword or dodging one. There had been no time, no space, for the study of Andt-Kyl's limited skyline.

That, at any rate, was what Adare had told herself, and every day that went by without someone asking questions, demanding answers, raised in her the hope that Valyn's death had gone unremarked, that it would remain undiscovered. It should have been a relief, that ongoing silence; the last thing she needed was a story of royal fratricide burning through the remnants of the empire. The absence of comment on the killing should have felt like a blessing; it did not.

History's brutal truths—the wars and famines, tyrannies and genocides—were a burden shared among millions. The truth of that murder atop the tower, however, was Adare's alone. The only witness, Ran il Tornja, was Csestriim, and for all his bonhomie and banter, incapable in his very bones of understanding what it had cost Adare to drive that knife between her brother's ribs. The story was hers, as was the silence, and there were days when both weighed more than she thought she could bear.

She shook her head. "I *wish* that we knew where Valyn was. I'd trade half of Raalte for a loyal Kettral Wing." She sharpened her gaze, fixed it on Kaden. "My spies told me that *you* might know where he is. That the two of you had some contact after he fled the Islands."

"Spies?" Kaden asked, raising his brows.

"Yes," Adare replied. "Spies. Men and women who pretended to be siding with you, but were really siding with me. Surely even your inept wreckage of a republic has spies."

He nodded slowly. "What did they tell you, exactly?"

"That Valyn fled the Islands in disgrace. That he came to you. Maybe that he rescued you. Is it true?"

Kaden nodded again. "True enough. And our spies tell me that there was a Kettral Wing at the battle of Andt-Kyl. They say that a woman with red hair took charge before the arrival of the Army of the North. There were explosions. Kettral-style demolitions. People saw a girl in Kettral blacks who looked almost like a boy." He watched her watching him. "The descriptions sound like soldiers on Valyn's Wing. Gwenna Sharpe. Annick Frencha."

Adare nodded. "I saw them from the tower," she said, cleaving as close as possible to the truth. "No one knew who they were."

"Not even il Tornja? He is the *kenarang*. The Kettral fall under his command."

"That doesn't mean he memorized the face of every cadet. And, in case your spies didn't mention it, there was a battle that day. Il Tornja was trying to stop Long Fist, not play Guess the Kettral."

"But there was no sign of Valyn? Up there in the north?"

Adare shook her head. "If he was there, I didn't see him. Of course, there was a battle going on, tens of thousands of soldiers. . . ."

Kaden hesitated, as though considering whether or not to press the issue, then frowned. It was the only real expression she'd seen from him since he joined her on the dock.

"What about Long Fist?" he asked finally. "Was the Urghul chieftain at the battle?"

It was a new line of conversation; dangerous, but not as dangerous as the discussion of Valyn.

"No," Adare replied. "A Kettral deserter named Balendin commanded the Urghul. A leach, evidently. He held up the bridges."

"I know Balendin," Kaden said quietly. "I almost killed him in the Bone Mountains. He is dangerous."

Adare clamped down on her surprise. She had heard no account linking the leach to Kaden, but there was a lot she hadn't heard in the madness of the months following her father's death. She tried to imagine Kaden killing anyone, let alone a Kettral-trained leach. He wasn't a warrior—that much was obvious at a glance—but those eyes . . . She shivered, then looked away, watching the ships swinging at anchor. Gulls gathered in the rigging. Every so often, one would scream, drop into a dive, then pull a fish, wet and writhing, from the waves.

"Dangerous doesn't begin to describe the leach," Adare replied after a pause. "He had his prisoners dragged out into the open, then torn limb from limb. Sometimes he watched. Sometimes he helped."

Kaden just nodded. "It is his well. He leaches off their terror of him, their hatred and revulsion, uses it to do . . . what he does."

"I'll tell you what he does," Adare said, the memory fresh and horrible even after so many months. "He raises up whole bridges for his army to cross. He smashes down walls." She shook her head. "He can squeeze his fingers from a hundred paces off, and a man's head will explode inside his helmet."

"It will only get worse," Kaden replied. "As more people come to fear him, his power will grow."

"Which is why il Tornja and I have been trying to *stop* the bastard. You're down here playing mapmaker with those fucking idiots on the council, but everything is happening in the *north*, Kaden."

"Everything?" he asked quietly. "I know about Balendin, but was Long Fist there?"

Adare hesitated, running her mind over the truth's twisting fabric. It was all woven together: il Tornja's identity and Valyn's death, the truth about Long Fist and the truth about Nira and Oshi. Once you gave up one of those truths, it was hard to stop. One thread led to another, and pretty soon you could find you'd ripped apart the whole fabric, find it scattered in tatters around you.

"Adare," Kaden said, eyes fixed on her. "I need to know what was going on up there. Horrible things could happen if we fail to act."

"Horrible things have *already* happened. To me. To you. To Annur." She waved a hand vaguely northward. "They are still fucking *happening,* Kaden. You haven't been to the north. You haven't seen the flayed corpses left by the Urghul. The charred bodies of the children. The women taken apart slowly, limb by limb. Have you even been outside the 'Kent-kissing capital since you returned?"

He shook his head slowly. "The work is here. . . ."

"The work is everywhere. Bandits choke off half our roads. Fishermen have discovered they can make more coin as petty pirates. Trade is down. Theft is up. You've lost half of Hanno and Channary to the Waist tribes, if anything I've heard is true. The Manjari are poking their noses over the Ancaz. Freeport and the Federated Cities are murdering us on tariffs. The whole thing is coming apart at the seams.

"You think I'm reckless because I rode into Annur alone, unannounced, and burned down your idiotic hall?" She stabbed a finger at him. "What about you? You and your republic have been cautious, you've been measured, you debate for eight or nine days about whether or not to fly more flags from the walls of the Dawn Palace, and you are getting *killed* for it."

She paused, breathing heavily, then corrected herself. "No. *You* aren't getting killed. Other people, other Annurians, people who don't have red walls to hide behind—*they're* the ones getting killed for the decisions you just make. Or fail to make."

If he was taken aback by the tirade, it didn't show. He gazed at her steadily, then nodded. "I understand your urgency. It will not save lives, however, to hurl ourselves heedlessly in one direction or another."

Adare was already shaking her head. "This is like something our father would have said. He thought everything through—thought it through far better than *you* have—tried to figure all the angles, had a 'Kent-kissing *plan,* and what did he get for it? A blade between the ribs." She bit down hard, partly to keep from saying anything else, partly to choke back her grief.

Kaden just sat there, hands folded in his lap, studying her as though she were a blue-fin striper dumped out on the dock to flop herself to death. The mention of Sanlitun's murder brought no expression to his face.

"It was your general who killed him," he said finally, quietly. "Ran il Tornja killed our father."

"You think I don't fucking *know* that?"

He blinked. "It's hard to know what to think."

"Yes, Kaden. It *is* hard. But that doesn't mean you can just *quit doing it.*"

"I haven't quit."

"Is that right?" Adare demanded. "What is it you've been doing then, these past nine months? You destroyed an empire that brought peace and prosperity for hundreds of years—I'll grant you that—and then what?"

Someone else, anyone else, would have responded to the challenge. Nira would have slapped her. Lehav would have argued with her. Ran il Tornja would have laughed at her, and Ran il Tornja was one of the 'Kent-kissing Csestriim. Kaden just shook his head.

"The situation is more difficult than you understand."

"And what makes you think," she demanded, bringing her voice under control, "that you have any idea what I understand?"

"There are other threats than the Urghul. More dire threats."

"Of course there are," she spat. "I just got done listing half of them. There are so many threats that the Urghul sometimes actually seem quaint. At least they're just a bloodthirsty horde with a fairly predictable plan to smash through the Army of the North and put the entire empire to the sword. It's really a somewhat old-fashioned notion, if you think about it."

"The Urghul may be a simple, bloodthirsty horde," Kaden replied, "but the man commanding them is not. And your general, Ran il Tornja—he is not simply a general."

A cold prickling ran up Adare's spine. She started to respond, then stopped. Just like that, they had returned to the dangerous ground of half-truths and qualified revelations. Kaden met her eyes. There was no eagerness there, no uncertainty. She couldn't see anything at all in those blazing irises. She had expected this, had planned for it, but she had not realized it would come so abruptly.

She glanced over her shoulder. The Aedolians were a hundred paces off, standing with their backs turned at the end of the dock. She lowered her voice anyway. "Ran il Tornja is Csestriim," she said.

Kaden nodded. "I know. Which means the child you bore him is also Csestriim, at least in part."

He delivered the words quietly, almost indifferently, as though he were a servant murmuring a message of little consequence. It took all Adare's restraint not to hit him.

"I did not bear *him* a child," she hissed, voice a blade honed against her rage. "Having a son was not something I did *for* il Tornja. Sanlitun is not some trinket, some prize that I produced from between my legs to please the great general. My child is my own."

Kaden didn't even blink in the face of her fury. "And yet your son links il Tornja more closely to the throne."

"Il Tornja doesn't *want* the fucking throne."

"Not as an end in itself, perhaps, but as a means, a tool. He is Csestriim, Adare."

Slowly, painfully, she shackled her pounding heart, choked back the words flooding up into her throat, forced herself to be still. Waves rustled beneath the dock like something alive and tireless. She watched her brother, trying to gauge her next play from the shifting fire in his eyes. After a moment, she decided to throw the dice. "As is the one you call Kiel."

"He is."

For a while they just sat, as though the truths they had both just uttered were too large to move past. The waves were growing colder as the sun sagged behind the palace, and Adare pulled her feet from the water, hugging her knees to her chest. An east wind had picked up, tossing her hair in her face. She shivered.

"Il Tornja warned me that Kiel would be here," she said finally. "He told me not to trust him."

"And Kiel told me not to trust il Tornja."

Adare spread her hands. "Sounds like an impasse."

"Not necessarily," Kaden replied slowly. "Beyond the opinions of the two Csestriim, there are the raw facts to consider."

"Facts," Adare replied warily, "have a way of twisting with the teller."

"We know this much, at least: the general you rely on so heavily is the same one who murdered our father, who sent close to a hundred Aedolians to kill me, who ordered a Kettral Wing to kill Valyn before he even left the Islands." Kaden shook his head. "If we're trying to decide who to trust, it seems to me we might want to look at what they've been up to, at what they have done to *earn* that trust."

Adare marshaled her thoughts. She'd known all this, of course, but it was different to hear it from someone else, to hear the bloody words spoken aloud.

"There were reasons."

Kaden didn't move. "There are always reasons."

Far out in the bay, a ship tacked against the wind, heeling

over to cut across the waves, first one way, then the next, approaching its invisible goal so obliquely that even after watching it for a while, Adare couldn't say for sure where it was going. After a long time she turned back to her brother.

She needed to tell him something—that much was clear. He already knew about il Tornja, knew that *she* knew her own general was a murderer. If she revealed nothing else, none of her reasons for everything she'd done, he would go on believing all the things he so obviously believed: that she had seized the throne out of some dumb lust for power, that she'd made common cause with il Tornja purely to consolidate that power, that she cared about her own station instead of the welfare of Annur. If he believed all that, there would be no working with him, and she needed to work with him, with the entire council, if they were to have any hope of saving anyone. She needed to tell him something, to explain. The question was: how much?

"When I took the Unhewn Throne," she said finally, quietly, "I thought you were dead."

"I don't care about the throne, Adare."

"If I'd known you were still alive, that you were going to return to the city, I wouldn't have made that move. I wouldn't have *had* to, but it had been months since Father's funeral, months with no word, and if I didn't take the throne, il Tornja *would* have."

"I don't care about the throne," he said again.

She studied him, tried to see past those eyes to something human, something true.

"Then why did you destroy Annur? If you don't care about the throne, why work so hard to keep me from sitting on it?"

"It wasn't to stop you. It was to stop il Tornja. Annur is his . . . his weapon, and I could not let him bring it to bear."

"Did it occur to you," she demanded, "that I might have already taken il Tornja in hand?"

"Taken him in hand?" Kaden raised his brows. "You slept with him, and then, with his support, you declared yourself

Emperor. Not only did you fail to take him in hand, you confirmed him in his post, and then you joined your own military force to his. If you've been anything but compliant, I haven't seen any evidence of it. The fact that you know he is Csestriim, that you know he murdered our father . . . that just makes it worse."

She wanted to hit him, to knock some expression into those expressionless eyes.

"Do you think there has been a day since I learned the truth," she demanded with a growl, "when I didn't dream of opening his throat?"

Kaden met her glare. "Then why haven't you?"

"Because sometimes it is necessary to suppress our immediate instincts, Kaden. Sometimes it is necessary to make sacrifices, to accept, if only for a time, the most loathsome situations." She shook her head, suddenly weary. "It would be nice, wouldn't it, to always speak the first words that came to mind. It would be a wonderful luxury to associate only with the honest and the upright. It would be so, so satisfying never to compromise, never to make decisions that led you to hate yourself."

She stared out to the east, to where the evening wind was whipping up the waves. Behind her, the council chamber would still be smoldering, but sooner or later, that clean east wind, salt-sharp and cool, would scour away the last of the smoke.

"Following your own heart might be a nice way to live," she said quietly, "but it's a disastrous way to rule."

Kaden blinked. "Fair enough," he said after a pause, then cocked his head to the side. "How did you learn the truth about il Tornja?"

"He made mistakes," Adare replied bluntly.

Kaden frowned. Those burning eyes went distant, as though he were studying something beyond the horizon. "That seems unlikely," he replied finally. "It is much more likely that whatever you know about him, he wants you to know."

"Why?" she demanded. "Because I'm just some stupid slut?

Because I couldn't possibly have any insight or agency of my own?"

"Because he is Csestriim, Adare. He is smarter than any of us, and he has had thousands of years to plan. He was their greatest general. . . ."

"You don't need to lecture me on his brilliance," she replied grimly. "You forget that I was on the tower in Andt-Kyl. I saw him command the battle. I know what he can do. I kept him *alive* because of that brilliance, because I know just how badly we need it."

Kaden raised his brows. "And you still think that you outsmarted him?"

"I think that even Csestriim can run into bad luck."

"Meaning what?"

"Meaning there are other factors in play here. Factors unknown to you."

"Tell me."

She barked a laugh. "Just like that, eh?"

He shrugged. "Why not?"

"Because I don't fucking *trust* you, Kaden. That's why not. The first thing you did when you got back to Annur was to destroy it. You're trying to stop il Tornja, or so you claim, but Ran il Tornja is the only one actually *defending* Annur."

"He is not defending Annur," Kaden said quietly. "He's trying to kill Long Fist."

"At the moment, it amounts to much the same thing."

"It would, if Long Fist were just an Urghul chieftain."

And so, after a long diversion, they were back to Long Fist. Adare had never even seen the man, and yet he seemed to be everywhere, the answer to every riddle, the fire beneath every column of smoke, the bloody battle at the end of every endless march. All paths led to him. Every scream could be traced back to his bright knives. Underneath every name she uttered—Kaden, il Tornja, Valyn, Balendin—underneath or above, she seemed to hear the name of the Urghul chieftain echoing.

"And you think he is what?"

Kaden took a deep breath, held it a moment, then blew it out slowly. "Long Fist is Meshkent."

Adare stared. The small hairs on her arm, on the back of her neck, stood up at once. The evening was cool, not cold, but she suppressed a shiver. Il Tornja had been saying the same thing for months, but she had never believed him, not really. "What makes you say that?"

He narrowed his eyes, studying her. "You knew."

"I knew it was a possibility."

"Il Tornja told you."

She nodded carefully.

"And did he tell you *why* he was so eager to see Long Fist destroyed?"

"For the same reason that I am," she said. "For the same reason that you should be. To protect Annur."

"Why would he want to protect Annur? He fought to destroy humanity, Adare. He nearly succeeded. Why would he care about one of our empires?"

"Because it is not *our* empire," she replied. The words were bitter, but she said them anyway. "It is his. He built it. He takes care of it."

"In the same way that a soldier cares for his sword."

"You keep saying that," she said, "but you never get around to explaining how he's planning to use that sword."

"To kill Meshkent."

"Why?"

Kaden hesitated, then looked away.

Adare blew out an angry breath. "If you expect me to believe you, Kaden, if you expect me to help you, then you have to give me *something*. Why are you so concerned about the health of Long Fist or Meshkent or whoever the fuck it happens to be? The bastard is putting our people to the sword and the fire, he's leaping around through these 'Shael-spawned gates—*your* gates, these *kenta*—lighting fires at every corner of Annur. I'm not sure il Tornja's reasons even matter, as long as he stops him."

For the first time, Kaden's eyes widened. Something she'd said, finally, had made it past that shield he used for a face.

"Long Fist is using the *kenta*?" he asked, a new note in his voice, one she couldn't place. "How do you know that?"

"I *don't* know it. It sounds impossible to me, but il Tornja insists it's true."

Kaden was shaking his head, as though resisting the claim.

"I know you thought you and your monks were special," she said, "but if il Tornja's right, Long Fist is a *god*. Evidently gods can pass through the gates."

"It's not the—"

Kaden clamped his mouth shut.

"What?" Adare pressed.

It had seemed, for just a moment, that he was about to talk to her, to *really* talk, without the evasions and omissions that had marred the rest of their conversation. It had seemed as though they were about to push past some unseen barrier, some awful, invisible wall that stood between them even in the limpid evening air. It had seemed, for just a heartbeat, that he was about to speak, not as one politician to another, but as a brother to a sister, as someone who understood the weight and texture of her loss, the awful, echoing emptiness, someone who shared it. Then the moment passed.

"It's surprising," he said brusquely. "Although it makes sense. The violence on the borders is too perfect, too well coordinated to be random."

Adare stared at him, willing him to say more, but he did not say more.

"Nothing about it makes sense," she snapped finally. "But that doesn't mean it can't be the truth."

Kaden nodded slowly.

"So," Adare said, breathing heavily, "are you *still* going to insist we should be worrying about il Tornja and not Long Fist?"

"It's starting to seem," Kaden replied, "that we need to worry about everyone."

"Well, I've done more than worry," Adare said. "I've got il Tornja collared. Under control."

"How?"

"I'll tell you when I trust you."

And suddenly, it didn't seem so impossible, trust. Kaden had known more than she realized. Her lies hadn't needed to be as wide as she had expected, nor so deep. The gap between them was just that, a gap, not a chasm. Intarra knew she could use an ally, one who wasn't immortal or half insane.

"Kaden," she said quietly. "We need to be honest with each other."

He held her eyes and nodded slowly. "I agree."

"You're my brother. We can figure this out together."

Again he nodded, but there was nothing behind the nod, no true agreement.

"I wish Valyn were here," he said after a pause.

It didn't seem like Kaden, like this *new* Kaden, to wish for anything. He was a monk now, and his monk's training appeared to have put him beyond wishing, in the way that fish were beyond breathing. On the other hand, the Shin couldn't have changed him entirely. He had confided in her. It was a start.

"Me, too," she said.

It was the truth. Scholars and philosophers were forever lauding truth, holding it up as a sort of divine perfection available to man. The truth in those old texts was always shining, glowing, golden. As though they didn't know, not any of them, that some truths were jagged as a rusty blade, horrible, serrated, irremovable, lodged forever in the insubstantial substance of the soul.

12

The deadfall was empty.

For the fifth day running, something had triggered the snare, something strong enough to shift the bait stick, but quick enough not to be there when the huge rock came crashing down. Valyn stifled a curse as he knelt in the soft, loamy soil, sifting through the brown needles and dry hemlock cones, searching for some sign of a print. The deadfall wasn't perfect. When he was too cautious in setting it, he'd find the bait stick licked clean while the snare remained untriggered. If he wasn't cautious enough, the whole thing would end up lying in a jumble on the forest floor with no sign that an animal had come anywhere near. Sometimes the stone came down wrong, pinning a hare or a squirrel without killing it. Sometimes the larger creatures— beaver, porcupines—could haul themselves free. It wasn't all that strange to find the snare empty. What was strange was finding it triggered day after day, finding animal tracks leading in and blood on the stone, but no carcass. No tracks leading away.

"'Shael take it," he cursed, resetting the trap with nimble fingers, trying once again to figure out what had gone wrong, how he could prevent it from going wrong again.

It had to be a bird. A red eagle would be plenty strong enough to haul a bloody carcass out of the trap. A red eagle or even a balsam hawk. Birds would take the catch without leaving tracks.

"But birds can't lift the stone," he muttered to himself, hauling with both hands on the flat slab of granite, grunting as he muscled it into position. Valyn could barely lift it himself—which seemed to rule out a bird after all. No—something else was stealing his catch, some creature strong enough to heave aside the huge stone, but smart enough to move over the soft ground without leaving a track. Valyn tried to puzzle out what it might be, tried and failed.

"Sure is a clever bastard," he muttered. "Clever, clever, clever."

As though speaking that word aloud, repeating it, could drown out the other word, the more honest one prowling the back of his mind: not *clever*, but *frightening*.

A cold wind gusted through the boughs. Hemlocks creaked, trunks packed so close together that even the dead trees still stood, forced to remain upright, supported by the living as they went to rot. Even at midmorning, sun filtered weakly through the branches, every lance of light casting a shifting shadow.

Normally Valyn didn't mind the gloom. He knew these woods better than he knew his own home, knew the softest, driest moss where he could catch a quick nap, the best trout holes in the meandering streams, the damp hollows where the mosquitoes swarmed most thickly, and the few sweet spots where the ferns and the breeze kept them at bay. The forest was his; he loved it. Today, though, as he straightened from the newly rigged snare, something felt off, wrong.

He paused just long enough to smear the bait stick with suet, then, crouching low, slipped through a gap in the rough trunks, wanting suddenly to be away from the dark thicket, to get to somewhere he could see more than a dozen paces, somewhere he could actually *run*.

It wasn't far to the Jumping Rock—a low, lichen-crusted granite shelf leaning out over a bend in the river, and when Valyn reached it, he paused, hunkering on the lip to catch his breath. The sun had climbed well above the jagged tops of the eastern trees, high enough to burn off the last of the mist above the meandering current, to warm his skin. A little upstream, a trout rose for a fly; tiny waves radiated out from the disturbance, perfect circles on the green-brown water. Suddenly, Valyn felt foolish. Here he was, a boy of eight, jumping at forest shadows as though he were a baby. He offered up a silent prayer of thanks that his brother wasn't along to witness his cowardice.

"It's a red eagle, sure," he muttered aloud, changing his mind once more as he pondered the mystery of the snare. Out of the shadows, sitting comfortably on the rock's rim, skinny legs dangling down over the water, it seemed like a reasonable answer. A rabbit had triggered the trap, then twisted itself partway free. The eagle could have seized the struggling creature without ever lifting the rock at all. He squinted, trying to picture the scene, the beak hooked in the blood-soaked fur. *Definitely a red eagle.*

He put the question out of his mind, rooting in his leather sack for a twisted length of dried venison, then sat gnawing it contentedly, looking out over the water. There were still a dozen more snares to check, and one of them, surely, would have a squirrel or a hare, maybe even a fisher cat. And if not, well, he wouldn't mind an afternoon going after one of those trout. There was still half a deer hanging up over the fire pit back in the cabin, and plenty of game in the forest. His mother might come home with another deer, or his father and brother with that bear they'd been tracking. It wasn't as though the whole family was relying on Valyn.

He had just settled back on the warm stone, half reclining as he chewed the dried meat, the morning's agitation all but forgotten, when something made him jerk upright, hand on his belt knife. Skin prickling along his arms, he scanned the forest around him. There had been no noise, no bear's growl or rabbit's dying scream. If anything, the woods seemed more still, somber. Even the birds had gone quiet, their light song chopped off mid-note. Sweat slicked Valyn's palms. He could feel his breath coming fast and ragged. Why were the birds so *quiet*?

"Leave your knife where it is."

Valyn spun, searching for the speaker, eyes ranging desperately over the dark wall of the forest. He had to turn in place three times before he finally found the figure, a man almost all in black, standing motionless maybe ten paces away, cloaked in the deepest gloom of the silent pines and hemlocks, face hidden in shadow.

Valyn's heart lunged inside his chest as he lurched to his feet. His fingers scrabbled at his belt knife, trying to pull it free as he raised his other hand in a feeble defense. The man hadn't moved, he had no weapon visible, but that hardly mattered. The simple fact of his presence was danger enough.

Valyn's parents had chosen this buggy, swampy stretch of nowhere precisely for the lack of people. After the Urghul arrived, and the Annurian armies, living in anything like a town became dangerous, even deadly. If the horsemen got you, they killed you, and they killed you slow. Valyn hadn't seen the corpses, but he'd heard the stories, how they'd take people, stake them out, and then start skinning. Just the way you'd take the pelt off a beaver, only you killed the beaver first.

The story was, the Annurian armies were there to protect the loggers and the trappers scattered through the northern woods. That was the story. The truth was, those armies were just as likely to take your winter's store of meat and mead as they were to do any protecting. Valyn's parents had tried to hide the worst from him, but he'd heard tales of Annurian soldiers demanding everything from blankets to bear meat, sometimes the coats right off those too defenseless to object. And that wasn't even the worst of it; Valyn had heard whispers, sick stories of soldiers insisting on having their way with kids like him, the sons and daughters of the frontier families. It wasn't right—it was a whole long way from anything even looking like something right—but if you refused, if you tried to fight back, the soldiers killed you. Killed you, or left you for the Urghul. Hard to say which was worse.

And so Valyn's parents had taken them away. Most folks who fled headed south. Valyn's mother, though, wouldn't hear of it. "What do we know about the south?" she had demanded of his father one night when the fire burned down to a few angry embers. "What do we know about cities? Or city people?"

"It's not all cities," Valyn's father had insisted. His father, who had never set foot outside the Thousand Lakes in his life. "There are farms."

"And what do we know of farming?"

Valyn was supposed to be asleep, tucked beneath his furs in the far corner of the cabin, but through slit lids he'd watched his mother take his father's face in both hands, pulling him close as though she meant to kiss him, then stopping short. "You're a tracker, Fen. A tracker, a trapper, and a hunter. You're a better man than any I've ever met, but you're no farmer."

He could see his father's jaw tense. "The forest isn't safe anymore. We can figure out the farming later. Right now, we've got to get out."

"No," she said slowly, shaking her head. "What we have to do is go deeper."

And so deeper they went, plunging north into territory Valyn had never seen before, untouched forest of balsam and hemlock and red spruce, territory only the hardest or the maddest had even tried to hunt or trap. They kept pushing until they were well north of the last logging villages, a week's walk clear of the lines of battle spreading across the forests of the north, beyond the reach of Urghul and Annurian both. Valyn was starting to think they'd walk forever—all the way to Freeport, maybe, and the oceans of ice beyond that—but one day, just as the sun was setting, the wind blowing cold and hard out of the north, they came to a tiny clearing in the trees, a quiet, mossy spot from which you could see the gray peaks of the Romsdals looming to the north.

"Here," his mother said, putting down her pack on a low granite boulder.

His father had smiled at that. "Here."

The next day they started building.

When it was done, the cabin was larger than the one they'd left—two rooms with a fieldstone fireplace built into the wall. The day they lit that fire for the first time, Valyn's father had taken his mother in his hairy arms, lifted her off her feet, then kissed her square on the lips despite her sputtering protestations.

"You were right," he said. "This is better than anything in the south."

Valyn had thought so, too. Exploring the new forests, choosing the best circuit for his own snares, claiming a portion of land that no one in the long history of the world had ever claimed— it was all a small boy's dream. If he sometimes longed for companionship, for other children to share his adventures, well, he had Kadare, two years older; Kadare, who had taught him even more than Mother and Father about hunting, trapping, and moving silently through the wilderness. Thanks to Kadare, these dark, dense forests felt like home. Until now.

"I told you to leave the knife in the sheath," the stranger said again, shaking his head grimly.

That voice—low, hard, rough and rusted as a long-neglected tool—made Valyn shrink back, and the voice was the least of it. The man facing him looked more dead than alive, lean as a starving wolf at winter's end, all the fat and softness scraped away until there was only skin stretched across corded muscle and bone. He wore something that might have been clothes once—leggings and a shirt of black wool so ripped and torn they offered less protection than Valyn's own crude hides. Beneath the cloth, his flesh was scribbled with scars, small puckered marks and long seams running over his chest and arms. The wounds that left those scars should have killed him half a dozen times over, but he wasn't killed. He was right there, standing just a few paces away, staring at Valyn, if staring was even the right word.

There had been a blind man in the village where Valyn grew

up, an old grandfather people called Ennel the Bent. Valyn had stared at Ennel's eyes whenever he could, fascinated and a little frightened by the milky cloud splashed across the pupils. It had been strange, queasy-making, but old Ennel's eyes were nothing beside those of the man who faced him now.

The stranger's eyes were . . . ruined. They looked as though someone had hacked straight across them with an ax. Blood, trapped somehow beneath the eyeball's surface, washed the part that should have been white. The dark part around the pupil—the iris, Valyn remembered vaguely—was black as burned wood, blacker, dark as the dot at the very center, except for a ragged line of star-white scar. They didn't look like a man's eyes. They didn't look like eyes at all. Valyn wanted to scream.

"Keep your mouth shut," the stranger said, stepping forward. He still hadn't drawn a weapon, but Valyn could see the axes now, two of them, handles lopped short, hanging from a poorly tanned leather belt. Dangling from the same belt was the corpse of a rabbit, skull crushed and bloody.

"My rabbit," Valyn said stupidly, words spilling out of him as he stared. "You been stealing from my snares."

The stranger grimaced. "You have bigger problems, kid."

Valyn took a step back, trying to keep some space between them, raising his hands. "I won't tell no one. You can have the rabbit. You can have all of 'em. I'll show you where the snares are. . . ." He was babbling, but he couldn't stop himself. He'd seen something he wasn't supposed to see, had caught this man who was barely a man with the stolen rabbit, and now he was going to die. Valyn glanced over his shoulder into the sluggish river. He could jump, could try to swim it out. Maybe the man in black didn't know how to swim. He turned back just as the hand closed around his throat.

Valyn felt his bladder give way. He tried to scream, but the hand wouldn't let him. The man might look starved, but his grip was iron.

"Quit squirming, kid. I'm trying to help you."

Stars screamed across Valyn's vision. Everything started to go dark. He aimed a kick at the killer's gut. *Like kicking stone,* he thought, just before he passed out.

A hard slap across the face brought him back. The stranger had laid him out on the granite ledge, was kneeling beside him now, hand poised at his throat.

"Don't scream," he said. "They're far off, but that's no reason to take chances."

He paused, raised his head. The movement—both wary and predatory—reminded Valyn of a lone wolf sniffing the air. After a moment, the man cursed quietly, then turned those awful, broken eyes back to Valyn.

"You know who the Urghul are?"

Valyn managed a weak nod.

"They're headed toward your cabin now. A small band of them. Maybe twenty. If you go back now, they'll catch you, too. Hurt you. Kill you."

For a few heartbeats, Valyn struggled to make sense of the words. There were no Urghul this far north. He was safe here, he and his family both. They'd come here so they would be safe. The stranger was lying to him, was going to kill him. . . . He stared up at the man. Those eyes were worse than a skull's hollow sockets. He was horrible, more terrifying than Valyn's worst dream, but he wasn't lying. A new horror bloomed inside Valyn. He tried to yank free, but the man held him down easily. It didn't seem possible he could be so strong.

"There aren't any Urghul here," Valyn protested. "They don't come up here."

The stranger grimaced. "They didn't. Now, it seems that they do."

"How do you know?"

The man hesitated. "I can smell them," he said finally. "Horses and blood. They reek." He turned an ear to the wind. "I almost believe I can hear them."

It didn't make sense. Valyn sucked in a huge breath. He didn't smell any horses. The only thing he could hear was his own desperate panting.

"If there's Urghul, I gotta warn my folks, my brother."

The man in black shook his head grimly. "Too late for warning. Your cabin's a long way off. They're almost there."

"Then I'll fight 'em!" Valyn said, trying again to twist free. This time, to his surprise, the man let him up.

"Four against twenty? All you can do is die, kid." He looked off blankly into the darkness between the trees, then shook his head. "Don't go back."

Valyn expected something else, something more, but the man just turned on his heel. He even moved like a wolf, stalking toward the trees. He paused at the edge of the forest, turned, yanked the rabbit free of his belt, and tossed it to the ground in front of Valyn.

"Yours," he said, then turned away again.

Valyn caught up with him a dozen paces into the hemlocks. Terror made him reckless, and he seized the stranger by the leather belt, pulled him back a moment, then found himself lifted by the front of his shirt, then slammed against the rough trunk of a tree. He could feel the jagged ends of the branches stabbing at him through his clothes as the man in black leaned close.

"Never touch me," he hissed.

Valyn could barely breathe, but he forced himself to speak. "I need your *help*."

"You already got it."

"I need more. I need to save my family. You can *fight. . . .*"

He couldn't say how he knew. Something about the way the man moved, about those twin axes hanging from his belt, about the terrible strength that kept him pinned against the tree. *He's a warrior.* The thought spun around and around in Valyn's mind like an autumn leaf caught in an eddy. *He's a killer.*

"I can't fight them alone," Valyn pleaded. "I need your help."

"I don't help."

The stranger held Valyn a moment longer, then dropped him.

Valyn struggled to catch his breath, to get to his feet. One of the branches had torn through his leather tunic, tearing open a gash across his back. He could feel it bleeding. It didn't matter.

"You helped *me*," he insisted. "You warned me. You're not Urghul. You're Annurian. You speak Annurian. And you warned me."

"It was convenient."

Valyn stared, aghast. He couldn't get the vision of his burning cabin out of his head. This time in the morning, they would all be there—his father and mother chopping firewood for the fall; his brother digging the new well. He imagined his family bleeding, sprawled out on the ground, cut open, bled out like wild game.

"Please," he said, staying on his knees, staring up at the horrifying figure above him. "Please help me."

The stranger ground his teeth so hard Valyn thought his jaw might crack, that the tendons of his neck might snap in two. It was impossible to read the emotion on that face: Rage? Regret? He didn't seem the type of person to feel regret, but he was hesitating, and that hesitation gave Valyn a faint, horrible hope.

"Please," he said again, voice barely louder than the breeze.

"I need you to guide me," the man said at last.

Valyn nodded eagerly, lurching to his feet. "All right," he said, stumbling down the low slope. "This way. Hurry!"

After a dozen steps, he turned, realizing that the man in black hadn't moved. He remained standing on the rock ledge, back turned to the morning sun, face lost in the shadow.

"Please!" Valyn pleaded. "Come *on*!"

The stranger shook his head slowly. "I can move through the forest alone, but I'm too slow." Then, with a movement that was the opposite of slow, a gesture so fast Valyn didn't have time to flinch, the man slipped one of the short axes from the belt at his side, spun it once in the air, then caught the haft below the head. He held the handle out toward Valyn. "Take the other end," he said. "Lead the way. It'll be faster."

For a moment, Valyn couldn't move. He was terrified of what the stranger claimed was happening at his home, and terrified, too, of the stranger himself. Touching that ax, even the harmless butt of the wooden haft, seemed dangerous. More than dangerous. "What?" he asked, rooted to the spot by his conflicting horrors. *"Why?"*

"Because," the man replied grimly, "I'm blind."

We're too late.

That was Valyn's first thought when they burst into the narrow clearing.

The cabin was still standing. Nothing was on fire. No one was screaming, but mounted men and women packed the small open space where Valyn's family had cleared the trees to let in a little light. The riders looked like monsters. Their skin was too pale, their hair too yellow, their eyes too terribly blue. *Urghul.* The man in black had been right. Somehow, impossibly, the Urghul had come. They'd found Valyn's home, Valyn's family, and now it was all over, all finished.

A scream scraped up his throat and out, shivering the late-morning air. Normally Valyn would have been ashamed of the thin, weak sound, but he was past shame, almost past fear, even. His legs shook beneath him, and he felt like he couldn't breathe, like the air was all tangled up inside his chest. He felt like that chest might explode. It felt like fear, and not like fear. Like something far worse than fear.

He dropped the wooden handle of the ax and stumbled forward a step, searching for his belt knife, wondering if it would hurt when the Urghul killed him. A hand on his shoulder brought him up short. The stranger's grip again, strong as stone. Valyn tried to twist free, but the man pulled him back.

"Knock it off," he growled. "Shut up. Get behind me."

"My family—"

"—is still alive." The man pointed to the shadow of the stacked woodpile, to where Valyn's mother and brother stood pinned against the logs by the lowered lances of the horsemen. His father lay sprawled on the ground a pace away, blood seeping from an awful gash across his forehead. "Your family's alive. Don't do anything stupid, and they might stay that way."

Valyn felt his legs collapse beneath him, then he dropped like a deadfall stone.

His mother jerked at the motion, noticing him for the first time, gave a strangled cry, tried to move forward, found steel at her throat, then subsided, tears streaking her cheeks. His brother met his eyes; he was trembling, either with fear or rage. Valyn's own tears smeared his vision. Again he knew he should be ashamed, and again, the shame meant nothing. He would live with a lifetime of shame and worse than shame if only the Urghul would just ride on, would leave his family to their life here in this tiny clearing.

"Huutsuu," said the strange man with the axes.

Valyn had no idea what the word meant, but most of the horsemen wheeled their mounts at the sound of this new voice. Spearheads glinted, bright in the unforgiving light. Bows creaked as the warriors took aim. There were enough to kill the man in black a dozen times over, but he didn't seem worried.

Of course he's not worried, stupid, Valyn realized. *He can't see them.*

"They have bows," he gasped. "They're going to shoot—"

Before he could finish the sentence, two of the horsemen loosed their shafts. They couldn't miss from that distance. At eight paces, Valyn could hit a chipmunk darting along a branch, and the stranger was a lot larger than a chipmunk.

And faster, too, as it turned out. So much faster.

Valyn stared as the man slashed his arm up and across, the motion too quick to follow, too quick to be *real* . . . and yet there was an arrow shaft clattering uselessly into the needles just a few paces away. When Valyn turned back, he found the stranger holding the other arrow, the shaft snatched from the air just inches from his chest. He clenched his fist, and the arrow snapped.

"Huutsuu," he said again. "Check your warriors, or I will kill them."

The archers didn't lower their bows, but they hesitated this time, obviously taken aback by what they'd just seen. Some were glancing over at a tall woman with streaming blond hair who was nudging her horse forward through the press. Valyn was no stranger to tough women—his own mother could spend half a day splitting rock maple with their eight-pound maul, then run her own circuit of traps before dark—but Huutsuu, if that was her name, made Valyn's mother look old, weak. He felt as though he had been raised by a feral housecat, and was only now seeing a mountain lion for the first time. The Urghul woman wore hide leggings and a hide vest that did nothing to disguise the scars carved into her arms and across the flesh of her shoulders. When she shifted in her saddle, Valyn could see the muscle move beneath her skin. She carried a bow across the front of her saddle, but had made no effort to nock an arrow or to bring it to bear.

She considered the man in black for a time, then shook her head.

"So. Kwihna has seen fit to test you," she said. "You are harder than when we last met."

The words sounded like a compliment. Valyn's stomach squirmed inside him. The man in black knew the woman. What if they were friends? What if he decided not to stop her after all? What if he was one of the Urghul himself?

Valyn glanced up at the stranger. His skin was too dark, and his eyes—but what did Valyn know about the alliances taking place beyond his family's own quiet corner of the forest? Who was he to say that there weren't Annurians—traitors!—in league with the horsemen? The Urghul had shot at the man in black, that was true, but then they'd *stopped* shooting. And the stranger had *lied*, lied about being blind. . . .

Valyn started to inch through the needles, away from the stranger, toward the dubious safety of the forest. If he could slip away, maybe he could double back. There was a narrow gap between the stacks of wood. They could sneak out that way, get into the dense hemlocks where the horses wouldn't be able to follow. . . .

Pain exploded, bright and baffling, across the back of his head. He was facedown on the earth, mouth open, gagging on pine needles, nose filled with the reek of wet dirt and rotting things. Someone had hit him . . . the stranger . . . he'd attacked. . . .

"I told you not to move," the man said.

Valyn began to raise himself up on his elbows, then caught his mother's gaze from across the clearing. She didn't speak, just shook her head slowly, carefully. She had a hand on his brother's arm, holding him back. Kadare was strong, angry, quick to act. If he was keeping still, letting himself be held back, then it was important. It was necessary. Valyn subsided against the cool ground. He wanted to vomit, whether from the pain or the fear, he wasn't sure.

"Why are you here?" the stranger asked.

Despite his claims about being blind, he had locked eyes with the woman. To Valyn's amazement, she was able to hold that awful, wrecked gaze without flinching. The silence lasted a long time, as though the man in black and the mounted woman were both leaning against it, seeing who would collapse first. Finally the woman—Huutsuu, her name was—nodded curtly, as though she had made a decision.

"We are looking. Hunting."

"Hunting." The stranger shook his head, then spat into the litter of leaves. "Hunting what? A family of trappers? Doesn't Long Fist have enough Annurians to murder down on the front?"

"Long Fist is gone," the woman replied.

The man in black frowned. "Gone. Where?"

"I don't know. He told us to obey the leach, your friend. Then he left."

"Balendin." There was rage in the stranger's voice now. Valyn could see his fingers tighten around the haft of his ax. "Balendin is leading your people?"

"Most of them," Huutsuu replied.

"Most?"

The woman glanced over her shoulder at the other riders, then nodded. "It is not right. Some of us have had enough."

"I didn't think you ever had enough. Pain is pain, right?"

"You are harder, but still stupid."

"So teach me."

"We worship Kwihna. This foreign leach worships only himself. His killing is not a sacrifice; it is a hoarding up of his own power. There is nothing ennobling in it. Nothing ennobling in following such a creature."

The stranger grunted. None of it meant anything to Valyn, but as long as they were talking, as long as they were focused on each other, no one was murdering his family. He glanced across the clearing. His father was still unconscious in the dirt, but his brother had slipped clear of his mother's grip, had used the distraction to pull a long log from the woodpile, wrapping his broad hands around it as though it were a weapon, as though he could fight his way free of two dozen Urghul with nothing more than a stick of firewood. Valyn's mother had noticed, was struggling silently with him, trying to stop him, but he yanked free, pivoted, searching for a target.

"Don't!" Valyn shouted, but the nearest Urghul was already turning, swinging his spear around. Valyn's mother lunged forward, trying to put herself between her son's body and the leaf-shaped blade. She was fast, but the stranger's ax was faster, flashing end over end through the center of the clearing, burying itself in the Urghul's back with the sound of steel striking rotten wood. The horseman went all loose in the limbs, then fell silently.

Before he hit the ground, Huutsuu was barking something in her own language.

The remaining Urghul looked angry, confused, but they didn't continue the attack. Valyn's mother wrested the log away from his brother, then dragged him back against the woodpile, her strong, sun-dark arm wrapped around him as he trembled with rage and shame, holding him close, whispering something in his ear that Valyn couldn't hear.

Huutsuu was watching the man in black, shaking her head. "Each time I see you, you kill my men."

"The last time I saw you, you told me they weren't men if they let themselves be killed."

If the stranger was bothered to have only one ax left, it didn't show. Nothing seemed to bother him. There was an angle to the way he stood, something in his posture or his face that seemed familiar. *Rabid,* Valyn realized suddenly. *He's like something rabid.*

Huutsuu's laugh broke through the thought. The sound was chilling, like the howl of coyotes late at night, when they were closing in on their kill.

"Why are you here?" she asked the man. "Where are your companions?"

The stranger shook his head, as though the word *companions* had no meaning for him.

"Keep going, Huutsuu," he said quietly. "Leave these people alone."

"There is a danger in leaving alive those who hate you." She smiled. "I thought that I had taught you this lesson."

"This family doesn't hate you, Huutsuu. I've been watching them for half a year. They hunt and trap. They cut wood for the winter. They're not part of the war. Leave them alone."

The woman hesitated, then shook her head. "I will kill them quickly."

"No," he replied, voice flat. "You will not."

Again she laughed. "You are only one man, Malkeenian."

"And barely that," the stranger muttered, so softly that Valyn almost missed the words. Then the man raised his chin and his voice both. "Ride or fight, Huutsuu. Ananshael can sort out the rest."

"Ananshael." The woman grimaced, then blew out a long breath. "You would die for these people? You would kill for them?"

"I've killed for less."

The Urghul watched him a long time. Valyn's palms were sweating. His heart galloped inside his ribs. He felt as though he might pass out, but he did not pass out. Finally a new expression crept onto the woman's face.

"These fools are harmless," she said, gesturing to Valyn's family. "I can leave them behind, leave them alive."

The stranger started to nod, but she cut him off with a raised hand.

"But *you*, Malkeenian, are far from harmless. You left me alive once, and it nearly killed you. I will not make your mistake."

"If you think you can kill me," he said quietly, "you are welcome to try."

He sounded ready, though to kill or to die, Valyn couldn't say.

"I don't want you dead. I want you to join us."

The man in black narrowed his eyes. "Why would I join a band of Urghul savages?"

Huutsuu smiled. "Because these Urghul savages will kill the leach who corrupts our people. Who profanes our god."

"Balendin." The name—if it *was* a name—sounded like a curse.

"Like us," Huutsuu replied, "you hate the leach. I remember this well."

The stranger hesitated, then shook his head. "I hate a lot of people."

She shrugged. "This is a start."

"I don't need a start."

"Yes," Huutsuu said. "You do. For half a year, you say, you have been prowling these forests like a diseased wolf. I offer . . . another path."

"I don't want your path. I'm delighted with my own."

Huutsuu's eyes flashed. "And if you do not join us, I will kill you, then offer this family to the god. Slowly."

The stranger studied her a long time, features expressionless as worn granite. "Why?" he asked, the word a growl.

She shrugged. "I need warriors. And whatever else you are, you are a warrior."

"If you need warriors, then what in Hull's name are you doing up here? You're miles from any kind of fight."

"We're looking for ghosts, Malkeenian. Three of them. People like you."

The stranger jerked as though struck, half raised his remaining ax, bared his teeth, as though he were about to leap upon the woman and hack out her heart.

His words, when he finally spoke, were cold as winter stone. "What people?"

Huutsuu shook her head slowly. "We have no names, but they wear black," she gestured toward the stranger's shredded clothes, "like you. Only three, but for many months they have plagued us. They attack our messengers and our warriors, sometimes come into full camp to do their killing. Those who give chase come back empty-handed, or they do not come back at all. They have no horses, these three, but they are fast, and they strike always at night."

"So . . ." Something that might have been a smile twisted the stranger's lips. "You want to join them? To help them? I thought Annurians were a weak, degenerate people."

"Not these. They are hard as any Urghul. More, they are Annurians, like the leach who leads my people. They may know how to kill him."

"It sounds like they've been trying," the man in black replied. "Failing."

Huutsuu waved the words away. "They are only three. It is a hard thing for them to move among my people. Together, though, we could open the throat of this leach."

"If they don't open your throat first. If they're so dangerous, they might find you first, kill you."

"Perhaps. Perhaps not. You will join us. You will explain the way of things to these Annurians."

The stranger lowered his ax, hesitated a long moment as though torn, then shook his head. "No. I am finished with all this."

Huutsuu shrugged. "Then we will fight, and when the fight is through, I will give this family to the god."

Valyn could only watch, aghast. He understood almost none of it. He didn't know who Long Fist was, or Balendin, or why this man had been hiding in the woods, or how he knew the woman, or why that woman kept calling him Malkeenian, as though he were some Annurian emperor. All he knew was that his own family's fate hung in the balance. If the man said yes, they might live. If he said no, something terrible was going to happen. He was sobbing, he realized, moaning into the dirt.

"It's all right, Valyn." His mother's voice from across the clearing. "Just stay still, son. It's going to be all right."

He looked up to see her staring at him, a hand half outstretched. Urghul spears blocked her way, and Urghul horses, but he could see her eyes, could hear her voice.

"It's all right, Valyn, my son. It's all right."

Off to his right, the stranger shifted. Valyn glanced over to find the man staring down at him.

"What's your name, kid?"

"Valyn," he stammered. "Named for the prince," he said. "The Emperor's oldest son."

Why the man cared, he had no idea, but talking wasn't killing. *Please,* he prayed inwardly, offering the words up to any god that would listen, *please let us just keep talking.*

And then, to his shock, Huutsuu was laughing. She was

watching the man in black and laughing uncontrollably. The stranger glanced up at her, then back at Valyn, studying him. Finally, something seemed to go slack in his shoulders. He nodded.

"Fine," he growled. "Getting tired of stealing the food from this kid's trap anyway."

"Of course you'll come," the Urghul woman replied, as though she'd known it all along, as though all the drawn bows and leveled spears had been just for show. "Your flesh is hard, but there is still a softness in your heart."

The man looked anything but soft when he fixed her with his gaze. "You may regret this," he said.

She smiled. "That's what makes it interesting." She turned away from the stranger, barked a few commands, and the Urghul were riding out of the clearing, ignoring Valyn and Valyn's parents as though they were no more consequential than dirt where they had fallen. Valyn could only stare as the man in black reached down, dragged him to his feet by the front of his tunic, then fixed him with that ravaged stare.

"You're brave, kid. And you're good. Whatever your name, you're better than any fucking emperor's son. You got that?"

Valyn nodded hesitantly. The man watched him a long time, then nodded.

"Good," he said roughly, then turned away to cross the clearing. He wrenched his short ax free from the flesh of the slaughtered Urghul, then kicked the body clear as though it were a piece of rotten wood, good for nothing; not building, not even the fire.

13

"Adare is lying," Kaden said.

Kiel studied him by the low light of the lamp. Kaden had returned to his study on the thirtieth floor of the Spear almost immediately after his conversation on the docks, pausing only to send a servant in search of the historian. The wait gave him time to mull over the conversation with his sister, staring out the ironglass walls at the city below while he worked through every gesture, every phrase, trying to see the truth beneath the words. By the time Kiel arrived, night had nearly fallen, and Kaden's darkest suspicion had calcified into certainty.

"About what?" Kiel asked, plucking an olive from a wooden bowl on the table, then joining Kaden at the clear wall.

Kaden paused to summon up the *saama'an* of his sister's face once more, examining her eyes, her mouth, the tension around her jaw. After considering the still image, he scrolled the vision forward slowly, pausing on the moments when she hesitated or looked away.

"Not everything," he said finally. "But where Valyn is concerned, she's holding something back."

Kiel kept his eyes on the city below. His expression was flat, impassive, as he waited silently for the rest of it.

"When I made contact with Gwenna and her Wing," Kaden went on quietly, "I learned a little more about Valyn. Talal—the leach—said that Valyn made contact with Adare in

Aats-Kyl—the town at the southern end of Scar Lake—days before the actual battle."

"And your sister," the historian concluded, "claims not to have seen him at all."

"That's right," Kaden said, then shook his head. "But why?"

Once again, he studied the image carved across his mind.

In some ways, Adare was instantly recognizable, the woman who had grown from the girl to whom Kaden had bidden farewell on the Annurian docks all those years earlier. The eyes, of course, were unmistakable—Adare's had always burned the brightest, the hottest, even when their father was still alive. The lines of her face, too, he recognized, long and lean, high cheekbones and a narrow jaw. All of her physical attributes, as he studied them one by one, seemed consistent with the slender girl he remembered from his childhood.

There was something else, however, a new cast to her face or her features, a look at once obvious and ineffable that had nothing at all to do with the girl she had been. Kaden stared into his sister's eyes, trying to shape their strangeness into words. She was more . . .

He closed his own eyes, blotting out the familiar sights of his father's study, focusing more intently on the image he had etched into his brain. There were Adare's scars, of course, a delicate red tracery seared into her skin by the lightning strike at the Everburning Well. Thousands of men and women accounted her a prophet for those very scars, for having survived the ordeal at the Well at all, and yet for all their strangeness, the scars were just scars—smooth, raised flesh bright in the day's remembered light.

"Adare has changed . . . ," Kaden began, then trailed off.

"It is natural," Kiel replied. "Your kind has always been . . . unstable, impermanent. Like all humans, like yourself, Adare is a creature in flux."

"No," Kaden said, shaking his head. "It's more than that. Or different than that. She's older, but she is also . . . deeper. Harder.

There is more to her, somehow, than I remember, and not just more, but different, as though she were broken, and that break were mended with something foreign to her nature. She reminds me of Valyn."

"Human nature is not fixed," Kiel said. "You are always shifting, changing. Normally your kind does not notice the alteration because it takes place gradually, over weeks and years. You, however, were separated from your siblings for a long time; now you are trying to accommodate that change, to make sense of it, all at once."

Kaden exhaled slowly, letting the *saama'an* go with the breath, then opening his eyes.

"According to Talal," he said, taking the facts, setting them carefully into place one by one, as though they were stones forming the foundation of a new wall, "Valyn wanted to kill il Tornja. Long Fist gave my brother both freedom and weapons to do just that. Valyn crossed the border with Talal and Laith. They found Adare and il Tornja at Aats-Kyl, draining the lake to allow the army to pass. Valyn spoke with Adare then. She convinced him that il Tornja was necessary in the coming battle with the Urghul. She convinced Valyn to spare him until after Andt-Kyl. According to Talal, Valyn lay in wait for the general, along with Talal himself, on top of the tallest tower in Andt-Kyl—some sort of signal tower for boats coming up from the south. Talal didn't see what happened next, he went down to fight Balendin, but we know from Adare that il Tornja was also atop that tower commanding the battle, along with Adare herself. . . ."

He let the silence say the rest.

After a long pause, Kiel nodded. "Your conclusion seems likely. Perhaps inevitable."

Kaden hesitated, then sloughed off his own mind, sliding first into the vast emptiness of the *vaniate,* and then, after a pause, into the imagined contours of a different mind, one that might have belonged to his brother. The *beshra'an* was an imperfect skill, especially when you weren't certain of the person you aimed to inhabit, of their actions and habits, the recurring patterns of emotion. Though they were brothers, Kaden knew almost nothing of Valyn. Their paths had forked too early in life, their reunion had been too brief and baffled by fighting and flight. Still, when he settled his own mind into the shape of Valyn's thoughts, a few things seemed clear: Valyn wanted il Tornja dead, and he wouldn't ever quit.

Kaden had never come within a hundred miles of Andt-Kyl, but he could imagine the tower, a precarious pile of roughly mortared stone at the north end of the lake. He could imagine Valyn lying on the roof watching the battle below, torn between a desire to take part, to fight beside his friends, and his determination to see il Tornja killed. According to Talal, he had sacrificed everything to stay on that roof. When the battle was finished, when he finally had the opportunity . . .

Kaden's eyes slammed open. He let his brother's mind go.

"He attacked. He tried to kill il Tornja, and he failed."

"It fits," Kiel said slowly, "with what you learned from Gwenna and Talal."

"And it fits with who he was. Even if Valyn knew il Tornja was Csestriim, even if he knew he couldn't win, he wouldn't have quit. He would have tried to carry out his mission."

Only when Kaden trailed off did he hear his own words: *who he was*. At some point, lost in the *beshra'an,* he'd started speaking of his brother in the past tense. He turned his mind once more to the memory of his sister. He contemplated her face, the way she averted her eyes when he asked her about Valyn.

"He's dead," Kaden said. "And Adare knows it. If she was on the tower, she saw him killed."

"Or killed him herself," Kiel added quietly.

Kaden felt a sick sorrow twist around him. For a moment, he began to reach for the *vaniate,* then resisted. Maybe the Csestriim was right about the dangers of living too long inside the emptiness, and maybe he wasn't, but this . . . if it was true . . .

was something he needed to face. What would it mean, after all, if his sister had killed his brother and Kaden himself felt no sorrow, no anger, no horror? If human beings were no more than the tangled sum of their experience, what was a person who had no experience, who sidestepped it, whose emotions remained unsnared by the cords of the world? Despite its allure, the *vaniate* of the Shin was a cold thing, alien, alienating.

"I don't think she *could* have killed him," Kaden said finally, shaking his head. "Not unless she put a knife in his back."

"Regardless of who wielded the knife," Kiel said, "it seems likely, more than likely, that Valyn tried to kill il Tornja. He failed, then died for his failure. Adare knows all of this."

"So ruthless," Kaden said, shaking his head. "And for what? So she can sit the throne? So she can wear the imperial title?"

He tried to inhabit his sister's mind, but he knew even less of Adare than he did of Valyn. The shapes of her actions and decisions made no sense. For several heartbeats he struggled to achieve some version of the *beshra'an,* then gave up. He had long ago accepted that there were some people—Rampuri Tan, Pyrre Lakatur, even his own father—that he would never really know.

"Adare was lying about Valyn," Kaden said finally, "but she was telling the truth about Meshkent."

"And what truth," Kiel asked, cocking his head to the side, "did she tell?"

Kaden took a deep breath. This was a part of the conversation that he had so far failed to parse. The facts were clear, but the implications remained beyond him. Which was why he needed Kiel's counsel.

"Long Fist—Meshkent—is using the *kenta.*"

The Csestriim studied him a moment, then leaned back, eyes suddenly elsewhere. Kiel was generally very good at hiding his true nature, but this look, one Kaden had seen before, always when the historian was trying to work through some intractable problem, was not human at all. "She knows this for certain?" he asked at last.

"She believes it. Il Tornja believes it. It explains the coordination of the attacks on Annur's borders, explains how everything seems to be falling apart all at the same time."

"It explains more than that," the Csestriim said quietly.

"Meaning what?"

"Long Fist is not simply Urghul." Kiel seemed to be studying the stars through the glassy walls of the Spear. "He is also one of the Ishien. Their commander, in fact."

Kaden stared. The words were simple enough, and the meaning behind them, but there seemed no way to thread this claim into the world's densely woven fabric. It didn't fit. And if it could be *made* to fit, the implications . . .

"Matol was the commander," Kaden said slowly, rehearsing his own beliefs, as though to speak a thing were to make it true. "Triste destroyed him with the *kenta*."

Kiel shook his head. "Matol was only a lieutenant, one who had been left in charge a long time, many years—but still just a lieutenant. There was another man they spoke of: Horm. I never met him."

Kaden ransacked his memory, sorting through the conversations. Tan had never mentioned the name, nor had Matol, but it was there, lodged in the back of his mind, recollected from an offhand remark of one of his jailors: *Rampuri Tan was a Hunter. Almost as tough as Bloody Horm, least in some ways.* In the moment, Kaden had been too curious about Tan's past to ask anything more about the man to whom he was compared, and there had been no reason to revisit the comment later. The Dead Heart had been filled with hard men, and he'd had no intention of getting to know them all.

"So Horm was on the steppe," Kaden said slowly, the stones of his thought locking into place. "He was Ishien pretending to be Urghul, pretending to be Long Fist."

Kiel shook his head. "Not quite. Long Fist, that physical

body, *is* Urghul—he has the skin, the eyes, the hair. It's hard to say when Meshkent inhabited that body—probably when Long Fist was still on the steppe, maybe after he'd joined the Ishien—but the Ishien piece is crucial." Oddly, he smiled. "I should have seen it so much earlier."

"You said you never even met Horm."

"It is hardly an excuse. The pattern was there."

Kaden frowned. "So Meshkent inhabited Long Fist, united the Urghul . . ."

Kiel shook his head. "No. His triumphant return to the steppe would have happened *after* he joined the Ishien, perhaps long after. The Ishien do this sort of thing all the time—take on new identities, worm their way into communities all over Vash and Eridroa, often for years. For decades."

"It's how they hunt you."

The Csestriim nodded. "They wouldn't find many of my kind if they never left the Dead Heart. To do that, they need to go out, to blend in, or in Long Fist's case, to return."

"Then why take the detour in the first place? Meshkent wants to destroy Annur, but the Ishien don't *care* about Annur. They don't care about anything except the extermination of your race."

"Your thinking is too linear," Kiel said. "Not every scheme leads directly to its goal."

Kaden's thinking felt anything but linear. His mind tumbled end over end, tossed like a stick in a turbulent stream. With an effort, he slowed that stream, tried to find an eddy where he could rest, take stock.

"The gates," Kaden said after a long pause. "Meshkent knew that to defeat Annur, he'd need to fight on more than one front, and to do that, he needed access to the gates."

"Indeed," Kiel replied. "Even with the full might of the Urghul behind him, Long Fist is unable to force his way past il Tornja and the Army of the North. He is winning because he's fighting on the other fronts. The pirates and rebellions, the proliferation of banditry and violence down in the Waist—it is a more subtle war than the one being waged in the north, but it is war all the same."

"And it is destroying us," Kaden breathed.

He felt, suddenly, like one of the raptors in the imperial mews. The birds were kept hooded when they weren't flying, and with a flick of his mind, he could imagine one of the creatures chafing against the constraints of the hood, eager to be free of the leather, believing that the hood was the whole prison. And then, to have the hood pulled off, to see that it had been the least of the constraints, to find the thick jesses wrapping the talons, to comprehend the bars of the cage, and beyond those bars, the implacable walls, and to find, nowhere in the deep rustle and gloom of the awful, man-made mews, any sign of the sky.

All this time, Kaden had known they were failing. He just hadn't seen how badly.

"And there may be another reason," Kiel went on, oblivious to Kaden's silence. "If Meshkent suspects that a Csestriim sits at the heart of Annurian power, he will have been wise to ally himself with the Hunters of Csestriim."

"Could he?" Kaden asked. "Could he know that?"

Meshkent was a god, after all. It suddenly seemed possible that he knew *everything*.

Kiel said nothing for a long time. He didn't move. Finally he met Kaden's eyes. "I cannot say. The gods are not omniscient, but what they know . . . or how they know it . . . is beyond me."

Inside the darkness of his own mind, Kaden studied the cold caverns of the Dead Heart, tried to imagine a god cloaked in a man's flesh walking those chill halls, eating the same soft white fish year after year, living among men whose minds were broken by the rituals they set themselves.

"And he likes it," Kaden said softly.

Kiel raised his brows.

"Meshkent," Kaden went on. "Long Fist. Bloody Horm. Whatever he calls himself, he might have joined the Ishien in order to use the gates, to get at the Csestriim, but he also *likes* it there. The Dead Heart—it is a temple to suffering."

The Csestriim nodded slowly. "So it is."

Kaden watched the historian for a moment, then looked out past the ironglass at the city of Annur stretched out below. The crescent moon, sharp as a blade, was buried in the rooftops to the west. The night was dark, and about to get darker.

"I have to go there," he said quietly. A part of him quailed at the words, but he found the fear, crushed it out. "I have to go back to the Dead Heart."

Kiel studied him. "You hope to find him. Meshkent."

"I need to," Kaden said. "I can't win against il Tornja. We brought Adare here hoping she might tell us his weaknesses, maybe even help us kill him. . . ." He shook his head wearily. "And now we know we can't trust her, that she's lying to us. For all we know, she's here to do il Tornja's work, whatever that is. At every step, he has outmaneuvered us. We destroyed the empire, and it didn't even *matter*. Not in the real fight."

"Don't be too certain," Kiel said. "If il Tornja had the strength of a unified Annur behind him, he might have destroyed Meshkent already. If you didn't control the Dawn Palace, he could have already come for Triste. For Ciena."

"We managed a delay," Kaden said, shaking his head. "Nothing more. Il Tornja *knew* about Long Fist, knew the Urghul chieftain was also the god. Meshkent isn't the only one fighting the war on several fronts, and worse, he might not even be aware of the danger he is in. He thinks he's fighting for Annur, but il Tornja doesn't *care* about Annur. All of this," Kaden gestured to the city, to the dark fields slumbering beyond, "is just a set of stones to be played, to be sacrificed if necessary."

"Ran il Tornja is quick," Kiel said, "and bright. But Meshkent is a god. He has played his own stones well."

"But he's playing the wrong game. He's trying to control the board, to wrest back control of Vash and Eridroa, to reinstate his own bloody worship. Il Tornja doesn't care about the board.

His victory hangs on the capture of just two stones: Triste and Long Fist. I can't help Triste any more than I have. She is as safe as I can make her, and more, she is *here,* inside the Spear, where she needs to be. There's nothing else I can do for her, but I can warn Long Fist. I can try to bring him here, too."

"To the Spear."

Kaden nodded. "Where else?"

Kiel watched him for a while, or seemed to watch him. Kaden had the impression that the Csestriim was actually looking past him or through him, at some truth more crucial and abstract.

"Long Fist is not like Triste," he said finally.

"They're both gods," Kaden replied.

"No," Kiel replied, shaking his head. "Triste as you know her is a young woman with a goddess trapped inside her mind. Meshkent is not trapped. He wears Long Fist as you would wear a monk's robe. He is in control, fully in control."

"That's why I need to talk to him. He can help. . . ."

"Why would he help?"

Kaden blinked. "Il Tornja is trying to kill Ciena, trying to kill *him.* We are trying to stop il Tornja. That puts all of us on the same side. At least as far as this fight goes, that makes us allies."

"You assume the god believes he needs an ally. You assume that he wants one. Do not forget, Kaden, that Meshkent came to this earth, took on this human flesh, to destroy Annur, to tear down everything your progenitors worked so hard to build."

"According to Adare, it was il Tornja who built Annur. The Malkeenians were just . . . puppets."

"And it is generally the puppets who pay the heaviest price. Meshkent may not know about il Tornja's involvement in your empire. And if he does know, he may not care. You are no longer Emperor, but you are still First Speaker of Annur, of the Annurian Republic. He has every reason to kill you. This notion of an alliance is a shield of glass. It will cut you when it shatters."

Kaden shook his head slowly. "You're wrong. My shield is not the alliance. It is my uselessness."

Kiel regarded him silently, waiting.

"I have failed here in Annur," Kaden went on, voice level as he faced the ugly fact. "The republic is a shambles. I could hardly have done more to help Meshkent if I had set out to support him from the very beginning."

"He may eliminate you nonetheless. He may kill you to simplify the battle, for no other reason."

"And if he kills me," Kaden asked quietly, "is that such a great loss to our cause? I have none of your understanding of history. None of Gabril's knifework. None of Kegellen's unnumbered underground army."

"You have Intarra's eyes."

"So does Adare, and she's the one sitting on the throne." Kaden smiled. The expression felt strange on his face. "I can go to Meshkent, I can die, if necessary, because I do not matter here."

Kiel spread his hands. "If you want someone who truly does not matter, send a servant. Send a slave."

"No," Kaden said, shaking his head slowly. "A slave cannot travel the necessary paths."

The Csestriim studied him with those empty eyes. "The *kenta*."

Kaden nodded silently.

"The Ishien control the gates," Kiel observed. "All of them. When you step through onto the island they will kill you before you say three words."

"Then I'll have to say what needs saying in two."

14

"There are two problems with recalling il Tornja to the city," Adare said, shaking her head. "First, if we bring him here, there won't be anyone to fight the Urghul."

She gestured to the ruined map below, as though it were possible to descry the movement of horsemen hundreds of miles away in the cinder and soft ash left behind when the tiny false forests of the Thousand Lakes burned. The council had abandoned the entire chamber after Adare's demonstration. She could hardly blame them. The place reeked of oil and char, half the lamps were shattered, shards of glass still littered the table, the catwalks, the chairs. Servants had come to clean it almost immediately, summoned by some unheard command. Adare had sent them away. She would see the map restored when she had restored Annur itself. In the meantime, the ruined hall provided a space where she could meet with Kaden and Kiel without interference from the rest of the council.

"There are other generals in the world," Kaden pointed out. "Warriors other than il Tornja who might fight the Urghul."

Adare looked up from the map to study her brother. He stood just a few feet away, almost close enough to touch, but everything about him—his posture, his gaze, that perfectly empty face—whispered of distance. There was no warmth to him. No human movement. Adare might have been watching him through a long lens while he stood alone on a far, far peak. Whatever rapprochement she had imagined or hoped might arise between them had vanished. The simple fact that he had insisted on bringing Kiel, the Csestriim, was evidence enough of that. Adare swallowed, unsure if the bitter taste on the back of her tongue was doubt or regret, then shook her head.

"There are no generals like il Tornja. The Urghul would have overrun us months ago if anyone else had been in command. They would have destroyed us in the very first battle."

"Annur was still divided then. We've healed that rift. . . ."

"Have we?" Adare arched an eyebrow. "The council might be willing to let me perch atop the throne, but it seems pretty clear, based on that last meeting, that perching is about the extent of my imperial powers."

"The point is," Kaden said, "that with our armies allied, we have greater resources to fight the Urghul. You can recall il Tornja without scuttling the northern campaign."

"You can recall him," Kiel said, voice soft as a leather sole scuffing stone. "He will not come."

Adare nodded curtly. "That was my second point."

She let the silence stretch as she considered the historian, trying to read him. She had expected someone like il Tornja—strong, confident, insouciant—but of course, that was all an act, a mask her general wore to make him appear human. There was no reason that Kiel should have chosen the same one.

According to Kaden, Kiel was older than the *kenarang,* older by thousands of years, although what such a difference meant among the Csestriim, she didn't care to guess. He certainly *looked* older. Partly it was the historian's manner—unlike il Tornja, Kiel moved and spoke deliberately, almost cautiously, and Adare associated such caution with age. Kiel had also been a prisoner for a very long time, and the marks remained—a nose and jaw broken over and over, a limp, hands shattered then poorly healed, fingers twisted as twigs. If il Tornja seemed too young and cocksure to be Csestriim, Kiel appeared too bent, too broken.

There was, however, something about his eyes, something old and impossibly distant that she remembered from that tower in Andt-Kyl. Like il Tornja, he tried to mask it, but for whatever reason, he hadn't been quite so successful, and there were times, as now, moments when he seemed to look right past her, *through* her, as though she were just a tiny point in some pattern so unfathomably vast she could never hope to understand it.

"He knows that I am here," Kiel continued after a moment.

Adare nodded. "He told me as much before I left. Said that you would tell me lies about him. He can't know that I'd side with you."

In truth, she wasn't sure that she *intended* to side with Kaden and the other Csestriim. The thought of il Tornja bending finally to Annurian justice was honey-sweet, but the brute facts of the matter remained: il Tornja held back the Urghul, and whatever Kaden had been about to say on the docks the day before— something about il Tornja and Long Fist, about the *kenarang's* insistence on seeing the chieftain destroyed—he hadn't said it. Just when Adare thought she saw a path, an open door, a chance at a connection, Kaden had folded back into himself like a paper fan clicking quietly shut.

"You're not telling me something," she said, careful to keep her voice level, firm.

Kaden raised his brows a fraction.

"I suspect," he replied, "that we are all holding something back. As you said before: you don't trust me."

That was true enough. It was more than true. Adare hadn't told her brother about Nira, about the noose of flame the leach kept around il Tornja's neck, about the fact that she could order the *kenarang* dead with a word, a gesture. Trusting and sharing were all well and good, but she wasn't about to go first.

"There is only one way to build trust," she said, holding Kaden's gaze as she spread her hands. "If we're going to do anything at all about il Tornja, about his stranglehold on military power, I need to know what he wants with Long Fist. You need to explain to me his . . . obsession with Meshkent. I can't do anything, I can't be an *ally* if you won't tell me the *truth*."

"The truth," Kaden repeated quietly.

They faced each other, a pace apart, eyes locked. That single word—*truth*—felt like a blade in her hand, something hard and sharp to hold up between her and this brother she barely knew. Of course Kaden had his own invisible sword, his own truth to parry hers. She could almost hear them scraping, grating against each other, as though the stillness were battle, their mutual silence were screams, as though that one syllable could cut, kill.

"If il Tornja destroys Meshkent," Kaden said at last, "we die."

Adare narrowed her eyes. This acquiescence was too sudden, too absolute to trust.

"Who dies?"

"All of us." Kaden glanced over at Kiel. Something seemed to pass between them, some unspoken agreement. Then he turned back to her and explained it all, explained in perfect detail just how Ran il Tornja, Adare's general, the father of her child, was plotting to destroy the human world.

"It doesn't make sense," Adare said slowly, when Kaden had finally finished. "Let's accept, for the moment, the premise that the young gods are the source of our feelings, our humanity. Let's say I buy that their existence is what makes us who we are. Meshkent isn't *one* of them. Why isn't il Tornja obsessed with Kaveraa or Maat or Eira?"

"He would be," Kiel replied, "if they were here. Unfortunately for him, fortunately for your kind, the young gods have not worn flesh since they came down to side with you in the long war against my people. That was thousands of years ago."

"So how does killing Meshkent solve his problem? How does ridding the world of pain suddenly usher in a second golden age of the Csestriim?"

The historian watched her a moment, gauging her question.

Then his eyes went distant in that way that made her stomach clench. She glanced over at Kaden, partly to see whether he had anything to add to the conversation, mostly to look away from Kiel. To her dismay, Kaden's eyes, too, were empty.

"The theology," Kiel said finally, "is nuanced."

Adare snorted. "In my experience, *nuanced* is a word people use when they don't know what the fuck they're talking about."

To her surprise, Kiel smiled. "I, too, have had that experience." He shrugged. "Meshkent and Ciena are the progenitors of the younger gods."

She shook her head. "So what? Il Tornja murdered my father, but I'm still around. So is Kaden."

"And Valyn, too," Kaden added quietly. "We can hope, at least."

"Of course," she said, heat rising to her cheeks. "Of course we're all pulling for Valyn, but the point is, the *relevant* point right now, is that killing Meshkent won't do a thing to limit the power of his progeny."

"Your analogy is limited," Kiel said. "Despite your burning eyes, the Malkeenians are not gods."

"And you're claiming that the gods die when their parents die?"

He shook his head. "As I said before, the theology is complex. My people studied the gods a long time, but those studies were, by their very nature, imperfect, incomplete. On many subjects touching the divine, we remain entirely ignorant. The corpus of knowledge is contingent. Uncertain."

"Wonderful," Adare said.

Kiel raised a hand, as though to stop her objection before it could begin. "One thing, however, *is* certain. The gods are more than us. Not just older and stronger, but *different*." He paused, as though searching for words sturdy enough to bear the freight of his thought. "We are *of* the world—you and I, Csestriim and human. We live inside it as a man lives inside a house. When we die, the world remains.

"The gods are different. They *are* the world. Their existence is built inextricably into the structure of reality." He shook his head, reformulated. "They *give* reality its structure. This is what makes them gods. To return to the analogy of the house—a most imperfect analogy, but one that might serve—the gods are the foundation and floors, they are the windows admitting light, they are the walls."

Adare tried to parse the claim, to make sense of it. "They seem a lot more opinionated than the walls."

Kiel spread his hands. "As I said, the analogy is imperfect. Reality is not a house. Foundational principles of order and chaos, being and nothingness . . ." He trailed off, shrugged again. "They're not just stones."

"The point," Kaden said, breaking into the conversation for the first time, "is that if you knock out the foundation, walls fall down."

Kiel frowned. "Meshkent and Ciena are hardly foundational. Not in the way of Ae and the Blank God, Pta and Astar'ren."

"I get it," Adare cut in. "For whatever reason, if you destroy Meshkent and Ciena, you destroy what's built on them. Shatter the parents and the children crumble."

The words made her think of Sanlitun, swaddled in his cradle in a cold castle at the empire's very limit. There had been no choice but to leave him. Annur was a den of wolves; Adare had no doubt that there were a dozen members of the council who would leap at the chance to see the child murdered. He was safer in the north, safer in Nira's care—and yet, what would happen to him if Adare herself were killed? How long would the ancient Atmani woman watch over him?

"It makes sense, in a way," Kaden went on, jolting Adare from her thoughts. "Imagine you had no capacity to feel pain or pleasure."

With an effort of will, she hauled her mind away from that castle, away from the son of hers who at that very moment might be sleeping or fretting, squirming or crying out, forced herself to focus. The only way to save him, the only true way, was to win.

"Physically?" she asked.

"Physically. Mentally. Emotionally. No pain or pleasure of any sort." He shook his head, staring down at the charred ruin she had made of Kresh, and Sia, and Ghan. "Why would you feel any of the rest of it? Why would you feel fear or hate or love? *How* would you feel them?"

Adare tried to imagine such an existence, to conceive of a life lived in the utter absence of . . . what? Not sensation. That wasn't it. The Csestriim could feel the wind when it blew, could hear the plucking of a harp as well as any human. Theirs wasn't a failure to apprehend the world. It was a failure to *feel,* as though the meaning, the importance were leached from all experience, leaving only the desiccated facts pinned to the mind like glittering insects, exotic butterflies—all bright, brilliant, dead.

She looked at Kiel, then shuddered. She had known the Csestriim were different—smarter, older, immortal. She had read all the most famous accounts, understood that they were creatures of reason rather than passion. Somehow, she had never quite realized what it all meant, the bleakness of it. The horror.

"We would be like you," she murmured.

Kiel nodded gravely. "If you survived at all."

"Why wouldn't we survive?"

The historian gestured to Kaden. "I have tried to explain this to your brother. Your minds are not built like ours. You rely on your loves and your hates, your fears and hopes, to move you, to guide you." He gestured toward Adare. "Why are you here?"

"Because this is where we agreed to meet."

"Not here in the map room. In Annur."

"Because someone has to fix this wreck we've made of the empire."

The historian raised his brows. "Oh? Why?"

Adare floundered. "Because people are depending on us.

Relying on us. Millions of them will starve, or succumb to disease, or end up on the blades of the Urghul. . . ."

"So what?"

"So *what*?"

Kiel smiled a careful, almost delicate smile. "Yes. So what? You're going to die anyway. All of you. It is what happens to your kind, how you are made. Does it really matter who does the killing? Or when?"

"It matters to me," Adare snapped. She stabbed a finger at the wall, a wordless invocation of the uncounted souls living in the city and beyond. "It fucking matters to them."

"Because an Urghul slaughter would pain you. A resurgence of the gray plague would hurt you . . ." He reached over to tap her very lightly on the head, just below the hairline. ". . . here."

"Yes!"

"Your general wants to make a world in which it would not. He thinks you will become like us, then."

Adare stared. "And you? What do you think?"

"You might change," he conceded, nodding to Kaden. "Some of you, those with the right training."

"And the rest?" she demanded. "The ones who actually *care*?"

Kiel looked down at the map, tilted his head to one side, then shrugged once more—a human gesture, but empty of all human feeling.

"There is no way to be certain," he replied. "I believe your minds would twist beneath the strain, crack, then shatter."

15

"All right," Gwenna said wearily, settling herself on a knobby mangrove root, feet dangling in the warm water, "now that we're all good and bloody, maybe someone can start explaining what in Hull's name is going on."

The woman, Qora, hissed in irritation. "We're not *safe* here. They'll have birds in the air—"

"Last time I checked," Gwenna said, cutting her off, "birds can't see through forest canopy, and neither can the people who fly them. Birds are excellent, on the other hand, at spotting the bobbing heads of desperate swimmers in full daylight, so if you want to keep swimming, then by all means," she gestured toward the bright light filtering through the seaward verge of the mangroves, "swim."

Not the most diplomatic approach, maybe, but it had been a long night. Gwenna had only counted ten or so of the Kettral—the ones with the blacks and the birds—in the central square. As she fled through the streets, however, dragging Qora along by the elbow, then the shoulder, then the back of the neck, the bastards kept turning up, leaping out of alleyways, dropping off rooftops. Gwenna killed at least three, Qora finished off one more, but they just kept coming. It made sense, in retrospect: if you were going to burn down a whole town, you wanted to bring enough soldiers to do the job right.

In the end, it was the night that saved them—Hull's darkness covering their retreat. That and the tortuous trail over the ridge. Gwenna could see the path just fine in the starlight, but Qora kept tripping, lurching into the thick vines to either side. Judging from the calls and curses behind them, their pursuers were having an even tougher time—more evidence that they weren't true Kettral, that wherever they'd scrounged up those smoke steel blades, however they'd managed to wrangle their way onto the birds, they'd never been down into Hull's Hole, never been bitten by the slarn, never chugged that disgusting slop from inside the egg. It was an advantage. A small one, but Gwenna wasn't in a position to be choosy.

Annick and Talal had met them at the beach in the dim hour before dawn. The leach was half carrying a young man with a head wound, the other half of Qora's sloppily laid trap. He was pale-skinned, his shaved head a white reflection of Qora's own. His shirt had torn away during the escape, and when he doubled over to puke, Gwenna noticed the spreading wings of a kettral tattooed across his broad shoulders.

"Jak," Qora had gasped, lurching across the sand toward the reeling soldier, clutching his shoulders as though he were made of dirt and starting to crumble, as though she meant to hold him together with nothing more than the force of her hands. "Are you all right?"

He'd nodded unsteadily, pushing himself free of Talal. Blood sheeted his face, obscuring his features. "Looks worse than it is . . ."

"Can you swim?" Gwenna asked.

Jak glanced at the black, lapping waves. "Normally, yes, but . . ." He raised his fingers gingerly to the nasty gash across his scalp, swayed, then shuddered. "I . . . maybe . . ."

"Maybe's not good enough," Gwenna replied. She pointed at the cliff above. Even in the dark, their pursuers were getting close. "If you can't swim, you're on your own."

"He's a liability if we leave him alive," Annick said.

Qora spun about to confront the sniper. "What are you suggesting?"

"That we bring him," Annick said, not bothering to look over. "Or we kill him. I'm fine either way."

The man named Jak stared at Annick, then turned to Gwenna. "Who in Hull's name *are* you?" he whispered.

"No one," Gwenna said. There was something about the man, about his voice or his bloody face, that nagged at her memory, but she couldn't place it. "Just sightseeing. Heard Hook was nice this time of year. Now get in the fucking water. Head north."

"Look at him," Qora demanded, leaning forward. "He can barely stand. We need a different plan."

"By all means," Gwenna said, gesturing to the ocean behind them, the tiered limestone looming above. "I always enjoy hearing plans." She paused, put a cupped hand to her ear. "If you wait just a minute, our friends on the ridgeline will be here. You can tell them about it, too."

Qora's jaw tightened. "Leave us, then, if you're scared. We'll take care of ourselves."

"Because *that's* been working out so well."

"Gwenna," Talal said, gesturing to the east. "Normally I'd take the time to talk, but . . ."

She nodded, turning back to Qora. "Look. I understand that you like this guy. Maybe he's your pasty brother. Maybe the two of you have been grinding hips when you should have been training. Doesn't matter. I'm not sure if you were paying attention back there, but he *abandoned* you. I was watching when those bastards in black tightened their net, and do you want to know what he did?"

Waves ground a thousand thousand small stones down the surface of the narrow beach. The west wind had picked up, flicking spray off the sea. The shouts on the cliff were closer, at least ten voices, male, angry, and confused. Annick half drew her bow and stepped out from the shadows, eyeing the rough trail they had just descended.

"Give the word," the sniper said. "I'll have a shot as soon as they come over the ridge."

Gwenna shook her head. "They're just guessing we're down here. No reason to confirm it." She turned her attention to Jak once more, trying again to remember where she'd seen him, how she remembered him.

"How about it, asshole?" she said, raising an eyebrow. "You want to tell your lady friend how you left her to twist in the wind?"

She had expected defiance or fury, expected him to snarl or come at her. Instead, his face crumpled. It took a moment for her to realize, shocked, that the star-bright lines carved through the drying blood smeared across his face . . . those were tears.

"I couldn't . . . ," he began. "I just . . . I *couldn't*. . . ."

Some old instinct shifted inside her; *pity,* she realized after a moment. Whoever the poor fucker was, he wasn't Kettral. Not everyone had trained half a lifetime to face down a dozen killers in a crowd. Clearly, Jak hadn't volunteered to battle men with smoke steel blades and murderous birds, and he was hardly the first person to freeze like a fawn when the blood started flying.

None of that mattered. What mattered was getting away, getting clear. Gwenna had always been a shitty card player, but it was time to bluff, so she took a deep breath and bluffed: "You can swim, or I can kill you quick. Your call."

Jak's head jerked up. She saw the fear blaze through his eyes, hot and bright as lightning. She might have felt bad, but there was no time for feeling bad.

She slid her knife from the sheath. "I'll count to one."

The man held up his hands. "I'll swim."

Gwenna ended up having to drag him the last few hundred paces, stroking with one arm and scissor-kicking hard while she kept the other hand clamped over his chest. It was a pain in the ass, but it worked. They reached a thick stand of mangroves just before dawn, slipping into the twisting waterways between the roots. Anyone trying to track them would need to do so over a mile of open ocean, and the mangroves themselves would pose even more difficulty for their pursuers.

As a cadet, Gwenna had always hated the mangrove stands—the trees were too thick to allow swimming, the water too deep for easy wading, the branches just the right level to take out an eye. You could spend half a morning covering half a mile, especially if you were trying not to make noise. Bad territory for training exercises, but a great spot to regroup. There'd been no sign of pursuit since the beach, but that wasn't a reason to get stupid. Whatever the next step, she planned to wait out the daylight among the knobby, twisted trees. Which gave them all plenty of time to get acquainted.

Gwenna eased back against one of the trunks, balanced a naked blade on her knees, then pointed a finger at Qora.

"So. Where should we start?"

"We can start," Qora spat, "with the fact that you blew our best chance at killing those bastards."

For a moment Gwenna could only stare.

"You have got to be kidding," she said finally.

"I'm *not* kidding. We had it set up, Jak and I. We'd figured the whole scene, and then you assholes showed up, whoever the fuck you are. . . ."

Qora trailed off, breathing hard. Gwenna looked over at Talal, wondering if she was losing her mind. The leach just shrugged. He was sitting on a twisted root a pace away, a hand on Jak's shoulder, steadying the man as he vomited up the last salt water from the swim. It was disgusting, but at least it kept him from talking. The more Qora talked, the more Gwenna wanted to spend a little time drowning *her*.

"You were about to get killed . . . ," Gwenna said, trying to keep her voice level, reasonable.

"No!" Qora said, eyes huge and furious. "I had an exit. You didn't see how we set it up."

"And did you see the men moving toward you through the crowd?"

The woman nodded. "I saw *both* of them."

Gwenna raised her brows. "Both? There were *five*."

"Henk and his gang were still on the dock."

Gwenna shook her head. "You were looking at the wrong thing."

"I was looking at the sons of bitches who have been hunting us like dogs for the better part of a year."

"Like I said," Gwenna replied. "The wrong thing."

Jak groaned, then raised his head. "What do you mean?" he asked quietly. The long swim had washed the blood from his face, and Gwenna studied him for a few heartbeats, tumbling his name over and over in her head. *Jak.* Who in Hull's name was Jak? The answer eluded her, as it had all night. She turned back to Qora.

"Look at this," she said, holding a hand above her head, fluttering the fingers slightly. Qora looked up. Gwenna drove a fist into her gut, caught the back of her neck, and shoved her head underwater. The woman struggled and splashed, clawed indiscriminately at Gwenna's leg, at the sprawling mangrove roots, battered pointlessly at the water. Annick shifted to avoid the thrashing. Qora was stronger than she looked, but strong didn't matter much when you couldn't breathe. Jak, eyes huge as plates, started to move, but Talal brought him up short with a knife at the neck.

"Don't worry," Gwenna said, satisfied to hear that she'd kept the anger out of her voice. "It's all right."

She counted to fifteen, then dragged the woman up, shoving her into one of the mangrove trunks just in time to avoid getting puked on. Qora choked and coughed and swore, looked like she was going to lunge for Gwenna, then subsided, jaw clenched with suppressed fury, brown eyes ablaze.

"If you keep looking at the wrong things," Gwenna explained patiently, "you're not going to make it."

The woman coughed once more, hacking up half a lungful of water. "Fuck you."

"Not my type," Gwenna replied. Her patience was fraying. She thought back to the Flea, tried to channel something of his unflappable calm. "We're trying to help you."

"By drowning me?" Qora spat. "By putting a knife to my friend's throat?"

Gwenna looked over at Talal. "He's all right."

The leach met her eyes, then slipped the blade back into its sheath.

"There," Gwenna said. "Can we talk like adults now?"

Qora shook her head. "Who *are* you?" she asked again.

"We are confused," Gwenna said. "Confusion makes us nervous, and when I'm nervous I start holding heads underwater. So maybe you could take the first turn answering questions."

On the whole, it felt like a very temperate proposition. Qora, however, didn't look at all pacified. She looked ready to keep fighting, if you could call having your head stuffed under the water and held there fighting. Gwenna blew out a breath and got ready for the next round, but Talal leaned forward instead, putting a conciliatory hand between them.

"We came to help," he murmured.

"That's what *I* said!" Gwenna protested. "I already said that."

Talal nodded, but kept his eyes fixed on Qora. "We came to help," he said again.

"To help who?" Qora demanded.

"Whoever's fighting the men with the birds. Soldiers flying kettral have already killed some of our friends. They tried to kill us. If you're against them, we're with you."

Gwenna leaned back against the narrow trunk of the mangrove. Probably she should have let Talal do the talking from the start. He had a way of bringing people around without holding their heads underwater. She forced herself to relax, to close her eyes, to feel the late-morning sun filtering down through the leaves, bright and hot. She might not be great with the talking, but at least she understood when to shut up and get out of the way.

"Those men with the bird," Talal said. "They set the fire because the townspeople were helping you? Hiding you?"

Qora nodded warily. "It was punishment. A lesson. They love their 'Kent-kissing lessons."

"And who *are* they?"

"Kettral." She spat the word.

Talal frowned. "I didn't recognize them, and I trained on these islands for almost a decade." He glanced over at Gwenna, then Annick.

"Nope," Gwenna replied.

The sniper just shook her head.

"They're calling themselves Kettral, anyway," Qora went on. "No better than us, really. Just Jakob Rallen's thugs."

"Rallen?" Gwenna asked, confusion getting the better of her.

Qora nodded grimly. "He's in charge now."

It made less than no sense. Jakob Rallen had been Master of Cadets for better than ten years, but no one had taken him much more seriously than the chair he sat in.

"In charge of *what*?" Gwenna asked.

"The Eyrie. He still calls it that, but really it's just his own personal racket now—raising yellowbloom over on Qarsh, using the birds to get it to market overseas, selling it for a massive profit, using the money to buy whatever he needs to cement his position here. He calls it the Eyrie, but it's just a yellowbloom operation."

Jak nodded. "Rallen styles himself a commander of the Eyrie, but he's just the one in charge of running the drug."

Gwenna spat into the water. "That useless bastard couldn't run a bonfire if the wood was already piled and someone else lit the match."

"Yeah, well, he's burned plenty," Qora replied. "As you saw last night. And not just buildings. He's tied people to poles, doused them with oil, and lit them ablaze. He's a vicious son of a bitch, and he's in charge."

"And you're the resistance," Talal concluded.

Qora hesitated, then nodded warily.

Gwenna glanced over at Jak. His broad shoulders were slumped, but he was watching her and seemed a good sight more cooperative than Qora.

"Where are the rest of you?" Gwenna asked.

He opened his mouth, but Qora cut him off before he could respond.

"Not a chance," she said, shaking her head.

"They saved us, Qora," Jak observed quietly. The man was obviously strong—he had the chest and shoulders of a serious swimmer, which was saying something on an archipelago where *everyone* could swim a mile or two before breakfast—but his voice was soft, deferential. If Gwenna closed her eyes, she could imagine a slender boy talking rather than a man grown. "Our plan went all wrong," he continued, "and they showed up to save us."

"Yeah, but showed up from *where*?" Qora stabbed an accusatory finger at Gwenna. "They already *admitted* they're Kettral."

"When we left the Islands," Gwenna replied grimly, "being Kettral wasn't something people tried to hide."

"Left the Islands to go where?" Qora demanded. "On what bird? On what orders? For all we know, you're working with Rallen."

Gwenna stared. "Would we be hip-deep in a mangrove swamp right now if we were working for Jakob fucking Rallen? If Rallen sent us to capture you, we would have captured you and brought you back to Rallen."

"Unless he sent you to spy."

Gwenna bit down on her retort. The woman was paranoid, but then, months living out of cellars and caves, of glancing up each time a hawk-shaped shadow slid across the sky . . . that would make a person twitchy.

"I killed three of those bastards back there," she said, keeping her voice level. She glanced over at the sniper. "How about you, Annick?"

"Three."

"Talal?"

"One," the leach replied. He nodded toward Jak. "I spent most of my time carrying him."

"Seven," Gwenna said, holding up her fingers, hoping the sight of something fleshy, something solid would finally reassure the woman. "If we were working with Rallen, would we kill seven of our friends?"

Qora watched her, worrying the bloody cuticle of her thumb with one insistent fingernail, lips pressed tightly together. For a moment, Gwenna thought she was about to crack, to talk, then she grimaced and shook her head.

"What did you say you were doing here?" she demanded.

"Sightseeing," Gwenna replied grimly. She glanced over at Jak. He seemed like he wanted to talk, but was taking his cues from Qora. It was tempting to seize them both by the necks, smash their skulls together a dozen times, rinse off the blood, ask the questions again, repeat as necessary. She could get answers that way, no doubt about it. Trouble was—they were likely to be pretty shitty answers.

Gwenna blew out a long, irritated breath.

"All right, look. You don't know who we are—I understand. You want to keep your friends safe—I respect that. Why don't you tell us about Rallen instead. How'd he get to be in charge? Why do those assholes follow him?"

Silence from Qora and Jak. The light slap of waves sloshing against the mangrove trunks. The shift and rustle of leaves, perfume of the small white flowers, heavy with their impending death.

"Look," Gwenna said, "I'm working on my attitude, and so I've been friendly so far. . . ."

She let the syllable hang. Then, to her shock, Annick spoke

into the stretching silence. "These two are insurgents," the sniper said without looking over. "If Rallen is the ranking Kettral on the Islands, he is in charge, according to the Code. Any resistance offered by Qora and Jak is treason. They are traitors, as are any allies they might have."

Gwenna turned to stare at the sniper. All morning she'd been trying to convince these two idiots that she had nothing to do with Jakob Rallen, that she was on *their* side, only to have Annick start rattling off passages from the 'Kent-kissing *Code*?

"Annick—" she began, but Qora got there first, rounding on the sniper, fury overmatching whatever fear she felt.

"Rallen came for *us,* you miserable bitch! We had no idea what had even *happened* at the Eyrie until he showed up, hawking his 'Shael-spawned *second chance!"*

Gwenna choked back her own objections, stilled her face, and settled back against the trunk. She stole a glance at Annick. The sniper was still staring out toward the ocean, an arrow nocked to her undrawn bow. She didn't say anything more, didn't even turn. If she knew what she had done, she didn't show it. Her words, though, that flat endorsement of Jakob Rallen, had rattled free a portion of the truth. The question now was whether to keep rattling, or to wait.

"Second chance?" Talal asked finally.

And then the understanding hit Gwenna like a slap upside the head. Suddenly she knew why she recognized Jak. "You're from Arim," she said. "Holy Hull, you're the washouts." From that point, it was easy to follow the logic's flight. "That's why you know how to fight, but you're shit at it."

"We're doing what we can," Jak said quietly.

"Quick Jak," Talal said slowly, looking at the man with new eyes. "Laith used to talk about you all the time. You're what, five classes older than us? Laith said you were the best flier on the Islands."

Jak grimaced. "You have to pass the Trial if you want to keep flying birds."

"And you washed out," Gwenna concluded. "We were too young to hear the details, but I remember the rumor—Quick Jak didn't make it. The Kettral's best flier wasn't going to be Kettral after all. I always thought you *died*."

The man laughed, a short, mirthless sound, like he'd been punched in the gut. "I'm alive, all right. I even made it through the first week of the Trial. But when we came to the Hole, when I saw those blind white creatures, I just . . . couldn't."

Like last night, Gwenna thought grimly, *when you froze in the alleyway. When the shit got thick and you left your partner to die.* This was the resistance, a group of men and women who had fizzled out at some point during their training, who had been kicked down enough times that they finally quit, skulking off to Arim to live out their lives in comfortable captivity. These were her new allies, her *only* allies.

"So while the Eyrie was destroying itself," Talal said quietly, "no one thought to come for you?"

"Why would they?" Qora demanded bitterly. "A few hundred washouts? The Kettral were focused on killing Kettral. We could see the birds fighting in the sky, could see the boats burning, but we don't have boats or birds over on Arim. We're not *allowed* them."

Annick nodded without looking over. "Makes sense. The whole island—all Arim—was a no-value target."

Qora nodded. "We were almost as irrelevant as the rotting town of rum-soaked thieves over on Hook."

"And so when it was all over," Gwenna concluded, "you were left."

She could see the guilt scribbled across both their faces. Quick Jak dropped his eyes, but Qora nodded again.

"Rallen was left, too," she said. The defiance had gone out of her voice.

"And for the same reason," Gwenna added. "When the shit hit, no one was worried about that useless sack of suet. I'd be more concerned about gull shit on my shirt than Jakob Rallen hoisting himself out of his chair to fight me."

"He's dangerous," Jak said, shaking his head.

"Maybe if he falls on you."

"Or shatters your face with a *kenning*," Qora snapped.

Gwenna blinked. In all her years as a cadet, she'd never paused to consider Jakob Rallen's weapons specialty. The idea that he'd ever been anything more than an overweening, power-hungry, third-rate trainer had seemed ludicrous. Even the Kettral made mistakes, and she'd always considered Rallen a perfect example. The thought that he'd once been deadly, that he was a *leach* . . .

She glanced over at Talal. "Did you know this?"

He shook his head slowly.

"How did you find out?" Gwenna demanded, turning back to Qora.

Qora, however, wasn't listening. Her eyes were far away, fixed on some distant, indelible memory. "When it was all done, he came to Arim," she said. "Claimed the Eyrie had been betrayed, betrayed from the inside. Said there would be a second chance for those of us who still wanted to serve. . . ."

When she fell silent, Jak took up the story.

"We had no idea what he was planning. All we knew was that he was Kettral, high-up Kettral, and here he was, telling us we could try again, could have one more opportunity to redeem ourselves. *Everyone flinches,* he said. *This is a chance to make it right.*" He blew out an unsteady breath. "He told me I could fly again. None of us knew what he really wanted."

"And what," Talal asked quietly, "does he really want?"

"Power," Qora spat. "His own little kingdom way out here in the middle of the ocean. At first it was all just drilling and training, new uniforms and new blades, burying the fallen and swearing oaths. We thought we were Kettral, thought we were fighting for the empire, thought we were finally doing what we'd trained all those years to do." She broke off, her mouth twisting into something like a sick, broken smile. "We were such fools. Such fucking fools. Took months before we realized we were just the thugs of some petty warlord who was setting up his fiefdom, the whole thing propped up on his yellowbloom crop."

Gwenna shook her head. "And when you *did* finally realize it, none of you thought to just slide a knife into his gullet?"

"We *tried*," Qora said, the two syllables grinding against each other.

"Evidently you didn't try very hard. That shit-licker can barely hoist himself out of a chair. He walks with a 'Kent-kissing *cane*. You could kill him with a brick and not break a sweat."

"You don't understand," Jak said. "By that point he had the Black Guard."

Gwenna shook her head. "The Black Guard?"

"Others like us. From Arim. For the first few months Rallen was watching us, testing us, figuring out who was really loyal to the empire, and who just wanted to get in on some killing. By the time we realized what was happening, he had a whole crew, five Wings loyal just to him. They had the birds. They controlled the armory."

"And you didn't fight them?"

Qora stared at her. "You ever try to fight a kettral from the ground? Standing on your own two feet?"

It was a sobering thought. Gwenna had spent her life around the birds, learning to fly them, to ride them, to trust them, and yet she'd never really grown accustomed to those huge dark eyes, the indifferent stare. Laith had claimed the creatures were never domesticated, just tamed, and even *tame* seemed like a stretch when you watched one rend a cow or a sheep to ribbons. Kettral-trained fighters were the best in the world, but a large part of what made them so deadly was the birds themselves. Fighting *against* a trained Wing in flight . . . it was a half step from madness.

"So," Gwenna said, trying to turn the conversation back to the current situation, "Rallen seized control. He has half of the wash—of the inhabitants of Arim fighting *for* him, while the rest of you are holed up somewhere."

"Those of us who are left," Qora replied. "Rallen put together his Black Guard, then demanded an oath of obedience."

"Kettral swear to obey and serve the empire," Annick observed.

"Not anymore," Qora spat. "Rallen's oath is to *him,* personally, as Supreme Commander of the Eyrie."

Gwenna shook her head. "What horseshit."

"Of course it's horseshit! That's why some of us refused. We just didn't realize he expected us to refuse, that he was ready for it. The oath wasn't just an oath, it was a test—a way to sort us, to winnow out anyone who might oppose him. The slaughter started almost as soon as he tallied up our names." She covered her eyes with a hand. "Only a few of us escaped."

Gwenna nodded slowly. It was hardly a subtle trap, but no less effective for that.

"Did any of you try to get free of the Islands altogether?" Talal asked.

Qora spread her hands. "How? We were never permitted ships on Arim. And if we managed to steal one, what then? Rallen has the birds. He has the munitions. The Black Guard could sink a ship from the air without ever coming close."

Just like the *Widow's Wish*. It had taken just a few hundred heartbeats from the first assault until the vessel slid beneath the waves.

"So you're fighting him."

"Trying. Failing, mostly. It's just about all we can do to stay hidden."

"I'm surprised you've managed it this long. There aren't that many islands, and they aren't that big."

Qora hesitated, then glanced over at Jak.

"Just tell them," the flier said after a long pause. He was staring down at his hands, strong hands by the look of them, but empty, fingers opening and closing as though hoping for a weapon, as though baffled at the lack of anything to grasp. "We're already losing. Maybe they can help."

"And if they're with Rallen?" Qora asked, voice tight.

"Then we'll get this whole 'Kent-kissing thing over with that much quicker."

Qora turned back to Gwenna, jaw clenched as though she'd nailed it shut. It took her a long time to speak, and when she did, her voice was rough and grudging as rust.

"We're not *on* the Islands. We're under them."

16

Nira had always looked old.

Ran il Tornja and his tiny cabal of Csestriim had made her immortal, or close enough. They'd found a way, in creating the Atmani, to keep human leaches alive for a very long time. *Alive,* however, was not the same as *young.*

When Adare first met the woman, she'd figured her age at eighty or ninety. Nira had an octogenarian's gray hair and lined face. Her brown skin was ashen. The decades seemed to weigh heavily on her, bending her spine, stooping her shoulders. Despite all that, however, the old woman had always been stronger than she looked—nimble, quick with her cane, capable of walking all day without flagging—so strong that Adare had started to think of her, despite the evidence, as young.

Now, she looked half dead.

Fire had burned away half her hair, seared her left cheek and jaw, licked sickening red weals down her neck. A thick bandage wrapped her left hand; Adare could see blood and yellow pus soaking through the cloth. One of her top front teeth was missing, two more were chipped nearly in half, and her nose was broken, then awkwardly reset. She looked as though someone had beaten her with a cast-iron skillet, then thrown her in the fire to die. The injuries were grim, frightening, but it wasn't the injuries that terrified Adare so much as the fact that the woman was there at *all.*

The word had come while Adare was holding court from atop the Unhewn Throne. She'd been there all morning, enduring a series of audiences by turns interminable and idiotic— busywork thrown up by the council to keep her from actually accomplishing anything—when a slave crept in, cringing and bowing all the way to the throne, carrying in her hand an urgent note from the guard captain at the palace's Great Gate: *A messenger from the north. An old woman, badly injured. She claims to be your Mizran Councillor.*

They were only letters—tiny and precise, dark ink on a roll of bone-white parchment—but they might as well have been barbs, every one of them lodged in Adare's chest as she read, lodged in her throat, tugging, then tearing. Nira was there, was wounded, and the guardsman's note said nothing about an infant. Nothing about Sanlitun.

Adare wanted to leap from the throne, to charge out through the huge doors, to find the woman who was supposed to be watching her son and wring the answers from her. She was the Emperor, however; there were forms to be observed. There was the whole ridiculous staircase—a one-ton piece of furniture, all dovetailed, polished teak set on silver wheels—to roll out from the shadows so that she could descend with imperial dignity. There were traditional phrases to intone, prayers to offer, then the endless fucking genuflection of the assembled ministers. Adare managed to keep her head up throughout it all, her eyes forward, her hands still at her sides. She managed to play her part, to speak the words that were hers to speak, while the same three questions carved through all other thought:

Why is Nira here?
What has gone wrong?
Where is my son?

When the great gongs finally shuddered the air and she finally walked from the Hall of a Thousand Trees, she could only hope that she looked like an emperor. She felt like a ghost.

The Sons of Flame escorted her to a small suite of rooms set into the red walls themselves just north of the Great Gate. It was a simple but elegant space, used for the entertainment of unexpected visitors, men and women of indeterminate rank or station, messengers or foreign ministers meriting a private space while more suitable arrangements could be determined. Nira sat just inside the door, slumped over a bloodwood table, ignoring both the pitcher of wine and the ewer of water glistening wetly on the polished wood.

Any other time, Adare would have been frightened for her councillor, furious. Any other time she would have been hollering for a physician, for a cot, for a change of clothes and bandages. In that moment, however, as she stood trembling just inside the door, she found all thoughts but one had been scrubbed utterly from her mind.

"Where is my son?" she asked in a voice dry as ash. "Sanlitun? *Where is he?*"

Nira grimaced. "He's alive."

"Alive?" Adare demanded, fear driving her voice high, then higher. "*Alive?* You were watching him, protecting him, and you show up looking like . . . like this, and all you can tell me is that he's alive?"

The Nira Adare remembered would have bristled at that. She would have bashed Adare's knuckles with her cane, or smacked her across the side of the head. Now, she could barely manage a nod.

"He was alive when I got out. He will be still. The bastard needs him."

"*Who?*" Adare demanded. "*What* bastard?"

The woman met her eyes, and Adare felt a hole open in her gut.

"Il Tornja," she breathed.

Nira nodded wearily. "He's got your son. Your son and my brother both."

For a moment Adare could only stare. She watched her hands reach for a glass as though they had their own mind, watched them fill a delicate flute to the rim with wine. *He has my son.* She started to pull the glass toward her, then looked again at Nira, slumped in her chair, and passed the wine to her. The old woman gazed at it with those defeated eyes as though she'd never seen a glass before. Adare poured one for herself, then drank deep. Nira twitched, as though waking from sleep, and followed suit. When she spoke again, there was a flicker of heat in her voice. Just a flicker, then gone.

"I'm sorry, girl."

Adare drained the glass, shook her head, then poured another. She could feel the questions pressing in, dozens of them, but couldn't bring herself to speak. Suddenly it seemed important to remain quiet, as though if she didn't ask what had happened, if Nira never answered, none of it would be real. As long as they stayed silent, it could be a dream.

When she'd drained a second glass, she placed her palms against the table, slowly, deliberately, as though the surface could hold her up. She studied the wood's grain, lingering on the delicate lines and whorls, as though she could lose herself in that imaginary topography. *Coward,* she thought grimly. *I am a coward.* Her gaze was heavy as a millstone as she hauled it back to Nira.

"Tell me."

The woman nodded, drank her wine down in a great gulp, then nodded again.

"I should have killed him," she said, her voice an angry ghost. "Should have killed him back in Aats-Kyl."

"But the collar," Adare protested. "That leash of fire. It broke?"

Nira snorted. "A thing like that doesn't break. It gets unmade."

"But he's not a leach."

"No. Oshi is."

Adare stared, baffled. "Oshi hates him. Oshi would have *slaughtered* him if you told him to."

"That was before the Csestriim started talking." Nira shook her head bitterly. "I was a fucking fool. I thought, because I put that noose around his neck and told him to help, to fix what he had done, that he was helping, fixing. They'd sit for hours, il Tornja asking his questions: 'What's the first thing you remember? What's the first face you remember seeing? When did you first cry? When did you first see your own blood?' Like that. Hundreds a' questions. Thousands."

She blew out a long, unsteady breath, winced as something shifted painfully inside her, then continued.

"Seemed useless to me—all that chatter. We weren't made what we are through a bunch a' questions, and I told him that. He just smiled—you know that smile—told me that before he could fix a thing, he had to see where it was cracked. I thought he was just stalling—that it was all useless but harmless. Thought it wouldn't hurt ta wait a little longer. . . ."

She trailed off, but Adare could already see what happened next.

"Il Tornja turned him," she said. "He turned your brother to his side somehow, and Oshi removed the collar."

Nira nodded. "My poor brain-buggered brother . . . He barely knew the sky from the sea on a good day. One time I had to persuade him not ta go ta war with the trees. He wanted to demand fealty from the fuckin' fish. He didn't know . . . anything, and all the time that Csestriim bastard was at work inside his busted head, twisting history, erasing memories, replacing them with his own lies. It must have been so easy."

"And you didn't try to stop it?"

"I didn't *know*. Not until the collar was off. Then I tried ta stop them both." She shaded her eyes with a withered hand, as though the memory of what had happened was too bright. When she spoke again, the words were a whisper. "I woulda killed him then—my brother. I tried. But he's strong. Oshi's broken, but still so, so strong."

She ran a hand absently over the burned stubble of her scalp, winced, then pulled her fingers away.

"He attacked *you*?"

"Yes. Maybe." Nira paused, shook her head. "The flames were flyin'—that's sure as shit—but I can't say he recognized me."

Nira was staring at the carafe of wine. After a moment, she took it in one withered hand and poured them both another drink.

"You used your own power," Adare said slowly.

The old woman snorted quietly. "Ya expect me to fight one a' the world's strongest leaches with my fingernails?"

"I thought," Adare replied, choosing her words carefully, "that you tried not to use your power. That dipping too deep and too often into his well is what drove your brother mad in the first place. That it's what drove all the Atmani mad."

Nira stared into her wine, swirled it, then raised it to her lips as though she hadn't heard. She finished off the glass in a single pull, and then set it back on the table so carefully the crystal made no sound against the wood.

"Yeah," she said finally, staring at the glass with rheumy eyes. "It was."

"And?"

"And what?" Nira asked, raising her eyes to meet Adare's.

"Is that a concern now?"

Nira laughed a sharp, jagged laugh. "Ya mean, have I gone mad?"

Adare studied the old woman. Nira had been there almost from the beginning, since the day Adare fled the Dawn Palace. She was the only person in the world who knew everything.

"I need you," Adare replied at last. "If we're going to survive this, if we're going to defeat il Tornja, I need you strong, and I need you sane."

"And what good," Nira asked quietly, "did staying sane do me? Hmm? More than a thousand years I didn't touch my well.

I could feel it all the time. Right *there*. I wanted it in a way you can't know, worse than any wet bride ever wanted a nimble tongue between her legs, worse than a dying woman wants water." She shook her head. "Sweet 'Shael, how I wanted it."

"But you didn't," Adare breathed, forcing herself to hold that horrible gaze.

"I don't need *you* ta remind me," the old woman snapped, "what I've done and not done." For a moment there was something like the old sharpness on her tongue, a hint of the familiar fire in her eyes. Then it went vague and distant all over again. "What good did it do?"

"You saved your brother," Adare said, pronouncing the words slowly, as though she were speaking to a small child.

"Saved him? Saved him from *what*? For more than a thousand years I watched him, fed him, kept him drugged half to dreamland, kept him from remembering the worst of what we've done, and for what? So I could hand him over to the bastard that broke him." She gritted her teeth. "I shoulda let him die centuries ago," Nira growled. "Shoulda dragged a knife across his gristly neck when I still could."

"He was your brother," Adare said, uncertain how else to respond.

"All the more reason ta show him mercy."

"A knife across the throat isn't mercy."

Nira studied her grimly. "Whatever you think you know about mercy, girl—it's wrong."

Any other time, Adare would have argued. Now, it hardly seemed to matter. Il Tornja was free, he'd twisted one of the Atmani over to his side, and he had Adare's own son. She could hardly bring herself to think about that last fact, as though if she ignored it long enough it might turn out to be a mistake, some misguided notion rattling about in an ancient woman's addled mind. Only Nira wasn't mad; not yet. There was still too much sense in everything she said. Too much regret.

"And Sanlitun?" Adare asked, the words meek, almost a

supplication. "Is he . . . all right?" She could feel the tears pressing, the rage welling, hot and purple beneath her tongue. "Has il Tornja hurt him?"

The thought of Sanlitun's fear and confusion had gouged at Adare like a knife the entire ride south. He had his wet nurses, but she was the only one who could reliably soothe him, the only one who could drive back the terrors he was too small to articulate. Her disappearance must have seemed like a betrayal, and now Nira was gone, too. Who would comfort him? Who would hold him close and whisper half-remembered lullabies while he fretted himself to sleep? Adare imagined him alone in some cold castle tower, darkness pressing in around him, his tiny fingers opening and closing hopelessly on his blankets, grasping them over and over as though the soft wool could offer any comfort, searching in vain for his mother's face, listening for her voice. . . .

"The child is fine," Nira said, her voice cutting through Adare's own waking horror. "More pampered by il Tornja's wet nurse than he ever was by you."

"But *why?*"

Nira grimaced. "Leverage. Same reason he stopped Oshi from killing me. He needs you. He needs us both."

"Needs us for *what?*"

"To get to the leach."

Adare shook her head, furious, baffled. "What leach?"

"The one your brother keeps locked up inside the tower."

Adare scrambled to think of the girl's name. "Triste?"

She remembered the reports. When Triste first appeared in the Dawn Palace in the middle of a mound of corpses, Adare's spies had tried to learn who she was, where she had come from. There was a swirl of rumors: the girl was Skullsworn, she was an Antheran spy, or an Aedolian-trained leach bound somehow to the new emperor. One witness to the massacre in the Jasmine Court swore that he saw the tattoo of a *leina* around her neck. None of it made any sense. All anyone could say for sure was that she had arrived with Kaden, killed more than a hundred people, then been locked away. Adare shook her head. "What does il Tornja want with Triste?"

"What does he want?" Nira raised her brows. "He wants the little bitch dead."

Adare stared at the older woman, trying to make sense of what she was hearing. For months she'd been juggling a hundred variables in her mind: the Urghul and the Waist tribes, the Sons of Flame and the Army of the North, il Tornja, and Kaden, and Long Fist. It was like studying a *ko* board as wide as the world itself, armies of thousands and tens of thousands, an empire of millions, the patterns ramifying across oceans and deserts, steppe and forest. In all those twisting lines of attack and retreat, Adare had barely glanced at the tiny stone that was Triste.

"She must be dangerous," she said slowly.

"'Course she's dangerous," Nira spat. "'Cording ta your report, took her less than half a morning ta turn your palace into a slaughterhouse."

Adare took a deep breath, tried to think through it slowly, calmly. "We knew she was a leach, but there are hundreds of leaches in the world. Thousands. Il Tornja isn't trying to kill them all. He must be frightened of Triste. . . ."

"The bastard is Csestriim. He doesn't *get* frightened."

"*Aware,* then . . . of something we are not. Maybe he knows who she is. Maybe he knows the source of her power, her well." Adare grimaced. "She could be another Balendin, and Intarra knows we can't handle another Balendin."

Nira nodded wearily. "That's how I read it, too. She's a knife. One your general doesn't want your brother to have."

"Kaden," Adare said, weighing her brother's name as she spoke it, "Kaden is not entirely the naïve monastic type I had expected. His republic is a disaster, but it was a surprise, one that nearly broke us for the war in the north. I can see why il Tornja would want to take away his knives."

Slowly, grudgingly, a shape began to resolve out of Adare's

initial terror and confusion. Her breath still came hot and ragged in her throat, but she no longer felt that the heart inside her chest might just explode. *My son is safe,* she said, the words like air in her lungs, like sun on her skin. *My son is safe.* Il Tornja had betrayed her, but a part of Adare had always expected the betrayal. If she thought too much about Sanlitun in il Tornja's clutches, her tiny, cantankerous, fire-eyed child swaddled at the breast of some complicit bitch of a wet nurse, if she let herself see all that, she might still collapse. But il Tornja had given her something else to look at, a problem to solve, an enemy to destroy.

"So I just need to get to her. To Triste. Get to her, then kill her."

"And then what?"

"Then I get my son back."

Nira stared, opened her mouth as though to respond, ran a tongue over her crooked teeth, then turned aside to spit onto the polished hardwood floor. "Ya still believe ya can bargain with him? After all this? Ya still think you can *trust* him?"

"Of course not," Adare replied, forcing her hands to unclench, her shoulders to relax. "But il Tornja has reason to keep our alliance. My name gives him legitimacy. Even after the situation with Triste is . . . finished . . . he needs me."

The words sounded true, but they tasted wrong on her tongue, poisonous. Bile rose in her throat. The truth was, she had no idea what il Tornja intended, no idea why he wanted Triste dead, no idea what he would do if Adare refused, or if she agreed. Not that it mattered. He had her son, and so she would kill Triste. The rest could wait.

"Kaden was right," she said finally.

Nira cocked her head to the side, the question unspoken.

Adare exhaled wearily. "He said il Tornja's mind was too wide for me to comprehend, for any of us." Her hands were clenched into white, desperate fists on the table before her. "He planned this," she went on. "When the offer of the treaty first arrived, he was planning this."

Nira nodded grudgingly. "If not before."

Adare's mind filled with the memory of Andt-Kyl, of the Csestriim general seated cross-legged atop the signal tower issuing orders no one could understand, commanding his men to flee, or fight, or lay down their arms, watching them slaughtered or slaughtering according to some logic only he could comprehend, studying a pattern in the bloodshed that only he could see. His men called him a genius, but it was more than that. Battle's chaotic scrawl was, to Ran il Tornja, a fully legible text. He had arrived in Andt-Kyl to fight a force assembled by a god, and he had won.

The spectacle had been terrifying enough when il Tornja still battled Adare's *foes;* even then, the ruthless, alien genius of the Csestriim general had made some mortal part of her quail. And now the tide had shifted.

Adare stared at Nira's ravaged face and scalp, at the burns and the dried blood where the cuts had broken open. In all the haste and confusion, one fact was awfully, perfectly clear: Ran il Tornja wasn't Adare's general anymore. The time had come to face him down, to fight him, to pitch her own mind and will against that monstrous brilliance, and Adare realized, her breath shaking in her chest, she *knew,* the certainty lodged inside her like a blade, that there was no chance, no hope, no possible way that she could win.

17

He could remember a time when darkness had been a quality of the world itself, a thing of the sky when the sun sagged below the horizon and the light leaked out; a thing of the sea when you dove deep enough for the weight of salt water to smother the shine; a thing of castle keeps and caves after someone snuffed the last lamp and the great stone space went black. Even the darkness of Hull's Hole, that absolute absence of light filling the cave's snaking chambers: you went into it, then you came out. Or if you failed to come out, if the slarn tore you apart, then you slid into the longer darkness of death. It had seemed an awful fate once, being stuck in that endless black. That was before the blade had taught Valyn hui'Malkeenian a greater, more terrible truth: the outer dark, for all its horrors—the old, cold dark of caverns or the bottomless dark of the dead—it was nothing when set beside the darkness carried inside, a darkness bled into poisoned flesh and carved across ruined eyes, a darkness of the self.

Valyn sat with his back against a balsam's rough trunk. He knew the tree from the sap's scent, knew the trees beside it: hemlocks and larch ringing the small clearing. There were a hundred smells on the air, a thousand—decaying needles and mouse droppings, thick moss and wet granite, horse piss and horse sweat, leather and iron—all woven into a rough fabric cast across his mind.

He couldn't see a fucking thing.

From overhead, through the branches of the trees, the sunlight filtered down, hot and dark. He turned his eyes upward, opened them as wide as he could, kept them open even as they dried out and started to sting. You could go blind looking at the sun, but he was already blind. Maybe if he stared long enough, something, some hint of fire, would sear through the scarred lenses. That was the thought anyway, the hope. Now, as always, he saw nothing.

A few paces off, the Urghul were preparing camp. Valyn could hear them hobbling the horses and rummaging in saddle packs. He could smell the newly kindled fire, the stolen whiskey passed from hand to filthy hand, the blood of the elk the outriders had brought down a few hours earlier. If he bothered, he could make out conversations, all of the individual voices rising and falling in tuneless counterpoint. He couldn't understand the language, though, and so instead of trying to untangle the words, he listened to the breathing of the Urghul as they went about their tasks, to the dozens of heartbeats. Those sounds were more useful than words, anyway. If the horsemen were going to attack him, they weren't likely to announce it. He would hear the approaching murder in a quickened pulse first, in breath rasping too fast between parted lips.

Not that anyone had come after him so far. On leaving the crude homestead that morning, the Urghul had given him two horses, then utterly ignored him as the small band moved north-west through the trees. He might have been a sack of grain rather than a foreign warrior in their midst. *Fitting,* he thought grimly. Without his sight, he rode about as well as a sack of grain, crouching low over the withers, guiding the beast by the sound of those before him, trying not to get knocked from the saddle by low-hanging branches. The forest was so dense that, aside from a brief canter up a stony streambed, the Urghul couldn't move much faster than a walk.

Valyn had spent all day trying to sift through the scents coming off the horsemen. Beneath their leather and iron, he could make out the thick musk of weariness and a brassy, hammered determination. A few of the Urghul were angry—a smell he'd come to associate with rusting steel. That soft, rotten stench was fear—mostly it came from the *taabe* with the reeking leg wound. The man would be dead within the week, though he didn't seem to realize it.

Huutsuu's scents were mingled almost too fully to decipher: there was rage mixed with a muddy cloud of doubt, thick and heavy, and there, hot with the heat of a summer pepper, something very close to excitement. She didn't seem to mind the endless, fly-plagued swamps of the northern forests, or if she did, she had hammered flat her own irritation.

As he sifted through her scent for the tenth time, Valyn realized the woman was approaching, bare feet almost silent in the fallen needles. He shifted his focus, shoving aside everything but the approaching Urghul. Her heart beat steady and even, but he could taste her wariness. Valyn put his hand on his belt knife, but made no move to stand.

She stopped two paces away, out of easy reach, then watched him silently for a while before speaking.

"You believe I gave you horses and water at dawn only to kill you in the dusk?"

Her voice was full and raw as the smoke rising from the strips of cooking meat. The memory of their first encounter on the steppe filled Valyn's mind, of Huutsuu standing naked outside of her *api,* scars carved into her pale flesh, yellow hair like fire lashed to a frenzy by the wind. She must have been twice Valyn's age, maybe even into her fifth decade, the mother of three children, but the years had done nothing to soften her.

Valyn left the knife in its sheath, but didn't take his hand from the pommel.

"What I believe," he said quietly, his own voice grating in his ears, a tool long neglected and running to rust, "is what I have seen. When you capture Annurians, you do one thing: you hurt them."

There was a quick whiff of irritation, then the soft sound of the woman shaking her head.

"You live one month on the steppe and you think you know a whole people."

"I saw what happened in Andt-Kyl."

"Andt-Kyl was a battle. People die."

"And after?" Valyn shook his head grimly. "For months, I was close enough to the front to hear your sacrifices. To smell them."

The woman paused. "This is what you have been doing since the battle? Cowering in the forest listening to the slaughter of your own people?"

The words would have stung once. They *should* have stung. Valyn just nodded.

"I'm done taking sides," he said. "Done with this fight."

"What about your empire? Your revenge on your war chief, the one who killed your father?"

"My revenge . . ." Valyn trailed off. His hand ached on the handle of the knife. The scene atop the stone tower in Andt-Kyl blazed across his mind, sharp as lightning: killing the Aedolian, fighting Ran il Tornja, Adare's knife in his side, the keen edge of the *kenarang*'s sword across his eyes, then the long fall to the water. His last vision had been one of blades and blood and betrayal.

"My revenge wasn't even mine," he said at last. The words sounded dull, dead. "It was a lie peddled by your chieftain in the hope that I would do his killing for him. And I did. I believed the lie, and good men died for it. I killed them."

Huutsuu paused. He could smell the uncertainty on her. "And your empire?"

"Is ruled by a murderous whore. I will not fight for her."

"And yet this morning you killed for a useless family of loggers."

"It's not their fault that my sister's a power-hungry bitch and il Tornja's a murderer. It's not their fault that Long Fist drove his Urghul vermin over the border."

Huutsuu's pulse tattooed the silence. Valyn wondered if she was going to attack. If she did, he wondered if the awful, inexplicable sight would come to him again, or if it would fail him. He didn't much care, either way.

"You are one man among foes," Huutsuu said at last. "You are fast, faster than you were, but not fast enough, I think, to be using words like *vermin*."

Valyn shrugged. "Scum. Rabble. Plague. Horsefucker." He paused, letting the words hang in the air. "Worthless, no-account, moon-pale, blood-drunk savages. Should I go on?"

Huutsuu's rage spiked, blood-hot and coppery. He could feel the air shift as she leaned toward him. He could hear, quieter than thought, her hand settling around the leather grip of her sword.

"Come on," he said, still refusing to stand. Either the darksight would come, or it would not. "Come on."

The moment balanced like a dagger set on its tip. Then Huutsuu leaned back on her heels, barked a derisive laugh.

"If you are so eager to die, why have you been hiding between the trees all these moons like a broken forest animal?"

"No reason to rush. You had to come sooner or later. You, or a band of riders just like you."

"A warrior finds his fight. He does not wait for it."

"I'm not a warrior," Valyn said, gesturing to the wreckage of his eyes. "I can't find anything. I'm blind."

Suddenly, she stank of suspicion.

"This is a lie."

Valyn shrugged. "Believe what you want."

Something in his voice gave her pause. Then he heard her shaking her head. "I saw you pull arrows from the air. I saw you throw the ax that killed Ayokha. These were not the acts of a blind man."

Valyn ignored the unspoken question; he had no answer to it. How could he explain to the woman that, though he lived in unrelieved darkness, though he was reduced to stealing game from the traps of a family of unsuspecting homesteaders, though he had spent the coldest months of the winter cowering inside a rough cave, eating strip by icy strip the carcass of the hibernating bear he had killed and left frozen in the snow . . . despite all that he could still, sometimes, impossibly, see? How could he explain that he was blind except for those moments when he most *had* to see, that when forced to fight his mind filled with a sight that was not sight, a vision of the world etched in layers of undifferentiated black? How to cram into words the inexplicable fact that when death loomed, his mind slipped into a kind of primal understanding buried untold fathoms beneath rational thought? And how to tell that whatever had done this to him had also made him fast, impossibly fast, far stronger than all his years of training? How could he explain to anyone, let alone this woman, that he was broken, broken beyond all possibility of fixing, but that, like a shattered blade, he could still draw blood? The understanding lay beyond words, perhaps beyond thought, and so he shirked it.

"So," he said instead. "You're looking for these Annurian warriors, these ghosts. You know that they're Kettral, right?"

He'd spent most of the day pondering Huutsuu's words back at the homestead: three warriors, dressed all in black, almost unkillable. They had to be Kettral; the question—the question that gnawed at his mind like a rat—was *who*?

"We know this," Huutsuu replied.

"Then you're an idiot. The Kettral, whoever they are, are going to want to help you even less than I do. They're not going to put aside the knowledge of what you've done here."

Huutsuu hesitated. A snow-cold breeze out of the north carried the smell of seared elk. Most of the Urghul were clustered around the fire, talking quietly between bites. It had always struck Valyn as strange that a people so brutal should speak in such a musical tongue. Listening to the horsemen was like listening to gentle chanting or birdsong. He could smell the stale sweat and leather of the sentries, four of them standing guard in a rough square around the camp. For just a moment the small patch of forest felt safe, warm, the kind of place you could let down your guard to enjoy the company of friends.

"The Kettral will not help us, even if it means killing this leach who leads my people?" Huutsuu asked.

"A man can hate two foes at the same time. Especially if one's a traitor and the other is a blood-soaked barbarian that loves to carve open kids."

"My fight is not with Annur."

Valyn stared stupidly into the darkness, toward where her face would be. "Then what the fuck are you *doing* here, Huutsuu? Why did you even cross the Black?"

Her frustration was bright, sharp. "We came to purge the world of your weakness, this is true. But now—the world has changed."

"The world doesn't change."

"There is much a man might miss while hiding in the forest."

Valyn shook his head grimly. "Did you torture Annurian citizens?"

He could feel the whisper of wind in his ragged beard as she nodded. "By the score."

"Then I haven't missed anything."

"We have stopped. I and my people put aside that fight. There is another, greater foe than the millions of people your empire raises into sheep."

"And because you realized you listened to the wrong lies, that you followed the wrong bloody bastard, you'll stop cutting Annurian throats for . . . what? A few weeks? Long enough to find a proper religious fanatic to lead you again? Then what? Back to boiling Annurian children in your pots? If you're really done with this then *go home*."

"I will not leave the leach at my back. I will not leave him alive to return to the northern grasses when his war is finished."

"And if you manage to kill Balendin, you will leave?"

"I will leave. This land was not built for horses."

Valyn breathed deeply, smelling her, searching for the lie. There was only the woman's sweat, her determination.

He shook his head, sick of it all. After more than half a year in the forest, lost, forgotten, dead in the minds of everyone who knew him, here he was again, getting tangled up in some formless war where no one was right, where everyone murdered and lied, where the ally you sided with might be worse than the foe you fought.

It doesn't matter, he reminded himself silently. *That family of trappers is still alive.* That's *why you're here.*

The rest of it would end in ugliness and blood. Saving that kid, though, him and his family, that, at least, had been good. Valyn hadn't expected, in the long months scratching an existence out of the forest, to have another chance to do a thing that was good, unfouled. As for what came next . . . well . . . it didn't much matter whether he died fighting a bear for next winter's cave or trying to put a knife in Balendin's heart.

"Fine," he said at last. "Tell me about these ghosts you're hoping to find."

"They wear black."

It was no more than she'd said that morning, but once more the urgency pricked at Valyn. The only other Kettral at Andt-Kyl had been those on his Wing. Immediately after the battle, when he was still struggling with the fact that Adare's knife had not killed him, he thought he'd caught Gwenna's smell on the lake wind, and Annick's, and Talal's. He'd thought about trying to rejoin them, had even tried for half a morning to force his way through the trees. Then he abandoned the course. His Wing, if they were alive, if his mind wasn't taunting him with warmedover memories, was better off without him. All he'd done was to lead them from ambush to disaster, and that was *before* il

Tornja carved out his eyes. They'd defended the small town just fine without him, better than fine. He'd taken one more long breath, dragging the air of those forests into his lungs, lingering over the distant smells of his companions, his friends, his Wing-mates, and then he'd turned his face away, to the north, pushing slowly through the trees until he couldn't smell anything but the forest and the wind off the mountains.

"Kettral," he said quietly. His palms were slick with sweat, as was his face, despite the cold air slicing between the trunks. Could it be his own Wing after all these months, Gwenna and Talal and Annick hiding in the woods just like Valyn himself?

No, he amended silently. *Not like me. Not hiding. Fighting.*

He half hoped that he was right. After so many months alone, he could almost hear Gwenna's tart laugh ringing in his ears, almost feel Talal's hand steady on his shoulder. But then, there was a reason he hadn't tried to find them immediately after Andt-Kyl. Even if they were his Wing, he had nothing left to give them.

"Describe them," he said.

Huutsuu hesitated, marshaling her thoughts. "The details are elusive; they attack only at night."

"Try."

"There are three, two men and a woman."

Valyn leaned back against the rough trunk of the tree, disappointment mingling with relief. It wasn't his Wing after all, at least not all of it. Maybe they weren't even Kettral after all. It wasn't as though the Eyrie had the only black cloth in the world.

"The leader is short," Huutsuu continued. "Shorter than me, and black-skinned. There is a tall, yellow-haired woman, almost Urghul-looking. Maybe Edish."

Valyn's relief evaporated. He leaned forward. Huutsuu paused.

"You know them," she said.

"The third," Valyn said. "An ugly bastard with a scraggly beard."

Her nod was a whisper.

"The Flea," he said. "Holy Hull. You're looking for the Flea."

Huutsuu repeated the name. "The Flea," she said slowly, as though tasting the word. "You are certain of this?"

"The description fits. It's perfect."

"Who is this Flea?"

Valyn shook his head, momentarily at a loss about how to respond. "The deadliest of us," he said finally.

"You know him?"

"He trained me," Valyn replied slowly.

"It was good to bring you, then."

"Not really. We fought later. It was my fault that his sniper died."

The memory of that desperate fight in Assare filled his mind, of Blackfeather Finn stepping from the open doorway, Pyrre's knife buried in his belly. Valyn had decided, over the course of the cold, lonely months, that that was the moment when his own life had turned. Everything that had gone before, even the horror of Ha Lin's death, even the flight from the Islands themselves—none of it would have led down the same path if only Valyn had managed to keep his people in check, to find a way to make his peace with the Flea instead of fighting him. He'd gone over the events a thousand times. Pyrre, of course, had been the wick that lit the whole explosive mess, but he should have found a way to control Pyrre. For some time he couldn't measure, he lost himself in it all over again. It was Huutsuu's voice, finally, that pulled him clear.

"So you fought him. Warriors fight. This does not mean you cannot ride at his side again."

Valyn frowned at the word *ride*. "Does he have his bird?"

"The bird is dead," Huutsuu replied. "Long Fist killed it the first time these Kettral attacked. He killed it and the woman flying on its back."

"Chi Hoai Mi," Valyn said, then shook his head. "The *first* time?"

"They came for Long Fist just before the battle at the lake, northeast of Andt-Kyl—the three of them with no bird, just like now. They killed many of my people, fought their way almost to Long Fist himself before they were stopped, taken. Then the bird came. Long Fist brought it down, but the other three escaped."

"Brought it down?" Valyn demanded. "With what?"

Huutsuu hesitated. He could taste her awe, bright and cold as the night wind. "His strength is not all in his limbs. He raised a hand, and the bird burst into flame. It screamed as it fell."

"A leach," Valyn breathed. "Long Fist is a 'Kent-kissing leach. Just like Balendin."

"Long Fist is blessed by the god," Huutsuu said. "Your Kettral leach . . . he is twisted."

"Twisted," Valyn growled. "We're all fucking twisted." He was holding the handle of his knife so tightly that his knuckles ached. With an effort he relaxed his grip. "Where did the Flea go? After."

"He disappeared. Into the forest. For months now, he has haunted our camps, striking, leaving a dozen dead in moments, then disappearing into the trees. I need him now; a Kettral to kill a Kettral leach."

"That's right," Valyn spat. "You need him. Not me."

"Two spears are better than one. I will use whatever weapon I can hold inside my hand."

"I'm not a weapon."

There was wariness on the wind now, and something else, something bright and hot that Valyn couldn't quite recognize. "I have seen you kill," the woman said finally. "I have seen this with my own eyes."

"I'm fucking *blind,* you stubborn bitch."

"Perhaps. And perhaps it is because of this that you cannot see what you have become."

18

"I hate this fucking place," Gwenna said, staring into the fissure in the limestone that marked the entrance to Hull's Hole.

They'd waited in the mangroves until dark, crossed the spine of Hook to Buzzard's Bay, stolen a boat from the harbor, rowed it three-quarters of the way to Irsk, scuttled it, then swam in the last few miles. The days since leaving Annur had pared away the moon, sliver by sliver, until only a slight crescent remained. Still, a slight crescent was enough to illuminate a boat on the waves, and Gwenna spent the entire passage scanning the sky, searching for some sign of pursuit.

If Qora and Quick Jak were right, if all of Rallen's thugs were washouts who hadn't passed the Trial, the darkness was plenty thick to hide a few swimmers. On the other hand, Gwenna herself could see just fine in the watery light, could make out the slow, graceful shapes of swells around them, the sullen bulk of Qarsh black against the horizon, a few high clouds thin as silver filigreed across the night. It would only take one flier who passed the Trial to make them, just one of those bastards with the slarn sight to turn them into chum. She'd felt exposed in the boat, then exposed in the water. The entire passage, she'd felt hunched and hunted, desperate to get under cover once more, and yet now that they were here, in front of the Hole, staring into that jagged black pit . . . well . . . the ocean didn't seem quite so bad.

Hull's Hole reeked in its subtle, sick-sweet way of guano, and salt, and mussels gathered by the seabirds then shattered on the rocks. Gwenna could still remember those mussels from the first time. Next to the slarn and the poison, it seemed like a trivial detail, but she could picture them inside the entrance, hundreds of purple shells burst open, the stringy, gelatinous flesh torn apart by the beaks of birds, what was left of the mollusks pierced through by their own shattered shells. There was something obscene about them, about that splattering of wet, helpless flesh, too dumb and busted even to squirm.

And that was just the *entrance*. She could smell more now than she had been able to then. Farther in, there was the thin, dank scent of wet stone, the keen smell of blood, and beneath these, faint as a remembered nightmare, the slick, oleaginous, rotten stink—like yesterday's vomit laid over rotting meat—of the slarn.

"How long have all of you been hiding here?" Talal asked, no more eager, evidently, to go down into the Hole than Gwenna herself.

"Months," Qora replied. "Manthe and Hobb had the idea."

"The idea to hide in a cave filled with poisonous hive lizards?" Gwenna asked. "Who are those two geniuses?"

"They're in charge," Quick Jak said. "Since we broke off from Rallen. They've been holding us together."

"And the slarn?" Talal asked. "You've found a way to keep them at bay?"

"Mostly."

The word spoke volumes. Gwenna hadn't forgotten the reptilian monsters—half snake, half eyeless lizard. She'd dreamed of them the night she escaped the Hole and passed the Trial, then nearly every night after that. If those dreams had grown less frequent, it was only because other horrors now vied with the slarn for her few restless hours of sleep. She hadn't forgotten the slarn, nor had she forgotten what the slarn did to people. When she closed her eyes, she could see Ha Lin's corpse, smooth skin pared open in long, fine gashes, flesh peeling back from the wounds. Some of that had been Balendin's work. Some, but not all.

"How many have you lost?" Gwenna asked.

Qora stared at her, held her silence like it was some kind of treasure.

"Twenty-two," Jak said quietly.

Gwenna stared at him. "Out of . . ."

"Close to fifty."

"And you're *still here*?"

"You don't understand," Qora snarled, turning on her. "We have nowhere else to *go*. You said it yourself. The Islands aren't that big, and there aren't that many of them. At least against the slarn we have a chance."

"Yeah," Gwenna replied, shaking her head. "A chance. About one in two, if I haven't totally fucked up the math."

"Should be higher," Annick said, switching from her longbow to a short horn bow more suitable to fighting in the tunnels. "Slarn are killable."

"And we've started killing them," Qora snapped.

"It's better now," Jak said. "Most of the people we lost, we lost early on. Manthe and Hobb found a new cavern, a place where we can keep them at bay."

"It makes sense," Talal said, stepping inside the entrance to the cave, then sniffing the air. "No one's going to come hunting here. Definitely not Rallen and his crew. They'd give up their biggest advantage the moment they left their birds to go in the door."

"They don't *have* to go in the door," Gwenna pointed out. She gestured to the broken limestone cliffs around them. "Set an ambush here. Kill anyone coming or going. Better yet, just block up the fissure and leave the poor fuckers for the slarn."

She could tell from the bleak expression on Jak's face that she'd hit a nerve, but then, maybe they *needed* someone banging on some nerves. Cowering in a lightless cave with a few hundred predatory monsters hungry for human flesh hardly seemed like anyone's idea of a sound strategy. She tried to soften her voice.

"They're going to *find* you sooner or later, you know."

"They've come to the island," Jak said. "They've even explored a few hundred paces inside the cave. . . ." He trailed off, shaking his head.

"No one wants to go deeper," Qora concluded. "That's why it's a good spot."

"Good," Gwenna said, "provided you're not one of the twenty-two."

"We all have to die of something."

"Yeah—but we don't all have to die *today*."

"You wanted to come here. You *demanded* it!"

Gwenna snorted. "Fair enough. Just seemed like a better idea when we were farther away."

It had been a year since the Trial, but she remembered the ordeal all too well. Life was like that—you tended to remember the times you almost died. She'd spent the first few hours searching the upper caverns and corridors, refusing any shafts that sloped down too abruptly, hoping she might come across one of the slarn eggs without diving too deep under the earth. It didn't work. The slarn preferred the depths, and so, as the fire from the poison burned its way up her arm, she had descended at last, torch in one hand, smoke steel blade in the other.

By the time she emerged, the torch was gone, the steel was bloody, and so was she—both arms soaked up to the elbows with her own wounds and those of the slarn she'd killed. A few hundred paces from the surface, she'd come across Gent. Another day, in another place, she would have been pleased to discover he was even more cut up than she was. Not in the Hole. The two of them had limped out together, leaning on each other, neither willing to speak. If there were words for what happened in that labyrinth, Gwenna didn't know them. She'd felt no relief at the sight of the sun when she emerged, just a faint slackening of dread. Whatever happened next, whatever miserable missions she undertook, whatever stinking shitholes she had to fight her way through, nothing would be as bad as the Hole.

And now I'm going back into the 'Kent-kissing thing, she thought grimly. Her chest felt heavy, tight, as though iron bands were constricting her heart and lungs.

"Let's just get in there, find out what the fuck's going on, figure out what we're going to do about it, and try really hard not to die while we're at it."

The only way to mark time in the winding passages of the Hole was by the burning of their torches. It was tempting to watch the flame twist and writhe around the pitch-soaked rag, but watching the flame played havoc with Gwenna's night vision, and so she kept her gaze on the ground before her, walking with one eye open, then the other, switching every so often to make sure she maintained at least some ability to see in the dark.

As they drove deeper into the cave, however, she started to wonder if eyesight was really all that important. According to Talal, drinking the slarn eggs had changed them, made them faster and stronger, more perceptive. Gwenna had witnessed the effects dozens of times since fleeing the Islands, both in herself and her Wingmates. She'd grown accustomed to her quickly clotting blood, to the fact that her ears could hear a bird rustling in its nest fifty paces distant, to her ability to run, or fight, or swim for hours without stopping. She'd grown used to her altered body, to what it could do. After all these long months, it was easy to forget what things had felt like . . . before.

And now, returning to the Hole seemed to have awakened something further inside her. As they descended into the bottom-less stone warren, she could feel each eddy of air shifting over the fine hairs on her arms. She could smell her companions, their sweat, the dried blood crusted on their clothes, scabbed over their skin. If she breathed deep, she could taste something else on the very back of her tongue, a rancid, bitter flavor. *Fear,* she thought. It wasn't impossible. Animals could smell fear. Maybe the slarn could, too. Certainly she felt some animalistic stirring within her, an awareness, a savage willingness that made her tighten her grip on her sword though there was nothing in the corridor to attack.

"Exactly how do you keep back the slarn?" she asked.

"Manthe and Hobb post a watch at each entrance to the cavern," Qora replied without turning. She was just a few steps ahead, but her voice sounded very far away. "They have us rotate every few hours. And we keep a large central fire up. That's a big part of the problem . . . the thing devours wood, but there's not all that much wood on the island. Pretty soon, we'll have to start crossing over to Harrask, which is risky with Rallen's birds in the air, but if the fire goes out . . ."

She left the rest unsaid.

Gwenna shook her head. "I don't remember those ugly bitches being all that scared of fire. I put out a torch in one of their faces and all she did was shriek like a boiling kettle and try to take my arm off."

"Sometimes they come past our fires," the woman admitted. "Then we fight."

"How does that work out?"

"Manthe and Hobb say—"

"I've had just about an earful," Gwenna cut in, "of Manthe and fucking Hobb. Who are these two idiots? How'd they end up running this sorry little show?"

This time Jak responded. "They're running things because they're the only real Kettral left. Aside from Rallen."

Gwenna frowned. "Never heard of them."

"That's because they live over on Arim. Lived there, I mean, before we came here. They haven't flown missions in ten years, not since half their Wing got killed down in the Waist."

"Fantastic," Gwenna said, the outlines of the rebel command

structure resolving themselves finally. "Not just washed-out cadets, but real, honest-to-'Shael Grounded. This is some operation."

The Grounded were unusual. The Eyrie had been perfecting its selection, training, and testing criteria for centuries. Most of the soldiers who survived Hull's Trial flew missions until they died or couldn't hang in the harness anymore. For those who survived to old age, there was a long row of small, unremarkable houses fronting the harbor on Qarsh. Command referred to the structures as Retired Veterans' Housing, but everyone else, including the scarred and limping old men and women who lived there, called it Lucky Fucks' Row. The buildings weren't much, but they were close to the arena and the mess hall, close to the action, and if there was one thing those old vets shared, it was a desire to be close to the action.

There was, however, another group, smaller, less talked-about, who survived the training and passed the Trial, who flew missions and then just . . . couldn't. Combat shock, the Eyrie called it, and though some of the afflicted had obvious bodily wounds, the real damage was somewhere inside, a breaking of the mind or heart, that left them unable or unwilling to go on. Gwenna had heard stories of women weeping at the sound of munitions, of men who shook as though palsied at the sight of a naked blade. The Eyrie offered them the choice to stay on Qarsh, but something about the island, the constant training and combat, the never-ending flyovers, the ceaseless stories of blood and brutality, sent them elsewhere, and elsewhere, for the Grounded, as for anyone trained by the Kettral, meant Arim.

As cadets, Gwenna and the others had tried to imagine what it must feel like, living on an island surrounded by the failed and the broken, an island that was at once a paradise and a prison, where every reasonable desire was met, where you would be killed without question for trying to leave. Five years ago, the notion had seemed inconceivable. Gwenna had sworn, they *all* had, that death would be preferable. Now that she was a little better acquainted with death, she wasn't so sure.

The washouts and the Grounded might be prisoners, but it was starting to feel as though everyone was a prisoner of something: duty or family, conscience or past mistakes. There were worse fates than a quiet life on a warm island far from the killing. Good people could choose to quit fighting—that was clear enough. The trouble was, sometimes you *had* to fight, and when the fight came, you didn't necessarily want the good people running the show.

"What made these two, Manthe and Hobb, get involved?" Gwenna asked finally.

Qora stopped in the passage ahead. "Do you still not *get* it?"

Gwenna resisted the urge to smack the woman. "I'm slow."

"*Everyone's* involved. You're either with Rallen, or you're fighting him."

"What about the rabble over on Hook?"

"They're an exception," Qora conceded. "But if you have any Kettral training at all, you're in this fight."

"Or you're dead," Jak added quietly, his words echoing inside the great stone throat of the passage.

"If those two are the only Kettral," Talal asked, "why were the two of you over on Hook? Why were you the ones doing the fighting?"

"We weren't supposed to be fighting," Qora replied grimly. "We were supposed to be hiding and watching. Learning their patterns."

Gwenna nodded, another piece locking into place. "And then the boys in black burned down your hideout. Still, you could have run. Could have just slipped away in the confusion."

"It looked like an opportunity," Qora said.

"Oops," Gwenna said.

She could smell the regret pouring off of Jak, dark as an old mold long lost to the light. Between the fear and the regret, it was a wonder the poor bastard had emotion left over for anything else. She wondered idly if he'd always been so tentative, so fearful, or if the years of training, training intended to harden him, had somehow had the opposite effect.

"And what were Manthe and Hobb doing," Talal asked, the question breaking into Gwenna's thoughts, "while you were running surveillance?"

A long pause, interrupted only by the sound of dripping water and their own feet scuffing the uneven stone.

"Planning," Qora replied finally. "Running things."

"By which you mean hiding," Gwenna said flatly. She hadn't even met these self-proclaimed leaders of the Kettral resistance, and they were already pissing her off.

"Manthe doesn't fight," Jak said. "She doesn't go out. She's been Grounded a long time. Vicious combat shock."

From the tone of his voice, he didn't share any of Gwenna's anger. He sounded, if anything, sorry for the woman.

"But you're *all* fucked up *somehow*. That's why you were on Arim."

"Gwenna . . . ," Talal warned.

"No. If we are going to be fighting our way out of this goat fuck together," she said, riding over his objection, "we're not going to do it tiptoeing around feelings like they're lit starshatters. The facts are the fucking facts—washouts aren't Kettral. They don't have the training and they never went down into the Hole. That's just a reality on the ground that we have to *deal* with."

"We may not be Kettral," Qora growled, "but at least we're *fighting*."

"*That,*" Gwenna said, wagging a finger at the back of the woman's head, "is exactly my point. You're out there risking your assholes, making a 'Kent-kissing mess of it, sure, but getting your hands bloody. And all the while your so-called leaders, the only ones with the full training to actually do the job right, are cowering in a hole." She blew out a frustrated breath. "I'm not pissing in your soup, you bitch. At least you're doing what you can. It's Manthe's combat shock that I'm finding tough to swallow."

She walked a few more paces before Talal broke the angry silence.

"What about Hobb?"

"He's fine," Jak said after a pause. "Angry, but fine."

"Then what was he doing on Arim?"

"Being with Manthe."

Gwenna sucked air between her teeth. It was almost inconceivable for a Kettral who still had the fight in his bones to stop flying missions voluntarily. Almost. She tried to imagine it, following someone she loved into uselessness and obscurity. Giving up everything she'd trained for, throwing away the chance at revenge, at redemption, for what . . . to sit on the porch with some poor broken bastard looking out at the sea? No wonder Hobb was angry.

"So he's in charge?"

"There isn't . . . a formal structure," Qora replied. "Manthe can't fight. Won't fight. Whatever. But she seems better than Hobb with a lot of things—tactics, knowledge of the birds, stuff like that."

"You have no birds," Annick observed. It was the first thing she'd said since entering the cave. "You are hiding in a cave being slowly decimated by slarn. It is time to shift tactics."

"My point exactly," Gwenna said. "If Manthe is the strategic genius behind this operation, you might want to rethink your leadership."

"They're Kettral," Jak protested. "The only Kettral."

Gwenna smiled grimly. "Not anymore."

The cavern stank of torch smoke and spoiled food, piss and wet wool. There was no ventilation. The air just sat, wet and sullen, fat and unmoving. The chill didn't feel invigorating. It felt dead. The large fire Qora had described was visible well before they

reached the cavern proper. Gwenna had expected something
warming, comforting, but from the tunnel in which they stood,
it looked like a hazy red maw, the ruddy light throwing everything beyond its scope into deeper darkness. And then there
was the blood, long dried but still acrid, a reminder, as if she
needed a reminder, that the darkness had teeth.

"Identify yourself," a man demanded as they stepped free of
the cramped, jagged passage. He was tall, but thin to the point
of emaciation, all bone and tendon and skin. The bare blade he
brandished a few feet from Gwenna's face looked like the only
solid thing about him, and from the way he held it—too far out
in front of him, too wide of the centerline—Gwenna doubted
he had either the skill or the strength to do much with it.

"It's us, Colt," Qora said wearily. "Plus a few new friends."

Gwenna shook her head. "Wrong place for a sentry. Anyone
who gets this far is already past the choke point. You want him
twenty paces back there," she added, jerking a thumb over her
shoulder, "where we had to climb up onto the ledge."

Colt's eyes bulged. He stared at her so long that Gwenna
wondered if he was right in the head. When he finally spoke,
he didn't lower his sword. "You don't know what's *out there*.
This isn't just some cave. . . ."

"It's Hull's Hole," Gwenna replied, the anger hot and unexpected in her throat, "and the slarn are out there. I know about
slarn because I spent the better part of a miserable day killing
them. The slarn are *more* reason to put guards in the right places,
not less."

"And just who in Hull's name are you?" a new voice
demanded. Gwenna pivoted to face another man, obviously
older than Colt—well into his late forties, by the look of him—
and bigger, and stronger. He stepped out of a shadowed alcove
by the entrance to the cavern, his sword, too, naked in his hand.
Unlike Colt, however, he looked like he knew how to use it, like
he was willing to. Something about his face—thick black beard,
wide-set eyes, heavy bones through the brow and jaw—looked

vaguely familiar. If Qora's timeline was right, he would have still been on Qarsh, still flying missions, when Gwenna herself first arrived on the Islands. Not that any of that mattered now. He stepped in front of Colt as though the other man were no more than a useless chunk of rock.

Qora moved forward, but he dragged her out of the way with his free hand, shoving her to the floor. "Get the *fuck* out of the way, you stupid, stupid bitch. You bring people here? *Here?*" Despite the fury in his voice, he never took his eyes from Gwenna. He reeked of anger and oiled steel. Beyond him, clustered around the fire, stood a couple dozen men and women, some on their feet, some caught resting, plenty of them hefting blades or bows, but hesitantly, as though they'd never considered how to face such a threat. Gwenna glanced at them, then turned her attention back to the bearded man.

"You must be Hobb. Qora mentioned you." He was tall, more than a head taller than Gwenna herself. Worth remembering if she had to kill him. "Your sentry's in the wrong place."

"I'll ask one more time," the man replied, jaw tight, "and then I'm going to start cutting. Who are you?"

"Never mind about the sentry, actually," Gwenna replied. "Qora told us you weren't the brains of the operation. Where's Manthe?"

It was a gamble, but it paid off. Toward the back of the rough chamber, in the shadows to the left of the fire, a woman jerked as though burned by an errant spark. *Still so scared after all these years,* Gwenna thought bleakly.

"Manthe," Gwenna said, looking straight past Hobb, raising her voice slightly. "You've got this poor idiot standing in the wrong spot. Take us, for example—we're already in the cavern. If you wanted to contain us, it's too late."

She hadn't been sure what to expect from the woman. She'd read accounts of combat shock, knew that it could scramble all reasonable responses, but even the most dire accounts failed to prepare her for the woman's panicked shouting.

"Get flatbows on them! Vessik and Larch, flank them, *flank them*!" Manthe's voice was high and desperate, about the furthest thing Gwenna could imagine from the standard-issue Kettral calm. And this when confronted with three strangers who hadn't even bothered to raise weapons.

The men and women inside the cavern, frozen by their surprise only moments earlier, lurched into motion, drawing blades and flexing bows, some scrambling to back up Hobb, others searching—as though they had just now considered the notion—for a clear line of fire on the intruders. The whole thing was a pathetic mess, but you could get killed easily enough in a mess, especially if one of the fools with a bow decided to start putting wood and steel in the air.

"Oh, for 'Shael's sake," Gwenna said, careful to keep her hands still at her sides. "There are only three of us. Knock it off with the theatrics. Talal . . . ," she added in a lower voice.

"On it," the leach replied quietly.

"Annick?" Gwenna asked, not bothering to look back.

"I have Hobb," the sniper said. Her voice came from a dozen feet up and to Gwenna's left. Clearly she'd climbed onto some sort of ledge, although when she'd had time to do that, Gwenna had no idea.

If Hobb was discomfited by the arrow aimed at his chest, it didn't show in his voice. "Put down the bow," he snapped. "Look around. You've got one shot. I have ten archers flanking you."

"Want me to kill him?" Annick asked. Hobb might not have spoken.

Gwenna shook her head. "No, I don't want you to kill him. He seems to be the only person here who knows how to hold a sword. We came to make friends with these fuckups, and besides, they're unarmed."

Hobb snorted. "Look, you idiotic bitch—"

"Talal," Gwenna said, raising a finger.

The twang of snapping bowstrings shivered the cool air, followed by the curses of the men and women holding them.

"You thought you had archers," she said, keeping her voice even, cheerful. "In fact, what you have is ten men holding curved pieces of wood. Annick, if Hobb moves, kill Manthe. Leave the rest alone. It's not their fault they're being led by idiots."

"It *is* their fault," Annick replied curtly. "They chose to follow them."

Gwenna waved away the objection. "As I understand it, the choices were limited."

Hobb shifted toward her. Gwenna looked at his blade, then shook her head.

"I really wouldn't," she said. "It'll take Annick about half a heartbeat to kill your cowering girlfriend. You think you've got something to prove, but the only thing you're going to prove by getting killed and dumped into a side tunnel for the slarn is that you have . . . *had,* I should say . . . terrible judgment."

For a few heartbeats she thought she'd misplayed her hand, that despite her warning the big bastard was going to limber up the sword and start swinging. There was no real danger—all that business about Annick wasn't a bluff—but if they were going to fight Jakob Rallen and his vicious little cabal, if they were going to get off the island with the birds and munitions, they needed these people to help them. The situation was ugly enough already, and a spasm of wholesale slaughter wasn't going to help.

After a moment, however, Hobb cursed, slammed the blade back into its sheath, and stepped up close, so close Gwenna could smell the rank fish on his breath.

"Don't threaten my wife," he growled. "Ever."

Wife. That was interesting. So Qora had the story straight, at least the important parts. Gwenna held up her hands in a mock surrender. "The only person I want to threaten is Jakob Rallen. Now, maybe we can put away the swords, and the bows, and the big words, and talk to each other about just what in Hull's holy dark is going on."

She gestured toward what seemed to be the center of the cavern. "Where do you sit around here?"

"Bare rock too hard for you?" Hobb demanded.

"Usually I bring a cushion," Gwenna replied, crossing the floor without waiting to see if Talal was following, "but I'll make an exception." She kept the words casual, kept her hands relaxed and far from her weapons. She tried to meet the eyes of Hobb's ragtag soldiers without glaring. It was hard to know, sometimes, if she was glaring.

The other soldiers were whispering, murmuring their confusion as though the words were prayer. What they were praying for, Gwenna had no idea. Probably that she would die before she started hurting people.

"So. I'm Gwenna . . . ," she began, lowering herself to the floor. Hobb was still standing, looming over her, really. The rest of the ragged band was scattered around the cavern, but someone had to sit first if they didn't plan to stand all night long. "This is my Wing. Sorry for the rocky start."

"Wing?" Hobb said, narrowing his eyes. "You're Kettral?"

"Of course we're Kettral. You think three friendly dockyard whores just wandered into Hull's Hole? We'd like to help, if we can all manage not to cut each other to pieces."

From the back of the cavern, Manthe burst in, voice ragged with almost-panic. "She still has the *bow*."

Gwenna shook her head. "What?"

"Your *sniper*," the woman insisted. "You said put down the bows and blades and talk, but she's still holding one, still aiming straight *at me*!"

"Oh," Gwenna said, waving a hand. "I meant everyone *else* should relax."

"What about *her*?"

"Annick never relaxes."

"Tell her to put down the bow," Hobb growled.

"Yeah. She doesn't do that either."

19

After five long days forcing the horses forward through miserable stands of tamarack and larch, they were still in the forest. Though the world remained unrelentingly dark to Valyn's scarred eyes, he could feel the cold wind, honed over the mountain stone and bright as ice. It cut through his leathers and the wool beneath. He could smell the snow, and the ancient ice of the glaciers hanging in the high valleys.

The Eyrie had flown his class of cadets out to the Romsdals once for a two-week exercise in alpine evasion and survival. He'd only been twelve at the time, but he remembered the great gray-black peaks well. Where the Bone Mountains around Ashk'lan were comprised of clean white granite, of rivers cascading over smooth sweeps of stone, the Romsdals were crumbling and dark. Year-round snow capped the highest mountains, but below that white blanket, everything was ankle-twisting scree and shattered schist. The Romsdals felt old, somehow, older than the Bones, heavy with the age and weight of the world. Even when the sun shone, they were cold.

"How far west have we come?" Valyn asked. He could smell Huutsuu at his side, her sweat and leather, the dried blood on her hands from butchering a pair of rabbits that morning.

"Far enough," she replied after a pause. "We are two days' ride from a river and just beyond that, a city."

Valyn studied his mind's map, a composite of the hundreds he'd memorized during his time on the Islands.

"Aergad," he concluded. "It's in northeastern Nish, near the headwaters of the Haag."

He could smell Huutsuu's indifference. "Stones piled on other stones. People crammed so close they live in the shit of their neighbors. In this, at least, I agree with your leach—such places should be burned."

"Balendin is here?" Valyn asked.

"He will be, either today or another day. He travels with his own guard now, joining the war at many places. The fiercest fighting is here, so he returns here often."

"And you're hoping the Flea will come hunting."

Huutsuu hesitated. "Your warrior friends strike in unexpected places, but never in the heart of our force. We will keep to the forests and hope that they find us."

It didn't seem like much of a plan, but he couldn't think of another. According to Huutsuu, the Urghul had been trying and failing to track the Flea for months. Even in deep snow, he and his Wing seemed able to simply disappear. The woman could hardly expect that adding a blind man to the mix would lead to more success, and Valyn had kept quiet about his hearing, about the fact that he could smell anything—a fox, a man, a bear—more than a mile distant. Maybe he could track the Kettral Wing if he got close enough, and maybe he couldn't, but he wasn't about to reveal that secret to Huutsuu.

"We ride south," Huutsuu responded after a pause. "Slowly. He hides, this friend of yours, in the deep forest. He looks for bands like this. If we present a target, he will come."

"The problem," Valyn observed, "is that he might cut all of our throats before you can tell him you've switched sides."

Huutsuu was silent for a while. "We are not cattle," she said finally. "Unlike your Annurians, we are not beasts who wait patiently for the carving."

Valyn felt the darkness twist, then tense inside him. The

memory of slaughtered loggers and trappers filled his mind, of men and women screaming as the Urghul held them down, cut them open. He dropped a hand to the head of an ax; the pitted steel was cool against his burning skin.

"They are people," he growled. "Not beasts."

Huutsuu snorted. "They are weak. We are not. When this Flea comes, we will be ready."

"Ready?" Valyn demanded. He could hear the rage in his own voice, but made no effort to harness it. "If you think because you bore three kids and can ride all day on a horse that you're ready for the Flea, you're a fool." He could hear the horsemen turning in their saddles to look at him. He smiled grimly, then raised his voice. "Which doesn't say much for these assholes following you."

None beside Huutsuu seemed to speak Valyn's language, but they understood a challenge well enough. They could translate the mockery if not the words. The horses, sensing the anger and confusion of their riders, shifted warily. Hooves ground against broken stone.

"I made peace with you," Huutsuu said, "to fight against this leach."

"You made peace with me," Valyn spat back, "because you thought I was a weapon. Well, let's find out." The blood slammed in his temples, in his ears, a roaring fire. He set a hand on the head of the other ax. "Who wants to find out? Anyone?" He hurled the words like stones into the jagged silence.

"Have a care," Huutsuu's voice was hard. "These warriors follow me, but it sits ill with them to ride alongside an Annurian."

"You're telling me you can't keep your people under control?"

"Control." She spat the word, as though it tasted bitter. "It is a thing for emperors and the sheep they keep penned. The Urghul are a free people."

"I've seen what that freedom looks like. I've seen the scars it leaves."

"It is a meager freedom that leaves no scars."

They made camp just before nightfall. On the steppe, the Urghul had been happy to ride in the darkness, but the ground of the northern forests was studded with stones and broken by twisting roots—dangerous ground, even for the small, sure-footed horses. The horsemen had gathered wood for a fire.

The faint heat was tempting, especially as the night's chill settled into Valyn's bones, but he didn't care to spend the night surrounded by Urghul. No one had tried to kill him yet, but that didn't mean they wouldn't. Maybe they agreed with Huut-suu's decision to find the Flea. Maybe not. He might have a better idea if he could understand their language, but he couldn't, and he didn't. He picked out a flat patch of ground fist-deep in brown needles, a narrow space wedged between two huge boulders. He explored it with his hands, then, satisfied that the only approach was from the south, settled in, his back to the stone. It was cold, but he was used to cold.

For a while he kept his eyes open, staring into the endless void of his blindness. The wind howled between the boulders, kicking up grit and tearing at the ratty leathers the Urghul had given to him. If he listened long enough, there seemed to be voices on that wind, screaming their warnings and their torments, maddened, just beyond the verge of syllables and sense. *Only the wind,* he told himself. *Just the icy fucking wind.* It kept tearing at him, however, indifferent to his wall of words, and after a while he gave up, opened his mind to the wind's wailing.

The people of Andt-Kyl had screamed like that, screamed as they fought and died, as Valyn crouched atop the signal tower, waiting, watching, and doing nothing. Over at the campfire, the Urghul were burning strips of rabbit, but the cooking reminded Valyn of the reek of human flesh, men and women charred to ash in fires they could not escape. Despite the night's cold claws scratching at his flesh, he was sweating, the ragged wool beneath his leathers—the last remnant of his Kettral blacks—soaked through.

Most nights it was like this. Plenty of days, too. Memory came with the darkness, horror with the memory, and he could never leave that darkness. Eventually, maybe halfway through the night, his body would shudder its way still and he would sleep, mind racked past endurance, the sudden unconsciousness violent as a breakage.

I fixed something, he told himself, remembering the child who bore his name, terrified but brave, demanding to go back to save his family. *I made that one thing right.*

The words did him no good. His body continued to tremble, his mind to turn in the same ruts like a rusted wheel. The Kettral had taught him to break out of a dozen types of fortress, but they'd said nothing about escaping from his own mind.

For a long time he sat there, trembling with memory; so long it was almost a relief to hear Huutsuu approaching through the darkness, her footfalls rough in carcasses of leaves and needles, her breathing a warm echo of the great wind all around them.

She paused a few paces from where he sat, watching him, probably. It was well past dark, but Valyn had long ago lost track of the phases of the moon. Perhaps it was hanging up there somewhere, bright as milk, lighting the stones around him.

"What is wrong with you?" she asked finally.

He'd stopped shaking, some part of his mind or body recognizing the threat, readying the flesh to deal with it. Rather than let the woman stand over him, he rose to his feet, settling a hand on the pommel of his knife. The weight of the twin, short-handled axes hanging from his belt was solid, real, a reassuring ballast that kept him from drifting off into his own darkness.

"Which part?" he replied.

"You have said already that you are blind. You ride like a blind man. You walk like a blind man."

"I guess it all fits then, doesn't it?"

"A blind man does not do the things I saw back at that trapper's cabin. He does not pull flying arrows from the air."

"Maybe you didn't see what you thought you saw."

"I saw this," Huutsuu replied grimly. "You put an ax in one of my *taabe* from fifteen paces. I will know how, or we will go no farther together."

For a dozen slow heartbeats Valyn didn't respond, though he could feel his body coiling, his heart slamming beneath his ribs. There would be no simple breaking of company, no riding off alone and unmolested. Not at this point. Splitting from the Urghul would mean fighting, and something inside him, something that had kept him alive in the waters of Scar Lake and then in the winters of the northern forests, was eager to fight, to limber his twin axes and begin carving. It would end in his own death, but for that, too, a part of him was eager.

But Balendin's still alive, he reminded himself grimly. He'd told himself that he was done fighting, but it was one thing to growl the words to himself alone, in the frigid dark of some northern cave, another to stay out of it when he was around so many others who were diving back in. Dying was fine. He was ready to die, but he might as well try to drag Balendin down with him.

"I'm not always blind," he said finally.

Wind whittled the silence to a point.

"I do not understand," Huutsuu said.

"Neither do I. Most of the time all I see is darkness. I can hear just fine. I can smell. But I can't see my own hand in front of my face."

"And the fighting?"

"The fighting is different. When it matters, when someone's trying to kill me, I can fight."

"You can see?" Huutsuu demanded. She sounded suspicious.

"Yes," Valyn said, remembering the shapes that were not shapes, those forms inscribed in black on his mind's broader blackness. "I can see to fight. To kill."

"So . . . ," Huutsuu began. The syllable was casual, laconic. It did nothing to cover the sound of her sword sliding free of the sheath, of her quickening pulse or her feet shifting on the stone. Even without the strange non-sight, Valyn would have known to move, to block, but for a moment there was more—a vision of the sword's blade carved across his blindness, moving and not moving, the whole thing so pathetically slow. It was less than nothing to slide beneath the blade, to slam his stiffened hand up into her jaw, knocking her teeth closed and sending her reeling back into the boulder behind.

And then it was gone. He could hear Huutsuu's breathing, he could smell the fresh blood, but he might as well have been standing in the bottommost pit of Hull's Hole, his only torch long ago burned out.

"So," he said. If his fist to her jaw hadn't explained it, more words weren't likely to do the job.

Huutsuu straightened, slid her sword back into her sheath. "I do not understand this," she said slowly. He could smell the wariness on her, even thicker than the smoke of the campfire blazing a hundred paces behind them. "I do not understand it, but there is much about this world I fail to understand."

Valyn just nodded. He felt suddenly weary, weary out of all proportion to the minimal effort of the scuffle. He wanted to sit, to lean his head back against the rock, to close his eyes against the stinging wind. He stayed on his feet instead.

"I'll tell you what you need to understand: my eyes are broken. That is all."

"Or perhaps," Huutsuu replied, "you are blessed. I have known women and men like this. . . ."

"Who could fight through their blindness?" Valyn demanded.

"No, not that. They were blessed in other ways. Blessed by Kwihna. This is like the touch of a god on your flesh. There is something sacred in your blindness."

"You don't understand the first fucking thing about sacred," Valyn spat. To hear the Urghul woman talk about sanctity after the chaos the Urghul had wrought in Annur made him angry in a way that went beyond human anger. He could feel his lips pulling back into a snarl. "You're twisted, all of you. Warped. Broken. I don't know how you ended up this way, but your worship of pain, it is an illness."

"What do you know of pain?"

Before he knew what he was doing, Valyn seized the woman by the throat. He could feel the tendons in her neck straining against his fingers as he pulled her closer. She was choking, he realized, hacking, strangling sounds clawing their way free. He smiled.

"Look at my face," he growled. He had drawn her so close that she could hardly do otherwise. Her ragged half breaths were hot against his lips. "Look at my eyes."

She was pulling at his clenched hand with both of hers. He took one and forced it down to his side, to the vicious puckered scar left by Adare's knife. "Do you feel that? *Do you?* What do you think? Did it hurt? Do I have some inkling of what pain is all about?"

Sickened suddenly by Huutsuu, by her savage god, by his own animal savagery, he loosened his grip. Instead of pulling back, however, she leaned closer, so close that her lips were at his ear. A moment later he felt the pain, the knife's frigid tip already past his leathers and his blacks, pressed against his chest, then severing the skin, skewering the flesh of his chest.

His first thought was that the strange sight had finally failed him. The violence had brought no vision.

His second thought, even as he seized her wrist, was that he'd been too slow and too stupid, and that the Urghul woman had killed him for it. No fear came with the realization. No regret. In a grim flash, he understood how Pyrre could be so indifferent to the prospect of her own death. And then he realized that he wasn't dying.

Huutsuu had threaded her blade through the muscle of his chest parallel to the ribs beneath. That knife was more than long enough to reach his heart, but she'd come in from the side; instead of driving it deeper, she was using it, using the pressure of the blade's flat against the striated muscle, to pull him closer to her. Like a water buffalo with a ring through the nose, Valyn obeyed the pressure, moving forward with it, until he could feel the woman's breath again, hot in the cold air.

"Show me," she hissed.

He seized her by the throat once more, whether to choke her or push her back, he couldn't say. There was pain, and there was darkness, and her ragged breathing.

"Show you *what?*"

"Show me," she said, pulling him to her with the knife hooked in his flesh, "what you understand about pain."

He started to respond, but her mouth was on his, hot and hungry, all lips and tongue and teeth and desperate breath. He tightened his fist, lifting her feet free of the ground, kissing her back, if something so vicious could be called kissing. In the endless blank of his blindness, there were two points bright as stars in dark night: the red pain of the blade buried in his chest, and the white fire of a lust that burned like rage. She shuddered when he slammed her back into the flat wall of the boulder, groaned with something that might have been pain or pleasure, then groped around his belt with her free hand.

The buckle was simple, straightforward, but she didn't go for the buckle. Instead, she pulled his belt knife free of the sheath, broke off the kiss to shove him backward, slid the knife through the leather of the belt, the action so quick and insistent she nicked his hip as she cut the leather. As the belt parted, she was already carving away the rest of his clothes, the keen blade parting the fabric, slicing careless, shallow cuts into the flesh beneath until the wool and fur and leather fell away and that glacial air was everywhere on his skin.

It was cold, bitingly cold, but the blood sheeting down his chest was warm, and Huutsuu's tongue was warm as she stepped forward again to lick the wound just where the knife plunged into his chest. When she kissed him again, he could taste blood, a taste that broke something inside him, some last, restraining civilized thread, and then both knives were in his hands, and the blood a hot wash down his flesh, and he could *see* her, see the rictus clench in her jaw as he cut her furs free, see the furrows he left in her flesh, fresh rents over the old webs of scar. He could see in shades of dark on dark her neck bent back, her back arching, her hands dragging him close, and then the sight blacked out and the ambit of his world became screaming, and blood, the blind pain and the searing, vicious bliss, unredeemed, unredeemable.

20

From the balcony of her chambers on the top floor of the Crane, Adare looked down. It was a hundred paces straight down to the courtyards, gardens, and temples of the Dawn Palace, but she didn't look straight down. Instead, she stared north, eyes wandering over Annur's roofs of copper and slate and teak shingle. Morning fog off the Broken Bay still filled the streets and alleys, and though Adare could make out the sounds of the city stirring—curses of carters and canal hands; the rattle of merchants opening their shops; strident cries of grocers and fishmongers hawking fruit and flowers, the day's fresh catch—she couldn't see anything in those streets but the still, white fog. The morning was all noise and no motion, as though the living had abandoned Annur to the ghosts.

The balcony easily overtopped the masts of the tallest ships, the gulls wheeling above the harbor, and yet from that balcony, even when she tipped her head back until her neck hurt, she could not make out the top of Intarra's Spear. That other, greater tower's wall rose like a curtain of slagged glass barely a hundred paces away, but the top was lost in the clouds.

Nira glanced up at it, then grunted. "Intarra's Spear, my withered ass."

"You don't believe it's a relic of the goddess?" Adare asked. She'd lived inside the palace her whole life, and yet some sights you did not grow used to. Could not grow used to. "It antedates all Csestriim records."

"*Antedates?*" Nira shook her head. "It's no wonder Lehav made you before we were halfway ta Olon. Ya never did learn ta quit talkin' like a princess."

Adare ignored the gibe. In fact, she would have suffered through a hundred more if only Nira would hold on to this tiny bit of her former fire. Adare needed her for the task ahead, of course; there was no way she could break into Intarra's Spear all by herself. Just as important, however, was having someone on her side, someone she could talk to, who would talk back. It had seemed in those first hours after her return that the Nira Adare had known was gone, the life drained out, all the rough edges scoured away by her brother's betrayal. The old woman had finished off a huge carafe of wine, and then, to Adare's despair, passed out on the table. When she woke, however, something had goaded her partway back to life. This morning she had climbed all the stairs to Adare's chambers with something like her usual vigor, and this discussion of the tower was the most animated she had been since returning.

"Even the name *Intarra's Spear* is ancient," Adare went on. "I spent weeks as a child sifting through old codices trying to find the source. The etymology—"

"Piss on your etymology," Nira griped. She hefted her cane, waved it over the balustrade at the huge tower, as though it had offended her. "What *goddess* is gonna give her name to the world's largest cock?"

Adare started to object, then stopped herself. They had come out to her balcony to plan an attack on the tower, or an infiltration, at least, not to bicker about history. She stared at the Spear a moment longer, then turned her attention to something closer, smaller, more manageable: the closed lacquer box that Nira had placed on the wooden table.

"So that's it."

Nira glared at her. "'Course it is. Think I'm in the habit a' using Csestriim lacquer ta pack my soiled underclothes?"

The box was small, just a little larger than Adare's two hands, barely deep enough to hold a pair of wine bottles. At first glance it was unremarkable—no gold or silver, no ostentatious scroll-work to the handle, nothing bright or shiny to draw the eye. When Adare lifted it gingerly to the light, however, she saw that Nira was right. Instead of a flat black, the lacquer was laid on in a thousand shades of gray—some inky and opaque, some smoke thin, some slick as the dorsal fin of a quickpike, some glinting like tarnished silver. From a distance, the cumulative effect was a simple black, but when you held it close, shifted it back and forth beneath the sun, elaborate shapes and beautifully crafted shadows ghosted below the surface. Adare thought she could make out an outstretched hand, a sun in near eclipse, a pair of twining dancers, but each time that she half glimpsed a shape, the whole scene shifted, like the surface of a fast-moving river, and it was gone.

"Hardly inconspicuous," Adare observed.

Nira shrugged. "Il Tornja didn't want anyone else gettin' at what's inside, and I wasn't about ta carry a locked iron chest all the way from Aergad."

Adare tested the weight, then set it back on the table. "How do you open it?"

The old woman laid the tips of her fingers carefully on the surface, scrunched her face in concentration, then traced a series of quick, precise gestures. With a click, the box popped open.

In spite of herself, Adare took half a step back. "A kenning?"

Nira smirked. "The Csestriim were a batch a' evil bastards, that's sure, but they weren't as squeamish about a leach's gifts as we are."

Adare nodded slowly. She'd read as much. After the wars, when men and women tore the Csestriim cities to the ground, they had discovered thousands of artifacts, blades and boxes, statues and stele that were not entirely . . . natural. Found them, and destroyed them—those that could be destroyed. A few historians, those who dared to touch the subject, traced the first seeds of the human hatred of leaches to those early purges.

Adare put the thoughts aside. Whatever the box's provenance, it was the contents that concerned her. She hooked a single finger beneath the lid, lifted it, and stared.

Arranged along one side in tiny beds of black velvet lay fifteen or twenty vials, each with a name etched into the glass. Adare recognized less than half the labels—*Sweethorn, Dusk, Itiriol*—but those few were enough to intuit the contents of the others. Il Tornja had sent her enough poison to destroy the entire council, maybe enough to kill everyone inside the Dawn Palace.

"He just . . . *had* this, lying around?" Adare asked.

"I've been alive more than a thousand years," Nira replied, "and the bastard makes me look like a child. He's probably got warehouses a' this shit piled up all over the world, hidden troves buried beneath the Romsdals, secreted on some unknown island in the Broken Bay."

All over again, the hopelessness of opposing her own general washed over Adare, dragging her down like a winter wave. The notion that she could ever steal a march on him, devise a plan he hadn't seen from years away—it was all hubris and stupidity. Was it likely, after the man had held Annur in his fist for centuries, that she, Adare, would be the one to wrest it away?

"Ya look like ya're thinkin' of drinkin' half those vials yourself," Nira said, her voice a rasp shredding Adare's thoughts.

Adare looked up to find the other woman studying her, an expression that might have been wariness or concern carved across her ancient features.

"He's just so far ahead of us, at every step."

"He hasn't won yet," Nira said.

"Are you sure? We don't even know what he wants. Not really."

"According ta what your brother told you, he wants ta kill Meshkent."

Adare grimaced. "I don't trust Kaden. And I definitely don't trust that Csestriim he keeps at his side."

"Well, whatever il Tornja wants," Nira snapped, "we know he hasn't got it."

Adare raised her brows. "We do?"

"A bull don't tend ta keep fuckin' after he's had his way with the cow. When a bull's done, he goes off with that sloppy slack sack between his legs ta eat or sleep."

"Il Tornja's not a bull."

"Men." The old woman shrugged. "Bulls. Csestriim. Point is, if il Tornja'd won, there wouldn't still be a war goin' on."

Adare stared north, toward Aergad, toward where il Tornja held back the Urghul. Things had come to a bleak pass when ongoing war was a reason for hope. The fact that il Tornja still wanted something made for dubious consolation, but it was the only consolation she had. She turned back to the box.

"What are these?" she asked, pointing at half a dozen metal tubes set into the velvet opposite the glass vials.

"Bombs," Nira replied.

Adare's hand jerked back. "Bombs?"

"Kettral make. Starshatters, moles, and flickwicks. Two apiece."

"And just what in Intarra's name," Adare breathed, still staring at the munitions, "am I supposed to do with Kettral explosives?"

"My guess is you're supposed ta blow shit up, but don't quote me. You're the prophet."

"They're stable?" Adare asked, studying the slender tubes.

"I lugged 'em here and I survived." She gestured at her body. "Two arms. Two tits, wobbly but still attached. Two legs." She shrugged again.

Adare blew out a low, slow whistle. "I'm starting to see why he didn't want anyone else to open it."

Nira nodded. "Question is, how do we use *this*," she jabbed a finger at the box, "ta get at the bitch in *there*?" Another jab, this time at the Spear.

"Yes," Adare agreed vaguely. "That is the trick." She turned back to the tower, then fell silent, baffled by the audacity of il Tornja's demand. "It's never been done, you know. No one's ever broken into the palace dungeon."

"I wish," the old woman replied, scowling, "we could quit calling it a dungeon. Dungeons are underground."

"Not this one," Adare said, shaking her head slowly. "People have tried to get at it before, tried to fight their way up from the tower's base. Skinny Tom made it to the thirtieth floor before the guardsmen cut him down, and Skinny Tom made it farther than anyone else."

"'Course, we've got an edge on Skinny Tom, whoever the fuck he was."

"A rebel," Adare said absently. "Two hundred years ago. A peasant."

"Hence the skinny. Point is, you're a princess, a prophet. I wager that gives you a leg up on some rebel peasant when it comes ta the gettin' into of well-guarded towers."

"The problem isn't the tower," Adare said, squinting. Most of the time the glass reflected back the sun, the sky, the copper and tile rooftops of Annur. If the glare wasn't too great, however, and you looked at it just right, you could sometimes catch a glimpse of the inside. From the balcony of the Crane, Adare could just barely make out the break, the point inside the Spear where the man-made floors gave way to that huge column of empty air. "I could go inside right now, climb all the way up to my father's study the way I did a million times as a child. The problem is what happens after, what happens *above*."

"I take it the whole place gets less welcoming."

Adare nodded. "There are guards where the stairs break free of the first thirty floors, then guards again, however many thousand feet above, when you reach the prison level."

"Last time I looked," Nira observed, "guards get outta the way pretty quick when the Emperor comes knocking. Snap your royal fingers, click your holy heels, and you'll have them all groveling."

Adare grimaced. "Not good enough. Triste is the most carefully guarded prisoner in all of Annur. I *might* be able to get close enough to kill her, but not without everyone in the 'Kent-kissing palace knowing."

Nira shrugged. "Let 'em know."

"No," Adare replied, shaking her head. "The council already hates me. They'll take any chance they can get to break the treaty. If I just walk in and murder the girl, I give it less than a day before they sling me into the cell to take her place."

"So . . . what? Ya want to piss yourself, quit, and go hide in a hole?"

Instead of responding, Adare studied the fields beyond the city's bounds, then looked past them, over them, to where distance scrubbed away all detail and she lost both the land and the sky in the morning's golden haze. How far could she see from this balcony atop the Crane? Fifty miles? A hundred? How far away were the walls of Aergad, the cold stone keep where il Tornja had her child? She could remember the distance if she tried, could pluck it from some map kept tucked tight in her memory. She did not.

Far. That was the simple, awful fact. *Too far.* All those horrible, indifferent miles, and her son at the very end of them.

"What if we don't kill her?" Adare asked finally, quietly.

Nira's eyes narrowed. *"Dead,"* she growled. "That was the deal. We kill the leach, and in return il Tornja leaves your son alive."

Adare nodded, dragging her gaze back to her councillor.

"I know," she replied quietly.

"You know. You *know*." Nira spat over the side of the balcony. "Then I'll go ahead and assume ya also know that if ya don't kill her, then *he* will kill *him*."

Adare closed her eyes. She could feel a tide of terror rising inside her, dark, icy, and undeniable. When she thought of

Sanlitun, of his tiny chest stilled, of those eager hands suddenly unable to clutch, she felt an almost physical compulsion to comply, to obey, to do exactly what il Tornja demanded. She would bully her way into the dungeon, then pour every one of those poisons down Triste's throat, she would hold the girl down while she blistered and thrashed, if only it would keep her own son safe.

Except that it won't.

Again and again, that was the thought that brought her up short.

"If we kill Triste," she said slowly, meeting Nira's eyes as she forced the thoughts into words, "what will il Tornja do? Will he surrender my son? Will he give your brother back?"

Nira's jaw was set. "He won't give Oshi back. He needs him too much."

"And he needs Sanlitun. As long as he has my child, he's turned the tables. He's cut his way free, and slipped a noose around *my* neck at the same time."

"I don't like it either, but that's the thing about nooses," Nira snapped. "Ya end up dead when ya start tugging on them."

"We're going to end up dead either way," Adare replied quietly. "All these alliances, all these deals—they're not real. If I've learned one thing about il Tornja, it's that. Whatever battles he fights, whatever wars he wins, he is not on our side. He will use us—you, me, Oshi, Sanlitun—then discard us. Now or later—whenever it's most convenient."

Nira spread her hands, weighing them as though they were scales. "If ya got a choice between dead now or dead later, later's better. There's a lot of time between *now* and *later*. Maybe enough time for someone to stick a knife in the bastard."

"And if they don't, we're done. You and me, Oshi and Sanlitun. I gave il Tornja what he wanted once. *More* than once—all the way from Annur to Aergad. I forgave him my father's death. I leaned on him to lead my armies. I thought I had him firmly by the reins—and now he's taken my son."

"I know the story, woman. Ya don't need to read it back to me. I'd like to drive a rusty knife into his eye, but I can't do that from here, and neither can you. He's got the noose around us both. We'll try to break free when we *have* to, but not over this. This is a stupid place ta make your stand, a dumb fight ta lose that boy a' yours over."

Adare stared at Intarra's Spear, trying to see past the sun-bright gleam. Somewhere inside that gleaming tower, well above the low fringe of clouds blown in off the sea, was the dungeon, and somewhere in that dungeon was Kaden's leach, this girl Triste, for whose life il Tornja had threatened Sanlitun.

Adare shook her head. "Is it?"

"Is *what*?"

"Is this—killing Triste—a stupid fight?"

Nira waved her hand in irritation. "She's dangerous, sure. I'll give ya that. But there's *lots* a' dangerous sons a' bitches in this world, and I'll go ahead and guarantee she ain't the worst of them. Take my brother—Oshi'd rip this little leach's head off her shoulders without botherin' to look down. She doesn't *matter*—not when ya look at the whole board. We kill her. Your kid stays alive. *You* stay alive. We fight later, when it's important."

"What if this *is* important?" Adare asked.

What am I missing? she wondered, imagining il Tornja sitting across from her, his immaculate boots up on the table. *What am I not seeing, you bastard?*

Nira narrowed her eyes. "How?"

"People call me a prophet of Intarra. Since this treaty, I am the acknowledged Emperor of Annur."

"Ya want me ta start kissing your asshole now, or wait 'til ya finish shining it up?"

"It's not *me* I'm talking about . . ."

"Oh?"

". . . it's the role. The roles. They are utterly unique. Il Tornja worked hard to position himself at my side *because* of these titles. It's valuable to him to have the support of an emperor, to have my stamp on his every action. It gives him freedom, power."

"He has plenty a' power without you, girl," Nira said, but for the first time she was nodding.

"Of course he does, but there's a *reason* he made peace with me in the first place. He knows that if I die or disappear, he won't be the *kenarang* anymore. Instead of being the highest-ranking Annurian general, he'll be just another warlord, and that will make things *harder* for him."

"What things?"

"His war against Long Fist, for starters," Adare replied. "Everything about that effort, from the troops to the supply lines, is predicated on Annurian might. Without me—"

"Without you he'll just prop another fool up on the throne."

"Maybe," Adare conceded. "But it won't be a Malkeenian. It won't be someone with the eyes. To prosecute this war, he needs Annur unified, and part of what has always unified Annur is the Malkeenian line."

Nira frowned. "I won't say you're wrong, but you're pissin' straight into the wind if ya think il Tornja needs ya so much that he won't give ya up."

"That's exactly my point!" Adare exclaimed. "He's *already* giving me up. Asking me to go after Triste, to kill her—it *is* giving me up!"

"Only if ya get caught."

"*Only?*" Adare demanded. "He's forcing me to break into the most highly guarded prison in the *world*."

"Us."

"Great. A princess-turned-Emperor and an insane leach."

Nira frowned. "Half insane."

"Regardless. Our odds are terrible." Adare shook her head. "I thought he wanted me dead, at first. That this was his way of seeing me finished off. But that doesn't make sense. He could have killed me a thousand times over when I was still in Aergad without anyone the wiser. Why send me hundreds of miles away to let someone else do the job?"

"Fine. He really wants Triste cut up like beef. Which we knew already."

"It's not *that* he wants her killed," Adare said, shaking her head, watching the pieces fall into place once more. "It's how *badly*. He's willing to sacrifice an emperor, an emperor he has effectively enslaved by stealing away her son, and for what? For the *chance* that together we might be able to kill a garden-variety leach? Does that seem like a smart trade?"

The old woman's scowl didn't go anywhere, but she was still nodding slowly. "Ya think Kaden's little leach is stronger'n she's let on."

Adare grimaced. "I don't *know*. That's the thing. I'm not sure *why* il Tornja's so eager to have her killed, but the fact that he is seems important. It makes me think that before we poison her or blow her up we might want to actually talk to her."

"Sounds true enough," Nira said grudgingly, glaring at Intarra's Spear as though a long list of il Tornja's goals were locked up inside along with Triste. "My old mind must be addled worse than I thought, not ta've seen it first." When she shifted her eyes to Adare, however, they did not look addled. "Y'understand what this means, right?"

"No," Adare said. "Not fully."

"I don't mean the girl herself; I mean breaking her out, disobeying that Csestriim bastard."

"He's all the way in the north, on the frontier. With a little luck he won't even *know* that we didn't kill her."

Nira snorted. "Just when you were creepin' toward the border a' smart, ya had to fuck it up by jumpin' back into a whole bucket a' stupid."

"He can't know everything," Adare protested, the words belied by the cold, heavy brick growing in her stomach. Il Tornja had been a full march ahead of her at every point. Even when she managed to surprise him, she failed. She had brought him

Oshi and Nira, had thought for months that they were *her* weapons, and then, when he decided the time was right, the bastard had taken one away, made it his own, as easily as a legionary might take a belt knife from a child.

A part of her ached to submit, to obey. If she did what il Tornja said, he would let her son live.

Maybe, replied a voice from deep inside.

"Ya know the facts," Nira said, "but ya don't *feel* 'em. Il Tornja's not human, girl. Your son is no more than a stone to him. So's Oshi. So are you and me. If we fit into his strategy, he leaves us be. If not . . ." She made a motion with the back of her hand, as though sweeping clean a cluttered *ko* board. "And it means *nothing.*" She shook her head. "I'm not against ya in this. I'm a crazy old bitch with nothing to lose. I *want* to fight him. But you . . ." She spread her hands. "You're bold, but by Ananshael's blackened asshole, ya can be dumb, girl. I want ta make sure ya understand."

To Adare's shock, there were tears in the old woman's eyes, small and bright in the sunlight, hard as tiny shards of glass, surprising as diamonds.

"You gave me your child ta protect," Nira said quietly. "And I let the bastard take him away."

"No," Adare said, laying a hand on her councillor's arm. "You didn't let him. You fought, and you failed, but you didn't *let* him." She realized she was trembling, and hated herself for it. Her father had never trembled, she felt sure of that, even when he sent his sons away.

"I know that opposing him is dangerous. Sweet Intarra's light, Nira, you think I don't know that? I'm even prepared to believe that it's hopeless, but I'll tell you something else I know: if we give him what he wants, we lose. Maybe not right away, but soon enough, and if I'm going to lose anyway, if I'm going to lose my *son,* I'm going to do it fighting back. If there's even a chance that this Triste girl can hurt that bastard, I'm going to take it, and maybe he'll kill me, maybe he'll kill my son, but I won't give him anything else. Anything else he gets from me, he's going to have to fucking *take* it."

Nira grimaced and glanced down at her shoulder. Adare realized that her own hand was twisted into a claw around the old woman's flesh, nails digging in through the cloth, knuckles purpling with the strain.

"That hurts," Nira said.

Adare didn't let go. "Will you help me?"

The tears were wet on the old woman's face.

"If ya have to ask," she said, her voice little more than a dried husk, "ya're even dumber than I thought. And I already thought ya were dumb."

The newcomer's laugh preceded her out onto the balcony, a light trill of girlish delight.

"Look at that *sky*! Oh, Your Radiance, it is altogether too blue! I refuse to believe that is the same sky I see from my own meager windows. Oh, and the *ocean*!"

Nira scowled. For half the morning, she had argued against adding another member to their nascent conspiracy. The old woman had tallied up and reviewed the risks from a dozen different angles, while Adare kept returning to the same simple fact: she and Nira couldn't break Triste out alone.

We need help, she had insisted over and over. *I don't like it any more than you do, but it's clear that we need help.*

It seemed less clear suddenly, now that the help had arrived.

"Welcome," Adare said, filing away her misgivings, turning to face their new companion as she glided out through the open doors. "Thank you for coming on such short notice."

"The honor is all mine, Your Radiance. An invitation to the topmost chambers of the Crane! How could I resist? I see now, though, that I should never have come. All at a glance, you've ruined me. I thought I was content before, snug in my humble house, but now I simply *must* have a *tower*."

The woman was all silk, and awe, and breathless gestures. Adare ignored it, as she ignored the talk of humble homes and meager windows. *If half of what I've heard is true,* she thought, *you could have a dozen towers like the Crane, and fill each one with golden suns.*

"Nira," Adare said, spreading her hands. "Please meet Kegellen, one of the three council members forming the delegation from Annur. Kegellen, Nira is my Mizran Councillor, recently arrived from the north."

"Mizran Councillor," Kegellen purred, bowing her head along with a graceful curtsy. "It is an honor."

Nira looked anything but honored. "You're the thief," she said bluntly.

The other woman straightened. Despite her massive bulk, she moved like a dancer, all grace and smoothness. She slipped a delicate paper fan from somewhere inside the sleeve of her dress, flipped it open, and fanned gently at her face.

"Oh, I'm sure I don't deserve the definite article. While I may be *a* thief, I could never claim to be the only one."

The words were mild, but Adare watched the woman's eyes. Adare herself had grown up around high ministers and visiting princes—shrewd, sharp, predatory men—and she had long experience reading gazes. Though Kegellen continued to smile, to fan herself absentmindedly, her green eyes were bright and still as she considered the older woman. She didn't look overawed or frightened. She looked . . . curious.

"I never thought," Kegellen said, shifting the subject, "that these old bones would live to see the day when a *woman* would sit on the Unhewn Throne." Her smile lit like sudden sunlight on Adare. "I couldn't say this in the council chamber without upsetting all those old men, but well played, Your Radiance. Well played."

"Maybe," Adare said. "And maybe not." She studied the large woman before her. "I think we can dispense with the charade. You don't know me. Don't trust me. I don't trust you. . . ."

"But ya called her here anyway," Nira said, shaking her head.

"Because," Adare said smoothly, "I believe we might *come* to trust one another. I hope we can forge a common cause. But only if we are frank with one another."

"Ooh," Kegellen replied, fluttering her fan. "By all means, let us be frank. I find frank talk so invigorating."

"How's this for frank?" Nira began, leveling her cane at the *akaza,* indifferent to the fact that the other woman was a full head higher and easily three times her weight. "You're a criminal. Ya shit all over Annurian law. You've made a life out of thieving and murder, intimidation and extortion, breaking free the slaves of others, then making them your own."

Kegellen listened to this tirade with pursed lips and an air of mild curiosity. When Nira paused for breath, she raised a stout finger. "Also, arson," she interjected cheerfully. "And I dabbled in whoring when I was younger, but found it tiring." She cocked her head to the side, as though a troubling thought had just occurred to her. "Is that a problem?"

"No," Adare said, shaking her head before Nira could object. "As far as I'm concerned, it's just perfect. It's why I asked you here, in fact."

"Your councillor seems markedly less enthused."

"Oh, I'm enthused, all right," Nira replied. "This face ya're lookin' at? This is my enthusiastic face."

"Nira . . . ," Adare began.

The old woman raised a hand. "Hold on. Ya've got all day ta scheme when I'm done, but there's somethin' this woman needs to know."

"Oh, I'm always interested," Kegellen said, "in learning new things. Please forgive me though, if I am slow. This fat old mind of mine is not what it once was."

Nira's smile was a knife. "A woman behaves a certain way when she believes she's the most dangerous bitch in the room.

Ya're used to it," she said, nodding at Kegellen, "ain't ya? Ya've been the most dangerous bitch in the room a long time, eh?"

The larger woman made a face. "*Bitch* is such an unpleasant word. . . ."

Nira chuckled. "Oh, I don't know. I don't mind it, myself, but then, I've had more time to grow into it."

"Surely you undersell your considerable charms."

Kegellen's fan had stopped moving. With her free hand, she patted absently at the wooden pins holding up her hair.

"I'll tell ya what I undersell," Nira said. "I undersell the number a' men I've killed. I undersell the times I've put a blade inside some traitor's ribs and fucking *ripped*. I undersell the thousands a' acres I've burned down to the ground. I got tired a while back of people screamin' when they heard my name, and so I undersell that, too, but because you're laborin' under some badly skewed impressions, I'm makin' an exception for you. Call it a courtesy, me sharin' this little fact: you are *not* the most dangerous bitch in this room, not while I'm standin' here." She cocked her head to the side. "I know your mind's fat and slow, so I hope I made that clear."

The mirth had vanished from Kegellen's eyes. She studied Nira in silence for a few heartbeats, then turned to Adare.

"It seems your minister thinks more highly of herself than she does of her own emperor."

Adare just shook her head. "Whatever wedge you're trying to drive, don't bother."

Nira's tirade was hardly a welcome introduction, but Adare had decided in the moment to let her run with it. The old woman was right about one thing: Kegellen was dangerous. Adare had been trying to unthread the massive net the woman had thrown over Annur's underworld even before she rose to Minister of Finance. The Queen of the Streets was excellent at covering her tracks, but if you spilled enough blood, you couldn't help but leave stains. Kegellen claimed now to be serving as a loyal representative of Annur, but whatever her pretensions of legitimacy, she hadn't given up her underground empire. Though it galled Adare to admit it, Kegellen was a far more effective ruler than Adare herself. It wouldn't hurt to blunt the woman's confidence, to make her second-guess any plans she might be laying for betrayal.

"Thousands murdered," Kegellen mused. "Whole fields aflame." She shook her head. "It strains even my rather generous credulity."

"No one said learnin' was easy," Nira replied.

The two watched each other like beasts newly thrust onto the bloody sand of some unseen arena. Kegellen had the weight, the reach, but there was a gleeful violence in Nira's eyes that gave the other woman pause. After a long time, Kegellen's fan started moving again. She smiled.

"Well, this is such a pleasure. I meet new people all the time, but find they so rarely surprise me."

"Oh, I'm fucking full a' surprises."

"How delightful," Kegellen purred. "And exciting. Maybe we could start with why you've asked me here."

Adare glanced over her shoulder at Intarra's Spear, turned back to the other woman, then gestured to a chair. "Please have a seat. This will take a while to explain."

21

"Look, Gwenna," Jak said quietly, "I know you didn't want me along for this."

She took a deep breath. As usual, she could smell his nerves, as though the skin had been flayed right off, leaving his raw flesh open to the salt air. She closed her eyes, hoping the darkness might blot out his anxiety, but she could still hear him picking at a ragged fingernail, the quick, convulsive motion a counterpoint to his shallow breathing, to his fast-beating heart. She opened her eyes again, staring up through the leaves of the mangroves at the low cumulus forming up to the southeast. Rain coming. Probably thunder, too. It would have been nice to bust out the long lens and get the scouting over with, but the morning sun was still too low in the east. Using the long lens now would be little better than flashing a mirror at Rallen's hastily built fortress. There was nothing to do but lie still, wait for the sun to climb higher in the sky, and try to ignore the fear that seemed to twist Quick Jak a little tighter with every passing heartbeat.

She considered falling asleep for a few hours. She'd been swimming and fighting almost every moment since the *Widow's Wish* slipped beneath the waves, and she could feel her muscles getting heavier, her mind growing more muddled. There was no sleeping, however, with Jak a few feet away, gnawing his nails down to the bloody quick, and besides, if she didn't say something to take his mind off the situation, he seemed likely to fall to pieces before they even started the swim back.

Should have sent him with Talal, she thought. The leach knew how to talk to everyone, even a washout, but Talal was with Qora and Annick on a different craggy, bird-shit-stained rock a mile to the east, scouting Rallen's fortress from a separate angle. Which left the talking to her. She took a deep breath.

"It's not personal," she said, hoping that would be enough, that they could both just leave it at that and get some shut-eye.

Instead she could hear Jak turning to face her. "I know what it is, Gwenna. You saw what happened back in Hook. You saw me freeze up in that fight."

"You weren't even *in* the fight," she replied, regretting the words even as she said them.

She expected resentment or rage. When he spoke, however, she heard only resignation in his voice. "I know. It's just . . . Never mind."

For a moment she lay still, her eyes closed. *Never mind.* It was a plausible break in the conversation, a reasonable end point. Maybe if she kept her mouth shut they could be done with all the chatter. Waves scraped over the stones a few paces away, soft, implacable fingers clawing at the shore.

Never was much good at keeping my mouth shut, she thought, then rolled onto one elbow, blew out an exasperated breath, and turned to face the flier.

"The thing is," she said, unable to blunt her glare, "I *do* mind."

He didn't turn away, but she could see him swallow quickly, heavily, as though holding her eyes required an effort of will. It was sad and it was fucking irritating. Quick Jak didn't *look* like a coward; he looked just as much Kettral as anyone else on the Islands—more so than most, actually. The shaved head, the muscle laid in carved slabs over his chest and shoulders, the scars cut into his forearms by half a dozen training accidents . . . He sure looked the part, and the bastard could *swim.*

It was two miles from the caves on Irsk to the craggy island of Skarn, where Rallen had built his fortress, two open miles unprotected by reef or shoreline, exposed to the huge swells rolling in off the ocean to the northeast. Kettral could make the swim easily, but then, Jak wasn't Kettral. Gwenna had seen him freeze up back on Hook, and she had visions of hauling a panicked, thrashing washout through the waves all the way out and all the way back. She need not have worried. Jak's stroke was so clean and languid it looked lazy. It was also strong as Hull and viciously efficient. Within a few hundred paces, Gwenna was working hard to keep up, gritting her teeth and measuring her breath while Jak sliced through the waves casually, only lifting his mouth to breathe every sixth stroke. *Going out fast,* she told herself. *Trying to prove something.* Halfway to Skarn, however, when Jak showed no sign of slowing, she was forced to admit that the pace, which seemed half a sprint to her, wasn't even straining him. He might be a coward, but he was a fucking *strong* coward.

She'd tried to keep up for a few hundred more strokes, battling her way up the steep green sides of the swells, straining to make the most of the downslope as the ocean slid beneath her. She wasn't about to call out—not that he could hear her anyway—but finally he paused, turned back toward her, and treaded water while she caught up. He wasn't even breathing hard.

"Tough passage," he said. Gwenna could feel her jaw tightening, but there was no hint of smugness in his voice. No sign of triumph. "These crossed swells," he said, nodding toward the northeast, "really slow things down." He hesitated a moment, then pointed at the inflated bladder Gwenna had been dragging behind her. "I'm happy to pull that. If you want."

She was about to refuse. Jak had his own float bag filled with dry blacks, weapons, and a spyglass. Gwenna was used to hauling her own shit. She was about to snap something about not needing a washout to take care of her gear for her, but Jak continued before she could speak.

"This is something I'm good at, at least," he said quietly. "It's a way I can actually help."

With an effort, she'd swallowed both her pride and her irritation. The flier might be a washout and a coward, but here he was all the same, in the middle of the 'Kent-kissing ocean, swimming *toward* a fort full of the same people who had been hunting him for months. That had to be worth something. Besides, something in his voice, some note she recognized but couldn't quite name, stilled her objection. She'd been lost since leaving the Eyrie, baffled and utterly out of her depth. She knew what it was like to want, want desperately, some job that you understood, some task that you'd actually trained for. One of her most confident moments at the battle of Andt-Kyl had been diving beneath the logjam, lit starshatter in hand. She'd been certain she was going to die, had known it in her very marrow, but she'd also been certain that she could blow the bridge, that that one problem, at least, was something she could solve.

"Thanks," she grunted, loosening the knot around her waist, then handing him the bitter end of the cord. To her surprise, he'd smiled in the starlight.

When they finally climbed clear of the water, out onto the barnacled rocks skirting a small atoll a few hundred paces west of Skarn, he hauled in the bag, untied the knot, passed it over to her without a word, and turned to his own gear, fishing out dry clothes. They'd made the swim over naked—no point struggling in soaked wool when you had a float bag to pull—and Gwenna snuck a glance at him while he was busy with his gear. He was breathing more deeply than he had at the start of the swim, the wings of the kettral inked across his back rising and falling with each breath. When he glanced over his shoulder at her, she realized she was staring, pulled her eyes away hastily, then cursed herself silently for the reaction. It wasn't as though she'd never seen a man naked before. The tropics were hot, water was wet. The Kettral trained to swim in their blacks, of course, but most of the year it made more sense to swim with no clothes. Thigh-slapping cocks and bare asses were part of the job, just like the sight of blood was part of the job. And yet here she was peeking and blushing like a first-year cadet.

She straightened up, ignoring her own nakedness, and studied the man openly.

"Where you'd learn to swim like that?"

He met her eyes, then looked away with a half shrug. "It was something to do. Over on Arim."

She frowned. "I thought they didn't let you off the island."

"We can swim," he said, pulling on his pants. "Could swim," he said, cinching the belt tight as he corrected himself. "Up to five hundred paces offshore. I circled the island every day, once in the morning, once in the evening."

Gwenna stared. "That's got to be what, ten miles a day?"

He nodded. "A little less."

"Why?"

"What do you mean?"

"I mean you're not Kettral. It's not like you're going to need to fly missions. It's not like people were going to die if you didn't swim fast enough. What the fuck possessed you to spend half of every day grinding through garbage yardage in rings around Arim?"

He stared at her. Dawn was just starting to bruise the eastern sky, but the night wind scudding in over the waves was still cool on her wet skin. A shiver ran through her.

Finally he gave half a shrug. "It was something to do." His voice was barely louder than the waves. "A way to forget about being locked up."

"If you didn't want to be on Arim," she said, the words pouring out of her before she could call them back, "then why did you *quit*?"

He watched her a heartbeat longer, then shook his head, turning away without a word, pulling his blacks over his head.

She could smell the shame on him, warm and cloying in the cool breeze, and after a moment she, too, turned away, shrugging into her own clothes, angry without knowing why.

They took up a position in the verge of the scrubby mangroves just before dawn, settled into the vegetation, laid out the long lens, which Gwenna planned to use later, and the weapons, which she didn't, then watched the sun rise without saying a word. She'd almost managed to forget about the conversation on the rocks, had almost bullied her squirming mind into something resembling sleep, and then he'd started up again with this shit about knowing that she didn't want him along. Well, if he was determined to talk, she'd fucking talk.

"You're right," she went on, more hotly than she'd intended. "I mind that you're here, not because I don't like you, but because I can't *rely* on you."

"You don't know anything about me, Gwenna."

"I know that you washed out during the Trial," she said, holding up a finger. "I know that you froze in the alleyway over on Hook, that you were about to let your partner die because you were too scared to make a play."

"Two moments," he replied quietly, "out of twenty-four years."

"The moments are all that *matter,* Jak. People talk about lifetimes, but lifetimes are built out of moments. The decisions we make, the ones that matter, the ones that get people killed or keep them alive . . ." She snapped her fingers. "They're that fast."

The memory of that first Annurian legionary she'd killed flooded through her, hot and awful and undimmed even after nearly a year. How long had it taken to decide she needed to kill him, to decide how and then to do it, to plunge that ridiculous stick through his eye as thousands and thousands of Urghul roared all around her? A heartbeat. Maybe two.

"It doesn't *matter* what you do in between those moments," she said, pressing ahead despite the hard wall of his silence. "It doesn't matter if you swim all day, or if you're kind to your aging mother, or any of the rest of that shit. What *matters,* when you're Kettral, is what you do"—she stabbed a stiffened finger straight down into the stone—"right now. Right now. Right now."

He watched her a moment, then rolled onto his back, staring up through the leaves.

"You think I don't know that?"

"Well, do you?"

"Of course I do. It's why I'm not Kettral."

Gwenna had clenched her hands into fists. With an effort, she relaxed them, then let her head drop back against a root.

"Fine," she said. "It's fine. Unless I've fucked up, and bad, we're not going to be fighting anyone today. We're just here to look at the birds, to learn what we can about what they've got and how we can take it."

That was why Jak had come in the first place. He knew about kettral, understood them better than anyone else left on the Islands. Gwenna could count the 'Kent-kissing things, could probably come up with a tally of the healthy and the badly injured, but that was about it. Before arriving at any plan worth the name, she'd need to know more: Which birds were the fastest? Which were the older and more experienced? If it came to a fight between the kettral, which were the strongest, the most likely to triumph?

According to everyone, Quick Jak was a genius with birds. Laith had said the man was the finest flier he'd ever seen, and Laith hadn't thought *anyone* was a finer flier than Laith. Maybe it was true, and even if it wasn't, Jak was what she had. Everyone could contribute something. That was the point of working in a team. The washout flier might still prove useful, even crucial. Gwenna just had to be careful to keep him out of a fight, to keep him well clear of any situation where he might lose his tenuous cool and get someone killed.

By the time the sun finally climbed high enough to use the

long lens without signaling everyone on Rallen's island, Jak had been quiet for hours, lying silently on his back, staring open-eyed into the thick-leaved canopy above. Gwenna had failed to fall asleep. Usually she could shut her eyes and be out in a few heartbeats. Certainly, the swim over had left her plenty tired. The morning's conversation, though, had irritated her. She kept going over and over what Jak had said, trying to understand how someone with a strong body and keen mind could be so useless, so resigned to his failures. That she wanted to like him only made it worse. She felt betrayed without even knowing the man, and it was with a long sigh of relief that she finally rolled onto her stomach, extended the wooden tube of the long lens, and began the scouting she'd come to do.

The main Eyrie compound—the command buildings, the barracks, the various training rings, the harbor, docks, and associated storehouses, the mess hall, Lucky Fucks' Row—almost everything that mattered to the day-to-day operation of the Kettral was on Qarsh, miles to the southwest. Rallen, however, had opted to move his base of operations off the island. It wasn't that hard to understand why. Qarsh was the largest island in the archipelago—nearly three miles across at the widest—and also the gentlest. Instead of crenellated limestone dropping straight into the sea, Qarsh had plenty of coves and beaches, mangrove stands and offshore reefs to break the worst of the swells. It was a great place to live but a nightmare to defend. Before the Eyrie ripped out its own guts, of course, defense hadn't been much of an issue. Anyone attacking would be attacking from somewhere else, and the regular Kettral patrols could see them at least two days out.

Rallen, however, was fighting a different sort of war. His enemies were already *on* the Qirins, hidden away in cellars on Hook, secreted in the tangles of jungle vines, lurking undiscovered in the endless warren of Hull's Hole. And then there was the question of numbers. On the day Gwenna fled the Islands with Valyn and the Wing, there had been hundreds of active-duty Kettral, half as many cadets, and at least that many retired vets living out their last years down by the harbor—more than enough for the minimal guard duty required. If Manthe and Hobb were right, however, Rallen didn't have more than thirty or forty soldiers at his disposal, not nearly enough to guard the whole perimeter of Qarsh.

And so he was here. Gwenna twisted the long lens, focusing it on the island half a mile to the east. *Skarn*. No linguistic relation, she hoped, to the beasts living down in the Hole, but the name put her on edge all the same. So did the 'Kent-kissing terrain.

"Well, this is unfortunate," she said, eyeing the cliffs that climbed straight out of the water on every side.

"You've never seen it before?" Jak asked.

"Of course I've seen it. I just never thought I'd have to *attack* it."

The truth was, she'd never paid the island much mind. It lay well clear of Qarsh and Hook, off the usual swimming and smallboat circuits, and while she'd sailed around it dozens of times, flown over it twice that many, the only people who spent any time on the island were the fliers, both active and retired. The fliers, and the birds themselves.

The kettral built their nests and raised their young over on the eastern end of Qarsh, where the ground was relatively flat. Once they matured, however, following some animal instinct no one at the Eyrie fully understood, they spread their wings and left the gentle island, searching, evidently, for something more . . . vertical. There wasn't anywhere in the Islands more vertical than Skarn.

"Are there *any* harbors or beaches?" Gwenna asked, sweeping the lens back and forth over the overhanging limestone.

Jak shook his head. "Not really. The only thing you can reach from the water is a little rocky shoulder on the far side. It's underwater at high tide, though."

"Can you get from there to the top of the cliffs?"

"No."

"So how did Rallen get in the supplies to build the 'Kent-kissing thing?"

She studied the fortress, or what she could see of it, at least. On level ground, Rallen's fort wouldn't have been much of a fort. It looked more like a series of stables strung along behind a large stone barn, the various structures connected by a wall no more than twice Gwenna's height. The trouble was, the fort wasn't set on level ground. The whole compound perched at the very brink of the cliff. The limestone crag on which it stood was so steep and high—at least forty paces, overhung for the bottom third—as to render the miserable walls at the top point-less, even ludicrous. It was as though the builders, having thrown together the hall and outbuildings, felt compelled to put up *some* sort of wall, all the time understanding the pointlessness of the gesture.

"Most of it's rock," Jak replied. "Quarried right there on the island. There was a crane to haul up the heavy supplies, the mast from an old ship anchored in the stone with a block and tackle at the end. That's how they hoisted up the timber for roof beams and the rest. Rallen had it torn down when the building was done."

"Why in Hull's name," Gwenna wondered aloud, "would you rip out your only means of resupply?"

"Because he's careful. The crane was a weakness. A potential entry point."

Gwenna put down the lens, then turned to stare at him. "Not if you remember to pull up the rope when you're done with it!"

Even as she was saying the words, however, she was thinking of ways she could have used that recommissioned mast. Annick could have shot an arrow over it, for one thing. Attach a light enough cord to that arrow—an unbraided thread of Liran rope, maybe—and you could use it as a pilot to drag up something more substantial. Then it was a simple matter of—

"Whatever else he is, Rallen's Kettral," Jak said, as though reading her thoughts. "He's lived on these islands at least forty years, and he knows what the Kettral can do."

"But there aren't any Kettral left."

Jak met her gaze. "Even the washouts have some training. We're not the real thing, Rallen knows that, but we're not completely useless."

Gwenna nodded slowly, then turned the long lens back to the fort.

"So the small buildings are storage and barracks, the large thing, that lopsided pile that looks like some farmer's first attempt at a barn, is mess and command?"

Jak shook his head. "I don't know. I've never been up there. This is the first time I've seen it."

"Who *has* seen it?"

"None of us. Not from the inside. When Rallen came for us on Arim, when he offered us all a second chance, we took boats over to Qarsh. Set up in the barracks there."

"You must have known he was building something out here."

"We did. He said it was the first in a series of fortifications to make the Islands safer, more defensible, more secure. Flew in a couple dozen craftsmen from over on Hook to build the place."

"Craftsmen," Gwenna snorted, peering through the long lens once more. "That's a generous term for anyone living over on Hook. Where are they now? Can we talk to them?"

"They're dead," Jak replied quietly. "When construction was finished, Rallen had them tied, ankles and elbows, and threw them off the cliff."

Gwenna shook her head slowly. "That sick fuck."

"You see why we have to stop him?" Jak asked.

"What I *don't* see is why you kept following him in the first place."

"He was Kettral. . . ."

Gwenna waved away the explanation. "I know. He showed up. He offered you a second chance. Fine. But when he started throwing civilians off cliffs? That didn't clue you all in to the fact that he was aiming at something other than the preservation of Annurian justice?"

"Of *course* it did." A new note in Jak's voice made her put down the lens again. She looked over to find his hands clenched into fists, knuckles gone bone-white, as though he were trying to throttle something.

I finally made him angry, she realized. *About fucking time.*

"Of course we knew it," Jak said again. "A lot of us were already planning to stop him, to stop helping, at least. That's why we refused his personal pledge of fealty the next day."

Gwenna watched the anger wither. The flier's eyes had gone wide and distant as he relived the slaughter.

"And that's when he killed you."

Jak nodded. "We didn't know it, but he'd already stocked this place. The munitions were here, his most trusted lieutenants were here . . ."

"And the birds were here," she finished quietly.

Jak nodded again, staring, rapt, into the past. That obsession, in its own way, was just as dangerous as what they faced atop the cliff. The flier was brittle enough when he wasn't reliving the blood and screaming of Rallen's purge. If he was going to survive, he needed to look forward, not back, and Gwenna needed him to survive.

"So where are they?" she asked, waving a hand at the cliffs. "The birds?"

For a few heartbeats he didn't respond. Then, slowly, his eyes refocused, found hers. She could still smell the fear on him, but there was something else there, too, something in those clenched knuckles, in the set of his jaw. *Stubbornness,* she thought. Not the same thing as courage, not by a long shot, but it would have to do.

"There," Jak said, pointing. "And there. And there. In those shallow caves, mostly."

Gwenna studied the cliff for a moment. She could make out

the hollows in the rock, huge holes carved from the stone by age after age of rain and prying wind. With the sun so bright overhead, however, she could barely make out anything inside. She put the long lens to her eye, studying the most obvious of the features. She could see the blocky shapes of the limestone wall in back, but no sign of a bird.

"It's empty."

"It's daytime," Jak replied. "They'll all be out, flying missions or hunting."

Hunting. That was a sight you weren't likely to forget. Early in their training, each class of cadets was hauled over to Qel, one of the only islands in the chain capable of supporting live-stock. Sheep, goats, and cows grazed on the stiff, thick-bladed island grass—hundreds of animals scattered over a few square miles. It was a pleasant enough scene, a warmer, more tropical version of the kind of pastoral landscape you could find anywhere from Sia to north of the Neck. Until the kettral showed up.

It was impossible to understand the birds, to really appreciate what they could do, without seeing them stoop from a few hundred paces up, fall on a full-grown cow like a boulder of avian feathers and flesh. Gwenna had almost puked on her blacks the first time she saw it. She'd grown up around hawks and falcons, of course, had seen them take field mice and squirrels caught out between the trees. The sight of kettral savaging entire cows, however, the vision of them rending to bloody ribbons beasts that weighed ten times what she did herself . . . that was a vision she'd been trying to put out of her mind during every flight for the past ten years.

"The timing is good," Jak was saying. His voice reeled her back to the present. "The birds are hungry when they wake up. They usually hunt in the morning, take a little time lazing on the thermals while they digest, then come back here for some sport."

"I thought the hunting *was* the sport," Gwenna said, thinking of sheep carved in half, split cleanly from spine to sternum as though with a massive ax.

Jak shook his head. "Killing a cow on open ground? That takes about as much effort for the kettral as it would take you to open a coconut with one of your blades. The sport is between the birds themselves."

Even as he spoke, he pointed south. Five kettral were gliding in, carried on some invisible shelf of wind, wings spread wide, pinions silently rippling. They might have been normal birds, small as Gwenna's outstretched thumb, until you realized they were still miles out and hundreds of paces up, that their scale was a trick of the eye, an untruth of the mind misreading the distance, a lie that made them, momentarily, a little easier to believe.

"Only five?" Gwenna asked.

"Six," Jak said, pointing up at the bird circling the rocky island in a high, silent spiral. "Rallen keeps at least one in the air at all times. Flying guard patrol for his fort."

Gwenna glanced up, then back at the approaching birds. "Even six. There must have been scores here a year ago. . . ."

"Eighty-seven," Jak replied. "There were eighty-seven before the Eyrie killed them."

The words were blunt, bitter. Gwenna could smell his grief. It made her mad.

"You realize," she said, forcing herself to keep her voice low, "that there were *people* killed, too. That Kettral Wings were *flying* those creatures. . . ."

"There are plenty more people," Jak replied grimly. "More than enough people." He gestured toward the incoming birds. "For all anyone knows, these are the last of the kettral."

Gwenna stared at him. She'd never considered that before. The destruction of the Eyrie itself, the mutual slaughter of nearly everyone she'd ever really known, that fact had eclipsed everything else. The birds were important, but important in the same way as munitions: valuable weaponry to be salvaged before it fell into unsavory hands. She'd never considered the kettral deaths themselves, never realized that the vicious battle on the Islands could well have scrubbed the creatures out of existence.

"There," Jak said, pointing at the two birds in the lead. "Sente'ril and Sente'ra. Young birds from the same clutch. We've seen them before, flying patrols. . . ."

Gwenna glanced at the two birds, then scanned past them to a group of three birds trailing a little behind, her eye drawn to the center of the group, a mottled female with the slightest stutter in her wingbeat. "Holy Hull," she breathed quietly. "She made it. Out of all of us, she was the first one back."

Jak glanced over at her, reading the situation. "Your bird?"

Gwenna nodded. "Suant'ra."

"I remember her," the flier said. "She was barely fledged when I . . . left for Arim."

"Laith raised her," Gwenna said, the memory of the dead flier like a shard of glass lodged under her skin. "He trained her."

"I remember him, too," Jak said slowly. "Good flier. Reckless."

Gwenna coughed up a laugh. "He was reckless, all right." She shook her head, as though the motion might shake clear the thought of her slaughtered friend. "Always thought nothing could kill him. At least not while he was mounted up on 'Ra."

"What happened to him?"

"He got killed," Gwenna replied, her voice flat. "Doing something stupid."

Jak glanced over at her quickly, then looked away, back to the approaching kettral. "And to her?" he asked quietly, gesturing.

"She took an injury fighting the Flea's bird up in the Bone Mountains. Something in her wing. Bad, Laith said. She couldn't carry us, and we were a seventy-foot target in the middle of the steppe as long as we stayed with her, so Valyn sent her south."

Valyn, too. Another one who would never come back to the Islands.

Jak glanced through the long lens for half a heartbeat, then nodded. "Looks like a patagial tear. She's lucky it healed up enough to fly."

Gwenna stared at 'Ra again. The wingbeat stutter was almost invisible, but she remembered Laith running his hands over his bird for what seemed like half the day, then coming up with the same diagnosis.

"You can tell that from this distance?" she asked.

Jak nodded slowly, half his attention on the remaining birds. "I was good at all of this," he said, voice little more than a murmur. "Just not the fear . . ."

Gwenna shifted uncomfortably on the stone. It was bad enough to be a coward; you didn't have to admit it. Didn't have to say the words openly.

"What about the others?" she asked.

"Kei'ta and Shura'ka," he replied after a moment. "I haven't seen either of them on patrols."

"Why not?" Gwenna asked. "Why would Rallen hold those two in reserve?"

"Maybe he's not. We're in the Hole, mostly. They could be flying every other day, and I might have just missed them." He shook his head. "It's a good thing I came. We have to get this right."

Gwenna turned at the unexpected note of determination in his voice. "Meaning what, exactly?"

Jak frowned. "We have, at most, three fliers."

"Including you."

"Yes," he replied, meeting her stare. "Including me. We're only going to have one shot at this, and we can't take all the birds. When the time comes, we need to make sure we get the right ones, the top flight."

"Top flight?"

He nodded. "Some birds are better than others. Like soldiers. Faster or stronger. More tenacious."

Gwenna nodded slowly. She'd heard plenty of chatter in the mess hall over the years, men and women comparing kettral, arguing endlessly over questions of maximum speed, talon length, beak strength. She'd never paid much attention. After all, if you were on a bird, and you were fighting someone who wasn't, the brute fucking fact of the bird itself was the deciding factor, not a few extra inches of talon. It had always seemed to her like quibbling over the raw tonnage of available warships when you were planning to go up against a nation whose best notion of a navy involved swimming.

Except that wasn't the case here. If she managed to find a way onto the island, if she managed to get the washouts mounted up, it would be birds against birds. The little differences suddenly mattered.

Jak just watched the kettral, panning back and forth with the long lens, sometimes taking it away from his eye to watch the whole group gliding toward them in loose formation. Then, as though responding to some unheard note on the breeze, he turned abruptly south, body stiffening as he stared through the wooden tube. Gwenna tried to follow his gaze, but she couldn't see much without a long lens of her own.

"What is it?" she asked.

"Holy Hull," Jak breathed, ignoring her.

"Jak," she snapped, reaching for the bow at her side.

"He's alive," the flier said. He lowered the long lens finally and met her glare. There were tears in his eyes. "Allar'ra."

Gwenna glanced back south. This time she could see a flash of gold in the high noon light.

"Another bird?" she said, shaking her head.

Jak nodded slowly. "My bird. The one I trained."

He passed her the long lens, but she waved it away. The creature was at least a mile behind the others, but closing at a furious pace. Already, she could see it was gaining.

"Never heard of a bird with golden plumage."

"Command didn't like it," Jak replied. "Said he was cursed by Hull. Too easy to see, especially at night. None of the other cadets wanted to train him, so I did. I called him the Dawn King."

Great, Gwenna thought, blowing out a long breath. *The Dawn King. The bird almost as broken as the washout who trained him.*

As Allar'ra drew closer, however, he looked anything but broken. He was larger than the others, for one thing, substantially larger, and though Gwenna was no expert on avian flight, there was something about his wingbeat, something horribly strong and smooth. It had taken him only a matter of minutes to catch up with the others, and she stared as they passed directly over-head, shivering momentarily as the dark shadows scudded over the ground, silent, and so fast. It was like some part of her remembered being a squirrel once, a mouse, remembered cowering in dense clover, willing the heart to stillness, refusing to look up as death passed on silent wings.

As the kettral drew closer to the cliffs of the rocky island, the golden bird suddenly beat his wings, just half a dozen powerful strokes, and he was a hundred feet and more above the rest.

"We want him," Jak said simply.

"What about the eye-catching plumage?" Gwenna murmured.

"Everyone's got flaws."

"Sure, but I'm not looking to add more to the group."

"We want him," Jak said again. "You have to trust me on this. I trained him."

Trained. It was not a word Gwenna would have used to describe the creature, not any more than she would when speaking of a crag cat or rabid brindled bear. Even silent, even gliding, the Dawn King looked wild, predatory, utterly unbrid-lable. Then he spread his wings, cracked his beak, and split the sky with a shriek that seemed one part challenge, one part rage.

The two smaller birds behind and below, the siblings Sente'ril and Sente'ra, split apart, screaming their answer to the challenge.

"*This* is their sport," Jak said, his voice soft with reverence.

It looked, at first, like a horribly lopsided contest. Sente'ril and Sente'ra set on the King from both sides at once, claws stretched out before them, raking, grasping. The larger bird, despite his altitude, looked cornered, caught as the siblings swept together. He couldn't face both at once, and if he turned to meet one, the other would have him. Gwenna had watched birds with fliers spar in the air, each trying to get behind and above the other, into a position where the Kettral stationed on the talons could loose their arrows at will.

That was nothing like this.

At the last moment, just as 'Ril and 'Ra closed on him, the King folded his vast wings and . . . rolled.

"What . . . ," Gwenna breathed.

"Most birds won't fight from that altitude," Jak replied, unable to keep the pride from his voice. "He will."

Suddenly upside down and just below his attackers, the huge bird could bring his own talons to bear. He locked claws with one of the siblings, then twisted viciously in the air, slamming one smaller bird into the other. Sente'ril and Sente'ra plummeted as the King pulled himself clear, righting himself as the water rushed up and his two assailants crashed toward the waves. They caught themselves at the last moment, swooping clear on outspread wings, no challenge this time, not even a glance back.

"He'll leave them?" Gwenna asked quietly.

"They're sparring," Jak replied. "He's not trying to kill them."

"Like blood time," she said. "In the arena."

"Considerably more civil than that, actually."

"It doesn't *look* civil."

"It does, once you know what to look for."

The second fight was more protracted than the first. Rather than two birds ganging up on one, Suant'ra, Kei'ta, and Shura'ka all battled each other. None had the obvious advantage, at least not at first, and the avian brawl seemed to stretch on half the morning, a savage display of beaks and talons, wings frantically hammering, huge bodies locked together, falling, then breaking apart. Somewhere in the middle of the fight, the smallest of the three, Kei'ta, peeled away, climbing clear of the conflict, then coming to roost on the stone cliffs. Not long after, Shura'ka seized 'Ra by the wing, claws clutching hard enough to hold, but not hard enough to break or tear. 'Ra twisted, let out an agonized shriek. Shura'ka let her go.

"I've never seen that," Gwenna said.

Jak shrugged. "Most Kettral don't. The fliers are interested, of course, but for the rest . . . it's a long swim over here, and for what? It's not like the bird's going to be doing any of this with a Wing strapped into the talons." He frowned. "Like expecting a horse to gallop with a grown man tied to each leg."

"So we want the King," Gwenna said. "And Shura'ka, clearly. Who's the third?"

Jak hesitated, then shook his head. "Not Shura'ka."

"She handled 'Ra and that other one easily enough."

"She's limited," Jak replied. "Slow rotation to the right, a stupid tendency never to check out and below her left wing. A dozen other things. . . ."

"And does any of it matter? I thought we were choosing the best birds, the ones that can *win* when things get bloody."

"The bird that wins fighting alone isn't the same as the bird that wins carrying a Wing," Jak replied carefully. "We want the King, Kei'ta, and your old bird."

"She's injured," Gwenna protested. "Even I can see it."

"And she's smart. She's wily."

"She lost."

"She lost today," Jak replied quietly. "Tomorrow is another chance."

22

Kaden studied the tall man standing at the stone altar, the man who was not just a man, but a god clothed in mortal bone and muscle. Long Fist may have taken a different name here, in the steaming jungle north of the Waist, where the men and women knew him as Diem Hra, but there was no changing his skin, milk-pale beneath the web of scars, no changing the blond hair that spilled past his shoulders. The flesh Meshkent had chosen for himself could not have been further removed from the bodies of the jungle tribesmen, all of whom were short and compact, their skin and hair universally dark. Long Fist towered above them all—he must have been a full head higher than Kaden himself—a god in the form of a blue-eyed monster come to offer his bloody sacrifice.

"Diem Hra," Kaden murmured to the Ishien guard at his side. "What does it mean?"

"Red Laughter," the man replied, then chuckled his own insane cackle. "It's a small local snake. The rattle sounds like a child's laughter."

Kaden was still amazed that the Ishien hadn't simply slaughtered him the moment he emerged from the *kenta*. He had stepped through from the stone chamber inside Annur's old Shin chapterhouse—a chamber he'd had guarded since returning to Annur—into warm salt air, the skirling of seabirds, and the surprised cries of armed men. The low sun seared his eyes, hot and bright, blotting out all but the vaguest shapes. He could barely see the forms of soldiers, dark and featureless as shadows, closing around him. A sharp point—either a spear or a sword—pressed against his back. Then there was another at his chest. He considered the pain from inside the *vaniate,* studied the jagged red shape of it, then set it aside. The pain was irrelevant. They hadn't killed him; that was what mattered. For a moment, he could not remember why.

He'd expected to have to convince them to bring him to Meshkent—Bloody Horm to the Ishien, yet another identity, another mask, another set of syllables that failed to name the god—but no convincing proved necessary. Meshkent had anticipated the possibility of Kaden's return. Or, if not Kaden's, *someone's.* The man had left orders to have anyone passing through the *kenta* brought immediately before him, and so, before he'd uttered two dozen words, Kaden found himself stuffed into a cloak with a hood deep enough to hide his face, his eyes, then bustled through another gate, off of the remote island and into the glistening, sodden green of the jungle.

The *kenta* stood just a few paces from a small waterfall, in a glade where the stream pooled momentarily before meandering away. Wide-leafed trees ringed the small clearing, their slender branches drooping beneath the weight of hundreds of flowers—red, and yellow, and orange—bright as any imperial finery and wide as his hand. A dense tangle of vines knitted the trunks and branches together, but beyond that verdant wall, Kaden could hear the buzzing of a million flies and the screeching of sharp-tongued birds. And then there was the heat, the thick air like a steaming broth in his lungs each time he inhaled.

"Where are we?" he asked, turning to one of his captors.

The Ishien grunted, then shrugged. "The Waist. Just north of it."

Kaden nodded. It was what he'd expected, what he and Kiel had guessed. Meshkent was using the Ishien gates to move all over the frontier, fomenting rebellion and war. Sometimes it seemed that all Annur was on fire, but the Waist had been blazing particularly brightly. It was no surprise to find Meshkent here, heaping more fuel on the conflagration.

"Where is he?" Kaden asked.

This time, instead of replying, the Ishien just shoved him forward, toward a small break in the trees and the shifting shadow of the jungle beyond. They walked for half the morning, following a network of streambeds and game trails down the side of a low mountain, deeper into the forest. The Ishien held to their silence as though it were a shield, and after two or three unanswered questions, Kaden, too, fell silent. It was tempting to remain in the *vaniate,* but Kiel's warning came back to him—*Your mind was not built for it*—and after a while he let the trance lapse. From what he could make of the light sifting down through the branches above, the sun stood almost directly overhead when he first made out the rumbling of drums, then, almost quiet as the flies, at first, the drone and hum of human voices chanting.

At last, they emerged from the trees into a huge clearing packed with men and women and children, hundreds of them, thousands, chests naked in the southern heat, skin glistening, bows, and spears, and stranger weapons Kaden didn't recognize clutched in their hands. Most were facing the center of the clearing, staring at a low ziggurat of pale stone. A few turned as the Ishien pushed Kaden forward through the throng, but they drew back at the sight of the men, as though they recognized them. A low mutter went up through the nearest, a quick patter of words in a tongue Kaden didn't understand. The majority, however, didn't even notice the new arrival.

Their attention was fixed on the ziggurat, and the pale man who stood atop it, high enough that even those at the very back of the throng had a clear view, low enough that everyone could make out the ritual about to unfold.

"Long Fist," Kaden said quietly, the name too quiet for even the Ishien flanking him to hear.

There was a limestone slab before the shaman, raised to waist level on four columns carved in the shapes of bound men and women. The stone faces wore different features, but each was distended, teeth bared, lips howling in private agony.

"How long has he been doing this?" Kaden asked. "Coming here?"

One of the Ishien guards—neither man had bothered to supply his name, but this was the one who occasionally responded to Kaden's questions—glanced over at him. "A long time."

"They're not surprised," Kaden asked, gesturing to the assembled throng, then to Long Fist atop the dais, "that he doesn't look like them?"

The man shook his head, his reluctance to speak giving way to the obvious awe in which he held his commander. "He turns this to his strength. They believe him to be singular. A prophet."

It was hardly subtle—a god posing as his own prophet—but Long Fist appeared to have won over the jungle tribes just as fully as he had the Urghul.

"How does he do it?" Kaden asked, shaking his head.

The Ishien snorted. "Bloody Horm was not given his Hannan name yesterday. This is his strength. He lives among a people, rising to a place of honor among them, a position from which he can hunt our foes." There was reverence in the Ishien's voice. He gestured toward his commander. "It is a great honor here to wield those snakes."

Kaden studied the snakes in question. One was a bright yellow, the other striped black and violet, each as long as his arm and writhing in Long Fist's grip. The shaman held one in each hand, fingers clamped just behind the heads, ignoring the bodies of the creatures as they coiled and uncoiled around his scarred, muscled arms.

"You've seen this before?" Kaden asked.

The Ishien nodded. "Once."

Before Kaden could respond, Hra raised the snakes above his head. The mass of men and women let up a great, ecstatic scream, all in unison, then fell suddenly, perfectly silent. Kaden could hear the cries of the jungle birds, high and accusatory, the croaking of a thousand bright-tongued frogs, the sweep and rustle of hot wind through the vines. Then the mob parted, men and women shifting aside to form a narrow avenue of sweaty flesh. After a few heartbeats, a prisoner, hands bound behind him, lurched forward on bare, unsteady feet. His shirt had been torn away, but Kaden recognized the filthy legion-issue breeches, the sloppy tattoo of the rising sun high on his right shoulder.

"Annurian," Kaden said.

His guard nodded. "These people won a battle against your republic." If an Annurian defeat mattered to the Ishien at all, Kaden couldn't hear it in his voice. "This is their offering of thanks."

The legionary approached the ziggurat, stumbling numbly on the uneven ground, then began climbing toward the stone slab and the man behind it. He moved slowly, as though something were already broken inside him, but he moved.

"Why doesn't he run?" Kaden asked, trying to make sense of the scene. "Why doesn't he struggle?"

The Ishien pointed with grim satisfaction to the thousands of men and women surrounding the altar, each with a bow or poisoned spear. They had fallen eerily silent, but each looked ready to rend the Annurian's flesh with their sharpened teeth.

"Why? He dies either way."

That seemed clear enough, and after a moment Kaden turned his attention back to the altar. The legionary stood on unsteady legs, staring out over the crowded clearing. The gathered thousands had gone perfectly still, as though paralyzed by their own anticipation. The soldier looked over the faces blankly, bleakly, searching from one to the next as though for someone he knew. His eyes widened when they fixed on the Ishien. Both men shared the soldier's complexion, a brown paler than the surrounding faces, and the man must have taken them for Annurians, perhaps even legionaries. For the first time, something like life seemed to flood his limbs. He opened his mouth to call out, to scream for help or cry his defiance.

Before the sound could twist free of his throat, however, the first snake—silent, quicker than vision—struck. The soldier's eyes went wide. His back arched. A sound like a strangled scream made it halfway out of his mouth, then withered on the hot air. Suddenly, awfully rigid, he toppled back onto the slab, where Long Fist laid him down.

"Paralytic," the Ishien announced.

Kaden nodded slowly, watching the man's fingers curl in skeletal claws. "And the second snake?"

Somewhere in the jungle behind them, a mortal creature cried out in terror, screamed its last, then fell silent. The Ishien's smile was like a rusted knife.

"Pain," he replied.

There was a monotony, Kaden had decided by the time the sun finally set, when the soldier's spent body was finally carved into parts and laid about the edges of the altar, to horror. Something ultimately pedestrian in the strangled protests clawing their way up from the soldier's frozen gut. The stomach could only twist so much at the sight of blood welling from the mouth and ears. The mind could only recoil so far.

When Kaden finally sat inside the hide tent, staring across the dwindling fire at the man who had done the hurting, the cutting, the man with all the names—Long Fist, Bloody Horm, Diem Hra, Meshkent, the man who was not a man at all—and when the tall man smiled at him, nodded, and asked, "How did you find our offering?" Kaden found himself answering without thinking.

"I found it boring."

Foolish words, perhaps, with which to address the Lord of Pain, but the tall man just watched him through the smoke, took a sip from his steaming wooden cup, then nodded. "In pain, as in all things, there is an art. I would not expect you to understand it any more than I would expect the tribesmen outside this tent to appreciate the polyphonic choral music of the Manjari."

Kaden blinked. Any mention of music seemed incongruous after the recent blood and brutality, and Long Fist's ease, the casual urbanity with which he discussed the famous Manjari choruses—it wasn't what Kaden had expected from someone who wielded poisonous snakes in his fists. Another reminder, as if he needed another, of an old Shin truth—expectation was the midwife of error.

"Where is the art," he asked quietly, "in a paralyzed prisoner bleeding out through his ears?"

His own question surprised Kaden even as he gave it voice. He had come through the *kenta,* had risked his life with both the Ishien and the tribes of the Waist, in order to *warn* the shaman about Ran il Tornja, not to argue the aesthetic merits of pain. And yet it seemed crucial, suddenly, to distance himself from the slaughter, from the savagery of the women and men just outside. This, after all, was the one figure responsible for setting fire to Annur, for kindling war on every front, for ordering the Urghul south and the tribes north, for ushering in the slaughter of thousands, maybe millions when the violence was finally finished. It seemed important to be clear on one central point: Kaden had come to warn the priest, not to follow him. Not to join him.

"Where is the art," he continued, "in peeling the skin off a man's body, one strip at a time?"

Long Fist—Kaden still gave him that name in his head—just smiled, as though the question were at once familiar and disappointingly dull.

"Where is the art," he replied, "in blowing air through a hollow reed? In smearing ink on a page? Reduce anything to its elements and the art . . ." He blew the pipe smoke slowly between pursed lips, watching it eddy in the hot air, then break apart. "It vanishes."

"No," Kaden said, shaking his head. "Music and painting are not like this. What you accomplish is just blood and suffering."

"There are more shades to the suffering of men than there are colors in the forest. I can draw more notes from a woman bound than a harpist can from her crude arrangement of wood and string." He gestured, a mere flick of the fingers that made something deep in Kaden's gut recoil. "There is no instrument like man, no musical counterpoint like the play of terror and hope, the bafflement and aching clarity that you can draw from his distended flesh." The shaman's voice was lower and slower than it had been. Reverential. Incantatory. "*This* is art. This is true beauty."

Kaden stared. A part of his mind moved, a part he thought he had long since tamed, something sluggish but powerful as a winter bear prodded from its slumber. The Shin had taught him to put away his terror, but here, in the tent's low firelight, seated across from the god, Kaden felt that terror stirring once more.

"I know who you are," he said, his own voice so low he wasn't certain that he'd spoken.

Long Fist just smiled. "Of course you do."

"And I know what you want."

"No," the priest replied. "You do not. You understand the edges, perhaps. You see the faintest outline, but the beating heart of it all—you are far from holding that in your fist."

"You want Annur destroyed."

"Annur." Long Fist nodded. "It is a perversion."

Something about the tent—maybe the sweet smoke, the heat, the closeness of the air—made Kaden's head swim. The shaman spoke flawless Annurian, but the words seemed new and strange on his tongue, the collected syllables threatening to dissipate like steam above a boiling kettle, to decohere, their meaning lost in the silty air.

Long Fist continued to sit as he had been sitting all along—cross-legged, one hand in his lap, the other holding the bone pipe—but he seemed larger somehow, or smaller, like a massive statue seen from a great distance. Though Kaden himself was also sitting, he felt suddenly that he might pitch forward into the fire, that the earth beneath him were shifting, lifting up, shoveling him toward the flames. The feeling was so intense that he nearly reached out a hand to arrest his nonexistent slide. With great effort he dragged his gaze from the glaciated blue of Long Fist's eyes to the fire's vermillion. When the sight of the fire had burned away his mind's smoke, he slid into the *vaniate*.

Inside the trance, the dislocation vanished. The smoke remained, but it was only smoke. He was still sweating in that dense, wet heat, but the sweat meant nothing. It slid down his skin, but his skin, too, meant nothing. The body he had worn for so many years—it was a feeble thing compared to this great roofless emptiness. He watched the flame for a few heartbeats. There was a stillness in that ever-shifting blaze, a stillness he recognized. When Kaden finally raised his eyes, Long Fist's pipe froze halfway to his pursed lips. For the first time he looked surprised.

"You remind me of your father," he said finally. "I did not expect this of one so young."

"What did you know of my father?"

The shaman spread his hands. "We met. Several times. Like you, the flesh weighed less heavily upon him than it does on the rest of your kind."

"Where did you meet?" Kaden asked. "Why?"

"On the hub where the gates converge. And *why*? This is a question with many answers. He wanted peace with the Urghul—"

"And you wanted to destroy Annur."

Long Fist took a long pull on the pipe, held the smoke in his lungs, then watched Kaden as he blew it out.

"It is difficult to hear a thing when your ears are filled with your own words."

"They are hardly my words," Kaden replied. "You said as much moments ago. Annur is a perversion. If you met my father privately, all alone on that island, why didn't you simply kill him?"

The shaman frowned. "Would he have been so easy to kill, Sanlitun hui'Malkeenian?"

Kaden hesitated. The truth was that he had no idea how hard his father had been to kill. Ran il Tornja had managed it, but then, il Tornja was Csestriim. Instead of responding, he shifted the conversation, tried to move it toward his original purpose.

"You took a risk in coming here, to take mortal form in this world."

Abruptly, unexpectedly, Long Fist smiled, revealing his canines, filed to white points. "You believe that this—" He raised a hand into the flickering light, studied the palm a moment, then passed it back and forth through the fire, fast enough that it didn't burn. "—is what I am?" His laugh, when it came, sounded like the purring of a massive cat, relaxed and predatory all at once. "Imagine, Kaden, that you are an ant. Your world," he went on, gesturing to the tent walls and beyond, as though offering up the jungle, offering up all of Eridroa and more, "is a scrap of grass. Your monuments are hills of sand, tamped down by a heavy rain. One day you are crushed beneath a ragged fingernail. As your mind darkens, you marvel at the strength of that nail. The speed. The way it came straight down from a clear sky. If you survive, you will worship it for the rest of your days, but what is a fingernail?"

The shaman's own nails were long and polished a deep arterial red. He set down his pipe, fanned his fingers, and contemplated those nails a moment. Then, with a quick, precise movement, ripped one clear of the finger. Blood welled in the recessed flesh. Long Fist ignored it. He held the polished nail up to the light, then tossed it into the fire. It was hard to be sure, but Kaden thought he could smell it burning, a dark, acrid scent woven into the sick-sweet smoke of the honey briar.

"You are not your fingernail," Long Fist said, "and I am not this body." He dragged that bloody finger over his chest, leaving trails of red over the pale scar, like a quick, hasty text brushed over another script, the older one more precise, inscribed in the skin itself. "This body is just the point where I intersect with your world."

"Then why did you take it?"

Again, he smiled. "Sometimes it is necessary to put a fingernail on the back of an ant."

Kaden wondered briefly how those words would have sounded to someone outside the *vaniate*. Unsettling, at the very least. Frightening. In the great blank, however, the emotions tied to those words had no meaning.

Years ago, during a severe winter penance, Kaden had sat naked in the snow outside Ashk'lan for the better part of a morning. When he was finally allowed back inside the refectory, stiff, dumb, and clumsy from the cold, he tried to cut a hunk of mutton from the shank, and ended up slicing open his palm instead. He could still remember staring at the wound, watching the bright blood flow, but feeling nothing from the cold-numbed hand. The limb may as well have belonged to someone else, and in the end it was someone else—Akiil, Kaden thought—who cursed, then wrapped it in clean cloth.

Long Fist's words were every bit as sharp as that knife, sharp enough to hack with, to hurt with, but the *vaniate* was far colder than Ashk'lan's snow, and whatever part of him the shaman hoped to harm had gone utterly, perfectly numb.

"If you wanted Annur dead," Kaden said, "if you wanted to crush it, then why didn't you kill my father when you had the chance?"

"Your father was not Annur. Not any more than you are. Than your sister is."

Kaden's own voice, when he finally spoke, sounded far off. "Ran il Tornja."

Long Fist nodded. "Your war chief is more than a war chief."

"He is Csestriim," Kaden said, the words he had rehearsed so many times, the explanation he had risked his life and traveled the length of a continent to deliver just tumbling out, almost unexpectedly, as though the words had just willed themselves into being. "Ran il Tornja is Csestriim, and his only goal is to destroy you."

Kaden wasn't sure what he had expected. Not laughter, certainly, but Long Fist laughed then, loud and long.

"Csestriim." He shook his head as memory slowly replaced the mirth. "I miss the arrogance of those creatures. It is almost a pity that your kind exterminated them." The shaman took a long drag on his pipe, eyes distant, as though watching something far away, or very far in the past.

"We didn't kill them all," Kaden said. "And il Tornja hopes to reverse the damage, to replace us with his kind again."

"Damage?" Long Fist said, pursing his lips. "*Damage?* No." He shook his head thoughtfully. "You men have only your fly-brief lives, but those lives are rich. The Csestriim—" He held thumb and forefinger together, lifted them into the air as though he held a diminutive figure between them, examining it before tossing it into the fire. "—the Csestriim were durable as stone, but there was no music to them. Ciena and I, we would strike them and strum them, drag our fingers over their flesh, and for what? A few dull thuds. Rarely, every hundred years or so, a single spark. Nothing more.

"*You,* though," Long Fist continued, gesturing to Kaden. "Humans. You are fragile as old harps. Always out of tune. Warped by the slightest change in the weather. A child could break you." He smiled, revealing those sharpened teeth again. "But the music . . ."

"I did not come here to talk about music," Kaden said. "I came here to warn you that—"

The shaman cut him off with a raised hand. "Let it go."

Kaden shook his head. "The warning?"

"Not the warning. That deadness you wear around you like a cloak."

"The *vaniate,*" Kaden realized.

Long Fist narrowed his eyes. "It is an ugly thing. An insult to what you are. To what you could be."

Kaden watched the tall figure seated across the fire. Inside the trance, he felt no fear of the god. No awe. He could remember, though, the sudden vertigo that had struck him when he first entered the tent, when Meshkent first spoke to him through the mouth of the Urghul chieftain. He remembered it—the dislocation, the sense of standing at the edge of some vast chasm as the earth tipped up beneath him—but the memory meant nothing.

"I am not your instrument," he said quietly.

Long Fist shook his head in disgust. "Not while you befoul yourself like this."

"There is nothing foul in the *vaniate*," Kaden replied. "It is freedom."

"Freedom?" The shaman shook his head. "And from what, do you imagine, are you freeing yourself?"

"From you," Kaden said. "From your touch. Your taint."

"You poor, stick-legged creature. What do you think you are *for*?"

A new log had caught, and the fire flared between them. Kaden found himself watching the other man through a veil of flame. It was hard to make out his features in the shifting light, but he looked less like a man. Or rather, he was still a man, but one made of planes and surfaces, as though the flesh catching the light were just a reflection of something impossibly larger. *This is the sun,* the Shin had told him many years ago, pointing to the bright circle reflected in the still surface of Umber's Pool, *and it is not the sun.*

"For?" Kaden asked, trying to place the word, to find some context for his own response.

"You belong to me, and to Ciena, and to our children. We made you, shaped you from the numb flesh of the Csestriim. Where they were bare, unwavering precision, we gave you resonance, and range, and timbre. You are a thing of beauty, Kaden, like one of these fine jungle drums, but you have defiled the wooden frame, smeared mud over the hide, sliced through the cords that should have held you tight, that let you vibrate to my touch." The face behind the flame grimaced. "It is an insult."

"I did not come here to insult you—"

"To *yourself*," the shaman said, cutting him off. Then he smiled. "Fortunately for you, it is an insult I can unmake." He raised a hand above the fire, placed the tip of his middle finger against the pad of his thumb, then snapped.

Kaden had felt the *vaniate* shatter before—when he stepped through the *kenta* into the frigid water of the Dead Heart, when the stone falling from the collapsing ceiling of the Dawn Palace smashed into his back, knocking him to the floor. The feeling was always disorienting, but it was nothing like this.

Instead of the silent bursting of the bubble he remembered, the snap of Long Fist's fingers ripped him, ripped him in a way that felt *physical,* from inside the *vaniate*. Suddenly, his own emotions, heavy as stone and studded with steel, pressed in from all around. He struggled to draw breath, closed his eyes, found the darkness thick and unbreathable as pitch, opened his eyes once more, found the shaman's unwavering gaze, and finally managed a ragged gasp.

It hurt. As though he were a fish hauled from the cool, weightless water into an air that burned like fire. Whatever he had learned among the Shin, it abandoned him. He could feel his mouth moving, gibbering with fear, could feel, buried deep inside him, the warm sweet hope that it would end, that the god would let him go. Briefly there was a hard cord of hope holding him up. Then Long Fist smiled more widely. The cord snapped.

"This is what you are," the shaman whispered. *"This is what you are for."*

"And if Ran il Tornja destroys you?" Kaden managed from between clenched teeth.

Long Fist waved a hand, brushing aside both the smoke and the warning. "He can no more destroy me than he can stab a star in the night sky."

"He can kill this body," Kaden ground out, hoping desperately that he was right, that he was making sense, that he understood the situation. The weight of his own emotion, ocean-heavy and pressing down, threatened to crush him, to annihilate the last walls of thought. "Destroy your hand on this world. How will you play your instruments then?"

The shaman watched him with narrowed eyes. "How do you know this?"

"Il Tornja knows who you are. He knows you are here and he is hunting you."

"It does not matter. He is no threat to me, not even in this diminished skin I wear to walk the ways of your world."

Kaden felt his mind might break beneath the strain. "What about Ciena?" he croaked. "She is here, too."

Long Fist went suddenly, perfectly still, his face bright with reflected fire, blue eyes unmelting in the heat. Kaden wondered if he'd actually spoken aloud, or if he'd only managed to think his final warning. He had no idea what the god was doing to him, no idea how to fight it, and then, suddenly, it was over. The crushing weight was gone. The fire was just the fire. The face of the shaman was just a human face, hard and intent, all signs of mirth or levity vanished.

"What did you say about my consort?"

"She is here," Kaden said. He was panting. Sweat poured in great sheets down his chest and back. His mind was his own once more, but it felt light, untethered from himself or the world. The heat in the tent, unbearable a moment before, was gone. Or it was not gone, but he no longer felt it. Or he felt it, but it didn't feel like heat. "She is here," he managed once more.

Long Fist's eyes bored into him. "Why do you believe this?"

"Because I was with her," Kaden replied warily. "With the girl whose mind she tried to inhabit."

"*Tried?*" The shaman leaned on the word as though it were a pry bar.

Kaden nodded. "It didn't work. I don't know why. She... the goddess... tried to do with Triste what you did with..."

He trailed off, gesturing at the flesh of the man who was no longer a man seated before him.

Long Fist shook his head. "This cannot be so."

"I saw her kill a man with a kiss—the man you left in charge of the Ishien."

The shaman's eyes narrowed. "Ekhard Matol. I was told that he lost his hold on the emptiness. That he tried to pass through the gates unprepared."

"He was unprepared because Triste—Ciena in that moment—stripped him of his emptiness. I watched her do it. It took her just a moment, a kiss. . . ."

"Bliss," Long Fist mused. "It is powerful as pain." He fell silent for a long time, staring into the flame. "This would be Ciena's way," he conceded finally.

"I spoke to her," Kaden said. "She is the one who told me you were here, on this earth. She said you were power-mad. That you were drunk on your own ambition. That it made you stupid and vulnerable."

The shaman laughed a long, rich laugh. "This, too, has the timbre of her voice." Then he sobered, shook his head slowly, eyes never leaving Kaden's. "And yet if I believe your tale, *she* is the one who lost control of her chosen flesh. *If* I believe this tale. If you spoke to her, then she is here, and this child—Triste—is gone."

"No," Kaden replied grimly. "Triste is very much alive; she is a broken woman, but your goddess was not the one to break her. I've seen Ciena only in crucial moments, situations of life and death, and then only glimpses. When Triste put a knife into her own belly—"

"The *fool*," Long Fist growled. "I spent decades preparing the earth, and she tries to follow me on a whim."

"I think she followed you to warn you."

"And instead, she ends up putting herself at risk." He bared his teeth. "The *obviate*. The girl must do it."

Kaden shook his head slowly. The balance in the conversation had shifted suddenly, powerfully. For the first time since entering the tent, Long Fist seemed unsettled, even agitated. Kaden had imagined the god would be something like the Csestriim writ large—passionless and rational, brilliant beyond human imagining. For the first time, he realized the error of that conception.

Meshkent was not Csestriim. He *despised* the Csestriim. Kaden had considered il Tornja's intellect and Kiel's to be godlike, but they were nothing like the gods, at least not like these gods. Why had he supposed that Meshkent and Ciena, the progenitors of all passion, would eschew that passion, that they would be untouched by the forces of which they themselves were the font? Long Fist was surprised, surprised and angry. Clearly Kaden's revelation had caught him like a fist to the chin.

"She won't," Kaden replied.

The man studied him through the smoke. "Does she understand what is at stake?"

Kaden nodded. "She doesn't care. Triste didn't ask to have a goddess lodged in her mind. She didn't want it. And she has suffered because of it."

"Suffered?" the shaman demanded, shaking his head. "She doesn't understand the first thing about suffering. None of you do. If this child is killed with Ciena inside, if Ciena's touch is severed from your world, *then* you will understand suffering."

"Triste won't," Kaden said. "She will be dead." He considered his next words carefully. "Can the *obviate* be performed without her consent?"

"No," Long Fist replied, the syllable like the tolling of some funerary drum. "The *obviate* is not just a killing, not even a self-killing. It is . . ." he frowned, "a voyage. If the girl does not cast off the moorings, the ship of my consort's soul . . . it will remain tethered to the shore as the dock burns."

He grimaced, eyes distant, watching some possible future that only he could see as the flames played across the pale skin of his face.

"The work I do here will wait," he concluded finally. "I must see this girl. Must speak with her."

"She is imprisoned."

"Take me to the prison."

Kaden hesitated, wondering how far he could press the shaman. "Stop the war," he said finally. "Stop the Urghul, and I will take you to her."

Long Fist watched him. "You dare to haggle with me?"

"You're attacking Annur," Kaden said. "Killing thousands. Tens of thousands. I want you to stop."

"And if I will not?"

"Then Triste stays where she is. The goddess remains trapped. Until someone kills her."

Long Fist moved with all the speed of a striking adder. Since Kaden entered the tent, the man had remained still, seated. The violence he had plied earlier was a violence of the mind. Now, however, as he uncoiled, Kaden had time to think a single thought—*impossible,* it was not possible that any human should move so fast—and then Long Fist was through the fire and on top of him, those long, elegant fingers with the painted nails closing around his throat, slamming him back against the damp dirt.

"You would trade Ciena as though she were some Urghul horse?" he demanded, the last word a hiss.

Kaden tried to respond, to shake his head, but that hand might have been cast from iron.

"You would barter her welfare like one of your copper coins?" The grip tightened until Kaden felt he was breathing through a thin reed, the hot, sweet air too little for his heaving lungs.

"I will tell you three truths," the shaman went on, "and I will shape them to your words so you can comprehend. First, the fact I wear this skin means nothing. That Ciena has robed herself in the flesh of some rebellious slattern means nothing. We are not what you are. We are so much more that your mind would break beneath the sight."

Darkness hemmed Kaden's vision. The light in the tent might

have been failing, and fast, only he could still feel the fire, hot against his right flank. He harnessed his heart, slowed it, parceled out his breathless blood, focused only on the moment.

"Next, Ciena will not die with this child, but *you* will. All of you. Your minds were built for our fingers. Without them, you will wither or go mad. Her death or mine, either one, will mark the end of your race."

He leaned so close Kaden could feel his breathing, smell the sweet root tea thick on the breath. Those blue eyes, sky-deep and ocean-cold, were suddenly the whole world, a universe awhirl with brutal blue, a blue so hot it burned, it seared. *How had people not known the truth?* Kaden's air-starved brain offered up that single thought over and over and over. *How had anyone ever believed those eyes were human?*

"Do you understand?" Long Fist demanded.

The hand relaxed fractionally, enough for Kaden to gasp a half breath, to nod. And just as quickly as he had struck, the shaman released his grip.

Kaden's body wanted to scramble backward, to claw through the walls of the tent, to get out and away. He forced himself to stillness. When he thought he could talk without gagging, he locked eyes with the Urghul.

"And the third truth you hoped to tell me?"

Long Fist watched him, his eyes human once more, or almost human.

"There is no calling it back," he said finally.

Kaden shook his head, his mind cloudy with the attack. "Calling back what?"

"This war," the shaman replied, nodding to the doors of the tent. "For decades, I have kindled fires beyond your border and inside it. Now they are beyond me."

"You are a god."

"There are older gods than I. Stronger gods. I took this flesh to set a single finger on the scales, to tip the delicate balance from order to chaos. That chaos stalks your empire now. It is beyond the grasp of any single man, so let us have no more talk of calling it back."

As Kaden dragged the jungle air into his lungs, breath after desperate breath, he tried to think. The leverage he'd so trusted had proven treacherous, illusory. Trying to move Meshkent with the truth about Triste was like trying to pry a great stone from the dirt with a branch of rotten pine. Maybe there was another way, something else he could do or say to regain purchase in the conversation. If so, he had no idea what it was, no idea how to twist the shaman to his will. No idea if it would matter if he could. He had spent enough time kindling fires, watching them burn, to recognize an immutable truth in the god's words. Maybe Kiel would have found a way, or il Tornja, but for all his skill with the *vaniate,* Kaden was not Kiel or il Tornja.

"All right," he said. The words were part plea, part confession.

"How will you make *all right?*"

"I'll get you into the Dawn Palace. I can probably even get you to Triste. . . ." He trailed off, despair, sudden as a hot summer gust, blowing over him, through him. Since Meshkent had wrenched him from the *vaniate* his mind was as disordered as that of the rankest acolyte. "But you won't be able to get her out. Even you. You have no idea what the dungeon of the Dawn Palace is like."

Long Fist just smiled that predatory, feline smile. "And you have no idea of the power slumbering inside me."

23

When Adare had asked Kegellen to acquire a thief, she'd had a few vague ideas in mind. A good thief, she'd always believed, would be inconspicuous, forgettable, bland as a stone wall, a creature of quick fingers and old clothes. Not a tiny, naked bald man with a hand-wide tattoo of the moon inked across his smooth brown face.

Adare glanced at Kegellen, then over the woman's shoulder, half waiting for some other, more suitable figure to slip in through the door. Over Nira's strenuous objections, she had agreed to meet in a modest mansion up on Graves, one of the dozens of properties belonging to the Queen of the Streets; if the whole plan went straight to 'Shael, after all, Adare didn't want anyone in the Dawn Palace remembering a parade of unsavory characters visiting her own chambers.

Kegellen's house, like the woman herself, was all elegance: quiet courtyards ringed with marble colonnades, delicate fountains, fine rugs from Sia and Mo'ir, tropical flowers that must have required an army of gardeners to maintain. The woman's taste in art leaned toward the erotic—sculptures of lithe young men twisting around their own muscled forms, Liran tapestries woven into scenes of pleasure and delight—but even the boldest pieces managed to be tasteful, restrained. It hardly looked like a den of thieves, but then, the naked man before her didn't look like a thief.

Adare raised a brow. "This is him?"

"Indeed, Your Radiance! Indeed." Kegellen made an elegant little flourish with her outstretched hand. "May I present to you Vasta Dhati, First Priest of the Sea of Knives."

The man didn't smile. He seemed to be looking at Adare and not looking at her, as though he were studying a portion of her forehead without realizing it was attached to a face.

"I wasn't aware," Adare said carefully, "that there *was* a priesthood associated with the Sea of Knives. Last I heard, the whole place was just a haven for pirates."

Dhati didn't blink, didn't shift his gaze, but he made a quick hiss, so loud and unexpected Adare took half a step back.

Kegellen spread her hands apologetically. "*Pirates.* It is a regrettable word that our landbound world uses to describe his congregation."

Adare blinked. "I asked for a thief who was good with climbing and ropes and you brought me a pirate priest of the Manjari?"

At the word *pirate,* Dhati hissed again. Then, without preamble, leapt into the air, folded his skinny legs beneath him mid-flight, and landed atop the table, ankles crossed onto the inside of his thighs in a way that made them look exceedingly likely to break. Adare stared.

"I think you will find Vasta Dhati's skills quite satisfactory," Kegellen said. "He has collaborated with me for quite some time."

"How long?"

Kegellen turned to Dhati, who, after his brief display of acrobatics, seemed content to sit atop the table, eyes fixed before him.

"Seven years, I think it is now."

"What about his flock?" Adare asked. "Back in the Sea of Knives?"

Kegellen spread her hands. "Regrettably, he is in exile."

"Exile? Exiled by whom?"

The small priest seemed disinclined to do any talking on his own behalf, and so Adare had addressed the question to Kegellen. Before the woman could respond, however, Dhati raised a single finger, pointed it straight at the ceiling, and began speaking in a rapid patter so heavily accented Adare could barely understand.

"Apostates and blasphemers. Those of unsteady breath. A plague of the unsanctified. Clutchers of anchors and coastlines, traitors to the swell of the holy wave. They"—Dhati's finger trembled here, and his eyes rose to the ceiling as though seeking confirmation from the huge chandelier—"will pay the full account on the day when I return."

He made some complicated sign in the air with that single finger, as though to seal the words, then fell so silent he might never have spoken. He wasn't even breathing hard. Adare stared. Despite his naked chest, it was hard to tell if the priest was breathing at *all*.

All right, she thought bleakly. *So he's insane.*

"Can you climb?" Adare asked hesitantly. "Climb ropes?"

Dhati hissed again. It seemed to be his preferred mode of expression.

"He is the finest climber in Eridroa," Kegellen replied for him. "Before he came to me, he lived an entire life in the rigging of his ship."

"Great," Adare replied. "But there's no rigging inside Intarra's Spear."

"Dhati believes a man should be his own rope."

Adare blinked, looked from Kegellen to the self-proclaimed priest, then back again.

"I have no idea what that means."

As if in answer, Dhati tipped his head abruptly back, his spine hinging perfectly at the neck until he was staring straight up at the ceiling. As Adare stared, he extended both hands before him, interlaced his fingers into a double fist, paused with his arms at their rigid full extent, and then, with a sound like a strangled, phlegmy roar, slammed the heels of his hands into his gut. The blow doubled him over. He remained in that position, motionless save for a wavelike rippling of his ribs.

"Is this . . . ," Adare began, looking over at Kegellen.

The woman smiled and raised a hand, pointing back at the priest with a brightly painted fingernail.

The small man bared his teeth as he straightened. They were crooked and yellow-brown, but there between them, caught between his right incisors, was a flash of bright red. Adare took it for blood at first, the product of that violent blow to the stomach, but after a moment Dhati reached between his teeth and took between his thumb and forefinger what turned out to be the end of a silken band. Adare watched, fascinated and repulsed, as the priest drew the silk out, hand over hand, length after length. It piled on the table before him, sodden and limp, coil after coil, until he finally pulled the last length free. When it was all out, he drew in a noisy breath, shuddered once, then shut his jaw.

"How long is that?" Adare asked.

"Ten times his height," Kegellen replied, beaming. "Not a trick to enjoy over the dinner table, I'm afraid, but from time to time it has come in terribly useful."

Adare looked from the red silk to the man, struggling to weigh the possibilities and the risks. Finally, she took a step to stand directly in his line of vision. He didn't twitch, didn't look at her, but she went ahead anyway.

"Did Kegellen explain what we need you to do? Did she explain the risks involved?"

Finally, the priest turned a dark, pitying eye on her. "The risk is what it is. I have been in prisons before, yes. And I have left them."

"This isn't just a prison," Adare said. "It is the imperial dungeon inside Intarra's Spear. To get you inside, you will be taken by the guards, accused of treason."

He smiled. "*Treason*? I am the First Priest of the Sea of Knives. It is a post far above any petty emperor."

"Right," Adare said, unsure if this was part of the coming show, or the man's actual belief. She suspected it was the latter. "So they'll have no trouble believing the treason part. You will be hung inside a cell."

"All the world beyond the Sea of Knives is a cell."

"Yes. Well. This one will be smaller. And steel."

"Steel is as smoke to me."

"Still . . ."

"The only question," Dhati went on, cutting straight through her words, "is one of price. Did the Priestess of the Streets explain to you my price?"

Adare cocked an eyebrow at the other woman. "The Priestess of the Streets?"

Kegellen spread her hands. "An honorific of his own invention. I make no claim to the divine, Your Radiance, I can assure you."

"Did she explain the price?" Dhati asked once more.

"No," Adare replied, shaking her head. "As a matter of fact, she didn't."

"When it is done," the priest proclaimed, "I will require a fleet."

Kegellen made a face, a sort of stretching of the lips that seemed to say, *Sorry! You know how priests can be.*

"A fleet," Adare said, wondering if the man was joking. "A fleet of ships?"

No, she thought, studying his face. *Not joking.*

"A dozen should suffice."

Adare shook her head. "Do you have any idea what you're asking?"

"The First Priest of the Sea of Knives understands the value of a vessel better than any grubby hugger of land."

"The council will notice if I start handing out ships. They will object. They will ask questions. I can give you gold."

Dhati hissed again, even more violently this time. Adare could feel the tiny drops of spittle strike her face.

She glanced over at Kegellen.

The woman shrugged. "He doesn't like gold. It sinks."

"What need," the man demanded, "does the First Priest of the Sea of Knives have for heavy metal clawed out of the earth?"

"Well," Adare said slowly, drawing out the syllable as she made an effort to keep her temper in check, "you can use gold to buy ships."

"I require ships."

"Yes, but with the gold you can—" She stopped herself. Dhati was staring at her forehead again. Glaring at it, really. "One," she said instead. "You can have one ship."

Dhati made a face, as though he had suddenly smelled something foul. "One is not a dozen."

"And you are not the only thief in Annur," Adare replied smoothly.

"There is only one First Priest of the Sea of Knives."

"While I'm certain that's true, I'm willing to make do."

The small priest sucked in a tremendous breath. Adare stared as his chest expanded and expanded, to the point where it seemed likely to explode. He held it a moment, and then, with frightening energy, began to hyperventilate. His eyes bulged. His lips turned a strange shade of purple. Adare took a half step forward, wondering if the man were having a seizure, but Kegellen put a hand on her arm.

"He is thinking," the woman murmured.

"He looks like he's dying."

"It is the way that he thinks."

And then, as quickly as he had begun, he stopped, sat stock-still on the table.

"Three ships."

Adare ran the numbers in her mind, considered the current deployment of the various fleets, reapportioned a few dozen vessels, then nodded slowly.

"Three ships."

"It is a meager fleet," Dhati said, "but am I not the First Priest of the Sea of Knives? It will suffice."

When the small man finally left, striding through the open door without so much as a glance back or a farewell, Adare turned to Kegellen, shaking her head.

"You know some interesting people."

The Unkillable Bitch smiled merrily. "I enjoy the company of unique souls."

Adare nodded, then glanced toward the door where Dhati had disappeared. "And were you able to find the other one; the . . . woman we discussed?"

Kegellen nodded. "I suspect, regrettably, that you will find her less interesting than Dhati."

"I certainly hope so. She's supposed to be dead."

"Hmm. Dead. Yes. Well, I hope that *dying* will be adequate. After all, we have two days to wait, and I understood you wanted the body to be fresh."

It was obvious at a glance that the young woman wasn't well. Though she leaned only lightly on the arm of the servant leading her into the room, her shoulders slumped, her hand trembled, and there was no missing the exhaustion in her short, uncertain stride.

So young, Adare thought, staring at the girl, *and already dying.*

That was the point, of course, but suddenly she felt sick, nauseated almost to the point of vomiting. She had ordered soldiers to their deaths, of course, sent them into battle dozens of times over, all along the northern front, signing their doom with a sweep of her pen. Every time, every battle, it felt awful. This was worse.

Adare had pored over reports of Triste's atrocities in the Jasmine Court, scouring them for physical details. It would have been easier just to go *see* the woman in her cell, but if things went wrong—and there was a lot about the plan that could go very, very wrong—Adare didn't want anyone remembering that she had visited the leach only days before. Which meant research in the imperial archives, a full night of reading the carefully compiled accounts from the day her brother returned to the Dawn Palace.

The most precise of them described "a young woman, staggeringly gorgeous despite her macabre appearance and the obvious perversion of her nature, a creature of the palest skin, the darkest hair, eyes of the deepest violet . . ."

The young woman Kegellen had found was pretty rather than beautiful, and her dark brown hair would have to be dyed. Otherwise, she seemed to fit the descriptions of Triste closely enough, although it was impossible to look at her, standing meekly just inside the door to the room, eyes downcast, hands clenched around the faded fabric of her dress, and imagine a vicious, murderous leach.

"Please sit down," Adare said. "Is there anything that you'd like? Anything that would make you more comfortable? Water? Wine?"

A slave hovered by the door, waiting to race to Kegellen's ample cellars, but the girl seemed not to have heard the question. She was staring at Adare in open amazement.

"You're here," she breathed. "Those eyes . . . You're her. The Emperor. Intarra's prophet."

"Mailly did not believe," Kegellen interjected, stepping forward gracefully, "that the Emperor of all Annur would have need of her."

"Do they hurt?" the young woman asked, touching the corner of her own eye absently. Then, as though just now realizing what it *meant* to be confronted by those blazing irises, she let out a tiny cry, bowed her head, and dropped unsteadily to her knees. "Forgive me, Your Radiance," she murmured to the bloodwood boards of Kegellen's perfectly polished floor.

Feeling sickened all over again, Adare crossed to the kneeling woman. "Please," she said, extending a hand. "Rise. We are alone here, among friends; there is no need for this formality."

Mailly stared at the hand, but made no move to take it. After a long pause, she rose unsteadily to her feet, slowly, as though she were lifting a great weight on her shoulders, then stood swaying, pale, her breath feeble between her lips.

She's got a case of the Weeping Sleep, poor thing, Kegellen had explained before the girl arrived. *She's fought it for more than a year, but she's losing now. Losing fast.*

"Please," Adare said again, gesturing to the empty chair. "How can we make you more comfortable?"

Mailly stared about her as though perplexed, then crossed to the chair, half sitting, half collapsing into it. When she finally looked back at Adare, she shook her head in disbelief.

"It's real," she murmured. "The Emperor and everything . . . it's all real."

Adare took a seat across the table, and Kegellen, after a murmured conversation with her servant, joined them as well. She had traded her white paper fan for a vermillion one, each of the wooden ribs stitched with fine gold thread. For a while, the only sound was its soft flutter.

"So," Adare began, choosing her words carefully. "I understand Kegellen has told you what . . . we need. And what I can offer in return."

The girl kept staring at her, her blue eyes wide as moons. *The wrong color,* Adare thought. *Though it shouldn't matter when this is done.*

"Mailly?" Adare asked.

Mailly took a shuddering breath, as though she'd been jolted from some waking dream. "Will it hurt?"

The simplicity of the question hit Adare like a slap. She had lived so long with misinformation, double meanings, and outright lies—her own and those of everyone around her—that it was easy to forget that some people just asked their questions, then believed the answers they were given. She felt a sudden knife-sharp desire to live in such a world, to cut away all the dizzying layers of her own schemes, to spend even a few days telling the naked truth, hearing it told.

She started to say *yes,* half opened her mouth, then shut it again slowly.

Do you love the truth enough, she wondered bleakly, *to let it kill Sanlitun?*

If Adare was going to free Triste, she needed this girl. Mailly had agreed to the meeting, but if she knew what was coming, if she understood the full truth of it, she could still walk away. She would, probably.

The sages and philosophers had a hundred metaphors for life: it was a path or a mountain, a voyage or a blooming flower, a harvest or a year with all the changing seasons. To Adare, however, life had always seemed like a simple series of trades. One woman could not have everything. She could sleep late only if she traded away the morning hours. Could trade an alliance with the Manjari for the goodwill of the Federated Cities. Trade a daughter's vengeance for a unified empire. Some trades were trivial, some so vast it was impossible to truly grasp the stakes, but there was always a trade. Pretending otherwise was folly.

When Adare didn't speak, Mailly turned to Kegellen. "Will it hurt?" she asked again.

The larger woman waved away the notion with her fan. "No. Of course not. A little sleepiness, a little trouble—"

"Yes," Adare said, cutting her off. "It will hurt horribly."

She prayed silently even as she spoke: *Please, please, Lady of Light, please let her still agree. Please say I have not traded away a chance to save my son.*

Slowly, Mailly turned back to her, lip quivering. She tried to take a half sip of her water, but was trembling too badly to hold the glass.

Kegellen pursed her lips. "Well. I suppose there may be *some* pain."

"First you will blister," Adare said, forcing out the awful truth. "On your palms and all over your face. They will form quickly and painfully. Then they will burn until they break. Then they will bleed. So will your eyes and throat."

Mailly was openly shaking now. "Is there no other way?" she asked. "No easier way."

There were, of course. Of the dozens of poisons couched inside il Tornja's lacquered box, *ayamaya*—the poison was named after the small Manjari spider from which it was extracted—was the worst. It was also the only one that would ravage the girl's face badly enough to obscure the truth, to hide who she really was. There was no point in leaving a body in Triste's cage if the guards could tell at a glance it wasn't Triste.

"No way that will work," Adare replied.

"It's possible," Kegellen suggested smoothly, "that your experience may be . . . more moderate than the Emperor suggests."

Adare shook her head again. She tried to imagine Mailly as an infant, but could see only Sanlitun's tiny features, his wide burning eyes. "It will not be moderate, but it will be short."

"How long," the girl asked, "from when I drink it until . . . until I die?"

"Half a day. Maybe a little more or less."

"And my little brother?" Mailly asked. "My mother? You'll take care of them? You'll give them the money you promised?"

Adare nodded. "I will."

"Because I won't be there," the girl said, shaking her head, scrubbing the tears from her cheeks. "To take care of them."

Kegellen stepped forward, placed a wide hand delicately on the girl's shoulder. "Death is never easy, child, but you are already dying. We are offering you a way to provide for the people you love, even after Ananshael has taken you."

"But fifty golden suns?" Mailly said, hope and disbelief warring in her eyes. "Fifty whole suns?"

The figure made Adare want to cry. Until that moment, she hadn't known the details of the offer Kegellen had made to the girl. She had just assumed she would have the coin—even in wartime, even with Annur falling to pieces all around her—to meet the girl's demands. A thousand suns, maybe? Five thousand? Vasta Dhati had required three fucking ships, after all. That the girl would sell herself for so little, that she should prize so highly fifty miserable suns—it seemed like a crime, somehow.

"We can afford more," Adare said.

"Mailly and I have spoken already," Kegellen interjected, "and agreed—"

"Five thousand suns."

Mailly stared, her skepticism carved across her face.

"Five *thousand* . . . For *what*? What do I have to do . . . for that?"

She was shaking again, caught in the grip of some imagined horror too vast to comprehend.

"Nothing more," Adare replied. "Just this."

Kegellen looked over at Adare, raised her brows, opened her mouth as though to object, then thought better of it and shaped her lips into a smile.

"Imagine your mother's delight," she purred. "Just think what this can do for your brother."

The woman sounded so sincere that Adare was genuinely surprised later, after Mailly had left, to find her shaking her head.

"Five thousand suns," Kegellen mused. She raised a beaded glass of Si'ite white to her lips, savored a sip, then set it down. "It strikes me as . . . excessive."

Adare stiffened. "It's not your coin."

"No!" Kegellen said, laughing. "It's most certainly not! Were it my coin, I would have bargained her down from fifty to twenty-five."

"You say that like you're proud of it."

"Pride," the woman replied, running her tongue over her lips. "It is a thing for women who have fought less hard than I have to survive."

Adare stared. "You're just as rich as I am. Maybe more, for all I know."

"And not, I assure you, Your Radiance, as a result of giving away whole piles of gold to dying girls for . . . continuing to die."

"It's for her *family*."

"I understand," Kegellen said, nodding.

"You told me yourself they're desperately poor. That you pulled Mailly straight out of some tavern in the Perfumed Quarter."

"They are," Kegellen said. "I did."

"Well, they can buy a mansion with five thousand suns. A small mansion with the slaves to take care of it."

"Another family in a mansion." Kegellen raised her brows sardonically. "How wonderful. And, oh yes, more slaves. I'm sure that they will be delighted with the gift, Your Radiance. As will the slaves."

Adare felt raked over by her own amazement.

"*This* is a mansion," she said, stabbing a finger straight up at the chandelier. "It must be worth at *least* five thousand suns. And I've stumbled over a dozen slaves since the moment I came in."

Kegellen nodded. "It is a comfortable life I have carved out for myself."

"And you don't think Mailly's family deserves the same?"

"I've found *deserve* to be an especially slippery word." She shrugged her shoulders. "Maybe it's just that my old brain is too slow."

"Do you think you deserve all this?"

Kegellen held her belly as she laughed, a long, rich sound. "Of course not. Everything I have, I stole!"

"Well, Mailly's family isn't stealing anything. I'm giving it to them."

"Such largesse," Kegellen murmured. "A truly imperial gesture."

Adare narrowed her eyes. "If you want to say something, say it."

"Forgive me, Your Radiance," the woman said, spreading her hands in supplication, "I meant no offense."

"Oh, fuck the offense, Kegellen."

The Unkillable Bitch watched her over the rim of her wine flute, then nodded. "It is only this: you can pull Mailly's mother out of the quarter, you can set her up as a merchant, a lady, a queen, but don't delude yourself. All gold comes from somewhere."

"Meaning what?"

"The coin you're so eager to give away was held by other hands before yours. For you to give it so freely, you had to seize it first."

24

"It's not a question of the plan," Gwenna said, shaking her head. "The plan's easy. We could come up with a *dozen* plans by the end of the night and still have time left over for drinking."

Talal frowned. "That might be overstating the case. Even without birds, Skarn is formidable. The cliffs alone—"

"Oh, I *know* it's fucking formidable, Talal," she snapped, exasperation getting the better of her. "It's not like I'm itching to spend an hour climbing ropes while my ass dangles in the wind. I'm just saying it's doable. It *would* be doable, at least, if we had a couple Wings of Kettral on our side, rather than this happy band of cowards and fools."

That last bit came out louder than she'd intended, but the cowards and fools were also deaf, at least by the standards of anyone who'd drunk from a slarn egg. They were all at the far end of the cavern, clustered close to the fire, and aside from the usual glances—part curious, part worried—no one seemed to have heard her outburst. *Except Manthe,* Gwenna amended. The woman was staring at her, a roasted gull wing still clutched in her hand, forgotten. She'd been through the Trial, of course, she and Hobb both. If she'd been paying attention, she'd heard Gwenna's estimation of her little rebellion, and she seemed always to be paying attention.

Let her, Gwenna thought. There was no point tiptoeing

around the basic fact: despite their various degrees of training, the washouts were a long way from being Kettral.

"They're not without skills," Talal said quietly.

"If you count *cowering* as a skill," Gwenna replied. "After that very first act of defiance, which got them absolutely decimated, they've done nothing but skulk around and try not to die."

"Not dying is a good first step."

"But it's not the *only* step. We came here to find out what in Hull's name was going on, and to get some birds. Well, now we know what's going on: Rallen, his yellowbloom trade, and his petty tyranny. Which means it's time to get the birds. The trouble is, we need a better team if we're going to have any kind of shot at it."

"No, we don't," Annick said.

The sniper didn't bother to look over; her eyes were trained on the two dozen men and women at the other end of the cave. They were all supposed to be working together, all on the same side, but Annick was watching them as if they were the enemy, as if she'd have to start putting arrows in eyeballs sometime in the next few heartbeats. At least she hadn't bothered to draw her bow. That always made Manthe twitchy, and Gwenna didn't need any more twitching out of the woman just at the moment.

"We are the Kettral here," Annick continued. "We'll take care of the mission."

Not for the first time, Gwenna considered it. The sniper's notion did have a certain appeal. After all, sheer numbers weren't everything, especially when your numbers didn't have any idea what in Hull's name they were doing. In theory it was better to have more bodies on the battlefield than the other guy, but when Gwenna ran her eyes over the bodies available—some barely older than her, two or three stooped enough to be grandparents—she didn't feel all that cheery about her prospects. A friend could put a blade in your back just as quickly as a foe, especially when the shit got thick. A fuckup on your own side could kill you just as dead as a stroke of tactical genius from the enemy.

"I'd love to take care of it ourselves," Gwenna replied finally, shaking her head, "but it won't work. The plan needs more people."

"Then change the plan."

"It's not that easy, Annick."

"Ease is irrelevant. Efficacy is what matters."

"Well, it won't be very effective either," Gwenna growled. "Not if the three of us go on our own."

Talal nodded slowly. "Even if we each took a bird—and when was the last time any of us flew a bird—we'd be easy targets for the pursuit. They'd have snipers down on the talons. We wouldn't."

"So we don't take the birds," Annick said. "We go after Rallen and his soldiers instead."

Gwenna stared at the sniper. "Three of us against all of them?"

"Why not?"

"Because three versus thirty or forty makes for shitty odds."

"Didn't slow us down with these," Annick replied, jerking her chin at the figures moving around the far end of the cave. "Rallen's troops aren't Kettral either."

Gwenna hesitated. The sniper was right. Rallen himself was an overstuffed bag of suet, even if he was a leach. He had the numbers, but if the story the rebels told was true, the bastards doing Rallen's fighting were culled from the same group of washouts as the semi-soldiers cowering in the cave.

"They're not the same," Talal pointed out. "Rallen handpicked his people. Don't forget, he was the Master of Cadets. He knows every single one. It's not a coincidence that there are no leaches down here. Or barely any fliers. He knew who he wanted, who would fight for him, who would fight *well*. Worse than that, when it came time to start killing, he would have gone after his most dangerous opponents first. The best soldiers are either fighting for him, or they're dead over on Qarsh. These are . . ."

He hesitated, probably searching for a delicate phrase to mask the ugly truth. "The leftovers."

"That is my point," Annick said, undeterred. "They have survived because of their incompetence, not in spite of it." For the first time she glanced over at Gwenna, blue eyes glacial. "And now you want to fight alongside them."

Gwenna started to respond, then stopped herself. It was sound thinking, all of it—Talal's analysis and Annick's objections. When she first set sail for the Islands, there had been no guarantee that she'd find anyone at all, certainly not anyone sympathetic to her own goals. She'd *expected*, from that first meeting with Kaden, that her own Wing would have to go it alone, that they'd have to find a way to face down whatever waited on the Islands with no help, no backup.

So what's the problem? she growled at herself.

The problem, once she'd wrestled it into a spot where she could get a good clear look at it, was simple: her goals had grown. When she wasn't paying attention—maybe when she was hauling her way through the waves, or lying in wait beneath the mangroves—she'd gone from wanting to find *one* bird and bring it out, to wanting something . . . larger. The Eyrie was destroyed, had destroyed itself, but the fact that there were still seven birds on the Islands, the fact that there were still Kettral-trained women and men holed up in a cave and willing to fight—it meant the Kettral weren't finished. Not fully. Not yet.

"They're the only choice," Gwenna said. "If we want the best shot at Rallen, we need more bodies." She paused, hunting for the words. "And after that, too . . ."

Talal watched her, his dark eyes grave. "We can't turn them into something they're not, Gwenna," he said.

"I know," she replied, chewing her lip. "I know."

"They failed," Annick said flatly. "They are failures."

Gwenna shook her head, remembering Quick Jak's relentless endurance on the long swim from Irsk to Skarn, remembering

Qora's stupid courage as she stood alone at the top of a flight of stone steps to face down Rallen's Black Guard.

"I'm just not ready to believe that the one thing means the other."

After the first three days trying to train some competence into the ragtag rebel band, Gwenna was starting to wonder if Annick hadn't been right all along. She'd gone into the task with a degree of optimism. Everyone hiding in the Hole had at least *some* training, and a handful, an entire Wing's worth, had made it all the way to the Trial before washing out. In theory, those few had just as much training as Gwenna herself.

The problem was, most of them were years, even decades past that training. Quick Jak was on the younger side, and he was six years older than Gwenna. Half the crew looked to be in their fourth decade, and one woman, Delka, must have been edging up on her fifties. She looked fit enough—evidently she enjoyed running laps around Arim's gentle coastline—but she hadn't held a bow or a blade in better than thirty years. Kettral instructors might have been able to polish the rust off all those half-forgotten skills, but the Kettral instructors were all dead, and so Gwenna found herself facing the woman, trying to keep her temper in check, to hide her desperation, as they worked through the basic shit all over again.

"Your high guard's too high," she said, knocking aside the woman's blade.

Delka nodded, shifted the weapon, then tried a tentative attack. Her hair—black and silver curls that she'd tied back with a leather thong—pulled free, flopping into her eyes. Gwenna shifted to avoid the thrust, not bothering to parry. Delka recovered, then lunged again, tried to brush back the hair with her free hand, failed, then lunged again. Again, Gwenna stepped aside.

"Stop announcing your attack," she growled.

The older woman cursed quietly. "I am, aren't I?" The lines on her face deepened around her frown, her narrowed eyes.

Gwenna nodded. "Half a dozen times over. You look where you're planning to thrust. You tighten your grip and pull back just before you lunge. You always plant your left foot, and just when you—"

She abandoned the words, slammed Delka's blade wide with her own, stepped smoothly into the gap, then buried a fist into her stomach. The older woman folded around the blow, groaning as she stepped back, raising a hand to surrender. Gwenna punched her in the jaw for that, then in the gut again, kept punching until the woman lashed out with her sword in a wide, blind arc. It was a shitty attack, but at least it was an attack.

"Don't stop fighting," Gwenna said. "Ever."

Delka was coughing, trying to seize her breath, but she kept her sword up this time, managing a passable approximation of a high guard. Gwenna worked through a couple of the standard gambits at half speed; Delka countered them warily.

"What was your specialty?" Gwenna asked. "As a cadet?"

"Flier." The woman shook her head. "You wouldn't believe it now, but thirty years ago, I was good with my blades, too."

"Why'd you quit?"

Delka stepped back, giving herself a little space, then smiled. That smile made Gwenna want to bury her head in her hands— it was a mother's smile, gentle and indulgent. It was hard to imagine Delka gutting a fish, let alone hacking a hole in a man's chest with a sword.

"I guess I was just . . . tired," the woman replied, shaking her head, brown eyes distant.

"Of course you were tired," Gwenna snapped. "That was the whole point. Everyone's tired. But you made it to the Hole. You just had to go *in*."

"I know," Delka said, shaking her head again. "I saw them do it. The others in my class. Huel, Tea, Anjin . . ."

Gwenna stopped her with a raised hand. "Anjin Serrata?"

Delka smiled that motherly smile again. "I hear they call him the Flea now." Then the smile flagged. "Or they did, anyway, before—"

"He wasn't here," Gwenna cut in. "Not when the Eyrie ripped itself apart. He was . . ." She hesitated. It wasn't as though this old woman was likely to go spreading state secrets. It wasn't even as though there was really a state with secrets left to spread. Still, it was best not to get in the habit of running her mouth. "He was somewhere else."

"Is he alive?" Delka asked. She still held her blade warily before her, still had her eyes on Gwenna, but she was seeing something else, something forgotten or lost.

"I don't know," Gwenna said quietly, lowering her sword. The woman's warmth, her openness, were disarming. "The last I saw him, he was going on a mission. A difficult mission."

"Then he's alive."

"I wouldn't be so sure."

Delka nodded. "You don't know him the way I did, Gwenna."

Gwenna stared. Then the words were half out of her mouth before she could call them back. "Were the two of you . . ."

The woman just laughed, a warm, rich sound. "Anjin and I? Oh, Gwenna. I was his friend. Would have been his flier, probably, if I'd passed the Trial. And maybe I did love him a little bit—young people love so easily." She shook her head. "No. Anjin's only love was . . ." She fluttered a hand, as though to wave away the memory. "Never mind. These aren't my tales to tell."

Gwenna watched her awhile in silence. The years had carved happy lines around Delka's eyes. She seemed to have none of Manthe's paranoia, none of Quick Jak's regret. She might have been sitting in a comfortable wooden chair looking out over the sea rather than standing on the damp cold stone of a cavern in the earth's gullet.

"Why are you here?" Gwenna asked finally. "The way the

others tell it, Rallen showed up on Arim and offered a second chance. Why did you take it?"

Delka's eyes went bleak. "And did you hear what happened, happened later, to those who *didn't* take his chance? It was fight or die."

Gwenna waved away the objection. "Sure, but from the way I hear it, a lot of people died. No one knew, then, that he'd be back to murder those who stayed behind. That wasn't why you joined up."

The woman hesitated, then shook her head. "No. I suppose it wasn't. I never liked Jakob Rallen—he was two classes younger than me. Never trusted him. But I didn't think he had this in him."

"Then why did you come back?" Gwenna pressed. "Why'd you take the second chance? It seems like you were happy over on Arim."

Delka watched her for a long time, so long Gwenna was starting to wonder if she'd actually asked the question or only intended to ask it. When the woman finally spoke, her voice was so soft Gwenna had to lean in to hear it.

"Most people, Gwenna, they get one life. For example, you're Kettral. You trained to be Kettral. Unless I've misjudged you, you'll die Kettral. Me, though—for the past thirty years I've been a wife; a mother, though my children both died young; a widow. . . . I had lived my life, lived it and loved it, made peace with the pains, framed a thousand thousand memories. It seemed all done except for the remembering. And then Rallen came and said that I could be nineteen again."

"You can't," Gwenna said, more harshly than she'd intended.

Delka just smiled. "I know that." She shrugged. "But can you blame me for wanting?"

The harm wasn't in the wanting, not for Delka, or Quick Jak, or Qora, or any of the rest of them. The harm was in the massive, seemingly unbridgeable gap between what they wanted, and what they were. Even those who'd made it most of the way through the training had deficits everywhere: they didn't know how to rig flickwicks in parallel; they couldn't remember the variations of a dead-man ambush; they botched even the most basic field repairs of their weapons. Several could recite whole chapters from Hendran's *Tactics,* a fact that Gwenna found encouraging until she realized that not a single one had real-world experience with any of those tactics.

The weapons skills were no exception. They could all swing a blade better than the average legionary. They could all hit the goat skull she propped up halfway down the cavern with either a flatbow or a longbow, but that wasn't saying much. A second-year cadet on the Islands—a kid of nine or ten—could do the same. And things got worse under pressure.

Gwenna had watched one of them, a stout, dark-skinned Bascan named Exte, put three arrows in a row through the skull's eye. She was starting to feel optimistic, even allowed him a slight nod. As he made to draw a fourth arrow, however, Annick stepped up behind him, then laid a bare blade against his throat. She didn't press hard, certainly not hard enough to draw blood, and she didn't shout. The words were mild, even quiet: "Now do it."

Exte swallowed hard, loosed the string, and missed the target by an arm's length.

"Again," the sniper said, pressing harder with the steel.

This time, Exte couldn't even nock the arrow to the string. Annick dismissed him silently, but the next shooter was trembling before he even raised the bow.

"It's not too late," Annick said after the first week was done.

She and Gwenna sat on the low stone shelf that had become both their bunk and command post. It afforded a good view out over the cavern. *At least it* would *be a good view,* Gwenna thought, *if there were anything encouraging to look at.* Talal was still finishing up with his part of the morning's training, drilling a dozen would-be warriors on the finer points of a windmill feint. Half of them couldn't do it at all, and the other half performed the sequence at something like quarter speed, their minds working through motions that Gwenna and the rest of the Kettral had entrusted to muscles years earlier.

"You can still change the plan," Annick went on. "We can do this ourselves. We *should* do this ourselves. This . . ." The sniper jerked her chin down the length of the cavern. "It's not working."

Gwenna cursed. "It's not, is it?"

The sniper glanced over at her. "Not your fault. If it were easier to become Kettral, there'd be more Kettral."

"I don't *need* them to be Kettral," Gwenna replied bleakly. "At least not yet. Not right away. I just need them to be *better*. To have just a few more skills . . ."

"Which ones?"

"I don't fucking know, Annick. The ones they're going to need."

"We could drill them all on bows for a week, make a little progress, then have the fight with Rallen come down to fists."

"Fists?" Gwenna snorted. "You'd be just as screwed as they are."

"No," Annick said, voice icy. "I would not."

Gwenna turned on the smaller woman. Annick might be death with her bow, but she couldn't weigh more than a hundred and ten pounds soaking wet.

"When's the last time you fought bare-handed?"

"In the Kwihna Saapi," the sniper reminded her.

Gwenna nodded slowly, the memory of the Urghul torment rolling over her like a storm cloud. She'd killed four men in the short time that Long Fist had kept them all prisoner, four Annurian legionaries. All of them had been taller and larger than her, probably stronger, too. Not that that had helped. She had murdered them all, murdered them in a matter of heartbeats. So had Annick, for that matter, and Annick wasn't even that *good* at bare-hand fighting.

Gwenna stared at the sniper so long that Annick finally glanced over.

"What?"

"The skills don't matter," Gwenna said slowly.

Annick frowned. "Of course they matter."

"Sure," Gwenna said, waving the objection away impatiently. "In an absolute sense, it all matters. Learning more sword forms is better. Learning more complicated demo rigs is better. Learning to shoot accurately from a moving deck, or a moving bird, or a moving horse, it's *all* better. . . ."

"Obviously. That's why we train."

"No," Gwenna said, shaking her head vigorously. "It's not. Not the only reason, at least. Not even the most important reason." The sniper started to respond, but Gwenna raised a hand, forestalling the smaller woman. "Think back to the men you killed during the Kwihna Saapi. What did you do to beat them?"

Annick frowned. "Different moves in each case."

"Yes, fine. But my point is that the moves were . . . secondary. The guys I killed—they were dead before I did a 'Kent-kissing thing. They looked at me, saw a woman in Kettral blacks, and they just . . . folded inside. I could see it, could see the hopelessness seep into their eyes. They fought—tried to, at least—but you can't fight when you don't think you can win. . . ."

She trailed off, wondering if she was remembering those battles clearly. She could hear the screaming of the Urghul, could feel the heat of the sacrificial fires, could smell the piss of the poor bastards she was facing down, see the hopelessness scribbled across their faces. She could see *all* of it, but was she reading it right?

The sniper studied her for a long time.

"And you think that's what's wrong with *them*," she said

finally, tossing her head toward the men and women at the other end of the cave. "That they don't think they can win."

"Of *course* they don't. That's why they're cowering down here, shitting in dark corners and being eaten by slarn."

"There is a massive logistical and supply asymmetry between Rallen's troops and—"

"I *know* that, Annick. But there's always *some* sort of asymmetry. The other guys always have more swords, or higher walls, or better intel, or whatever. When's the last time you studied a battle between perfectly balanced forces? The point is, you can fight *through* all sorts of tactical and strategic imbalances. You can win. But you're not going to *win* if you don't think winning is possible."

The sniper picked at her bowstring with an idle finger, sounding that same note over and over and over. "All right. The psychological element is important. Hendran writes about it more than everything else combined. But a confident blacksmith is still just a blacksmith. The mind is not everything."

"We don't need everything," Gwenna said. "We need *enough*. And they're not blacksmiths. They already *have* Kettral training, *years* of it, in most cases. They just need to believe they can use it."

"And what's your plan for getting them to believe?"

Gwenna blew out a long, unhappy breath, wondering suddenly if she was wrong, if she'd gone crazy. "It's going to be tricky."

Annick shrugged. "It's all tricky."

"And it's going to get some of them killed. Maybe a lot of them."

The sniper shook her head. "I thought the point was to toughen them up *before* sending them out to die."

"We're not sending them out," Gwenna replied, smiling grimly. "We're sending them *down*."

*

"No," Manthe hissed, shaking her head so hard Gwenna wondered how it stayed attached to her neck. "Are you insane? Absolutely *not*."

"No one's asking *you* to do it," Gwenna pointed out. "The two of you have already been through the Trial. You passed. Remember?"

Manthe just shuddered, her eyes distant, focused on some remembered horror. Gwenna had the feeling she could reach out and knock the woman over with a gentle push. She could have, that was, if Hobb wasn't standing there, looming over Gwenna, a protective arm around his wife's shoulders. Since that first showdown in the cavern, neither of the two Kettral had challenged Gwenna again. When she decided to go scouting, she went scouting. When her Wing started trying to train the rebels, Manthe and Hobb stayed out of the way, watching the long sessions of archery and bladework with cautious, guarded looks.

Early on, Gwenna had tried to enlist them. "Feel free to help," she'd suggested. "Even after spending the last decade on Arim, you've got more experience than the rest of this lot."

"We have more experience than *you*," Hobb had pointed out, his voice hard.

Gwenna had managed not to hit him. She didn't even retort. She just spread her arms, a gesture she hoped looked welcoming. "As I said, I could use your help getting the others up to speed."

Manthe had only glared at her, eyes bright, almost feral behind her stringy, graying hair.

"I don't think so," Hobb had replied slowly. "You wanted to run this show. You run it."

Those had been their last words on the matter.

It was just as well, Gwenna concluded, when her anger finally cooled. The older Kettral had gone through the training, had passed the Trial, had even flown actual missions, but they were broken, shattered. Hobb was too protective of his wife, and Manthe saw monsters in every shadow, heard death and disaster on every breath of air eddying through the cavern. The rebels needed backbone more than they did bladework, and they weren't likely to get it from Manthe and Hobb. The two veterans didn't go anywhere—there wasn't anywhere to go—but they kept to their corner of the cave, to their own grimy blankets. They watched constantly, dark eyes flickering with the firelight, but they had made no move to interfere. Until now.

"You cannot *do* this," Manthe hissed again, half raising a clawed hand, as though to ward off a physical attack.

"I can," Gwenna said, "and I'm going to. I already said you don't need to be part of it."

"It's not about us," Hobb said. He gestured the length of the cavern, to where the would-be soldiers were paired up, sparring. "These kids . . ."

"They're not kids," Gwenna said. "Every one of them is older than I am. A few of them are older than *you*."

"Doesn't matter," Hobb insisted, jaw tight. "They're not ready."

"They'd be a lot *more* ready, you idiot," Gwenna snapped, "if you quit telling them they're not."

The man stared at her with open contempt. "Listen to yourself. You lucked through the Trial. You managed to survive barely a year off the Islands—a year in which half your Wing *died*—and you come back thinking you're Kettral. Thinking you know the first thing about what it is to be a soldier. What it takes."

"I'll tell you one thing I know," Gwenna shot back. "Until we got here, you were fucking hiding. You were losing."

"There is a difference," Manthe snarled, still clutching her husband's arm as she leaned forward, "between courage and recklessness."

"And which one is it when you hide in a cave letting your people get killed by slarn?"

"We are *assessing*," the woman hissed. "There is *intelligence. . . .*"

"We gathered more intelligence in the last week," Gwenna snapped, cutting her off, "than you did in all the months since Rallen took over. At some point you have to stop assessing and start killing people."

Manthe stared at Gwenna, thin lips parted in disbelief. Gwenna could hear her panting, her heartbeat galloping along just at the edge of panic. Then she turned to her husband, voice low and beseeching. "She's going to get us killed, Hobb. She's crazy, and it's going to kill us all."

Hobb grimaced, then shifted slightly in her clutches. *Trying to keep his sword hand clear,* Gwenna observed. Talal and Annick were working with the washouts at the other end of the cave, the leach murmuring quiet advice, Annick smacking knuckles and elbows with the flat of her blade to emphasize the price of error. Gwenna thought she could kill Hobb in a fair fight, but that might be exactly the recklessness Manthe was ranting on about. The man had the height, the reach, and judging from the muscle corded in his arms, the strength. *Save the fight for Rallen,* Gwenna reminded herself. *This is not a risk you need to take.*

"Look," she said, holding her palms up. "All I want is to beat Rallen and those sons of bitches he has flying for him. To do that, we need every advantage, and you both know that the Trial confers major advantages. You've been bitten by the slarn and eaten the egg. You know what it does to you."

Hobb glanced over at his wife. Her eyes were wide as lamps and her lips twitched silently.

Gwenna ransacked her memory for recollections of the Flea, for that quiet voice that always rode the edge between confidence and indifference. "I'm not asking permission," she said. "This is happening." It didn't come out sounding like the Flea, but it would have to do. Hobb wasn't going for his blades, at least. "I told you first," she continued quietly, "as a courtesy. You're Kettral, and I thought you might want to help."

Manthe shook her head frantically. Hobb looked down at her for a long time, then put an arm around her shoulders, smoothed her hair back from her furrowed brow. The gesture was incongruously soft, private, as though they were alone somewhere, standing on the veranda of a house, maybe, or in front of a quietly crackling fire. Gwenna had been ready to fight Hobb, even to kill him, but the sudden and unexpected intimacy caught her off guard.

"I could use your help," she said awkwardly.

Hobb kept his arm around his wife, but when he met Gwenna's eyes again, his voice was hard. "Something wrong with your hearing?" he growled. "I already told you: no."

Gwenna stared at him a moment, then shook her head. "Then stay out of the fucking way."

25

Every day, as they nudged their horses forward through the mossy trunks of the old trees, Valyn swore to himself that it was over, that he was finished, that when the sun's heat dropped beneath the western peaks he would shackle his sick lust, wrap himself in bison hide, close his ruined eyes, and sleep. Almost every night, he failed.

Traveling with Huutsuu was like standing chest-deep in the surf as a hurricane approached; between the swells he could keep his feet, hold his head above water, breathe freely, but when the waves came there was no way to avoid the whole oceanic weight tugging him under, under and out, away from familiar footing, far from any shore he might hope to recognize. Half the time he thought that she would drag him down and kill him. That first night, for instance, when she finally pulled the knife free of his chest. Or the second night, when they fucked so close to the fire that the heat blistered his skin. Or the third, or the fourth . . .

Sometimes he thought *he* would be the one to kill *her,* even that he *had* killed her. One night, as the wind scythed down off the mountains, cutting through the rough trunks of the trees, he wrapped a leather belt around her neck, dragging it tighter and tighter as she shuddered, arched her back, choked out a moan, then went suddenly slack. She was only out for heartbeats. Valyn remembered his training well enough to know the lack of air wasn't going to kill her unless he kept going, kept pulling, and yet he discovered, horrified, that there was a part of him that *wanted* to keep going, wanted to break her, destroy her.

Or to have her destroy him. Hurting or being hurt, killing or being killed—it was all part of the same desperate currency, the same cold, heavy coin.

Most nights he half hoped she would just finish it, finish him. It would be a relief to be cut free finally from the tatters of his own life, a release, and for some reason that release seemed to lie through Huutsuu. The Kettral had offered him a path—a straight road of discipline and sacrifice—but he had strayed from that path. His only road now, the only way through the wilderness, was one of violence and pain, but even as he walked it, a faint voice whispered in the back of his brain, a human voice trapped inside the beast he had become, asking the same questions over and over: *What kind of man does this? What kind of man* enjoys *it? What have you become, Valyn hui'Malkeenian? What have you made yourself into?*

When he let the belt drop, Huutsuu would lie corpse-still and warm a long time, reeking of blood, and sex, and leather, then shudder into life all over again, her strong hands seizing him, twisting, scratching her demands into his ravaged skin, and he would grind out that questioning voice like a fire's last ember.

Sometimes—when her knife cut too deep, when he bent her arm behind her to the point of breaking—he could see. It was the same sight that came with mortal violence, that precise etching of darkness on darkness, Hull's twisted vision, a rush every bit as strong, as overwhelming, as the final convulsions of their sex. Just as fleeting. When the gravest danger passed, so did the engraved blackness of his non-sight, leaving him in darkness once more, with only Huutsuu's growling voice to guide him.

The Urghul woman knew her work. She understood just where to put a blade to hurt a man without crippling him, without killing him. When she bit his neck, her teeth closed just wide of the artery throbbing beneath the skin. Still, without the slarn's strength in his blood, Valyn's wounds would have left him unable to travel most days. As it was, he found himself limping to the horse each morning, fire from a dozen cuts blazing over his skin as he hauled himself into the saddle. That Huutsuu, likewise, managed to press ahead spoke volumes of her acquaintance with pain. Valyn could remember her mocking him back on the steppe when they first met, mocking him and the rest of his Wing for their softness. He had placed little stock in the words then. Now, at last, he understood; the woman did not simply endure her pain, she wore it like a cloak of fine cloth. She was a savage, worse than savage—but she lived her faith.

For all the carnal fury of the nights, the long, chill summer days riding north and west were mostly given over to silence. Valyn's horse followed a few paces behind Huutsuu's, and yet they barely spoke. The animal lust that he smelled pouring off her in the night vanished when the sun rose, replaced with a granitic resolve, a fixed and unwavering purpose. If she shared any of his confusion, his regret, his turmoil and shame, he couldn't hear it in her even breathing or steady heartbeat, couldn't smell it on her skin. Beneath the bright eye of the sun, they were warriors going to do the work of warriors, nothing more.

"You understand," Valyn said to her one day when he grew tired of listening to the horses' hooves on the stone, to the steady swish of their tails, to the breathing of the Urghul all around him, "that if we ever find the Flea, he'll probably kill us all."

"Not all," Huutsuu replied. "It takes time to kill thirty warriors, time I will use to speak."

"Fine. It will still mean buying that time with the lives of your warriors."

"So there will be a price." She shrugged, leather sliding over skin. "Only a fool believes a thing of value will be laid in her lap with no reckoning." He could feel her eyes on him. "Still.

Your presence here may slow this Flea. He may pause before killing."

"Maybe," Valyn conceded. "Probably not. Kettral tend to come in fast and brutal. There's not a lot of exchanging names or studying faces."

Huutsuu shrugged again. "Then women and men will bleed." She smelled almost eager.

Halfway between midnight and dawn, Hendran wrote, *most people are either sleeping, fucking, or drunk. It's a good time to attack.*

It was old advice, but sound, and the Flea took it, hitting the small Urghul camp sometime between midnight and dawn. Huutsuu had posted guards, but guards were little use against men and women trained to move silently through the dark, whose own senses were heightened beyond all normal proportion by the eggs of the slarn. Valyn himself was asleep, shivering through nightmare after nightmare, when a starshatter exploded fifty paces distant, ripping him from his dreams.

His eyes slammed open at the sound. An old reflex—useless now, stupid, just opening a door from darkness into darkness. He extended a tentative hand, groping in the black until he brushed the rough bark of the hemlock's trunk. He'd climbed a dozen feet into the fork of the old tree just after nightfall, wedged himself there before falling asleep. It was hardly the strongest defensive position, but it was what he had. The Urghul camp would have been warmer, but he had no intention of sleeping among the horsemen—Huutsuu might kill him, but he didn't intend to offer himself up to the other bastards, or to the Flea, if the Wing leader finally came calling. Outside the camp, he'd at least be able to make a fight of it. Now, it seemed, the decision had saved his life.

The Urghul were shouting, screaming, and Valyn could smell blood in the air, thick, and hot, and wet, as he dropped out of the tree, landed awkwardly, then straightened up. He half drew one of the axes at his belt, then let it be. If he'd wanted to stay alive, he could have stayed in the fucking tree. The whole point in coming all this way was to try to make contact with the Flea. If it didn't work, well then, he would die.

"Anjin Serrata," he called out, moving too slowly through the low branches, shielding his face with his hands. It was the first time he'd ever used the Flea's real name. He couldn't say why he thought to speak it now. "Anjin Serrata!" he shouted again, pitching his voice to carry above the screams of the injured and the dying. The starshatter had done its vicious work, shredding limbs as it had broken apart the silence, leaving those Urghul who had gathered too close to the dying embers of the fire broken, burning, or both. The Flea's Wing was already moving among them, cutting hamstrings and slitting throats before anyone had a chance to regroup or recover.

Valyn couldn't see them, of course, but he could hear steel parting flesh, the grinding of blade against bone, the reluctant sucking sound when the weapon was wrenched free. He could smell the Flea, his leather and determination, and Sigrid sa'Karnya, his leach, who might have bathed in lavender and jasmine that very day. Newt was there, too—pitch, and lice, and nitre. Valyn could hear him muttering to himself, quiet but insistent, as he went about his work. All of the Flea's people were quiet.

Huutsuu, on the other hand, was bellowing orders in her strange, musical tongue. Like Valyn and a dozen others, she had made her bed outside the range of the fire. The decision had spared her the ravages of the starshatter, but she wasn't likely to stay alive if she kept shouting.

Valyn tried to redouble his pace, stepped into a hole—some sort of burrow, maybe—cursed as he twisted his knee, half fell, caught himself on an outstretched hand, and forced himself up again, lunging forward in spite of the branches stabbing at his face and arms.

"Anjin Serrata," he called out again. "Sigrid sa'Karnya."

He started to say more, then stopped himself. Any plea or demand would only muddy the message. Either the names would be enough, or nothing would. This time, if only for a moment, the sounds of violence paused.

"Valyn," the Flea said finally. "Newt said he smelled you. I didn't believe him."

Nearly half of Huutsuu's Urghul were dead or dying, and the man didn't even sound winded.

"We need your help," Valyn said.

He was still a dozen paces from the guttering fire; close enough to take an arrow in the chest, but not close enough to fight. It would have to do. Unless the Flea had gone horribly soft, one of the three Kettral would have taken up a position just outside the fray, would be picking shots with a shortbow while the other two managed the close work. Even as Valyn spoke, someone—probably Newt—would be training an arrow on his chest. His flesh felt hot beneath his blacks. It itched, as though eager for the steel to strike, to punch past his breastbone and into his heart.

The memory of that night in Assare burned. Seared across his mind's unblinded eye, the whole disaster played out again: the dead city of stone, acrid smoke filling the air, Gwenna's deafening explosives, the Flea's Wing surrounding them, and Blackfeather Finn, the best sniper on the Islands, stumbling into the crumbling chamber with a Skullsworn knife in his chest.

That was the moment, Valyn thought again. *That was the moment I lost it.*

He had thought he was finally ready to face the Flea again, to put right what had gone wrong in Assare. Now, though, locked inside his own private darkness, one arm outstretched helplessly before him, the whole notion seemed so desperately stupid. He hadn't known the right words then, and, for all he had rehearsed this moment over and over, he didn't know them now. Worse, the stench of blood on the air had woken something inside him, something vicious and bestial, the same creature that Huutsuu dragged from him each night, an animal eagerness indifferent to all negotiation, whispering over and over the same silent syllable: *Kill. Kill. Kill them all.*

"Listen," he said again, choking back his own savagery. "Just listen."

The Flea's voice was hard in the darkness. "You have five heartbeats."

Valyn counted two before he found his voice. "They want to kill Balendin. These warriors want to kill Balendin."

Over by the fire, someone was groaning, the same incomprehensible Urghul word over and over. The sick crack of steel against skull cut it abruptly short. Piss mingled with the blood and smoke and hemlock.

"If they want to kill the leach," the Flea asked quietly, "what are they doing here? He's three days to the north, or he was three days ago."

"They are looking for you."

The silence was cold as winter's first ice; at any moment it would break, and people would start dying all over again. Valyn ached to reach for the axes hanging from his belt. His empty hands hungered for their weight. Some part of him buried deep inside his brain was thirsty for the blood; it hardly mattered whose. The last time he'd fought the Flea, he'd lost, but he was stronger now, and faster, so much faster. For a moment the scene around the fire resolved in his mind's darkness: the other Wing leader back-to-back with Sigrid, all four of their blades drawn and dripping, the Urghul scattered like dolls. One of the nomads had fallen into the fire's last embers. Valyn's stomach moved at the scent of the burning flesh; he couldn't say if he was nauseated or hungry. Then the vision was gone, scrubbed away.

In the vertigo of darkness, he could hear his body's song, keening to the drumming of his blood: *Kill. Kill. Kill.* He started to reach for his axes, then, hands twisted into fists, he checked himself again.

"Looking for us why?" the Flea asked warily.

"An alliance. They can't kill Balendin alone. They need Kettral."

"Looks like they've got you."

Valyn's pulse flared. Fire raged beneath his skin. "I'm not Kettral."

"It's not always up to a man," the Flea replied quietly, "what he is, and what he's not. Some things you don't get to choose." Valyn could hear him shift, could imagine him scanning the darkness between the trees. "Who leads here?"

Huutsuu was somewhere off to Valyn's right, still hidden. She smelled wary but ready.

"I do," she replied after a moment.

"Drop your bow and blades. Tell your warriors to do the same."

"You are the ones surrounded," Huutsuu observed. "In the open."

It was true enough. The Flea's entire attack was predicated on speed, surprise. To succeed, even to *survive,* he needed to be out of that tiny clearing before the Urghul fully awoke, before they could bring their numbers to bear. The Wing leader had taken a grave risk in pausing halfway through the assault. Even as they spoke, Valyn could hear the Urghul—those who had slept farther off from the fire—moving in darkness, readying their bows.

"I wouldn't quite say surrounded," the Flea replied. "There's a hole in your net there, and there, and there. We killed your guards to the north, so that's a way out as well." He paused to let the point sink in. "But you can't see that, can you? It's a new moon. You can't see anything at all."

And that was the crux of the matter. The stars splattered across the northern sky would be plenty of light for the Flea and his Wing. They could move through the trees as though it were full day, killing Urghul who were almost as blind as Valyn himself.

"I can hear you," Huutsuu replied. "So can my warriors. If we put enough arrows in the air, you'll die."

"Not much of a way to open a parley," the Flea replied wearily. "But you're welcome to try it."

It seemed a foolish taunt, an insane gambit, until Valyn realized that what he'd seen in that moment of darksight didn't coincide with the voice. He inhaled deeply. Sigrid and the Flea were at the far side of the clearing now, well wide of the source of the Wing leader's voice when he spoke. *A kenning,* Valyn realized. *The leach is throwing his voice.* He could hear Huutsuu moving forward, searching for better light maybe, or just a better position if it all went to shit. She was being quiet, but not nearly quiet enough.

"Huutsuu," he said. "Stand down. I know this man and his team. I've seen what they can do. If you want to make peace, do as he says."

"I would have a peace between partners, not between masters and unarmed slaves."

"Don't have much interest in slaves," the Flea replied. "I came to kill, so the fact that I'm not killing is a pretty good hint I'm willing to talk. I'm getting tired of arguing, though, and my back's getting itchy between the shoulder blades, so I'll say it one more time: drop your bows, drop your blades, and then we can decide who else needs to die and who maybe ought to stay alive."

Huutsuu's shame and rage were so thick Valyn could taste them. The Flea's casual demands, his obvious indifference to whatever threat she posed, cut more deeply than any knife. Her blade slid from its sheath, steel whispering against leather. She reeked of readiness.

"Do you want Balendin dead, Huutsuu?" Valyn demanded. "Or do you want to destroy that chance right now, here, for the sake of a meaningless fight in the forest?"

In truth, his own hands were still trembling to grasp the hafts of his axes. His body ached to attack, to let out a roar, then come out of the trees swinging. Whether he took the side of the Urghul or the Kettral hardly seemed to matter. Fighting brought that awful sight, and he had lived inside the darkness for so long. He started speaking, then kept going, because his own words were the only wall he could build to hold back the violence clawing inside of him.

"Even if you win, you lose. You came here to find the Flea. What are you going to do if you actually manage to kill him? Go back to the front? Try to take down Balendin, fail, spend your last day screaming as he opens your chest and holds up your beating heart?"

"I have no fear of that leach," Huutsuu replied, voice tight. "Not of him or of his pain."

Valyn ground his teeth. "I don't know what they say on the steppe when a woman dies in a hopeless, pointless fight, but back on the Islands we called it stupid. Useless. You don't need to go looking for pain; the pain finds you."

Huutsuu didn't respond. The other Urghul were moving carefully in the woods beyond the clearing. None of them would have understood the exchange, but that hardly mattered. The challenge in Huutsuu's voice was obvious. The bodies of the dead scattered around the fire were fucking obvious. Even cloaked in the darkness, even with Sigrid throwing his voice, the Flea was taking a risk by waiting, by listening, by letting the Urghul wake up fully, get their bearings.

Then a naked blade clattered against gnarled roots in the clearing—Huutsuu's weapon, Valyn realized. A moment later, her belt knife followed, then her bow. She barked something curt in her own language.

There was a long, tense pause. Then, from the far side of the clearing, one of the Urghul—a man—responded angrily, defiantly, a string of quick syllables rising with his rage. Before Huutsuu could respond, the words twisted into a long, guttural moan.

"Sorry," the Flea said, not sounding sorry at all. "I don't understand your language, but he didn't seem eager to talk."

"He was a fool," Huutsuu replied curtly.

"How many more fools are there?"

As though they'd heard the taunt, two *ksaabe* launched themselves howling from the trees, charging blindly at the spot where the Flea wasn't. Newt's bowstring hummed once, and then, after a pause, twice. He wasn't anywhere near as fast as Annick, but he was fast enough. The bodies tumbled to the dirt, a dozen paces apart by the sound of it.

Then Huutsuu stepped into the clearing. *"Piat!"* she spat. Valyn didn't know the word, but the intent was plenty clear. "Enough!" she went on, switching languages, turning slowly in place, making her body an offering to the hidden Kettral. "This quarrel can do nothing but brighten the heart of the leach we hope to kill. We will sheathe our swords and speak as equals."

"Great," the Flea replied. "We'll talk when your swords are sheathed and you're all out here in the light. That means you, too, Valyn."

"There is no light," Huutsuu said. "The fire is long dead."

Before she had finished speaking, however, there was a great inrushing of air, a roar like a house-high wave crashing on a rocky shore miles distant, and then the heat of a large blaze played over Valyn's face and chest, warm even through the layers of wool and leather.

"There's the fire," the Flea said. "Get warm. See to your dead. When you're ready, we'll talk."

"And you?" Huutsuu asked warily.

"I'm here," the Flea said. Valyn could hear him approaching the newly kindled blaze.

"And the others? Your sniper? Your leach?"

"I think they'll stay in the trees," the Flea replied. "Just in case the talking doesn't go so well."

*

It took the better part of the night for the surviving Urghul to collect the bodies, wash them in the small stream winding through the trees off east, then carry them back to the fire's verge. When they were laid out on the ground, Huutsuu spoke over them, her voice low and hypnotic, halfway between chanting and prayer. When she was finally finished, Valyn could smell the wet wind that always gusted up just before dawn. Rather than letting the fire burn down, the Urghul heaped it higher. There were no graveyards on the steppe; scavengers would just dig up the buried bodies. Instead, the Urghul dead were given to the flame.

The scent of burning flesh was thick, cloying, foul as the smoke that had filled the air of Andt-Kyl for days after the battle. Valyn stood a few paces from the fire, trying to keep his face still, his hands from shaking at the memory. Hundreds had burned alive in the small town, loggers and Urghul alike, trapped inside log buildings or pinned beneath flaming barricades. The hissing and steaming of the green branches blazing in front of him sounded like screaming.

Not screaming, he told himself over and over. *They're dead. The fire can't hurt them.*

Then one of the *taabe* stepped forward.

Valyn could hear him chanting at the very edge of the fire. The words were raw with grief. Then the man bellowed his defiance into the huge night, and Valyn heard the pyre shift, collapsing in on itself in a shower of sparks as something was pulled free. The stench of burning flesh grew suddenly stronger, sharper.

The Flea had been silent throughout the ceremony, but he spoke now.

"We're going to have a tough time killing Balendin if none of your men can hold their blades."

Huutsuu stank of contempt. "One of the warriors we just burned was Moahe's brother. The Coward's God has taken him to a place where he cannot feel pain, and so Moahe holds the burning brand for him. He feels the pain for his brother, who has gone beyond all feeling."

The Flea grunted, but fell silent.

After that first cry, the *taabe* was silent. Valyn tried to imagine it, to understand how it might feel to clutch a smoldering log in his hands as the skin blistered, cracked, then sloughed away. *Clean.* The word came unbidden to his mind, shocking as a knife in the eye. *The burning is clean. The pain is clean.* It was an awful thought, but one he could not deny. Somewhere in the wide, cold northern forests he had become like these creatures, bowing before the most brutal of gods, as though life's beauty had been utterly burned out of him, leaving only anger, hunger.

Finally it was over. Valyn heard the crash of the log landing back in the fire, then the sound of a body collapsing to the dirt.

Huutsuu said something in Urghul—Valyn thought he caught the words for *warrior* and *hand* before hearing her turn slowly to face the Flea. "Now," she said, "we will talk. Balendin—"

"Before we get to Balendin," the Flea said, his voice quiet but sharp, slicing right through Huutsuu's own, "Valyn and I have one or two questions to work out. The last time I saw him, one of my people died."

Valyn nodded, but didn't move. He was close enough to the fire for the Flea to see him. That would have to be enough.

"Ask your questions."

"What happened in Andt-Kyl?"

"Laith died. Gwenna and Talal managed to blunt Balendin's attack before Adare and her pet general arrived to finish the fight."

"I meant what happened to you."

Valyn took a long breath before answering. "I tried to kill il Tornja. Adare put a knife in my side and then the bastard blinded me."

"You're carrying a lot of weapons for someone who can't see."

It wasn't a question, and so Valyn didn't reply.

The Flea sighed. "You went after il Tornja because you think he killed your father."

"I *know* he did," Valyn growled. "Adare told me herself. She admitted it."

"All right," the Flea said. "He killed your father." He didn't sound surprised. "So you decided to join up with the Urghul?"

"He didn't join us," Huutsuu said.

"He's here," the Flea pointed out. "You're here. I'm looking at both of you."

"We ran into each other," Valyn said. "More than a week back. She told me there was a Kettral Wing attacking her people, that she wanted to find you, to join up in the fight against Balendin. I agreed."

"I get the feeling there's a little more to the story."

"There's always more to the story."

The Flea snorted. "That's truth. Fine. Balendin. We'd all love to see the bastard dead. Last time I checked—and I check pretty often—he was still alive. How's our own budding friendship going to change that?"

Huutsuu shifted beside the fire. "You know him. You know where he is weak. Tell us this, and we will kill him."

To Valyn's surprise, the Flea chuckled. "That's the plan? Not long on details, is it?"

"These details," Huutsuu replied coolly, "will depend on what you tell us of his weaknesses."

"Well, that's the trouble," the Flea said. The Wing leader paused to suck loudly at something stuck in his teeth. After a moment he spat into the fire, then continued. "If Balendin has a weakness, I don't know it. The kid was dangerous back on the Islands, but that was nothing compared to what he can do now. If you've been anywhere in the north or west, you've seen it."

When Huutsuu responded, her voice was caught between hatred and grudging awe. "I saw him hold two bridges in the air while hundreds of horsemen rode across. I saw him burn a palisade of half a mile to ash. We have leaches among our people, but not like this."

"His well—" the Flea began.

"Is us," Valyn said, the words heavy on his tongue. "Balendin's an emotion leach. He feeds off of us, off anyone who feels anything about him."

For a while no one spoke. The fire snapped into the blackness. The Urghul had taken up wary positions almost directly across the fire from the Flea, though they couldn't understand the conversation taking place.

"Sig," the Flea said finally. "Newt. Might be you can join us after all. Looks like we already killed everyone who needs killing."

The two Kettral had flanked the fire moments after the fight. Valyn could smell them—the Aphorist as muddy and filthy as Sigrid was inexplicably clean. When Sigrid stepped into the clearing behind him, he could hear the mutters of surprise, could taste confusion on the cold air. He could imagine the Urghul staring, as though an atrep's wife had stepped out of the trees in her full finery, condescending to walk among them.

Valyn had been a boy of nine when he first met Sigrid—if "met" was the right word. He'd spent most of the day running navigation drills down in the mangrove swamps off the west coast of Shirrin, covered in mud and leeches most of the time, bruised everywhere from clambering over the twisted roots. When he finally got back to Qarsh just before dusk, he was wiped, aching for a bowl of fish broth and a few hours passed out in his bunk. Just as he was approaching the mess hall, however, a group of cadets came racing through the compound.

"Come on," Ha Lin called, seizing Valyn by the arm of his soaked blacks.

"Come on *where*?" he'd protested.

"The Flea's Wing is fighting in the ring—part of it is, at least."

The *part,* as it turned out, was a single soldier: Sigrid sa'Karnya. It wasn't all that odd for the vets to take a turn sparring, but the Flea wasn't just another vet, nor were the men and women who flew with him. The man had been a legend, even back then, and he and his Wing were out flying missions most weeks of the year. Valyn never got a straight answer about what Sigrid was doing in the ring that day, but he never forgot the fight.

The woman wore blacks, but unlike the serviceable wool favored by the rest of the Kettral, Sigrid's clothes were immaculately tailored from fine silk. They were fighting clothes, but someone had cut and stitched them so they hugged and hung on her in the same way as the elaborate gowns Valyn remembered from the women in the Dawn Palace. And Sigrid moved like those women, at least partly; her grace was a hybrid of courtesan and killer. Valyn had seen pale-skinned women before, both in Annur and on the Islands, but he'd never witnessed anything like this golden-haired leach, who stepped into the ring with all the scorn of a goddess deigning to set foot upon the earth.

The Flea had been in the rapidly gathering crowd that day. He'd looked tired and a little impatient, not at all the way a legend was supposed to look. The rest of his Wing seemed more enthusiastic. Blackfeather Finn was reclining with his boots up, gesturing to the ring and chatting expansively with some other vets. Chi Hoai Mi was drunk, sloshing around her wooden cup as she argued with anyone who would listen. The hideously ugly demolitions man that people called the Aphorist was even taking bets, stacking and sliding small piles of coin on the rough stone that formed the circumference of the fighting space as he dispensed his incomprehensible wisdom.

"Who's she fighting?" Laith asked, standing on his toes to try to see above the crowd.

"Felp's Wing," someone replied.

Valyn knew the name vaguely—the woman was in her thirties. Evidently she flew a lot of missions into Manjari territory.

"*Who* from Felp's Wing?" Lin demanded.

"All of them," Valyn said slowly, staring as five grim-faced

Kettral filed into the ring. "Holy Hull. She's squaring off to fight all of them."

And fight them she did, if you could call it fighting.

The soldiers from Felp's Wing arrayed themselves in a rough circle, blunted weapons brandished warily before them. Sigrid shook her head, drew her belt knife, then ran the steel along the pale flesh of her arm. Even from a distance, Valyn could see the blood bloom, so dark it looked black in the blazing sunlight.

"That's her well," Laith hissed. "Blood!"

Lin cuffed him on the back of the head. "No one knows what her well is."

"But she always *does* that," Laith protested. "Everyone says it. She always cuts herself before a fight."

And indeed, a spiderwork of scars twisted around the woman's arms all the way to her shoulders.

"But she's not allowed to use a kenning inside the ring," Valyn pointed out. "It's against the rules."

"I don't think she cares," Ha Lin whispered, obviously awed, "about the rules."

The leach didn't look like she cared about anything, not the raucous crowd of Kettral screaming at her from all sides, not the five soldiers arrayed in an arc before her. She raised the bleeding arm to her lips, ran her tongue along the wound. It came away red and dripping. Valyn could see the red smeared across her perfect white teeth. The woman glanced over at the Flea, who made an impatient gesture with his hand—*Get on with it*. And then madness descended on the ring.

Even when it was all finished, Valyn couldn't quite say what he'd seen. There were no impossible kennings, no sheets of fire erupting from the ground, no swords of ice coalescing out of the air. Sigrid fought with her twin blunted blades, the same as any other Kettral, moving through the same forms that Valyn and the rest had been learning since they first arrived on the Islands. She was faster than some of the other Kettral, but not *that* much faster; she was more accurate, but not *that* much more accurate. The five soldiers arrayed against her should have taken her down in a matter of moments, and yet somehow, impossibly, they failed.

It was like watching a year's worth of bad luck strike Felp's Wing in the space of a hundred heartbeats. Every blow was just a touch too slow, every attack just a hand's breadth off target. Lunges that should have struck home slid past the leach, inexplicably wide. Knees buckled at crucial moments. Feet slipped. There was nothing that Valyn could identify, no one specific thing he could point at and say, *There! That's a kenning.* Sigrid fought at the center of a whirlwind. Her blades were a blur, her feet constantly shifting on the sand, but her face never lost that look of casual disdain.

She was barely winded by the time the five other Kettral lay groaning in the dirt. She looked down at them, shook her head, then made a horrible, tortured hacking sound deep in her throat. It took Valyn a long time to realize she was laughing, that those mangled, guttural sounds were all she could make with her severed tongue. After a moment she looked up, raised her chin, spat blood, and spoke to the crowd. The words came out broken between those beautiful lips, incomprehensible.

"My esteemed companion," Newt translated, "would like to thank Commander Felp and her soldiers for a challenging fight."

Sigrid's mouth quirked up at the corner. The Flea sighed as she stepped from the ring, and Newt began collecting his coin in great glittering piles.

Sigrid sa'Karnya was, in her own way, more dangerous than the Flea, and she was standing right behind Valyn in the small forest clearing. He couldn't see her, of course, but he could smell her, could smell, beneath the jasmine and lavender, the woman's blood, and hotter than that, redder, her rage.

"What do you think, Sig?" the Flea asked. "Is Balendin leaching off our emotions? Is that even possible?"

For a long time, the woman didn't reply. When she did, the Aphorist translated the shredded sounds from across the fire.

"My charming companion says yes."

"Yes to what?" the Flea asked.

"Yes to all of it. It's not just possible. She believes Valyn is right."

"Balendin admitted it," Valyn said. "Back in the Bones. He tricked us, trussed us up, said it straight out: the only reason he was keeping us alive was to leach off our emotions."

"All right," the Flea said. "What does it mean?"

Sigrid choked up a handful of sounds.

"He's strong," Newt said. "Stronger than Sigrid. One of the strongest leaches alive."

"And he's getting stronger," Valyn said. He'd been over it a thousand times since Andt-Kyl. Leaching off the terror of a single person—poor Amie back on Hook—had given Balendin enough power to rip down an entire building. Now, however, as the war leader of the Urghul, he was feared by tens of thousands—nomads and Annurians alike. "As his fame grows," Valyn went on grimly, "so does his power. The more foes he faces, the greater his strength, as long as they know who he is."

Sigrid spoke a few sentences, then fell silent. For the first time, Newt was slow to translate.

"What is it?" the Flea asked finally.

Valyn could hear the Aphorist shaking his head: "Dark words dim even the brightest fire."

"We've been in the dark before," the Flea replied. "Just tell us what she said."

"She says that if Valyn is right, then Balendin's well is so deep he could bury a legion with a flick of his little finger."

Valyn frowned. "So why hasn't he?"

"Because," the Flea mused, "someone is stopping him."

26

All morning they climbed through the vast column of light and air inside Intarra's Spear. Adare's legs ached after the first ten floors, then throbbed, then burned. Whenever she stopped to catch her breath, they quaked uncontrollably. Her mouth was dry, her throat raw, her hands twisted into claws from so much clutching of the banister. Halfway to the dungeon, she felt as though she might simply collapse, and yet her own struggle was nothing compared with Mailly's.

In the three days since Adare had last seen the girl, the Weeping Sleep had continued its vicious work. Mailly's eyes were sunk in their bruised sockets, jaundice stained her skin, and the disease had scraped away all healthy flesh, leaving skin tight around the smooth bone beneath. She didn't look as though she could stand, let alone climb, and yet climb she did, slowly and with gritted teeth, pausing often to gasp or cough, dropping to her knees whenever she stumbled on the steps, but always rising once more, shaking, fighting, gutting it out, ascending through interminable degrees toward her own horrible death.

Adare's guards—Sons of Flame in half armor—escorted them, two ahead and two behind. The men could have helped—Mailly was a small woman, small enough that the soldiers might have carried her between them without too much effort—and yet Adare had refused that help. She trusted the Sons as much as she trusted anyone else—which wasn't much. Mailly wore a deep hood to hide her face, but Adare wasn't taking chances. Soldiers talked, even loyal soldiers, and the less they had to talk about, the better. Adare had ordered them to take up positions well before and behind, where they could see little and hear less. Of course, that left only Adare herself to help Mailly back onto her feet each time she stumbled.

Gripping the girl's arm was like holding a brittle stick. Adare could feel the fever blazing beneath her skin. Kegellen had assured her that the Weeping Sleep wasn't contagious, but there was something about being so close to such sickness, about holding a person who, by the end of the day, would be dead, that made Adare queasy. She'd been forcing the feeling down all morning, guiding the girl by her elbow or shoulder, running a hand over her back when she rested. If Mailly could keep climbing, Adare could keep helping her. Not that *helping* was the right word.

More like a shepherd leading her sheep to the slaughter, Adare thought grimly. The climb was just one more torture to add to the young woman's suffering.

Near the end of the morning, when the sun filtered down from above rather than lancing straight through the wall of the Spear, they finally reached the prison, or the start of it, at least. The steel floor was still a dozen flights above, but the landing where they stopped was the last one before the steel walls encircled the staircase, blocking out all light, all access to the cages hanging above. Past this last landing, there would be no room for mistakes.

"Mailly," Adare began, turning to the girl, touching her lightly on the elbow. "Are you ready? Are you all right?"

For a long time, Mailly just stared out into the bright, limpid column of empty air. Almost close enough to touch, a pair of swallows turned lazily on an unseen breeze, but she didn't seem to be looking at them. It was hard to tell, with her eyes hidden in the hood, but Mailly didn't seem to be looking at anything.

"It's so . . . light," she replied finally, quietly. "I've never seen so much light."

"That's why it is named for Intarra," Adare replied, unsure what else to say.

Slowly, as though in pain, Mailly shook her head, then turned. Always before, she had tried to avert her gaze around Adare; now she stared straight into her eyes. "And she loves you," the girl said quietly. "Intarra, I mean. She *chose* you."

Adare nodded, mute.

Mailly shook her head again. "I wonder why."

There was no malice in the words, no doubt or condemnation. Just genuine perplexity. Perplexity and resignation.

"So do I," Adare replied quietly, her mind sliding back to that moment by the Everburning Well, to the crack of thunder and the lightning's all-encompassing flash, to the single syllable ringing in her head—*Win*—a syllable she'd taken for the voice of Intarra herself. It seemed unreal now, like something she had dreamed, or a story she'd found in an old book, a story about someone else. Adare glanced down at her own hands, at the delicate scars burned into the skin. The glabrous whorls reflected the noon light, seemed to burn with it, but what did that mean? Everyone had scars.

"Is it really hers?" Mailly asked, gesturing to the walls of the Spear. "Did Intarra really make this?"

Adare shook her head slowly. "I don't know. No one knows."

Mailly turned, her face twisted with pain and confusion. "But you're her prophet."

Am I? Adare wondered. The Chronicles of Annur held dozens of accounts of prophets, men and women rabid with their faith. They had always struck her as tragic figures—deluded, often deranged.

"I am," Adare replied, "but even a prophet cannot comprehend the whole mind of a goddess."

"Does she speak to you?"

Not since the Well, Adare thought bleakly. *Not a single fucking word.*

"Yes," she replied. "Although her messages can be obscure."

Mailly held her eyes a long time, then nodded. "I'm ready," she said, sounding stronger than she had all day. "I'm ready to go up."

"I am here," Adare announced, "to see the prisoner."

For a moment, shocked stillness ruled the chamber. After the brilliance of the Spear itself, the steel room seemed dim, even with the light of a dozen lamps reflecting off the polished walls and ceiling and floor, as though the whole place were buried underground rather than suspended thousands of feet above it. The people, too—the scribes at their tables, pens poised above their records, the guards posted at the doors—seemed subterranean somehow, wide-eyed, startled as troglodytes by her arrival, staring at her burning irises as though they'd never seen the sun.

Then, in a moment, everything tumbled into motion. Scribes were standing, knocking over chairs, bowing low while a wave of stiff salutes ran through the guardsmen. The Sons of Flame had offered to climb ahead, to provide word of her imminent arrival; Adare had refused. She was relying on this surprise and confusion. She wanted the dungeon guards and jailors shocked and off-balance, too busy staring at *her* to pay much attention to Mailly's slender figure at her side.

"Your Radiance." One of the older jailors bowed formally, then stepped forward. Lamplight glinted off his immaculately polished armor, glittered in his dark eyes. *Shrewd eyes,* Adare concluded grimly. She had been hoping for a fool. "My name is Haram Simit," the man continued, "and I am the Chief Jailor here. You honor us with your presence."

"I didn't come to honor you," she said brusquely. She had put on her Emperor's face before entering the chamber, and she used her Emperor's voice now. "I came to question the spy."

Simit pursed his lips. "We have a number of spies, Your Radiance."

"Vasta Dhati. The Manjari. The one who broke into my brother's study. The one who somehow managed to elude you until just days ago."

The rebuke was unfair, but she had hoped it might unsettle the Chief Jailor. Simit, however, did not look unsettled. He shook his head slightly.

"The prison staff does not apprehend the criminals, Your Radiance. Our charge is limited to their imprisonment." He gestured to a set of chairs. "Please. If you and your companion would rest, I will send someone for water and refreshment. The climb is long, even for those who make it often." The chairs were bare wood, hard and unupholstered. Adare ached to collapse into one, to rest her trembling legs. The last thing she needed, however, was to sit in a 'Kent-kissing chair while Simit scrutinized her further. The sooner they were into the prison and out again, the better. She shook her head.

"As you say, the climb is long. Too much time has been wasted already. We will see the spy now."

Simit's lips tightened, and he shifted his gaze to Mailly. "And may I ask, Your Radiance, who is your companion?"

Mailly twitched at her side. Adare reached down and took her by the elbow.

"No," Adare replied, careful to keep her voice brusque, level. "You may not ask. She has knowledge of the spy that may prove useful—that is all you need to know."

Simit studied Mailly for two or three heartbeats, as though if he watched her long enough, he might see straight through the fine wool of her hood.

"Forgive me, Your Radiance," he said at last, "but is this not a matter for the First Shield and his Aedolian Guard?"

"The same so-called *guard*," Adare snapped, pouring as much scorn as she could into that last word, "that let the bastard into the Spear in the first place? The same guard that allowed three of their number to be subdued by a single spy? Is *that* the guard you want me to trust?"

She let the question hang there, cocked her head to the side and raised an eyebrow. The other scribes and jailors might have been statues. No one moved. They barely seemed to breathe. There was no way, however, to stop them from watching, and when the whole thing was over, when Adare was gone and the corpse was found, they would remember what they'd seen. They would spend hours pondering Adare's visit, going over and over all the details, debating the tiny nuances of what she said, the way she held herself. She needed to get out of the chamber soon, get away from all those eyes before she let something slip, or Mailly did. Rushing, on the other hand, was a good way to cause just such a slip, and so she forced herself to stand still, to keep her face aloof, to wait for Simit's reply.

"Forgive me, Your Radiance," the man said again, "but I was given to believe your brother declared the Aedolian Guardsmen free of any guilt."

My brother, Adare reflected grimly, *who seems to have disappeared from the palace.* Kaden had been seen days earlier, departing through the Ghost's Gate, but after that . . . nothing. Kiel had assured both Adare and the council that the First Speaker would be absent only temporarily. Adare was not reassured. She had sent twenty of the Sons into the city to search for her brother; they had returned empty-handed. Kaden's absence was a vexing and dangerous riddle, but breaking Triste out of the Spear afforded no leisure to consider it further, and so Adare had set the question aside, where it gnawed quietly at a corner of her mind like a rat at a bit of gristle.

"I am not bound by the whimsical declarations of my brother."

"And yet he *is* the First Speaker of the council."

Adare made her voice cold, hard. "And I am the Emperor." Simit acknowledged that with a shallow bow, but Adare was bulling ahead even before he had a chance to straighten. "This matter is more important than my brother knows, and I will not see the handling of it botched any further."

Simit bowed lower this time. The man was all respect but no submission. Even as he acquiesced to her demands, she could feel him watching, could see his mind moving behind his eyes. The room wasn't hot, but Adare was sweating. She could feel it running hot and slick down the skin beneath her robe, glistening on her brow.

It's a long climb, she reminded herself. *Everyone must be dripping with sweat by the time they get here.*

Simit glanced at Mailly again. "Your Radiance, if I might just—"

"The Manjari," Adare said, smashing through the man's voice with her own, "attacked us here. In the very heart of Annur. You may not find that troubling, but I do, and I will not hand away Annurian advantages to assuage your idle curiosity. I will not have my companion compromised."

"My scribes and guardsmen are sworn to silence," Simit protested, "as am I. The truth of what transpires here does not pass beyond that door." He pointed discreetly at the steel slab behind Adare.

"I have every trust in your circumspection." Adare smiled grimly. "Still . . ."

She let the word hang there, the silence stronger than any threat. After a pause, Simit bowed again. "I will have the prisoner transferred to a standard cell for questioning."

Adare's heart bucked like a panicked horse. Everything, the entire plan, depended on meeting Vasta Dhati *below,* where the steel cages hung in the vast emptiness of the Spear.

"No," she barked.

Simit's eyes widened a fraction.

Adare strangled her fear, took a deep breath, and shoved it aside. "I am done with waiting, with incompetence and delay. We will see him now, wherever he is."

Simit shook his head, then pointed down through the floor. "He is in a cage, Your Radiance. Hanging below us."

"And you're telling me you have no way to reach these cages?" she demanded, arching an eyebrow.

"We do," Simit replied. "A sort of steel basket, but it is not fit for an Emperor. It is precarious."

"So is sitting on the Unhewn Throne."

"But the basket will accommodate only two," Simit said.

"One," Adare said, pointing to her own chest, then shifting her finger to Mailly. "Two."

"You wish to see the prisoner *alone*?" Concern fringed the jailor's voice, and his eyes were troubled as he met hers.

Adare forced herself to meet that gaze, to nod. "Perhaps I was not very clear earlier. There was a breach in palace security. Until I have the answers I seek, I will believe there is *still* a breach, and while there is a breach, I will trust no one. Including you."

Simit studied her. "This is most irregular, Your Radiance."

"We will see the prisoner now," Adare said. "We will see him alone. And if there are any more delays, I will see you removed from your post, stripped of your armor and honors, and put out of the palace."

The man held her gaze a moment, then bowed a final time. "As you say, Your Radiance. If you will follow me . . ."

Adare let out a long, unsteady breath when the man finally turned. Maybe there had been a more graceful way to handle the jailor, a subtler way, but grace and subtlety carried their own risks, risks she couldn't afford to take while il Tornja had her son. The blunt force of imperial prerogative wasn't pretty, but it worked.

It works, she reflected bleakly, *provided you're willing to burn through all normal human bonds.*

Simit's metal "basket" looked more like some obscure machine of torture than anything meant to carry apples or cotton. Adare and Mailly stood on a slab of cast iron barely wide enough for the two of them, grasping a waist-high metal railing that might have been hammered out on some drunken blacksmith's forge. The thing was all warped angles and rough edges, a baffling contrast with the clean lines of the rest of the prison.

It's meant to frighten them, the Chief Jailor had explained, just before he lowered them through an open trapdoor in the steel floor. *The journey to the cages below should not be an easy one.*

The whole thing hung from wrist-thick chains—obviously strong enough to hold up half a dozen oxen—but Adare felt nauseous all the same as the basket dropped through the floor in a series of jolts and lurches. The chains rattled over the pulleys above, setting the basket swaying. After a moment of dizzying vertigo, Adare closed her eyes. She could feel Mailly beside her. The girl was sobbing silently, trembling inside her robe, the sound muffled by the clanking of the chain. Adare felt her own fear begin to give way, shoved aside by her shame. Things could go awry for them all, horribly awry, but Mailly was the only one who had come to this place to die.

How does it feel, Adare wondered, *to know you won't live to see another sunrise?* Soldiers marched to their deaths all the time, of course, and old people lying in their beds could surely hear Ananshael's quiet steps. Almost no one, however, could foresee with any certainty the actual *moment.* A soldier might survive a vicious battle. A grandmother with the gray pox might live for five more years. It was that *chance* of survival, the not knowing for sure, that kept people moving forward, even at the end. That chance had been denied to Mailly. Adare was denying it. She carried inside a small pocket of her robe the poison that would destroy the girl. Mailly knew it, had climbed all the way to the dungeon knowing it.

The basket jolted suddenly to rest, throwing Adare into the twisted railing. She opened her eyes to find a steel cage hanging in space just half a pace away. Like the basket in which she stood, it hung from chains, but when she traced those links back up, she found them fixed in the floor above. There was no raising and lowering of the hanging cells. Prisoners went down in the basket, and usually they didn't leave until they were dead.

If any of that bothered Vasta Dhati, it didn't show. The pirate priest sat cross-legged in the center of his cage, his only clothing a single scrap of sailcloth around his loins. The man was more battered than the last time Adare saw him—something had split his scalp just above the eye, and a huge bruise spread like a stain across his shoulder. He didn't appear to notice; not the wounds nor his new visitors.

"All is well, Your Radiance?"

Adare craned her neck to find Simit leaning out over the open door, staring down at the swaying basket.

"It is. You may leave us now."

Simit hesitated. "Call out loudly—very loudly—when you are ready to ascend." His head disappeared, and then, moments later, the trapdoor above slammed shut. Adare ignored her roiling stomach and the recriminations of her mind, turning back to face the priest.

"Are you all right?" she murmured. The sight of his wounds had filled her with sudden foreboding, and despite his earlier assurances, the whole thing suddenly seemed impossible. How could he keep track of the cloth for three days, through arrest and transport, beatings and interrogation? Could he eat, with that silk rope snaking down his throat? Could he sleep? "Do you have it?" she demanded, suddenly convinced she should have found a way to carry the rope herself, whatever the added risk.

"You are speaking to the First Priest of the Sea of Knives," Dhati replied serenely, raising his eyes. Before Adare could respond, he tipped back his head and, as he had in Kegellen's home days earlier, vomited the silken rope into his hands. The cord was a slick, twisted mess, but it was *there*. When it was done, Dhati spat onto the steel floor of his cage. "This is no prison for the First Priest of the Sea of Knives."

"What about the cage?" Adare asked, eyeing the steel grid-work. Instead of the simple vertical bars she had seen in other prisons, bars ran both horizontally and vertically over the front of the cell. The resultant empty squares were barely larger than the priest's head, certainly far too narrow for his shoulders, a fact that seemed to bother him not in the slightest.

For a moment he stood still as the steel walls. Then, with no warning, he began to windmill his arms in frenetic circles, all the while breathing in and out so quickly and violently that Adare thought he might snap his ribs. Mailly had pushed back her hood, and was staring at the tiny man, amazement replacing, if only for a moment, the pain that was usually scrawled across her face.

"What is he doing?" she whispered.

Adare grimaced. "Escaping." She hoped.

Suddenly, Dhati went still again. He closed his eyes, muttered a few words in a language Adare didn't understand, then stepped forward to the bars. He put an arm through first, an approach that seemed obviously doomed to failure. Before Adare could lose hope, however, the priest let out a deep *humph,* and the arm seemed to pop free from the body, the shoulder liberated from its socket. The sight was both sickening and fascinating. Adare could do nothing but stare as the man distended his own flesh, twisting his limbs into positions of torture, horror, his body writhing in the impossible postures of nightmare. He didn't seem to climb through the metal grate so much as *pour* himself, as though there were no muscle or bone inside his skin, but an amorphous, gelatinous ooze. For a moment Adare thought the man was a leach, but she realized as she stared that there was no kenning involved—only a staggeringly violent subjugation of the flesh. It took a matter of minutes, but when Dhati was finished he stood outside the cage, perching easily on the bars as he retrieved his rope. Then, with an acrobatic flip, he tossed himself up onto the roof of the cell.

Adare shook her head in amazement. "Now what?" she managed, when she finally found her words.

Dhati bared his teeth—a feral expression that might have been a smile. "Knots."

The First Priest of the Sea of Knives was fully fluent in his knots; his thin fingers flew through the whorls and twists as easily as Adare might write her own name on an empty page. It took him only a matter of moments to tie a series of small, fixed loops into the length of silk—holds for hands and feet, evidently—then just a heartbeat more to attach the end of the silk to one of the bars on his cage. When he finished, he looked up at Adare, then pointed beyond her shoulder.

"I will get the girl."

Adare turned slowly, warily, shifting her grip on the railing as she moved. She'd managed not to look down, had managed not to look at anything but Dhati and his cage. Now, however, she was forced to confront the full scope of the prison. Dozens of cages hung from the floor above, most at different levels, facing different directions. She had a brief vision of the architect or mathematician responsible for solving that particular problem, for packing in as many cages as possible without offering any one prisoner a clear line of sight to any other.

In a way, the whole place was ludicrous. Holes hacked into the stone would have been cheaper and easier, and no one was likely to escape from a cave built straight into the bedrock.

But then, Adare reflected, staring at the hanging cells, at the light reflecting off the steel, *it's not about ease. Not any more than this tower we decided to occupy. It's about power.*

Anyone who saw the sunlight glinting off the tower—sailors miles out to sea, travelers down the coastal road, visitors to and citizens of Annur itself—knew that it belonged to the Malkeenians. Somehow a single family with blazing eyes had taken the greatest structure in the world for its own, then built a prison inside it, a dungeon so high, the story went, that even if a prisoner managed to leap from his cell, he would die before striking the ground. It was worth a logistical hassle to have the whole world believe a thing like that.

Atop his hanging cage, Vasta Dhati pulled the last of his knots tight, grunted in satisfaction, and then, without even a glance down, leapt the gap between his cell and the hanging basket. The whole thing swayed dangerously as he landed on the railing, but while Adare and Mailly scrambled to hold on, Dhati balanced easily, shading his eyes with a hand as he squinted to the west.

"How long will it take," Adare asked, "to search the cells?"

The First Priest hissed, then shook his head. "No search. The girl is there."

He pointed at a cell just twenty or thirty feet distant.

Adare stared at it. The gleaming steel walls stared blankly back. Presumably the cell had an open side, a gridwork of bars like those through which Dhati had just escaped. *It had better,* she thought. Even Dhati couldn't drag Triste out through a sheet of solid metal.

"She's in there? How do you know?"

"You want me to free a leach," Dhati replied. "To keep the leach safely, she must be drugged. That is the only cage the guards visit, even in the middle of the night."

I should be grateful, Adare thought. The information was an unexpected windfall, as was the simple fact of the cage's location. After so much scheming and second-guessing, Triste hung inside a cell just a stone's throw away. Dhati, as promised, was out of his cage. Improbably, it was all working. *I should be grateful,* she told herself again, and yet, instead of gratitude, she felt only her heart's hammering, dread rising in her throat to choke her.

"You have the grapples?" Dhati asked impatiently.

Adare started at the question, then nodded. Hidden in her piled hair, masquerading as lacquered pins, were the three hooks the priest had given her days before. In retrospect, she could have simply carried them in her pocket, but there had been no way to be sure that Simit wouldn't search her, Emperor or no. Her fingers felt numb, clumsy, as she pulled the hooks free, and as she passed the final one to the priest, she felt it slip from her sweat-slick hand, tumbling into the void. Adare could only stare, but Dhati lashed out, viper-quick, snatching it as it fell, then hissing his disapproval as he straightened. It took him only a moment to lock it together with the other two, then to thread the rope through the triple eye of the grapple.

"How . . . ," Adare began.

Before she could finish the question, he tossed the steel hook. It was a casual motion, almost indifferent. It reminded Adare of the way she herself might toss aside her robe when she undressed for the bath. She watched, amazed, as the silk fluttered out behind the hook, as the enameled steel flashed with the sunlight, then landed with a *clank* atop the far cell. The sound seemed horribly loud, the kind of thing that would surely bring Simit and his guards running. She stared up at the closed trapdoor for a dozen nervous breaths. The steel panels didn't move. The Chief Jailor did not appear. Adare let out a long, slow breath, then turned back to the silken cord hanging in a shallow arc between the cells.

"Stay here," Dhati said. Then, without even a glance down, the priest swung out onto the silk, hanging spiderlike beneath it, suspended from his hands and the backs of his ankles, then moved along its length, nimble and frighteningly fast. He reached Triste's cell in moments, rolled onto the roof, then tipped his head over the far side. He looked up a moment later, then signaled.

"She's there," Adare breathed weakly. "She's there."

"And he can get her out?" Mailly asked, her voice faint. "He can get me in?"

Adare kept her eyes fixed on the far cell, but nodded slowly. "You saw how he did it. You're just as small as Dhati—smaller, actually."

"But my body," the girl protested. "It doesn't *move* like that."

"It will," Adare replied. "He can help you."

Help, in fact, seemed like entirely the wrong word for what the priest would have to do. He had demonstrated his uncanny ability back in Kegellen's mansion, his strong, nimble fingers finding a series of points halfway between Adare's neck and shoulder, then pressing so viciously she thought he would break the skin. She'd cried out in alarm just as her shoulder went slack, then numb, the whole arm dangling stupidly at her side.

"Your soft emperor's body would not last a day on the Sea of Knives," the priest had said, gesturing, "but it can be trained to obey."

Then, before Adare could protest, he popped her shoulder from its socket. Whatever he'd done to relax the muscle also deadened the pain, at least in that moment. The ache came later, when she'd recovered the limb's use and feeling, a bone-deep sense of the wrong that had been done. Kegellen, of course, had been all apologies and solicitude, but Adare had brushed aside the woman's concern. "All that matters is that it works, that he can get Triste out, and Mailly in."

"He's going to relax your body . . . ," Adare began. Before she could finish, Mailly collapsed at her side, shaking her head in the slow cadence of terror or regret. "I can't do it. I'm sorry, Your Radiance. I'm so sorry. But I can't do it."

Adare took a deep breath, knelt on the hard iron slab, then draped her arm over Mailly's shoulders. She could feel the girl's thin frame shaking, racked with terror and disease.

"It's not so far," Adare said, forcing a calm she did not feel into her voice. If Mailly refused her role, the whole thing was finished. They might still escape with Kaden's leach, but the guards would know within the day—the very next time they descended to force the adamanth on Triste—that she was gone, and Adare had little doubt that Simit would make the obvious connection. Everything hung on Mailly's cooperation, and yet, it was an awful thing to coax a young girl to her death.

"Dhati will take you over," Adare said, gesturing.

Even as she spoke, the tiny priest had removed the grapple and tied the far end of the silk to the chains supporting Triste's cell. With the steel hooks in his teeth, he made his way back hand over hand, swung up atop the basket railing once more, then dropped down next to Mailly.

"Be quicker," he hissed, lifting her robe over her head. "Speed is safety."

The girl, still half dazed, raised her arms. She wore only a light linen shift beneath the robe; the cloth had been washed so many times it was nearly sheer, and Adare winced at the gaunt angles of the girl's body. Once she was in the cell, she would exchange garments with Triste. At least, that had been the plan before Mailly's courage faltered.

Dhati, oblivious or indifferent to the girl's terror, tossed the robe aside, then began work on a harness. He had an extra length of silk, one he'd untied from the longer swath, and as Mailly stared at the far cell, he wove it deftly into a kind of saddle around her bare legs. In moments it was finished, tied off to the grapple hook.

"Climb," Dhati said, leaping up onto the railing once more, taking the long rope in his hands. "Hook over this. I will pull you."

"Not yet," Adare protested, pulling the glass bottle from the pocket of her robe. "She has to drink this first."

"I can't," Mailly protested, shifting her gaze from the gap between the cells to the bottle in Adare's hand. "Oh, Sweet Intarra, no. I *can't*."

The words were desperate, panicked, but almost inaudible, as though there were no air left in the girl's lungs for speech.

You have to, Adare wanted to scream. *You said you'd do it, and now you have to!*

Instead she hauled in a slow breath of her own, then forced herself to meet Mailly's terrified eyes. "Tell me why you're afraid."

Mailly stared at her. "I'm afraid to die."

"So am I," Adare replied quietly.

The words just tumbled out, but they weren't quite the truth. It wasn't Adare's own death that terrified her, but her son's. When she closed her eyes to shut out Mailly's face, Sanlitun filled her mind, the tiny child with his small hands grasping for her hair, her face. If she failed here, he was gone. Il Tornja would learn she had defied him, and he would kill her son with the indifference of a fisherman hacking the heads from his catch. The simple fact felt like a knife nestled right beside her beating heart. She opened her eyes to Mailly's tear-streaked face, so different from Sanlitun's and yet bathed in the same bafflement, twisted by the same helpless need.

And where is her *mother?*

Living in some squalid hovel, no doubt—a rat-infested basement or a leaking garret in the Perfumed Quarter. Wherever it was, it couldn't be good, not if Mailly was willing to drink poison to save her from it. Adare imagined the woman for a moment, imagined her in the cramped room as the sun's last light flamed on the sill, then died. She would be confused about her daughter's absence at first, then concerned, then sick with worry. Adare couldn't picture her face, but she could see the hands, skin rough with a lifetime of scrubbing, clenched in the woman's lap, the knuckles pale, bloodless.

"You don't have to do it," Adare said. She glanced down at the bottle in her hand, suddenly tempted to toss it over the railing of the basket, to watch it disappear in the dusty light.

"But the money," Mailly moaned. "Five thousand suns . . ."

"I'll make sure your mother gets it. And your brother."

"You would do that?" the girl asked, shaking her head in disbelief, then dropping to her knees, clutching at Adare's legs in gratitude or supplication.

Adare nodded mutely. It was ruined. The whole fucking thing was ruined. She wanted to scream, but screaming wouldn't do any good. *I can delay,* she thought, mind racing, *tell il Tornja that I need more time. He won't kill Sanlitun until he knows I've turned on him. . . .*

"Why are you crying?" Mailly asked.

Adare stared at the girl, confused, then touched her own face with her fingertips. It was wet, soaked with tears.

"It's fine," she said, scrubbing them roughly away. "We need to get out of here."

From his perch atop the railing, Vasta Dhati frowned.

"You would stop now?"

"Things have changed," Adare snapped. "Take down the silk. Quickly."

The Manjari narrowed his eyes. "And my ships? This failure is nothing of my doing."

"I'm aware of that," Adare snapped. "You make your own way out, as we arranged before, and you'll have your ships."

"A weak people," Dhati muttered, shaking his head. "What about the leach?" he asked, tossing his bald head toward Triste's cell.

Adare shook her head. "Leave her."

"She's seen me. She could talk."

"Who would believe her?"

Mailly changed her grip on Adare's knees. She was still kneeling, but had shifted her gaze from Adare's face to the far cage.

"Who is she?" she asked, voice weak, as though it had been broken somewhere deep inside her throat.

"It doesn't matter," Adare said, reaching down to grab the girl by the elbow, pulling her roughly to her feet. "We need to get out of here. *Now.*"

Horror propelled her, horror at abandoning the plan, at what it would mean. Despair darkened her vision, pressed down on her heart. If she paused, it seemed, if she hesitated even a moment, it would crush her.

"Put your robe back on," she said, dragging Mailly toward her. To her shock, the girl pulled away.

"Who is she?" she asked again, voice stronger this time.

Adare met her gaze. "She is a leach. She killed over a hundred people here, in this palace."

Mailly blanched. "And you want to get her *out*? Why?"

"We need her."

"But she's a *leach*."

"She is a weapon," Adare said wearily.

"But you're the Emperor," Mailly protested. "You're Intarra's prophet. You have whole armies to fight for you."

"Those armies," Adare said tersely, "are losing. We are losing."

She wasn't sure whether she meant losing to the Urghul, or to her own *kenarang*. Of course, there was more than one war, more than one kind of defeat. A woman could lose over and over, could fail in a thousand different ways.

Mailly shook her head. "I didn't know," she whispered finally.

"How would you know? It's all happening in the north, or along the coast, or down in the Waist. Everywhere but here. The whole fucking empire could collapse, and Annur would only notice when there were no more boats, no more wagons piled high with food and supplies."

"And this leach," Mailly asked, nodding toward Triste's cage, "can stop it? Can save Annur?"

"I have no idea," Adare said. She could feel the long climb up the tower stairs like lead in her legs. She wondered if she would be able to descend from the Spear without collapsing. It didn't seem to matter. "Maybe not. I had hoped so. Maybe there's another way."

Mailly looked at Triste's cage, tears in her wide eyes, then turned her gaze beyond it, past the hanging cells, through the clear walls of the Spear, out and away, to where Annur lay sprawled thousands of feet below. The towers glittered with their miniature beauty. The canals caught the noon light, throwing it back. From this height, even the slums looked beautiful, a collection of tiny dwellings stripped of the stench, the sobbing, the disease.

"I'll do it," Mailly said at last. She was crying again, but the shaking was gone.

Adare stared.

"I'm dying anyway," the girl whispered. "And what good are five thousand suns to my mother and brother if there's no food to buy? If there are Urghul riding through the streets?"

Hope bloomed in Adare like a sick-sweet flower. She hated herself for it, but she'd hated herself for a lot of things for a long time now. She could live with a little more hatred. She glanced up at the trapdoor twenty feet above. It was still closed. How long had they been hanging in the basket? She'd told Simit that she needed time, but how long would the man wait? Not all day, certainly. Was there still time to make the switch?

"Are you certain about this?" she demanded, gripping the girl by the elbow more firmly than she'd intended.

Mailly flinched, but she nodded, dragging her gaze from Adare's eyes to the brown bottle in her hands. Kegellen had mixed the *ayamaya* with strong Breatan spirits. *It might dull the poor child's pain,* she had suggested, studying the bottle as she handed it over. Adare didn't believe that for a moment.

Mailly stared at the glass as though it were a viper, then grabbed for it, clawing at the cork with shaking hands like a drunk desperate to get at whatever was inside. The glass, slick with her tears, half slipped from her grasp. Adare lurched forward, catching it before it could tumble through the basket railing. When she raised her eyes, Mailly was staring at her.

It seemed like there should be something to say. Emperors were always making speeches, after all, extended declamations on patriotism and sacrifice. Generals addressed the men before sending them into battle, and the fate that Mailly faced was at least as awful as an Urghul spear to the stomach. Surely there was something to say, something both comforting and ennobling, but Adare found the words would not come. She was gambling away the girl's life, and for what? The shadow of a shot at Ran il Tornja. There was no nobility in the sacrifice, only desperation.

Adare studied the bottle in her hands. Then, with a nudge of the thumb, popped free the cork.

Mailly gave a little gasp, like the sound a girl makes when she steps into the ocean for the first swim of late spring—a small sound, almost the start of a laugh. Adare could imagine her standing knee-deep in the waves, eyes wide with the excitement and the cold, ready to dive in, but waiting, maybe, for her friends. Only Mailly had no friends, not here. There was only Vasta Dhati, perched impatiently on the railing, and Adare herself, the woman who had brought her here, not to brave those bright spring waves, but to die alone, her awful pain utterly unwitnessed.

"Mailly . . . ," Adare began, but before she could think what to say next, the girl seized the bottle in both hands and raised it to her lips, drinking desperately, almost greedily, the brown spirit trickling down her bare neck. Adare stared at the girl's throat as she swallowed, and swallowed, and swallowed again, then suddenly convulsed. Mailly grimaced, lips twisted back, eyes squeezed shut. It seemed for a few heartbeats that she would vomit it all up.

Does it work so fast? Adare wondered. *Is the poison so violent?*

But after a heartbeat more, Mailly trembled herself free of the liquor's grip, fixed her eyes on the bottle's rim, and began drinking again, more slowly this time, but with a quiet determination, pausing between each sip.

"How much?" she gasped when she'd had a third of the bottle.

"No more," Adare said, reaching out to stop the girl, to take the poison back.

According to Kegellen, a single swig would do the necessary work, but only if Mailly held the liquor down. For a moment the two just stared at each other, both frozen. Mailly's eyes were wide, as though she'd just now realized what she'd done, was only now understanding that she could not take it back.

But she can, Adare thought grimly, some cold part of her own mind, a part she loathed, working through the logistics of the girl's death. *'Shael only knows what might happen if she gets sick now.* She had a vision of Mailly in Triste's cage, vomiting but not dying, her skin spared the worst of the coming blisters, her eyes unbloodied by the poison's violence. The next time the guards descended with the adamanth, they would find her, would know that Triste had escaped somehow, and Simit, with those careful eyes of his, would put the pieces together easily.

"Are you all right?" Adare asked.

Mailly's mouth moved, framing the shapes of silent words.

"Mailly?"

The girl locked eyes with her. "I'm really going to die."

Adare nodded gravely. "You are. But you saved your family. Your mother and little brother and . . ." She hesitated, uncertain how to phrase the rest. "And maybe more. Maybe, in some strange way, all Annur."

"She's that important?" Mailly asked, staring at Triste's cell. "The leach?"

I don't know, Adare almost said. It was the honest truth. *I don't know who she is. I don't know why my own general wants her dead. I don't know what threat she poses or to whom. I have no play in mind, nothing even resembling a plan. All I can do is deny him his demands, and even that might prove pointless.*

"Yes," she said instead. "She's that important. And so are you. You're crucial to this whole rescue."

And then, to her shock, Mailly smiled. *"Crucial."* She shook her head ruefully, suddenly even younger than her few years. "Will you tell my brother that?" she asked. "That I was crucial?"

"Of course," Adare said. "I'll make sure—"

Before she could finish, a convulsion doubled Mailly over, violent as a fist to the gut. She groaned, then clamped her teeth shut on the sound.

"Is this it?" the girl asked, half straightening, face tight, stitched with pain.

Adare nodded helplessly.

"So fast," Mailly marveled.

"Now," Dhati said. "We go."

The priest reached down, and, with surprising strength, hoisted the girl up onto the railing, held her there as she seized the chain, then tossed the hook from her harness over the silken rope.

"Go," he said again, gesturing.

Mailly stared down, swallowed a sob, and tightened her grip.

"Let go," the priest said again.

"Wait," Adare said.

The two looked down at her, the priest impatient and disdainful, Mailly with her tear-streaked, terror-blighted eyes, and Adare realized she had nothing to say. She had brought the girl here to see her dead, to leave her behind, and the time had come for leaving. Dhati watched her a moment longer, then hissed his irritation, shoved Mailly squarely in the chest, and they were both over the edge of the railing, the girl dangling from her makeshift harness, the priest hanging from his hands, his knees locked around her waist as he pulled her out over the abyss.

Adare started, half stretched a hand toward Mailly, some stupid, human effort to touch her, as though that touch could bring any comfort. They were already away, though, Dhati's hands moving fast, his wiry arms drawing them toward Triste's cage.

Thank you, Adare realized. *That was what I should have said. Just* thank you.

She opened her mouth to call to the girl, but they were too far, the risk of raising her voice too great. Mailly's gaze was fixed on her, her eyes wide, as though she were waiting for something, but Adare forced her own mouth closed, painfully aware of Simit waiting, just a few paces away through the steel ceiling above.

It's over, she told herself. *The whole thing is long past words, anyway.*

She wanted to turn away, to shut her eyes, but she held Mailly's terrified gaze until they reached the far cage and Dhati lifted her clear of the silk, guiding her onto the roof of the cell, where he paused, running his strong hands over her skin, driving his fingertips into the wasted flesh in just the right places to make the girl go numb, limp. Then, with a savage tug, he jerked her arm from the socket and lowered her over the side.

For what felt like forever, Adare stood alone in the basket, bathed in the afternoon light, strangled by her own emotion. *It's taking too long,* a part of her thought, but the part of her that could still feel fear seemed wrung out, too exhausted to respond. There was only a cold, broken feeling, like a shattered knife lodged in her chest, driving deeper each time that her heart beat.

When the pirate priest finally emerged, dragging a different woman up into the light, Adare barely noticed. It was the leach, Triste, the one they had come for. They were so close to the very end of the whole insane plan. It was going to work. Adare discovered that she didn't care. All she could think of, as Dhati hauled this other creature back across the silken cord, was Mailly alone in that cell, suspended in the air so many thousands of feet above everyone in the world who loved her, shaking as the poison raked its sharp claws through her flesh.

"Here," Dhati said, jolting Adare from her thoughts as he deposited the leach unceremoniously inside the basket. "Remember. Three ships when I escape."

Adare stared at the woman before her. Triste and Mailly were roughly the same age, close enough to the same size and build that, after the poison's ravages, the guards wouldn't notice the difference. The similarity, however, ended with those basic dimensions.

Mailly was pretty, if strangely pale. Triste was . . . perfect. Adare could arrive at no other word. Violence had scribbled scars across her skin. Red weals marred her face and arms. Something that looked like a burn spread across the flesh of her left hand. Her black hair was utterly unkempt, matted to her scalp as though she'd long ago gone mad. None of that mattered. *She's too beautiful.* That was Adare's first thought. It seemed wrong, somehow, impossible.

"You have his eyes," Triste said. Her voice was quiet, drugged, but bright enough to slice through Adare's thoughts.

Adare was used to power. She was the daughter of an emperor, the sister of princes, the one-time consort of a Csestriim, and the protégé of one of the Atmani. As she locked gazes with the young woman, however, as she stared into those hooded violet eyes, something inside her quailed. For half a heartbeat she wanted to bow, to grovel, to leap from the basket if that was what it took to escape that gaze. It went through her like a knife, and then it was gone, leaving her knees weak and her mind reeling.

"Kaden's eyes," Triste said again. "You have them."

Adare steadied herself on the railing, straightened her spine, filled her voice with all the iron she could muster. "You will find I'm nothing like Kaden."

Triste started to reply, then shook her head as though the effort were too much, as though the whole enterprise of speech was pointless.

"You're breaking me out. Why?"

"I need you," Adare replied.

"For what?"

"I'll explain later."

Triste shrugged, as though the answer didn't really matter, as though the whole escape were no more amazing than the arrival of the evening meal. *The drugs,* Adare realized. *She's drugged almost thoughtless.*

"Put this on," she said, holding up the hooded robe that Mailly had worn into the tower.

Triste studied it, then slipped it over her head. The gesture was casual, indifferent, but there was a grace to it that would make most women ache with jealousy.

"Who was she?" the leach asked, tugging the fabric into place.

"Someone who agreed to die in your place."

"Why?"

Adare opened her mouth, but found she lacked the language to respond. The truth was too large for words, too necessary and too cruel. What finally came out, when she managed to speak, was the barest brutal shadow of that truth, a shadow that settled down on Adare's heart like a cold winter sickness.

"Because I fucking paid her."

27

"I can't do it," Quick Jak said quietly, staring at the milk-pale monster flailing on the stone floor of the cavern.

The creature was fully trussed, and yet even captive, even tied, the slarn was a nightmare to turn the strongest stomach, slick, and twisted, and twisting. *Like some sick fuck grafted together the worst parts of a wolf, a snake, and a man-sized salamander,* Gwenna reflected. The slarn's raking claws were long as her thumb, the teeth too many and too jagged for that gaping mouth, but the teeth and claws weren't the worst of it. The worst part was the eyes, or rather, the blank swath of skin where the eyes should have been.

Men and women the world over revered Bedisa as a gentle, loving goddess, the tender midwife of all living things. It was worth remembering, however, that in addition to the beasts of the forests and the light-winged birds of the air, Bedisa also made monsters to prowl the cold, dark places of the world, that she who knit the stuff of human souls had also sculpted this horrific vision with its too-white, glistening flesh. It seemed to Gwenna that if the goddess wanted to fill the world with life, she might've gone a little heavier on the feathers and lips, a little lighter on the poison and claws, but then, there wasn't much point in second-guessing the gods. The world was the way it was; some parts of it you could relax and enjoy; some parts you just had to kill.

The other rebels had gathered in a rough circle around the slarn, staring at it silently, awe and horror scribbled on their faces, amazement in their eyes. They'd fought the slarn before, but in the mad fury of a fight people didn't always really *see* a thing. *Well, they're seeing it now,* Gwenna thought. Seeing it, and, judging from the horror on their faces, wishing they weren't. They'd heard about the slarn over on Arim, but hearing about it was useless. Words might manage to capture something of the way the creatures looked, how they moved, but you could never describe to someone how those things made you *feel* deep in the soft inner part of you.

"I couldn't do it then," Quick Jak continued, taking a half step back from the writhing slarn, holding his hands up in surrender. "And I can't do it now."

"Yes," Gwenna said grimly, "you can. You will. We didn't haul that fucking thing out of the guts of this cave just to play touch and tell."

It had taken her, and Annick, and Talal hours to find the slarn. When they finally got it out and up into the cavern where the rebels had made their camp, Gwenna was ready to throw the 'Kent-kissing creature on the bonfire and have done with the whole idea of the Trial. The slarn was only a young adolescent, Talal had worked up some sort of kenning to keep its jaws locked for a few breaths, and the beast had *still* almost taken her arm off when she jumped on top of it.

Killing the creatures was tricky enough. Capturing the fucking thing had almost finished her. She'd barely managed to keep hold of its back as it thrashed, barely managed to stay clear of the jaws and the claws as the beast smashed her into the walls, tried to scrape her off on the floor, barely managed to wrap an arm around the slarn's throat, then roll so the writhing creature was on top of her, belly-up, raking the air with furious claws. Another couple heartbeats and it would have broken free, but Annick and Talal didn't give it a couple heartbeats. While Gwenna cursed and clutched the thing tighter, they managed to truss the long rear legs, then the shorter front ones. By then Talal was sweating like an ox, and his kenning, instead of fading, just *snapped*. Then, of course, the miserable beast went at Gwenna all over again, ignoring its trussed limbs, twisting and snarling, trying to sink a tooth into her as she rolled free.

And of course, after all the wrestling, dragging the slarn half a mile upward through the twisting passageways of the Hole had taken a toll on all three of them. One of the claws had hooked Talal, leaving a long gash down his arm; the long, muscular tail knocked Annick a dozen feet off a ledge; and the sheer weight of the thing falling on her over and over had jammed two of Gwenna's fingers, fingers that blazed with pain as she wrenched them back into proper alignment, then settled into a dull, constant ache. The physical effort, however, did something to distract from the horror of the slarn itself, and it was only as they lugged the writhing creature into the light of the bonfire, only when Gwenna saw the shocked and horrified expressions on the faces of the washouts, only when she smelled their fear, hot and rotten, that she felt the full weight of what she meant to do.

"You want it to *bite* us?" Qora asked, pulling Gwenna's attention away from Quick Jak. The woman's shaved scalp was slick with sweat, dark skin glistening in the firelight. "You want us to *let* it bite us?"

"You wanted to be Kettral?" Gwenna asked. She nodded toward the slarn. "This is how you get to be Kettral."

Qora was staring, they were *all* staring, but only a few were looking at the beast pinioned in front of them. Most of them were looking at *her*, Gwenna realized; they were staring with a mixture of awe and fear, as though some vicious killer had suddenly appeared in their midst, some implacable warrior they were powerless to resist. The whole thing made her sick.

"What the fuck did you *expect* from Hull's Trial?" she demanded. "A short essay on your favorite line from the *Tactics*?"

"It's poison," Manthe said from beyond the ambit of the

circle. She refused to come within twenty paces of the creature, but she'd risen to her feet as though getting ready to flee, had one hand on the pommel of her sword while the other kneaded the filthy hem of her tunic over and over. Her eyes burned, fever-bright behind her tangled hair, and though her voice trembled, it was loud enough for everyone to hear. "You remember Carl over on Arim? Poor old shaking Carl? This is what happened to him. *This.*"

Gwenna made herself nod calmly, made herself meet the frightened eyes of the washouts. "Manthe is right, but she's not telling you the whole story. The bite of a slarn is poison, but there is a way to cure it. There are eggs in this cave, slarn eggs. Those eggs are the antidote. Find one, drink it, and the poison goes away."

"Then why do it at all?" Qora demanded. "It's pointless."

"No," Gwenna replied. "It is not. Something about the poison and the egg, about the combination of the two . . . it changes a person. It makes you stronger and faster. You can feel things, hear things you've never heard before. It's those advantages that make the Kettral the Kettral—those just as much as the birds and the blades. They're part of the *reason* we were able to go down there and drag this one out."

A murmur of shock, of disbelief ran around the circle.

"Tell them, Manthe," Gwenna said.

The woman backed away, shaking her head, out of the firelight and into the darkness. "This is madness. I'll have no part of it."

Talal stepped forward instead. The ugly seam down his arm had already clotted and begun to scab over. He held it up to the firelight, where everyone could see, then ran a finger along the damaged flesh. "It's true," he said simply. "I took this wound barely an hour ago. We are asking you to believe a shocking thing, but we can offer our own bodies as testament to the truth."

As usual, Gwenna marveled at the steadiness in his voice, the grave, quiet confidence in those dark eyes. *If I had any brains,* she thought, *I'd let him do* all *the talking. I'd only open my mouth when we really needed to piss someone off.*

The fear-stink still rolled off the assembled soldiers, but there was something else there, too, a smell she couldn't quite place: awe, maybe, or hope.

Then Jak started up again. "I know that you're telling the truth," the flier said quietly. "It's what they told us at my own Trial. But we could *die* down there."

And just like that, it was impossible to keep quiet.

"You could die just about anywhere," Gwenna snapped. "You could die right here in this cavern. The fire could go out and the slarn could come. Rallen could smoke you out or starve you out. You could eat a hunk of rancid gull meat and die curled up on the floor shitting out your own guts."

Strangely, suddenly, she thought of Pyrre, of the woman's casual indifference to her own inevitable doom. For the first time, it actually seemed sensible, enviable. Maybe it was even beautiful to live so close to the ugly fact of death and yet to feel so little fear. Gwenna racked her mind for what Pyrre might say to these terrified soldiers. Probably nothing. She'd probably just laugh at the lot of them and walk off.

She took a deep breath, gathered her calm, tried all over again to sound reasonable. "The thing is—" she began.

Hobb cut her off. "The thing is, these people aren't Kettral." Manthe still trembled in the far shadows, her back pressed against the rock wall. Her husband, however, had approached the group while Gwenna was haranguing Jak. He stood just beyond the circle now, thick arms crossed over his chest, surveying the washouts scornfully. "They're not ready for the Trial. They might never be ready. I told you this before."

Gwenna turned to face the man. The slarn thrashed on the floor between them, but she stepped forward anyway, straight over the flailing beast, taking the straightest line toward the other Kettral. The other soldiers, sensing the danger, parted to give her room. Hobb didn't step back, but he dropped a hand to the handle of the sword at his waist. Gwenna didn't bother with her own sword, flicking free her belt knife instead when she was a pace and a half away.

To his credit, Hobb was just as quick with his own weapon, but a sword is longer than a knife, and takes longer to draw. Just as he pulled it clear of the sheath, Gwenna slammed it aside, stepped into the gap, and laid her knife's edge against his throat. "You *did* tell me before," she said. "I remember. You told me they weren't ready. And I told you they *are*. They trained as Kettral, every single one of them. When Rallen came with his second chance, they stepped forward to take it. When Rallen played his cards and started his killing, *these people* were the ones who fought back, who resisted, and who got away."

Hobb started to respond, eyes wide with rage, but Gwenna pressed her knife deeper into his neck.

"And it wasn't because of you and your fucking wife, whatever you told them. They're not alive because of you. They are alive because they are strong. Because they are survivors. What you have helped them to do is *hide*. You've convinced them to quit hunting and allowed them to become *hunted*. They are fucking *losing* because of you. And so if I hear another word about how they're not ready, how they're not Kettral, how they can't do what they need to do, I am going to cut your throat, and then I'm going to cut your wife's throat, and I am going to feed both your useless, cowardly carcasses to the slarn."

If Hobb was frightened of the knife at his neck, he didn't show it. Instead, his lip curled up in a sneer. "You fool," he said, shaking his head slowly. "You little fool."

Gwenna met the man's furious eyes, wondering if she was going to have to make good on her threat, but before she could respond, Qora spoke from behind her, the woman's voice quiet but clear above the sounds of the slarn scraping against the floor, the crackling and shifting of the fire. "I'll do it."

Gwenna didn't turn. She kept her knife on Hobb's throat,

ready to open it if he twitched. Hobb's eyes, however, moved past her, toward the washouts gathered around the slarn.

"Listen to this, and listen good," he spat. "The fact that one bitch barely past her own Trial tells you you're good doesn't make you good. I flew missions with the Kettral for more than a decade, with real Kettral, and I'll tell you something you don't want to hear: you're not Kettral. You're slower. You're weaker. You're dumber. And if you follow her," he raised his chin toward Gwenna without bothering to look at her, "Jakob Rallen is going to cut you to ribbons."

Again, it was Qora who replied. "Then I'll die fighting. That's what Kettral do, right? They die fighting, not hiding."

For once, Gwenna managed to keep her own mouth shut. She waited for Hobb's eyes to return to her, then she just smiled. The man spat past her, onto the stone, then turned, indifferent to the small slice her knife left on his throat, stalking back to the far end of the cavern where his wife waited in the shadows. Manthe hissed something urgent and desperate when he reached her—all Gwenna could make out was . . . *careful* . . . and . . . *my love* . . . and then Hobb wrapped a brusque hand around her shoulders, ignoring Gwenna and the rest as though they'd ceased to exist.

Gwenna exhaled slowly, sheathed her knife. When she turned, Qora had already taken a step into the human circle, a step toward the thrashing slarn.

"I'll do it," she said again. Then, before anyone could respond, as though dragged forward by her own fear, she darted the last few paces, baring her arm to the creature. Gwenna watched as the slarn, scenting flesh, twisted in its bonds, then brought those jaws to bear. Startled by the movement, Qora jerked back with a shout. She was fast, but not fast enough. The beast snagged two fingers on her left hand, severing them at the second joint, shrieking that high, hair-raising shriek just at the edge of hearing. Qora straightened, staring half in shock at the blood welling from the stumps of her fingers, then pulled back.

Gwenna swallowed her curse, and crossed to her. It wasn't a bad wound—clean, tendon neatly severed, no crushed bone—but it was a wound, all the same, worse than required for the Trial, and it was bleeding badly. The others had gone abruptly silent, as though the horror was lodged in their throats. Gwenna could smell the fear, hot and rotten. They were ready to break.

"Look," she said, seizing Qora by the wrist, pressing down on the artery even as she held the woman's hand in the air for the others to see. "This is what you're afraid of."

"Her fingers . . . ," someone gasped.

"I know," Gwenna replied. "It got two of her fingers." She looked slowly from one to the next, pronouncing the next words as clearly as she could. "So what?"

They gaped at her, unable to parse the question.

"So what?" Gwenna said again. She could hear Talal moving behind her, stirring at the fire for some reason. She ignored him, turning to Qora instead.

"You can still stand, right?"

The woman nodded shakily.

"And you can talk?"

Another nod.

"Let them hear you talk."

After a long pause, Qora ground out the words between gritted teeth. "I want to gut that fucking thing."

Gwenna smiled.

"Hear that? Not only can she walk and talk, she wants to *fight*. You're all frightened. I understand that, but I want you to look at this, and to keep looking until you understand." She gave Qora's mangled hand a little shake. "This is what you're afraid of and it is *nothing*. Am I right, Qora?"

Please, Hull, she prayed silently, *let me be right.*

Qora licked her lips, then, after a moment, she nodded.

"We need to cauterize it," Talal said quietly. The leach had come up behind Gwenna's shoulder. He held a red-hot belt knife in his hand. Gwenna grimaced. Qora had shown some grit so far, but the burning was going to hurt a lot more than the original wound. To her shock, however, Qora looked over at Talal, met his eyes, then nodded. "I'll do it myself."

Talal started to object. "It'll be—"

"She'll do it," Gwenna said. "She's earned it."

And they need to see this.

Talal hesitated, then handed the woman the knife. Qora stared at the glowing steel as though it were a snake. Then, with a bellow of defiance, pressed it against her ravaged flesh. Blood hissed, bubbled. The stench of seared meat filled the air, and after a moment she dropped the knife, sagging to one knee. Then slowly, painfully, she stood again.

"All right," she said quietly, meeting Gwenna's eyes. For once there was no bluster in her voice, no anger. "I did it. Now what?"

Gwenna nodded, clapped the woman on the shoulder. The extra stiffness in Qora's spine, the proud tilt of her chin—it was worth a couple fingers. Gwenna studied the other washouts, pausing on Jak. The flier's face had gone pale as the slarn's belly. Qora might have found resolve in her wound, but clearly the sight had only sickened the flier further.

"I go down now?" Qora asked. "Go looking for the egg?"

Gwenna shook her head. "No. You don't go in alone."

"That's the way they did it during my Trial," Jak said. "One at a time."

"Yeah," Gwenna said. "We got that shit, too. And it was stupid. You're going to fight as a Wing, you're going to die, if it comes to dying, as a Wing. I figure you can do this, too, as a Wing. Now . . . who's going to join Qora?"

There was no sound but the fire and the hammering heartbeats of two dozen washouts. Gwenna looked from face to stricken face, hauled in a deep breath, trying to catch a whiff of the resolve, or anger, or courage they so desperately needed. No one moved. No one met her eyes.

I was wrong, she thought bleakly. *I played it all wrong.*

From the far end of the cavern came Hobb's low, derisive laugh. "I told you," he growled. "They're not ready."

Gwenna considered killing the man. It wouldn't fix any of the washouts, but it would feel good to tackle a problem she knew how to solve. She couldn't fix cowardice, couldn't fix a lifetime of failures, couldn't find the right words to forge pig iron into true steel. She could, however, face a live man with a sword in his hand and make him dead. That, at least, was something she understood.

Before she'd moved, however, Delka stepped forward quietly. "I'm ready," she said.

Gwenna turned to stare at her, this woman in her early fifties, her hair more gray than brown, the wrinkles deep around her eyes, dark skin spotted from long days in the sun. She smelled frightened, but she didn't flinch as she rolled up her sleeve, baring her arm for the slarn. She studied the monster for a moment, then met Gwenna's eyes, and, shockingly, she smiled.

"I'm ready," she said again. "I've been getting ready for this a long, long time."

In the end, amazingly, they all stepped forward. All but Quick Jak, who stood trembling like an autumn leaf, eyes fixed on the blood-spattered stone. Most of the rebels were already below, hunting in groups of four or five for the slarn eggs that would save them. Three of the bitten soldiers stood at the gaping mouth of the tunnel, clutching their fresh wounds, waiting impatiently for Jak to step up, bare his pale skin for the writhing slarn, then join them. Jak, however, was not stepping up.

"It's time," Gwenna said, trying to balance her voice on the narrow edge between encouragement and scorn. "Your turn, Jak."

He didn't respond, didn't even seem to hear her. Instead he watched the slarn, staring at that hideous, eyeless face, his own eyes pried wide with the horror, helpless as a mouse caught in the snake's cold gaze. He'd watched the others, watched every one of them as they stepped up to be savaged by the creature. Gwenna had taken that for a good sign; he hadn't looked away, hadn't even flinched, really. Now she wasn't so sure. That stare of his seemed locked to his face. He wasn't looking because he wanted to; he was looking because his fear compelled him.

"Jak," she said, crossing the rough stone floor to grab him by the jerkin. "It's time."

She had to shake him to break his gaze, to get him to look at her instead of the blood-soaked slarn. When he did, she knew that it was hopeless. The terror had him, had him utterly. It was seared into his eyes. She could smell it, thick in his fetid sweat. She could hear it in his rapid breathing, shallow and far too fast as it rasped between bared teeth, chapped lips. He wasn't going to do it, *couldn't* do it. In another circumstance, she would have let him go, would have shoved him away, indulged briefly in her own pity and disgust for the failure of a man who could have been a soldier, then let it go.

But we need him, she thought. *Hull help us all, we need him.*

There were two other fliers in the group: Delka and a fat, ginger-haired idiot named Corantan. The fight against Rallen, when it came, might well rest in large part on the birds and the people flying them.

And so you want a coward in the mix, a busted-up excuse for a man who lets his panic paralyze him?

She didn't, but then, wanting didn't much come into the question. According to everyone, Quick Jak was a genius when you put him on a bird's back. He'd made it all the way through training, after all, made it all the way to the Trial. Despite his current paralysis, he couldn't be a complete fuckup. She needed him in the battle against Rallen, needed someone to wrangle the Dawn King, to make the best use of the fastest, most powerful bird, and after that . . . Gwenna had tried to put the thought out of her head, but the truth was there, bald, ugly, and undeniable: after Laith's death, her own Wing needed another flier. Delka might be all right, but Delka seemed too old, too soft, too gentle.

Gwenna just couldn't get out of her mind the memory of Jak swimming the midnight swells, that strong, efficient, almost effortless stroke, the way he wasn't even breathing hard when he climbed out of the ocean and shook off the last of the spray. He could be so *good*. . . . It was like finding a beautiful blade, perfectly balanced but gone to rust on the surface. You didn't throw away a blade like that. You got a stone and you scoured it clean.

"It's time," she said again.

He looked at her, then dropped his eyes. She could almost taste his shame, sick-sweet in the back of her mouth. Those strong shoulders slumped forward as he shook his head.

"I can't, Gwenna. I couldn't then, and I can't now. I'm sorry."

"I don't care what happened then, and I don't care how sorry you are, you need to do this. Your friends need you to do it." She almost admitted that *she* needed him to do it, but stopped herself. "Let's go," she said instead.

"I *can't*," he insisted, his voice quiet but horribly tight. Anger roughened those syllables now, and he jerked away from her hand on his shoulder. "Just leave it, all right?"

"No," Gwenna said. "It is not all right, and I won't leave it."

"Gwenna," Talal said. The leach stood a few paces away, his arms crossed over his chest, dark eyes grave.

"Don't interfere," she snapped.

"Hull's Trial is a voluntary crucible," Talal continued. "To make it anything else is to turn it into a sort of torture."

"Do you see me forcing him?" she demanded, holding her hands up.

Over by the tunnel mouth leading down into the dark, the others watched them, urgency and reluctance warring on their faces. Gwenna could remember what they felt, the slow, mesmer-izing burn of the poison gnawing its way up through the flesh, up, up, up, like some awful, mindless acid stupidly seeking the heart.

"Every heartbeat you delay," she said, leaning in so close that Jak couldn't avoid her face, "is killing your Wing."

"They're not my Wing."

"They are until this Trial is over," Gwenna spat. "And you are *letting them down.*"

His explosion happened instantly and without warning. One moment he was hanging his head, shame and terror steaming off of him. The next, he'd seized her by the shoulders, was screaming into her face, his lips drawn back in a rabid rictus, his spittle hitting her in the face.

"That's why I'm not going to do it, Gwenna! I'm not Kettral. I've never been Kettral. I was good with the birds and that was *it*! And if you think I'm letting someone down now, wait until it comes to a real fight. You saw what happened back on Hook, but you don't understand. It's like that *every fucking time.* I don't want it to be that way. I hate it. I *hate* it. But I can't *help* it, Gwenna. The fear, it just . . . gets me. It's like a claw closed tight around my heart, and I can't move, I can't *breathe,* all I can think about is getting *out*. Getting *safe*! If this was something I could cut out of myself with a knife," he said, dropping her shoulders to bare his chest, as though exposing some treacherous organ, "I would start cutting. I would carve it out if it killed me. But it's *not*." He shook his head, and finally his voice subsided. "It's been there all my life, since I was a tiny boy. This fear is part of every memory I have."

"I don't accept that," Gwenna said finally.

"It doesn't *matter* if you accept it," he said. "It's real. It's an ugly, disgusting fact, but it's a fact."

"Well, I'll tell you another fact," Gwenna replied grimly. "If you want to save yourself, if you want to survive, you've got to go down in those tunnels."

"Gwenna," Talal said, voice harder this time.

"I'm not going down there," Jak said. "I quit. I refuse the Trial."

"No," Gwenna said, spinning easily on one foot, sweeping the flier's ankle, catching him in a half lock before he hit the ground, wrapping her legs around his chest, then flipping him toward the thrashing slarn. He tried to resist, made a good show of it, actually. He was *strong,* and if they'd been wrestling to a pin, or a blackout, he would have given her a run for her money. She didn't need to pin him, though. Didn't need to knock him out. All she needed to do was hold him half a heartbeat as the slarn's jaws snapped shut on his forearm, tearing away a flap of skin and muscle. Jak bellowed, and she let him loose, rolling away and to her feet, dropping into a fighter's crouch in case he came after her.

Instead, he was staring at his arm. Blood wept down the skin, puddling on the floor. The creature gnashed its teeth, searching for more, and the flier pulled back, eyes wide with disbelief.

"Hull's Trial is voluntary," he said quietly. "You can't force someone to do it."

"No one's forcing you," Gwenna replied. "You have a choice. You can let the poison gut you, or you can go with your fucking Wing."

"That was wrong," Talal said.

"Spare me the lesson in morality," Gwenna spat. She stared into the bonfire, following the shifting shapes as logs turned to embers, then the embers caved under their own weight, sending showers of spark and ash into the air. They'd fed the hungry fire half a dozen times since the last poisoned Wing, including Quick Jak, disappeared down Hull's gullet. It was impossible to gauge time down in the Hole, but it seemed someone should have come back. "I know it's not the way the Eyrie used to do it, but we *need* him, Talal."

"We do not," Annick said. She had her bow in hand. Whether

she was guarding against a sudden appearance of slarn, or against Manthe and Hobb, who were crouched in whispered conversation over at their corner of the cavern, Gwenna couldn't say. "He is the weakest of the entire lot. And they are all weak."

"He's not weak," Gwenna insisted. "He is *afraid*."

The sniper shook her head as though the statement didn't make sense. "Fear is a weakness. A dangerous weakness."

"We *all* have weaknesses. I'm not saying Quick Jak is going to be the Flea someday, but he deserves a chance."

"Chances are something that people need to take for themselves," Talal pointed out. "Part of your reason for sending them down into the Hole in the first place was to build their confidence. It doesn't build a man's confidence to knock him down, then offer him up as meat for a beast that terrifies him."

"I know," Gwenna said, putting up a hand as though she could block the objection. "I understand that. But we all need a nudge sometimes. I was terrified my first barrel drop, couldn't make myself undo the buckle. You know what Adaman Fane did? He cut the straps and shoved me off the talon. And I realized, as soon as I hit the water, that I could do it, that I'd *done* it. The next time, I did the buckles myself."

"You are not Quick Jak," Talal said quietly.

"Of course not. We're all our own people."

"That's not what he means," Annick said.

"Well, what the fuck does he mean?"

"I mean you're . . . better suited to this," Talal said.

"I'm not *suited* to it. Every 'Kent-kissing thing I've learned has been a struggle."

"Maybe," Annick said, cutting her off. The sniper pursed her lips, flicked her bowstring with a finger. The note echoed in the empty chamber. Annick waited for it to die out before she continued. "And still, you are what the Eyrie aims for when they train us. You're the perfect Kettral."

Gwenna stared at her. For a moment all words failed. "Are you fucking *mad*?" she managed finally.

"No," Annick replied evenly. "I was there when we fought our way free of Long Fist. I saw you command the defense of Andt-Kyl. I saw you pull Qora out of the mess over on Hook."

"I was *improvising*. Annick, I was *making that shit up*."

Talal just laughed. The sudden mirth was both welcome and disconcerting. "That's the point," he said. "Kettral improvise. They fight on the fly. When the Flea put you in charge of the Wing, he did it for a reason. You're good at this shit."

Gwenna stared from one to the other, unsure what to make of the lump in her throat. Before she could get too emotional, however, the smile slipped off the leach's face, and he was shaking his head.

"That's what we're trying to tell you about Jak. Just because something worked for you doesn't mean it will work for him. I like the guy, too, Gwenna. I'm sorry he's broken, but he *is* broken. You're a great demolitions master and an even better Wing leader, but that doesn't mean you can fix him."

Annick nodded. "Keep trying, and someone's going to get hurt. Killed."

"That *happens* to Kettral," Gwenna retorted. "We get killed."

"Quick Jak's not Kettral."

Gwenna turned away, staring into the tunnel where it snaked away into the labyrinth below. When she finally managed to speak again, her own quiet words sounded strange in her ears, half desperate, half defiant:

"Not yet."

By the time they'd heaped the central fire with wood another half-dozen times, the sniper's warning was starting to look horribly prescient. All of the Wings had returned from the Hole—bloody, with broken fingers or twisted ankles, limping, leaning on one another, glancing over shoulders at some remembered terror, at a recollected triumph—all except for Quick Jak's.

The rebels clustered around the fire, too exhausted, mostly, for the sharing of stories or the comparing of wounds. Some dozed off, while others went at the stores of dried meat and fruit with a vengeance. They looked more like weary workers at the end of a long harvest week in the fields than they did soldiers, but Gwenna could smell the satisfaction on them, could hear the new note of pride in their voices. Sure, she'd changed the rules of the Trial; sure, she'd given them plenty of light and sent them down in groups; sure, it was ten times easier than what Gwenna's own class of cadets had faced. None of that *mattered*. Not to them. Not now. They'd faced the slarn, had gone down into the Hole panicked and poisoned, and then they had found what they were looking for and come back out. They had *won*.

All of them but Quick Jak and his three companions.

Gwenna had taken to pacing impatiently over by the tunnel mouth, eighteen steps to the ledge, turn, eighteen steps back. She'd tried stepping into that darkness and listening, but that made it worse. For someone with her hearing, there were a hundred sounds whispering up from the depths of the cave, water washing the cold stone, wind etching the stalactites, underground rivers rumbling in the rock's throat. The sounds of Hull's darkness—none of them human.

After she'd paced off the distance four or five hundred times, Delka came over to join her. Talal was busy tending to the wounded—wrapping bandages and splinting fingers—while Annick continued to stand watch against any number of hypothetical threats, the seen and the unseen. Both of them had given Gwenna her space when she finally shoved her way free of the fire and the questions both, leaving her to stalk back and forth in a cloud of her own doubt. Delka, however, had gone into the Hole before the whole scene with Jak. She had no idea what had happened, and a smile creased her lined face as she approached.

"Thank you," she said simply.

Gwenna stared at her. The punctures in the woman's arm had scabbed over, but she had other wounds—a gash across her scalp that left her face streaked with blood, a huge contusion on her left shoulder, purple so dark it was almost black except at the red, angry edges. Blood smeared her teeth. She looked like she'd spent half the night losing a rough fight, like she ought to be sleeping it off somewhere dark and quiet, not standing in front of Gwenna grinning. Not fucking *thanking* her.

"For what?" Gwenna demanded.

"For letting us do it. For encouraging us."

"Encouraging . . . ," Gwenna said, shaking her head, remembering Quick Jak's frantic thrashing as she held him down, imagining him and the others lost in the tunnels below, maybe dead already, ripped to fleshy ribbons by the slarn.

"You see anyone else when you were down there? Any of the . . . others?"

Delka met her eyes, shook her head slowly. "Just slarn. But we weren't really looking, Gwenna. They could be finding the egg right now. They could be on their way up already."

"Or they could be dead," Gwenna said.

To her surprise, Delka nodded. "They could be dead," she agreed, voice matter-of-fact. "That's what it is to lead soldiers, Gwenna. Sometimes you make the right decision and people still get hurt. Sometimes they still die."

"I understand that," Gwenna growled. "I understand it better than *you* do. While you were eating sliced firefruit over on Arim, I was up to my elbows in blood fighting the Urghul in Andt-Kyl." She could still hear Pikker John's screams as the horses lashed to his limbs pawed the earth, tearing him apart. She could still see the captives, bound hand and foot, heads bent toward the dirt, helpless as statuary in the moment before her starshatter rent them to pieces. "I know you lose people in a fight, but this isn't a fight."

She glared at Delka a moment longer, then glanced into the darkness of the Hole once more. She could hear the river down there, groaning over the stone like something huge and in pain. She smelled blood, thick and hot on the back of her tongue; some of the stench came from the cavern behind her, where the returning men and women nursed their wounds, some from the warren of tunnels below.

"The Eyrie has always sent men and women into the Hole," Delka said quietly. "They don't always come out."

Gwenna shook her head. "When the Eyrie sent us in we were trained. We were *ready*."

The older woman laid a hand on Gwenna's shoulder. "I don't know the other three well, but Quick Jak and I used to run together over on Arim. He's strong. He's smart."

"Is that enough?" Gwenna growled.

Delka spread her hands. "We'll have to wait to find out."

Gwenna shook her head curtly, seized a burning torch from its makeshift sconce near the entrance to the tunnel, then slipped a blade from the sheath on her back. "No," she said quietly, stepping into the darkness before anyone could call her back. "We won't."

As it turned out, Delka was right. Gwenna found Jak less than a quarter mile below the cavern where the rebels made their camp, limping up the uneven stone, one blade bare and bloody, his own torch burned down to a guttering stump.

Thank Hull, she thought, relief flooding through her like light, like air. Then she saw his face, the awful shock scrawled across his features, looked past him into the deeper dark, listened for those other footfalls, for the three other soldiers who had gone down into the Hole with him, who weren't coming out.

"They're dead," he said. His voice, too, sounded dead.

"How?" Gwenna asked, covering the distance between them at a lope.

Jak just shook his head.

"How?" she demanded, shoving her torch almost into his

face, trying to read what had happened in the spatters of blood, in the dark soot smeared across his skin.

He stared at her, incredulous. "What do you mean, *how?* There are monsters down there, you bitch. Bigger than the one you dragged up into the cavern, the one you fed our blood to."

She shook her head, as though to refuse the truth. "The others all made it. The others came back."

"Maybe the others were *better*."

"No," she said. "They weren't. You're one of the only wash-outs who actually made it all the way to the Trial. You're younger than most of them, and you're stronger. I've seen you swim."

"It's not swimming down there," he said, staring at the naked blade as though he had woken up only moments before, had just now discovered it clutched in his hand. "It's a lot uglier than swimming."

"What happened?"

"The slarn happened," Jak said, shaking his head, eyes wide, mind obviously lost in the memory. "Half a dozen of them. We found the nest. Enough eggs to go around. Thought we got lucky. We were actually laughing as we drank from them, slapping each other on the back." He closed his eyes. "Then they hit us."

"And did you fight back?"

"Of course," he said quietly. "What else could we do?"

What else could we do? Gwenna stared at him. The flier was spattered with blood, but not much of it seemed to be *his*. There was that initial wound, wet and messy on his arm, and a handful of scratches. Nothing more. Nothing to indicate a bare-knuckle fight to the death.

What else could we do?

"You could run," Gwenna said. Even in her own ears, her voice sounded like a knife sliding across stone.

Jak opened his eyes, met her stare. "There was no need. Not in the end."

"You killed six slarn?"

"I didn't do it by myself. Helli killed at least three before the big one tore out her throat. Gim got one, I think. All I know is that they were all dead, finally. I was the only one left. Me and the largest of those monsters, and he was already all cut up. Dumb beast, practically dead on his feet and didn't know it. I finished him."

Gwenna studied him. She could smell the grief, but grief for what? For seeing his companions killed or for leaving them? He'd frozen up that night in Hook, had all but abandoned Qora to the mercy of Rallen's thugs. Was it really likely that he'd behaved any differently, that he'd behaved *better* in the tight, twisting darkness of the Hole? Gwenna had shoved him down into the cave's gut hoping that could be true, but all those hours pacing back and forth in front of the fire had eroded her hope. Despair had had hours to whisper its own sibilant song, insistent as a river undercutting the bank: *He's a coward. He's a coward, and you were a fool.*

"You don't believe me," Jak said, shaking his head wearily. "You think I ran."

Gwenna took a deep breath. "Take me to the bodies. They deserve to be burned."

Not just that. A few minutes studying the dead, and she'd know what had happened, who had fought and who had fled.

"I can't."

"We'll find them," Gwenna insisted grimly. "Just a matter of a little backtracking."

"I didn't forget the way. The bodies aren't there. I threw them into a river that carved its way through the cave."

Gwenna's jaw throbbed. She realized she was grinding her teeth together, biting down so hard on her anger that pain lanced down the back molars.

"Why did you do that?"

"I wasn't going to leave them for the slarn. They're people. Not meat."

And now they're gone, Gwenna thought bleakly. *The bodies and the truth with them.*

"I didn't run," Jak said, eyes weary but defiant.

She opened her mouth, ready to press the point, then shook her head, turning abruptly on her heel. There was no way to get at the facts, not anymore. And even if the flier *had* run, even if he had frozen up or abandoned his companions, it was Gwenna Sharpe who had forced him down there in the first place.

28

Nightly, when evening's keen knife carved away the light, Valyn felt rather than saw the coming darkness in the air, which cooled to ice against his skin. He heard night in the silence of brighter birds, jays and woodpeckers giving way to the muttering of bats, the owl's long cry. Night had its own smell—harder and more grudging than the scents of the day, as though every flower had closed, every leaf furled against the cold. And Valyn could feel the night inside himself as well, feel his own body answering the rhythms of the larger world, muscles tensing, hands closing into fists, breath faster in his lungs, hearing honed to such a point that every woodland crack and rustle cut.

It was almost impossible to believe that there had been a time when darkness meant relaxation and rest, that there were still millions of men and women the whole world over who turned down the lamp, snuffed the candle, then curled comfortably into their blankets. Since his blinding, Valyn's whole body had rebelled against sleep's surrender. Most nights he managed only a few fitful bouts of nightmare, waking sweating more often than not, trembling, clutching the haft of his ax. Most nights, he fought sleep as hard as he could, back to a boulder or tree, staring into the cold dark, and so, despite the late hour, he was awake to hear the Flea approaching, boots quiet in the dried hemlock needles.

The Urghul had made camp under a stand of pines a hundred

paces to the north. Valyn could still hear a few of them talking quietly, eating and dicing. Huutsuu was among them, her rich laughter threaded on the breeze. If she came to visit him at all, it would be later, much later.

A quarter mile to the south, the Kettral had hunkered down in their own bivouac. Valyn could smell Sigrid and Newt, the leach's delicate perfume twining strangely on the night air with the Aphorist's half-rancid stench. Valyn couldn't say whether they were awake or asleep, but they were far off and staying there. The Flea was approaching alone. Valyn wasn't sure how the man knew where he had bedded down, but the Wing leader was making straight for him, slowly but inexorably as the falling of night itself.

Valyn had been expecting this encounter, dreading it from the moment he realized the Flea was still alive. He'd half expected the Wing leader to just kill him, to find him wandering around the forest with a band of Urghul and cut his throat. Some broken part of him had been hoping for that. Dying was easy, after all—a little pain, and then nothing. What had to happen now—that was hard.

When the Flea was half a dozen feet away, he paused. He smelled like leather, and wool, and good, sharp steel. They'd talked earlier, obviously, but this was different. This time there was no Urghul band surrounding them. This time there would be no hiding from the past.

"So," the Flea said quietly.

"So," Valyn replied, parrying the syllable with his own.

"Time to talk."

"We talked this morning."

"That's not what I mean."

Valyn shook his head. "You already talked to Gwenna months ago. Gwenna and Annick. I'm sure you heard it all from them."

"I want to hear it from you." The Flea didn't raise his voice, but there was something dangerous in the words, something that made Valyn lean back against the tree, his body trying in vain to put a little more space between them. He didn't want to go over it all again, to say it aloud, to explore the dismal chronicle of his own failure, but then, sometimes wanting didn't really come into it. After Finn's death, he owed the other man an explanation. That much, at least, was clear.

He blew out a long breath. "We got to Assare just before dusk—"

"No."

Valyn hesitated.

"Start earlier," the Flea said. "Start on the Islands. Why did you leave?"

Valyn shook his head silently, trying to find the words. His life on the Qirins—Ha Lin and Gent, barrel drops and mess hall slop—it all seemed like something from a dream. Worse, when Valyn thought back on himself, on the self he had been before losing his eyes, he barely recognized the man. Valyn the Kettral cadet, the Wing leader—he had died somewhere between the Bone Mountains and Andt-Kyl. What he had become, he had no idea.

"There was a conspiracy . . . ," he managed finally.

It was a twisted, tortuous tale, but it didn't take long to tell it: how Balendin had killed Ha Lin, had tried to murder Valyn himself; how the Aedolians had come for Kaden; how Valyn's rage at the *kenarang* had blinded him to all the rest; how he had sat atop the tower in Andt-Kyl while his friends fought, while they died. He'd lived every detail of the story over and over, waking and in nightmare, but it was another thing to say the words aloud, and when he finished, he was trembling. If he hadn't been sitting already, his back pressed up against a huge hemlock, he thought he might collapse.

"It's no easy thing," the Flea said finally, "losing a Wingmate."

It seemed a strange thing to focus on, after all the rest. After all the talk of Csestriim gates and imperial treachery, Valyn hadn't expected the man to return to the simple fact of a soldier fighting, dying. That was what soldiers did, after all. It was the least of the tale. And yet it was Laith's death, Valyn realized with a cold shock, that remained lodged inside him like a poisoned arrowhead the medics had been unable to pull free. He'd had moments of success—killing Yurl, making sure Kaden got free—but who were Yurl and Kaden? Strangers. Valyn had slaughtered one and saved the other, but both actions seemed small now, trivial. Laith, on the other hand, had been a friend and a Wingmate, more a brother than Valyn's real brother. And Valyn had left him to die, fighting alone on a bridge.

He wanted to say all that, to force his own guilt and regret into words. After recounting the whole sick story, however, he found he had no more words to offer. Instead he just shook his head. "We're all going to die one day."

"Still," the Flea replied, his voice low and cold as the night wind. "The day matters."

Valyn let out a long, shuddering breath. "About Blackfeather Finn," he said finally. "I didn't . . ."

He trailed off. The Flea hadn't moved, hadn't even twitched, but the man smelled suddenly of grief, bright red grief twisted with rage, the scent so powerful that for a moment Valyn thought he might choke on it. The man's voice, however, when he finally spoke, was flat, level.

"Tell me about your eyes."

"No," Valyn replied. "I have to say this. About Finn . . ."

He wanted to talk about the fight in Assare, wanted to explain the whole context, how he couldn't have known the Flea's allegiance, how even after he'd decided to trust the other Wing, Pyrre had come out of the darkness. He wanted to explain that her killing wasn't his killing, that he hadn't ordered it, hadn't wanted it. . . .

"We're done talking about Finn," the Flea said, cutting into his thoughts. He hadn't raised his voice, but for just a moment Valyn could *see*. The other Wing leader stood a pace away. He'd moved his hand to his belt knife, but his eyes weren't on Valyn. He was looking up between the boughs, as though there were something to read in the night's black bowl. Then, as quickly as it had come, the vision was gone. Valyn suppressed a shudder. Vision meant danger, always and inevitably—mortal danger—as though there were more violence pent up in the Flea's few quiet words than in any number of bared blades. Wind blew down cold out of the north, raising the hairs on Valyn's neck. There had been no threats, no rage, but suddenly he felt certain that death had blown past him, just barely ruffling his hair.

Words were useless to stitch together some wounds, and so Valyn left behind the subject of Blackfeather Finn's death. "I can see," he said after a long pause. "Not most of the time. Only when there's a fight, when I'm about to die." He omitted the nightly violence of his sex with Huutsuu. "Like another sense, a new sense that isn't quite vision, shades of black on black. . . ." He trailed off, shaking his head.

For a long time the Flea said nothing. Valyn could smell the grief fading, dissipating on the night wind, replaced by the old steely focus. "Something that happened in the Hole?" he asked.

Valyn nodded slowly. "I think so. Maybe. At first it was the same . . . abilities as the rest of my Wing, only better, more. Talal thought it was because I ate from the black egg."

"And then?"

"Then il Tornja cut out my eyes."

The Flea was silent for a long time. At last he grunted. "Makes sense, I guess."

Valyn stared into the endless void of his burned-out vision.

"How," he demanded quietly, "does it make sense?"

"Slarn move just fine in the darkness. So do bats. Talal's probably right—you got it from the egg."

"If that was true, I would have had the sight from the moment I came out of the Hole."

"Not necessarily. You were busted up then, but you weren't broken."

"What's being broken have to do with it?"

For a while, the Flea didn't respond. Far off, somewhere to

the east, an owl's screech shredded the silence. Valyn could just make out the sounds of struggle, of some small forest creature writhing in the claws of the bird, screaming as it died. It was done in moments, and then the night clamped down again, cold and unbroken.

"Sometimes you need to break a thing," the Flea said finally, "in order to see what's inside it."

29

"I don't want it," Triste said, shaking her head as Adare slid the small glass of adamanth across the polished table.

"The world is filled with things we don't want," Adare replied. "Drink."

The leach glanced warily at the glass, then raised her violet eyes to study Adare.

"Things *we* don't want?" She shook her head. "Are you and I on the same side?"

"That depends on your side."

Triste didn't respond. She held Adare's gaze for a few moments, then looked away, examining the room in which they sat. Kegellen's wine cellar was small by imperial standards, barely a dozen paces square, but the modest space was more opulently appointed than most formal entrance halls. Cedar racks along the walls cradled thousands of bottles—bloody reds and sparkling whites, rose-pale vintages from Sellas and icewine from north of the Romsdals, rich and lustrous as gold. At a glance, the collection looked to be worth a lifetime's wages for most of the city's citizens, but Triste wasn't looking at the wine. The leach's gaze had drifted past the racks to snag on a statue in the corner.

The marble piece was one of a set of four, each gazing inward from its solitary plinth, two gods, two goddesses, clean-lined, pre-Annurian, slender-waisted, and naked. Intarra was there, of course, stern-browed and regal, her crown a towering sunburst carved in stone, and Hull, his eyes gouged into deep, shadowy sockets. The rendering of Meshkent made Adare's skin crawl; the Lord of Pain was gaunt, almost emaciated, all extra flesh chiseled away as though he were the victim of famine or some wasting disease. The statue's face, however, was ecstatic, the knife-sharp smile sickeningly wide.

But Triste wasn't looking at Hull or Meshkent. Her eyes were fixed on the depiction of Ciena. The Goddess of Pleasure was a popular subject in both painting and sculpture. Adare had seen more versions than she cared to remember; most imagined the goddess as little more than a wide-hipped, full-breasted slattern, her tongue poised coquettishly between her parted teeth, or her eyes closed, mouth half open in a silent moan. This Ciena was different, frank-eyed and direct, hard and unyielding beneath her marmoreal curves.

"What is this place?" Triste asked. Her eyes lingered on the statue a moment longer. Then she turned slowly, almost grudgingly back to Adare. "Where are we?"

"A private home."

"Why did you take me outside the palace?"

"Because everyone inside the palace wants to kill you."

If Triste was disturbed by the revelation, it didn't show. That scarred, perfect face didn't show much of anything. The girl—and she *was* barely more than a girl—reminded Adare of the stones players she used to watch growing up, silent figures bent over tables tucked away into mossy corners of the palace gardens. There was no obvious similarity. Those players were old, Triste was young, they were all men, while the leach was undeniably a woman, and yet the girl had learned, in her short years, had learned as well as those canny stones players, how to keep her face closed, how to scrub away any expression that might be read and used against her.

"And you *don't* want to kill me?"

"I don't want to kill you," Adare replied. *What I want is to*

know who you are, and why il Tornja needs you dead so badly.
"Obviously."

The leach shook her head. "Nothing is obvious. You were supposed to be in the north. Losing the war."

Adare ignored the barb. "I came back."

"Kaden allowed that?"

"He requested it. He brokered the treaty."

"And the council?"

"Is a collection of idiots."

Triste studied her. "Even idiots can kill. When they threw me in prison, most of those idiots were as eager to see you slaughtered as they were to watch me burn."

"That was nearly a year ago. Things change."

Triste shook her head again slowly, as though denying the possibility of change. When she spoke again, it was with a new wariness, her scarred, delicate hands closing into fists.

"And your general—Ran il Tornja—has he returned with you?"

Adare hesitated, wishing she could hear the question again, hear the girl's voice as she asked it. There was a connection between il Tornja and the leach, an important connection, there had to be—that was why he had risked so much to have her killed. Adare had expected Triste to be ignorant of it all, however; just another mortal stone in the Csestriim's plans. Triste's question, though, the sudden tension in her shoulders as she asked it, suggested otherwise, suggested that she knew that he wanted her. Maybe even *why* he wanted her.

"Do you know the *kenarang*?" Adare asked.

Triste stared at her. "How would I know him?"

"Do you?" The question came out harder than she'd intended, the words sharper, and Triste sat back in her chair, eyes hooded once more.

"No. I don't. Is he here?"

Adare shook her head, trying to see past the girl's words to the truth beneath. "The *kenarang* is still in the north, fighting the Urghul."

"But he sent you." The statement cut a little too close to the bone, and Triste smiled grimly, as though she'd seen the answer in Adare's face. "He sent you here for me."

"I came here," Adare replied, keeping a tight rein on her voice, "to heal the rift dividing Annur."

Triste shook her head slowly. "You just risked your life, you just *killed* a girl to get me out of there. You came for me."

And suddenly, Adare thought, *I'm answering the questions rather than asking them.*

She gestured to the glass in the middle of the table. "Drink."

Triste lifted the glass in one hand, raised it to the light, but made no move to take a sip.

"What if I won't?"

She had seemed half addled by the drug when Adare first dragged her from the prison. There was no way to know how much adamanth the guards had been giving her—according to Nira, a dose could last for a few minutes or a full day, depending on a dozen factors—and Adare had forced the girl to take several long swigs from the bottle during their long descent through the Spear. Triste had been quiet then, pliable, sipping absently from the flask as she stared over the banister of the spiral stairs into empty space. That compliance had evaporated, however, almost as soon as they were outside the red walls. Once they were free of the Dawn Palace, as soon as the leach began to believe in her freedom, she grew more defiant.

"If you won't drink it yourself," Adare replied, "someone will hold you down, and I will pour it down your throat."

Triste nodded, as though she'd expected as much. "So—I'm not out of prison after all."

Adare gestured to the room. "Do you see bars around you? Have I shackled you to the bottom of a steel cage?"

"Not all shackles are chains. When you tell me I can go, when you open that door, and the one beyond it, then step aside, when I'm miles away and no one has stopped me—*then* I'll begin to believe that you don't have me in a cage."

Adare scrubbed a hand through her hair. The climb had taken its toll on her legs, and the climb had been the easiest thing she'd done all day. If she closed her eyes, she could still see Mailly clutching her knees, drinking desperately from the bottle, then doubling over as the poison began its work. Through the whole descent, whenever Adare heard a steel door slam open or shut, the echo of boots over metal, the clanking of chains, she imagined that behind it, underneath it, she could hear the girl's screams. Even when they reached the ground, even after they exited the tower, she half expected Simit and his guards to come pouring out after them crying treason, demanding that Triste should pull back her hood. Only when she'd finally stepped inside the gate of Kegellen's carefully guarded compound—a different mansion than the one in which she had first met Dhati and Mailly—had Adare allowed herself to relax a fraction. That was when she realized how exhausted she was.

"Fine," she said quietly. "You're not free. I didn't break you out of the middle of the Dawn Palace just so I could drop you off at the nearest tavern with a pile of coin. I need something from you. A girl died so I could get it. And so, until I do, you're not going anywhere, you're not seeing a 'Kent-kissing thing but these walls." Triste's lips tightened, but Adare was beyond caring. "I don't trust you," she went on. "You're a leach and a murderer. I read the reports of what you did inside the Jasmine Court, how you paved the way for Kaden's return. . . ."

"I wasn't—"

"I don't care," Adare said, cutting her off. "Later, I might need to know why you did it. Later, I might need to know all kinds of fucking things. Right now, however, what I need is for you to drink what's in that glass. You can do it on your own, or, as I just got done saying, I can have someone pour it down your throat. It's your choice."

Triste met her gaze. Her face remained still, but Adare could see a new light in those flawless eyes—anger, maybe. Or hate.

At least she's not just staring at the 'Kent-kissing lamps anymore.

Without looking away, the leach raised the adamanth to her lips, drank deep, finishing it in a single swallow, then slammed the glass back to the table so violently it cracked.

Triste grimaced, shuddered, then shook her head. "Well, one thing's clear—you're nothing like your brother."

Adare almost laughed. "No. Not aside from the eyes."

"Even the eyes. They both blaze, but his are . . . colder."

It was a slim opening, but better than none.

"How do you know my brother?" Adare asked. "Where did he find you?"

She stopped herself from adding, *And do you know where in Hull's name he's disappeared to?* No need to give the girl any information she didn't already have.

Triste snorted. "Kaden didn't find me. I found him. I was *given* to him."

"Given?" Adare turned the word over in her mind, trying to fit it into some comprehensible narrative. "By whom?"

"Tarik Adiv." Triste's eyes went distant as she pronounced the name. The syllables sounded strange in her mouth, as though they weren't words at all, but the sort of incomprehensible incantation so often attributed to leaches in children's tales. The girl lingered over them as though they were a prayer or a curse. Another mystery Adare found herself powerless to plumb.

"So," she said, trying to work it through, "my father's Mizran Councillor brought you to Ashk'lan? Why?"

"Bait," Triste replied, violet eyes brilliant and bruised as the day's last light. "I was supposed to keep His Radiance . . . entertained, to make sure he was fully occupied when they sprang their trap."

"What trap?" Adare asked, shaking her head. "According to Kaden, there were scores of Aedolians. He was unarmed. If

Adiv was so eager to see him dead, why didn't someone put a blade through my brother's belly the moment they arrived?" She studied the girl across from her. "Why didn't you do it yourself?"

"You think I knew?" Triste demanded. "You think I understood why my—why Adiv dragged me there?"

Adare spread her hands. "Did you?"

"I'll tell you what I knew," Triste growled, leaning so far over the table that her arms trembled with the effort of holding her up. "I was supposed to fuck your brother. *You will let him do whatever he wants.* That's what Adiv told me. *You will please him, and you will keep pleasing him. If you fail, then your mother dies.* That's what they told me. As far as I knew, *that's* why I was there."

Adare studied the girl. The drug had started to reassert its hold. The answers were coming faster now, pouring out of her, the words slightly slurred. If she was lying, she was a brilliant liar, every bit as good as il Tornja. It seemed unlikely, and yet what was the alternative? If Triste was telling the truth, she was just a whore, a piece to be used and thrown away. But why would il Tornja risk so much on a single worthless stone? There was something more, something Adare still wasn't seeing.

"What about your family?" she asked, coming at the question from a different angle. "Where are they?"

The girl nodded dully. "My mother's name was Louette Morjeta. A *leina* in Ciena's temple."

"Was?"

Triste waved a hand as though to clear the air of smoke. "She's dead."

For a moment, it seemed that there were tears in her eyes. It was hard to tell in the shifting lamplight. Triste blinked once, twice, and they were gone.

"What happened to her?"

"Kaden claims she killed herself. After . . . the Jasmine Court."

Adare narrowed her eyes. "Claimed? It doesn't sound like you believe him."

Triste shrugged. The motion was sluggish, reluctant. "I was in prison by the time it happened. She might have. She had enough reason to, I guess."

"What reason?"

"Selling me to my father. Betraying the Emperor. Learning her daughter was a leach and a murderer. Take your pick."

"Who was your father?"

Triste coughed up a mangled laugh. "Kaden didn't tell you?"

Adare's heart beat a little faster. "Tell me what?"

"Holy Hull," the girl said, shaking her head. "Sweet Intarra's light, have you even *talked* to Kaden since you returned?"

"We spoke," Adare replied warily.

"So he doesn't trust you. Even though you're back, he's not telling you things."

"Why don't you tell me?"

Triste met her gaze. Though her eyes were vague with drug, there was no compromise in them. "Or what? You'll beat me until I do?"

Adare wanted to hit the girl, to stand up, lean across the table, slap her across the face, and growl that she, Adare, was the only one in the whole fucking capital willing to help. *Kaden locked you away,* she wanted to say, *and then vanished. The council wants you tried and killed. Il Tornja wants you killed without a trial. In all Annur, I am the only one willing to help you.*

Instead, she took a deep breath, then another, keeping her mouth shut until she had shackled her anger.

"The question," she said finally, planing the edges from her voice until it was perfectly level, perfectly smooth, "is not about my relationship with Kaden. It is about my relationship with you. My brother locked you up. I set you free. I thought that might have earned me a measure of trust."

"Freedom," Triste said, tipping over the cracked glass in front of her. It rang against the table like a bell. A few final drops drained from its rim as it swung across the bloodwood in a lazy arc. "How wonderful."

"I will tell you something," Adare said, deciding in that moment to try the truth. "You were right. Il Tornja wants you dead. He took my son, threatened him with harm if I failed to kill you in your prison."

For the first time, the leach's eyes widened.

So, Adare thought. *Chalk up one point for the truth.*

"You have a child?" Triste asked.

Adare nodded. It was hardly a secret. Even if it had been, there was no calling it back now. "His name is Sanlitun, after his grandfather."

"His grandfather," Triste said, shaking her head sadly.

Adare stared, trying to parse the sudden change in the girl's mood. "My father," she clarified, as though anyone in Annur could be ignorant of the late Emperor's name.

"Your father," Triste said, nodding slowly, almost drunkenly, "who was related to my father."

Adare opened her mouth, but found she had nothing to say.

Triste, seeing her shock, just nodded again. "Tarik Adiv wore that blindfold all his life because beneath it, he had eyes . . ." She trailed off, gesturing vaguely toward Adare's face. ". . . just like yours."

"How do you know?"

"Kaden told me. He found out the truth, and then he killed him, killed my father."

"How do you know it was the *truth*?" Adare demanded, her mind racing to deny the claim. "How do you know Kaden wasn't lying?"

"It just fit," Triste said, head lolling to the side, "with everything. Besides, why would Kaden lie about *that*? What would he get out of it?"

"It's not what he would get," Adare said slowly. "It's what

he could keep *me* from having. Holy Hull," she breathed, something like a pattern falling finally into place.

The Malkeenian claim to preeminence rested on divine blood, blood claimed by every emperor since Terial himself. The Malkeenians were the lineage of Intarra; their burning irises blazed with that undeniable proof. The difficult thing about lineage, however, was the fact that it forked. Every dynastic chronicle Adare had ever encountered involved rival cousins and brothers, far-flung relatives returned from exile or obscurity to make their own claim to one throne or another.

Annur had been spared such trials by the blazing eyes. The Malkeenians produced as many brothers and bastards as any other royal family, but none had the burning irises. There were gray-eyed offshoots and brown-irised by-blows scattered across two continents, maybe farther, men and women who might also trace their ancestry back to Intarra, but the burning eyes, that unmistakable gaze of fire, that, it seemed, was reserved for the purest stock, for the true inheritors of the blessing of the goddess.

There were stories, of course, outlandish tales of men and women far flung from the capital itself, whose eyes also burned. As a child, Adare had devoured those tales with a mixture of horror and fascination. On the one hand, any ramification of Intarra's blessing would make her own family's claim a lie; on the other, Adare liked to imagine another child like herself, a girl her own age raised in Mireia, or Sarai Pol, or Mo'ir; not a sister, exactly, but a cousin, another person who understood what it was like to live with those irises. Adare had spent days imagining the friendship growing between them. Valyn and Kaden had each other. Why shouldn't she have a companion, too, someone to share her own worries and delights?

She had put the question to her father once, asking if he could send imperial messengers to search for the almost-sister she'd grown certain that she had. Sanlitun shook his head. "If another child had the eyes, we would know. That is the nature of the blessing. It is not something one can hide."

"But the *stories*," Adare had protested.

"Are stories," he said. "Tales people tell, that they cultivate in their own boredom or confusion. There are always such stories—hidden princes, lost kings, princesses raised as swineherds. They are rarely tethered to the truth."

"So there are *no* other branches of our family?"

"There are branches," he replied soberly. "But we are the only Malkeenians."

So ended Adare's hope of a long-lost cousin. She had put the notion away like an outgrown childhood toy, and focused in earnest on her education, on whatever training her father could give her. And now this.

"Another line of the family," Adare said slowly, studying the girl across from her. Triste looked nothing at all like the distant cousin she had imagined as a child, nothing at all like Adare herself, but then, why would she? Adare and Valyn barely resembled each other, and they shared the same parents. "Could that be why il Tornja wants you dead?"

Triste stared at her a moment, then looked away. Adare waited, but the girl remained silent, that glazed gaze of hers cold as a fortress wall.

"You understand," Adare said finally, "that I'm trying to help you."

"You're trying to help yourself," Triste replied, still not looking at her. "And you think I might be a useful tool. I'm through with that. Through being someone else's tool."

No, Adare concluded, still chewing on her earlier hunch. *That's* not *it. It's not about succession.*

Even if Tarik Adiv *had* possessed Intarra's eyes, Triste did not. The Mizran Councillor was dead, and his orphaned daughter was a leach with violet eyes and no allies. She hardly posed any threat to Adare *or* il Tornja. Which meant the *kenarang* wanted her for some other reason.

"What does it feel like?" Triste asked, reaching out unexpectedly to touch the scars on Adare's arm. Her motion was slow, deliberate, in the age-old manner of the very drunk. She ran a cool finger over the crimson whorls, then pulled away. "What does it feel like to be loved by a goddess? To be chosen?"

The words were quiet, but the girl's question burned, as though it mattered more than anything else she'd said since her escape. Adare pulled her hand back, half burying it in the sleeve of her robe. Prophets were supposed to be bold, unflinching in their faith. It was a role she'd been trying to play for months now, in front of the Sons of Flame and the Army of the North, in front of Lehav, and Kaden, and the council. She'd hit on a set of platitudes that seemed to satisfy most audiences, a brief statement of conviction thick with terms like *blessing* and *sacred trust, divine right* and *responsibility*. For a moment she started to trot it all out again; then she stopped herself. The only thing Triste had responded to so far was the truth, and so she gave her the truth.

"It's baffling. Half the time I don't believe it's even real."

Triste's face twisted into the echo of a smile. Adare watched her, waiting for more, but nothing more came. She just closed her eyes, as though she were too weary to go on. Adare forced down her frustration, trying to come at the question from a different angle.

"I understand," she began slowly, "that you don't want to be a tool. You were eager enough to help my brother, however, when you came back to the city. You were willing enough to help him break into the Dawn Palace."

Adare wasn't sure what she expected in response—quiet defiance, maybe, or more of the same drugged lassitude. When Triste's lids flicked open, rage burned in her eyes.

"I didn't even know we were *going* to the Dawn Palace."

"You must have. You killed all those people for him."

"I didn't do it for *him*."

Her lips curled, baring her perfect teeth, and Adare leaned back in her chair, her own body quick to put distance between them even as her mind scrambled to stay balanced on the shifting conversation.

"Then why? Why murder a hundred people you didn't even know?"

Triste shook her head, but her only response was a sort of dying growl deep in her throat.

"If you didn't do it for Kaden," Adare pressed, "who *did* you do it for?"

"No," Triste replied finally, drawing out the syllable, shaking her head warily from side to side. "No."

Adare gritted her teeth. The answer was there, *an* answer at least. She could sense it the way she could sense the coming dawn sometimes, even when the sky was still flat black. Somewhere in the mess of words, tangled up among all those intertwining facts, lay il Tornja's reason for wanting the girl dead, a reason that might also be a weapon, something Adare could use to fight the Csestriim general, something she might use to save her son.

"I'm done," Triste said, planting her palms firmly on the table before her.

"What do you mean, done?"

"I don't want to talk to you anymore."

"You stupid, stubborn fool," Adare spat. "Kaden put you in prison. Il Tornja wants you dead. I'm the one who *freed* you. Why do you want to help them and thwart me?"

"I don't want to help anyone," Triste said, her voice dry as ash. "Certainly not you."

Adare blew out a long, exhausted breath. "If you're right about your father, then we're family. Very distant family, but family."

"Family?" Triste stared at her. "What does family mean to you? Kaden is your *brother*, and the two of you have been trying to kill each other for a year."

"Kaden betrayed Annur. He did everything he could to

destroy it. You and I . . ." She studied the girl, that perfect face etched with scar. "We could be allies."

"No, we couldn't. To have allies, you need equals, and an emperor doesn't have equals."

Adare started to respond, to point out that the world was filled with asymmetrical alliances—empires allied with independent city-states, kings with aristocrats, warlords with the peasantry they protected—then stopped herself. Whatever Triste cared about, whatever her reasons for refusing Adare's overtures of peace, they weren't likely to be altered through some academic discussion of power structures. The problem was the chasm of distrust running between them, a rocky gap that the trusses of logic would always be too weak to bridge.

"Fine," Adare said. "If you don't want to talk today, we'll stop."

"You expect tomorrow to be different?"

"I don't expect anything," Adare replied. "But I know what I need, and I'm willing to take the time necessary to get it."

It was partly true, at least. The jailors would have already found Mailly dead inside her cell. With any luck they would take the body for Triste. They would be confused, no doubt, at how the girl had contracted such an awful disease inside her cell, but there were half a dozen possible, if unlikely, vectors— bird shit piled high in the corners of the cages, contamination of the food. . . . There would be an investigation. They would cut the poor girl's body apart searching for the cause, but they would be looking in the wrong place, looking *inside,* and each cut they made in Mailly's skin would only obscure the truth.

As far as anyone knew, Triste was dead, and Adare planned to report as much to il Tornja. She hardly expected him to return Sanlitun—he had played his hand, and there was no unplaying it now—but the lie would buy her time.

"Whatever you believe," Adare said finally, "I'm not your enemy."

Triste's laugh was light, bitter. "Then let me go."

"No. There is something about you, something dangerous to il Tornja. If I intend to fight him, I need to know what it is."

"Fight him . . . ," Triste said quietly. For just a moment, for a heartbeat or two, something bloomed in her eyes, and the lines of her face softened. She looked years younger. Younger and lost and almost hopeful. Then she blinked, shuddered, and her face slammed shut.

"I hope you fight him," she said, enunciating carefully.

"I intend to—" Adare began.

The girl cut her off. "I hope you fight him, and he fights back. I'll still be locked up somewhere, but I hope I hear about it."

"About what?"

"About his death," Triste said, violet eyes ablaze. "And Kaden's. And yours. About your son's. That's the only way this ends. You know it, but you're too stubborn to believe it. All of you scheming bastards are going to cut each other down, and though I don't pray often, when I do pray, I pray for this: that I get to hear how it all happened."

30

Gray deepened into green as the eastern sky brightened with the watery light of the still-unrisen sun. Unseen frogs along the river's bank began their monophonic chorus. Fish rose to the water's surface, took flies, then disappeared, the silent ripples of their passage growing, spreading, fading. Kaden could make out flashes of color between the trees and vines—red and cerulean, sky-white and green—bright-plumed birds swooping down from their night's roost.

A part of his mind—the part that remained unmoved by Kiel's sudden arrival and dire news—catalogued the creatures, their songs and cries. The life of the jungle was so different from the life of the Bone Mountains—bolder, louder—but it was life all the same, millions of creatures moving through the stations of hunger and fear, lust and confusion, pleasure and pain.

"It will all go away," Long Fist said, as though reading his thoughts, "if my consort's host is killed."

"Triste is not Ciena's host," Kaden replied without looking up from the river. "She didn't invite the goddess into her mind. She doesn't want her there."

"The girl's invitations and desires are irrelevant. The world you know is fragile as glass. Her death will shatter it."

Kaden turned to study the man. They sat—Long Fist, Kiel, and Kaden himself—on a large boulder at the river's edge. Dawn Rock, the local tribes called it, for the fact that it was there, from the top of the rock, looking east down the river's course, that you could first see the morning sun. Kaden would have preferred to be already on the way back to the *kenta,* but Long Fist's hieratic duties required him to be at the river just before dawn, to spill the blood of a small, black-haired monkey down the stone and into the swirling current as the sun rose. Unlike the sacrifice of the night before, this was a private ceremony, but a necessary one, evidently, and so the three of them sat on the rock as wide-mouthed fish rose for blood from the river's unseen bottom, and the morning's hot light ignited the white mist.

"Triste is not dead yet," Kiel said. "She is simply missing. Gone from the dungeon."

The Csestriim had arrived unexpectedly late the night before, escorted into the jungle camp by a pair of wary Ishien, just as Kaden had been.

Kaden shook his head. "The dungeon was the last thing keeping her safe."

The Csestriim nodded. "She is at greater risk now. Grave risk."

Whatever that risk, Kiel's voice was calm. He seemed indifferent to Triste's fate or that of the goddess trapped inside her. The girl's disappearance was a fact, no more or less than the other myriad facts of the world. Like Long Fist, Kiel sat cross-legged, gazing down into the current, but unlike the Urghul shaman, whose stillness spoke of coiled might, of strength gathering for an attack, Kiel might have grown from the stone itself. He might have planned to sit there forever.

"How did you know it wasn't her in the cell?" Kaden asked.

"I looked at the body," the historian replied simply. "It was not her."

"And no one else noticed? None of the jailors?"

"Your kind has always struggled to see clearly, and the girl's face was disfigured by the poison that killed her. There were blisters and sores everywhere. Discoloration. Bleeding and black pus obscuring the sclera—"

"Sclera?"

"Her eyes. They were unrecognizable."

Kaden could remember perfectly his first encounter with Triste. Her eyes had been sharp and clear, bright as the jungle flowers unfolding to the sun all around him now. She'd been younger then, younger in more than years, and terrified, trussed up in Tarik Adiv's ostentatious bonds as though she weren't a woman so much as a gift, an object, a beautiful bauble for the new Emperor. It was her eyes—those layers of violet laid one over the next—that had first jarred Kaden from his speechless stare. He tried to imagine them blackened, tarred over with poison, but of course, they weren't. It wasn't Triste that Kiel had seen inside the cell, but someone else.

"Who?" Kaden asked. "Who was she?"

"The dead are nothing," Long Fist cut in. "We must find the living girl, the one whose flesh conceals her goddess."

"And our best chance of finding her," Kaden replied, "is discovering who broke her free, and why."

Kiel nodded. "The body in the cell is an obvious place to start. I was unable to learn her name. . . ."

"But?" Kaden asked, hearing the pause in the historian's voice.

"Your sister visited the dungeon the day that Triste disappeared, the day this strange girl's corpse appeared inside the cell."

Surprise knocked faintly against the bronze of Kaden's calm, and then, a heartbeat after the surprise, anger, scratching with almost-silent claws. He held both feelings in his mind a moment, then put them away. There was no time for surprise, no room for the error that waited on human anger. What he needed was the bottomless calm of the Csestriim, but even as he reached for it, Long Fist was standing. "We will go to Annur then, and take the girl from your sister."

As though it were that simple. As though the problems of the world could be solved just by going, by taking.

Instead of following the shaman to his feet, Kaden stared down into the river's slow eddy. The current had carried away the monkey's blood. There was only the water, muddy and dark, carried down from some distant hillside, traveling all the way to an unseen sea.

"How did Adare do it?" he asked. "Get her out?"

"I can't be certain that she did," Kiel replied. "It is only an inference."

Long Fist let out something that might have been a growl. Kaden glanced up to see the shaman's lips drawn back from his sharpened teeth. "She visited the girl the day she disappeared—"

"No," Kaden said, cutting him off. "Kiel said she visited the *dungeon*."

The Csestriim nodded. "She was there to see a man named Vasta Dhati, a Manjari prisoner."

"Imprisoned for what?"

"The attack on your study."

"That was Gwenna."

"Indeed."

Kaden took a breath, held it for a dozen heartbeats, then let it out.

What does my sister want? What is she trying to accomplish?

Answering the questions was like trying to find shape in the shifting clouds, but then, Adare's mind was smaller than the sky, more ordered. Understanding was no more than a matter of seeing through her eyes. Kaden closed his own, let his own thoughts go, and tried to slip inside Adare's conception of the world. She'd planned Triste's extraction well. Brilliantly, in fact. Had it not been for Kiel's perfect memory, no one would have realized Triste was missing at all.

"There is no time for talk," Long Fist said. "Your sister has bound herself to this Csestriim, Ran il Tornja. She will deliver the girl into his hands, and he will destroy her."

Kaden considered the claim. "No," he said slowly. "That doesn't work."

The shaman's gaze settled on him, hard and sharp enough to cut. "He twisted your sister to his purposes months ago. This was known, even on the steppe."

"Maybe," Kaden agreed, "but things change."

"How are you certain?"

"Il Tornja wants Triste dead," Kiel said.

Kaden nodded. "It is easier to kill a woman than to smuggle her out of the most closely guarded prison in the world. If Adare was taking orders from il Tornja, the jailors would have found Triste's body in that cell. We would have already lost. Adare went to great trouble, great risk, to take the girl out alive."

Long Fist's hand had clenched into a fist at his side. His jaw was tight as he spoke. "Why?"

Kaden frowned. "That is what I will have to ask her."

31

The barrel was cramped, and dark, and hot. It reeked of rum. The rum wouldn't have been so bad if it hadn't also smelled like pickled herring, and curdled goat's milk, and the rancid oil that Gwenna had dumped into the harbor shortly before climbing into the fucking thing. The residents of Hook reused their barrels. Gwenna herself was only the most recent cargo, and whatever happened in the following days, she was unlikely to be its last. She imagined herself shattered on the rocks at the bottom of Skarn's limestone cliffs, or floating facedown in the waves. People were expendable, especially on the Islands, but a good barrel ... you didn't just let a good barrel go to waste. She tried to imagine what it might hold next.

The question was, in its own odd way, relaxing. Better to think about those wooden staves brimming with whale oil or bootlegged ale than to spend too much time dwelling on the fact that she had willingly let herself be nailed into a cylindrical wooden coffin. She'd done hundreds of barrel drops in training, but never from inside of the 'Kent-kissing barrel.

Of course, the plan wasn't to get dropped fifty feet into the waves. The plan was to be set down as slowly and gently as an actual barrel of rum, to sit silently until nightfall, and then to carve her way free of the cramped space with the chisel, hand brace, and belt knife she had secreted beneath her crunched-up knees. She would have preferred to bring more weapons—her smoke steel blades, at the very least—but there wasn't room in the barrel for more, not if she didn't want to risk cutting off her leg in transit.

In theory, it wouldn't matter. She was going to Skarn to steal birds, not to fight Rallen and his men. In theory, she would connect with Quick Jak and Talal, both of whom were tucked inside barrels of their own, slip out of the storeroom, find the birds they wanted, and get in the air. In theory, Rallen wouldn't even know they'd come and gone until they were back again, the bird loaded with a full Wing this time, to gut the treacherous ex-Kettral leach and his bloody band.

That was the theory, anyway.

It had sounded good back in the Hole. She'd gone over it with Annick and Talal at least a dozen times. Now that she was nailed into the reeking barrel, the whole thing seemed a lot more likely to end in a quick, vicious death. There were dozens of ways the plan could go awry. The birds tasked with hauling the supplies—"tribute and taxation" as Rallen called the stacked crates and barrels—might drop her into the surf. Rallen's soldiers might decide to inspect the goods before flying them over to the island stronghold. Some of the rabble from Hook, furious at the burning of their homes, might decide to set the barrels ablaze out of sheer rebellious spite. It wouldn't matter much, once she started cooking, that they were all supposed to be on the same side.

And then there was the question of what would happen over on Skarn, provided they landed safely and were able to break free. It had been more than a week since the makeshift Trial, enough time for all but the worst of the wounds to knit closed, for bruises to fade, for the consumed albumen of the slarn eggs to begin its slow, subtle change in the flesh of the newest Kettral. Whether they were aware of their keener senses, of the fresh strength threaded through their muscles, Gwenna couldn't say.

She could see the difference, though. They had come out of the Hole harder, more willing to stand straight and keep their eyes up. It was more than Gwenna had dared hope for, actually, a reward commensurate with the risk, and yet she found herself dwelling, not on the triumphs of the living, but on the silence of the dead, on the three who *hadn't* come out of the caves. They had paid the price for her gamble. The three of them, and, in a different way, Quick Jak.

After their tense exchange on the day of the Trial itself, Gwenna had avoided another confrontation with the flier. She was worried she might hit him. Hurt him. Try as she might, she still couldn't bring herself to believe his story, not all of it. It seemed too easy, too pat, that he should come out of the darkness alone, nearly unharmed, when the others were cut to shreds. There wasn't anything to be gained, though, from badgering him. You couldn't shake the truth out of a man. Cut it out, maybe. Burn it out. But then you might as well be Jakob Rallen. Then you might as well be the 'Kent-kissing Urghul.

The simplest solution to the problem of the flier's cowardice would have been to ground him, to keep him in the caves until the fight was finished, then dump him off over on Arim, let him live out his days somewhere he couldn't get anyone killed. As Annick kept pointing out, some people just weren't meant to be Kettral. The trouble was, Gwenna didn't quite believe that. Or she believed the general principle, but couldn't convince herself that it was true of Jak. Every time she was ready to give up on him, she remembered just how easily he'd made the grueling swim to Skarn, how thoughtful he was when he wasn't terrified, how rational. And then there were Laith's words rattling around in the back of her head. Laith had said Quick Jak was the best flier on the Islands, and the truth was, she needed a flier.

Others could learn, of course, once they'd taken back control, but in order to *do* that, in order to kill Rallen and his batch of thugs, Gwenna needed fliers *now,* needed someone she could nail in a barrel, who could take control of a bird as soon as they broke out over on Skarn.

She'd almost chosen Delka. The woman was older than Jak, weaker and slower, but she was steady, reliable. When Gwenna went to talk to her, however, Delka had convinced her otherwise.

"You're in command," she'd said, shaking her head, "and if you tell me to go, I'll go. But I think you're making a mistake."

"The mistake has a name," Gwenna'd spat. "Quick Jak. He'll start shitting himself the minute someone draws a sword."

"But no one's supposed to draw swords. That's the plan, right? Sneak in, get the birds, sneak out. Jak freezes when he has to fight, but there shouldn't be any fighting."

Gwenna ground her teeth. "*Shouldn't* isn't the same as *won't*. I can't be certain what's going to happen once we get over there."

"Of course you can't," Delka said. "You play the odds. I was already over on Arim when Jak started his training. We heard the stories, even over there. A flier like him comes along once in a generation, if you're lucky, and if Rallen comes after you while you're in the air, you're going to need the best flier you can get."

Gwenna glanced the length of the cave. Quick Jak was in the shadow of a large stalactite, working through his sword forms over and over. The moves were good, fluid, but it was easy to be fluid when someone wasn't hitting you back. "Fuck," she said.

To her surprise, Delka smiled. "Fuck, indeed."

"You think he can do it?"

The older woman shrugged. "I don't know. But there's one other thing, right? That bird, the huge one?"

Gwenna nodded slowly. "Allar'ra."

"It's Jak's. He trained it."

And that settled the question, to the extent that it could be settled. Gwenna spent the next nine days swinging between irritation and impatience, trying to beat a little last-minute training into the heads of the men and women newly under her command, trying to hammer out a plan that wouldn't get them all killed, and all the while worrying that right now, when they were so close to go-time, Rallen would discover their hideaway, blow shut the entrance in the stone above, and leave them all to rot. It was almost a relief to climb finally into the barrel. At least the time had come to *do* something, even if doing meant sitting in the hot, cramped dark, trying not to vomit from the smell.

When the bird finally arrived, that relief had faded to a dull ache pervading muscle and bone. There was no real way to mark time inside the barrel. For a while she tried counting heartbeats, but they were too loud, too jarring, and after a hundred or so, she tried focusing on something else—the waves washing the rocks, the indignant screeching of the gulls, anything to take her mind off the staves squeezing her from every side.

Even focused on the world outside her tiny wooden prison, she almost missed the bird's approach. Kettral tended to screech when they stooped—a habit encouraged by most fliers—but there was no need for such a precipitous dive to pick up a load of cargo. The bird came in low and quiet from the east. Gwenna caught the *whrrr* of wind feathering the great wings, then felt the barrel's sickening lurch as the kettral caught the cargo net in its claws, lifting the whole load into the air.

It took a few moments to get used to the motion, to the creak of the heavy ropes, and the groaning protestations of the cargo. The load was too large for one bird, and there was no way of knowing whether Gwenna had been bundled into the same grab net with Talal or Quick Jak. Not that it ought to matter. The whole stack of goods was bound for Skarn. They could rendezvous when they arrived.

The flight was short, a lot shorter than the swim, and there was no more warning for the drop than there had been for the pickup—just half a heartbeat of sick, sudden weightlessness followed by a tooth-rattling thud.

Gwenna twisted inside the barrel, trying to ease the pain in her cramped legs. Hours of motionlessness had wrapped a thick strap of tension across the muscles of her back. It would be a bitch drilling her way out, and she could already feel the lead-heavy ache that would make an awkward mess out of her first few steps. Those were problems she'd anticipated, however, problems she could solve. The first hurdle was behind her.

She wondered how the others were faring. Talal was slightly taller than Gwenna, but Jak would have the hardest time of it. He'd gone in first, knees, then elbows, then shoulders scraping against the barrel's rim. Gwenna had watched him, trying to decide if he'd make it through half a day trapped inside the thing, trying to read his face for any hint of panic, any sign that he'd lose it once they hammered the lid shut. The flier grimaced silently as the rough wood tore open the slarn scab on his upper arm, then, as though feeling Gwenna's gaze upon him, glanced over. He didn't do anything when she met his eyes. Didn't scowl, or nod. Didn't even blink. If he looked ready to be locked inside the barrel, it was only because he looked half dead.

But he's here, Gwenna reminded herself. He'd managed to remain silent during the long wait and the short flight. The rest of it, the stealing of the birds, the flying . . . that was the shit he was supposed to be *good* at. That was why she'd risked bringing him in the first place.

She shifted, trying to get a better grip on the hand brace, then froze at the sound of voices approaching. Three of them. All male. *No,* she realized, listening more intently. *Four.* The fourth wasn't talking, but she could hear his footfalls alongside the others': soles scuffing over rough stone. The men paused just a few paces away. She imagined them standing at the edge of the piled barrels and crates. Slowly, silently, she pressed her hands against the wooden staves, bracing herself for the jostling to come.

"Which ones you want to start with?" A deep voice, and loud. The man sounded amused for some reason.

"Up to you, Ren. We gotta move 'em all in the end."

"Not necessarily," said a third voice, high-pitched and sly.

"We could just . . . lose a couple. Right over the edge of the cliff."

A pause, then laughter all around.

Gwenna tensed. They were joking, clearly. There was no point in hauling supplies all the way from Hook only to chuck them off the limestone cliffs. Even Rallen's thugs couldn't be that lazy.

"That's our food, you fuckin' fool. Whatta'ya want to get rid of it for?"

"Not all *our* food, is it? Rallen's going to eat half a' what's here. I'm not sayin' we chuck anything good, but surely we can do without half a ton a' . . . say . . . squash."

Squash. That was Jak's barrel. The rebels had filled two burlap sacks with the yellow and green vegetables in order to make enough room for the flier. She tensed, a slow, cold dread creeping up her spine. Suddenly, horribly, she felt the full weight of her helplessness. Training didn't matter if you couldn't move, and combat nerves weren't worth much if you couldn't get to the actual combat. Worse, she wasn't the only one listening to the lazy banter. Quick Jak would be able to hear the men as well as Gwenna herself. He'd know better than she did that six letters—S Q U A S H—were stamped in bold red ink on the lid of his barrel.

Stay cool, Jak, she prayed quietly. *They're just joking. Just fucking around. Stay cool.*

"I like squash," one of the men was saying. "You're not tossing my barrel of squash."

"We're not tossing anything," the first voice cut in. "We're going to do what we're told to do. Let's go. One man to a barrel. Get 'em rolling."

Something was wrong. A voice was screaming inside her skull to abort, abort, *abort*. Only there was no aborting. There was no doing anything. As the barrel lurched onto its side, she tightened her grip on the chisel. It wasn't much of a weapon, but it would kill a man quick enough if you put it in his eye.

The 'Shael-spawned thing almost ended up in her own eye

when the barrel lurched into motion. Whoever was pushing it wasn't making any effort to save the wooden staves, and the whole thing bounced over the rough ground, jolting against the rocks, jostling into larger obstacles, all with Gwenna spinning inside it, trying not to vomit into her own mouth. They couldn't have covered more than a hundred paces, but by the time it was done, she felt bruised in a dozen places, battered at the knees, back, and elbows.

While Gwenna tried to sort up from down, a door creaked open, salt-rusted hinges shrieking. She just had time to locate the ocean behind her, waves breaking against the stone, and then she was moving again. There was no light inside the barrel, but the shift from uneven stone onto smooth wood planking told her all she needed to know—they'd entered the warehouse.

Suspicion and unease still coiled around her chest like a huge snake, constricting each time she drew a breath. She kept the chisel clutched in her hand, but clutching it was about all she could do as she listened to the other barrels jolting over the stone, the cursing of the men as they hauled in other crates and containers. Then there was only silence, thick and hot. Then a voice, Jakob Rallen's, that sullen anger of his as instantly recognizable as the sound of the waves.

"Which one is the leach?"

"Not here, Commander. Must be in the next load."

He knows, Gwenna realized with horror. *He knows the whole fucking thing.*

"You're sure?" Rallen demanded. "He didn't slip away?"

"I don't think so, sir. The bastard's nailed inside a barrel. Hard to slip away from that."

Rallen just grunted his agreement, then, with an imperious gesture Gwenna couldn't see but could picture perfectly, pointed at her barrel.

"Get her out."

The blows started before she could come up with anything resembling a plan, before she could even protest. Someone was hitting the barrel with a heavy hammer, two or three people really, the brutal blows landing over and over, splintering the wooden staves, driving the shards of oak into her skin. The heavy steel hammers came down again and again, bruising her hips and shoulders. One particularly vicious strike sent a spike of pain shooting down her leg. There was nothing to do. No way to fight. Even as the hammers smashed holes in the barrel, the metal hoops held, trapping her inside. She wondered if Rallen intended to see her beaten to a meaty pulp right there on the wooden floor, struggled to cover her head with her arms, then realized that for all their ferocity, the men wielding the hammers were avoiding her head. They weren't trying to kill her. At least not yet. Not quickly.

With some difficulty, she brought her arms down, tucking her hands into the safe space in the hollow of her knees, protecting them. If there was ever a weapon close to hand she wanted to be able to grab the fucking thing. It was tempting to close her eyes, but closed eyelids weren't going to stop an eight-pound hammerhead, and she forced herself to keep them open, trying, through the haze of pink pain and the barrel's wreckage, to piece together the layout of the cavernous room.

The space was large, but dim and windowless. When her head stopped spinning long enough, she caught a glimpse of wooden boxes stacked all the way to the eaves. So they *had* brought her to the warehouse. She stifled a grim laugh. At least that part of the plan had worked out. Of Talal, there was no sign. A few paces away, however, stood the tall barrel stamped *Squash*.

Not only did Rallen know we were coming, she thought as the hammers rose and fell, *he knew which 'Kent-kissing barrels to go after.*

Finally, after what seemed like an age, the staves around her collapsed. She could hear Rallen's panting, hear the hammering hearts of his soldiers, and below that, another sound, a low,

angry groaning. It was her own voice, she realized, and she went
to work stopping it.

Three steel hoops still ringed her folded body. She tried to
straighten her legs, failed, strangled a scream before it clawed
its way out of her throat, then tried again.

Between the long, motionless hours and the beating, she
wondered if it was still *possible* to straighten her legs. She'd seen
ex-Kettral before, men and women who took a bad fall during
barrel drops or on a botched extract, who couldn't move from
the waist down. Terror at the prospect took her by the neck,
tried to shake her, but she forced it away, focused on her legs
once more. At last, agonizingly, she managed to get them to
twitch. They burned, throbbed, but she kept going, trying to
loosen tendons twisted to the breaking point.

These assholes better watch out, she thought, twisting her
neck, hoping that the exploding pain there didn't mean anything
important. *At this rate I'll be able to attack some time around
the middle of next month.*

Rallen, however, was taking no chances. "Get back!" he
snapped at his men. "*Back!* All of you. She is not some useless
washout, she is Kettral. *Real* Kettral."

Gwenna might have taken more satisfaction from the warning
if she'd been able to stand up. She rolled onto her side, managed
to get her bloody knees beneath her, then to lever herself up
onto her elbows, raising her head enough to look around. Rallen
had left nothing to chance.

Two soldiers in blacks—one man, one woman—covered her
with flatbows from five paces away. Too far to lunge at before
they got off a shot; too close to even hope that they might miss.
And they weren't the only ones. Two other men had put down
their hammers and drawn their double blades. They'd been
enthusiastic enough in breaking her out, but now that she was
free, they watched her as they would a viper, eyes fixed on that
chisel in her hand. She debated throwing it. She could kill one
of them, at least, but there wasn't much point in killing just one.

"Five on one?" she said to the men with the swords, packing her voice with as much scorn as it would bear. "You didn't want to bring a few more, just to be on the safe side?" She locked eyes with the nearer of the two soldiers, smiled, then snapped her teeth at him. He jerked back as though stung, then, realizing his folly, started forward, anger bright in his eyes.

"Stand *back*, you idiot!" Rallen snapped. "She is *baiting* you. Trying to force a mistake."

Not that it would matter much. Rallen's men could make a dozen mistakes, and they'd still have the odds. Still, it was nice to know she'd put them on edge. Despite the birds, the blacks, and the blades, these soldiers weren't true Kettral, and they knew it.

Gwenna turned from the men with the swords and bows, neck shrieking with pain, to face Jakob Rallen himself. A year earlier, the Master of Cadets had been the fattest man on Qarsh. He'd broken his leg during a botched drop shortly after his own Trial, and the bone had set wrong, making it impossible for him to run or swim. He'd barely been able to walk without his cane, in fact, and in all Gwenna's years as a cadet, she'd rarely seen him outside his office. He ate at his desk, shoving aside his papers to make space for a piled plate carried in by whatever young soldier had been unlucky enough to earn that particular punishment, and he went outside only for the short trek between Eyrie command and the small cottage afforded him as a top-ranking officer.

Despite the extra weight, however, it had been possible back then to see that Rallen had been a soldier once. There had still been slabs of muscle under the fat, thick arms and legs that would have been punishing in the arena. And his keen dark eyes had missed absolutely nothing.

All of that had changed. The fat was gone, gone so fully it might have evaporated, leaving his gray-brown skin hanging loose over his bones. It was hardly a healthy transformation. He sat on a single crate that someone had hauled out into the center of the room as though it were a makeshift throne, but he displayed none of the effortless ease one expected of men on thrones. The cloth of his blacks was soaked. Sweat glistened on his bald head, despite the shade of the warehouse. And his eyes—they were bright but glazed as he stared at her.

Still dangerous, she thought as she studied him. *Maybe more dangerous, but not as sharp.*

She couldn't help shaking her head. "You're all taking your orders from *this* piece of shit?"

Rallen just smiled, a thin, mirthless expression, raised a clay cup to his lips, drank deep, then widened his smile. "Gwenna Sharpe. You always had too high an opinion of yourself, too little respect for anyone else. Here you are hurling insults, but it is *you* whose training appears to have been worthless. *You* who have stupidly delivered yourself to me like a side of pork."

That got a chuckle from a couple of the soldiers. Gwenna could feel her cheeks flushing, the anger burning through her bones. Her muscles tensed for the lunge. She could kill him. If he weren't a leach. Even with a couple arrows in her side she could live long enough to choke the life out of the bastard. Jaw clenched, she throttled the urge. He *was* a leach. For all she knew, he could burn her to ash if she blinked the wrong way.

"How did you know?" she demanded. "About the barrels?"

The man took another long sip from his cup. His pupils widened as he watched her, as though drinking in the sight. "You have a lot to learn, Sharpe, about leadership. About loyalty."

The words carved a sick pit in her gut.

"Who talked?"

Rallen pursed his lips. "You don't want to guess?"

Half a dozen names came to her at once, rose halfway up her throat before she swallowed them. It might be a game to Rallen, but that didn't mean she had to play.

"Not really," she replied, sucking the blood from her split lip, then spitting it out in a slick bolus on the wooden floor.

Even that minimal defiance made the nearest soldiers twitch. Gwenna looked over at the two with the flatbows, focusing, after a moment, on the woman. She was noticeably older than most of Rallen's other recruits, maybe around thirty, though her arms were firm and her shoulders wider than those of most men.

"You're holding it wrong," Gwenna said, nodding to the flatbow.

The woman's lips twisted. She took a hesitant step back, gaze darting between Gwenna and the weapon.

"Don't *listen* to her, Pol," Rallen growled. "She's testing you. That's all. Just trying to find a weakness."

The woman named Pol colored, half lifted the flatbow to her shoulder, and stepped forward again menacingly.

"You want to play with me?" she demanded, fear transmuted to fury in that strange, sudden way Gwenna had seen so often in the arena. "You still gonna want to play with me when you've got a flatbow bolt shoved halfway down your throat?"

Gwenna shrugged. "Probably. Why don't you try it and we'll find out."

"Enough," Rallen snapped, half rising to his feet. "Pol! Stand back." The woman hesitated, then cursed under her breath and retreated several steps. Rallen turned his attention to Gwenna once again. "I know what you're doing. You're trying to drive a wedge between me and my people. It's sad, actually, because you're too stupid to realize that is precisely what I've already done to *you*." He spread his hands. "Hobb? Remember him? He *gave* you to me. For free. A gesture of goodwill, he said."

Rage burned in Gwenna's throat, hot and bilious, so thick she thought she might choke on it. Rallen, however, was watching her above the rim of his cup, and so she forced her face to remain still, indifferent.

"Thanks for sharing. I'll be sure to kill him first. After you, I mean."

The man coughed up a disgusted laugh. "Don't bother taunting me. It won't work. As for why these loyal men and women follow me . . ." He half raised a languid hand, twisting his fingers as he did.

Gwenna felt a great invisible fist close around her, the empty air suddenly harder than the barrel staves had been. Harder and far, far tighter. She could barely breathe inside Rallen's invisible grip, couldn't even kick when he lifted her clear off the floor, held her twitching in midair.

"They follow me for the same reason that men have always followed other men: power."

He rotated a lazy finger and Gwenna found herself revolving slowly in midair. The awed, frightened faces of Rallen's soldiers told the whole story. *So,* Gwenna thought grimly, *I guess he can reach his well from here.* When she was finally facing Rallen again, he smiled. She stopped spinning, a puppet yanked short by a string.

"Wait there," Rallen said, sipping from his cup as he turned his attention to the other barrel. "While we get this other idiot out."

This time, his words were slightly slurred. Gwenna eyed the cup, wondering if the man were drunk barely halfway through the day. Then the hammering started again, the crack of steel against stave followed by the sickening thud as the blows connected with human flesh. Gwenna couldn't turn her head to look behind her, but she could smell the fear on Jak—acrid as burning tar—and she could see Rallen's eyes, glazed but greedy as he watched the unfolding violence. There was blood on the air now, mixed with Jak's terror.

When the blows finally stopped, Rallen smiled.

"Tie him," he said, gesturing toward the flier. As the soldiers set to work, Rallen reached out to refill his clay cup from a cast-iron kettle set on a crate beside him. "I'm enjoying this."

The acrid steam made Gwenna want to sneeze. It took her a moment to ransack her memory, but when she finally recognized the smell, she understood a dozen things at once: the fields of sun-bright flowers spread across the land around Hook; the slurring of Rallen's words; the weight loss; the slack, grayish skin hanging off of him in folds; that unfocused, abstracted look in his eyes. In a snap, it all made sense.

"Yellowbloom," Gwenna said. Her voice sounded all busted up. Rallen's invisible bands wrapped so tightly she had to force the words out. It hardly seemed worth the effort, but she'd be shipped to 'Shael if she'd wait patiently for the bastard to have his way. The taunting took all her breath, but it was worth it. "Drinking up your own profits?"

Rallen's gaze sharpened for a moment, as though she'd actually managed to land a blow. Then he relaxed, laughed, raised his cup in a mock salute, and drank deep once more.

"The flower is much maligned," he said, swirling the cup and considering the steaming liquid within. "Properly cultivated, it is fine as the best wines. And yet," he said, setting the vessel down, "I don't want to dull my enjoyment of the coming entertainment."

The former Master of Cadets was obviously pretty dulled already. Yellowbloom was weaker than whiskey, but the effects were less predictable. Some people reported visions, others nothing more than a vast lassitude settling over them, like a silk sheet spread over the mind. Gwenna had tried it once in some shithole over on Hook, just a small cup. It made her skin burn. Then it made her want to fight.

That Rallen was drinking it now, in the middle of a crucial operation, was massively, inexcusably stupid. Clearly, he had moved on from enjoyment of the plant to *need*. This was the sort of error that could get people killed.

So figure out a way to kill him, you useless bitch.

She tested her bonds silently, straining against emptiness that might have been iron. Behind her, Jak groaned once, then fell silent. They'd drag Talal in soon enough, then smash apart his barrel, too. Gwenna could still talk. If she was fast enough, she could warn the leach before they started in with the hammers. *Not much of a fucking warning.* Talal's well wasn't that strong, and there wasn't that much steel in the room. She'd never seen him manage anything like the kenning that held her motionless in the air.

His well, she thought, turning her attention back to Rallen. If she could figure out his well, find a way to—

The truth hit her like a shovel-butt to the stomach. She stared, first at the leach, then at the cup at his side. *The yellowbloom.* Rallen wasn't keeping ahold of his twisted power in *spite* of the drink; the drink was the source of his power. *Holy Hull,* she realized, *the yellowbloom is his well.*

All those fields on Hook, the long rows of sun-bright flowers— Rallen wasn't growing them to sell, at least not entirely. He was tending to his own supply. He could never have used the drug so aggressively when the Eyrie still existed. He would have been found out in a matter of weeks, and ousted from his post. Since the fall of the Kettral, however, everything had changed. He could glut himself on the leaf. He *had* to, in fact, if he wanted to keep the soldiers under his own command awed, cowed. A fat man with a busted knee was weak, vulnerable, even to the sort of half-trained washouts that Rallen had assembled around him. The only way to hold them under his heel was to show— as he was doing now, just by holding Gwenna motionless in the air—that he could reach his well at any time, that with a flick of the finger he could destroy anyone opposing him.

It left the man walking a delicate line. The ravages of the yellowbloom were already clear, after no more than a year. He needed the leaf, needed his well, but a drug was still a drug. It would be dulling his mind, making him slow, even as the power poured through his veins. On the other hand, he seemed to have found a workable balance. No one on the Islands had managed to topple him.

But then, Gwenna thought, eyeing the leach, *maybe they just didn't shove hard enough.*

If she was right, if Rallen relied on the yellowbloom in diffi-cult situations, he would be hitting it extra hard today. He would want to make an example, not just of Gwenna and the rest, but of his own power. It was working. Two of his soldiers were guarding Jak, but the others had lowered their bows and blades, were watching Gwenna with smug satisfaction. They had ceded their own vigilance to the leach. It was an opportunity, if only a slim one. . . .

"So," Gwenna asked, raising her brows, trying to keep her voice casual despite the iron bands around her chest. "How do you want to die?"

Rallen's lips tightened for a moment. He reached for the cup at his side. Gwenna forced her face into a smirk. *Go ahead,* she thought. *Reach for it. Keep drinking.*

The leach took a small sip. It seemed to settle him. He watched Gwenna a while, then shook his head.

"Your sad little gibes are tedious."

"Then kill me, you impotent fuck."

As gambits went, it seemed safe enough. Rallen could have tossed her barrel off a cliff the moment she landed. The fact that she was alive meant that he wanted her alive, at least for a while longer.

"I will be delighted," he said, "when the time comes. For now, there are still a few things we need to discuss."

"I'm not much for discussion."

The Kettral commander exhaled heavily. "You know how this goes as well as I do, Sharpe. I was the one who trained you. Do we really need to walk through all the steps?"

"Trained me?" Gwenna raised an eyebrow. "You sat behind a desk and gave orders. You were weak then, and you are weak now. The women and men who *trained* me could break you across a knee."

"And where are they now?" Rallen demanded. "They are dead. Surely you remember your Hendran: *All that matters, when the fight's over, is who is still alive.*" He looked around as though appreciating his own survival for the first time. "Looks like I win."

The words were confident, undeniable, but he raised the cup to his lips again.

"Oh, the fight's not over," Gwenna replied airily, trying to shape her face into something that might read as amused indifference.

Rallen frowned, drank. "Actually, I would say it is. Here you are, bound like a bitch for the Manjari flesh markets. In fact, the idea of selling you when this is done entertains me. Of course, you'll be horribly mutilated. It's a shame, in a way—"

"Save your pity for yourself," Gwenna said, cutting him off, meeting his stare with her own. Let him think she had a plan. Let him think he needed even more strength to meet it.

Rallen narrowed his eyes, chewed at the inside of his cheek as he studied her warily. "You think you're clever." He raised his cup to his lips, found it empty, frowned, then reached over to refill it from the kettle. When Gwenna had tried yellowbloom, a cup smaller than her closed fist had made her feel crazy. Rallen, on the other hand, had likely been drinking it every day for a year. There was no telling how much he could handle. It was altogether possible that her goading was only making him more powerful, that it wasn't compromising his judgment or timing at all. Not that she had any other ideas.

"Luckily, I don't need to be clever," Gwenna said. "Not when you're the target."

The final word had the intended effect. Rallen's soldiers shifted uncomfortably, glances sliding from the leach to Gwenna and back. Whatever show Rallen had hoped to put on, Gwenna clearly wasn't playing her part.

"Let me explain this to you in a way that might penetrate," Rallen said, more loudly now. Was she just imagining that the slurring had grown worse? "I am going to hurt you. Then I am going to hurt you worse. . . ."

"Then hurt me," Gwenna said. "Start hurting. What's with all the talk?"

Rallen's lips pulled back in a snarl. He tightened his fist, and

Gwenna felt her ribs bend painfully. He stabbed a finger at her. "I'm looking forward to driving a knife between your tits, but first you're going to satisfy my curiosity on a number of points. If you were the type to take advice, I'd make a suggestion: answer my questions directly, and I'll kill you quickly. But then, you've always been dumb and stubborn, so it seems we're going to have to go back to the *Uses and Methods.*"

Rallen smiled, as though he could see the fear he'd kindled inside her burning like a hot, silent ember.

The real title of the volume was *On the Uses, Methods, and Limitations of Torture.* When Gwenna was first introduced to it as a third-year cadet, she'd thought it the most horrifying book she'd ever seen. Page after page of hand-inked illustrations comprised a catalogue of agony: men flayed or burned, bruised or broken, cut open so slowly and carefully that they remained alive even as the torturer removed the various organs. . . . She'd known this was coming, but still felt her guts go watery at the mention of the title.

"In fact," she made herself say, shoving aside the fear, filing her voice flat, "you're wrong. You're already dead." She forced herself to smile. "You just don't know it yet."

It was an insane claim, beyond madness. Rallen stared at her blearily, glanced up into the rafters, then toward the doors, as though expecting the warehouse to implode at any point. Then he raised the cup to his lips again.

32

Returning through the *kenta* to the island hub, and from there to the quiet, musty basement in the Shin chapterhouse, was easy. Convincing Long Fist to remain behind proved far more difficult. The shaman seemed to think he could stride straight into the Hall of a Thousand Trees, demand answers, and start picking people apart at the seams when he didn't get them. For all Kaden knew, maybe he could. He wasn't about to second-guess the raw power of the Lord of Pain.

On the other hand, there were some problems that couldn't be solved by any amount of power, and this appeared to be one of them. There was no telling where Adare had hidden Triste, no telling who was guarding her or what they would do if an Urghul chieftain suddenly appeared in the throne room, sword in hand, scarred flesh flexing beneath his leather vest. Long Fist might be a god, but the price of his power seemed to be a kind of blindness about the limits of his chosen flesh.

"Adare won't talk to you," Kaden had insisted. "She loathes you. She's been fighting *against* you for a year."

Long Fist had smiled grimly. "Her warriors have been fighting my warriors. It is not the same thing."

"You think she's likely to be more cooperative in person?"

"Pain has a way of limbering the tongue."

"And while her tongue is being limbered," Kaden replied, "what will be happening with Triste? There is no quick way to bring you into the Dawn Palace without dozens of people seeing. There are guards outside the *kenta* chamber. They will speak to Adare before you reach her. She could have Triste smuggled out of the city before you make your first cut in her skin."

In the end, the shaman loathed the logic, but he saw it.

"You have one day," Long Fist had said, laying the words out before him as though they were knives. "One day to wrestle the truth from your sister and return. If you are not here, I will come myself."

He didn't need to speak the rest.

It had been night on the *kenta* island, the stars glistening like tiny points of ice. Back in Annur, however, the sun hung halfway down the sky, filling the pavilions of the Dawn Palace with a golden light, casting long shadows from the cypresses lining the paths. The timing was good. Adare had left the Hall of a Thousand Trees for the afternoon, and Kaden found her in her study, poring over a sheaf of documents.

"Kaden," she said, glancing up from the papers on the table before her, then pushing back her chair. Dark hollows ringed her eyes, and though she would be expected on the Unhewn Throne within the hour, her hair hung loose around her face. In a way, it wasn't surprising—the strain of ruling a crumbling empire could wear on anyone—but Adare was hardly a stranger to strain. She'd been fleeing or fighting someone for more than a year, had faced at least as much danger as Kaden himself. For her to look so weary now ; . . it meant something had gone wrong. Something important enough to shake her in her bones. She almost looked like a different woman, although her voice was still strong, almost sardonic. "So you decided to come back after all. I was starting to think you gave up on the whole Annurian experiment."

He shook his head. "I haven't given up."

Adare chuckled. "I'd find that more comforting if I understood what in Intarra's name it is you're trying to accomplish."

Kaden glanced over his shoulder. The heavy, engraved doors

to his sister's study were closed. He turned back, studied her blazing eyes for a moment, trying to read something in those shifting flames. There were priests of Intarra who claimed to see things in their fires—the future, or the truth. Looking into his sister's irises, Kaden could find no trace of either. The fire was the fire, cold and bright, utterly unknowable.

"Where is Triste?" he asked quietly.

He'd debated taking a more subtle approach, but he wasn't sure he had either the time or the skill for subtlety. Every hour Triste remained unaccounted for was a danger. If Kaden couldn't trick the truth out of his sister, maybe he could shock it out, and indeed, his question seemed to shock. Adare's eyes widened a fraction. The breath caught silently in her chest.

"Dead," she responded after half a heartbeat, shaping her face into a frown. "I cannot mourn for a leach, but I know that she was close to you, and so for your loss, I am sorry."

It was a good act. A great act. Kaden ignored it, keeping his eyes on hers as he seated himself across the table.

"She is not dead. You replaced her with a different woman, one you killed to cover her disappearance."

Adare shook her head slowly but relentlessly. "How would I do that?"

"I don't know, and it doesn't matter. What matters is that you took Triste out of the prison where she was safe."

Kaden's last doubts evaporated as he watched his sister. Though she tried to hide it, the truth was scribbled in a hundred tiny ways across her face.

"Why do you *care* so much," she demanded after a pause, "what happens to some murdering leach?"

Kaden ignored the challenge, considering one final time what he was about to say, the peril of it. Whatever he and Adare had shared since her return to the city, she was still lying to him, lying about Valyn, maybe about a dozen things of which he was still unaware. She didn't trust him, and he certainly didn't trust her. She'd stopped trying to tear apart the republic, but that didn't mean they were on the same side, not by a long shot. If there were another choice, he would have taken it, but he couldn't see any other choice.

"She is not an ordinary leach," he replied finally. "Just as Long Fist is the human vessel of Meshkent, Triste carries Ciena inside of her."

Adare opened her mouth to reply, then shut it. For a long time, she just watched him, her eyes hooded, wary. Kaden held the gaze, schooled his pulse, and waited. His claim was, on the surface of it, outlandish. He could imagine Adare's laughter, her scorn, her curt refusal to say anything about the missing leach. And where would that leave him? He could go back to Long Fist, tell him that he'd failed, throw wide the doors of Annur, offer up his sister to the Lord of Pain in the hope that the shaman's savage ministrations could tease out the truth. It was a bleak path, but they seemed to have come to a place where all paths were bleak, where all led through cold, and shadow, and doubt.

"Well, that," Adare said finally, quietly, breaking him from his thought, "is a fucking disaster."

There was no disbelief or mockery in her gaze, only a deep, unplumbed weariness.

"You believe me?"

Adare hacked up a laugh. "For two reasons. First, it's an insane story to make up. And second, it fits."

"Fits with what?"

"The risk il Tornja took."

Kaden shook his head. "Il Tornja?"

"It was *his* idea. He wanted her dead. Badly."

"And what risk," Kaden asked, dread welling inside him, "did he take?"

Adare gestured to her chest. "Me. The Emperor. He risked my life, my station here inside Annur, my endorsement of him and of his command—all to see the girl dead."

To see her dead, Kaden repeated silently, fear's cold claw running along his spine. He drained the feeling from his flesh.

"But you didn't kill her."

Adare scrubbed her face with her hands. "No."

"Why not? You couldn't have known the truth."

"I didn't need to. Il Tornja wanted her dead badly enough to risk me, to threaten my son's life."

Kaden raised an eyebrow. "He has Sanlitun?"

Her face froze at the question, lips drawn back as though she were about to snarl or to scream. Her hands had curled into fists on the table before her, trembling with some unbearable strain. For a half-dozen heartbeats she stayed like that, almost motionless, a mute sculpture of rage and pain, caught in the grip of passions Kaden had spent his whole life learning to evade. Then, with an effort that seemed to tear something free inside of her, she closed her eyes, dragged in a breath, held it a long time, then blew it out. When she opened her lids, tears glazed those burning irises.

"Yes. He has my son."

Annurians considered Eira the gentlest member of the pantheon. In statuary and painting, the Goddess of Love was universally doe-eyed and open, slender arms spread, as though offering her embrace to the weary and worn. Men and women prayed to all the gods, even Kaveraa and Maat, but they prayed to Eira most often and most fervently, as though she were an old friend or a loving parent, a figure of universal understanding and infinite compassion.

And they're wrong, Kaden realized, staring at his sister.

Love's brutal truth was there in those four words, in the crack of her voice as she spoke them: *He has my son.*

Whatever tenderness the goddess offered had to be set in the scales against this: the fear, the desperation. Love's open-armed embrace hid blades. Her ministrations could be counted kind only by those who had not lost what they loved.

"I'm sorry," Kaden said.

Even as he said the words, he doubted them. It was inconvenient that il Tornja had seized his sister's son. It was dangerous.
Certainly, Kaden would have preferred it not to be the case. But
sorry? Sorrow? Did he feel that?

As though in response, Adare shook her head.

"I was an idiot," she said, voice rough as sand dragged over
steel. "I thought he would be safer in the north."

"Surely he won't hurt the child."

Adare stared at Kaden as though he'd lost his mind. "Il Tornja
is Csestriim. If you are right about Triste, and I'm starting to
think you are, he wants to destroy *all of us*. You think he'll balk
at cutting one tiny throat? Do you think it will give him a
moment's pause?"

She shuddered, fell silent.

"Then why did you defy him?"

Adare shook her head. Her fists had fallen open, and she was
staring at her palms, as though trying to remember something
they had once held. "I thought I could at least make it a fight."

Kaden studied her. Whatever lies she had tried to tell him
earlier, this was the truth. Her face was naked, unpremeditated,
all the guile finally, for this one moment, scrubbed away. She
might have schemed with il Tornja a year earlier, might even
have been in league with him when she returned to the city, but
they were in league no more. She hated the *kenarang* in a way
that Kaden, tutored so long among the snow and the stone,
could not begin to imagine.

He nodded slowly. "All right then. Let's make it a fight. Where
is Triste?"

Adare looked up at him then. Horror burned in her eyes.

"She's gone," his sister whispered. "She escaped. I lost her."

For a long time, Kaden didn't respond. Instead of following
a logical train of thought, his mind probed that one word: *lost*.
Strange that a single syllable, such a small sound, could bear so
many meanings. *Lost:* it might indicate a person who, journeying
through a dark wood, had stumbled from the path; it could

point to a defeat, either in battle, with thousands dead, or on a game board, the stones lying in some final, silent, inevitable configuration; or it could mean, simply, something gone—gone only for the moment, or utterly, beyond all retrieval.

"How?" he asked finally.

Adare shook her head. "Her well. I had her in Kegellen's mansion. She threw up the adamanth. . . ."

"No," Kaden said. "That wouldn't be enough. Triste isn't a leach. It's *Ciena's* power, and Ciena only comes out when their shared body is in mortal danger."

"It was," Adare said wearily. "Triste *told* the guards she'd thrown up the adamanth. Showed them. They panicked, came after her. Kegellen had six men on that door, and only one survived."

Kaden studied his sister. She was telling the truth.

"I have to go," he said.

"Where?"

For a heartbeat, he considered telling her everything—about the *kenta,* the island lost in the thundering sea, the god inside the body of a man who waited for him there. The barrier between them, so insurmountable when she first returned to Annur, looked feeble now. He could crush it with a handful of words. They could fight the *kenarang* together, brother and sister, as he had thought to do with Valyn once. . . .

Valyn.

Slowly, he shook his head.

Adare watched him. "You were going to tell me."

"I was."

"But you think you still can't trust me."

"It is not something I think. It is something I know."

Adare covered her burning eyes with her palms. The gesture kindled some old memory inside Kaden, a vision of his childhood, of playing hide-and-find with his brother, how they had believed somehow as tiny little boys, believed foolishly, madly, that by covering your own eyes you might disappear, as though

if you could not see the seeker, then you could not, in turn, be
seen.

What is it, Adare, he wondered silently, *that you don't want
me to see?*

When she finally dropped her hands, her gaze was like the
fire's heart.

"I killed Valyn."

The words might have been uttered in some foreign tongue
for all the sense Kaden could make of them at first. Even when
his mind had translated, linked the three together, they made
no sense, as though she'd claimed to have doused the sun. He
started to respond, then stilled himself, falling back, baffled,
into the old Shin discipline of listening and observation.

"He was waiting on the tower in Andt-Kyl," Adare went on.
She stared at the empty space between them, as though she'd
forgotten Kaden entirely, as though she were talking only to
herself. "He surprised me, murdered Fulton, and then he tried
to kill il Tornja. I thought we needed the *kenarang,* thought we
needed him to save Annur, and I panicked. I picked up a knife,
and I slid it between his ribs. I killed him. I saw him fall. . . ."

She fell silent.

Kaden scrambled to build the scene as it had been, to popu-
late the tower with the necessary bodies, to put them all in
motion, then to see inside their minds, inside Adare's mind most
of all, to understand what she had done, and how, and why. At
first it would not come. His brain was like a bright bird
squawking out the same pointless syllables: *brother, murder, why.*
He silenced it, studied that tower's top, and at the same time,
his sister's eyes as she stared into the awful chambers of her
memory.

She had none of Kaden's training, no ability to set aside grief,
no ability to smooth the cruel edges of confusion. She had lived
with this memory as though it were a rusted blade lodged inside
her, hiding it even as it bit deeper. Kaden himself might betray
a whole world of brothers and never feel the same pain. The

Shin had trained it out of him. Whether that was good or not, he could not say.

"What are you going to do?" Adare asked finally. Her eyes were on him once again, so hot it seemed impossible they should not burn out.

"I'm going to try to stop il Tornja," he said quietly. "And so are you."

He told her then, explained the *kenta* and his training, the Dead Heart and the Ishien, Long Fist's hatred of Annur and the strange alliance Kaden himself had managed to strike up with the shaman. Adare had given him the truth, finally, and so he gave her his own truth in return.

It was strange the way that people venerated truth. Everyone seemed to strive for it, as though it were some unalloyed good, a perfect gem of glittering rectitude. Women and men might disagree about its definition, but priests and prostitutes, mothers and monks all mouthed the word with respect, even reverence. No one seemed to realize how stooped the truth could be, how twisted and how ugly.

33

There was a passage buried in the middle of Hendran that Gwenna had always thought deserved more attention. Not really a passage, actually—just a couple of sentences: *Change is dangerous. The change of guard on a fortress wall. A change of a prisoner from one cell to another. A change of command in the middle of the battle. In every case, there will be a moment— sometimes no longer than a single heartbeat—when everything goes slack, when no one is in control. Strike then.*

Gwenna was waiting for that moment.

It hadn't taken long for Rallen's thugs to return to the ware-house pushing the barrel with Talal inside. Gwenna couldn't see it. She was still pinned against the empty air by Rallen's kenning, and the leach hadn't allowed her the freedom to turn her head. She could hear the barrel rumbling over the stone outside, however, the staves protesting each crunch and jolt. She could hear it hit the ramp into the warehouse, then bump the threshold, then roll smoothly over the level floor before coming to rest somewhere off to her right.

Close now, she thought, trying to keep half a dozen possible scenarios in her mind at the same time. The kenning didn't allow her to move, but she could flex her muscles against the invisible bonds, tensing, testing. *Readiness is everything.*

If they were going to crack out of Rallen's trap, it would have to be in the next few moments, and Gwenna was the only one in a position to start the cracking. Talal didn't know what was going on, not yet, and Quick Jak . . . She could hear his breathing behind her. The last glimpse she'd had of the flier he'd been kneeling, frozen, a knife against his neck. He'd appeared more ready to die than to fight. Even now, she could smell the panic pouring off him. The rank scent made her want to spit.

Another mistake to add to the growing list.

If she survived, she'd be able to write her own text, a rival to Hendran's. She'd call it *Error and Improvisation: How to Learn From a Total Goat Fuck.* It was starting to look like she'd need an entire chapter for her idiocy when it came to Quick Jak. Handling him would be crucial when everyone started swinging steel. . . .

No, she told herself, pulling her focus back to her bonds, to the three guards readying their weapons. Jak was a problem for *after* she was free.

"Right there," Rallen said, licking his lips warily, looking past Gwenna to the new arrivals. "Bows on the barrel. The leach inside has nothing like my power, but until he's drugged, he's dangerous."

That was what Gwenna was counting on. Rallen might be strong, but he wasn't invincible; he couldn't look at everything at once. Standard Kettral protocol would have split the prisoners up from the very start, but Rallen couldn't do that. Or wouldn't. He didn't trust his soldiers, certainly didn't trust them to go toe-to-toe with real Kettral, and so here they were, all packed into the same space, and if Rallen was going to handle Talal, there would be at least a few moments when he couldn't handle Gwenna herself.

"You three," the leach said, waving his hand toward the soldiers ringing her. "Close in, but be wary. I'm going to put her down."

As he spoke, the air around Gwenna slackened, as though some invisible rope had been cut. Then slowly, slowly, she began to sink toward the floor. The nearest of the three soldiers took an eager step forward, raising his sword.

"Not too close!" Rallen snapped. "You're not here to fight her. You're here to just *watch* the miserable bitch while I deal with the leach."

That's right, Gwenna thought, suppressing a smile as her feet touched the floor. *Just watch this miserable bitch.*

And then, as Rallen was shifting his attention and his kenning to Talal's barrel, as the guards were still raising their blades, uncertain how to configure themselves, Gwenna hurled herself into motion. She smashed aside the nearest blade, aiming for the sword's flat with the palm of her hand, hitting it slightly wrong, feeling the steel slice across her skin. The pain didn't matter. She was inside the bastard's guard, and she crushed his windpipe with a fist.

She turned into the collapsing body, shrugging the corpse over her shoulder with one arm as though he were a heavy coat, turning, heaving him around so that the desperate blows of the other two sank into dead flesh, lodging against the bone. When Gwenna dropped the body, it pulled the blades down with it, wrenching them from the hands of the baffled soldiers. She put two stiffened fingers into the eyes of the nearest man, pulled away as he screamed, then lashed out, shattering the kneecap of the other with her boot. As he lurched toward her, she stepped aside, stripping his belt knife from the sheath, cocking her arm, then throwing, watching the blade tumble over and over toward Rallen's throat.

It had taken her only heartbeats to destroy her guards, but heartbeats should have been plenty of time for Rallen to hurl another kenning at her—to tie her in invisible chains all over again, to shatter her skull. Even as that blade hung in the air, as his glassy eyes widened, Gwenna was half waiting for his own killing blow, for that attack she had no way of stopping, the one that would smash the life out of her.

Only the yellowbloom saved her—those few extra swallows

she had taunted him into taking. The tea might have given the leach power, but it had dulled his reflexes, and, sluggish with drug, his reaction was the most basic of any man facing his own death. Instead of attacking, or striking back, he flung up a desperate hand in the oldest motion of self-preservation. The knife careened off an invisible wall just feet from his face, then skittered off across the floor.

"Four men standing," Gwenna shouted, turning toward Talal's barrel and the stunned soldiers beside it, stooping to snatch one of the short blades from a fallen body. "Bows and blades . . ."

Before she could finish the warning, the roof fell on her. That's how it felt, anyway—as though a crushing weight had been dropped onto her head and shoulders from a great height. Her knees buckled, then she caved, head smashing against the floor, darkness gnawing the fringes of her vision.

Rallen's bellow, slurred and furious, filled her ears. ". . . kill you, Sharpe. I'm going to feed your blood to Hull's twisted tree. . . ."

She fought the pain and nausea, tried to twist free of the leach's grip, to find some break in whatever held her. There was nothing but air above, but she might have been lying under a pile of rubble. Breathing was almost impossible.

She'd fallen facing the doorway, toward Quick Jak. The flier was still on his knees, hands bound behind him, the knife still at his throat. The soldier guarding him was obviously shocked, distracted, so stunned by the sudden violence that it would have been a simple matter for the flier to roll free, kick the knife away, get on his feet, and start fucking fighting. Jak didn't even try. Instead, his eyes fixed on Gwenna, wide and horrified, and though his shoulders strained against the bonds, it was just some animal impulse. He wasn't actually trying to break away.

Gwenna tried to shout at him to *go,* but she could barely draw enough breath for a moan. Out of the corner of her eye she could see motion; Rallen, she realized, approaching her, his cup of yellowbloom discarded in favor of a naked blade.

"You thought you could defy me, Sharpe?"

She tried to growl something vicious and defiant. All she managed was a groan mixed with drool, and so she clamped her mouth shut.

"I was going to hurt you," Rallen went on, "in order to learn what I needed to learn." He waved the knife in the air between them in satisfied admonition. "Now, though? Now I'm going to hurt you for that, and then I'm going to keep hurting you just for the sheer—"

Before he could finish, the steel hoops ringing Talal's barrel snapped. The sound echoed in the closed space of the warehouse, crisp as a series of cracked skulls, and then, a moment later, the staves split. Wood shattered, splintered, tore into jagged fragments along the grain, pushing up, and out, and away as Talal, sweating, bleeding, eyes wide, teeth bared, like something awful hatching from its massive shell, shoved his way clear, then stumbled to his feet.

The soldiers facing him reeled. One tried to back up too quickly, tripped, then fell, losing his sword, crab-crawling away from the leach, struggling to find his feet or his freedom or both. Talal took a step after him, belt knife half raised, then noticed the other threat, the woman in his blind spot who was also backing up, but raising her flatbow as she retreated, sighting hastily along the quarrel. He tried to turn. . . .

Too slow, Gwenna wanted to scream.

Talal's movements were leaden, awkward—despite the violence with which he'd broken free—as though he'd forgotten how to use his legs. Like Gwenna herself, he'd been in the barrel too long. That he was standing at all, that he was fighting, was testament to his will, but you couldn't will the feeling back into legs gone numb half a day earlier. You couldn't will blood into starved muscle. Talal twisted halfway to face this other foe, then stumbled. The stumble saved his life.

The flatbow had been level with his chest. When the soldier pulled the trigger, however, she panicked, yanking the weapon back and up. As Talal dropped to his knee, the bolt just cleared his head. His eyes widened, then he lunged. It was fucking ugly—the sort of thing you'd see from first-year cadets in the ring—but Talal was no first-year. Unlike those kids fumbling with their wooden swords, he was fighting for his life, for *all* of their lives. He managed to snag the spent flatbow with one hand, wrench it free of the woman's grasp, then smash it across her face. Once, twice, three times, quick and vicious, until her head snapped back, dangling limply from the broken neck.

That was enough to stop Rallen in his tracks. In less time than it would take to recite a quarter page of the *Tactics,* he'd lost four of his six soldiers. One was half crawling, half groveling in his effort to get clear, and the other, the one guarding Quick Jak, instead of watching the flier, was staring at the bodies sprawled across the floor, at the blood seeping into the dry, eager wood.

Talal glanced over at Gwenna. He couldn't see the kenning holding her, but seemed to understand the situation all the same, and pivoted to hurl the bloody flatbow at Rallen. As attacks went, it wasn't much. Talal's aim was good, but if the other leach had been thinking clearly he could have blocked it, or simply stepped aside. Instead, he let Gwenna go, swinging his empty hand around, palm out, blocking himself from the bow with the same kenning he had used against the knife moments earlier.

Gwenna heaved in a breath, felt the life flooding back into her crushed limbs.

"He can't . . . ," she tried, fell off coughing.

"I know," Talal said, snatching up a dropped sword, then moving wide, away from Gwenna, toward the far wall. Her own stolen blade tight in her hand, she lurched to her feet, circling the opposite direction, forcing Rallen to choose a target, denying him the chance to hit them both with the same kenning. Rallen watched them glide to the flanks, his eyes wide, lips drawn back in a rictus. Gwenna debated hurling her blade, but she'd tried that twice already.

Time to be thorough. Time to finish it.

She took a step forward, keeping her gaze on Rallen, following Talal out of the corner of her eye. There was no need to talk. They'd been fighting side by side long enough to slide into the plan without any need for words. She took another step, another. Then, before she could close with him, Rallen bellowed and swung his arm in a wide, desperate arc. The kenning was like a massive hammer on a long chain swinging silently through the room. It hit Talal first, slamming him across the open floor and into the wall, then smashed into Gwenna a quarter-heartbeat later.

The corner of a stacked crate caught her in the ribs. She felt something break, but people fought with broken ribs all the time. She shoved the pain aside, twisted around—she could move this time, although it was like struggling through almost-frozen water—to find Rallen stumbling for the warehouse door. He was faster than Gwenna remembered, but then, he was also a hundred pounds lighter. Still, sweat streamed down his face. She could hear his breathing, labored, almost painful. She strained, trying to bring her sword to bear, to break free, to give chase, but Rallen was already framed in the doorway, and then he was gone.

The kenning shattered just half a dozen breaths later. Gwenna shoved herself off of the crates, was halfway to the door when she realized someone was shouting at her, the same desperate syllable over and over: *Stop! Stop!*

It was the last guard, the one with his knife at Quick Jak's throat. He'd lost his chance to slip out in the madness, and now his fever-bright eyes darted from Gwenna to Talal, then back. He was shaking his head. His hand trembled, scraping the blade against the stubble of Jak's neck. He hadn't drawn blood, not yet, but he was so obviously terrified he could easily slit the flier's throat without even noticing.

"Stop," he said again, begging now, voice barely more than a whisper.

Jak's face was bleak. His mouth hung half open, as though he wanted to protest, but couldn't remember how. A wave of loathing washed over Gwenna. She and Talal had been fighting—getting their asses handed to them, but still *fighting*. Jak hadn't moved, hadn't even raised his voice. The soldier guarding him was so lost in his own horror that the greenest cadet on his first day of training could take him down, and yet the flier stayed on his knees.

And this, Gwenna thought bleakly, *is why you should have brought Delka.*

On any other day, she would have been tempted to leave the flier, to take Talal and go after Rallen. The ugly truth, however, was that she still needed him. The plan had gone straight to shit, but then, that was the nature of plans. It was still possible to win, but to win they needed Annick and the others. Which meant they needed a bird to go get them. Which meant they needed Jak.

She shifted her eyes from the coward to the man guarding him.

"Let him go," she said slowly. "And I won't kill you."

"Don't come any closer!" the soldier insisted, pressing the knife harder against Jak's throat. A thread of blood ran down the flier's neck. He closed his eyes.

Gwenna ignored the warning. "If you kill him, I will take out your eyes and feed them to you off the end of my knife. I'm not much for horse trading, but this seems like an easy one: let my man up, and I will let you walk out of that door."

The soldier stole a panicked glance over his shoulder, out the bright rectangle into the open air. Rallen was getting away, but Gwenna forced down her own impatience. Part of any battle was picking who to fight and when. Choosing who to save and who to let die.

Slow down, she told herself, *and do it right.*

"What's it going to be?" she asked the guard.

Horror etched the man's face. "How can I trust you?"

"You can't," Gwenna replied grimly. "Now I'm going to count to one."

"What?"

"One."

The soldier shoved Jak to the floor, then hurled himself backward, stumbling as he reached the door. For a moment, he was just a silhouette against the sun, all detail blotted out in the glare. Gwenna waited for his second foot to clear the threshold before she threw the knife. It hit him square between the shoulders, and he tumbled to the ramp with a wet groan.

Jak stared at her. "You said . . ."

"I said he'd leave this room alive," Gwenna replied. "He did. Now get the fuck up."

The flier just stared at her.

She turned to Talal. "Get him. I can't carry him, and we're dead if we can't fly out of here."

She reached the doorway in half a dozen strides, then pulled up, blinking in the sudden brightness. Jak's guard was dragging himself down the ramp, crawling toward the brilliant shape of his own death, leaving a smear of blood on the wood. Gwenna glanced at him, then looked away, scanning the land to the east.

Rallen's fort wasn't a single fort at all, but a compound of half a dozen buildings arranged in a vague L near the island's edge. The warehouse from which she'd just escaped stood inland, back from the ocean, at the very end of the short leg of the L. A few dozen paces away stood a small, open-walled shed, and beyond that, a large, barnlike structure that Gwenna took for the livery. The long leg of the L stretched along the seaward cliff, and those buildings—thick, defensible stone structures— were surrounded by a stone curtain wall maybe twice as high as Gwenna's head.

The leach himself had disappeared behind the walls. She could hear shouting—orders and questions—the urgent chorus of soldiers scrambling to meet an attack. Her lips tightened. Rallen had at least two dozen men back there, even after the soldiers she'd killed in the warehouse. From what she could hear, the whole fort seemed to be in momentary disarray, but soon enough the idiots would get their asses under them and come out swinging. Which would make it two dozen against three.

"What's the play?" Talal asked quietly.

He was half a step behind her, holding Jak around the waist. The flier didn't seem to be injured, but he was paralyzed, lost in his own fear.

"The livery," she said, stabbing a finger at the low stone barn just outside the compound walls.

The original plan had involved more waiting and sneaking, less fighting and fleeing. For all the changes, though, everything still revolved around the kettral, and to have any hope with the kettral, they needed to find the whistles.

Every bird on the Islands was trained to respond to a particular pitch. Without that training, the entire Eyrie would have dissolved into chaos, kettral quartering the sky at random with no way to respond to their fliers. The whistles were a simple solution, louder than a human voice, more precise, small enough to carry in a pocket or on a thong around the neck, and almost indestructible. Those whistles simplified day-to-day logistics on the Islands, and in battle, their piercing shriek, higher than any human cry, could cut through the clash of swords and the roar of fire, calling the bird down at the crucial moment, saving soldiers' lives. After nearly a year, the birds would be accustomed to Rallen's soldiers, but they would accept new riders. All you needed was the right whistle.

When Gwenna first arrived on the Islands as a cadet, those whistles had seemed like an oversight, a weakness. "What if a soldier's captured?" she'd demanded. "What if an enemy gets her hands on the whistle and calls the bird?"

The Flea had just raised his eyebrows. "And then what?"

"Calls a bird. Climbs *on* the 'Kent-kissing thing. Starts killing the wrong people."

"Climbs on?" the older man asked, raising a bushy eyebrow. "Do you remember the first time you saw a bird? Would you have known how to climb on?"

That was the crux of it, after all. Kettral were accustomed to fighting a foe that was *not* Kettral. Accustomed to dropping unseen straight out of the sky, cutting throats, and disappearing beneath the beat of massive wings. There was no point in devising tactics to fight other Kettral, no point to guard against them. Until now. There were always extra whistles in the livery, hanging up beside the harnesses and barrel straps, each labeled with the name of the bird that would respond to its call.

That, at least, was the way it had been back on the Eyrie before the Kettral destroyed themselves. How Rallen handled things was anyone's guess. Gwenna had hoped to have time to snoop around, to keep hunting if they came up empty-handed in the livery, but hope was a weak shield, one that had shattered the moment Rallen's thugs started bashing the outside of her barrel.

Maybe the whistles weren't in the livery at all, but one thing was clear—the three of them were standing in the open, asses in the wind. Almost no vegetation grew from Skarn's rocky soil, certainly no trees, nothing that might provide any real cover. Whistles or no, the livery was shelter, and they were going to need shelter soon—partly from the arrows that Rallen's thugs were sure to put in the air, but mainly, crucially, from the patrol that would be circling somewhere above.

Gwenna glanced skyward. It took only a moment to find the bird turning in a lazy gyre around the island, a few hundred paces up and maybe half a mile to the north. Neither the bird nor the soldiers patrolling from her talons seemed to have noticed the violence breaking out below. They were searching the waves, most likely, if they were actually searching at all. A year of unopposed tyranny wasn't likely to lend vigilance to the daily watch. Still, you didn't need to be vigilant to notice the madness that was doubtless unfolding behind Rallen's wall. You didn't need to be vigilant to notice three assholes standing around looking confused.

"The livery is close to the fort," Talal pointed out.

"It's where the whistles are," Gwenna said, breaking into a run. "And if we're still out here when that bird spots us, we're dead." She turned to Jak. "Can you fly?"

He stared at her with blank eyes. Gwenna slapped him full across the face.

"You said you could do this, you bastard, and now I need to know: *Can you still do it?*"

Even as she asked the question, she was trying to find some way to tweak the plan. There were a dozen options, all equally bleak.

Jak stared at her. "I'm sorry. I don't . . ." He shook his head.

"Oh, *fuck* this," Gwenna spat. "Just get to the livery. It'll buy us time."

They barely made it. The airborne patrol noticed them moments after they started running, banked for a closer look, then dropped into a half stoop. The arrows started raining down—from the fort and the bird both—just a few paces later. Rallen's snipers had nothing on Annick, but the range wasn't bad, and the shafts were landing all around, steel heads striking sparks from the rock.

Gwenna kicked open the door to the livery, shoved Talal inside as a broadhead clattered off the stone a few feet from her head, then dove for the opening. She rolled into a crouch as Talal slammed the door shut behind her, then dropped to a knee, chest heaving as he shrugged out from beneath Jak. Gwenna seized the flier by the throat, dragged him to his feet.

"Time to start fighting, you piece of shit. You freeze again and we're leaving you."

Slowly, the flier's eyes focused on her face. After a moment, he nodded unsteadily.

She wanted to say more, wanted to beat the blood out of him, actually, but there was no time.

"Let's just find the whistles. Talal—hold the door."

The leach didn't need an order. He was already dragging a crate out from the corner, a wooden box large enough to slow anyone trying to force their way in. Gwenna left him to it, turning toward the gloom. The ranks of window didn't admit much light, but she didn't need light.

Dozens of flight straps and harnesses hung from the iron hooks set into the wall. Flight nets had been draped neatly over the rafters to dry. Reinforced cargo barrels lined one wall, two ranks deep. Above them were shelves packed with all the necessary apparatus of flight: training blinders and drag hooks, stitch kits and wet-weather slicks. All the necessary apparatus, that was, except the crucial whistles.

Outside, just above the thatch roof, the kettral screamed. The bird's cry was like a hot knife torn through the air. Something inside of Gwenna quailed at the sound, some childlike part that could never be entirely trained away.

Jak's head jerked around. "Shura'ka," he said.

Gwenna forced aside her fear. "She's the patrol bird?"

He nodded.

"All right," Gwenna said. "What does that mean for us? For the plan?"

The flier closed his eyes, dragged in an unsteady breath. "She's strong," he replied finally. "Reliable." Something about the conversation seemed to be bringing the man back to life. Or maybe it was just the fact that they were under cover finally, that for at least a few moments no one seemed likely to kill them.

"What about the others?" Gwenna asked. "Any chance they're here already? Roosting somewhere? Can we get to them without the whistles?"

Jak shook his head slowly. "Probably not. This time of day, they'll be feeding, all but Shura'ka and whatever bird's hauling the cargo over from Hook. We weren't supposed to be doing this until later."

"I fucking *know* that. Just in case you haven't been paying

attention, quite a few things have happened that weren't supposed to happen."

The sound of shouting was louder outside, louder and more
organized. Gwenna took a few steps toward the windows, risked
a glance toward the fort. Rallen stood just outside his walls,
furious, reeling, leaning heavily on his cane and screaming at
his men. They were maybe twenty-five paces away. Gwenna
didn't bother trying to count them. Twenty? Thirty? Too many.
They weren't attacking, though. Not yet. A few were looking
south instead. There was a high, clear whine, then another, and
another, the whole dissonant chord pitched just at the edge of
hearing.

"*They* have the whistles," Jak observed quietly, "and they just
put out the call."

The abattoir where the kettral fed was miles to the south.
Gwenna couldn't make out the low, fertile island behind the
walls of Rallen's fortress, but she could imagine the massive
birds perched on the bloody soil, beaks rending the sheep to
ribbons.

"They can hear the whistles?" she asked. "Even at that
distance?"

"Of course they can." The flier followed her gaze out the
open window. "There might be—"

Gwenna cut him off. She'd already done the quick math, not
that she really needed it.

"We failed," she said. The words hurt, but not as much as
being torn apart by what was coming. "We need to get clear
now."

Jak shook his head. Uncertainty twisted his face. "I might—"

"We are *leaving*," Gwenna snarled.

Talal studied her, his face grave. "How?"

She gestured toward the door. "Make a break for it. Get to
the cliff and jump."

The leach shook his head. "There are rocks at the base,
Gwenna. There's no way we'd make it."

"Not here," she said. "Northeast, on the far side of the island. It's open ocean up there, and the cliffs are lower."

"It's still fifty paces down."

"You can work on your swan dive."

"No," Jak said. His voice was quiet, but surprisingly hard.

Gwenna rounded on him. "You're welcome to stay here."

He shook his head. His brown eyes were wide in the darkness, frightened as he stared out the window, but the shock was mostly gone.

"There's another way," he said.

Gwenna glanced out the window again. Another bird was approaching from the southwest, from Hook, a huge, black shadow backlit by the afternoon sun. It bore a single flier on its back and carried a net laden with barrels in its claws.

"Great," Gwenna spat.

Talal followed her gaze. "We're not going to beat two kettral to the far side of the island."

"We weren't likely to beat one," Gwenna growled. "It's the only play we have."

"No," Jak said once more. "It's not."

For a heartbeat, she considered hitting him again. Not just a hard slap this time, but a punch, a hundred punches, vicious blows to the face and stomach that would double him over and shut him up. They'd be faster without him anyway, and if it came to dying, she'd rather do it without a coward at her side. Something in his tone, however, brought her up short, some bleak determination that hadn't been there before.

"Talk," she said. "Fast."

He opened his mouth to reply, then broke off, shaking his head. "There's no time. It's Allar'ra." He ran to the door, seized the crate, and, muscles straining, hurled it aside.

"Jak . . . ," Gwenna began.

The flier ignored her, wrestling instead with the rusted latch. *"Jak!"*

Before she could finish, he slammed the door open, and

stepped outside. For a moment he stood stock-still in the sunlight and the flashing steel of the arrowheads. Then he ran west, putting the livery between himself and Rallen's soldiers. Gwenna cursed, started to follow him, but Talal raised a hand.

"Wait."

She stared at the leach. "For *what*?"

"You said we should bring him."

"Yeah. And I was *wrong*."

"Maybe not."

"He's been less use than a side of rotting beef, Talal. He hasn't done a fucking thing since Rallen sprung his trap."

"He's doing something now."

Gwenna stared at her companion.

Talal met her gaze. "You said we could trust him. So trust him."

She hesitated, then turned back to the window. The flier stood still as a post a few dozen paces from the cliff. Shura'ka, the patrol bird, was to the east, on the wrong side of the livery to see him, at least for the moment. That would change quickly, though, and there was nowhere to hide on that bare, sun-parched rock. Over Jak's shoulder, in the distance, she could still see the silhouette of Allar'ra. The bird was closing, closing fast, despite the huge load of cargo it carried in its claws.

"When this goes to shit," Gwenna said grimly. "We run."

Talal just nodded.

A quarter mile out, Allar'ra dropped the net. The bird screamed, flexed his claws, and then, to Gwenna's shock, rolled smoothly upside down. It was the same maneuver she'd seen weeks earlier when she and Quick Jak came to scout the fortress, only this time there was a flier on the creature's back, and the sudden twist flung the man free. He tried to hang on, dangled from both arms for a heartbeat, flailing desperately, then failed, fell. The bird had just reached the island, and the flier shattered on the uneven stone. The scream and the crunch reached Gwenna just a moment later.

"Holy Hull," she said as Allar'ra righted himself with a flick of the wing and tail.

Quick Jak didn't flinch, didn't flee. Instead, he raised a hand even as he fell into a crouch. She couldn't see his face, but there was something in the motion, a confidence, a certainty that she'd never seen in him before, as though he were Kettral after all, had been Kettral all along, and she'd just never noticed. Then the bird was on him.

"That's it," Gwenna murmured, stomach lurching inside her. "He's dead."

She couldn't see exactly what had happened, but *dead* was the only real possibility. When it came to smash-and-grab maneuvers, fliers weren't very good to begin with. They were generally on the bird's back, after all—it was the other members of the Wing who had to be able to catch the straps in a hurry, and that was when there *were* straps to catch. Allar'ra was fitted out for cargo carry, not for human transport. The bird had come in far faster than Gwenna had ever seen, his claws at all the wrong angles—canted forward for attack, rather than backward, as they should have been for any sane mount. She couldn't see past all the kicked-up dust and shadow, but one fact was clear—Jak had botched the grab, and badly.

"It was too fast," she growled. "Too fucking fast."

Even the Flea couldn't make a grab at that speed, at *half* that speed. A human arm and hand and shoulder could only take so much. Gwenna couldn't see more than the narrow patch of land outside the window, the stone and the sea beyond, but Jak was gone. She processed the fact, then set it aside.

"Let's go," she said, waving to Talal. "He gave us a distraction."

The leach joined her at the open door.

"We run straight north," Gwenna went on, "use the shed and the warehouse for cover from the kettral if we have to. . . ."

Talal, however, didn't seem to be listening. He was looking

toward the eastern sky instead, shading his eyes with a cupped hand.

"Holy Hull," he breathed after a moment.

Gwenna followed his eyes, half expecting to find Shura'ka circling back, low enough this time for the soldiers shooting arrows or hurling starshatters, or Allar'ra, those vicious claws outstretched. She found the huge golden bird all right, but it wasn't stooping for the kill. It was climbing, climbing hard, wings hammering the air. And there, clutched in one claw— Quick Jak.

"Holy Hull," Gwenna agreed, wondering if she was really seeing what she thought she was seeing.

Kettral snatched up sheep and cows in their claws all the time, of course. That was how they hunted. Gwenna had seen the birds sink talons into a full-grown heifer and haul it screaming into the air as easily as their diminutive cousins might take a hare or a mouse. Allar'ra had snatched up Quick Jak in almost the same way, but unlike those bleeding, bleating beasts, the flier didn't seem hurt. In fact, it looked like he was . . . climbing, climbing free of the great bird's grip, moving nimbly, fluidly between the talons, then over them as his kettral soared higher.

"Have you ever . . . ," Talal began.

"No," she said. Then, because it seemed worth saying again, "No."

It was the kind of story you wouldn't believe if you heard it straight out of the Flea's mouth. Laith had always said that Quick Jak was the only flier on the Islands better than he was, but he'd never mentioned *this*. Gwenna had never even considered the possibility of letting a bird seize a soldier in its claws. No one had. The first shot at that would be the last; a human would be sliced into ribbons of meat—the end of a bold, stupid experiment.

Jak wasn't meat, though. He was alive, had even managed to climb out of the cage of claw. As Gwenna stared, he was holding on with one hand, leaning back and out, like a sailor hiking over the rail. Instead of waves beneath him, though, there was only empty air, fathoms of it, and hard stone at the bottom. Then he jumped.

For just a moment the flier seemed to hang, arms spread, caught between the speed of the bird's climb and his own inescapable weight. In that moment, Allar'ra screamed, twisted, tucked his wings and fell sideways, rolling into the empty air. Jak reached out, easily as if he were floating at the top of an ocean swell, and caught the harness that had held the other hapless flier. The movement was casual, almost lazy. Jak pulled himself in close, pressing his body against the bird's back, and then, as the Dawn King rolled upright once again, settled into his seat, tucking his legs behind the straps of the harness. The whole thing took less than five heartbeats. Gwenna had been raised on the Islands, trained among men and women who made a daily habit of the impossible, and it was the most astounding thing she'd ever seen.

"All right," she said, still staring. "I'm glad we brought him."

"Down!" Talal shouted, slamming into her from the side.

A few feet above, right where Gwenna's head had been, an arrow shivered in the wooden doorframe. *I guess Rallen's done waiting,* she thought, half crawling, half rolling through the open door, back into the dubious safety of the livery. Talal dove over her as a handful of arrows and crossbow bolts clattered against the stone to either side of the door. The archers had flanked them, venturing around the east and west sides of the livery to find an angle of attack.

"We're pinned down," the leach murmured.

Gwenna eyed the archers, then shook her head. "No, we're not. Now we have a *bird*."

And then, as though summoned by the word, Allar'ra fell on Rallen's men. One moment the archers had been moving steadily, warily closer, covering one another with heavy fire through the open approach. Then a massive shadow blotted the sunlight, a bird's predatory scream split the afternoon air. This time when the kettral swept past just a pace above the stone those claws *did* cut, slicing through muscle and bone, killing a soldier on the approach, then snatching two more, crushing them between the talons, tossing the limp bodies into the dry dirt.

The closest of Rallen's minions made a panicked rush on the livery. Gwenna stabbed the first man in the throat, kicked the second in the crotch, then watched as Talal's blade came down in a quick, sharp blow, smashing open his skull. Gwenna tossed her sword behind her, grabbed a corpse in each hand, hauled them inside, out of the way.

"Get it closed," she growled, dropping the bodies, then seizing the crate Quick Jak had moved aside, dragging it back into place as Talal slammed the door shut. "Another," she grunted, gesturing. "Two more." When they were piled three high, she drove the swords of the dead soldiers into the wooden floor just behind the crates, bracing them.

"It won't hold long," Talal said, backing up, eyeing the barricade.

"You're welcome to build a fucking portcullis. I'm taking the high ground."

Even sore, even tired, it was easy enough to climb the unmortared wall and into the rafters. Below her, Talal frowned, then made a little flicking gesture with his hand. The blades sunk deeper into the wooden floor, all the way to the hilts. He kicked them once, seemed satisfied, then followed her up. By the time he was standing in the rafters, she'd already hacked a hole in the thick thatching of banana leaves.

"Hold on," Talal said, laying a hand on her arm. "Jak's up there, but so is the other bird. Shura'ka."

"So let him kill her," she snapped, slicing and stabbing at the stubborn thatch. "That's why we brought him, right? When it's time to make the grab, I want to be ready. Besides—we blocked the door, but there's about to be an armory's worth of arrows flying in those open windows."

She'd barely finished the words when the first steel-tipped

bolt thudded into one of the posts below. After a pause, two more followed. And then it was chaos. Rallen's men weren't trying to force the door, weren't even bothering to get close enough to pick targets out of the shadowy darkness. They were just filling the livery with arrows and hoping to get lucky. It wasn't much of a strategy, but then, you didn't need much of a strategy when you had your foe pinned down and outnumbered.

"They're not using munitions," Talal said.

"Not yet," Gwenna replied grimly. "I want out of here before they start lighting fuses."

With a final, vicious shove, she cleared the last of the thatch from the ragged hole she'd hacked in the roof. There were no birds in the visible patch of sky.

"Come *on*," Gwenna muttered, forcing her way up through the opening. She glanced down at Talal. "Stay clear. I might be coming back through, and fast."

The leach nodded, then moved along the rafter.

It took her a moment, once she was up on the uneven thatch, to find the two birds. Shura'ka was low in the sky to the north, close enough that Gwenna could make out the faces of the men and women strapped in on the talons. They were leaning out in their harnesses, trying to see above them and failing. Like the rest of the Kettral, they'd never trained to fight a foe coming down from above, and that was just where Quick Jak and the King had positioned themselves.

The golden kettral was higher and behind the other, wings spread wide. As Gwenna watched, the creature shrieked, tucked those wings close, and fell on Shura'ka like a stone. The smaller bird, alert to the danger, ducked and twisted in the air, but she was barely two-thirds the size of the King, and lower, and heavy with the weight of the four soldiers strapped in to her talons. Allar'ra hit her hard, one talon tearing the rider from her back, the other raking across her starboard wing.

The women and men on the talons were shouting, screaming. They couldn't see past their own bird's wings, but they knew what was going on well enough, and they understood how it would end if Shura'ka didn't pull herself free. 'Ka twisted desperately, but Allar'ra held on, stabbing down with his huge hooked beak into the back of the smaller bird's neck, a vicious shredding motion, over and over and over, until his beak was slick with blood. On his back, Jak was shouting something, but Gwenna couldn't make it out, not at the distance. Both creatures were falling fast, crashing toward the stony ground of the island.

"Get free," she growled. *"Get free."*

At the last moment, the King did just that, tossing the other bird aside, spreading his massive wings, and leveling out just a few paces above the stone. Shura'ka didn't. One wing flapped desperately, weakly, but the other had gone limp. All she could manage was to roll halfway over in the air before she hit. Distance delayed the sound, but Gwenna could see the creature's rib cage burst beneath its own weight. It was easy to forget, watching the birds soar on the thermals, that they were heavier than a dozen horses. Shura'ka crumpled on impact, crushing the men and women beneath her. She twitched once, half raised a mutilated wing, then fell still.

High overhead, the Dawn King's scream sliced across the sky.

Gwenna glanced over her shoulder. Rallen's soldiers hadn't realized that she was on the roof. Like her, most had been staring north, watching the violence play out across the sky. As Allar'ra broke free, they began to retreat, slowly at first, then sprinting toward the safety of Rallen's compound. It was a slim opportunity, but then, the Kettral were used to slim opportunities.

"Now," Gwenna said, turning back to the golden kettral. "Come on, Jak—get us out of here."

She had no intention of trying Jak's version of the smash and grab, but there was time to make a short touchdown. Allar'ra wasn't wearing talon straps, but she and Talal could hold on for the short flight back to Hook. The bird banked south, back toward the livery, and Gwenna reached down to haul Talal up through the hole in the thatch. When they were both standing on the roof, however, she realized that the bird wasn't coming for them after all. It was too high, winging out to the south and west. Gwenna stared as Jak took the creature down over the island's edge, out over the waves and away.

"He's going for the others," Talal said quietly.

"Or running away," Gwenna replied.

There was plenty to run from. Despite the carnage wrought by Jak and his bird, despite their obvious mastery in the skies, Rallen still had more than twenty soldiers at his disposal, soldiers with bows and explosives. Rallen's own kennings, if he managed to focus them, might be enough to cripple even the King, to bring the bird down, and then there were the other kettral, the ones that Rallen had summoned. Gwenna could just barely make them out, a handful of specks winging their way north even as she watched.

"He's not running," Talal said, pointing toward the low-lying island where Annick waited with the rest of the Kettral. "He's picking up the others."

Gwenna sucked air between her teeth. "It's gonna be close," she muttered. "If the other birds get here while Rallen's still holding the whistles, we're fucked. I don't care how good Jak and his bird are, they can't go five against one."

She shifted her gaze from the sky and the waves to Rallen's fort. After the undisciplined madness of the initial attack on the livery, the leach had finally done the smart thing, pulling his people back behind the walls. There was no point attacking Gwenna and Talal from the ground, after all, when they could wait just a little bit longer and then put five Wings in the air. From the top of the livery, Gwenna could get a better sense of the courtyard shielded by those walls.

"The birds can land in there, under cover. If that happens, we're done." She took a deep breath, glanced over at the retreating figure of Allar'ra, tried to figure the angles and flight times in her head, then gave up. There was really only one play left. "We've got to force the gate. Get inside that compound."

"We'll have a better shot when Jak gets back here with the others."

"We don't have *time* to wait for the others. By the time they get back, Rallen'll have five birds loaded and airborne. Our people'll never even get a chance to land." It was a nasty truth, but it had to be faced. She glanced down through the hole in the roof, then stepped through, dropping the twelve feet to the floor and landing with a grunt. The pain in her ribs lanced up through her chest. Talal was smarter—he landed on the rafters first, then leapt down from there.

"The door," Gwenna said, grimacing as she straightened up. "Punch out the hinges."

Talal looked at her, then nodded. While she heaved aside the crates, Gwenna heard a quiet *ping* as the hinges snapped beneath some invisible force.

Gwenna seized the door in both hands. The thing was heavy, but then, she'd be glad enough of that when Rallen's men started filling it with arrows.

"Get that," she grunted, nodding toward the narrow wooden ladder leading into the loft.

Talal raised his brows, then sheathed one sword to free up a hand for the ladder.

Gwenna met his eyes. "Ready?"

"We've got a door and barn ladder to assault a fortified position. How could I not be ready?"

Despite his bruised face, despite the blood trickling down from his scalp, despite the fact that they were probably about to die, Talal smiled.

Gwenna found herself grinning back. "And all these years I thought you weren't funny."

"It's all right. All these years, I thought you were a bitch."

"A bitch, hunh? Watch this."

And then she was out of the livery, wooden door held up and at an angle before her, heart thundering in her chest, boots pounding over the broken ground. She could hear Talal just behind her, running in the shelter of the door, his breathing heavy but steady. She could smell him. Whatever he'd said moments before, he smelled ready. The first arrows punched into the door, staggering her for a moment, but she found her footing and charged on, borne up by the bellow rising from her chest.

There was no way to see where she was going, and she wasn't about to stick her head into the thicket of falling arrows to look. She tried to run in a straight line, but ended up hitting the fort's wall at an angle anyway, hitting it so hard that the corner of the door cracked and her head smashed up against the wooden boards. The thing was riddled with arrows; they'd been driving down like a heavy rain in the middle of the insane dash. Now that they were close to the compound, however, the wall actually shielded them from the worst of the attack.

Talal threw the ladder up against the stone. The wall was a dozen feet high, and the ladder's top rung didn't quite reach, but then, that would be a problem to deal with if she ever got to the top rung.

"Go," the leach said. "I can hold the door up above you for a few heartbeats."

Gwenna nodded. When she released the heavy door, it didn't fall. Instead, it floated up a few paces, wavered in the breeze, and held, like a narrow roof just above her head.

"Don't drop that 'Kent-kissing thing on me," she shouted as she started climbing.

A few more arrows and at least one stone showered down. The door lurched beneath the assault, but held. Gwenna glanced back. Talal was sweating, panting, eyes fixed on the slab of wood he held suspended above her.

"Go," he growled.

She'd just reached the top rung and set a hand on the top of the wall when the leach groaned and the whole door lifted away and fell, as though tossed aside by the wind. Gwenna found herself staring over the wall into the courtyard below.

Two of Rallen's guards had raced down the narrow walkway to meet her. She stabbed the first in the throat, twisting the blade free as he fell, then parried the attack from the second as she scanned the courtyard. There were at least twenty soldiers, half holding bows, all of which were aimed directly at her. Right in their midst, leaning heavily on his cane, stood Jakob Rallen himself. He was bleeding from a cut on his cheek, but his lips parted in a rictus of a grin.

"You're done, Sharpe," he snapped. "You're a useless fraud, and you're finished." He glanced at his men. "Shoot for the legs. I want her alive and twitching."

Gwenna ducked under the guard of the second soldier, slid an arm around his neck, put a knife to his throat, then hauled him around in front of her, a crude human shield.

"Not done yet," she called back.

Rallen spat into the dirt. "Shoot at will."

A few of his soldiers exchanged worried glances. Evidently it was one thing murdering innocents over on Hook. When it came to killing their own, however, when it came to cutting down someone they'd lived, feasted, and trained with for the past year, things got a little more tricky.

"Not great leadership," Gwenna shouted, "calling for the slaughter of your own men. But then, you're not really a leader, are you?"

"Leadership," Rallen hissed, "is the ability to make hard decisions. Not that I would expect you to know anything about that." He turned back to his soldiers. "The last one to loose an arrow dies."

So much, Gwenna thought as the bowstrings sang, *for keeping them talking.*

The bolts and arrows sunk into the soldier's flesh in a series of wet, sickening thuds. The man groaned, choked up his own blood, tried to pull free, but Gwenna held grimly to him, even after the body stopped twitching, waiting for the first volley of shots to fall still. Then, in the momentary pause that followed, she shrugged the corpse away and leapt from the narrow wall.

She hit the packed earth hard, and rolled to her feet expecting to take a broadhead to the face. There was too much open ground to cover before she could bring her blade to bear. Rallen's men held too many bows. *No winning this one,* she thought, fixing her eyes on the leach. The man smiled at her. *Please, Hull, just let me carve that smile off his face before they bring me down.*

Before she could reach him, however, before the leach could speak, before anyone could loose another arrow, a great shape exploded over the compound's far wall. It was a bird, but seemed bigger than a bird, the twin golden wings wide as the sky, blotting out the sun, throwing the whole courtyard into shadow. Below, hanging from the talons by a tangle of makeshift rope, hung half a dozen Kettral, Gwenna's Kettral, the men and women she had trained or tried to train—Qora and Delka, Fruin and Chelt—their eyes wide with anger and horror, knuckles white where they clung to the madness of straps, and where they hung on, also, to another figure, small as a boy, utterly untethered to the bird's talons, relying only on the hands of the others to hold her as she leaned so far out it seemed she had to fall—Annick, her bow a blur in her hands, her eyes still as stone as she drew and fired, drew and fired, drew and fired, her bowstring's twang lost in Allar'ra's ear-shattering scream.

34

Long Fist stood beyond the ring of *kenta,* at the very edge of the island, half a pace from where the cliffs dropped away into the surrounding sea. He was looking west over the waves, his back to Kaden, as though he could stare straight through the miles, around the curvature of the world, all the way to Annur—if, indeed, Annur lay in that direction—into the Dawn Palace itself and the events unfolding there. Gusts of hot wind tore at him, snarling his long blond hair, threatening to hurl him into the surf. He paid them no mind. Legs spread, arms crossed over his chest, he looked as much a part of the island as the ancient gates flanking him—rooted, immovable.

Kaden made no noise as he approached, but the shaman turned anyway, fixing him with that glaciated stare. The salt wind howled between them.

"You failed," Long Fist said after a long pause.

Outside the *vaniate,* the words might have carried some vague sting. Kaden had held on to the trance since passing through the gate, however, and inside the chapel of emptiness, Long Fist's accusation was a simple statement of fact.

"Yes," he replied.

The shaman studied him a moment longer, then turned away, back toward the sea.

"I will go myself."

"There is no point. Adare isn't hiding anything. She broke Triste out of the prison."

"So where is she?"

"Escaped," Kaden replied.

Long Fist shook his head. The bones on the leather thongs around his neck clacked quietly against his chest.

"Then we will do this the other way."

"What is the other way?" Kaden asked.

"I will kill the Csestriim before he finds her."

It was a reckless plan—if *plan* was even the right word. Il Tornja didn't care about the Urghul or Annur, didn't care about Kaden, or Adare, or the Unhewn Throne. All he wanted was the gods, to have them within the compass of his sword, and now Long Fist was talking about giving him precisely that. Maybe the shaman had enough power to get to the Csestriim general, to kill him . . . and maybe it was all part of the trap.

"You can't kill him," Kaden said.

The shaman turned to Kaden once again, lips drawn back in a snarl or a sneer. "You would dictate to me the limits of my own strength?"

"It's not a matter of strength, it is a matter of planning. Whatever you feel about the Csestriim, you know the scope of il Tornja's mind. You know how thorough he is. If killing him were a simple matter of walking into his camp, you would have killed him months ago and seen your Urghul trample all Annur."

Long Fist bared his teeth, but he did not reply.

"You know this for the truth," Kaden went on quietly. "If you go after il Tornja now, on his own ground, you will lose. He will destroy this body you have taken and sever your touch from this world."

"You claim to know the mind of a creature you have never met?"

"There are many ways to know another mind," Kaden replied.

And what about your mind, Triste? he thought. *What are you thinking? Where have you gone to hide?*

He closed his eyes, then slowly, almost delicately, shed the infinite skin of the *vaniate,* moving from unbounded emptiness into a model of the young woman's mind. For a time, the space of her thoughts remained inchoate, unknowable. Kaden set aside his impatience, resigned himself to the long effort of imagination, ignored Long Fist's massive, silent presence at his side, and then, slowly, slowly, like the spring's first warm, blind bud, Triste's mind began to grow inside his own.

For a long time, the *beshra'an* was just a matter of emotion, huge swaths of rage and pain binding and confining. Kaden knew little of Triste's childhood, but her most recent years had been built from suffering and betrayal. The world had brutalized or abandoned her. Her goddess had betrayed her, as had her father, and most cruelly, her mother. Triste couldn't even confront them: Ciena was buried too deep, and Ananshael's strong hands had delivered her parents beyond all human reach forever.

That's where I want to go. The thought was Triste's, blooming inside Kaden's mind. *Beyond all human reach. Somewhere I am no one, at the edge of the world . . .*

And then, strange as a leach's kenning, the words, *her* words, took form. The imagined became the real, the *remembered,* Triste's voice, speaking weeks earlier from the shadows of her cell, drugged past wariness, drugged into something like honesty: *I'd go somewhere. Somewhere as far from your 'Kent-kissing palace as possible. There's a place my mother used to talk about, a little village by an oasis in the shadow of the Ancaz Mountains, just at the edge of the Dead Salts. As far from the rest of the world as you can get, she used to say. I'd go there. That village. That's where I'd go.*

Kaden's eyes snapped open.

It wasn't much to go on. Less than a hunch, really—a few drugged phrases spoken in regret and rage. And yet, when he let himself settle back into the currents of the girl's emotion, it made *sense.* The wastes of western Mo'ir were about as far from Annur as she could get; and more, going there would be a way of reaching out, reaching back, trying to grasp some fragment of her mother, of something Morjeta had told her in a moment of intimacy before all the betrayal began.

Kaden turned to Long Fist.

"She's going to the Ancaz," he said, surprised at the certainty in his own voice. "To an oasis there, on the edge of the Dead Salts."

The shaman's gaze was a hammer.

"How do you know this?"

Kaden shook his head, unable to explain it all. "She told me."

"She told you where she was going, and you *forgot*?" The words were low, dangerous. "Or is this some mortal folly. Do you believe you can lie to me and survive?"

"This is no lie," Kaden replied. "Nor is it folly or forgetting. A human mind holds more than we can know. Her words were there, lying silently inside me, like a closed codex in some forgotten attic. I did not know what I had. It took time to find it. To open it."

Above them, gulls circled, gyring higher on the damp ocean air. The island might have stood at the center of the world, or it might have been severed from that world entirely. It was easy to believe, staring out over the sea, that those waves stretched on forever in all directions, that there was no Annur, no empire, no Urghul . . . only the slow swells of the ocean, the ragged island sward, and the tall, pale figure at Kaden's side, a man hollowed out to hold a god.

"Why would she go to the Ancaz?" Long Fist asked.

"Because she wants to go somewhere empty and beautiful, somewhere no one will ever find her." It seemed as sane a wish as any other. "We need to get there first."

"You would play all of your stones on this hunch?"

"It is not a hunch."

Long Fist turned to him, placed a finger beneath Kaden's chin, then lifted, hooking the sharp nail just behind the jaw, lifting slowly, smoothly, with awful strength, until Kaden's feet were dangling above the ground. The pain was a bright fire. The pressure threatened to choke him. Kaden's hands ached to reach up, to claw at the scarred arm that held him aloft, but he forced down the impulse, waiting for the Lord of Pain to say what he would say.

"If you are lying to me," Long Fist ground out at last, "or if you are wrong, I will open you like a fish. I will hold your lungs in my hands. I will work them like bellows as you scream."

"If I am lying," Kaden managed, each word an agony, "or wrong, then I am dead. We all are."

Those blue eyes held him a heartbeat longer, then Kaden was falling. He hit the stony ground, lurched seaward, managed to stop himself just inches from the cliff's brink. Long Fist watched him, as though wondering if he would fall. When he did not, the shaman nodded slowly.

"We will go to the Ancaz, then."

With an effort, Kaden shook his head. "Not yet."

The Urghul's eyes narrowed to slits.

"We are two men," Kaden said, shaking his head, "and the world is large. We need more."

"The Ishien," Long Fist said after a pause.

Kaden nodded. "They can pass the gates—some of them, at least."

"And if the Csestriim is hunting the girl with his soldiers, we may need soldiers of our own."

Kaden blinked. "If il Tornja has heard anything by now it will be that Triste is dead. Only Kiel knows the truth. Kiel and Adare."

The shaman's eyes bored into him. "Are you willing to bet so much on the *kenarang*'s ignorance? Were you not just lecturing me, moments ago, on his formidable mind?"

"All right," Kaden said. "That's another reason. It might be useful to have men who trained to kill the Csestriim. That's why you joined them in the first place, right?"

"One of the reasons." The shaman nodded curtly. "We will bring the Hunters."

Kaden took a deep breath. "And one more," he said quietly, steadily. "Rampuri Tan."

The shaman's face hardened. "The monk is an apostate. He killed his brothers."

"He was helping me escape."

"Indeed. And for this he has been imprisoned."

"Then get him out."

The Dead Heart stank of salt and spoiled fish, stale breath and stone, smoke and blood and urine. The stench didn't stop at the nose. It coated the skin and tongue, chafed the lungs, soaked into the pores, until it felt as though no scrubbing could ever scour it all away. Kaden remembered the smell, of course, from his long weeks locked inside the Ishien fortress, but memory, even for a Shin monk, was imperfect, a leaky vessel, a smudged mirror. The fact of the place, its presence—cold, ancient, and implacable—weighed down in a way no memory ever could.

And then there were the Ishien themselves. Their hate was palpable. Long Fist's orders kept them in check, but Long Fist had disappeared down some side corridor almost as soon as he and Kaden arrived, leaving Kaden in the hands of two men that he recognized, men who had been on the *kenta* island the day that Tan was taken, the day Triste had slaughtered Ekhard Matol, using his sudden lust as a blade to hack the man apart. Whatever Long Fist's orders, the Ishien had been honing their hate for a long time, and as they escorted Kaden down the corridor to the prison levels, one man before him, one behind, it was hard not to feel as though he had made a grave error in coming back. Hard not to feel that he was descending through the stone throat of the fortress, not to save Tan, but to become a prisoner himself.

When the Ishien finally stopped before a heavy wooden door,

Kaden wondered if the cell was to be his own. Fear scratched at the edges of his calm, and he was tempted to slide back into the *vaniate*. With an effort, he pushed back the temptation, Kiel's warning echoing in his memory.

"Be quick," snapped the taller of the two men. "Horm wants to be gone before night."

How the Ishien could divide day from darkness while buried inside the Dead Heart, Kaden had no idea. He nodded, though, and after a pause, the two men retreated, leaving him to find his own way back to the levels above.

Despite their admonition, Kaden remained still for a long time. The lantern hissed angrily in his hand, the impure oil burning grudgingly, fitfully. Kaden set it on the stone, but made no effort to lift the steel bars blocking the door. The whole thing all seemed suddenly too simple. If he could free his old *umial* simply by asking, why had he not asked before? Why had he left the monk who covered his escape to languish in the chilly dark, or worse, to writhe beneath the knives of the broken men he had once called brothers?

It was strange, in a way, to dwell on this regret. The world was filled with people Kaden had failed—thousands of them, tens of thousands, who had starved or suffered or died because of decisions he had made. Unlike those tens of thousands, though, Rampuri Tan was not some abstract figure inked on a page by an overtired scribe. Whatever Kaden had become, the fact that he'd survived at all, survived Ashk'lan's burning, and the Dead Heart, and everything that followed—he owed it to Rampuri Tan. It was an unpaid debt.

And yet, if Tan had taught him anything, it was that such sentiment was meaningless.

The fact that Kaden could set aside his own guilt, sequester it in a dim, unfrequented corner of his mind—that, too, was a legacy of the monk's brutal tutelage, and when Kaden finally lifted aside the bars and hauled open the door, he felt nothing— no guilt, no fear, nothing—having let the feeling go after all, sliding into the *vaniate* despite Kiel's warning, armoring himself in emptiness as he stepped into the darkness to face the man who had trained him.

At first, Kaden thought he had the wrong cell. The figure seated cross-legged at the chamber's center looked tall enough to be Rampuri Tan, but was far too thin, almost emaciated, dark skin pulled tight around muscle and bone. He was naked, completely naked, and Kaden could see the scars carved into that skin, puckering the flesh of the chest and arms—Meshkent's ancient script etched in the body's imperfect palimpsest. Rampuri Tan, in keeping with Shin tradition, had always kept his hair shaved to the scalp. This creature's hair, however, a greasy, tangled mess of gray and black, hung almost to his shoulders, obscuring his bearded face. The boulder of a man that Kaden remembered was gone, replaced by this withered thing. The voice, though, when the prisoner finally spoke, was Tan's voice, rough and rock-hard.

"You were a fool to come back."

Kaden considered the words from inside the *vaniate*.

"The world has changed," he replied finally.

Tan shook his head. "You are tricked by the shifting of surfaces. The river is the same, regardless of the waves."

"Meaning what?"

"This place is dangerous."

"Everywhere is dangerous," Kaden replied quietly. "Annur is dangerous. The Dawn Palace is dangerous. I came because I had to come."

For the first time, Tan looked up. Lamplight glittered in his dark eyes. Slowly, he unfolded his limbs and stood.

"Why?"

It took less time than Kaden had expected to explain it all. It seemed as though it should have taken longer to anatomize the dissolution of an empire, to recount the return of the gods, to set in the scales the whole human race, to watch all humanity teeter over the abyss. Inside the *vaniate,* however, it was all a matter of timelines and facts, observation and inference, the possible annihilation of millions nothing but a desiccated conjecture. Kaden set his account between them like a species of strange beetle, killed and pinned to the board.

Tan evinced no shock at the revelation. No alarm. He listened silently, still as the stone walls of his cell as the lantern's light played over him. When Kaden finished, he didn't move, stood staring into the darkness for a dozen heartbeats before speaking.

"And you believe this."

Kaden nodded. "I do."

"And if you are wrong?"

"About what?"

"About all of it. What if these gods are not gods at all?"

Kaden studied the empty space between them. "I have heard Ciena speak. And Meshkent . . ."

"You heard words. You assumed divinity."

"They pass the gates. They wield massive power."

"The Csestriim pass gates," Tan countered. "The Csestriim, too, have their leaches."

"Long Fist is at *war* with Ran il Tornja—"

"He appears to be at war," the monk cut in.

Kaden blinked. "Thousands have died on the northern front," he managed after a moment. "More. This war is more than a mirage."

"The deaths of men mean nothing to the Csestriim."

"But *why*?" Kaden asked. "Why would they feign this?"

Tan met his eyes. "To destroy us."

Kaden shook his head. "That doesn't make sense. Kiel is helping me to *stop* il Tornja. Long Fist didn't even know about Triste or Ciena until I told him. . . ."

"Stop listening to their words. Stop watching their faces. Look at the world as it is, at what they have caused to happen."

"I have been looking at it. While you've been locked in the darkness, I have been looking at it every day."

"Then the light has blinded you."

Kaden stared at the figure of his former mentor. Tan had not shifted at all from the cell's center. The heavy door hung open at Kaden's back, but the monk had not looked toward it even once. If anything, he seemed indifferent to his sudden freedom.

"Blinded me to what?" Kaden asked. Even inside the *vaniate,* he almost felt like an acolyte once again, scrambling to answer his *umial*'s questions, trying to follow the thread of the logic and falling short.

"They are all Csestriim," Tan replied. "Il Tornja and Long Fist, Kiel and Triste. They are Csestriim, they are allies, and they are winning."

Kaden shook his head. "No."

"Il Tornja and Long Fist appear to be foes, but who are they destroying?" Tan let the question hang between them. "They are destroying you," he said finally. "Us. Humanity. Listen to what you have told me: Long Fist seized control of the Ishien decades ago. He took the name of Bloody Horm, rose through the ranks until he ruled the Dead Heart and the men inside it. But has he used this power to attack il Tornja? He has not.

"Il Tornja took control of your throne, and to do what? To fight a perfectly balanced battle against Long Fist, a battle in which men and women die in droves while the two of them survive, often miles from the field of war itself. Triste and Kiel convince you to gut Annur from the inside, killing untold citizens, and then, when Triste is imprisoned, Ran il Tornja finds a way to break her free. They dance around each other, growling and feinting, but it is the humans who suffer, humans who die."

The monk fell silent, but the emptiness trembled, around Kaden and inside him like a great, invisible bell tolling in his bones. It seemed impossible. The entire fabric of the past year was stitched from the conflict between Long Fist and il Tornja, between a god made flesh and the Csestriim trying to destroy him. But then, where had Kaden first heard that notion? From Kiel, another Csestriim, one who, for all his protestations of loyalty to Annur, all his alleged fascination with humanity, had been languishing in an Ishien dungeon when Kaden found him.

Or had he?

If Long Fist ruled the Dead Heart as Bloody Horm, Long Fist could have planted Kiel. The two of them could have colluded to ensure that Kaden returned to Annur with a Csestriim advisor at his side, an advisor who would convince him to destroy the very foundation of his own empire, an empire that had played a crucial role in holding the ancient gates against the return of the Csestriim. . . .

"It's not possible," Kaden murmured. Even as he spoke the words, however, they sounded wrong.

The memory of Kiel at the stones board filled his mind. The Csestriim had spent countless hours at those solitary games, warring against himself, laying one stone after another on the polished surface, each landing with a quiet click—black, white, black, white. Kaden knew the game, of course—everyone did—but Kiel's play was baffling, almost nonsensical. Instead of the classical forms and attacks, the historian pursued moves so arcane as to seem suicidal: solitary stones placed deep inside enemy terrain, broken formations with obvious flaws, scattershot attacks that seemed built to fail. Never until the endgame could Kaden see the true shape, the structure beneath the chaos toward which both sets of sides had been aiming all along.

"They have played you, Kaden," Rampuri Tan said quietly. "They have played us all."

For a long time the words sat there, cold as the surrounding stone. Kaden studied Kiel's face, clear and motionless in the amber of memory, then Triste's, then Long Fist's. Was it possible the shaman's rage was all an elaborate act, one for which he'd trained a thousand years? Was Triste's grief all feigned, her fear and agony a calibrated farce? Inside the *vaniate* it seemed possible, probable, and after a long pause he let the trance go.

He felt naked outside the emptiness. Cold. A shiver ran over his skin, and deeper, somewhere between the muscle and the bone, emotion moved, fear and confusion burning like poison. It was tempting to slip back into the *vaniate,* but Kaden thrust the temptation aside, searching the memory of his flesh for what he had felt when he confronted Triste, when she touched him, when she sobbed or screamed.

Regret, he realized. He felt regret, and something else, something more, a warm bewilderment to which he could not put a name.

"No," he said slowly.

Tan just watched him, dark eyes reflecting back the lantern light from behind the mess of hair.

"You're wrong," Kaden said again, remembering Triste's desperate sobbing that first night in his tent, the fear in her violet eyes, her fury when Pyrre killed Phirum Prumm in the mountains above the monastery. "There are things you cannot fake."

"It is dangerous," Tan replied finally, "to believe you understand the Csestriim. Their minds. Their abilities. I studied the creatures half my life, and I do not understand them. Our minds cannot encompass them."

"Then how can you think you know Triste? Or Long Fist? Especially when you've been locked inside this prison?"

Tan shook his head. "I make no claim to know them. I am reading the facts of the world, facts you have conveyed to me."

"The bare facts about what's happening in the world outside don't capture the whole truth." Kaden thought of Triste's arms wrapped tight around him that first night back in Ashk'lan, of the tears streaking her cheeks in Assare, of those awful moments of hope when, from inside her cell, she seemed to actually see him. "There are other ways to know a thing," he concluded quietly.

"No," Tan said. "There are not. These 'other ways of knowing' are the blindfolds of your hopes and fears. Remove the blindfolds. The world is the only truth."

"Not always," Kaden replied, shaking his head. "Not all of it. The world I've returned to is packed with lies."

"The lies, too, are the truth."

A grain of irritation scratched at the edge of Kaden's calm.

"I have begun to question the value of the old Shin paradox."

"It is not a paradox. The blacksmith makes blades: a truth. The liar hammers out lies: a truth. All that is real is the thing made." Tan crossed slowly to the stone wall, then laid a hand against it. "I know nothing of the creature who built this cell— male or female, old or young—but I know it is a cell."

"Triste hasn't put me in a cell. Kiel broke me *out* of one."

"The world is larger than one blindfolded prince."

"And you think, based on what you just learned, that they've turned the whole world into a cell."

Tan shook his head grimly. "Not a cell. A slaughterhouse." He watched Kaden with those dark eyes before continuing. "You cannot see inside their minds, not even with the *beshra'an*. You can only see what they have done. What they have made. This is what the monks of Ashk'lan tried to teach you, but you are a novice no longer. Now there is a price for your blindness."

Kaden stared past Tan, into the cell's far corners. It was easy, too easy, to remember Triste crouching in a cell exactly like this, her face cut and scabbed, her fingernails ragged and bloody from trying to claw her way free. An act? It seemed impossible.

More impossible than the Goddess of Pleasure come again? a voice whispered in his ear.

Finally Kaden shook his head. "The only way to know is to find Triste."

Tan's silence was stone.

"I need your help," Kaden pressed.

"To save the creatures? Or to kill them?"

"We can't do either until we find them. Come with me, help me track down Triste, and we will find il Tornja, too. When you've seen her, seen Long Fist, you can tell me if you still think they're Csestriim."

Tan made no move toward the open door. Water dripped from the stone, marking its own inscrutable hours.

"And if this is, in fact, what I tell you?"

Kaden considered his old *umial,* trying to read something in that unreadable face. "Then it will be good," he replied finally, quietly, "that I am with a man long trained in the killing of Csestriïm."

35

Whatever reason the Csestriim had for building a *kenta* on the cracked, arid plain of the Dead Salts, that reason had been whittled to dust by the wind, or swallowed by the land. The sun, nailed high overhead in a cloudless sky, baked the soil until it was hard as stone. The few plants were stunted, spiky, nearly as brown as the earth itself, and widely spaced, as though anything growing too close would choke. There were signs of rain, Kaden realized with surprise—sharp drainages and spattered dirt crusted up around the base of the bleached-white rocks—but even those marks were sharp and harsh, carved, scored, scarred into the dirt by vanished water sharp as any knife.

The *kenta* itself stood at the bottom of a man-made trench. The gouging of shovel and pickax were clear in the baked clay flanking the gate, although the material of the *kenta* itself remained unscratched.

"The Ishien keep it clear?" Kaden asked.

Long Fist nodded, but ignored the gate. The shaman had climbed immediately clear of the hole. His eyes were fixed on the horizon to the northwest. The land stretched away, flat as an iron pan in all directions, but there, just at the limit of vision, the jagged tips of the Ancaz broke the horizon, bloodred against the cruel blue of the sky. Somewhere in that direction, in the evening shadow of the stony cliffs, there was an oasis, a palm-fringed patch of green amid all the brown, home to a few dozen herders and hunters. Triste's destination, if Kaden had read the situation right. For the hundredth time he called to mind the *saama'an* of their final conversation.

I'd go somewhere, she'd said, clutching the bars of her cage, *as far from your 'Kent-kissing palace as possible. There's a place my mother used to talk about, a little village by an oasis in the shadow of the Ancaz Mountains, just at the edge of the Dead Salts. As far from the rest of the world as you can get, she used to say. I'd go there. That village. That's where I'd go. . . .*

There was no doubt about the words. He could hear them so clearly Triste might have been standing at his ear. He could see her face twist as she spoke. The question was one of interpretation. Did she truly want to find the oasis, to hide away there, or was it just an empty wish, a vaguely articulated longing for *any* desolate spot away from the prying of human eyes? If that was the case, the hunt was hopeless. She could be anywhere, walking the wide ways of the earth with the goddess lodged inside her, utterly unfindable, one highwayman's knife from the destruction of all humanity.

"Why here?" the shaman asked, studying the sun-blasted land, a hand shading his eyes. His strange, pale skin would blister beneath that sun, but he paid it no mind, focusing instead on the distant mountains.

Kaden shook his head. "Not here."

"The mountains," Long Fist replied. "I understand. But why? What ties her to this place?"

"It's empty," Kaden replied. The answer was more complicated, but he wasn't sure he had the words to fit the truth.

Long Fist shook his head. "The world is filled with empty places. In your greatest cities there are holes, openings, places no one goes."

"Her mother was here once. I think she wants to see what her mother saw."

The shaman frowned. "And this girl, does she always speak the truth? Is she incapable of deception?"

Kaden wished he had the answer to that question, and not just regarding Triste. Tan's suspicions still rasped in his ears: *They have played you, Kaden. They have played us all.* Of course, he had managed to convince the older monk to suspend judgment, to play his part in the hunt until they could learn more. Tan himself was somewhere to the east now, leading all the Ishien who could pass the gates through a different *kenta,* one east of Mo'ir. Their hope was to pick up some sign of Triste's passage, to follow her, or, barring that, to somehow intercept il Tornja.

Provided Triste was coming this way at all. Provided the *kenarang* had left his post in the north to hunt her. It was all guesswork, a mixture of *beshra'an* and desperation, but it was the best plan they'd been able to devise, and any plan was better than sitting in Annur or the Dead Heart, waiting for Ran il Tornja to finally spring shut his trap.

"Triste had no reason to lie," Kaden said after a pause. "She couldn't have known she would be free in a matter of weeks."

The shaman spat onto the parched ground. "But once she *was* free, she would remember this conversation. She would go anywhere but here."

"No," Kaden said, studying his memory of the woman. "She was drugged. Half delirious. It was a trivial remark, almost inconsequential. Not the kind of thing she would remember."

"It is a thin thread to follow," the shaman said. "If it snaps, we will be far from what matters with no fast way to return."

Kaden nodded, then turned to consider the *kenta* once more. They had crossed from the Dead Heart to that nameless island lost in the ocean to here, two or three days' hard march east of the Ancaz, all in a few dozen paces. It was enough to make the mind quail. Kings would kill for the power. Emperors had. And it was not enough. This was the closest gate, and it put them at least a hundred miles from the oasis, provided they could find it at all.

"Is there no way," Kaden asked, studying the arch, "for you to create another?"

Long Fist turned to him. "You do not understand what it is that you ask."

"No. I don't. But the Csestriim made them, and you are more than the Csestriim."

"The Csestriim did not make these any more than they made the emptiness between the stars."

Kaden shook his head. "Meaning . . . what? The *kenta* were always here?"

"The *kenta* are not like stones or steel," Long Fist replied. "They are not things. Not a part of this world."

The arch glinted, that silvery substance strangely dull in the blazing overhead light. Through it, beyond it, Kaden could see only the same cracked clay, half rock, half dirt.

"I don't know what that means," Kaden said.

"Your world," the Urghul replied, "is like a wall. The Csestriim punched holes in it, but those holes are not the wall, and the Csestriim did not build what lies beyond."

"And you cannot punch another hole?"

"It destroyed them," Long Fist said, voice hard and flat as the surrounding waste. "All of them and utterly. I will not meddle more than necessary in the domain of the Nameless."

There was a new note in the shaman's voice, something Kaden could not parse, and after a moment, as though by some silent accord, they both turned away from the *kenta* toward the diminutive western peaks, toward the hope that somewhere there they would find a girl who was also a goddess, that she would be alive when they found her.

The urgency dug at them both like a sharp burr against tender skin, but they could only move so fast. Long Fist set a brutal

pace, and Kaden was amazed by the betrayal of his own body.
A year earlier he had run through the Bone Mountains, run for
days in his desperate attempt to escape the Aedolians. A year
of sitting, however, of spending each day debating in the council
chamber rather than running the Circuit of Ravens, had left him
with soft legs and lungs that labored in his chest. The shaman
was impatient. They walked all day, then all night, making the
most of the low, fat moon and the delicious cool, and then again
all the next day, stopping only to eat the dried fruit and meat
Kaden carried in a small pack over both shoulders. By the end
of that second day, however, even the god was forced to submit
to the weakness of his chosen flesh, and as the sun bled out into
the west, they made a rough camp on the featureless plain.

The night was surprisingly cool, but there was nothing to
burn, and so Kaden drank long and deep from his waterskin,
settled the pack beneath his head, and leaned back. He'd spent
harder nights in the Bone Mountains a hundred times over, and
expected to fall asleep at once. Instead, his body, still for the
first time since stepping out of the *kenta,* cooled, stiffened, then
began to ache. The bands along the outsides of his legs were so
tight that they felt like stone when he tried to knead the flesh
with his fingers. He worked at the muscle for a while, then gave
up, lying back, letting the pain wash over him, warm in the cold
night.

Long Fist did not lie down. He sat cross-legged, staring
northwest, hands folded in his lap. The posture was a familiar
one. Kaden had spent half his life like that: sitting, chanting,
painting, breathing his measured breaths. The Urghul chief was
not chanting, however, not painting, and there was something
in his posture, something Kaden couldn't quite articulate, that
seemed predatory rather than restful. His open eyes were bright,
sharp in the starlight.

Kaden watched the other man, unease coiling and uncoiling
like a restless snake twisting about his innards. Since the Waist,
the calm he had mastered among the monks had proven elusive.

Each time he reached for the *vaniate,* it was slippery in his fingers, almost ungraspable. Even inside the trance, he could feel his own fear and hope like vibrations pitched too low to hear. On the back of his tongue, like something overripe, almost rotten, he could taste his own desperation.

For the most part, the shaman had ignored him, striding over the broken ground with his eyes fixed on the horizon. Whenever Long Fist turned that gaze on Kaden, however, something quailed inside him. The *vaniate* offered an escape, but Kaden had not forgotten the ease with which the other man had shattered the trance, had little doubt that Long Fist could do it again if he chose, do it at will. Walking with the chieftain was like walking alone through the parched land beside a crag cat; Kaden's body wanted to run, but there was no point. Nor was there any point to fighting. The best you could do was to keep quiet and hope to remain unnoticed, and so Kaden had remained quiet, had kept his eyes on the fissured ground, and turned his attention from the dozens of questions swarming like summer flies to the mindlessness of his own movement.

Now, however, there was no progress to distract either him or the shaman. Night leached color and contour from the land, reducing the brown of the flats and the red of the approaching mountains to planes of gray and black. The stars were bright with their silent violence, but irrelevant, meaningless, and after watching them for a long time, Kaden looked away. Long Fist was just a shape, a sharp-edged shadow chiseled from the surrounding dark. Kaden could not see his face. That absence made it easier to speak.

"Who was he?"

For a moment Long Fist did not respond. Then he slid a finger down the center of his chest, as though slicing open the flesh and the bone beneath.

"The creature who inhabited this body before me?"

Kaden nodded.

"It does not matter."

"You could have chosen anyone?"

"Of course not," the god replied. "Human minds are cramped, filthy. I could no more slide into them than you could inhabit a barrel filled with rocks." His voice hardened. "Ciena was a fool to try to force herself inside the head of one so unprepared, so fat and swollen with her own self."

Wind winnowed the stony ground as though it were grain, as though there were something there worth saving, something that could be saved.

"Unprepared?" Kaden asked.

This time Long Fist raised the finger to a point between his eyes. "It is possible for your kind to carve away a portion of what you are. Possible, but rare. It is into this emptiness that I stepped."

Kaden blinked. "The *vaniate*."

"A perversion," Long Fist growled. "A mockery. The space I'm describing doesn't come from your desiccated mantras and endless sitting."

"Then what?"

"Devotion. Worship. Prayer and sacrifice. The most devout give away something of themselves. This creature, through the fervor of his faith in me, made of himself a vessel."

Kaden studied the still form of the chieftain, then turned away to stare at the star-stabbed northern sky. The language was close to the language of the Shin—emptiness, space—but there was Long Fist's talk of passion to consider, too.

"Triste," Kaden said finally. "She was raised in Ciena's temple. She was trained to serve. . . ."

"Not every woman who moves through the stations of prayer is a priestess," Long Fist said. "If she had been devoted to her goddess, truly devoted, Ciena would not be trapped inside the polluted prison of her too-human mind."

A falling star sliced a white scar across the night.

"How will it happen?" Kaden asked. "If il Tornja catches Triste, if he kills her, what will it feel like?"

The shaman didn't respond, didn't move. Kaden wondered for a moment if he'd actually spoken aloud, or only thought the question. When Long Fist finally spoke, he didn't turn his head, as though his words were directed to the night and the horizon.

"The death of the goddess would fill past the brim the cup of your suffering."

Kaden frowned. "Isn't that what you want? You took this form to wage your wars against Annur, to spread your suffering across Vash and Eridroa both."

"I took this form to reestablish a world that had lapsed."

"A world of brutality and violence. A plague of suffering and slaughter."

Long Fist shook his head slowly. "It is your empire that is the plague. It twists what you are. In the dry flesh of the Csestriim, we built something beautiful, Ciena and I. We made them into something better, freed from inside them the twin screams of bliss and misery. We offered them this gift."

"Gift?" Kaden asked. "What gift?"

"A gift of the world. Like a man touching a woman through thick leather gloves, the Csestriim felt nothing. We removed the gloves. We made you feel the world as you moved through it and it moved through you. For thousands of years after the death of the Csestriim, humans were naked in the forests. You were beautiful and bloody as you moved over the plains. Then Annur took that away, forced you to be mute and ugly. Reduced you to slaves."

"Is it slavery to outlaw the slaughter of children on some bloody altar? To put a stop to the rape of the innocent?"

Long Fist laughed, a sound like distant thunder on the horizon. "The alleys of your cities reek with the corpses of children. Your fields crawl with the violated; they hunch over the memories of their rapes as though those memories were green, growing things. They suffer, but there is no glory in the suffering. You have taken a sacred thing and profaned it, made it a matter of offices and laws."

"Annur's offices and laws are there to protect people."

"Your offices and laws are blindfolds. They are methods of looking away, of not seeing. You have endless blood—more than the Urghul and the people of the Waist combined—but there is no reverence in it. An emperor waves a finger and a whole people is put to the sword. A merchant moves a pile of coin and a thousand men become slaves. The rich man in his tall house does not know their names. He does not see their faces as the manacles slam shut. He does not feel the warm blood on his hands. He does not hear the screaming, does nothing to tune it. There is no music in his violence."

Kaden felt that he had come unmoored in the wide ocean of the night. Long Fist's talk of music and violence, exaltation and profanation, was baffling but hypnotic, the language a landscape all its own, dark as the salt flats surrounding them, a place where a man could become lost. Annur wasn't perfect—Kaden understood that clearly enough—but surely it was better than a hundred rival warlords rending the land and the people who lived there. Surely the sufferings of the countless Annurian slaves weighed less, when you put them in the scales, than the broken infants torn from their mothers' breasts and killed; than the defeated armies castrated, mutilated, mocked, and massacred; than the annihilation of whole nations because they spoke the wrong language, wore the wrong clothes, worshipped at the wrong altar. Surely, set in the scales, Annur was an improvement over what had come before, over the world to which Long Fist struggled to return them all.

But then, what did Kaden know of Annur? What did he know of the world? He had passed his early childhood cloistered inside the opulence of the Dawn Palace, and the rest of his life in a monastery so remote that goats and ravens outnumbered men. Of Dombâng and Sia, Mo'ir or Ludgven, of the city of Annur itself, he knew nothing. The fishing villages and logging towns, the mining camps perched on the slopes of the Romsdals and the terraced rice patties of Sia—he might be able to gesture to them on a map, but nothing more. What did he know of the lives lived in such places? What could he say of Annurian justice, Annurian peace, Annurian prosperity that was not simply an echo of the self-congratulatory words he had overheard from ministers and scribes a thousand times over as a child?

He put his palms on the hard dirt beside him, as though the solidity of the ground might give foundation to his tottering thoughts. He tried to focus on the silhouettes of the mountains, but it was impossible to be sure, in the gathering darkness, what was the land, and what was thick cloud, piled up on the horizon. Sailors navigated by the stars, but the stars were different here than they had been in Ashk'lan, the familiar constellations perched strangely in the sky, and besides, the stars moved.

"If you believe all this," he said finally, "if you think we are not present enough in our own suffering, that we don't take adequate delight in the misery of others, why do you care what happens to Triste? To Ciena?"

It was the question that had started the conversation, and he asked it again, as though by returning to that first place, by beginning again, he might find once more the path that he had lost.

For the first time the shaman turned to stare at him. "Ciena is what makes you what you are, she and I together. You would be shattered without her, a million lutes dashed on the rocks. Whole octaves lost. What agony could I sustain without hope? What hatred without the promise of love? What pain is there when there is only pain?"

Kaden tried to make sense of the words. "Hope and love," he began hesitantly. "They are the work of Orella, Eira. The young gods—"

"They are nothing without us."

"Your children—" Kaden began, and again Long Fist cut him off.

"Your words are boxes built too small to hold the truth."

"Which is what?"

"We are not this flesh," the shaman replied, touching the shadow that was his chest with a dark finger. "We are not beasts squeezed out screaming from between the legs of other beasts. A woman might rut with a dozen men, birth a dozen children, and then die. The flesh born of her flesh is not her flesh. Her children will survive her death. It is not so with us."

Kaden realized he was holding his breath, and slowly, silently, he let it out. When he inhaled once more, the night air was cold in his throat, in his lungs. He could imagine the darkness of that almost-desert inside him like an inhuman child, heavy as flesh but not flesh, chill as the night itself, still as something already dead.

"If the young gods are not your children," he asked, voice little louder than a whisper, "then what are they?"

"They are something we dream," Long Fist replied.

Kaden shook his head. "They can't be. They're real. They took human form in the war with the Csestriim, just as you have now."

"Dreams are real."

"But you're saying the young gods are just a part of you? That they do what you say?"

"Do the creatures of your own dreams follow your desires? Do the creatures of your nightmares bend to your will? They obey their own nature, these children of ours, but they are our dreams all the same."

"And without you," Kaden said slowly, the words raising the fine hairs from his skin, "without you, they die."

"Death," Long Fist spat. For the first time that night, he sounded angry, disdainful. "That hoarder of bones has no lordship over gods."

"But the young gods are in peril, too," Kaden insisted. "By threatening you and Ciena, il Tornja threatens them."

The shaman inclined his head slightly. "Without the dreamer, there is no dream, at least not one strong enough to touch your world, to color your minds."

"That's what he wants," Kaden said. "Il Tornja. If he destroys you, we would be Csestriim once more. Kiel was right."

"You would be Csestriim or mad."

"And what if you survive," Kaden asked, "but Triste does not? What happens to us then?"

"You are puppets, all of you. We hold your strings. You move through this world because there is a balance—Eira and Maat, Kaveraa and Heqet."

"And if il Tornja breaks that balance?"

"Imagine a puppet," the shaman said, "tangled, twitching, struggling to move, strangling slowly in its own severed strings."

When Kaden finally fell asleep, he dreamed of strings strong as ropes of steel twisted around his throat. He woke to a sandstorm blowing up out of the south. At first, he thought he might be imagining it. The sky above was still scraped perfectly clean, the sun a pitiless blazing eye in the midst of that unblinking blue. Any change in the weather seemed impossible, but there it was, a brown wall looming up out of the south, moving so fast they barely had time to assemble the tent.

When they were finished, Long Fist stood, baring his teeth as he stared down the storm. The wind tore at his hair and hides. "The people of the Dead Salts call this Hull's Scourge. The worst of these storms have destroyed whole caravans."

Kaden could taste the dirt, rough and rusty on his tongue. "We have the tent. You told me it was built for this."

Long Fist turned those blue eyes on him. His gaze was fervid, almost rabid. "I am not worried about us. The tent will hold, though the storm may pin us down for a week or more. If the girl is moving west as you claim, however, if she is caught unprepared in this, the Csestriim will not need to find her. The wind and sand will flay her to the bone."

36

Close to its headwaters, the Haag ran fast, and white, and cold, pouring down from the high, glaciated valleys above. This, too, Valyn remembered from his training years before, and from the maps he had studied back at the Eyrie. Over uncountable eons, the river had carved a deep course between the banks to the east and the west. It wasn't as wide as the Black River at Andt-Kyl, or the White just above the confluence, but it was wide enough to form a boundary. More importantly, it was violent.

He could hear the river when they were still half a day's ride off, below the noise of the horses moving through the thick forests of pine and tamarack: a churning, grumbling current. At first it was no more than an itch in the ear, some vibration buried so deep in his bones he might have imagined it. As they drew closer, however, the growl grew to a roar that all but obliterated the softer sounds of the forest: it was as though all the squirrels scuttling along branches, all the woodpeckers and snuffling porcupines had fallen silent together, as though they'd all died.

The sound brought back his memory of the sight: the river's current smashing down against house-sized boulders in the rocky bed, tossing spray fifty feet into the air. He could smell it now, the schist and iron on the damp morning air. Aergad stood on the western bluff, almost a mountain itself, dark stone slammed up against the skyline. It had been a fortress before it was a city, a single castle guarding the northeastern marches of Nish. Over time, as war faded, a city had grown up around it, an entrepôt for traders coming through the Romsdal passes or linking up the northern atrepies. It hadn't seen a battle in two hundred years, and yet the city, when Valyn had last seen it, still looked built to take a siege—all windowless walls and arrow loops glaring down on the river below.

A single bridge spanned the river. All those years ago, Valyn's instructors had spent a whole morning lecturing the cadets about that bridge, pointing out the methods of construction, the weak points, the economic value to the city itself. . . . Valyn had forgotten most of it, but one point remained, the most basic: that bridge was the only place to cross the Haag above Lowan. Whoever held that bridge held the whole southwestern corner of Vash.

Judging from the furious sounds of battle echoing off the river's banks below, Valyn wasn't the only one who had learned that lesson. The Haag was still almost a mile from where he stood, hidden in the shadows at the forest's edge, among the last fringes of firs, but even at that distance he could make out the vicious clash of steel against steel, the thunderous drumming of hooves churning the dirt to mud, the brutal chorus of thousands of voices shouting, bellowing, screaming out their rage, and bafflement, and pain. He had lived so long in the quiet of the northern forests that he had almost forgotten the deafening noise of war's thousand-throated roar.

Valyn let it pour over him, tried to find some structure, some order in the serrated wave of sound. Sometimes a word or phrase would rise out of the swell, like a stone tossed up on the beach by the sea's storm—an order, a plea, a dying scream. Everyone was down by the river, but it seemed the Urghul were concentrated at the northern and eastern ends of the battle, sounded as though they were trying to force their way west.

"The bridge," Valyn murmured quietly. "The horsemen are trying to take the bridge."

The Flea just grunted, started rummaging in his pack. A

moment later, Valyn heard the metallic click of the long lens snapping open.

"Give two men the wide world," Newt observed, "and they will still kill each other over a single scrap of land." The words were bleak, but if he was concerned about the violence unfolding below, Valyn couldn't hear it in his voice, couldn't smell it on him. The Aphorist reeked, as he always did, of smoke and nitre, wet wool and rancid sweat.

"What I'm concerned about," the Flea said after a moment, "is that the Annurians don't seem to be doing their share of the killing."

Valyn shut his eyes, let himself sink more deeply into the sound. If the panicked shouts of the Annurians were anything to go by, the Army of the North was losing. Valyn could hear the legionary drums beating out conflicting orders to conflicting companies—*Stand firm. Retreat. Dig In.*—the skins trembling out the bass to some greater music whose treble registers were the screeching of steel against steel, the screams of the frightened and the dying. He could imagine them pressed back against the river's bank, forced onto that single, crucial bridge.

"A week ago, the fight was further east," the Flea observed grimly. "Higher up in the foothills. Something has changed."

The northwestern corner of Raalte was a strange place to be fighting in the first place. Long Fist's initial strike at the empire had been far more direct, aiming to cross the Black close to the steppe, and from there to drive straight into the heart of Raalte. After the defeat at Andt-Kyl, however, after Long Fist's disappearance, Balendin had taken charge, and he'd pulled the Urghul back, all the way into the icebound empty land north of the Black. They'd been able to make good time up there, pushing west past the source of the streams that fed the wetlands below, until they reached the apron of the Romsdals. The shattered scree didn't favor the Urghul horses much more than the dense forests of the Thousand Lakes, and il Tornja met them there with the Army of the North. According to both Huutsuu and the Flea, the two forces had locked horns and barely moved in the long months since. The winter had taken its toll on both armies, but the Annurians had supply lines running back through Aergad; the Urghul were left hunting deer, elk, and beaver through the chest-high snows.

"I thought the Urghul were too weak for a major push," Valyn said. "Too hungry."

"They are," Huutsuu replied.

"Not that weak, if they managed to force the Army of the North back to the Haag."

"It is a matter of only miles."

"Important miles," the Flea said. "Before, it was just rocks and gravel. Now they're fighting for something that matters. It's the first time since Andt-Kyl. Il Tornja has made a mistake."

They fell silent at that. As he listened to the thunder of hooves, the high cries of the nomads, the grudging, barked commands of the legionary soldiers, Valyn tried to imagine Ran il Tornja, *kenarang* and Csestriim, making a mistake. After watching the battle of Andt-Kyl, he thought it seemed unlikely.

"My people will not take the bridge," Huutsuu said. "The Annurians have fortified it fully."

"They don't need to take the bridge," the Flea replied. "They're not trying to cross. At least, I wouldn't be. If they can bottle up the Annurians over in Aergad, on the western bank, it's a straight shot south along the east bank of the Haag, a straight shot all the way to Annur."

"The Thousand Lakes back up to the river," Valyn said, trying to remember the details of his geography.

"Not quite," the Flea replied. "There's a strip of high ground separating the drainages. We're at the edge of it now. It's not more than a few miles wide in most places, but wide enough for the Urghul to ride and to ride hard. They could be in Annur in days."

"And the legions aren't blocking that southern passage?" Valyn asked. "How are they deployed?"

He could hear the battle well enough, but it was maddening

not to be able to see, not to be able to make more sense of the riot of sound.

"Shittily," the Flea said. "If they form up to stop the Urghul from going south, they won't have enough men to guard the bridge, or Aergad for that matter. If they protect the bridge and the city, they leave the path to Annur wide open."

"Better to sacrifice one city than the whole empire," Valyn said.

"They don't appear to agree. Whoever's in charge has a screen of men across the southern route, not nearly enough. The rest are on the bridge or west of it, where the Urghul can't get at them. It's a strong defensive position, but they're defending the wrong thing."

"Where is this war chief of yours?" Huutsuu asked. "Ran il Tornja?"

She smelled wary, suspicious. Even while surveying the battle below, she was careful to keep a few paces between herself and the Kettral, as though she half expected them to come after her at any moment.

"The *kenarang* seems to have disappeared," the Flea said after a long time.

"Disappeared?" Valyn asked. The word felt like Adare's knife buried in his guts all over again, a cold, serrated betrayal.

They'd come for Balendin—that had been the plan from the start—but now that Valyn stood on the edge of the battle, just a mile from the Army of the North, he realized that during every step of the long ride, even when he thought he wasn't thinking, even asleep, a part of his mind had been revolving one image over and over, the last thing he'd seen with his unbroken eyes: il Tornja's blade, and behind the blade, his face. Valyn was ready to kill Balendin, eager, but killing the leach was just a beginning. Once the slaughter started, there would be no reason to stop, not while il Tornja remained alive, or Adare. . . .

Valyn realized he was trembling. He balled his hands into fists around the horse's reins, forced himself to breathe slowly, steadily, until the shuddering stopped. When he finally spoke, his voice sounded old as good steel gone to rust.

"Where is he?"

"Gone," the Flea replied simply.

"Not every man you cannot see is gone," Huutsuu said. "He could be somewhere in this city. He could be meeting with his chiefs."

"No," Valyn said. He dragged in a long breath, testing the air. It was impossible to unthread one man's smell from the stench of piss, and mud, and shit, and bleeding meat, but an awful certainty had settled in his gut all the same. "The Flea is right. Il Tornja is gone. That's why the Urghul were able to force their way west, why they were able to get *here*."

Sigrid made a vexed, violent sound. She shifted in her saddle, gesturing to something, and for half a heartbeat the delicate jasmine scent of her hovered on the air, unsullied by the battle's reek.

"This flawless woman at my side," Newt said, "would like to point out that even if the *kenarang* is gone, the man we came to kill is very much present."

"So he is," the Flea agreed quietly. "So he is."

Valyn turned his head pointlessly to the north, opening his eyes from darkness to darkness, as though that might do the slightest bit of good.

"Where?" Valyn asked. "What's he doing?"

"Balendin is doing what he always does," the Wing leader replied. "Standing at the edge of battle, beyond it and above it, tearing people apart."

"He has the high ground?" Valyn asked.

"Sure does. About half a mile northwest of us. Staked out the best command post on this side of the valley. On top of that rise, he can see everything."

"He's not *trying* to see everything. He wants everyone *else* to see *him*. He wants the Annurians to witness him murdering his prisoners, skinning them, or cutting out their hearts, or threading their eyes on string. He wants the legions terrified and the Urghul in awe. It's how he builds his power. He did the same thing back in Andt-Kyl."

"For what?" Huutsuu asked. "What does he want to do with that power?"

Valyn spread his hands angrily. "I can't . . ."

"The bridge," the Flea said.

"My people cannot take that bridge," Huutsuu said again. "Even with the leach, they cannot seize it."

"Balendin doesn't want to seize it," the Flea replied grimly. "He wants to destroy it."

Valyn cocked his head to the side. There was another sound, a new one, something that hadn't been there when they first arrived at the battlefield, a low, bass scraping of stone over stone punctuated by percussive cracks. Those cracks were far apart, at first, as though someone incompetent were struggling to set off Kettral munitions. Then they came faster, the sound growing louder, shifting into a higher register.

"He's tearing it down," the Flea said.

The bridge's collapse came just moments later, the slow groan of stones that had stood for centuries caving beneath some new, unnatural weight. Valyn's blindness spared him the sight of the men falling from the crumbling span, of the soldiers trapped and crushed as the huge blocks shifted, of legionaries pulled under the standing waves by the weight of their armor or pinned against stones to drown more slowly. He couldn't see it, but he could hear it all, even the individual voices: the most plaintive, the most strident. Some submitted quickly, lives quenched in an instant. Others took a long time to die.

"We have to move," the Flea said. There was no awe in his voice, no sorrow or anger. *We have to move.* It was a fact, nothing more.

"The bridge . . . ," Valyn began.

". . . is gone. Or will be soon. When it's done, Balendin will hammer through the poor bastards set up to screen the southern approach."

"Unless we kill him first," Huutsuu said.

"Hopeless," the Flea replied.

Sigrid spoke, and Newt translated. "He's filled with his power. We would never get close."

Valyn could feel Huutsuu's anger spike, then subside as she brought it back under control.

"So we go back to the woods," she said. "Wait for him to pass, then strike at his back."

"No good," the Flea said. "Newt, get up there to the line. Order half the legionaries screening the southern approach to fall back on my position. And get me messengers, at least two."

The demolitions master kicked his horse into motion without bothering to reply.

"What is not good?" Huutsuu demanded. "We came to kill the leach. It is his death that matters, not the dirt where his blood drains out."

The Flea ignored her. "Sig," he said, voice calm, quiet. "Can you hold here 'til nightfall?"

There was a long silence as the leach took stock of some context known only to herself. Valyn could feel the sun on his face. It was low in the sky, maybe an hour until dusk. Sigrid must have made some sign in reply, because the Flea grunted. "Good. Don't die."

She rasped out a few syllables.

"I'll tell you when it's time to make our stand, and this isn't it," the Flea said. "Buy us time, but not with your life."

Like Newt, the woman didn't respond, just wheeled her horse and galloped off to the north.

"Your leach will make no difference," Huutsuu said. "My people will shatter that line. They will ride over your soldiers like grass."

The Flea shook his head. "Sigrid might not have Balendin's strength, but she's been at this game a lot longer. If she says she can hold until night, she'll hold. It's our job to make use of the time."

"How?" Huutsuu demanded.

"Is there any kind of choke point farther south?" Valyn asked. "Anywhere we could hope to bottle them up?"

"We'll talk in the saddle," the Flea said. "As soon as we have these two."

"These two?" Valyn asked, then listened. After a moment, he realized that two runners were approaching. He could hear their footfalls and ragged breath even over the noise of the battle. They stopped a few feet from the Flea. Valyn could smell the wariness on them, even stronger than the sweat and blood. Wariness and deep, bone-bruising weariness.

"Messengers?" the Flea asked.

"We are," one of them replied. "I am Jia Chem. This is Ulli." He hesitated. "And you . . ."

"Just another soldier trying to hold this mess together," the Flea replied.

"Are you—"

"Kettral," the one named Ulli cut in. "You're Kettral, aren't you."

"We are," the Flea said.

And suddenly, there was hope. Valyn could almost taste it, thick and viscous on the cold breeze.

"The Kettral are here?" Chem asked. "How many . . ."

"We're it," the Flea said. "Sorry. Take four horses and ride hard for Annur. Tell whatever idiots are on or around the throne that the Urghul are coming. They have days to get ready. Weeks at the most."

To the messenger's credit, his shock lasted only a moment. "Who should I say sent the order?"

The Flea snorted. "Doesn't much matter who's giving the order, does it? What matters is that there's an Urghul army coming."

"Understood, sir."

"And just so we're clear—you're it."

The messenger hesitated. "It, sir?"

"The two of you are the only messengers. I won't tell you how to do your work, but remember that for every moment you rest, Annur will pay in lives. No one else is carrying this word. There are no birds. There are no other riders. You are it."

"Understood, sir. What about you?"

"Us?" the Flea asked. "We're going to ride with you for a while."

"And then what?"

"Well, at a certain point, we're going to stop riding, turn around, and do some fighting."

The ride south was punishing. In the forest, Valyn had been forced to guard constantly against the low-hanging boughs that threatened to sweep him from the saddle, but at least they'd rarely been able to move at much more than a walk. The uplift between the Haag and the eastern forests, however, was all grassland, open enough to allow the horses their heads, and although his beast was more sure-footed than any Annurian steed, Valyn still found himself thrown about roughly in the saddle, blind to the land ahead, unable to anticipate the thousand tiny adjustments of his horse.

He soon discovered, however, that if he could see too little, he could hear too much. They couldn't have been much more than a mile south of the ragged Annurian line when Balendin ordered the attack. He couldn't hear the leach, of course, but he didn't need to. At that distance, the individual cries all washed together, Urghul and Annurian, killer and killed, the rage and the terror, all caught up in the same swell of sound, punctuated by the crash of steel against steel. Given the scene the others had described, it seemed impossible that the legionaries would survive even that initial charge, but as Valyn galloped south, away from the fight, he began to hear the screaming of horses woven into the other sounds. Which meant that the legions were hurting the Urghul after all, holding them back, if only for the moment. The battle raged, but it didn't seem to be following.

The Aphorist caught up another mile on.

"Got half of them," he said.

"And the other half?" the Flea asked.

Valyn could hear the Aphorist's shrug, the shift of stiff wool over skin. "Dying. As all men must."

"Sigrid?"

"Making the dying take longer. She'll hold the line until night."

"Good," the Flea replied. "Double back to the Annurians coming south. Stay with them. Keep them moving at a double march through the night. You'll catch up to us around midday tomorrow."

Newt whistled quietly. "These soldiers are not Kettral. They do not have our training. Every man has a point beyond which he will break."

"They can break later. Right now, they're all that stands between the Urghul and Annur. Explain that to them. Go ahead and promise them all estates on the Channarian coast when this is done."

"We have no estates to give," Newt observed. "Regrettably."

"That's fine," the Flea replied. "When this is all over, there won't be any soldiers left alive to give them to. Regrettably."

The Aphorist chuckled, as though it were all a fine joke. "A vital lie can shine more brightly than the truth."

"Sure," the Flea replied. "Just keep them moving."

Huutsuu shifted in her saddle as the Aphorist rode off.

"Urghul can ride at night," she said. "Ride fast enough to catch these soldiers, if they have to."

"But they don't have to," the Flea said. "Balendin might have a straight shot to Annur, but even the Urghul aren't going to ride all the way there without stopping. There's no reason for him to risk a night gallop now when he has hundreds of miles to cover."

He kicked his horse into motion once more, and after a moment, Valyn followed.

"What is our plan?" he asked.

"Plan?" the Flea replied. "I thought you heard me when I told the two messengers. We ride south for a while, then turn around, then fight."

"For a great warrior," Huutsuu said, "this seems very foolish."

"Yeah," the Flea said. "Well. I didn't end up all the way out here because I was smart."

As it turned out, the Flea did have a plan after all. After a full night riding, eating strips of dried venison in the saddle, and stopping only to change mounts, they crossed a shallow stream early the next morning. The Wing leader called a halt just beyond it. For a few moments the only sounds were the water washing over the stones, the breathing of the weary beasts, and the shifting of men and women in the saddle, stretching sore muscles after so many hours.

"What is this?" Huutsuu asked finally.

"A fort," the Flea replied.

"It looks like a ruin."

"You're welcome to stand out in the middle of the grass when your people arrive."

Valyn pored over musty memories of battles he had studied back on the Islands, trying to remember what a fort might be doing out here, in the middle of nowhere.

"Something left over?" he ventured. "From when Raalte was an independent kingdom?"

"It was the northernmost of Mierten's forts. A bulwark against the barbarians beyond."

"How did you know it was here?"

"I memorized the map of this area years ago."

"Lucky for us."

The Flea shrugged. "Not really. I memorized them all."

Valyn stared into the darkness.

"There are hundreds of maps at the Eyrie."

"Yep," the Flea said. "It was a pain in the ass."

Valyn turned south, toward where the old fort waited. More than ever, his blindness chafed. Around people, he could use his other senses. He could hear them approaching, could listen to their breathing or their heartbeats. He could smell them, their fear or hope. Their confusion. Here, however, facing the dilapidated wall, there was nothing to hear but the wind, nothing to smell but the vague cold scent of stone.

"Can we hold it?" he asked.

"Not a chance."

"Then why . . ."

"We're not fighting to win. We're fighting to buy time. This old wall is worth a day. Two days, maybe, if the dice come up our way. It's hard to ride a horse through a wall."

"What's anchoring it? Why don't they just go around?"

"The river to the west," Huutsuu replied. "And something that looks like a bog to the east." It was hard to tell from her tone if she was happy about the terrain or not.

"That," the Flea agreed, "and the fact that Balendin's not going to want to leave a fort full of enemies at his back."

"*Full?*" Valyn asked. "We've got what, a hundred Annurians on the way, plus a dozen of Huutsuu's Urghul?"

"No," the woman said. "This is not our fight. It means nothing to me if your empire of cowards falls. We came to kill the Annurian leach, not to make war with our own people."

"So go kill him," the Flea replied.

Huutsuu reeked of anger. "Our pact—"

"—remains," the Flea said quietly. "We need to get a good fight going, first. Without a fight, Balendin has no reason to reach for his well, and we have no way to get close."

"A distraction?" Huutsuu asked, incredulous. "It will not work. Even in battle, this leach guards himself. If he could be killed with a spear in the back, he would be dead already."

"A spear wasn't what I had in mind," the Flea replied. "More like an explosion. He can't be guarding against everything. A mole right underneath his feet might do the job."

Huutsuu's suspicion hung in the air, sickly sweet as the stench of overripe fruit. "If you have these . . . devices, if you are able to make these explosions, why did you not kill him months ago?"

"Not the right ground," Valyn said, seeing the strategy despite his blindness. "In order for the explosion to do any good, you need to know where Balendin's going to be and when. The front was too wide before. The timing was too uncertain."

"That," the Flea agreed, "and all the spots we knew he would go were in the middle of an Urghul army. Didn't think they'd take kindly to us burying munitions in the center of their camp. Here, though, we have it all. We know when, and we've got a pretty good idea of where."

"The hill," Huutsuu said, stirring in her saddle to point in a direction Valyn couldn't make out.

"The hill," the Flea agreed. "It's high enough for him to see and be seen. He'll drag his captives up there, and start slaughtering them, hoping to pull more power from the Urghul and from our people on the wall. But that means," he went on, turning to Huutsuu, "that we need to *have* people on the wall. We need to make it a fight. If not, he'll have no reason to bother getting up on that hill. We'll end up blowing a few clods of dirt fifty feet into the air. That's it."

Huutsuu didn't reply at first. Valyn could hear the other Urghul behind her, the restlessness of the riders in the shifting of their mounts.

"All right," she said at last. "We will stand here with you. We will make this place a great sacrifice to Kwihna. And you will kill the leach."

Only when she had wheeled her horse away, calling out to the Urghul in her own tongue, leading them south to the fort itself to begin the preparations, did the Flea turn to Valyn.

"Will she betray us?" he asked.

Valyn hesitated, poring over his memories of Huutsuu. "No," he replied finally. "She's too proud."

"We're risking a lot on one woman's pride."

"When I first captured her on the steppe, she looked me straight in the eye and told me that if I didn't kill her, she would hunt me down."

"That was dumb."

Valyn nodded slowly. "Maybe. But it was brave."

"Brave usually has some dumb mixed in."

Valyn shook his head, trying to see the situation clearly. "She hates Balendin. To her he is a . . . perversion of everything sacred."

The Flea grunted. "Enough of a perversion to make her turn traitor?"

"She doesn't see it as treachery. The Urghul don't share our notion of command or duty." Valyn thought of Huutsuu killing the Urghul warriors who had opposed her, the way she'd opened their throats without hesitation or regret. "For Huutsuu, it is the result that matters, not the path. If she needs to fight other Urghul in order for Balendin to die, she'll do it. It's not as though they've never fought one another before. I don't see very many things clearly, but I'll tell you this: she will stand on that wall and fight."

The Flea sucked at his teeth, spat into the dirt. "And what about you? Can you fight?"

Valyn took a deep breath. His hands were suddenly sweating, the blood and death of Andt-Kyl scrawled across his vision. All over again he could hear the screaming, the men and women carved apart, burned alive, crushed beneath falling homes, choking as the river's current dragged them down.

"I'll fight," he managed finally. "I'll fight."

37

The low, narrow space of the tent was hot and dark. It reeked of poorly cured hide and human sweat. Outside, sand scraped over the leather with a million tiny claws. The wind screamed, trying to tear it free of the rocks holding down the corners. It was almost impossible to mark the passage between day and night; the hide shut out whatever meager, watery light had seeped down through the maelstrom, and so at noon and midnight both, Kaden and Long Fist sat or slept in an almost perfect darkness, even the sounds of their breathing scrubbed out by the raging storm.

After a while, it started to feel to Kaden that the world outside the tent had ceased to exist. Annur and Ashk'lan, the Dead Heart and the Waist—they might have been places that he had imagined or dreamed, and indeed, that line between dreaming and waking became harder and harder to trace. Long Fist refused to speak, refused to do anything but sit, staring northwest, a silent weight inside the hot darkness of the space. Two or three times, Kaden dreamed of walking free, of throwing open the leather folds and wandering into the storm. Each time he choked to death on dust, then woke again to the darkness of the tent.

When the storm finally broke, a week later, when he stumbled out of the battered hide on unsteady legs, the sudden light was like a spike driven straight into his eye. For a while he could do nothing more than stand there, bewildered by the brightness.

For all its violence, the storm had left no trace. The land was still bleak and blasted. The blazing blue stretched drum-tight across the sky. Kaden took a deep breath, savored the clean air, morning-cool in his chafed and painful lungs, then realized what that meant.

"She's still alive."

Long Fist nodded. "For now. We must move quickly to find her before the Csestriim."

Kaden stared at the rusted peaks to the west. "We don't know for certain he is hunting her."

"We know," Long Fist replied, pointing to the southeast, back the way they had come.

Kaden squinted. Just on the horizon he could make out a wisp of sand rising like smoke against the blue.

He shook his head. "Another storm?"

"Men," Long Fist replied, shouldering his pack. "Going toward the *kenta*."

Kaden stared at that tenuous smudge, wishing he had one of the Kettral long lenses. "It could be anyone."

"It is il Tornja. Or men under his command."

"But Triste isn't going for the *kenta*. She doesn't even know where it is."

"He has the soldiers to play all sections of the board at once. That," Long Fist said, leveling a long finger at the plume of dust, "is not the head of his spear. It is a wall to block our retreat."

Kaden nodded slowly. He had seen a snake from the Shirvian delta once. A rich Channarian merchant had presented it to his father as a gift, and Kaden and Valyn had both been mesmerized by the creature, the sheer size of it: twenty feet long and as thick as Kaden's chest, a monster of scale and coiled muscle. For all its size, though, the snake killed slowly, twisting its prey into an embrace. Kaden had watched it take a pig once, a massive sow that must have weighed eight hundred pounds. The snake wrapped it almost gently in its coils and then, each time the screaming beast exhaled, it curled imperceptibly tighter.

The great snake's weapon was its patience. It killed by waiting, by taking the space it was given, and refusing to relinquish it. Il Tornja's games of *ko* were like that, Kaden realized, as was this march to block the *kenta*. There would be no frantic rush to catch Triste all in one forced march, no desperate frenzy of eagerness that might lead to a mistake. Il Tornja would deny her space little by little, draw his slow coils close, destroy every avenue of escape, every person who might get her out, squeeze and squeeze until there was nowhere she could go, no way for her to breathe.

"And yet," Kaden said slowly, "he came here, to this part of the world, for a reason. He can't have soldiers everywhere. Not across all two continents. He's following her somehow. Or following us. How?"

Long Fist hissed. "It is irrelevant. We are ahead of him. This is what matters. If we want to stay ahead of him, we must run."

And so they ran.

For a day, and a night, and the start of the next day they ran, pausing only to drink from the flaccid skin that Kaden carried, and then later, to piss away whatever meager fluid remained after so much sweat. When they stopped, it was all Kaden could do just to stand there without collapsing.

Long Fist might have become a god, but he was a god locked inside a man's flesh, and despite the shaman's long limbs, the lean muscle rippling in his legs and arms, he was struggling even worse than Kaden. A limp had crept into his left leg at some point in the night, some tightening or slackening of a tendon, judging from the change in his gait. Kaden recognized the type of injury from his years in Ashk'lan, knew that it would only stiffen further, twist the shaman's stride more violently, until he could do little more than lurch over the uneven stones. What Long Fist needed was rest, but there was no time for rest.

The mountains, which had been no more than tiny red teeth

against the western sky when Kaden first emerged from the *kenta,* were so close now that they cast half the land in shadow as the sun began to set. Somewhere in that shadow was a tiny village clustered around a reedy pool of water—Triste's oasis—maybe somewhere close, although it was impossible to know precisely where to look. If Kaden and Long Fist continued west, they would hit the cliffs by dawn, but then what? Turn north? South? They might spend days scouring the wrong patch of desert, and the plume of dust rising to the east whispered at their backs that they did not have days.

In the end, it was il Tornja's own mistake that saved them. Evening's cool shadow had settled over everything when Kaden saw the tracks. At first, he barely noticed them, his exhausted body plodding on, driven by little more than its own momentum as his mind worked through what his eyes had seen. A dozen paces on, he finally slowed to a trembling stop. The desert air burned in his lungs as he called out to Long Fist, gesturing wearily for the shaman to wait as he made his slow way back, bent over the broken ground, searching.

The tracks were easy to find, once he knew what he was looking for. The Dead Salts were not Ashk'lan; the ground was dirt rather than stone, and though the sun had baked it to a brittle clay, that clay still took a print, especially when that print was sharp, jagged, the result, not of paws or hooves, but claws.

Ak'hanath, Kaden thought, staring at the scarred dirt.

He wanted it to be a mistake, for the shapes not to be tracks at all, or to be tracks, but from some other creature. Only there were no other creatures, not like that. Kaden could still see their segmented bodies scuttling over the granite ledges of the Bone Mountains, could hear their shrieks pitched at the very edge of human hearing. The *ak'hanath* might have looked like spiders—spiders the size of large dogs—save for the dozens of bloody eyes grafted into every clicking, twitching joint of the carapace. He remembered the way his stomach had twisted at that sight, as though his body understood the awful truth before his mind:

the *ak'hanath* were no creation of Bedisa's art. They were not born, but made, spawned, built thousands and thousands of years ago by the Csestriim to track their human prey.

"What?" Long Fist demanded, doubling back. His long hair, drenched with sweat, hung heavy around his shoulders. His eyes were hard, glittering like stars in the gloaming, but his breathing was heavy and uneven.

Kaden pointed at the dirt.

"The answer to a question. Triste came this way."

The shaman studied the tracks, then shook his head. "The girl did not leave these marks."

"No," Kaden agreed grimly. "She did not. It is the track of the *ak'hanath* that Ran il Tornja has tasked with following her."

It made perfect sense, of course. It was the *only* thing that made sense. The *ak'hanath* could never creep into Intarra's Spear, but the creature could have been lurking inside Annur itself, could have been standing watch. When Triste escaped, it would have known, and so il Tornja would have known. The girl might have eluded all human pursuers, but the creations of the Csestriim were far from human. The *ak'hanath* needed no physical trace, no human track or mortal scent. Tan had explained it all what seemed a lifetime earlier: the spiders could taste the self. That was what they hunted. Triste could flee through the mountains or take to the sea, and the thing would follow, follow her across entire continents if necessary. And then il Tornja would come.

They reached the oasis and the tiny village of reed and thatch just as the eastern sky began to fill with a watery light. From the top of a low rise, Kaden could make out the shapes of twenty or thirty huts—little more than shadows in the tall, shifting grasses—most clustered right up against the small body of water. He glanced east, over his shoulder. The column of dust was closer. It seemed il Tornja's soldiers, too, had marched straight through the night, and while Kaden and Long Fist had been slowed by the effort of pausing to find faint tracks in the fickle moonlight, the men behind them had come on at a steady, unhalting pace. They were, at most, two miles back. As dawn resolved the eastern horizon, Kaden could see the dark shapes shimmering with the morning's heat.

He squinted, trying to make out more detail. "Where are Tan and the Ishien?"

Long Fist didn't look back. "Lost. Dead. It doesn't matter."

Dead. Kaden tried to imagine Rampuri Tan dead. He failed.

After a moment he set the thought aside, took a deep breath, held it in his ragged lungs, then blew it out. "There's not much time," he said, gesturing to the oasis. "We get Triste. Then we get out. Away somewhere."

The shaman was breathing hard, panting really, but he smiled a lean, predatory smile. "No." That single syllable bristled with violence. Then: "We kill."

Kaden shook his head. "There are two of us. Three, with Triste. We can't fight."

The Urghul smiled wider, baring those perfect teeth. "There will be no fight. I will destroy them."

And suddenly Kaden was back inside the Jasmine Court, breath heaving in his lungs, wounds afire, staring in bafflement at the scattered dead, then turning to find Triste standing there, ancient-eyed and vacant, hands clenched into fists at her sides as though she had torn out those windpipes and shattered the skulls with her own small hands, one at a time.

"Your well . . . ," Kaden began. "You can reach it?"

"What do I need with a well? Where there is pain, there is power," Long Fist replied. "And there is suffering in every hovel, misery in the beating of every creature's heart."

Kaden looked into his own flesh, tried to weigh the ache in his calves and thighs, the dozens of tiny agonies driven like invisible spikes into his knees, his ankles, the soles of his blistered feet. He hurt, but he had hurt worse.

"Is it enough? The pain that's here, that you can reach?"

"Here?" Long Fist looked around, eyes narrowed, as though he were just now seeing where they stood, just at that very moment noticing the desert sprawled out to the south and east, the mountains towering to the west. "I am not this body. Where there is screaming, I am there. Why will this truth not put down root inside your mind?"

"You don't need to be near your well," Kaden said slowly. The consequences were terrifying: a leach with no weakness, no moments of ordinary impotence. It seemed impossible, but then, when he sifted through his memories of Triste, it fit. She had drawn on her own powers at need, indifferent to her surroundings, as though the whole world were her well, as though she could plunge her hands into that arcane strength wherever she stood and they would emerge full and flowing over.

"It would be a small thing," Long Fist continued, oblivious or indifferent to Kaden's shock, "to snuff out those lives."

He held up a hand, sighting east between thumb and forefinger, as though il Tornja's soldiers, made small by distance, were no more than the charred wicks of so many candles. Kaden waited for him to squeeze those fingers shut, stared at the distant figures, wondering how slowly they would die. After a moment, however, the shaman shook his head, lowered his hand.

"No."

Kaden felt a strange relief wash through him. The soldiers were dangerous. They had killed, would kill again, would keep killing until they came to Triste and cut her throat. Without Long Fist's power it would come down to little more than a race, a desperate gamble that they could find the girl, warn her, and escape. Kaden should have been grateful for the shaman's strength, and yet at the man's words—*Where there is screaming, I am there*—he had experienced a strange and sudden vision, as though his mind had been split open and pried wide as the world. He saw a million people twisting in their private agonies, bleeding or not bleeding, screaming or not screaming, dying or not dying, each person's pain a single red thread, pulsing like living tissue in a thick lace laid across the whole face of the earth. He saw all that awful fabric gathered in the shaman's fist, the pain inextricable from the power. They needed it, if they were to win, if they were to *survive,* but a question prowled the edge of Kaden's mind: *And if we win . . . what then?*

Kaden looked from the shaman to the approaching soldiers. "Why are you waiting?"

Long Fist leveled a finger over the blasted land. "The war chief will be with them. This petty creature with his schemes to lay me low."

"Il Tornja."

The shaman smiled. "I want him. He is no great instrument, but I want to hear the sounds he makes as I carve him apart."

"What if he's not there?"

"For thousands of years he has aimed at this moment. He will be there."

Kaden nodded slowly. The Csestriim was hardly likely to leave the killing blow to any hand but his own. Which meant that the man who had murdered his father, who had tried to murder him, the creature who had turned the whole Annurian Empire inside out—he was just a mile away, guarded by no more than a few dozen men.

"So we get to Triste," he said. "Find her. Then what?"

"Then," the shaman replied, "I will show this petty Csestriim what it is to war against a god."

Whatever weariness Long Fist had felt seemed to have left him. His breathing was even now, steady, his face eager. When he broke suddenly into a run, it was the ground-covering lope of a hunter who has sighted his prey. After a pause, Kaden followed, unsteady on his own trembling legs.

38

Adare sat at her writing desk, though she made no effort to write. She had returned to her chambers at the top of the Crane late the night before after an evening arguing with Nira and Kegellen, had fallen onto her bed still clothed, dropped into a blank sleep, then woken to the midnight gong. For a while, she'd tried to go back to sleep, but sleep proved every bit as elusive as Triste. The girl's face filled Adare's mind, those violet eyes drugged but defiant, her words quiet but horribly final: *All of you scheming bastards are going to cut each other down.*

If the girl were no more than a leach, her escape would still have been a disaster. According to Kaden, however, she was the vessel of a goddess, the human incarnation of Ciena herself. It seemed impossible, and yet it fit too perfectly with il Tornja's claims about Long Fist and Meshkent, with the fact that the *kenarang* had been willing to give up Adare herself in order to see the creature dead. Certainly, Kaden seemed to believe the tale he had told her days before. Which meant, if it were true, that Adare's mistake in letting the girl escape may have doomed them all.

Finally, she cursed, got up, and crossed to the doors leading out to her balcony. She unlatched them, then threw them open. The summer air washed over her skin, lifted her hair, then let it fall. She'd intended to write, to toil away at the backlog of imperial business waiting at her desk, but instead she'd just been sitting there, sitting there for half the night, the lamps unlit, the inkwell unopened, staring out those open doors from the darkness of her chambers into the larger darkness of the world beyond.

According to Kaden, the *kenta* were doors of a sort, gates, impossible passages from one land to the next. He could step from Annur to Sia as easily as Adare herself might walk from room to room. At first, she hadn't believed him. Surely, her father would have told her, would have trained her in the way he had trained her about so much else. That he had neglected this most crucial fact of his rule, the secret of the entire Malkeenian line, seemed both cruel and pointless. Then Kaden showed her.

It didn't look like anything, really, a strange arch in the basement of an abandoned Shin chapterhouse in one of Annur's backwater neighborhoods. Certainly it didn't look like the relic of a vanished race, the worst weapon of their genocidal war. It might have been nothing more than the folly of an eccentric architect until Kaden, his eyes cold as the winter stars, stepped through and vanished.

"I won't come back," he'd said. "Not right away."

And he did not.

That should have been a relief. He was searching for Triste, after all, using the network of gates to hunt down and reclaim the leach. If he succeeded, if he brought her back, there might still be some hope of thwarting il Tornja, of rescuing the gods and the millions of men and women who depended on them. The stakes were almost ludicrous, far too large for any human mind to comprehend, but Adare didn't find herself thinking of all those millions, not really. When she thought of what hung in the balance, it wasn't humanity she pictured, not Annur, not her brother, or Nira, or Lehav: there was only one face, her son's, those tiny blazing eyes, the pudgy hands; though to her horror, the memories she had of him were fraying.

Just another thing I can't keep hold of, she thought, as she stared out the doors into the night.

In the dark hours, she tallied up her failures: her father, her mother, her son, one brother murdered, another, at least for now, beyond a set of gates that she could never pass. She'd lost control of the general she'd hoped would hold the northern front, and for all she knew, she was losing the front as well. She'd managed to reclaim her family's throne, but to what end? Every day, the good she'd hoped to work, the security and safety she'd hoped to bring to all Annur, crumbled like clay in her hands. Partly it was the council's fault, but another emperor, someone stronger, wiser, would have found a way to take the recalcitrant bastards in hand, to trick them or twist them into acting for the public good. Another emperor would have done what she had not.

And then there was her miracle, her blessing, the touch of the goddess laid into her very flesh. Adare ran a finger along the smooth whorls of scar. In the days following the lightning at the Everburning Well, she had believed, really *believed* for the first time in her life, that Intarra was something other than a name, a myth, a convenient fiction to cement her family's rule. The people had called her Prophet, and with the exhortation of the goddess ringing in her ears, she had accepted the title, worn it like an armor in her righteous fight. That righteousness, though, had seeped away—partly when Fulton died, then Valyn, partly when she forgave her father's murderer—and the title felt too large for her now, shining, ostentatious, hollow.

While Adare claimed to speak for Intarra—a goddess she could neither hear nor understand—there were others who walked the world, Triste and Long Fist, whose gods lived in their very flesh. Adare made speeches, accepted the genuflection of the Sons of Flame, of all Annur, but the words were her own. They were mortal, fallible. Whether she spoke the language of the Lady of Light, she had no idea. Not much more than a year earlier, she had seen a man destroyed for such a profanation of his faith. It had felt good to watch Uinian pinned there, burning in the awful beam of light. It had felt right. It was only justice, she had told herself, to unmask a traitor and a false priest, a man who invoked the name of the goddess for nothing greater than his own gain.

And if the false priest deserved to burn, she asked herself grimly, *what of a false prophet?*

Before she could fashion an answer to the question, a sharp rap sounded at the door. She glanced at the hourglass at the desk's corner—more than an hour remained before dawn. It would be urgent, for someone to disturb her now. Slowly, methodically, she put away her doubts, her fears, set them inside the drawers of her mind, then closed those drawers. Perhaps she was a fraud. Perhaps she would be unmasked one day, burned alive as she had seen Uinian burn. Fine. It didn't change the fact that there was work to do, and no one else to do it.

Instead of a legislative session, Adare might have been looking at the moments immediately before a battle. By the time she arrived in the hall, most of the others were already there, despite the fact that the sun had yet to rise. Her own stomach twisted sickeningly inside her, as though the news were rancid meat that her body refused to digest, but she managed to keep her face still. On that front alone, she was a step ahead of almost everyone else on the council.

They had gathered inside the Hall of the Chosen—the vast chamber they had selected as the legislative seat after Adare burned their map and the catwalks above it—but instead of seating themselves around the massive wooden table, almost everyone was standing, gathered in small knots by atrepy or alliance, all talking at the same time, a few of the delegates doing quite a bit more than that, bellowing in the faces of their ostensible friends and loudly cursing their enemies. No weapon longer than a belt knife was allowed inside the council chamber. Otherwise, Adare felt sure, blood would have spilled already.

There should have been a herald at the door to announce her, but either because of the chaos or the early hour or both, he was missing. As a result, despite the Sons of Flame at her side, almost no one noticed her arrival. She might have been a slave carrying a plate of roasted firefruit, a fact that had its advantages: it meant she had longer than she'd expected to gauge the situation, not that there was much to gauge. The men and women tasked with leading Annur through her darkest days were baffled, terrified. If they had a plan to deal with the coming catastrophe, Adare saw no sign of it.

As Adare studied the crowd, Nira approached from behind her. Whether a messenger had woken the old woman, too, Adare had no idea, not that it really mattered. She was here, now, glaring at the assembled council as though they were a herd of swine that had broken into her home.

"This is a disaster," Adare muttered quietly.

"Been a disaster all along," the small woman snapped. "Like a cracked glass no one notices until the day it shatters."

"Il Tornja didn't say anything about leaving the front?"

"No," Nira replied. "He did not. You think I would a' skipped that part when I first arrived?"

Adare shackled her impatience. "Were there any hints—"

"If there'd a' been hints, you'd a' known 'em. Now, you want ta keep up with the dumb questions, or you want ta do something about this?" Nira waved her cane toward the madness, almost taking out the eye of the senior delegate from Aragat. The man was saved by the endless slope of his nose, but he blundered backward all the same, rounded on Nira in a rage, recognized her belatedly, then turned to Adare, lips pulled back as though he were ready to bite.

When he finally found his words, they came out loud and all at once.

"Your 'Kent-kissing general has betrayed us!"

Nira did hit him then, swinging her cane up in a clean arc that took the man square across the throat. It was impossible to tell if he'd been about to say something more because he dropped to one knee, hacking up an awful cough, clutching at his neck.

"When you speak to the Emperor," Nira said, standing over the Aragatan, "you will use her proper title."

"Nira...," Adare began, then let it drop. There was no restraining the old woman, and besides, the people standing nearest had already turned. They stared at her for one heartbeat, two, three, then the questions began—demands, really—crashing over her like waves. It was impossible, in the shouted chaos, to make out more than a few words at a time—*why did you let ... if he's a traitor ... not warned ... a betrayal of the greatest proportion*—but the gist was clear enough.

Time to be Emperor, Adare thought bleakly.

Ignoring the cries, she stepped up onto the massive wooden table. There was something to be said for being above everyone else, and when you didn't have a throne handy, well, you just had to improvise. Usually, she wore thin silk slippers inside the palace, but after learning the dire news, some part of her had wanted to dress, not for debate, but for war. In addition to a severe tunic and split pants, she'd thrown on riding boots, and now, as she strode to the center of the table, the heels punched out a grim rhythm against the wood.

It was tempting to try to raise her voice above the chaos, but Adare was no battlefield commander. There was nothing to be gained by entering a screaming match she was sure to lose, and so she waited, turning in a slow circle until she was sure she'd caught every eye. Then she started talking in her normal voice, exaggerating the movement of her lips slightly, but making no effort to compete with the general din.

"Early this morning," she began, "I received grim tidings of events taking place to the north." The opening words weren't important. No one could hear her anyway. The important thing was to be seen talking. "I came here in all haste," she went on, "because this is obviously a matter of the greatest import."

One by one, then in small groups, the assembled legislators fell silent. A few of the councillors were still rattling on—Adare could make out Bouraa Bouree baying his displeasure somewhere toward the back of the room—but for most of the delegates, the desire to hear what she was saying had, at least for the moment, overcome the desire to be heard. Adare paused, shook her head, fixed in place her imperial visage, felt her eyes blaze.

All an act, of course. Her legs felt weak beneath her. Aside from half a cup of *ta* gulped down as she dressed, she had put nothing in her stomach, and her guts twisted viciously. *Don't puke,* she growled silently to herself. *And don't shake.* They were all silent now, even Bouree, and when she finally raised her voice, it came out clear, carved from the stone of some confidence that was not her own.

"This is a disgrace," she said, gesturing to the chamber with a hand.

"It's not your place—" someone began.

"Not my place to *what*?" Adare demanded. "To come into the council chamber? To berate you all for behavior that would shame a group of children?"

Ziav Moss stepped forward, his face grave. "According to the treaty that you signed, Your Radiance, the Emperor, bright be the days of her life, has no place in the affairs of the council. This body decides policy. It is your part only to put it into action."

"And what policy is it that you have decided?" Adare demanded. She held Moss's cold gaze for a moment, then slowly shifted her eyes over the other women and men. "Please tell me, because evidently our general has disappeared, the Urghul are south of the Thousand Lakes, and I am eager, as the one responsible for taking action, to *take action*."

"These tidings are fresh even to us," Moss replied. "We must sort fact from hearsay. We must take the necessary time to consider all available options. The work required here is nuanced, Your Radiance, sophisticated in ways few would understand. Rushing headlong into a battle we don't fully understand will look like bravery in these early days, but I fear it will seem like folly later."

A few heads had started nodding along with Moss. *They play nice with each other only when the monster has arrived,* Adare thought. *And I get to be the monster.*

"Far be it from me," she said, raising her hands in mock surrender, "to stand in the way of deliberation. When I arrived, however, the scene looked more like a screaming melee."

"We are, all of us, understandably upset—" Moss said.

Adare cut him off before he could finish. "You cannot *afford* to be upset. *Annur* cannot afford it." She shook her head. "Let me tell you something. You are the legislators of an empire, the lawmakers who will decide the fate of millions. Fishwives can scream when they are upset, loggers can brawl in their northern camps, merchants can rail at one another over brimming cups of wine, but you are not fishwives, nor loggers, nor merchants."

She shook her head, letting that point sink in. It was a delicate dance, chastising them while also appealing to their pride. "The reason you sit around this table, *you* instead of any of the other millions of souls whose asses would fit those seats as well, is precisely this: you are *better.*

"This, at least, is what I had hoped. I had hoped you would be better than drunken sailors in a crisis, that you would keep your heads where others would run mad. I had hoped to come here, to this room, to find the leaders of Annur already assembled, already seated, already well on the way to the formulation of a plan. I had hoped you would be impatient with *me,* chafing at my absence, ready and eager to share the outlines of a response to this disaster." She raised her brows. "Did I hope for too much?"

For a moment, there was only silence in the room. Then

Bouraa Bouree bulled his way forward, lips twisted in a snarl as he leveled his finger at Adare.

"I will not . . . will not . . . *stand* here," he barked, his words tangling in his anger. "I will not stand and listen to a . . . to this . . . *chastisement* from a woman who has sat upon the throne barely a month." It was clear that he wanted to say more, and worse, but whatever the full fury of his thoughts, Adare was still the Emperor, and the man had retained at least a modicum of caution. "I suggest you tend to your work, Your Radiance, and we will tend to ours."

"By all means," Adare said, gesturing to the empty chairs, inviting them all to sit. "Start tending. We might start with the messengers. Where are they?"

"Here, Your Radiance," said a new voice, weary but firm, off to the side of the room.

As the members of the council grudgingly sat, the two men who had carried the word stepped forward. They were both obviously legionaries, and older than Adare had expected, well into their early forties, creased and hard as riding leather, lean from lives lived in the saddle, quartering whole continents on horseback bearing messages of death: battles lost or won, armies marching, towns lost. Someone had chosen these older men, the most experienced, to deliver the most dire tidings.

"Your names?" Adare asked.

They stiffened, raising knuckles to brows in the type of military salute rarely encountered inside the Dawn Palace. "I am Jia Chem, Your Radiance," replied the shorter of the two, "and this is Ulli, who men call the Coyote."

Both men kept their eyes fixed straight ahead.

"Who is your commanding officer?"

"Jan Belton, with the Seventeenth."

"Where is the Seventeenth stationed?"

"We've been northeast of Aergad since the winter, Your Radiance."

Aergad. Where she had left her son, thinking him sheltered behind the crumbling walls. If the Urghul broke through, it would be the first place they razed. Brutally, she shoved the thought aside.

"What was the state of that city when you left?"

For the first time, Chem hesitated, glancing over at Ulli.

"Speak," Adare said impatiently. "We are not in the habit, here in Annur, of hurting those who tell a painful truth."

"Of course, Your Radiance," the rider replied, bowing his head. "Of course. Aergad survives, but the bridge over the Haag is destroyed."

Aergad survives. Relief flooded Adare, then disgust at herself that she had felt such relief. There were other lives than her son's at stake.

"And your legion?" she pressed. "And the rest of the Army of the North?"

The man grimaced. "Alive, but west of the river. On the wrong side."

At that, the whole chamber erupted into shouts and cries. Adare started to raise her own voice, then shook her head and just waited for the furor to subside. It moved on finally, violent as a summer squall, then faded to hissed whispers and shaking heads, as though everyone in the room had collectively rejected the messenger's words.

Silence finally settled back over the room, glassy and fragile.

Adare spoke into that silence, trying not to shatter it. "Deliver your full report."

Jia Chem bowed again, then began.

"All winter, we were able to hold the Urghul with help from the snow—"

"We don't need a three-volume history," Adare cut in. "Start with what matters, with what's happening now."

Chem nodded, reframing his message, then began again. "The *kenarang* is gone. No one's sure where. He left orders with his generals to hold the Urghul in the foothills as long as possible, then to fall back on Aergad. Our men fought, but without the *kenarang,* it was hopeless. We were forced back almost immediately. No one knows how to stand against the Priest."

"The Priest?" Randi Helti demanded, teeth clamped on the stem of her unlit pipe.

"Meaning the leach," Chem replied, his weathered face grim. "The Kettral traitor. His name's Balendin, but the men just call him the Priest. Short for the Priest of Pain. Supposedly it was Long Fist, an Urghul chief, who united the blood-loving savages, but no one's seen him in half a year. The Priest, though . . ." He shook his head. "He's everywhere. For a while, he was with the nomads east of Scar Lake, then he disappeared briefly, then turned up in the west, where he's been trying to force a way through in the foothills of the Romsdals. There's a little strip of land up there between the mountains and the forest, an east-west passage high and dry enough to ride horses over, and that's where the worst of the fighting's been since late winter. We've got legions upon legions plugging that tiny gap, and men are still dying by the hundreds and the thousands.

"No one can stop the Priest—no one can even get near him— and somehow it seems that each week, he's stronger. The Urghul are little better than beasts, but when he's leading them, they're mad, almost rabid, insane in their eagerness to get at us. I've watched their warriors, their weapons gone, climb over piles of bodies, then hurl themselves on our soldiers, biting, snarling, clawing, fighting like animals until we put them down.

"And sometimes it seems that the horsemen are the least of it. The Priest . . ." He paused, eyes bleak with some remembered horror. "He can make the rivers burn. He can flick a finger and send rocks the size of cattle crashing through our lines. He can turn the sky to ice, shatter it, so that chunks the size of stones come crashing down into our army. I saw a sergeant's skull crushed inside his steel helmet. His face was . . . pulp."

The soldier seemed to have forgotten his audience. His gaze was fixed on empty air, his hand opening and closing convulsively at his side, as though reaching for something he could never quite find.

"You can usually see the Priest. He finds a knoll with a vantage of the field—just laughs at our archers—and he has a dozen captives dragged up after him. Sometimes they're just loggers, but more and more he has Annurian troops, our men still in their own armor, and he . . . does things to them."

"Things?" Adare asked. She could have spared herself the account. During her months in the north, she'd heard in horrific detail of Balendin's depredations. The other members of the council, however, were staring at the soldier, shocked. After almost a year prowling the borders of the empire, the war was suddenly close. Jia Chem's tales—tales that might have met with disbelief or indifference a month earlier—were suddenly, awfully relevant. *They need to hear this,* Adare thought. *And maybe I do, too.* Since Nira's unexpected arrival in the city, she'd been too wrapped up in her own private terrors and hopes. While plotting to free Triste, to find a way to save her son, she'd all but ignored the larger war. And now, suddenly, she was losing it.

"I watched him once," Jia Chem went on, driven somehow to tell it all. "I watched him take a man, a soldier about my size, and just . . . turn him inside out. That poor fucking bastard—he was still *alive.* I could see his lungs heaving, pink-white, strong at first, then weaker, and weaker. The Priest held the beating heart awhile, held it the way you or I might hold an apple, then he handed it to the soldier, made him hold his own heart. . . . It took forever for him to die, and all the time our men were fighting, trying not to look up, but *knowing* what was happening up there on that hill. Another time the Priest held a man's head in his hands while his pet falcon pecked out the tongue, the cheeks, the eyes. . . ."

"Stop calling him the Priest," Adare said finally, snapping the trembling cord of the man's story. "His name is Balendin. He's sick, twisted, filthy, but like any other leach, he's just a man. He has weaknesses." She pointed at the riders. "You held him back, you and the rest of the legions. Whatever vicious little rituals he enacts, you *stopped* him."

"No, Your Radiance," Jia Chem replied. He bowed his head again, but the words were hard. "The *kenarang* stopped him. For months now, we've been pressed desperately, but wherever the Priest appeared, there was our general. He's not a leach, but he *sees* a battle, he sees . . ." He trailed off helplessly. "I can't explain the genius."

You don't need to, Adare thought. *Not to me.* It wasn't until that day atop the stone tower in Andt-Kyl, watching il Tornja command his army, that she finally realized the kind of creature she had spared. He was shaped like a man, had a man's face and hands, but when she looked into those perfectly empty eyes, instead of any human feeling, she had found only a great, implacable immensity, frigid as the coldest winter night, alien as the space between stars.

"Are we to understand," Moss demanded, "that your general has abandoned his post?"

"Abandoned?" Chem pronounced the word as though the action it described couldn't possibly apply to il Tornja. "No. The *kenarang* would never abandon us." Ulli, too, was shaking his head.

"But he is gone," Adare said bluntly.

Where? That was the crucial question.

Adare didn't believe the general was dead, not even for a heartbeat. He hadn't lived through all those long millennia, through wars, and purges, just to die falling off his horse, or from a stray arrow to the eye. He was alive. The certainty was solid and undeniable as a jagged stone lodged in her mind. If he had disappeared, it was for his own reasons, in order to act out some scheme that Adare herself had always failed to see. He could be anywhere by now, could be allied with Balendin himself for all Adare understood the fucking situation.

She felt like a child staring at the great book of the world, diligently, stupidly studying letters she could not read. Il Tornja had created the Atmani; what did that mean? He seemed intent on waging a vicious war against an Urghul chief that he claimed was the God of Pain; what did that mean? He wanted Triste freed. . . .

Adare paused, then beckoned to Jia Chem. "When?" she demanded.

She could barely hear her own voice over the room's din, and the rider hesitated, shook his head, then bowed and stepped closer.

"Beg pardon, Your Radiance?"

"When did he disappear? The *kenarang*? What *day*?"

"It's hard to say, Your Radiance. The *kenarang* has always moved along the front, riding through the night from one legion to the next, arriving unexpectedly where he is needed most, then disappearing again. We thought his most recent absence was just that . . . part of a larger stratagem that none of us could ever understand."

"Estimate."

He pursed his lips, shook his head. "It must have been . . ." He closed his eyes, calculating. "Maybe ten days back?"

Adare took a slow, shuddering breath. *It's just a guess,* she told herself. *He just got done saying he can't be certain.* But the coincidence seemed too strange, too perfect.

The same day, Adare thought. *He disappeared the same day we broke Triste free.*

"And then?" she asked.

"Then the Urghul broke through in the foothills. We kept fighting, made a strategic retreat, but order started leaking out. Once enough men knew we were going to fall back on Aergad anyway, get behind the bridge and the river and those high stone walls, they lost stomach for the fight—no point dying over ground you're planning to give up."

"But if the army's in Aergad," Adare said, consulting her

memory of the map, "there's nothing standing between the Urghul and Annur itself."

Jia Chem nodded bleakly. "Commander Belton understood that. He refused to cross the bridge, insisted on staying on the east side of the Haag."

"With how many men?"

"A couple hundred."

Silence settled on the room, heavy and cold.

Finally, Kiel spoke. "Two hundred men," he said quietly, "against Balendin and the entire might of the Urghul? They wouldn't last an afternoon. They wouldn't last the first charge."

Jia Chem nodded. "Belton expected to die. *Our place is fighting for our land and our families, not hiding.* That's what he said to the men. The other commanders believed that the *kenarang* had a plan, that il Tornja'd find a way, even with the army on the wrong side of the river, to stop the Urghul before they pushed too far south. I was there, at Belton's shoulder, when they argued with him to retreat. They said that disregarding the *kenarang*'s order was treason. He just shrugged. *The* kenarang *comes and goes,* he said, *but my conscience never leaves me.*"

"And what happened," Adare asked, dreading the answer, "to Commander Belton and his men?"

Jia Chem shook his head slowly. "I don't know. Not for sure. The Kettral sent us south before the battle began."

"Kettral?" Adare asked sharply.

Mention of the fighting force sent a shiver of excitement and confusion through the room, and it took some time before the tumult subsided.

"They were Kettral," the messenger said. "Four of them . . ."

"With a bird?"

Chem shook his head. "If they had a bird, they could have flown here to warn you. Ulli and I can ride, but we're nothing compared to those creatures. No. They were on horseback, riding with a small group of Urghul, maybe two dozen, a group that had broken off from the main army, traitors to their own people, I guess. I don't know—the one in charge told us to ride south. We'd planned to stay, to fight along with Belton and the others, but this man," the messenger shook his head at the memory, "he wasn't the sort you disobeyed."

Adare's skin had risen into gooseflesh. *Four Kettral.* Valyn had died in Andt-Kyl, but the rest of his Wing might have survived.

"Can you describe them?" she asked.

Jia Chem glanced at Ulli for the second time. The Coyote's face was tight, frightened.

"I'd never seen Kettral up close," he said finally. "And I hope I never do again. They were all different—the leader was coal-black and short, there was a woman, she was beautiful, even though her skin was sickly pale and she didn't have a tongue. One of them was blind, one seemed to be missing half his teeth. They were all different but they were all the same—they didn't look at you, they looked *through* you. Like they could already see you dead, and were just trying to decide whether it was time to make it so." He shuddered. "They rode up out of the woods. No warning. No nothing. Their commander told us to ride south, to bring you word of what was coming.

" 'What are you going to do?' I managed to ask him.

"He just smiled. 'We'll try to hold 'em long enough to give those idiots in the south a head start with the defense.'

"There were only four of them, not counting the Urghul." He held up his fingers, stared at them as though he couldn't quite believe what he was saying. "Four. And he talked about holding back the Priest and the whole Urghul army as though it were an irritation. An inconvenience."

Adare tried to make sense of the story and failed. Aside from Valyn, she didn't know any of the Kettral by face or name. The soldiers in question sounded older than the remnants of Valyn's Wing, but beyond that, there was little else to be learned. Grimly, she turned her attention to the larger question.

"How far away are the Urghul now? How fast are they coming?"

"I can't be sure, Your Radiance," Chem replied. "The Kettral—"

"Assume the Kettral failed. That they are dead."

"Still, there are so many factors. . . ."

"Estimate."

"Any estimate I make—"

"—will be miles better than anything we could come up with," she snapped impatiently. "You know this foe. You have watched them, fought them."

Jia Chem hesitated, glanced over at Ulli, then nodded.

"A whole army—even an Urghul army—is slower than two men. We've stopped only to change mounts, haven't really been out of the saddle since Aergad." He shook his head wearily. "If they pushed *hard,* they might be halfway to Annur, but that's not the Priest's way. He likes to stop, to hold his sick ceremonies— it's like he wants to savor all the pain he's caused." He frowned. "I'd say they're still four or five days out."

Four or five days. The words went through Adare like an icy blade.

The council chamber erupted into madness once more, but this time Adare made no effort to impose order. For months, the Urghul had pressed against the Annurian lines all along the northern front, and for months, the legions had held them off. The battles were savage. The northern swamps ran red with blood in a dozen places, but each time the horsemen had attacked, the legions threw them back. The horror remained, but Adare had started to believe it was contained. She had even allowed herself to hope, after signing the treaty with the council, that the newly unified Annur might finally crush the horsemen once and for all. And now there was an Urghul army five days from Annur.

Even as she sat there, bafflement and rage playing out all

around her, men and women were dying, sacrificed on Balendin's blades and in his fires.

All while I schemed and meddled, spent my energy on freeing that leach so I could see my son again.

She wanted to be sick. Sick for all the tens of thousands she had failed, and for her own child, if he was even still alive. It seemed suddenly, violently important to go over it all again, every choice, every decision she had made. Somewhere along the way, she had made a mistake, maybe dozens of mistakes, but she found that just exactly *where* she had gone wrong, she couldn't say. In fact, whatever her errors, whatever her flaws, it was starting to seem that she might be irrelevant. She was the Emperor, accounted Intarra's prophet by an army of the faithful, but what had she done? Il Tornja had held back the Urghul and their bloody priests. Not the council. Not Adare. Not even the legions, really. It all hinged on il Tornja, and now he was gone.

"Five days," she said, the words rising like bile to her tongue.

"We do not know precisely what's taking place up there," Moss observed. "This account is vague."

"It is what we *have*," Adare spat. "We know what we know. Il Tornja is gone. The Urghul have broken past the Army of the North, and are pushing south out of the lakes. I've seen these horsemen with my own eyes, seen what they do. Even now, while we are talking, they are hurting Annurians, burning, raping, rending, and killing the people we have sworn to protect. Right now, there are babies—" She hesitated half a heartbeat, the memory of Sanlitun's face filling her mind again, then forced herself ahead. "Right now there are children hanging from the trees. There are men staked naked to the earth, their bellies open to the sky."

She could see the horror seeping into their eyes, as though that simple syllable—*war*—were a relic of another tongue, something to be puzzled over, debated, but never truly faced, as though they were only now, after almost a year, starting to understand what the word actually meant.

"And I will tell you something else," she said, forging ahead before they could regain their balance. "Those horsemen are coming here, to Annur, to this city, and right now we have no force in place to stop them."

"Well," Kegellen said, speaking into the stunned silence, patting at her chest with her hand as she surveyed the room. "All this excitement has strained my fat old heart."

She didn't look strained, Adare thought. She looked ready, almost eager.

After another moment, Bouraa Bouree stumbled to his feet. "We must move the council. Move it immediately. Evacuate those of us crucial to this government . . ."

The other voices spoke over and around him in a grim chorus of fear and denial.

". . . we go to the eastern coast . . ."

". . . Sia is well provisioned. We could defend . . ."

". . . the fortresses of the northwest . . ."

The panic moved like fire from one voice to the next, blazing higher, brighter. Adare heard it roaring around her, felt it hot and urgent in the air. There was something inside herself, however, that would not catch. It felt as though her heart had been scorched already, burned down to the roots by so many months of fighting and fear. There was a strange safety in that blackened desolation. She imagined herself standing on a wide patch of charred earth while the world burned around her. The cries of the others didn't frighten her. They made her angry.

"We are staying," she said.

No one heard. The fury raged.

"We are staying," she said again, more quietly this time.

Ziav Moss was on his feet calling for calm. He, too, was failing. For a moment, he met Adare's eyes, then looked away.

They can't face it, she thought. *None of them will face what is coming.*

Il Tornja was gone. The council was falling apart, readying

itself to flee. Annur was tearing itself apart, and all the while the Urghul were coming, a world of war and fire at their backs.

"*I* am staying," Adare said after a long pause, the words loud enough for her ears alone.

39

Justice, as it turned out, was a lot harder than war.

War was largely a series of technical questions, a matter of taking living human bodies and making them dead. There were infinite variations in the tactics and the strategy, of course, nuances in weaponry and technique, but the basic premise was bedrock: you'd done it right if you were alive at the end of the day, and the other poor fool was not. Jakob Rallen, for instance— Gwenna had put a knife through his neck the day before almost without thinking, hurling the blade even as Annick and the rest of the Kettral swept low over the compound. It was almost easy, when it came down to it. Trivial.

Gwenna had never really enjoyed killing. She still had night-mares about the Annurians she'd cut down in the brutal Urghul pits, awful dreams from which she woke soaked in a sweat that felt, in the midnight hours, like hot blood. Even what came later, the men and women she'd killed in proper battle, were hard to stomach when she pondered them from the still, cool darkness between waking and dawn's first light. She could see the pale blue eyes of a horseman she'd stabbed in Andt-Kyl, the way they went suddenly wide as her blade slid past his ribs, then flat, lifeless as broken crockery. In her dreams she tried to talk to him, to scream at him, to urge him to go the fuck home.

The thing about those fights, though, was just that: they had been *fights*. Even at the bloodiest, *especially* at the bloodiest, a combination of rage, and righteousness, and training had carried Gwenna through, her own thudding pulse holding her up even when her mind quailed at the madness of it. What she faced now was something different.

A score of men and women knelt before her in the soft earth beneath the tenebral oak: Rallen's soldiers—the ones that were left—and there at the end, Manthe and Hobb, the traitors. Most kept their faces down, avoiding Gwenna's gaze, avoiding the eyes of the Kettral who stood behind her. Looking at them bound and bruised, it was tough to believe that so few soldiers had tyrannized the Islands so effectively, so brutally, for so long.

The kid at the end had been in Gwenna's own class of cadets—a pale-skinned young woman named Urri. She'd been training to be a sniper, but wasn't very good, and had washed out a year before the Trial. Beside her knelt a middle-aged man. He was weeping silently, tears carving through the grime on his face. Every so often he'd raise his red-rimmed eyes slowly, tentatively, as though hoping Gwenna might have disappeared; every time he found her standing there, fists on her hips, he'd cringe, fold a little further into himself, as though his own dread had cored him out. It went like that straight on down the line.

Gwenna stared at them a moment longer, then, disgusted, raised her eyes to the branches of the ancient tree. Instead of leaves, ten thousand bats hung from the tenebral's twisting limbs. They would wake at dusk in a great rustle of wings, take to the air, harry the creatures of the night, both the large and small, sinking fangs into bird or beast, any creature with hot, beating blood, drinking deep before returning at dawn to roost. The ground beneath Gwenna's feet was soft with the blood that dripped from the bats' fangs. It squelched beneath her boots. The massive oak had no need of sunlight; it drank the spilled blood in through the roots.

The old bastard's going to drink deep today, Gwenna thought grimly, returning her eyes to the captives bound before her.

Justice. It sounded like such a noble word. Clean. Polished.

It seemed strange that justice should come to this—a brutal bloodletting in the shadow of a blood-hungry tree. It would have been easier, in a way, to cut the throats and have done with it, but that was not justice. Justice allowed the accused to speak, to explain, to plead. That was what made it so 'Kent-kissing hard.

"You," Gwenna said, gritting her teeth as she pointed at Urri. "Did you serve with Jakob Rallen?"

The woman's eyelid twitched. Her mouth dropped open, revealing crooked teeth. Language seemed to have abandoned her.

"Of course she did," Qora snarled, stepping forward beside Gwenna. "They all did—you know it as well as I do. You were there when we hauled them out of Rallen's fucking fort. Quit this horseshit, kill them, and have done with it."

Gwenna turned to face the other woman. Of all the newly anointed Kettral, Qora was the one who most reminded Gwenna of herself, of herself before Hull's Trial, before she fled the Islands. A part of her wanted to agree, to slip her blades free of their sheaths, and go at the mass execution as though it were war.

"This is a trial," she said to Qora grimly.

The blood vessels bulged beneath the skin of the woman's shaved scalp. "Fuck your trial. These sons of bitches have been hunting us for months." She slipped a knife from the sheath at her belt. "They've been killing us, murdering people over on Hook, stealing and raping. And now you want to hear them talk? Now you want to give them a chance to *explain*?" She shook her head. Her dark eyes were bleak, fixed on the prisoners. "No. If you won't do it, I'm going to—"

Gwenna's backhand blow took her across the face, knocking her to the ground. The woman snarled as she rolled into a crouch. Despite the blood pouring from her split lip, she'd managed to keep a hold on her knife.

She'll make a good fighter someday, Gwenna noted in the back of her mind, *if she can ever put a rein on that rage.*

The rest of the Kettral were still, staring, unsure what to make of Qora's challenge and Gwenna's sudden violence. Talal raised an eyebrow, but Gwenna shook her head incrementally. She could keep knocking Qora down all day if necessary, but she didn't want it to be necessary. She could feel her own blades, heavy in their sheaths across her back. She made no move to reach for them.

"When we're finished," she said, holding Qora's gaze with her own, "you can tell me if I let them off too easy. When we're done here, you can tell me if there was justice. If you think I've betrayed either you or the Eyrie, you are welcome to come after me with everything you have." She raised her eyes to the other Kettral. "All of you are. *After.*

"Now, we are going to have a trial, and if you get in the way of it, I swear to you, no matter how tight your ass might happen to be, I will put my boot all the way up inside of it and keep kicking until you shut up. The Eyrie has protocol for this, and we are going to follow it."

Qora spat blood into the moist earth beneath the tree. "The Eyrie was *destroyed.*"

"Well," Gwenna replied, "now it's back."

I didn't know.

When it was all finished, that was the phrase uttered more often than any other, uttered in nearly endless variations—screaming, sobbing, pleading.

I didn't know about the murders on Hook.

I didn't know who to trust.

I didn't know about the builders he killed.

I didn't know about the ships he sank.

We were Kettral. . . .

We were just soldiers. . . .

We were fighting for Annur. . . .
I didn't know. . . .
I didn't know. . . .
I didn't know. . . .

Some of the men and women reeked of deceit, eyes shifting away from Gwenna every time they opened their mouths; not everyone could be ignorant of the violence that had held the Islands in thrall for nearly a year. Some of the others, though, seemed genuinely perplexed, baffled to find themselves bound beneath the bloody tree.

"Of course we killed people," said one skinny man with a birthmark across half his face. "That's what Kettral do. We're soldiers."

"It matters," Gwenna ground out, "*who* you kill. And why."

He shook his head blankly, perplexed. "We followed orders. We didn't know—"

"If you say that one more time," Gwenna replied quietly, "I will cut out your tongue." She jerked a thumb back over her shoulder, toward Qora, and Quick Jak and the others. "They came from Arim, too. They were washouts, just like you. Jakob Rallen tried to give them orders, but when they realized what was happening, they refused. A lot of them *died* for refusing the orders you so happily followed."

The man just stared at her. "They were traitors."

He was still saying it, hours later, still in utter disbelief, when she finally cut his throat.

In the end, they killed all of Rallen's soldiers. Gwenna did some of the grisly work herself, partly because it seemed necessary to acknowledge her role in the whole affair, partly to set an example for the other Kettral: "This is not about vengeance," she said as the first body dropped. "It is about justice. You will kill quickly, cleanly, or you will join the dead."

It didn't take long. That fact, as much as the blood itself, made Gwenna sick. It should have taken longer, it should have been *harder* to turn two dozen men and women into meat. She forced the thought aside, turning her attention finally to Manthe and Hobb. She'd left them for last partly so that they could see the fate brought on them by their own betrayal, mostly because Gwenna herself wasn't sure what to say. They'd tried, after all, to fight against Jakob Rallen, had endured the same dangers and privations as the others for so long. . . .

"Why?" Gwenna asked quietly.

She expected screaming from Manthe and bluster from Hobb. That was what she'd faced, more or less, since first descending into the Hole. Instead, they were both silent. Despite the ropes binding their arms behind their backs, Manthe had sagged against her husband's side, and he'd managed to shift slightly to let her lay her head against his shoulder. Gwenna realized, as she stared at the married couple, that she'd never seen them outside the flickering firelight of the cave. They looked older in the sunlight, exhausted. Even Hobb, who had seemed so strong in the shadows, was obviously well past his best fighting years. Manthe didn't look terrified anymore; her dark eyes were weary, resigned.

"Spare us the charade," Hobb murmured, meeting Gwenna's gaze. "We all know where this ends."

"I want to know why," Gwenna said again.

For a long time, she thought he would refuse to answer. He turned away, pressed his lips to his wife's head, just where her graying hair met her brow. She closed her eyes and smiled weakly—the first smile Gwenna had ever seen from the woman. After a long time, Hobb sighed, and turned back to Gwenna.

"You think you understand good and evil. Right and wrong. Justice and betrayal." He shrugged. "I don't know. Maybe you do. I'll tell you one thing, though, that you don't understand: love."

He shook his head, as though he himself were surprised at the notion.

"I would do anything for Manthe. I thought your idiocy was going to get her hurt. Killed. I did what I could to protect her."

"You were *wrong*," Gwenna said, forcing down whatever stone was rising in her throat.

He shrugged again. "That's clear now. It wasn't then."

"But . . ."

"I'm done explaining," he said, shaking his head. "It's not something you can explain."

He turned away. His wife looked up, met his eyes, and smiled wider.

"I'm sorry," she said.

"As am I, my love," he replied gently.

They kissed tenderly and for a long time, ignoring Gwenna, ignoring everyone, as though for just that moment they were alone, unbound, free, as though the bright, unfeeling blade of justice were not waiting just a pace away.

"If I never have to do that again, it'll be too soon," Gwenna said.

Talal nodded, refilled her wooden tankard, and passed it back to her.

After the executions, Gwenna had spent the entire afternoon in the ocean. She swam the circuit from Qarsh to Hook and back three times, until she finally felt the salt waves had washed the blood from her skin, her scalp, from beneath her nails, until the trembling was gone from her arms, replaced by honest exhaustion. When she finally waded out of the water onto the beach by the Kettral headquarters, Talal and Annick were waiting. The sniper was holding tankards and, instead of her bow, a long staff of something that looked like bone. Talal had a small wooden barrel beneath his arm.

"Someone please tell me we're going to get fantastically drunk," Gwenna said as she slicked the seawater from her skin.

"We're going to get fantastically drunk," Talal said.

Gwenna glanced at Annick, then down at the tankards—three

of them. "The last time I checked, you didn't drink beer. You always claimed it messed up your shooting."

Annick shrugged. "That's when we're training. Or on a mission."

"Which is pretty much always."

"Not tonight," the sniper said. "Besides, I could drink half that barrel and still shoot better than anyone within five hundred miles."

Talal chuckled quietly. "Was that a boast, Annick?"

"Just a fact."

"What about *that*?" Gwenna asked, pointing at the pale staff.

"Kettral bone," Annick replied. "Stronger than wood, lighter. All Kettral snipers make their own bow after the Trial. I never had the chance."

Gwenna stared. "Tell me you didn't slaughter one of our very few remaining birds so that you could have a slightly better bow."

"It's from the storeroom. And the bow will be much better. Not slightly better."

Talal just shook his head, while Gwenna tried to imagine what that might mean.

"Do you think there's a limit," she asked finally, "to the distance from which you'd like to be able to kill people?"

The sniper's brow wrinkled, as though she were pondering a nonsensical question. "No."

They spent the evening and the first half of the night out on the breakwater at the harbor's head. Gwenna threw stones into the waves, Annick worked her bone bow stave with her belt knife, and Talal kept refilling the tankards when they were dry. For just a while, it was possible to forget the corpses of the traitors they'd burned, the people they'd lost, the justice they'd meted out. It was almost possible to forget everything, to believe they were still cadets shirking some miserable assignment, that when they finished the barrel they would stumble back along the uneven stones of the breakwater to find the Eyrie whole and buzzing with life—men and women in the ring, in the mess hall, coming and going from the barracks. They might run into Valyn and Laith, the Flea or Gent or Blackfeather Finn. They might pull third watch for absconding, but that would be the worst of it. No one would ask them to settle the big issues, to solve the questions of life and death. That was what command was for.

Only now we are *the command,* Gwenna thought, staring at the lights of Hook where they reflected off the black water of the sound.

"How did it happen?" she muttered drunkenly, aloud.

"Which part?" Talal asked.

Gwenna waved a hand around her, trying to indicate Qarsh, the Islands, the whole busted world. "This."

"What?" the leach asked, nudging her in the ribs. "A year ago you didn't expect to be running the entire Eyrie?"

"I'm *not,*" Gwenna protested.

"You are," Annick said, without looking up from her bow.

"That's insane."

The sniper just shrugged.

"Annick's right," Talal said, voice sober, subdued. "According to Kaden, Daveen Shaleel made it out, but she's down in the Waist somewhere, if she's even still alive. We are here."

"So *you* run it," Gwenna snapped.

The leach shook his head. "You're the Wing leader. You're in charge."

"I don't *want* this."

"When did that start mattering?" Annick asked. "We're soldiers. We do what we have to. Wanting doesn't come into it."

"What a comfort."

"I wasn't trying to be comforting."

"I *know* that, Annick," Gwenna snapped. She hurled another rock into the water. It disappeared, the splash swallowed by the relentless wash of the waves. Behind them somewhere, bunked down in the old Eyrie barracks, were seventeen men and women, cadets who had become washouts who had become, finally, Kettral. They'd survived the fight against Jakob Rallen, but that was hardly the last fight.

"They're gonna wish they'd never left Arim," Gwenna muttered.

"Maybe," Talal said. "Maybe not."

Annick slipped a bowstring from her pocket, bent the newly finished stave, and fit the string to the bow. She'd carried an arrow with her, all the way out to the end of the breakwater. Gwenna watched as the sniper nocked it silently, drew the bow, then let fly directly at the moon. The feathered shaft climbed against pale light, climbed higher than any normal arrow, impossibly high, then dropped out of sight.

"Well, that was a waste of an arrow," Gwenna said.

Annick shrugged. "It's nice, once in a while, to shoot at something you can't hit."

Talal chuckled.

After a moment, Gwenna kicked back the last of her ale, then set the tankard on the stone. "All right. We've got five birds. Which means five Wings."

"The numbers don't quite work out," Talal observed.

"So they don't quite work out. We stock up tonight with munitions, blades, and blacks. We're in the air at first light."

The leach raised his eyebrows. "Where are we going?"

"We're going where they need us," Gwenna replied. "We're going where the fight is."

40

The short, sturdy horses penned inside a wide corral at the edge of the village whickered nervously as Kaden and Long Fist passed.

They smell the strangeness on us, he thought. *They know that something's wrong.*

Cook fire smoke mixed with the thick, wet smell of the mud and reeds. It rose in twisting plumes from a dozen fire pits before the open doors of the reed huts, hovering for a moment, then torn apart by the warm wind blowing down out of the mountains. Men and women in loose tan robes tended those fires, cooking fish and plantains over the open coals. They watched the two strangers approach silently, their dark, weather-battered faces betraying nothing. They raised no voices, either in challenge or welcome.

"This could take time," Kaden murmured. "If Triste is even here."

"A matter of moments," Long Fist replied. "There are only so many huts."

"At least two dozen. She could hide for half the morning, especially if the locals are helping her. Searching—"

"We do not search."

Before Kaden could ask what that meant, a couple of children came darting toward them, chattering a strange babble as they swooped in, then doubling back quick as swallows, shouting to friends or companions Kaden couldn't see. They couldn't have been much more than five, a girl and boy, siblings maybe, dark hair and eyes, brown skin made browner by hours playing in the dirt. They were the sort of village children you might find anywhere from the Romsdals to the Waist.

When Kaden and Long Fist reached the town's central square, they found a knot of men and women drawn up before the largest of the thatched huts, all facing them warily. A couple of the men held axes—the sort of thing they might use on the cedars up in the mountain valleys—and one of the women clutched a long knife at her side, blade still bloody from the antelope that hung half gutted from a low branch a dozen paces distant. Tools, not weapons. It was possible that the villagers had just been surprised going about their morning's work. There was something in those postures, however, that looked guarded, and when Kaden shaped his face into a smile, no one smiled back.

"We're looking for a girl," he said. "A young woman. Black hair. Violet eyes. Striking. Probably very tired."

It was tempting to say the rest of it, to warn these people that even as he spoke soldiers were coming, well-trained men who would burn the village to the dirt to find their quarry, men who would not be deterred by a pair of axes and a skinning knife. Such an announcement, however, would cause almost as much confusion as the attack itself, and if Triste *was* here, he didn't want to lose her in the ensuing panic.

"Have you seen her?"

No one spoke. Kaden studied their faces, their hands. The tightness around the eyes was obvious, the slight twist in the lips, the whitening knuckles. One woman glanced over her shoulder toward a cluster of other huts, then jerked her head back as though burned. Kaden's heart beat faster. He forced it to slow. Triste was here—that much was obvious. They just needed to get her out.

"We are her friends," he said, holding up his hands, palms out, as though in surrender.

The silence held for a moment. Then a man with a headscarf piled high on his head stepped forward. He might have been thirty-five or forty, thin, barefoot beneath the hem of his robe. Even in the morning's weak light, Kaden could make out the ropy strength in his shoulders and arms, the scars webbing the backs of his hands.

"There's no one here," he said in imperfect Annurian, voice surprisingly soft, like the wash of wind through the reeds.

Kaden suppressed a grimace. "Please," he said. "She's in danger."

The man met his eyes. "We say a thing here: Beware sand from the south, rain from the west, news from the north, and strangers walking out of the east." He pursed his lips, glanced up at the sky. "There is no news. No sand or rain . . ." He turned his attention pointedly to Kaden, then to Long Fist, leaving the rest unsaid.

Kaden glanced over his shoulder. The scrubby trees obscured the dust kicked up by il Tornja's soldiers, but they would be closer, closing.

"We know that she is here," Kaden said, turning back to the group, "or that she has been here recently. . . ."

Before he could finish, Long Fist stepped forward. The shaman didn't talk until he stood just a hand's breadth from the man who had spoken. When the villager took an uncertain step back, Long Fist moved forward to fill the gap. It reminded Kaden of a dance he'd seen years ago in the Dawn Palace, only there was no play in these movements, no flirtation. The Urghul was a full head higher than the other, and he had to crane his neck to look down at him.

"What . . . ," the slender man began, raising his hands.

Long Fist lifted a single finger, pointed it straight up, then pushed the other man's jaw shut. Kaden thought for a moment that the shaman was leaving his finger there, the nail pressed into the soft flesh just behind the chin, to keep the other from speaking. Then he saw the blood, saw the man's body twitch, saw him rise up onto his toes as Long Fist drove that finger up and up, through the skin and the muscle folded beneath. Another heartbeat and the bloody finger appeared in the opening mouth, behind the lower teeth and beneath the tongue, curving up and out, like a hook through a fish's jaw. The villager twitched, a series of spasmodic convulsions, but made no move to pull back or to fight, as though he were too shocked by the abrupt attack to do more than dangle from the Urghul's crooked finger.

Kaden stepped forward, started to object, but a woman's scream cut him off. She was the one with the knife. While the others stared, paralyzed, she lunged, staggering across the dusty ground with her blade outstretched, small features smeared with fear and fury. Long Fist glanced toward her, smiled, then pursed his lips as though he wanted to blow her a kiss. She covered another two paces. Then he whistled—a high sound slicing through her scream—and she collapsed, knife clattering to the gravel. The shaman watched as she thrashed at the dirt, suddenly blind to everything but her own agony. She clawed at her ears, pressed her palms hard against the sides of her head as though trying to block out that piercing whistle. As she rolled into a tiny ball, blood seeped between her fingers.

Long Fist ignored the man dangling from his finger, turning instead to his horrified neighbors.

"Where is the girl?"

A dozen of the villagers ran, darting away into the high scrub like panicked rabbits. The rest just stared, eyes scrubbed blank by their terror. One man started sobbing.

"No," Kaden said, raising his hand as though there was anything in the world he could do with it. "We don't need to do this. Let him go, let him—"

"You forget the stakes," Long Fist said, turning to Kaden. "The game is about more than these few ragged souls."

His blue eyes had gone a gray so dark it looked black. Kaden was reminded suddenly, incongruously, of Valyn. He shoved the memory away, hauling his mind back to the moment.

"They are not our *enemies*."

"I said nothing of enemies." Long Fist returned his attention to the man suspended from his finger. The villager had gone into spasms. "The Urghul would account this a great honor."

"We're not among the Urghul," Kaden said.

"Indeed. And so here, it is merely an expedient." He glanced over the crowd. "Bring the girl. Now."

And then, as though responding to the shaman's words, the door to one of the reed huts slammed open. Triste stepped from the dark square under the wooden lintel into the day's dwindling light. Her violet eyes blazed with the sun's reflected fire, and she held an arm out before her, palm up, as though she planned to take Long Fist in her fingers and crush him.

"*Stop,*" she said. For a moment Kaden didn't know if the command was hers, or if it came from the goddess inside. Then he saw the fear painted across her face, saw that her legs were shaking. Not the goddess then. Just the girl. Her gaze snagged on Kaden. Anger blazed there, and betrayal, and hopeless bafflement, then she was rounding on Long Fist, pushing her way through the assembled villagers.

"I'm here," she said. "I'm *here*. These people have done nothing but help me, hide me when no one else would. Leave them *alone*."

Long Fist didn't speak. He tossed aside the villager without a glance, ignoring the man where he fell writhing to the dirt. His eyes were fixed on Triste, his lips pulled back to reveal his sharpened teeth. He tilted his head back, dragged a long slow breath in through his nose, then blew it out between pursed lips.

"Ciena," he said. The word started in a snake's hiss, ended with a vowel drawn so thin it was little more than air. Then, again, shaking his head. "Ciena. How did you lose yourself in such a creature?"

Triste looked terrified, but she didn't shy away. *She never has,* Kaden realized. Not in Ashk'lan or the Bone Mountains, not in Assare or the Dead Heart.

"I know who you are," she said quietly.

The shaman shook his head. "You have no idea what I am. Your mind could not hold it all."

"What about *her*?" Triste demanded, tapping at the side of her skull. "That's what you came for, right? That's why you're *both* here," she went on, including Kaden in her gesture. "To carve her out? Well, I guess that means my mind was large enough for your fucking wife."

"Wife." The shaman seemed to find the word amusing. "She is not my wife. And you have seen only the smallest shard of what she is."

Triste opened her mouth to respond, but no words escaped her throat. The things that happened next took place so fast Kaden could only catch the fragments: a low, fluttering whir; a breeze just at his ear, as though a small-boned bird had flitted by; a slight shape catching the morning's light, flashing it back; a blur as Long Fist turned; his shudder, then stumble; a bright splash of blood across the dirt.

For a heartbeat the details refused to cohere. Kaden could see the hilt of the knife, see the Urghul chieftain pitching forward, but his mind balked at the meaning tangled up inside the motion. All this time they'd been trying to save Triste, trying to get to the goddess trapped inside her.

And we were looking at the wrong thing.

As Long Fist reeled, Kaden spun, searching for the attacker, suddenly certain that il Tornja's men had been faster than he expected. Or they'd managed to get to the village first, somehow, to lay an ambush. As he struggled with the raw facts of the attack, the head-high reeds fringing the clearing parted, and a man with a spear stepped out into the open.

No, Kaden realized. *Not a spear, a* naczal.

Rampuri Tan stood a dozen paces distant, studying the

bleeding figure of the Urghul chieftain with that hard, unreadable stare Kaden remembered so well from his years at Ashk'lan. Long Fist stumbled to one knee, groaned, tried to stand, then dropped again. The knife wasn't large, but it was buried to the hilt in the shaman's side—more than deep enough to puncture a lung, to reach the heart, even. Kaden stepped between Long Fist and Tan.

"You just destroyed us all."

The older monk shook his head slowly. "I told you already. The creature behind you is not what he claims."

"He is a god," Kaden said, "and you have killed him."

Long Fist wasn't dead yet—Kaden could hear the wet, labored breathing just a pace behind him—but he was dying, and fast. The villagers, transfixed by the sudden violence, bore shocked and sickened witness to the scene. One woman vomited onto the ground. The man Long Fist had hoisted into the air just moments earlier kept twitching in the dust, moaning quietly.

"He is Csestriim," Tan said, stepping forward into the clearing. "Just as il Tornja is Csestriim."

"No," Kaden replied. "I explained it to you in the Heart. . . ."

"You painted a picture of your own error." The monk shook his head as he approached. "This creature," he continued, lowering his *naczal* toward Long Fist, "sent us through the *kenta* into a trap, a slaughter. Dozens of il Tornja's men were waiting with bows and blades."

"Il Tornja is sending soldiers to *all* the *kenta*," Kaden protested. "He's *hunting* Long Fist, not colluding with him."

"Then where were the men," Tan asked, spinning the spear in a curt arc, as though testing its balance, "when you stepped through the gate to the Dead Salts?"

Kaden stared, uncertain how to respond. The cold, stone memory of Ashk'lan flooded his mind, the years sitting on ledges and running the vertiginous trails, trying to scrape away the last remnant of the self. Tan had taught him the lesson a hundred times in a hundred ways: *The mind is a flame. Blow it out, or it will blind you.*

"Ran il Tornja and Long Fist," Tan continued implacably, "have just destroyed the Ishien. They have gutted the last order that remembered the old war, and they have done it posing as foes to each other all the while."

Tan reasoned like a man building a stone wall: *Here is a fact. Here is a fact. Here is a fact. The world is no more than this.* Kaden shoved at that wall, attacking the individual blocks with the crowbar of his own logic. Nothing budged. Il Tornja had freed Triste. Triste and Long Fist passed the *kenta*. For all his alleged loathing, Long Fist had never struck directly at the *kenarang*.

"No," Triste said. Her eyes blazed violet. "You're wrong."

Tan turned his gaze on her. "And now this creature leaps to their defense. The truth is clear as the sky. Open your eyes to it."

Open your eyes. Clear away the blindness of the self. After half a lifetime, Kaden had mastered the Shin method, and what wisdom had it brought him? Tan's wall was unassailable, but a wall was not the world.

"Surely," Kaden said quietly, "there are other ways of knowing the truth."

The monk shook his head. "This is the babble of mystics and fools."

He lowered the strange spear's blade to Kaden's chest. Kaden could feel the cold gray metal on his skin.

"Move," Rampuri Tan said quietly.

Kaden looked down at the spearpoint. There would be no fighting against his old *umial*. Tan had destroyed a dozen *ak'hanath* alone in the Bone Mountains. He had stood against Ekhard Matol and his Ishien as Kaden escaped from the Dead Heart. The monk was as deadly with that *naczal* as any fighter Kaden had seen, and Kaden himself didn't even have a weapon.

There could be no fight, but neither could he simply stand aside to allow the slaughter to play out.

"No," he said.

Tan's eyes were dark, unreadable. "You should have stayed at Ashk'lan."

"Ashk'lan was destroyed."

"You would have made a fine monk." Tan drew the spear back, "But this is no world for monks."

He is going to kill me, Kaden thought. Fear and anger scrabbled against his composure, cats dropped in a steel bucket to drown. Kaden broke their necks, one, then the other, using that quick motion of the mind that Tan himself had taught him during those cold, gray-blue days among the peaks. The calm that came was glacial, older than all human struggle, a final gift from a *umial* to his last pupil. *It does not matter,* the wind whispered. *It doesn't matter.* The words seemed wrong somehow, but Kaden could find no error in them.

Rampuri Tan opened his mouth to say something else—a last demand, a farewell—then stiffened. Instead of words, blood gushed out, hot and thick as vomit, so much blood that Kaden could only stare as it splashed over the thirsty ground. Tan half bent, swaying on his feet. Blood poured from between his teeth, running down his chin, as though some invisible blade had ripped him apart inside, from the gut straight through the heart in one vicious, inexplicable stroke. It seemed that so much blood erupting so suddenly should have dropped him where he stood, but Tan was still standing—leaning on his *naczal,* but standing—eyes fixed on something just beyond Kaden.

Kaden half turned to find that Long Fist had shoved himself into a seated position. The knife remained buried in his side, but he had leveled a scarred hand toward Rampuri Tan, seemed to be squeezing with it, twisting, as though those long fingers were wrapped around human organs rather than empty air. Rage illuminated his face.

Tan groaned, a sound like stone sliding over stone. Blood ran from his ears now, from the sockets of his eyes, but he took a halting step forward, then another, ignoring Kaden entirely, ignoring the blood and pain, his gaze, his whole body bent toward the wounded shaman bleeding out into the dirt. Long Fist snarled, wrapped his hand tighter, and Tan stumbled to a knee.

"You are finished, monk," the shaman said. There was a sound like snapping wood. Spasms took Tan's flesh, shook it violently. *His bones,* Kaden realized, stomach lurching into his mouth. *Long Fist is breaking his bones.* Blood smeared the shaman's white teeth when he smiled. "This is your end."

But it was not.

Somehow, impossibly, Tan forced himself back onto his feet, swayed a moment, then stumbled forward, one halting pace, then two, then three, until he stood within reach of the wounded Urghul chieftain. Kaden watched, lost in the stillness of his own amazement. Slowly, agonizingly, Tan raised the *naczal*.

Long Fist was sweating now, the hot sheen mixing with his blood. He grimaced, snarled, then twisted his hand again. Tan's leg buckled beneath him. He dropped, but kept the *naczal* raised. The shaman's blue eyes went wide.

"It is finished," Tan managed, choking the words out through the blood. "I am ending it."

For half a heartbeat, the two men were still, silent as a painting. The pale leach half-sitting, one hand pressed into the dirt, holding him up, the other cast out before him. The dark-skinned monk knelt, spear held in both hands above his head, as though it were a splitting maul. Blood glistened on both faces, bright with the rising sun. The whole scene might have been a fresco in the Dawn Palace, or a tapestry.

Or a saama'an, Kaden thought, staring at the motionless tableau.

It was as though the action were already over and he were just remembering it, as though everything that had to happen had already happened long, long ago. The morning wind had fallen away. The clouds hung still, nailed against the sky.

Kaden stepped forward into that stillness. He caught the cool, smooth shaft of the *naczal* as it hung there at its height, then pulled it free of his *umial's* trembling hands. It was easy. Horribly easy. Tan's broken grip was weaker than a child's, the bones of his wrist and arm shattered beneath the skin. How he had managed to keep holding the weapon at all, Kaden had no idea.

"You can't kill him," Kaden murmured, dropping to his knees beside the monk. Some sensation he could not name had caught him in its jaws. "He is a god. Our god."

Tan dragged his gaze away from Long Fist. His eyes wandered over the land as though lost, over the huts and reeds, over the still water of the oasis, then settled finally on Kaden. The first time he opened his mouth, nothing came out. He ground his teeth, hauled in another breath, then managed a single word, weak as the wind: ". . . wrong . . ."

With all context pared away, there was no saying who was wrong: Kaden, or Long Fist, or Tan himself. Kaden started to reply, to protest, but the monk's eyes had already moved past him once again, past the village this time, past the branches of the trees, to the great space of the sky, the unplumbed blue depth of it, the cool, unrelenting emptiness. One heartbeat Rampuri Tan was there, a mortal creature shaking in his own shattered flesh . . . and then he was gone.

Kaden ignored the cries that had erupted behind him, the mad panic of the villagers finally tumbling into motion. He stared at Tan's face. . . .

No, he reminded himself, the word cold as winter stone. *Not his face. Not anymore. Just meat and bone.* With a gentle motion he closed the drying orbs that had so recently been eyes, then turned away, from the dead back toward the dying.

Long Fist had fallen over into the dirt. He was breathing, but blood flecked his lips, dribbled down his chin. Kaden turned him slightly. Found the blade buried in his side. He knew next to nothing about the treatment of wounds in battle, but he had seen sheep die, and goats, had wielded the knife himself a hundred times. Long Fist was hurt, and badly, was bleeding into the dirt even as Kaden watched.

The thought was too big and so Kaden shoved it aside, focusing instead on the immediate situation. The soldiers were still coming. They were off to the east, somewhere, but they would be closing. Even more urgent, the townsfolk, loosed from their terror by the monk's attack, were circling like jackals, growling and shouting, stabbing fingers at Long Fist, the man who moments before had held their own so cruelly in his hands. They wanted to see him finished, but fear still held them back; the lion was dying, but he was not dead.

That fear might buy us a hundred heartbeats, Kaden thought, scanning the small crowd. *No more.*

"Can you move?" he asked, glancing toward the paddock with the horses. "Can you ride?"

Long Fist twisted his head to meet Kaden's eyes. Kaden had expected to see something human there, pain or fear, but there was nothing human in the shaman's gaze. His voice, when he spoke, did not sound like a broken thing, but like something that had done the breaking.

"Not like this. Not with this in me."

He forced himself up from the dirt. Then, slowly, deliberately as a violinist taking up his bow, the shaman wrapped a hand around the shaft buried in his side, then tightened his grip. He closed his eyes as he pulled the knife free, but the expression playing over his face was not one of agony but of careful attention, as though he were trying to make out some terribly beautiful, terribly distant music. When the knife was clear, blood welled from the wound, surging with each heartbeat, soaking his clothes and pooling beneath him. Long Fist ignored it, turning instead to Tan's body.

"He hid it until the very end, but there was music in your monk. Most of your kind would have folded beneath the note

I sounded in his bones. I wish I could have drawn out longer the great chord of his agony."

"He's dead now," Kaden said. "He's not important. We need to get out of here."

He glanced over his shoulder as he said the words. The villagers were circling. One of the men had half lifted his ax, as though testing its weight. Even the empty-handed among them had balled fingers into fists or claws.

Long Fist rose slowly to a knee. Too slowly. Kaden seized him by the elbow, dragging him roughly upright, then searched for Triste. The girl stood a few paces away. She was wringing her desert robe between her hands, but made no move to step forward. Kaden started to shout to her, something about getting on the horses, escaping, then stopped himself. Shouting would do nothing but drive the villagers more quickly toward the coming violence. He took a half breath, ordered his thoughts, and turned to the townsfolk instead.

"Soldiers are coming," he said. "They will be here before the sun crests these trees, and they will kill you all."

The warning was for them, but not just them. He needed to talk his way clear of the town, and he needed Triste to follow. Seizing the girl was no option. He might be able to drag her screaming for a mile, maybe two; certainly not far enough to outpace il Tornja's men. If they were going to escape, she needed to hear what was coming, needed to believe it.

"What happened here was wrong," Kaden said, gesturing to the twitching body of the man Long Fist had hooked through the throat. It was hard to say what was wrong with him. The wound would have been painful, excruciating, but the mindless writhing was the product of something more. The woman beside him still bled from the ears, and the shaman hadn't even *touched* her. "It was wrong. It was a mistake, and we will fix it."

Long Fist gave a jerk at his side. Kaden turned, half expecting to find the Urghul dying on his feet, finally losing control of the flesh he had so thoroughly possessed. Instead, Kaden realized with horror, the shaman was laughing, a low, slow sound, almost a growl.

"What would I fix?" he asked, gesturing with a bloody hand to the man and woman, both obviously lost in their own pain. "I have kindled something bright inside their minds. I will not put it out."

"They haven't done anything. . . ."

"They did nothing," Long Fist agreed. He seemed barely able to stand, but his voice was strong. "They lived gray, quiet lives, and I have made them sing."

Triste shouldered her way forward angrily. "You're *killing* them."

"No," the shaman said. "I never break an instrument." Despite the hemorrhaging wound in his side, he glanced at the mound of flesh that had been Tan, then smiled. "Almost never."

It was that smile, Kaden thought later, that goaded the villagers out of their hesitation. They understood nothing of what was happening—how could they?—but two of their number were writhing like fish hauled out of the water, tossed onto the shore to flop themselves dead, and they knew who had done the tossing. Someone toward the back, a woman, Kaden thought, started screaming, and then those in front tumbled toward them like a wave.

They're going to kill him, Kaden thought. *They're going to finish killing him.*

He hauled on the shaman's arm, but Long Fist might have been rooted to the dirt, might have been some piece of statuary carved from the bedrock itself.

"Run," Kaden growled, but the Urghul chieftain shrugged him off.

Standing straight for the first time since Tan's attack, he faced the fury of the townsfolk, raised a hand, and flicked his fingers outward, as though to sling clear the blood that had been pooling in his palm. It was a small gesture, almost delicate, and it hit the men and women of that nameless town like a wall. Flesh ripped open on some invisible fence. Bones shattered, the rough ends stabbing through ragged flesh. Suddenly, from the dark spaces between the reeds, a hundred dark-winged desert birds burst screaming into the sky. The villagers screamed too, men and women, young and old, screamed, then collapsed, clawing with the wreckage of their hands at their own bodies, as though there were some burning coal buried deep inside, as though they would rather die than keep it in a moment longer.

Only Triste remained upright.

"Why?" Triste demanded, stumbling toward the villagers, then half kneeling, stretching out her arms as though she were about to gather them all into her embrace, to lift them clear of their suffering.

"It is only what they would have done to us," Long Fist replied, nodding to that awful tangle of flesh. "I have visited their own fury upon them."

"You *attacked* them," Triste screamed.

Kaden shook his head. A part of him was as shocked as she was, but he cordoned it off, set it aside. There was no time for shock. Not if they wanted to escape. Not if they wanted to survive. He glanced east, past the last huts, to where the sky had grown bright as bronze. He could just make out soldiers, dozens of soldiers, coming over the headland maybe a mile distant.

He stabbed a finger at them. "*Triste.* Those are il Tornja's men. They have been marching west for days."

She wrenched her eyes from the carnage at her feet. The soldiers were small, but impossible to miss. Her voice, when she could speak, was a whisper, that same word she seemed unable to avoid: "Why?"

"For you," Kaden snapped. "For the goddess inside."

"How did they know?" she asked. "You told them. . . ."

"The *ak'hanath*. Those huge spiders that tracked us through the Bone Mountains."

Triste let out a wail, a high sound close to breaking.

"We have to *go*," Kaden insisted.

"These people," Triste protested, turning back to the fallen villagers.

Kaden shook his head, kept his eyes from the faces. "We can't help them."

"No," she said. Then, with more conviction, leveling a finger at Long Fist's chest, "*No*. I won't go anywhere with him."

Kaden cut her off, surprised at the edge in his own voice. "You were worried about these people?" he demanded, gesturing to the mangled bodies of the villagers. "You were worried about two dozen souls at the edge of the desert? You carry a goddess inside you, Triste. So does Long Fist. If you do not survive, both of you, then this human destruction will be nothing. If you do not survive this day, then *no one does*."

Triste's face twisted, caught between one horror and another. She stared at Kaden a moment, then looked over at Long Fist. The shaman's pale brow had gone ash-gray. His blue eyes burned in their sockets, as though with fever.

"Can you stop them?" Kaden asked the man. "The way you did with . . ." He gestured to the still-twitching villagers.

The shaman tilted his head to one side, as though listening to his own beating heart. "Not all of them," he said finally. "This body is weak and bleeding."

"Can you fix it?" Kaden asked. "Use a kenning to stitch up your own wound?"

"No. It is not permitted."

"Permitted by *whom*? Who's stopping you?"

"There are rules. I did not sculpt the shape of the world. This flesh cannot mend itself." He turned to Triste, ran a tongue over his lips. "The goddess inside the girl, however—she could hem the wound with a flick of her smallest finger."

"No," Triste said, taking a step back. "Never."

"Triste is not Ciena," Kaden said. "And she cannot call her forth."

Long Fist grimaced. "Then we flee." The last word sounded

like a curse on his lips, as though such surrender bothered him more than the life leaking out of him.

"You can't," Triste spat, half defiant, half triumphant. "Not with that. You'll bleed out."

Long Fist studied her. Despite the approaching soldiers, he showed no urgency. "How can you hold her inside and still understand so little?"

"I know you're dying," Triste snarled.

"Dying," the shaman replied, "is not dead."

He turned from the girl, then beckoned to the knife that lay, bloody and forgotten, half a pace away. It flew to his hand like some sharp-beaked bird of prey. Long Fist held it delicately between his fingers, examining the steel as though reading some lost text etched into the blade. Then the metal began to glow a dull, sullen red. Long Fist pursed his lips and blew on it, like a man before a dying fire. At the breath, the red flamed into russet, then sun-hot gold. The shaman smiled, then pressed the glowing blade against the wound. Kaden could hear the sizzle and scorch of blood, could smell the burning meat. Any man would have collapsed beneath the pain, but Long Fist was not a man, not really, and instead of collapsing, he straightened, stiffened, back arching as though with pleasure or bracing cold. Then he threw the knife aside.

"Quickly," he said, leveling a long finger toward the west. "There is a *kenta* in the mountains. The soldiers and the *ak'hanath* cannot follow us through."

Kaden stared. "Il Tornja has moved to seize the *kenta*. That's what Tan said. We've seen it ourselves."

Long Fist shook his head. "He would have to get ahead of us. There has been no dust."

"How far?" Kaden asked.

"A night and then a day."

"Will you make it?"

Long Fist glanced down at his body as though it were an old robe he intended to throw aside. "The flesh is flagging, but there is strength in it still. And this body was riding horses long before I took it for my own."

"I won't go with you," Triste whispered.

Kaden extended a hand to her, but she jerked back. "It's the only way."

"I could stay here," she said quietly. "Die on my own terms."

"Are these your terms?" Kaden asked.

Triste bit her lip.

Kaden pointed east, toward the soldiers. "These are *his* terms. Il Tornja's. Everything that's happened to you since you left Ciena's temple happened because of *him,* and if he finds you here, he wins."

She shook her head, lips drawn back in a rictus of indecision, eyes fixed on Kaden.

"And what about me?" she demanded quietly. "How do *I* win? You don't care at all about that, do you?"

"Right now," Kaden replied, "just living a little longer . . . *that* is winning. And to do that, we need to move west, move *now,* put a little space between us and danger."

Long Fist's rough laughter cut through the silence that followed.

"Oh, there is danger everywhere."

Kaden turned to stare into the fevered eyes of the shaman. "Meaning what?"

"There is a reason il Tornja has not tried to reach the mountain *kenta* with his men."

"What's the reason?"

"To reach it, we will need to pass beneath the shadow of the fortress of the Skullsworn. Ananshael's priests are blind to the fact, but the Csestriim gate stands less than a day from Rassambur."

41

All Adare's life, the ancient wall surrounding Annur's inner city had been the haunt of lovers rather than warriors. She'd never been there herself, of course, not until now—the old wall was no place for a princess—but she'd heard of how young couples would stroll hand in hand along the wide walkway at the top of the stonework, whispering quiet nothings to each other as they admired the city stretching out to either side, ducking into the old guard towers that punctuated its length, taking advantage of the shadows. There was even a phrase—*to walk the whole wall*—usually offered up with a knowing wink and a sly smile, that had nothing to do with the lonely watch of long-dead sentries.

That wall had marked the edge of Annur once, centuries earlier. Terial's soldiers had built and manned it to defend against the raiders that would ride down out of the north. That had been before those lands were incorporated into the empire, before the kings and queens of Raalte, Nish, and Breata lost their hereditary titles and their heads, before their scions saw their territory annexed to Annur. After that, the soldiers went north or south or west, where the new wars were, and the city grew, bulging out beyond its walls. Adare had studied the old maps. There had been just a few buildings at first, like barnacles on a ship's hull, then more and more built up over the decades and the centuries until a third of Annur lay beyond the ambit of the wall: temples and squares, markets and thoroughfares, whole neighborhoods, the homes of tens of thousands.

It was, Adare thought, as she stood atop one of Terial's towers, a measure of Annur's success that the architecture of war had been given over so fully to the demands of love. *And a measure of my failure,* she added silently, *to have to seize it back.*

Even as she stared, the Sons of Flame were hard at work north of the wall destroying homes and markets, turning back the progress of centuries, tearing down smithies and stables, rendering temples to their constituent blocks and beams, then erecting those parts again as barricades across the streets and alleyways. Anything valuable, anything that might provide even the most minor succor to the coming foe, they burned. Huge, charred heaps smoldered in every square, in the center of every street, smudging the warm summer air with a sickening, greasy smoke.

Oddly, awfully, Adare found a strange sort of resolve in the destruction. She wouldn't have believed it a year earlier. Razing half of her own city would have seemed, back then, like the rankest defeat, the most ignominious capitulation. And it was, but at least commanding this defense was something she could *do.*

Triste had disappeared beyond her reach, and Kaden, and il Tornja, playing out the last moves of a game she barely understood, a contest on which the future of the world hinged and in which Adare herself was useless, superfluous, or worse. She had no idea how to save the gods or stop the Csestriim, but suddenly, it didn't matter, or didn't matter quite as much. The Urghul were coming, coming to destroy Annur. The council had disbanded, fled, for the most part. Which meant the city's defense had fallen to her, and with it, the terrible need to see so much of that city destroyed.

It was necessary work, but ugly. Even as she watched, a knot of ragged men burst from one of the alleys, their arms piled high with bolts of fine cloth. What they planned to do with the muslin and velvet, Adare had no idea. Probably they didn't either. All they knew was that large swaths of Annur were about

to burn. The rest—the violence, the looting, even the suicides—
it was inevitable from the moment Adare gave the orders.

"Your Radiance."

She turned to find Lehav at the top of the tower steps, one
hand in a stiff salute, the other resting on the pommel of his
sword. Judging from the blood spattered across that hand, the
blade had been out of its sheath, and recently. Despite his spear-
straight posture, the commander of the Sons of Flame looked
exhausted. Dark hollows ringed his eyes. Smoke and charcoal
marred his usually immaculate uniform. Cuts and scrapes criss-
crossed his knuckles and arms.

Adare tensed at the sight of him. "More?"

He nodded.

"All right," she said. "Let's go."

The man hesitated, obviously torn between his military discipline and the need to speak. "It is not necessary, Your Radiance,"
he said finally. "Not every time. It is a pointless risk. The Sons
are seeing to the evacuations and the defense. We can tend to
the executions as well."

"You could," Adare replied. "But these people deserve to
hear what's happening and why. They deserve to hear it from
me."

"Will hearing it from you make them happier when we loop
the nooses around their necks and hang them? Will it matter
to them that the Emperor herself descended from the wall to
explain their misdeeds?"

"I'm not doing it for the condemned," she said quietly.
"They've chosen their course. I'm doing it for the rest."

The soldier shook his head. "And what will they take away
from it?"

"The chance to stay alive."

Adare studied the neighborhood square from atop her horse. It
was unremarkable. Two bakeries, their proprietors probably

locked in lifelong rivalry. A tailor's shop. Three taverns. A small temple to Bedisa. There were hundreds of squares just like it all over the city. By nightfall, the whole swath of houses had to burn, and though Adare knew something of the population living here, she had no way to calculate the lives she would destroy, the dreams she planned to tear down with those old teak homes, the families she would rip apart. It had to be done, but there was no way to tally up the harm, not fully. Not truly.

Behind her, to the east, an oily smoke was already rising into the sky. She could hear the vague roar of fire punctuated by the smash and clatter of buildings that had stood for a hundred years cracking, then collapsing into their own rubble. To the west, in the streets she hadn't yet reached, came shouts and bellows, screams and the high sound of steel scraping against steel. More people were resisting. Which meant this would not be the last of the executions.

The Sons had hung two dozen people already for defiance of Adare's edict. There should have been trials, but there was no time for trials. Anyone who attacked a work crew was killed, the body tossed inside a fallen home to burn with the wood and plaster. Anyone who preached defiance was hauled before Adare herself to hang. It made her sick, but so did the thought of Balendin and the Urghul taking Annur. This was what her life had become: a choice between degrees of sickness.

Gritting her teeth, she turned to face the crowd that had gathered in the square. The Sons had been at their work for days, leading a conscripted crew of slaves and laborers in the brutal work. Even before that, Kegellen's shadowy network of runners had been spreading the word: *All structures north of the old wall are coming down. Take your families. Take what you can carry, and get out.*

The men and women facing Adare now—a crowd of three or four hundred—looked angry, frightened, confused. One woman had a baby in a sling across her breast and a chicken held upside down by the legs. It wasn't clear whether she wanted to rescue the creature or slaughter it; the bird gave a weak flap every so often, but for the most part it hung still, as though it had already accepted its fate. Most people had some sort of bag—clutched to the chest, slung across the back, hanging down dumbly from a slack arm. One old man had held a dozen dogs on leashes, but nothing else—no food for either him or them. Adare had ordered the conversion of hundreds of warehouses by the harbor to shelter these sudden refugees, but there would be no room for the dogs. She wondered who would tell the old man that, wondered who would kill the beasts.

The dogs were sniffing the ground, but the people in the crowd were all staring at her, caught between awe and anger. They lived far from the Dawn Palace. Most would never have seen a Malkeenian or those burning eyes. In a city the size of Annur, people could live, work, and die without ever venturing more than half a mile from their homes. Adare herself might as well have been a myth to them, a subject for speculation rather than outright belief. And now here she was, tired, sweating, sitting atop her horse, about to tell them everything they'd ever known was going to be destroyed, that those who had tried to defend it would be killed.

She shifted her gaze from the crowd to the prisoners who knelt at the square's center, guarded by a dozen Sons of Flame. There were six of them. Two had been beaten so badly that blood streamed down their faces while their heads lolled drunkenly to the side. Were it not for the soldiers behind them, they would have collapsed. Those soldiers stared straight ahead, a portrait of military discipline, but Adare could see the bruised knuckles, the blood spattered across armor. Whether the prisoners at their feet had earned their beatings, she had no idea. Maybe they'd attacked the Sons—dozens of soldiers had already been wounded by roving mobs of angry Annurians—and maybe they'd done nothing more than refuse an order. Adare found herself wishing she knew who to blame—the soldiers or the citizens—found herself wishing she knew who had started it.

But you do *know, don't you?* she thought grimly. *Whatever happened here, it was* you *who started it,* you *who gave the order to clear the streets,* you *who pitted these men with their bronze and blades against people who wanted only to keep their homes, who were just trying to resist the destruction of everything they'd ever known.*

"We are at war," Adare said, raising her voice to block out that other voice inside her mind. "We are at war with the Urghul, and we are losing."

"Haven't seen no Urghul," someone shouted from the crowd. "Just these bastards burning down the city."

"These bastards," Adare replied, "are preparing for a battle. The Urghul have broken past the Army of the North. They are riding on this city even as we speak. Each structure we leave standing beyond this wall is a shield behind which they might shelter, a mask for their movements, an infirmary for their wounded. If we leave this portion of the city standing, we risk the rest, and let me assure you, if they take Annur, we will all die, horribly and in unimagined pain."

"We?" someone shouted from the crowd. "You'll sail out on the last tide, go to one of your other palaces."

The defiance would have been inconceivable a year earlier, when Adare's father still ruled, but that year had played havoc with Annur.

The Emperor's power was an illusion. It always had been. There was the palace, and the palace guard, the Aedolians sworn to guard the royal family, and the legions, and of course Intarra's blazing eyes, all militating for the divine right of the Malkeenian line. None of it mattered. Not really.

That was the mystery at the heart of all power. Power appeared to be something that a ruler had, that she held, that she had taken from the people. The appearance was false. Power was something people *gave,* gave willingly, even if they didn't know it, even if they resented it. The wealthy merchant who paid a tax on every bolt of cloth, the slave who lived day after day under the yoke, the sailors who allowed their boats to be searched by crown officials, the soldiers who refused to break ranks even when their orders were ridiculous, insane—it was these people who gave a ruler her power, offered it up like a sacrifice.

Adare had read more than enough history to be baffled by the fact. Even the greatest writers seemed unequal to the explanation. Maybe people were frightened of chaos, those writers stipulated, frightened of violence. Maybe they were too stupid to rise up. Maybe they were too happy and sated. Too beaten down. Whatever the reasons of ten million men and women for giving up their freedom, history painted one lesson clearly over and over: people obeyed . . . until they did not.

Adare had read about it in tome after tome: that moment when a whole people, as though waking from a collective dream, stopped giving away their power. Sometimes the spark of change was obvious—a murder, a famine—but more often the causes were obscure, endlessly debated. Really, those causes didn't seem to matter. *Something* caused a crack in the veneer of power. The crack spread, ramified, until it was deep enough and wide enough for everyone to see. Then the whole edifice crumbled. When that happened, people died, millions of people, including those who had risen up to defy their rulers in the first place.

This is how it begins, Adare thought, studying the crowd, wondering if this would be the moment the glass bauble of her own rule shattered in her hand.

"You'll burn our homes," someone else shouted. "And then, when the Urghul come, you'll disappear, go somewhere soft and comfortable, leaving us to sleep in the ashes."

Already, the grumbling had gone on too long. Beside Adare, Lehav shifted in his own saddle, testing his sword where it rested in the scabbard. Behind her, she could hear the Sons of Flame preparing. She laid a gentle hand on the general's wrist, holding him back even as she spoke.

"You are wrong," she said. "There is nowhere else to go. Nowhere soft and comfortable. The whole world is on fire, and even were it not, I would stay here. I will stand at the wall when the Urghul come, and though I am no fighter, if it comes to that, I will fight."

"And if the wall falls?"

Adare nodded. "Then I will retreat into the city. I will hide in attics and cellars. I will sneak out at night to poison the food of our foes, to cut their throats, to hobble their horses. When the grain stops arriving, and our fleets stop fishing, I will eat rats. I will sleep wedged beneath floorboards. I will fight until they kill me, and after that, I will become a ghost. I will haunt their dreams, and drag claws across their flesh so that every time a shadow falls across an Urghul face, they will know fear. I will not leave this city, even in death, because it is mine. It is mine, just as it is yours, and regardless of the army arrayed against us, *I will not go.*"

She paused, chest heaving, air burning in her lungs, thighs trembling where they gripped the saddle. She shifted her gaze from face to face, waiting for more bellowed defiance, for the mob to finally fall on her. It did not. Instead, the silence stood like a great stone in the center of the square.

"I will fight the Urghul," she said quietly. "I will kill them." Then, slowly, she turned to the slumped forms of the condemned, the six who had to hang. "And I will see those killed who would jeopardize that fight."

She forced her face into the shape of determination and resolve. The bile rose in her throat.

She'd told Lehav that she came down from the wall to warn the living, but that wasn't the truth, not all of it. A part of her *wanted* them to rise up. She imagined it each time, imagined the thousands of hands clutching her, pulling her from the saddle, slaughtering her on the flagstones. It was a coward's thought, but each time, as the soldiers pulled the nooses tight, it consumed her: if she died, if the mob tore her apart, she would be freed from doing it again, freed from everything that had to happen next.

42

Impossible, Kaden thought.

For the better part of the day they had pressed west on the backs of the desert horses, away from the oasis, across the open flats, then into the first foothills of the Ancaz. As the mountains steepened into cliffs and canyons, however, the exhausted beasts began to lose their footing.

"We have to go on foot," Long Fist had groaned.

It was impossible. Kaden could make it a few miles over flat ground, maybe ten at the outside, tottering forward on exhausted legs, but here in the mountains? The bloodred cliffs loomed up in front of them, thousands of vertical feet stabbing straight into the bleached-blue belly of the sky. Canyons broke the serrated wall, offering tenuous access to the high country beyond, but even those canyons were steep, boulder-choked where they weren't flooded with storm runoff. The terrain would test even rested, healthy runners, and the three of them were anything but rested or healthy. They'd be navigating those canyons all day and all night, provided Long Fist knew the way, fleeing il Tornja's soldiers, hoping to avoid the eyes of whatever guards the Skullsworn posted at the approaches to Rassambur.

Maybe a year ago, Kaden thought grimly, focusing on the ache in his thighs, the twinge in his left ankle that bit a little deeper every stride. *I could have run this as a monk, but I'm not a monk.* Tan had been clear enough about that. Still, there was nothing to do but run or turn back into the swords of the soldiers behind them, and so they ran.

The memory of his slaughtered *umial* dogged Kaden as he hobbled up the canyon, a twinge in his mind, a catch in his chest more painful than the aches of his knees and feet. He could set it aside as Tan had trained him, could slide into the smooth, cool halls of the *vaniate,* but doing so seemed wrong somehow, an evasion. Strange, that unexpected imperative to embrace the suffering. As though what Long Fist had been claiming all along was right, as though pain were ennobling, as though the *vaniate,* the ease of its promised escape, were indeed a profanation.

Kaden glanced over at Long Fist, wondering how long *he* could hold on. The shaman was moving fast, despite his uneven, shambling stride, the wound in his side cauterized and forgotten. As for Triste, Kaden had seen just what she could manage a year earlier, during their flight through the Bone Mountains, and she was fresh now, rested, far more ready than Kaden himself for this desperate trek westward.

And yet, as they ran, he found a strange strength returning, the stirring of the body's memories of all those endless days climbing the high peaks or running the Circuit of Ravens. It wasn't that the ache receded, but that he grew familiar with its contours, as though exhaustion were a home to which he had returned after a long time abroad. The strides which had at first threatened to break him grew increasingly plausible, and though his body throbbed with the effort, as the sun crested overhead, Kaden felt, to his surprise, that he could keep going all day.

Even when they reached the cliffs and began climbing the streambed, scrambling over the broken stone, fighting their way up, up through the choking briars that clustered around the water, he found himself able to keep moving, even to speed up. When he glanced back down the canyon, he could sometimes catch a glimpse of the soldiers, twenty of them at least, laboring up the defile behind. Mostly, he tried not to look back, keeping his eyes on the ground in front of him instead, shrinking the task at hand to a matter of the next few steps.

He lost himself so thoroughly in the landscape of his own motion that when they finally reached a saddle between the peaks, he almost didn't notice it. The sandstone canyon had tightened until it was only shoulder-wide, then too narrow to pass, and when he climbed free, he found himself looking down the other side of the mountains, into a smooth, sweeping valley, red, and yellow, and gold sweeps of unbroken stone. Without thinking, without pausing, he lengthened his stride, loosened his arms for the downhill, chose a line through the chaparral and scattered stones, and started down.

Triste's shout brought him up short. He thought, at first, that something had gone wrong, that il Tornja's soldiers had managed to close the gap, and he skidded to a stop. When he turned, however, Triste wasn't looking back the way they had come. She was pointing at Long Fist. The shaman was still running, but his gait had faded to a rough stumble. He didn't seem to be paying any attention to the ground before him. His eyes were empty, fixed on the far horizon or on some vision only he could see. The endless run would have been a brutal trial for a healthy man, and Long Fist was not healthy. Though his wound was burned shut, the blade had done its damage; purple blood pooled beneath his pale skin. While Kaden and Triste had been grinding out the miles, the Urghul had been dying on his feet by slow degrees.

"We need to take a break," Kaden said, lurching to a halt on wobbling legs. "Drink something."

Long Fist didn't seem to hear him. He continued on, stumbling down the slope until Kaden snagged his arm. The shaman's weight almost brought them both down, and when he did finally stop, he swayed on his feet, then came to rest leaning against Kaden. Triste caught up to them, shook her head in mute exhaustion, then bent over, hands on her knees, lungs heaving in the dry air.

"He needs to stop," Kaden said again.

Triste wasn't looking at him, gave no indication, in fact, that she was listening to him at all, but Kaden addressed the words to her anyway. At some point during the long day, a balance had shifted. Since the Waist, the shaman had held the unspoken threat of pain and madness over Kaden's head like a bright blade, one he could bring down with a snap of his fingers. Even after Tan's attack, in the few hours after they left the oasis and the village, Long Fist had been the meager party's undisputed chief.

No more. There was still a god inside the body, but it seemed as though Meshkent had been baffled to silence by the weakness of his chosen flesh.

He has not felt this, Kaden realized, studying the Urghul. *It is a simple truth that all men die, but he has never lived inside it.*

"We . . . ," Triste gasped, waving a vague hand backward, the way they had come, ". . . can't stop. They . . ."

She trailed off, panting. Kaden turned, shading his eyes from the noonday sun, peering down the canyon they had climbed. There was no sign of the soldiers, but he couldn't see far, not more than a quarter mile, and with the mountain wind keening over the stones, he couldn't hear much more than his own breath rasping in his throat.

"Where is the *kenta*?" Kaden asked, turning back to Long Fist. The shaman didn't respond. Kaden reached up, took him by the shoulders. "How far?"

Slowly those bottomless blue eyes focused. The Urghul looked at Kaden first, then turned to consider the red stone walls and canyons of the high Ancaz mountains.

"That way," he said finally, pointing southwest. "There is a side canyon. It will take us in, then down."

Kaden stared at the shattered land. He could count dozens of canyons from where he stood, a labyrinth of sandstone cuts and defiles. All of them led down eventually, but only one would reach the *kenta*.

"How will we know which canyon to take?" Kaden asked, staring south. "What do we look for?"

"Pillars," Long Fist said. Then, as though goaded on by his own words, he lurched into a run.

"What kind of pillars?" Kaden asked, but the shaman did not turn. Triste looked over, her face a mask of exhaustion, shook her head, then followed.

Kaden didn't follow, not at first. As he struggled to regain his breath, he watched the two figures laboring down the mountain's steep side. From a little distance they looked so human—the blond Urghul beside the black-haired girl, both stumbling, both exhausted. From a distance, you couldn't see the scars webbing Long Fist's skin, or his eyes, couldn't see how terribly beautiful Triste really was. They might have been refugees fleeing some ugly corner of the larger war, two people plucked from the many millions, just trying to survive.

Not at all like gods, Kaden thought, watching them. *How could they possibly be gods?* And then, hard on that thought, another, darker thought: *How can they possibly survive?*

That they had escaped the small village behind them was something of a miracle, as was the fact that they had made their way up and into the mountains. Suddenly, however, these miracles seemed meager, unequal to the coming fight. Even Long Fist's effortless devastation of the villagers seemed inadequate, and as Kaden turned his gaze from the retreating figures to the great maze of the Ancaz, a thought, thin as the dust rising in the east, spread across his mind: *We can't win.*

The despair settled down on him, lead-heavy, fitted to his flesh like a finely tailored coat. At Ashk'lan, he had not felt despair. Or if he had, it had been little more than an echo, a lassitude in the bones, a slowness of the mind that he had learned to recognize and escape. Back then, he had not fully appreciated the gift of the Shin, had not understood the gray weight under which most men labored the length of their days. Even in Annur, sparring pointlessly with the council while the fabric of the republic frayed and tore, he had not felt this hopelessness.

Or the hope, he thought. *Or the hate.* Il Tornja had betrayed him. So had Adare. But they had been stones, pieces to surround, to overpower and remove from the board. Even the prospect of Kaden's own defeat, of his death, of the eradication of all humanity, had been clear but colorless, like frost etched across a winter pane.

Since joining Long Fist, however, his emotions had come back in a hot, bright flood. Anger and fear bathed him, battered him, smashing up against all rational thought like logs caught in the spate. He felt like a child again, lost in the wash of feeling, carried along on a current that was nothing of his own making. Only the *vaniate* offered escape, and so as he stood in that high saddle, cliffs falling away on all sides, wind tearing at his clothes, his face, legs quivering beneath him, he shrugged off his emotion, slid into the emptiness, and was able to breathe free once more.

Suspended in that blankness, he watched Long Fist and Triste struggling south, carrying the gods buried in their battered flesh.

And if they were destroyed? he wondered, cool and light inside the space of the *vaniate*. *Would that be so tragic?*

He turned his face slowly from the retreating figures to the huge sweep of the canyon below. A pair of hawks circled silently upward, wings outstretched and motionless, lifted on some distant, invisible wind. Those hawks followed their own ancient imperatives, ignorant of love or desperation. And the peaks themselves, carved from reds deeper and fuller than human blood, built from yellow, and white, and russet sandstone by forces stronger than any human hand—what did those mountains care for women, for men, for the gods on whom they depended? What did the sky care? Or the sun?

What if the world were like this? Kaden wondered.

Unbidden, his mind filled with the vision of a great, still space, the stone of the mountains, and beyond that stone the whole downward sweep of the earth west and south all the way to the ocean, the whole world empty, hill and stream and stone utterly untouched, unblemished by the scrabbling of men and women. There were no houses, no gouges in the dirt where quarries had cut free the rock. There were no roads carved across the land. There were no ships, no boats.

Would that be worse?

How hard would it be for him to simply step aside? He studied the cuts and valleys. A quarter mile off there was a pinnacle, a sheer-sided needle of stone. He had climbed formations like that back in the Bone Mountains. There would be space at the top of it to sit, to study the canyon, to watch the sun shift its slant while il Tornja's soldiers followed the *ak'hanath* to a final slaughter. Long Fist and Triste would be far south by that point, almost out of sight, certainly too far for him to hear their cries. Inside the *vaniate,* he would feel nothing when they died. And later? He would emerge from the emptiness into a larger emptiness, a vacancy wide as the sky. He wouldn't even need to fight for it.

This is what Kiel warned me of, he thought. *That one day I might just walk away.*

He could remember being wary of the possibility once, not long ago, but staring at it now he could not remember why. The world was brimming with worse fates than stillness and silence. At that moment, scattered all across Annur, soldiers were driving swords into skulls; pox-plagued children sobbed, bleeding in their sleep; men stole and women stole, heaping up their shining piles, screaming and snarling whenever anyone else came close. Why *not* walk off into the peaks?

Kaden took a deep breath. The air was bright in his lungs. Then, from the south, he heard a cry. He turned slowly from the great gulf of empty air to find Triste, thin as a sapling in the distance, waving her arms above her head, gesturing to him. Her voice was thin when it reached him, just a thread of sound: ". . . with me. *Please.* Please hurry."

It was nothing, that thread, the thinnest wool, but it snagged on a corner of his mind. Slowly, he blew out the bright air, let go of the *vaniate,* sagged again beneath the weight of his own hope and pain, then started south, following in the footsteps of the feeble and stumbling gods.

They need not have worried about missing the pillars. The landscape of the Ancaz was littered with stone, huge boulders carved by the wind into strange, unwieldy shapes—giant saucers, blasted lumps that could almost pass as faces, top-heavy balanced forms with the attenuated waists of wasps—but even amongst that menagerie of stone, the pillars drew the eye. They flanked the entrance to a canyon, just a gradual, natural ramp at first, little more than a cut in the ground that deepened and widened quickly, dropping out of sight between sheer stone walls. Like the rest of the stone, the pillars had been whittled by the wind, thinned from perfect cylinders to vaguer shapes, but both were tall, five times Kaden's height at the very least, and in the hard glare of the overhead sun he could just make out the shape of writing twisted around their length.

"What are these?" he asked.

No one replied. Kaden turned just in time to see Long Fist totter, put out a hand, and then collapse into the dirt. Triste let out a quiet whimper, but made no move to approach. Kaden glanced over his shoulder, north. It was hard to say, but he thought he could hear the clatter of rocks knocked free, falling hundreds of feet to shatter on the ledges below. He crossed to the shaman, then dropped unsteadily to his knees.

"We made it," he said, gesturing to the looming pillars.

"To the canyon," Triste said. "Where is the *kenta*?"

Long Fist didn't respond. His breath was shallow and fast, his pale skin ashen. Sweat beaded his brow, matting the long blond hair to his scalp.

"This body," he panted. "It is giving out."

Triste stared, bafflement and anger warring across her features. "You healed the wound," she protested.

Long Fist shook his head. The movement was weak, as though all the muscles of his neck had suddenly gone slack. "I burned shut the skin," he replied. "It kept the blood in, but did nothing to stop the bleeding inside."

He reached down with a feeble hand, scrabbled at the hem of his vest, as though his fingers could no longer grasp, as though he had forgotten what it was to hold a thing. Kaden pulled back the cloth, then stopped. Dried blood flaked from the shaman's skin, but that was hardly the worst of the injury. Long Fist was right; the hot knife had seared shut the wound, but the blood beneath had pooled in a wide band from armpit to hip, from the center of the chest all the way around to the man's back. The pale skin bulged, the bone and tightened cord of the shaman's torso little more than a bag of blood.

He's dying, Kaden realized. *It doesn't matter if we make it to the gate or not. He is already dying.*

Panic scratched and scratched in a corner of his mind, like a mouse with one foot caught in the trap. Kaden turned his focus inward, took the terrified part of himself between his mind's fingers, then crushed it. The scratching fell silent for a heartbeat, then reappeared, louder and more insistent. The emptiness beckoned, but he shoved it back.

"What can we do?" he asked, gently probing the shaman's wound with his fingers.

"You?" Long Fist raised his brows. "Nothing. This is beyond whatever little skill you have. It is beyond all mortal instruments." He turned to Triste, but coughing swallowed up his words, spattered bright, arterial blood across his chest in great gouts. There was more now, much more, as though something crucial had torn free inside. When the spasm finally subsided, pink phlegm trailed from his chin. When he spoke, it was a single word, sibilant as the wind's whisper: "Ciena."

Triste stared at him. Then, understanding, recoiled as though slapped. "I can't. . . ."

Long Fist half lifted his hands. Kaden couldn't say whether it was supplication or some weak spasm.

"This flesh fails," he said, lip curling above bloody incisors. Then, again, "Ciena." He wasn't simply naming her this time, but calling, calling across the barriers of their two human bodies, across the wall of Triste's mind into whatever cramped space Ciena had carved out for herself.

Kaden put a hand behind the shaman's head, lifting it slightly, as though that might keep the life from draining out his mouth along with the blood. When he turned back to Triste, he half expected to find the girl gone from her own face, to hear the goddess speaking in that huge, implacable voice. It almost seemed it *must* be so, that the extremity of the situation would call her forth as it had each time before. Triste's eyes, however, remained her own. The expressions ghosting over her face, her mouth opening in silent lamentation, her forehead creasing . . . Kaden had seen those expressions before, seen them scores of times. The girl was angry, baffled, terrified, but she was herself. Of the goddess inside, he could discover no sign.

"We have to draw her out," Kaden said. They had pared away the other choices. The other choices had been stolen from them. It hardly mattered. Only this remained.

Triste's lips were trembling. She took half a step back.

"The only way to do that . . ."

". . . is to hurt you," Kaden said. "I know." There was no time left. Whatever indifference he had felt an hour earlier, it was gone, vanished. Outside the *vaniate,* unshielded from his own emotion, he felt almost sick with urgency. His heart hurled itself against his ribs again and again. He laid the shaman's head down against the stone, straightened up, then reached for the knife at his side. "Ciena will respond," he said, fixing Triste's eyes with his own. "She will emerge. She always has."

Triste took another step back.

"It won't work."

"It will. It *has*. In the Crane, that time you stabbed yourself—"

"I meant to *kill* myself. That's what brought her out. It's like she can smell it, can smell the real threat. That's the *only* time the wall between us breaks."

Long Fist groaned, a low sound like an animal might make. Kaden shook his head. "There is no other choice. Triste. If he dies, we are done. *Everyone* is done. Everyone you love—"

"Who?" she screamed, the word a broadax cleaving his own. "Who do I love?"

In a moment, Kaden saw his mistake.

"My parents are dead," Triste snarled, voice caught somewhere between a shout and a sob. "And when they were alive, they traded me away. They *sold* me."

"Your parents betrayed you," Kaden said, nodding. He took a step toward her, and she took another step back, a dance modeled from blood and distrust. "Does that mean everyone in the world should suffer?"

"Suffer?" she demanded, incredulous. She stabbed a finger at Long Fist where he lay against the rock, blue eyes unfocused on the sky. "He's *why* they suffer. *He's* where it all comes from! And you want to save him. You want to stab me in order to *save* him."

"Not him. Humanity."

"And what do I care," she asked, voice dropping to a whisper, "about humanity?"

There is no time for this, Kaden thought. He tried to measure the distance between them, tried to weigh the knife in his hand. The shaman shuddered behind him, back arching in obedience to some command of the ruined body. *Careful,* he told himself. *Careful.* It was a narrow window. He needed Triste frightened, desperately frightened, but the girl was right—the goddess inside seemed only to break out in moments of the most violent need. How close would he have to be to induce such need? How deep would he have to cut?

Long Fist groaned. Kaden glanced over his shoulder. Just a glance, just a fraction of a moment—too long. Triste, legs lightened by her fear, darted past him, between the twin pillars, down the canyon and into the shadows. He was after her in an instant, hurling himself into a sprint, following half a dozen steps down the defile before he stopped. He could hear her feet scuffing the stone as she fled. He could catch her— he thought he could catch her—but how far down the canyon? And then what? Stab her? Put the knife to her throat and drag her back up? He couldn't kill her, not without destroying the goddess in the vain attempt to save the god. Triste knew that as well as he did. If Ciena were going to emerge, wouldn't she have done so already, wouldn't she have shoved her way to the front of Triste's mind the moment Long Fist called her name?

Kaden turned. The shaman was curled in the dirt behind him. He looked small, suddenly, as though death were already diminishing him.

I could carry him, Kaden thought. *Get him as far as the* kenta.

What good that would do, he had no idea. Maybe if he carried the man back to the Dead Heart . . . The Ishien were a military order. They would know something of the healing of wounds, if only because they had grown so adept at dealing them. It was a sliver of a hope, fingernail thin, but it was better than leaving Long Fist for the crows and the soldiers closing in from the north.

Hope's edge, Kaden thought, remembering the old Shin expression, *is sharper than steel.*

He had never felt the emotion so strongly before. Strange that for so many millennia it had been so praised by so many men and women. Strange that there were innumerable temples raised to Orella all across the world. In that moment, the weight of Kaden's own hope seemed more horrible to him than hate, or rage, or the blackest despair.

*

He could see Triste's tracks clearly enough as he carried Long Fist down the canyon, but those tracks didn't matter. What mattered was the weight slung over his own shoulders, the incremental movement of the shaman's ribs that told Kaden he was still breathing, the ache in his own legs that threatened to buckle beneath him every step, and the fight against that ache. Mile after mile he carried the man, following Triste's tracks across sunbaked stone and washes filled with sand. As he descended, the canyon grew warm, then hot. The dry air raked his lungs with every breath and his lips began to crack. When he first heard the roar of the river, he thought he was hallucinating, imagining the sound of water where no water should be, but a hundred paces later he broke from the walls of the narrow side canyon to find himself standing on a wide ledge. Below, a hundred paces straight down, a froth-white river tumbled past.

Triste's footsteps led off to the right, following ancient stairs carved into the stone, but Kaden paused for a moment to adjust the shaman's weight across his shoulders. That was when the voice started.

It was so strange that for the first few syllables he could ignore it. Then, as he stood there, gasping his ragged breaths, he began to understand the words.

There is another way.

He thought at first that Long Fist was whispering to him, and he held his breath, waiting for the shaman to speak again. There was only the roar of the river, the low moan of wind threading its way through the canyon, and the clatter of rocks from somewhere above; the echo twisted the distance until he couldn't say whether his pursuers were far or near. When the words came again, Kaden realized with a shudder that they were not a matter of the ear, not something so pedestrian as sound, carried on dry stony air. They were inside his head.

There is another way.

Kaden could feel the language like the pressure deep in his ear when he had climbed a peak too quickly, or like a stone inside his mind, small, painless, smoothed by the long motion of a stream, but heavy, displacing something else. Reflexively, he pushed back. The voice dwindled to the barest breath, but he could still make out the words.

Submit, it whispered. *Serve.*

It was Long Fist—the same indifferent conviction, the same certainty, the same cadence—and yet not Long Fist. The syllables, as Kaden heard them, were shorn of all Urghul accent, filed down until there was no intonation left, as though they were not actually words at all, but only the idea of words.

You will not survive, if you do not serve. No one will survive.

Again, that pressure, and stronger now. It was an unfolding inside the mind; an awesome flower, sun-bright and blossoming too quickly; a hatching egg, the insistent beak cracking the smooth shell. Kaden could feel the shards breaking apart, shattering, slicing through his own thoughts. He put a hand against the canyon wall to steady himself, closed his eyes, felt himself falling into bottomless darkness, as though the whole world had become a well with that voice echoing up from the bottom.

You can be more than this—a vision of Kaden's own burning eyes—*more than the contents of your skin*—another vision, this time from a great distance, of a pitiful figure kneeling on a sandstone ledge. It took a long time to find a name for that huddled, mortal creature: *Kaden.* The syllables were familiar, but irrelevant. The sad little man bore, on his bent back, a figure of such perfect radiance that it burned.

You can be this, the blazing figure said. *You can be this if you submit.*

A burning, as of cold fire sliding across the mind.

A desire, strong as week-long hunger, to burn.

Yes, the voice said. *Let yourself burn. I will take this flesh and make of it a god.*

A great conflagration, blue-bright as the noonday sky, divine, undeniable.

Yes, the god said. *Yes.*

But laced beneath that voice, there was another voice, barely the whisper of yesterday's wind, dirt-poor and cracked, too-human, doomed. Defiant.

The mind is a flame, it insisted. *The mind is a flame. The mind is a flame.*

And then the part of him that heard, that recognized the words, that was still Kaden, whispered in response: *Blow it out.*

He opened his eyes. The sun had shifted overhead. The line of light and shadow, inscribed as though with a chisel, fell across his face. Long Fist was still alive, breathing weakly beside his ear, but the god inside had fallen almost quiet.

"You tried to take me," Kaden said aloud. His own voice sounded strange in his ears, dry as stone. His tongue was swollen. "Tried to take my place in my own mind."

It is the only way.

The voice was still inside his head, but weaker now, as though whatever fuel had fed that first fire were all but burned away.

"I am not a priest," Kaden said. "I am nothing like the Urghul that you inhabit now. I never worshipped you. You explained it yourself. My mind is unprepared. You could not enter it."

There are other ways than worship. Polluted ways, but ways all the same.

And then, as though the god spoke over himself in awful polyphony, Kaden heard his words from days earlier: *It is possible for you to carve away a portion of what you are. . . .*

"No," Kaden said, shaking his head, seeing all over again the bafflement and self-loathing in Triste's eyes, understanding it for the first time. "Not for this."

If you do not submit, the Csestriim win.

Kaden heaved the Urghul chieftain from his shoulder, struggled briefly to hold the limp body, then lowered him to the stone at the very edge of the drop. Long Fist's lids were closed. Breath rasped between his bloody lips. He was nearly dead, but then, what did that mean? Long Fist, if he had even been *called* Long Fist as a child, before his flesh was seized by his god, had been dead a long time, or if not dead, then gone, subsumed inside the mind of the divine.

Long Fist gave himself, the god said, *as you must give yourself.*

Kaden tried to imagine it. Not the quiet annihilation of the self that the Shin pursued. Close to that, but something worse: a twisting, a transmutation into something vicious and immortal, a creature of bloodletting and screams. Better to be gone than that. Better to simply cease.

Unless . . .

Triste had resisted. No one seemed to understand quite how, but she had resisted her goddess, taken her in, then locked her off in one of the mind's forgotten corridors. She had kept hold of herself while she carried Ciena, and she had no training in the *vaniate,* no quiet years studying the shape and movements of her own mind. If she could find a way, then perhaps he could, too.

The dying god saw the shape of Kaden's thought before he spoke.

No, Meshkent said. *I will not be penned.*

Kaden could feel the pressure starting again inside his head, trying to force him out.

Submit.

Kaden shook his head grimly, pushed back. It was easier, this time, almost trivially so. The god was growing weak, fading from the world.

Why would you choose to be what you are? Why be the flute when you could play the music?

"I know your music," Kaden replied. "I have heard it."

He could see the people burning, could see Annur replaced by an empire of pain, men and women and children manacled to ten thousand altars, bleeding, screaming. He could see them harnessed to their own agony, forced to drag it behind them like great stones, to bear it upon their shoulders until it broke them, and ruling over it all, seated on the Unhewn Throne, he saw himself, but not himself. A god wearing his face.

"No," he said, shaking his head. "No."

Then this body will give out, my touch will fade, and you will break, all of you. You were not made to live without me.

"We won't," Kaden said.

He turned his vision inward, considered the shape and space of his mind. The Shin had trained him to step outside the ambit of his own emotion, counseled him in the abdication of both his pleasure and his pain. What was the *vaniate* but empty space, a bubble's perfect sphere beneath the surface of the world's great sea? He couldn't step into the trance, not without risking the blank indifference of his own addiction, but he could carve a part of him away without entering his own emptiness. There was room inside for his own mind and the god's: Triste was proof.

It was a simple thing to clear the space—he had done the same a thousand times before—but much harder to remain outside of it, to live in his own mounting anxiety rather than diving into the *vaniate*. The blankness beckoned.

"There," Kaden said. "I will not be your slave, but I will carry you."

Nothing. Silence from the mind of the god.

I am too late, he thought, searching Long Fist's chest for some sign of heartbeat or breath. *He died while I stood here debating.*

Then, vicious as a sword slammed into its sheath, the god was there. Kaden reeled beneath the violence, pressed a desperate hand against his eyes, certain he had erred somehow, ceded whatever self he had to Meshkent. He waited for the pain, then realized slowly that there was no pain. He straightened up, studied the body of the Urghul chieftain. Long Fist was dead, dull blue eyes staring stupidly skyward.

Gingerly, Kaden looked in. He could feel the edges of the god's mind lodged inside his own, bright, startlingly sharp, but yes . . . sheathed.

I will not be your slave, growled something older than the world.

When Kaden finally replied, he spoke aloud, as though to
the stones and the sky, to the slope of the canyon floor, to the
wind, to something, anything beyond himself.

"You have no choice."

This, too, the Shin had taught him: to look at the fact beyond
the passion. He could hold the god, could pen him. It was all
a matter of building the right walls, of draping the right chains,
of being sure they would not break when the Lord of Pain threw
his weight against them.

43

Before any fight, there was the waiting. In the moment of violence, Valyn could kill as well as anyone else, but in the long hours of preparation, he was lost in his own blindness. He could hear Huutsuu and her riders chopping trees in the forest somewhere to the east, could feel the earth vibrate as they hauled the huge logs into place to block gates in the old fortress, and doorways. He could smell the sweat pouring off of the men and women, the lather of the horses, the sweet resin of the newly felled firs. He felt it all around him, the coming violence building like a summer storm, and yet he could do nothing to prepare.

While the Urghul worked, he walked the length of the old stone wall—108 paces from the embankment on the west, where the land fell away sharply into the Haag, to the squat tower in the east, beyond which the ground grew mossy, then spongy, so soft that he sank halfway to his knees. Old Mierten had understood terrain—that much was clear. Hundreds of years on, it was still a good place to fight.

The fort itself was another matter. Valyn could pull crumbling mortar from between the stones with his bare fingers. The wall was high enough to stop the horsemen—ten feet in most places—but when he climbed atop the walk, loose stones rocked beneath his feet. Half the ramparts that would shield the defenders from arrows and spears had fallen away, leaving only clusters of stone to crouch behind, and those were tenuous at best. He dislodged one with a casual shove, listening to it scrape against the north face of the wall, then thud into the dirt. It might be possible to drop a few more on the Urghul when the assault came, but that would mean destroying the wall even further, like ripping off your own arm to use it as a club.

Squat towers punctuated the wall every thirty paces. Originally they would have offered archers a little extra range, provided elevated platforms for the fort's commander or a welcome shelter for the wounded. Now, they were mostly falling down. The jumbled stones blocked easy passage along the top of the wall, passage that might prove crucial to the defenders as the battle ebbed and flowed. Valyn couldn't build barricades or dig trenches, but he could clear the battlements, and so that was what he did for the better part of the morning. Those blocks he could lift, he placed on the ruined ramparts. The stones would be good for a few shattered skulls at the very least. Some of the pieces were too heavy to lift, but Valyn did his best to muscle them out of the way.

The work left his shoulders sore and his hands bloody, but he kept at it, even when the towers were more or less passable. It was that or sit in the midday darkness and wait. He was kicking the last of the gravel off the ledge with his boot—even an egg-sized stone could mean lost footing or a broken ankle— when the Annurians finally arrived. He'd heard them when they were still a mile off, boots thudding into the earth. As they drew closer he could smell the blood- and sweat-soaked wool, the leather and polished steel. And the fear. The Annurian soldiers reeked of fear.

It seemed impossible that they were able to keep going. That much fear should have crushed them, unstrung their legs, left them gibbering in the dirt to be ground beneath the horses' hooves when the Urghul rode south. Valyn paused his work, stretched his neck and shoulders as he stared into the darkness that was the north. *What's keeping them going? How have they not quit?*

As they drew closer, he could hear the ragged breathing, the pounding of dozens of hearts, quieter than the boots, but more frantic. And he could hear their voices. They weren't really talking—none of the men had the breath left for conversation—but every so often one would offer a word, a fragment of a phrase:

Steady there, Tem.

When we gonna start running?

Told you you were gettin' fat. . . .

It was all mixed up, the earnest exhortations with the bleak jokes, the choked-off curses when soldiers stumbled followed immediately by the goading of the others urging their fellows on. Valyn stood alone at the wall's top, the wind cold on his face, listening. *And there's your answer,* he thought. He could remember that feeling, the strength that came when you stood shoulder to shoulder with someone else, sharing the struggle. He could remember swimming the sound between Qarsh and Hook with Gent, running punishment miles all night long with Laith, sitting long, shivering watches with Ha Lin during their training missions in the north. He could remember that strength, but it had been a long time since he stood beside a friend or ally. What had kept him alive, in the long night since Andt-Kyl, was something deeper and darker than any human bond, something stitched into his flesh, something he could never share.

As the legionaries clattered to a halt in front of the fort, Valyn glanced down. His knuckles throbbed. He realized he'd been punching the top of the wall over and over, lightly but persistently, testing his flesh against the stone. *Stupid,* he thought, wiping the blood on his furs. There would be plenty of fighting soon enough with no need to war against the heedless walls.

From below, the Flea's voice cut through the wind. "Welcome to Mierten's Fort."

The Wing commander was on the ground north of the wall, had been working on the barricades. Even as he spoke, he kept working. Valyn could hear him pounding yet another spiked stake into the earth, parceling out his greeting between the blows. For a moment there was just silence. Then a new voice responded, a voice thick with wariness.

"Who are you?"

"My name is Anjin," the Flea replied. "You have the command here?"

"I do."

"You have a name, Commander?"

The man hesitated. "Belton," he said after a moment. "You have a rank?"

"Kettral," the Flea replied.

A wave of murmurs ran through the troops at that. The Flea didn't elaborate, didn't stop working.

"If you're Kettral," Belton demanded after a pause, "then who are they?"

"Those are the Urghul," the Flea said. "On our side. The good Urghul."

Belton spat. "No such fucking thing. What are you doing with a batch of horse-fuckers? Where's your bird?"

"Bird's dead. And as I said, these particular horse-fuckers are on our side."

"I don't like it."

"There's not much to like. We have less than a hundred and fifty men to defend this wall. The wall itself is falling down and the gates rotted away two hundred years ago. We have maybe a day to get ready. We have no reinforcements. No one knows we're here, and if they did, they couldn't get to us in time." Even blind, Valyn could imagine the Flea's tired shrug. "Given the situation, I'd say having a dozen extra fighters is one of the only things *to* like."

"Kettral are one thing," Belton said warily. "We're proud to fight with the Kettral, but we've been putting blades in these Urghul sons of bitches all year. You ask me, we'd do better chopping off their heads and shitting down their throats while we've got the chance."

"I did not ask you," the Flea replied quietly. For the first time, his ax had fallen silent. The Urghul were a quarter mile to the east, felling more trees, but they would be back soon. Valyn settled a hand on the cold steel head of one of his own axes.

Belton shifted his feet on the rough ground. Valyn could taste the tension pouring off his men. Back on the Islands, he'd seen brawls break out over less, but this wasn't going to be a brawl. If it came to swords, people were going to die.

Good, whispered some dark part of him.

With violence came sight.

Men were loosening swords in sheaths. The returning Urghul were muttering angrily in their liquid tongue. They, too, had stopped working, as though they were watching the confrontation unfold. There were only a few heartbeats before it all went straight to shit.

Good.

Valyn gritted his teeth, shook his head. It *could* be good, but not yet, not until Balendin arrived. He wanted, even more than a wash of mindless violence and the darksight that came with it, to hear the leach scream, to be there when the man who murdered Ha Lin in the depths of Hull's Hole was finally torn apart.

He set a boot against one of the stones he had balanced at the top of the wall, then shoved. It grated against the stone, then fell, cleaving in half with a sharp crack against the jumbled rubble below. Shouts of alarm erupted from the assembled legionaries. Steel scraped over steel. Valyn pitched his voice above it all.

"Your friends are dead," he said, pointing north. "They held the line so that you could be here."

For just a moment, everyone fell silent.

"Of course, you're dead too," Valyn went on. He could feel the eyes turn to him. "You're walking and talking like living soldiers, but you're corpses, all of you. You're as dead as the men you left behind yesterday, and the only reason you're here and standing rather than there, getting trampled into the dirt, is because the Flea brought you here. This wall is just a different place to die."

"Who in Hull's name are you?" Belton growled warily.

"Just another dead man. And I'll tell you this, one corpse to another: the dead don't get to decide much, but you've got one choice left. You can be dead from saving your empire, your republic, whatever the fuck we're calling it these days, or you can be dead for nothing, for a stupid scrap in the middle of nowhere, fighting people who want the same thing you do. Maybe it doesn't matter—dead's dead, after all—but you've got a choice to make, probably your last one, so you might as well make it."

For a long time no one spoke. Then the Flea started laughing, a low, wry chuckle barely louder than the breeze.

"You know," he said after a moment, "that the speech before the battle is traditionally more upbeat. Less death, more pride and defiance."

Valyn snorted. "Want me to try again?"

"Nah. You already fucked it up." Valyn could hear the Wing leader turn back to the legionaries. "So. You want to fight the good Urghul now, or the bad Urghul later?"

Wind carved through the stones. Men shifted, coughed.

"I'm asking," the Flea went on, "because there's a lot to do. If I need to kill you, I want to do it now, so I can finish this palisade."

"All right," Belton said finally, grudgingly. "We'll fight beside you. Just keep your pet savages on their chains."

Sigrid reached the fort a little before dark. The woman had fought in a battle, then run all day long, but as usual, she smelled of delicate perfume—lavender, this time, and rosewater, and something Valyn couldn't name. The legionaries stopped working as she approached, staring, waiting for word of the others, the Annurians who had stayed, the friends they had left behind. Sigrid ignored them, found Newt and the Flea up on the hill instead, where the two men were studying the ground and laying charges. Even with the wind, Valyn could hear their conversation easily enough.

"How much time do we have?" the Flea asked.

Sigrid coughed up her own mangled language.

"Better'n I thought," the Flea replied. "I figured they'd be here tonight. Good work. Anyone else make it?"

Valyn didn't need to see to know Sigrid was shaking her head.

"No man can escape his fate," Newt mused.

"Let's hope that applies to Balendin."

The Aphorist paused for a moment. "There's enough explosive here to kill half a dozen oxen, but it's all about how he sets up. If he's dead center on the hill, we've got him. If not . . . probably not."

"I'll take it," the Flea replied. "How long will the fuses burn?"

"Half a morning," the Aphorist replied. "I'll light 'em when we hear the horses. The flame will be underground. He won't see anything. Won't smell anything."

"Half a morning," the Flea said grimly, "means we need to hold that wall for half a morning. How much you have left, Sig?" he asked.

Newt translated the leach's response. "She'll be flooded in power when the time comes, but she's been awake two days now, and on the move for all of it. She'll only be able to pull a little from her well. Any more would drown her."

"All right," the Flea said. "Get behind the walls. Get some sleep. Newt—let's see about rigging some scare charges down in the field, see if we can get the horses to balk."

Valyn was so intent on the conversation that he didn't notice the steps approaching along the top of the wall until they were a dozen paces off. He turned, half expecting Huutsuu, but the gait was all wrong, as was the smell—raw nerves rather than

Huutsuu's characteristic resolve. Instead of the warm, rank scent of horse and fur, the person smelled of oiled steel, weariness.

"I'm sorry to interrupt, sir." One of the Annurian legionaries. "I was ordered to this section of the wall."

Valyn spread his hands. "All yours."

He didn't feel like talking, but he didn't feel like moving. If the poor bastard wanted to guard the wall, he was welcome to it. For a long time the two of them stood a couple of paces apart, unmoving. Valyn tried listening for the horses that would be thundering down out of the north, but he could hear only the hack of axes and the cursing of soldiers as they worked, the rush of the river off to the west and the intermittent shrieking of the wind.

"You really think they're dead?" the soldier asked finally. "The men we left up north?"

He offered the questions slowly, quietly, as though afraid to ask them, as though he didn't really want to hear the answers. Valyn blew out an irritated breath.

"Yes."

"All of them?"

Valyn pointed over the wall toward Sigrid. "She's here, which means she's not there, which means your friends don't have a leach to shield them anymore. You've seen Balendin and the Urghul fight, so you tell me: You think your friends are alive?"

"There's always a chance. A hope."

"You're hoping for the wrong thing. You should be *hoping* they're dead, because if they're not, then Balendin has them, and you know what he does with his prisoners."

They were cruel words, maybe too cruel, but there wasn't anything to be gained by dodging the facts. The man sounded young, but half the people wrapped up in the fucking war were young. The legionary had fought the Urghul. He could hear the truth. He could face it.

Valyn wanted to turn away, to forget the man, to take up his silent watch once more, but behind him the soldier's breathing had gone rough and ragged.

"Those 'Kent-kissing bastards," the legionary managed. The air smelled of tears and sweat. "I'll kill them. *I'll murder them.*"

Valyn closed his eyes. The young soldier's grief was thick as early morning mist. Valyn wanted to step clear of it, to find some other place on the wall where there was only the stone and the wind, but there was no other place. The Annurians were preparing, readying weapons, testing out the jagged rocks that Valyn himself had balanced on the ramparts in preparation for the attack. There were people everywhere. There was grief everywhere. You could walk forever and not escape it, could cross rivers, continents, seas, only to find new cities filled with the bereaved, every life shattered in some awful way, every man and woman weeping.

"They kill your friend?" he asked. His own voice sounded rough, callous, half a step from mockery.

The soldier didn't reply. Sobs rocked him. Nothing unusual there—men cried in battle, before, during, after—and if Valyn was lucky, the crying would be the worst of it. The guy would cough it out and move on. If he was lucky, there wouldn't be a story to go with the sobs. He wasn't lucky.

"My brother," the soldier said finally. "My brother was with them."

As though that single word—*brother*—were some kind of kenning, the darkness plastered across Valyn's eyes shifted, filling with the memory of Kaden. According to the Flea, he was still alive, had made it back to Annur somehow, had even managed to pull the empire out from underneath Adare's feet. Before Andt-Kyl, the discovery would have filled Valyn with relief, with pride. Now, when he probed his mind for those emotions, he found nothing, just a dark pit where the emotion should have been, lightless, bottomless, cold as winter stone. He could see Kaden's face, could hear his brother's voice in his mind, but behind it there was only that emptiness.

"What was your brother's name?" Valyn asked.

"Oberan," the soldier replied.

Valyn turned to face the young man. "Well then, you'd better hope that Oberan is dead."

The thunder started at dawn, not a thunder of the sky torn apart by lightning, not an intermittent growl punctuated by silence, but a low, constant rumbling: the thunder of hooves so far to the north that Valyn had to strain to make it out, but growing always closer. He rose from the chilly corner of the fort where he had spent the night alone, felt his way along the broken passage, then outside and up onto the wall. Mist was rising off the swamps to the east—thick as smoke, wet and vegetal—but either the sun was obscured by clouds or it was still too low to feel the heat.

The legionaries had spent the night on the walls—their snoring a softer counterpoint to the rumbling in the north—and as he walked among them Valyn thought about sounding the alarm, then discarded the idea. By his own vague reckoning, the Urghul were at least ten miles off. Probably there was something else that could be done to the fort, some final preparation to make, but all the crucial work was finished, and besides, the odds were against any of the sleeping men ever walking away from those walls. The dreams they dreamed as the morning mist shifted over the fort—their nightmares or the bright and fragile worlds to which they had escaped—those dreams would likely be their last.

Valyn stepped carefully over the snoring forms, past them, continuing along the top of the wall until he reached one of the towers, then climbed the crumbling stairs to the top. There was nothing to see, not for him, but the air smelled lighter there, less like dirt and piss and hopelessness.

The Flea found him there just after the sun finally broke through the morning cloud. Valyn recognized the Wing leader's gait as he climbed the stone stairs to the tower—a little heavier on the right foot, as though some old wound had never fully healed—recognized that solid, steady heartbeat. The man joined him at the crenellations. He stood just a pace away, but remained silent a long time. The eastern forest was alive with birds—nuthatches and chickadees, jays and nightjars—a thousand threads of song. Valyn tried to untangle them, to pick one melody apart from the rest.

"You should go," the Flea said finally. "There's nothing you can do here except get in the way."

Valyn let go of the birdsong. The hooves to the north were drowning it out anyway.

"I won't get in the way."

"You're blind."

"Only when I'm not fighting. Only when I'm not about to die."

The Flea fell silent for a while, then handed him a strip of dried meat. "Then eat."

Valyn shook his head. "I survived in these forests a long time before we came to find you."

"Good for you. You still need to eat."

Valyn turned to face the man, measured out the next words, trying to keep his growing rage in check. "You have no idea what I need."

Anyone else would have recoiled at his tone. The Flea didn't flinch. There wasn't even a hint of fear-smell on him. "Yes," he said quietly. "I do. I watched you grow up, Valyn. I trained you."

"You trained an idiotic kid who was soft as summer grass. Trust me when I tell you this: *I am not him.*"

"I know that. It's a shame."

For a moment Valyn lost his words. "A shame?" he managed finally. "It's a *shame*? That kid was weak. He was slow. He was stupid. I may not have eyes, but back then I was fucking *blind*. I lost my bird, lost my Wing, sat by while Laith died, and for what? So I could let my sister stab me. So I could fail to kill il Tornja, and fall off a tower."

His breathing was hot and ragged in his chest, his heart

pounding as though he'd just raced five miles, but there was no stopping.

"I'm broken now, busted all to Hull, but I'm not *dumb* anymore. I'm not soft. If we fought now, you and I, the way we did in Assare, I'd take you apart, I'd cut you to fucking pieces."

He hadn't meant to say it, but it was true. Even as he raged, he could feel the part of him that was not quite him, the part that was tainted by the slarn's strength gathering, coiling to strike. No one, not even the Flea, could stand against that.

"You trained me," he went on, voice little more than a growl. "It just took me a year too long to learn what you were teaching."

"No," the Flea replied. "This is not it."

"You don't believe me. That's fine. Wait until the Urghul get here."

"I'm not talking about fighting."

Valyn shook his head. "Then what *are* you talking about?"

The Flea was silent a long time.

"You know why I joined the Kettral?" he asked finally.

"Don't shovel me a steaming pile of shit about defending the empire, about Annurian justice."

"I won't. I was a kid in Ganaboa. I barely realized I *was* part of the empire. I joined the Kettral because of Finn."

Valyn's stomach lurched inside him. "Blackfeather Finn."

He could hear the Flea's nod, the scrape of whiskers over wool. "He was from Ganaboa, too—the son of a ship captain. People forgot about that, that Ganaboa part, because his skin was so light. Anyway, when the Kettral showed up looking for recruits, Finn went. And because I loved him, I went."

Valyn was mute. The forest birds had gone quiet, as though they, too, heard the distant rumble of the coming horde. *Love.* It was a word he'd never heard from the Kettral, something the Eyrie worked hard to train out of them long before the Trial.

"I didn't have the words for it then—we were kids. He was my best friend. I couldn't imagine staying in Ganaboa without him. Finn was brilliant with that bow of his, even back then.

When the Kettral came to the island, came with their contest and their offer of training for the winners, Finn was certain the Eyrie would want him, and he was right.

"I, on the other hand, didn't know shit, barely knew what end of a knife to hold. Everyone told me I was stupid, that I was going to get the life kicked out of me in the ring while half of Ganaboa laughed, and that would be it." He paused for a moment at the memory. "They weren't wrong. Not about the ass-kicking, anyway. Thing was, they didn't realize how bad I wanted it. I figured if I just kept getting up, if I just kept fighting, the Kettral would have to take me, and if they took me, I could stay with Finn. By the end of that fight I'd broken three ribs, two fingers, and an ankle. I had half of some older kid's ear in my mouth when they hauled me off. I couldn't walk for a month afterward, but it got me onto the Islands.

"I thought I was done, then, but you know how it is—I wasn't close to done. There was the training, the Trial, the early missions, more training. It's enough to drive a person crazy. I watched it drive men crazy, and women. I watched it break them."

"But it didn't break you," Valyn said, his voice rusted.

"For me it was easy."

"Easy." Valyn coughed.

The Flea paused. "Uncomplicated, at least," he amended. "There was only ever one thing to think about: if I trained hard enough, if I was good enough, I could be with Finn. If the shit hit, I could keep him safe. That's what I thought about every single morning swimming those 'Kent-kissing laps around the sound. That's what I thought about all those long days swinging blades in the ring. All the barrel drops. All the quick-grabs and map study and language lessons. *This might be the thing,* I thought, *that keeps him safe. This might be the thing that saves him.*"

He fell silent. Along the wall, the legionaries were calling out questions and orders, readying themselves for the attack. The Flea didn't seem to notice.

"And now?" Valyn asked quietly.

"Now? I'm old. Finn's gone. But the habits are there. I don't think I could wake up late if I tried." The words were soft, but Valyn could hear the grief vibrating in the other man's voice.

"Why are you telling me this?" Valyn asked.

The Flea waited a few heartbeats before answering. "A couple reasons, I guess. The first is to apologize. It didn't have to go down like that in Assare, even after Finn died. I lost control, of myself, then my Wing."

"You didn't lose control," Valyn said. "I dropped my blades, and you let me *live*."

"I was after the Skullsworn, not you." The Flea shook his head again. "But I would have gone through you if I had to. I would have killed you all to get at her. It was a mistake. If that night had played out differently, we might have saved a lot of other lives."

Valyn couldn't speak. He'd been carrying Assare inside him like a jagged stone for months, the guilt of it weighing him down, its edges shredding anything that it touched. In all that time he'd never once paused to consider another possibility—that maybe the blame wasn't all his. He opened his mouth to say something, anything, but the Flea was already talking again.

"The second reason I'm telling you this, the more important reason, is that you've got it wrong. I know how people see me now, even on the Islands. I'm a killer, supposedly the best killer we've got. Maybe I am. I've opened up plenty of people, some that deserved it, some that probably didn't. I'd never argue that we are *right*, not me, not my Wing, not the Eyrie, but I was fighting *for* something."

He fell silent.

"And?" Valyn asked. He'd been half holding his breath, he realized. His chest burned as though with a slow fire.

"You, Valyn, you're just fighting."

44

It was simple enough for Kaden to lever the limp body of Long Fist over the edge of the cliff, into the roiling river below. It should have been easier to run without the Urghul chieftain across his shoulders. Long Fist had been a tall man, and strong, but his flesh had been made of honest weight. Carrying him had been no different, in its way, from lifting stones, or lugging buckets of water, and though Kaden's frame had grown weak during his year back in Annur, his muscles and bones remembered the feel of such physical work. Nothing, however, had prepared him to carry the weight of a god lodged inside his mind.

The thought was too large, too bright to stare directly at, and so Kaden tried to put it aside. Il Tornja's soldiers weren't far behind; Triste had vanished somewhere ahead. If he didn't reach the *kenta* before the Annurians, they were all dead. The god was silent—maybe baffled, maybe preparing a stronger, more deadly strike against the man who carried him—and yet even silent, even insubstantial, the alien weight bore down on Kaden until he felt he might collapse.

Just get to the kenta, he told himself, staggering after Triste's footsteps. *Get to the* kenta. *You can face what you've done when you're safe on the other side.*

Canyon gave way to ledge, ledge to ramp, ramp to rough-hewn steps, worn almost smooth by centuries of wind and rain.

Who had built them, or when, or why, Kaden had no idea. It didn't matter. What mattered was that they offered a way out, a way free, and so he followed them down, down, as they flanked the soaring sandstone wall, a hundred steps, two hundred, and then he was there at the bottom, in a maze of ancient buildings the size of a modest town.

The whole thing was built on a long, rocky shelf only a little higher than the river itself. Debris from the floodline marked the lowest stones of the buildings that were still standing. Most of those by the river had been washed away; several teetered out over the current, as though caught in the act of crumbling. Everything was built of huge sandstone blocks, evidently quarried from the local cliffs. The heavy clay that had once cemented them together, chinking the gaps, had mostly crumbled away, rotting the foundations, leaving huge holes in the walls.

Triste's footsteps led straight down the central avenue, but Kaden hesitated, some sense honed in the glacial cold of the Bone Mountains pricking the skin along the back of his neck. Something was wrong about this place. He ran his eyes over the fallen façades and gaping entryways. Obelisks and great plinths lay shattered and askew, toppled either by the river's seasonal rush or their own unrelenting weight. In recessed grottoes carved into the canyon wall stood a series of blocks that looked like altars, though no text remained to name the gods for whom they had been built. The old stones were strange, unexpected, but it wasn't the stones that had set Kaden's mind on edge.

Behind him, he could just make out the sound of the Annurian soldiers, boots clattering over the ledges above, shouts echoing off the cliffs. He closed his eyes, inhaled deeply, exhaled, then opened them again. The whole exercise took precious moments, and he still couldn't say what it was about the ancient buildings that had given him pause.

More looking does not mean more seeing. The quiet voice was Scial Nin's, conjured from the depths of his memory.

Swallowing his misgivings, Kaden stumbled into a run once

more, following Triste's tracks between the ruined buildings. She couldn't know where the *kenta* was, but her footsteps showed no sign of hesitation. If anything, she was running faster, panicking, trying to put as much distance as possible between herself and the soldiers behind. *Trying to escape from me, too,* Kaden realized. The sheathed belt knife slapped against his thigh as he ran, a reminder of the violence with which he'd threatened the girl.

"Triste," he called, pausing for a moment to listen for her response. Stopping now was a risk. Calling out was a risk. On the other hand, if she overshot the *kenta,* there would be no time to double back.

"Triste!" he shouted again.

There was no reply but the echo of his own voice, thin and hollow above the raging of the river. Somewhere in the vast labyrinth of his own mind, Meshkent stirred. There were no words, but Kaden could feel the god's urgency, his rage. Thoughts and emotions that were not Kaden's own pressed out, testing, searching for a way free.

"No," he murmured, shoving away all other concerns to focus on the prison he had made. The walls were there, solid and strong, but even in the short time since Long Fist's death, the god had begun to wear down the barriers. It was an assault as wordless and violent as the river's flow, and Kaden could feel that, like the river, it would never rest. Meshkent was inside him now, the impossible current of the divine carving into his own walls, searching for a freedom as wide as the sea. "No," Kaden said again, taking a heartbeat to fortify himself, to buttress those invisible walls, then hurling himself into motion once more.

He rounded the next corner at a run, and for a few steps into the small plaza he kept running, his legs going through their motions even as his mind struggled to parse the sight: there were armed men in the open square, dozens of them, their bows half drawn, their blades naked in their hands. They wore no uniforms, but something about their deployment, both the organization and the way they stood, whispered the same word over and over: *soldiers. Annurian soldiers.* Kaden stumbled to a halt, his mind scrambling to make sense of the scene, to come up with another plan, eyes scanning for some escape.

"Hello, Kaden." The man who spoke sat on a wide block of fallen stone, half reclining on one elbow, a booted foot propped up on the stone. Unlike the soldiers around him, who looked ready to fight, to kill, this man seemed like he ought to be playing the harp, or eating ripe papaya from a porcelain bowl.

No, Kaden realized, his bones going cold, *not a man.*

Though he'd never seen the creature in person, he knew that face, had studied it back in the Temple of Ciena what seemed like years ago. Triste's mother had made the painting. *But she didn't get it right,* he thought bleakly. *Not quite.* The courtesan had captured the sharp eyes and the casual smile that bordered on a smirk, she'd inked in the same amusement and disdain, but she had missed the emptiness behind it all. She had painted Ran il Tornja, the human general, without ever realizing that the mind behind that face was alien and inimical, that it was Csestriim.

"Run," the general said, smiling, waving a lazy hand.

In truth, Kaden had been about to do just that, but the single syllable brought him up short, triggering some primitive wariness.

Il Tornja's smile widened, as though he'd expected that precise response. "Or don't. It doesn't really matter."

Kaden felt Meshkent go dangerously still inside his mind, an animal trapped in the back of a cage. While the Csestriim studied him, Kaden piled layers of his own thought on top of the god's cell, heaping on his terrors and regrets, his confusion and still-born hopes, any scraps of self to hide the mind he carried inside. He had no idea what il Tornja could see with those inhuman eyes, but one thing was clear—the Csestriim could not be allowed to catch even a glimpse of the god.

"You weren't—" Kaden began.

Il Tornja cut him off, finishing the sentence with a grin. "Chasing along behind you? No. Chasing is tiring, especially in this heat. It's so much more effective just to go to the right place at the start."

"How did you know we'd come here?"

The *kenarang* pursed his lips as though considering the question, then shook his head. He almost looked regretful. "I could tell you something about patterns and probabilities, but it wouldn't mean much. Like trying to explain mathematics to an ant." He shrugged, as though that settled the question. "Anyway, you're here. More importantly, *she's* here." He jerked a thumb over his shoulder.

Triste.

The girl slumped between a pair of soldiers, hair falling forward over her face, chin lolling against her chest. There was no sign of violence, but something had knocked her unconscious.

"Not the most hospitable greeting," il Tornja said, as though reading Kaden's thoughts, "but from what I hear, she's pretty dangerous. I didn't want to end up a smear of blood and flesh like those poor people back in the Jasmine Court." He cocked his head to the side. "You were there for that, right? Was it as bad as people say?"

Panic surged inside Kaden, a rabid dog hurling itself against its chain. The *vaniate* beckoned, but he couldn't trust himself inside the trance. Instead he seized the panic, choked it until it stopped squirming, until he could think. Facts tumbled over him like cold rain: Triste wasn't dead. Maybe Kiel was wrong. Maybe il Tornja didn't know about the goddess. Maybe he didn't want to kill her. Maybe they could escape. She could wake up. Ciena could fight her way free the way she'd done before. It wasn't over. It wasn't over. It couldn't all be over.

Il Tornja drummed his fingers against the stone and smiled. "Anyway, it was a good lesson, and I owe it to you: always have a leach on your side." He pointed lazily.

Kaden followed the gesture to an old man, bent and balding,

who stood half a dozen paces from the *kenarang*. Kaden hadn't noticed him at first, surrounded as he was by soldiers with their weapons drawn.

"Everyone thinks that leaches are insane," il Tornja continued, shaking his head. "It's not fair, really. They just see the world . . . differently from you or me."

"You and I do not share a view of the world," Kaden said, surprised that his own voice came out steady.

The general raised his brows. "Oh, I'm not so sure about that! Those monks who trained you, those Shin—I think they're really on to something. I'll bet, if we sat down, you'd find that you and I see eye to eye about a lot more than you realize." He winked, held Kaden's gaze a moment, then turned his attention back to the old man. "Roshin, though, he's a little different. Loyal, though, and that's important to me."

Roshin. Kaden struggled to make sense of the name. Who would name a son after one of the most hated creatures in recorded history? The world had mostly forgotten the Csestriim, but it remembered the Atmani, remembered the horror they had wrought, the devastation. Across two continents and beyond, the names were still spoken with loathing.

The truth resolved so suddenly, so violently, it felt like a leather belt whipped across Kaden's naked brain. Some part of his mind buried deep beneath all rational thought made out the pattern: Roshin wasn't *named* for the Atmani. He *was* the Atmani.

Il Tornja had leaned forward slightly, as though eager to watch the understanding play out in Kaden's eyes. "You see?"

Before Kaden could respond, however, the soldiers behind him clattered into the courtyard. Sweat streamed down their faces. A handful of men toward the back doubled over, hands on their knees, chests heaving. They snapped to attention quickly enough, however, when the man leading them hammered his fist against his heart and barked out a salute.

"Sir!"

Il Tornja nodded casually. "Sarkiin. Good work." He scanned

the men behind, then his eyes narrowed. "Where's the third? The one who was with them?"

It didn't seem possible, but Sarkiin went even more rigid. His eyes were fixed on empty air half a pace in front of him. He looked like a man readying himself to die.

"Gone, sir. Over the cliff just above and into the river."

If il Tornja was angry, it didn't show. *Of course,* Kaden reminded himself, *he's not capable of anger, not really.*

"Interesting," he said finally, shifting his attention from his lieutenant and back to Kaden. "Who was he?"

Kaden scrambled for a plausible lie, one this immortal creature might believe. "Ishien," he said after a heartbeat. "He came with me to find Triste. Before she could do more damage."

"And why," the *kenarang* asked, "did he decide to leap into a river knowing he could not possibly survive the current?"

"He died," Kaden said, hewing as close as he could to the truth. "I tried to hide the body."

"Sarkiin?" il Tornja asked.

The soldier nodded brusquely. "The man was injured, sir. Badly. I am surprised he made it as far as he did."

"Describe him."

Kaden tensed. It was impossible to say just how much the Annurian soldiers had seen. They'd been miles off during the entire chase, but if one of them had a long lens, if they'd managed to find a line of sight somewhere in that canyon . . .

"Tall," Sarkiin replied. "Couldn't make out much more."

"His race?"

The soldier shook his head slowly. "The light was wrong, sir. We only caught a couple of glimpses and couldn't make out much more than shapes."

"Send a team downstream. The body may have washed up in an eddy, or caught on a snag." Il Tornja paused; his eyes went distant for a quarter heartbeat, then refocused on Kaden. "You tell an interesting story, and this is only the start of it."

"Not really," Kaden replied. "We came to find Triste. We found her. Then you came."

"Triste," the *kenarang* said, his voice brimming with a mirth he couldn't feel. "Is that what you call her?"

"It is her name," Kaden replied.

"Names," il Tornja mused, "are even easier to put on and take off than faces." He glanced over his shoulder at Triste. She hadn't woken, hadn't even moved. "I will speak with her first." He pointed to the shell of an old temple. "There."

That Triste was alive at all was puzzling. Il Tornja knew about the goddess in the girl. It was the only explanation for the fact that he had abandoned his war with the Urghul to come here, chasing her to the very edge of the empire. He knew he had Ciena in his grasp, yet he held back. . . .

Because he doesn't know, Kaden realized, that awful hope slicing him up inside. *He doesn't know he has us* both.

As far as il Tornja was aware, he'd captured half his quarry, but only half. Meshkent was still out there, and if the Csestriim wanted to trap the Lord of Pain, he would need bait. Which meant that Triste was safe, at least for the moment. The moment the *kenarang* understood that he had won the game, however, when he realized that he had both gods in his hands—at that moment it was over.

Meshkent raged silently in the locked corner of Kaden's mind.

"I don't know about you," il Tornja said, turning his attention back to Kaden, "but I find this all very exciting."

Kaden studied the eddy. He was bound at the elbows, wrists, and waist, tied to a huge stone behind him, but he was free, at least, to look, to watch the river play out its elegant violence half a dozen feet below him. As an acolyte in the Bone Mountains he had spent hours studying the eddies of the mountain streams. It was the sort of inscrutable exercise the monks might have assigned, but the truth was, Kaden had enjoyed it. There was something relentless in the twisting currents of those small rivers, so much inevitability in their onrushing course. The eddies offered the only reprieve. Kaden had never quite understood why the current would pause, slow down, double back on itself, but the whole retrograde motion seemed, in some odd way, like a type of forgiveness, the river escaping, if only momentarily, from its own ineluctable nature.

It was a lie, of course.

The water might pause, but it would empty into the sea all the same. The world was built from a thousand examples of such inevitability. Thrown stones fell unerringly to earth. Flesh left unfrozen would always go to rot. The days would grow short, then long, then short again. Without those truths, the whole framework of reality would tremble and break apart. You could forget for a while, caught in the eddy's beguiling spiral, that the world's current raged all around. That it could not be denied.

Submit, Meshkent whispered inside his mind, the voice quiet but ripe with fury. *You risk everything if you do not. Submit.*

It was impossible to be certain how much the god understood of what was happening. Kaden had tried to respond to the commands, to explain the bare outline of their situation, while at the same time keeping that other, divine mind buried so deep that even he himself could barely hear it.

Give yourself to me, the god grated again, then fell silent.

Kaden weighed the possibilities. Meshkent could fight—he'd shown that much already when still wearing the flesh of Long Fist. The crucial question was: how well? A single monk with a knife and the element of surprise had nearly killed the shaman and the god inside him—*would* have killed him if Kaden hadn't taken the Lord of Pain into himself. Meshkent was strong, but his strength was his weakness; even now, he seemed incapable of imagining failure, or conceiving a world that did not end in his own victory. *And why would he be?* Kaden thought wearily.

What setback had Meshkent encountered that could serve as a model for his own destruction?

Submit to me, the god growled.

Kaden shook his head as he stared into the slowly circling eddy.

No.

It was well past midnight when he finally heard boots approaching over broken stone.

"Go," il Tornja said to the soldiers who had been standing guard. "I'll talk with our new friend alone."

After the others had retreated beyond earshot, the *kenarang* stepped in front of Kaden, set his lantern down on a low wall, and half sat, half leaned beside it, arms crossed over his chest.

"So . . . ," he said, nodding genially, as though they were old companions sitting down to dinner after a long time apart.

"Where is Triste?" Kaden asked. "What did you do to her?"

"What did *I* do to her?" il Tornja asked, touching a finger to his chest as though perplexed. "It looked an awful lot like she was fleeing from *you.*"

"She was terrified," Kaden said, brushing aside the truth. "Confused. I didn't knock her unconscious or drug her. I didn't tie her up."

"Actually," il Tornja replied, drumming his fingers on the stone, "you did. You let the poor girl secure your return to the palace, then you threw her inside that ridiculous prison of yours. All things being equal, I'd say she has a lot more reason to hate you than me."

Kaden shook his head. "She knows who you are. So do I."

Il Tornja raised his brows. "And who am I?"

"Csestriim," Kaden said, locking eyes with the man. "The general who led the war to destroy humanity. The architect of the genocide against your own children. The murderer of gods."

"Oh," the *kenarang* replied, waving a lazy hand, "that."

Kaden hesitated, uncertain how to respond. He wasn't sure what he had expected. Denial maybe. Defiance. Almost anything but this jocular indifference.

"The thing is," il Tornja continued, "you can make anything sound bad if you pick the right words: genocide, murder—that sort of thing. You slap a word on something you don't like, and it excuses you from having to think about it any further."

"What is there to think about? Kiel told me how you killed the gods—Akalla and Korin. He explained it all to me, how after you murdered them a whole part of what we are—the reverence for the natural world and the heavens—just . . . went away. I know the whole story. You've been searching all these thousands of years to find a way to destroy more gods, *older* gods, to annihilate our race. . . ."

"Sure. Of course. But did he tell you *why*?"

Kaden stared. "Because you hate us . . . ," he began, realizing his mistake as soon as the word left his mouth.

Il Tornja shook his head. "Don't be dense. The word means nothing to me, and you know it." He sighed ostentatiously. "I have been trying, all these years, to fix something that is broken."

"We are not broken."

"Oh?"

"We are different. Not every living creature needs to be like the Csestriim."

"Of course not. Kettral aren't Csestriim. Dogs aren't Csestriim." He paused to wag a finger at Kaden. "But *you* . . . you *were* Csestriim once, before the new gods broke you."

"It is no breakage to feel love, loyalty, joy. . . ."

"Those are just the chains," il Tornja said impatiently. "The new gods broke you, made you weak so they could enslave you, and then, in the greatest insult of all, your new masters made you worship them. Look at the temples you've built: to Ciena and Eira, Heqet and Whoever. Listen to your prayers, 'Please, goddess, give me joy. Please, lord, spare me pain.'" The general shook his head. "I expected better from you, Kaden. You, at least, had the chance to understand."

Kaden took a slow breath, tried to steady his thoughts. "What chance?"

"The Shin!" il Tornja exclaimed. "You studied with the Shin. You weren't there long enough, obviously, but you must have at least glimpsed the truth. You must have seen at least a piece of the beauty of a life lived free, unenslaved by all those brutish passions."

Kaden hesitated. Whatever twisted game the Csestriim was playing, his words hit close to the truth. Kaden had, in those long years at Ashk'lan, come to cherish the freedom from his own human weakness, from all the relentless *need*. It was an imperfect freedom, of course. Even the Shin still looked out at the world through the dirty window of the self, but the absolute emptiness of the *vaniate* suggested something greater. A life more pure, more clear.

"Let's be frank with each other," il Tornja said, settling back against the wall. "You know there's a goddess locked inside the girl, and so do I."

Kaden blinked, tried to keep his thoughts from showing in his eyes.

"You've been brainwashed and blinded like the rest of your kind, twisted all around by the shape of your own brain," il Tornja went on, "but you're not an idiot, Kaden. You know I wouldn't have left the northern front, wouldn't have come all the way down here just to chase a leach." He raised his brows, waiting for Kaden's response.

"What do you want from her?" Kaden asked finally.

"I want to kill her!" il Tornja said brightly. "I'm *going* to kill her."

Deep inside Kaden's mind, Meshkent twisted, writhed, hurled himself against walls that were not walls. In the early iconography, the Lord of Pain had been depicted as a tiger, or giant cat, and it felt as though a tiger were slavering, pacing, growling inside

Kaden's brain. Just keeping company with Meshkent had been enough to unsettle whatever equilibrium Kaden had won among the Shin; having the divine inside of him was worse. He felt infected by the god's presence, disturbed, as though Meshkent were a huge stone thrown into the still lake of his thought. Fighting back the god, keeping him caged, was battle enough. Doing that while guarding his face before il Tornja proved nearly impossible.

"What are you waiting for?" Kaden asked, voice tight.

Il Tornja sighed. "I need her."

"For what?"

"For bait."

So, Kaden realized. *I was right.* There was no satisfaction in the thought.

"You think you can lure Meshkent to her," he said, shaking his own head this time, forcing a measure of scorn into his voice. "You really think a god would be that stupid?"

Il Tornja just smiled. "Of course I do. You're forgetting that I've fought them before."

"You lost," Kaden pointed out.

The *kenarang* shrugged. "The battle is not the war. I have Ciena now. Meshkent will come. Then I'll kill them both."

Kaden gritted his teeth. "Are you trying to frighten me?"

"What could be frightening," il Tornja replied, "about a world without suffering? What's frightening about a world without pain or hate? Without people being dragged around by the clanking chains of their lust? What's frightening about a world in which no one needs to weep over a child's grave?"

"We would not be what we are," Kaden said. Even to his own ears, the answer rang hollow.

"Surely the Shin taught you *something.* Surely you learned you can be better than your self."

"Why do you care?" Kaden asked, desperate for the conversation's end.

Submit, Meshkent whispered. *Submit, and I will rip out his lying throat.*

The pressure inside Kaden's mind was almost unbearable, but he could still hear his own baffled reply: *He's not lying.* However tortured il Tornja's version of the truth, it *was* truth. Meshkent's province was pain. That was his only gift. What kind of man would submit to such a master? In this much, at the very least, the Csestriim was correct—the young gods came, and they made men and women into slaves.

"Why do I *care?*" il Tornja asked, cocking his head to the side. "Why am I telling you this? Because I want you to help me."

"Help you? How?"

"You could start by telling me the truth. How did you know that Triste would be here? How did you find her? You have no *ak'hanath.* . . ."

"She told me," Kaden said simply. "When she was still in prison. She told me where she'd go if she escaped."

Il Tornja stared at him, that gaze measuring, weighing. Then he burst out laughing. "I'll tell you, Kaden—it's amazing. You'd think, after all these centuries, that I'd get used to just how stupid people can be, but I just . . . I'm still surprised." He composed his features. "I'll admit it. It's a weakness. Now. Tell me how Meshkent escaped."

The question landed like a slap. Kaden's stomach seized inside him.

"I don't know who—"

"Of course you do. You didn't arrive here with some lone Ishien soldier, as you claimed. You came with Long Fist, the Urghul chief, and you know as well as I do that that name, that flesh, is just a mask. He came with you to find his consort. You arrived through one *kenta* and you attempted to flee through another."

Kaden realized he was shaking his head. "You're wrong," he whispered.

"No," il Tornja replied patiently. "I am not."

"You're guessing because you're desperate."

Even as Kaden spoke, however, he was remembering the stones board, remembering Kiel playing out the *kenarang's* games. Even the most basic moves had been utterly opaque, following a logic beyond anything Kaden understood.

"I'm neither guessing," il Tornja said, "nor am I desperate. I am, however, vexed."

"You can't be. You don't have the capacity for anger."

The general waved away the objection. "A figure of speech. The point remains—you came here with Long Fist. He is not dead, as you claimed. If the river had killed him, we would know, the *world* would know. He is alive. He survived. You spent time with him. You can tell me what he wants, how he thinks."

"You think you can turn me to your side the way you turned my sister."

"Of course not. You and Adare are nothing alike. She conspired with me because she genuinely thought I'd help her save Annur, save the *people* of Annur. You don't care about the people of Annur."

"I do . . ."

"Of course you don't. Not really. You are free to help me in a way she never was. You can help me willingly."

"Why would I do that?"

"Because," il Tornja said, smiling wide, his teeth moon-bright in the lamplight, "you know that I am right."

Kaden took a long, shuddering breath. Meshkent raged inside him. His own mind was a maelstrom. The *vaniate* beckoned, the only calm in the chaos. He turned his face away. "Kiel told me that you'd lie."

"Kiel," il Tornja said, shaking his head. "Of course he did."

"This face, this argument, all these human gestures . . . none of it is true. You're doing it so I won't see what you really are. What you really want."

It was barely convincing, but it was all he had, the only resistance he could summon. For the first time, however, il Tornja's face went serious, still. He studied Kaden for a long time, then stood abruptly, turned away, and approached the river, walking to the very edge of the low cliff fronting the current.

The water was black in the lamplight. It looked cold, bottomless. For a long time, the Csestriim just stared into the moving depths. When he finally turned back, Kaden found himself looking into the face of a creature he did not know. The jocular, indifferent Annurian general was gone, scrubbed utterly away. This creature wore his face, the flesh hadn't changed, but the eyes were impossibly cold, hard. They were formed like a man's eyes, but the thought that moved behind them was unknowable as the river at night.

Kaden had faced gods, had spoken with the lords of all pleasure and pain, and yet there had been something in those immortal spirits that he recognized, a posture of feeling and thought, a core of emotion that he shared even with the divine. This, the emptiness in that stare, the distance of it . . . the sight made Kaden's heart fold inside of him. It was all he could do to keep from crying out.

"I thought to spare you from the full truth," il Tornja said. "It was a mistake."

Meshkent howled inside Kaden's mind.

This time, the Csestriim's smile was the smile of a skull.

45

The leach spoke to his prisoners as he murdered them, spoke in the soft, almost soothing voice that a man might use with a balky horse, or a petulant child:

"I'm going to take out your eye now," he purred. "I will pop it from the socket, like husking a pea. It will hurt, hurt horribly, I'm afraid, but I'm going to ask you to hold it carefully in your hand. It's amazing, but you'll still be able to see out of it. Do you understand?"

Valyn stood atop the crumbling wall, hundreds of paces from the small hill where the leach stood, and yet he could hear it all, every word a window into memory. In the battle's lull, he was blind, but he could remember Balendin all too well, the blue ink twisting up his arms, the long, dark braids hung with fragments of bone, the rings piercing his ears—iron and ivory, bronze and silver and steel. Valyn's mind stitched the old images—scenes from the Islands, from Andt-Kyl—onto the land he imagined lying to the north. He could see the man's easy slouch, the cruel hook of his smile, the arms bathed to the elbows in blood as the prisoner whimpered.

"Do you understand what's going to happen next?" Balendin crooned.

The whimper broke into open sobbing. Overhead a raven screamed, then another, and another. Balendin had always had a way with animals, even back on the Islands, though it was impossible to tell if the birds above were tamed somehow, or just waiting for the promised offal.

"If you don't talk to me," the leach went on, "I will make it worse. I will make it hurt more. Do you understand?"

"I understand. . . ."

"Thank you. Try to be brave. . . ."

The prisoner's scream cleaved through all other words, an endless, animal howl divorced from all language and reason, a perfect expression of agony and terror and despair. As though in response, the Urghul raised their voices, thousands of them, tens of thousands, so many that the whole dark world to the north seemed nothing but a wall of sound. It grew louder, higher, more frenzied, and then, as though cut with a knife, snapped. Behind the sound, there was only silence, high as the sky and hard as stone.

After a moment, Balendin spoke into that silence.

"A shame. I thought he would live longer. Bring out the next."

It had been going on like that for the better part of the morning.

The Urghul vanguard had ridden down out of the north a few hours after dawn. Most armies, confronted with a long wall manned by an unknown number of defenders, would have called a halt, sent scouts into the swamp to try to get behind the enemy lines, maybe arranged a parley in the hope that the other side would give something away. Not the Urghul.

When those early riders were still half a mile to the north, instead of stopping, they kicked their horses to a full gallop, swinging wide to the west, almost to the river itself, then looping back to the east, charging along the face of the fort just a pace from the defenders above. At first it had made no sense to Valyn. There was no way the horses could jump the wall; all the maneuver seemed to do was bring the Urghul pointlessly within reach of the Annurian spears. It took him a moment to piece it together from the alarmed shouts of the legionaries on the wall:

the horsemen weren't sitting, they were standing on the backs of their mounts, then leaping from the horses onto the crumbling ramparts.

The darksight came to Valyn then. Each time one of the horsemen gained his section of wall, Valyn would have a few heartbeats of razor clarity, the whole scene etched in shades of black against black—the howling face of the woman or man, lips drawn back from the teeth, sword or spear raised. Each time, the sight came long enough for Valyn to make the kill, but the Urghul made it onto the wall only rarely, and the resulting vision proved flickering, inconsistent, unreliable. As the battle raged around him, Valyn found himself hungry for *more*. More danger, and the vision that came with it. More death. It hardly mattered whose.

Instead, after what might have been an hour, the Urghul pulled back. Throughout the assault, more warriors had been arriving from the north, arriving constantly, until it seemed that they must fill the narrow space all the way from Mierten's Fort to the ruined bridge at Aergad. When Valyn finally lowered his axes to listen, he heard the whole land brimming with voices, thousands and tens of thousands, enough to come against the feeble wall day and night in successive waves without ever abating. The northern front was wide, but it seemed to his blind eyes that the whole Urghul nation was here, in this one place, ready to break through and into Annur.

"Stupid," he muttered. "If those first idiots had just waited . . ."

At his side, Huutsuu made an irritated sound deep in her throat. "There is honor," she said, "in being the first warrior over the wall."

True to her word, the woman and her tiny band had fought alongside the legionaries all morning. Valyn had caught glimpses of her spear flashing out, catching riders as they passed, the weapon's tip snagging a jaw, a neck, then Huutsuu lifting them from the backs of their horses as though they were so many fish to haul struggling from the water. If she felt bad about killing her own people, Valyn couldn't smell it on her.

"Trouble is," he replied, "none of them made it over the wall."

"There is honor in the attempt."

"What they got for the attempt was a stone to the skull or an ax to the face, then a short fall back into the bloody mud."

"Honor comes at a cost."

Someone on the Urghul side seemed to have decided, finally, that the cost wasn't worth it. After hours of furious, unpremeditated attack, the riders had finally fallen back. They didn't go far—just out of bow range. Valyn could hear them regrouping, checking horses and binding wounds, muttering to one another in their musical tongue. Closer to the wall, the wounded were turning into the dead. Some were dragging themselves over the ground, some lying still, their breathing wet, shallow, rapid. For the most part, they died quietly—no sobbing, no groaning, no protestation against the pain.

"Is anyone going to help them?" Valyn had asked.

"Those able to crawl out of bow range will be treated."

"And the rest?"

"Will endure their hardening in silence."

Endure they did, but not in silence. Balendin shattered whatever quiet had come with the battle's lull, emerging from out of the massed warriors to take up a position on the hill, just where Newt and the Flea had predicted that he would. Then, after a long pause to let everyone notice his arrival, the leach began his macabre bit of theater. One after another, men and women were dragged from the train of prisoners, hauled before Balendin, and carved apart. Valyn was no leach, but he could smell the horror reeking off the legionaries along the wall, the awe of the Urghul riders, hot as fanned embers, glowing brighter with every sacrifice. He could hear, in Balendin's smugly satisfied brutality, that it was working, that the leach was finding what he sought in the reverence or loathing of the massed humanity, that his power was growing.

Valyn dragged in a breath, trying to catch some hint of the wicks of the Kettral munitions smoldering silently beneath the ground. No use. There was only blood and horse sweat, piss and horror. He could only trust that the fuses were still burning somewhere under Balendin's feet. Newt knew his work, of course, but if he'd made any mistake, if those charges failed, then the battle was finished. The leach would punch a hole straight through the wall, and the Urghul would pour through, murdering everyone they found.

"Bring me someone strong," Balendin said, his voice carrying over the bloody ground. Valyn could hear the smile, the certainty. "Bring me someone who won't break the moment I put a knife in his flesh. I want to take my time with this. I want the soldiers on those walls to plumb the full depths of their despair."

The words were Annurian, of course. The leach had learned the Urghul tongue, but he was speaking to the legionaries, speaking directly to their fear. The realization hit Valyn like a slap.

"We need to distract them," Valyn said.

Huutsuu shook her head. "The Urghul?"

"The soldiers. *Our* soldiers. We need to give them something to look at, to think about, that's *not* Balendin. He needs their fear, their horror, but we can take it away."

Too late.

As the leach's captive screamed, a massive section of the wall of Mierten's Fort collapsed. There was no explosion, no concussive blow, nothing like what a Kettral starshatter might do. Instead, there was a grinding of stone against stone, slow at first, almost reluctant, maybe forty paces to Valyn's west, as though some implacable giant had put a shoulder to the huge blocks, dug in his heels, and shoved. There was time for the Annurians atop that chunk of wall to shout the alarm, to give voice to half a dozen baffled questions and desperate warnings. Then the structure hit some invisible point beyond which it could not stand, and the whole thing crumbled inward, the sound of falling stones mingled with the screams of those crushed beneath.

"There," Balendin said, when the noise finally subsided. He lingered over the word, as though he were trying to choose the juiciest pear from a marketplace stall. "Now we can finish with this foolishness."

The Flea was already shouting orders, sprinting toward the breach. Sigrid coughed up something that might have been a curse, and then the world exploded into sound once more, the panicked shouting of legionaries mixing with the vicious, triumphant screams of the Urghul as they wheeled their horses for the final attack.

"Where is the explosion buried by your Flea?" Huutsuu demanded.

Valyn shook his head. "It's too soon." He turned blindly toward the sky, but the sun had passed behind a cloud and he could no longer feel it, no longer gauge its height. It might have been noon or midnight for all he could tell. "We need to hold the wall. Need to *keep* him there."

Huutsuu spat. "There is a hole in the stones wide as ten men. My people will ride through—"

"No," Valyn said, cutting her off, turning away before she could finish. "They will not."

He planted a foot on top of the wall, hefted his axes, and leapt to the ground in front of the fort. The blind landing almost broke his ankle. He hit with one foot on the ground, one foot on the soft flesh of some dead warrior. His body responded more quickly than his mind, rolling over and away even as his ankle absorbed the strain. When he rose, he stood in darkness, the wall behind him, the Urghul a wordless thunder rolling in from the north.

His first steps toward the breach were blind, uncertain. He could hear Huutsuu cursing on the wall above and behind him, but she didn't matter. All that mattered was reaching the hole, the gap, and the killing that had to happen there. He needed it suddenly, needed it in the way a man struggling for days in the desert needed water. He could already feel the violence tugging at him, as though every death were a tiny hook hauling him onward. He stumbled over stones and corpses, caught himself on his axes, and ran on, westward, into the darkness as though it were light, life, freedom.

Just before he reached the hole, just before the Urghul hit, the darksight came.

Balendin's kenning had brought down a dozen feet of wall, but there was still a pile of rubble for the Urghul to struggle over. The Flea had taken up a position atop the heap, Sigrid a few paces behind him, the Aphorist just at his side. The Wing leader was shouting orders to the legionaries. Some were stumbling, some covered with their own blood, but they tried to form up, to make some sort of line as the Urghul hammered down out of the north.

"Valyn," the Flea shouted. "Fall back on me."

Valyn hesitated, caught between the line of Annurians and the approaching storm. Then slowly, his axes light in his hands, he turned away from the legions, away from the dubious safety of the wall and the other men, turned north toward the galloping horses even as he spoke: "No."

The fight that followed was a dream of blood and bliss. For the first time since il Tornja had taken his eyes, Valyn was able to see for more than a few heartbeats at a time, and not just see, but move through the violence that buoyed him up, lashing out and pulling back, stabbing and hacking until the blood ran down his face, his arms. There was no saying how long he fought. Sometimes Huutsuu was at his side, sometimes not. He could hear the Flea calling out orders behind him, well behind, but the Flea had given him up to the fight. The man's words weren't for Valyn, but for the line of Annurians still struggling to hold the wall, and Valyn made no effort to listen to them, to understand. Words were crooked, useless things beside the clarity of blood. He waded in it like a warm sea. He'd been fighting forever, but he wasn't tired. As long as they kept coming, he would keep killing, and killing, and killing.

He buried his axes in one Urghul after another, slaughtering man and beast alike, throwing the weight of his shoulder behind heavy steel wedges, pivoting and rocking, shattering skulls, then pulling free. He was laughing, he realized, had been laughing for a long time, the joy horrible inside him.

When the hill finally exploded, the force of the blow knocked Valyn back half a step. Stones and dirt fell all around him like rain. It took him a moment to realize what it meant.

Newt's munitions, he thought. *Balendin's dead.*

There was no joy in the understanding. If anything, that explosion meant an end to the battle. It felt like something stolen, like a great door closing. It was victory, and it tasted like rust.

46

A low stone plinth—the altar, maybe, of the ancient temple—stood at the room's center. Triste sat atop it. She wasn't chained, wasn't tied up or tethered in any way—evidently il Tornja considered the thick stone walls and the half-dozen guards outside the only door ample protection against her escape. The space was nothing compared to the subterranean cells of the Dead Heart, or to the steel cages of the imperial prison inside the Spear, but then, it didn't really need to be. Triste wasn't likely to fight her way past three dozen armed Annurian soldiers, and if she did, what then? She could search for ages in the ruined city without finding the *kenta*.

He has us, Kaden thought. *We raced straight into his trap.* They were alive only because il Tornja thought they might still be useful: Triste as bait, Kaden as a willing traitor to his race.

The failure should have stung, but Kaden found himself beyond stinging. The confrontation with the Csestriim general had left him numb, exhausted to the bones. The effort of holding up the lie, of maintaining his own face while hiding the god inside, had burned through the last of his reserves. He felt like the blackened, twisted scrap of wick left at the bottom of the clay pot when all the wax was gone, the flame guttered out.

Meshkent, at least, had fallen finally, mercifully silent. Kaden could still feel the god inside his mind, shifting, testing, searching for a way out, but now that il Tornja was gone, the urgency had subsided. Sooner or later, Kaden would fail. He was built that way. He would fail, and the god would claim him completely.

And why not? he asked himself.

Meshkent might be blinded by his own pride, but he was strong—Kaden could feel that strength like a bright, awful weight. More importantly, il Tornja, for all his planning, did not know the truth. He kept Triste drugged, but there had been no point in forcing Kaden, too, to drink the adamanth. It would be easy, so easy to just . . . give himself up, let the Lord of Pain take his mind and body both, let Meshkent have his fight with the Csestriim. Let him win.

It would mean not being Kaden anymore, but what was that worth? He'd spent half a lifetime trying to snuff out the embers of his own thought, and now he could achieve it, achieve that sublime annihilation instantly, absolutely. All it would take was a simple acquiescence of will.

"Did you come to finish killing me?" Triste asked.

The words were quiet, but they snapped the thread of Kaden's thought. He shifted his attention from the invisible landscape of his own fragmented mind to the room in which he stood. The guards had left a single lantern burning on the floor, but the flame was too small to illuminate the entire space; the corners and vaulted ceiling were lost in shadow.

He started to protest, then thought better of it. Il Tornja would have men listening, and besides, what could he say? He'd drawn a knife on Triste, had threatened to drive it into her flesh in an effort to flush out the goddess. It hadn't been an empty threat. He would have done it, if he'd been faster.

"Il Tornja wants you alive," he replied finally.

"Alive?" Triste asked. She stared at him a moment, then lay back on the stone slab, arms flat at her sides, her whole body limp with drug or exhaustion. Only her eyes moved, shifting back and forth as though searching for something in the darkness above.

"Bait," Kaden explained. "For Long Fist."

"Better be careful," Triste said, sounding indifferent to her own advice. "You don't want to give anything away to whoever's listening."

"There's nothing to give away," Kaden said. "He knows everything. He knows that you carry Ciena inside you. He knows that Meshkent and I came to find you, to help."

Triste made a wry, bitter sound that might have been a laugh.

"He knows the whole thing," Kaden said again. "He figured it out before I told him."

"Of course he did. He's Csestriim. All of this . . . it's just a game to him. We're just stones on the board." She shook her head wearily. "So Long Fist got away. He wasn't dying after all."

She might have been talking about some made-up character from a tale in which she had long ago lost interest.

"He got away."

"And I'm the bait. For Long Fist. Or Meshkent. Or whoever wants to bite."

"At least you're still alive."

Triste raised her head just slightly, staring at Kaden as though wondering whether to believe what she had just heard. When she let it drop, he could hear her skull against the stone. She didn't grimace. Didn't even seem to notice.

"Bait is not alive, Kaden. A worm on a hook *thinks* it's alive—it keeps wriggling and wriggling and wriggling—but you only need to look a few heartbeats into the future to see what happens to that worm: either the fish kills it, or it dies, still squirming on the hook. The 'Kent-kissing creature was finished the minute it became bait. Worms are dumb, so they don't know that. I'm not a worm. I can see what's coming."

"It's coming for all of us," Kaden replied quietly. "If you wait long enough, we're all dead."

"Well, that's not exactly right, is it?" Triste demanded. "Your sister's general—he's not dead. This bitch inside my fucking head—she's not going to die."

"They are Csestriim and gods. They are made differently from us. Bedisa wove our fate into our bones."

"I know that, Kaden. You think I don't know that? The thing I don't know yet is why we don't all just get *on* with it." She shook her head. It lolled back and forth sloppily over the weathered rock. "All it takes is one little blade to end a life. You don't even *need* a blade. You don't need anything. You can just not eat for couple of weeks. . . ."

Kaden studied her, the perfect skin laced with scar, the blazing violet of her eyes. "If you were so eager to die," he said finally, "you would have performed the *obviate* back in Annur, when we had the chance."

"It's not the dying I care about; it's helping *her*. She's in my *mind,* Kaden. You don't understand what that's like. You can't." She took a long, deep breath, then blew it out. "Growing up in the temple, there was always talk about rape."

Kaden shook his head. "The *leinas*—"

"Will you stop talking for just once?" At least there was heat in her voice now, a hint of the old fire. "You might have learned to be quiet in all those years with the monks, but you never learned to listen, did you?"

Half a dozen replies came to mind. Kaden set them aside. If Triste wanted him to listen, he would listen. After a long silence she continued in a whisper.

"Just because a woman is inside the temple walls doesn't mean she's safe. Demivalle and the other *leinas* who run the temple try to have guards in place, there are ways of doing things that are supposed to protect the priestesses, but you can't protect against everything all the time. Sometimes the women can't cry out, and sometimes they can but they don't. You're told you're supposed to please, that pleasure is the apotheosis of your faith. There's no space for second-guessing. No space to say, *'Wait.'* It's the clients, half drunk and emboldened because they paid, *donated,* whatever—but it's not just the clients, it's the *whole place*. If you're not a conduit of pleasure, you don't *belong,* and so the priestesses and priests suffer what's done to them. The clients go away, but Ciena's most holy carry their wounds inside."

She fell silent, lips parted as though she were short of breath or about to cry. Kaden's mind filled with the memory of Louette Morjeta, Triste's mother, the woman who had given her daughter up when her father came and demanded her. Had Morjeta wanted to lie with Adiv? Had she wanted to carry his child?

"This is like that," Triste said, breaking into his thoughts. "What the goddess did to me is like that, like what happens to women the whole world over, but it is *worse*. She's inside my mind. She didn't just fuck me and leave, she tried to *become* me. She's probably *still* trying. Do you understand?"

Kaden considered his words before replying. "Many people would embrace the presence of their god. To be taken in this way—it is an honor. That is what the man who was Long Fist must have thought before the Lord of Pain took on his mortal form. The acceptance is an exercise of devotion."

"That's disgusting," Triste said. Her eyes were far away. Dead-looking. "That's what men tell women after: *Actually, you wanted it. I am a king, a minister, an atrep, an emperor—you must have wanted it.* Well, I'll tell you something, Kaden," she said, her voice rising, rising with her body as she shoved herself up onto her elbows, shoved herself up until she was sitting, glaring at him, a finger extended, trembling. The words, when she finally managed to finish them, came out a scream, *"I didn't fucking want it!"*

She was panting, breathless. Although the night was cool, her face glistened with sweat. He considered crossing the space between them, trying to offer some comfort, but what comfort could he offer? His words were all unequal to the task, and any human touch seemed suddenly obscene.

"It's not the dying I mind," she said. They were the same words as before, but this time there was iron in them. "But I'll let that Csestriim creature flay me alive, I'll let him take me apart joint by joint before I do a thing to help this goddess who thought she could just take me, tame me, make me into her."

"I understand," Kaden replied finally.

"No," Triste said, shaking her head. "You don't. You can't."

Meshkent moved silently, massively inside Kaden's own mind. The pressure, the presence, the constant effort required to fight back against it, to keep the god from seizing control, was almost overwhelming, and Kaden had *allowed* him in, had managed to control him. He felt ashamed, suddenly. After half a day, he'd been almost ready to give himself over to the god, had been tempted to let the corridors of his mind just . . . fold, and here was Triste at the same time, still fighting, still defiant. The goddess could seize everything she was, had wrested her from herself half a dozen times at least, and still she hadn't given up. For all her talk of dying, she wasn't dead.

"You would have made a good emperor," Kaden said. He had no idea where the words had come from. As he spoke them, however, he realized they were true.

Triste just stared at him, baffled. "What do I know," she asked finally, "about the running of empires?"

"As much as I do."

"From what I heard, you made an utter mess of it."

Kaden nodded. "I did." He wondered what had happened since he left the Dawn Palace. Maybe Adare had managed to right Annur's listing ship. It didn't seem likely. The water had been pouring in in too many places. The whole vessel had already sunk too deep in the waves. Besides, Adare was hardly the benevolent leader she pretended to be. Il Tornja claimed she was doing what she did for the people of Annur. Maybe that was true, and maybe she was interested only in her own glory. Kaden didn't know her well enough to say. What he did know was that she had lied to him even as she tried to make her peace. Lied about Valyn, about her own brother.

It doesn't matter, he reminded himself. A liar could rule an empire. A traitor could rule an empire. Either one would be better than a half-trained monk.

"Why did you go back?" Triste asked.

Kaden realized he'd been staring at her without seeing her.

"Go back where?"

"To Annur. To try to take the throne."

It was a simple question. He had no answer. Looking back, words like *duty* or *tradition* seemed too weak, too dry and abstract to explain the things that he had done. The throne itself had carried no allure. He knew no one in Annur, not even his sister.

He shook his head. It was as though he were a stranger from his own life, incapable of explaining his own decisions, even to himself.

"Look . . . ," Triste began.

The night's quiet shattered before she could finish. Over the low moan of the wind and the lisp of the river's current, men began shouting, voices etched with anger and surprise. Annurian voices. Il Tornja's soldiers, though Kaden couldn't make out the *kenarang's* orders in the sudden chaos.

Steel smashed against steel, ground over stone. Men were screaming now. Dying, by the sound of it, the crisp urgency of command and response mixed with an animal panic, high keening notes of pain and desperation. As if in response, Meshkent shifted inside Kaden's mind, testing the boundaries of his cage all over again.

Slowed by drug, Triste rose slowly.

"Who—"

The wall exploded.

One moment, lamplight had been playing over the rough red stone. The next, a sheet of flame, bright as the midday sun, blazed across Kaden's eyes. Something punched him in the chest, knocking him back across the chamber and into the stone altar.

A shard of rock, he thought blearily, trying to keep hold on his own consciousness even as he groped at his chest with a clumsy hand. Surely there would be blood. Surely beneath that massive ache, there would be something broken. Either he had gone blind, or the world was suddenly, absolutely dark. Meshkent seized that moment to claw at his prison, growling, raging, larger than the sky and bent on escape.

Kaden closed his eyes, threw the whole weight of himself against the walls he'd made. The god inside him wanted out, ached to join whatever battle raged outside, but Meshkent misunderstood the weakness of his human vessel. Fighting was hopeless, pointless. Kaden couldn't see, couldn't stand, couldn't even hear beyond the high, bright ringing in his ears. If Meshkent got free, he would fight, and if he fought, he would die.

No, Kaden whispered.

The god bore down, furious and huge. Kaden gritted his teeth, marshaled what strength he had, and pushed back.

Between the battle beyond the temple walls and the desperate struggle raging in his mind, it took Kaden a long time to realize someone was clawing at him, a small hand, panicked and desperate. *Triste.* He reached out to seize her arm. Smoke and stone dust filled his nose, but the ceiling hadn't fallen. No great corbels had crushed them. Instead, cold night air poured through the hole in the shattered wall. Flame ravaged the streets outside, though what was burning Kaden had no idea. Against that blazing background of orange and red, a dark figure stepped into the breach.

Kaden blinked his eyes furiously, trying to make out more than the shape against the blinding flame. Then, abruptly as it had come, the fire was gone, leaving him staring into blackness. He raised his fists—a pointless gesture, but he could think of no other.

"*Triste,*" he called out.

There was no time to find out what was happening outside, no opportunity to sort the battle into sets of tactics or clearly labeled sides. The only thing he knew was that chaos had come, and with it, an opportunity.

"Triste," he hissed again.

The girl's answer was a scream.

Kaden spun toward the sound, trying to blink back the afterimage—filigrees of red and yellow flame—stitched across his eyes. He could make out no more than two shapes in the darkness: Triste, and someone at her back, someone taller and evidently stronger, pinning the girl's arms to her sides. Triste lashed out with a foot, started to scream again, then fell silent. Another fire roared to life beyond the temple's shattered wall, farther away this time, but close enough that Kaden could see the flame reflecting off a blade at Triste's neck.

"Kaden," said a new voice. "Triste. It's lovely to see you both looking so well."

Whatever madness was unfolding in the streets beyond, the person holding the knife didn't sound worried, didn't sound rushed. It was a woman's voice, low and throaty. She sounded . . . amused. Inside Kaden's mind, Meshkent went suddenly, utterly still. Wariness poured off the god, wariness that could be explained only by the woman with the knife, a woman Kaden remembered all too well, though the last time he had seen her had been a year and two continents distant. They had been lost in another ancient city then, in another range of peaks, fighting for their lives against a different group of Annurian soldiers. . . .

"I'm not sure what it says about the two of you," the woman went on conversationally, "that every time I see you, you're being chased by men with swords. Some people might take that amiss, I suppose, but I'm inclined to think it means you're special."

"Pyrre," Kaden said quietly.

So Rassambur had noticed their arrival in the Ancaz after all.

"What is going on out there?" he asked.

"Oh, you know," she replied breezily. "Death. Dying. A great offering to the god. And what a spot for it! Just a couple dozen miles from Rassambur, and we had no idea this place was even *here*. Very atmospheric."

As though to underscore the point, the air beyond the broken wall burst into another sheet of flame, illuminating for half a heartbeat both Triste and the Skullsworn assassin, who continued to hold the knife against her neck. Fear and confusion played over Triste's face, but Pyrre looked cheerful, despite blood dripping down from a gash at her hairline. It was almost a loving pose, that arm wrapped around the girl's chest, the two heads close to touching. Minus the knife, it was the sort of thing you might find between a mother and daughter, although the two looked nothing alike. Pyrre was obviously older, her face lined by long years in the sun, her hair as much gray as black. Older, and harder, leaner beneath her leathers. She wore the blood smearing her face as though it were makeup.

"We have to go," Kaden said, glancing toward the broken wall once more. Boots clattered somewhere in the streets beyond, steel continued to scream against steel, but there were no soldiers just outside, at least not for the moment. Pyrre had said nothing about a rescue, but she was a priestess of death. If she had come to kill them, she would have killed them already.

"Indeed," the assassin replied, cocking her head to the side. "The tide has shifted. My brothers and sisters came to make an offering to Ananshael, but it sounds as though they have become the sacrifice." She didn't sound bothered by the development.

He listened to the fighting. "How do you know?"

"Less screaming," she said. "Ananshael's adherents die quietly." She shrugged. "They have a leach—a strong one. We didn't figure on that."

Triste twisted in the woman's grip. Pyrre let her go.

"Where is the other one?" the assassin asked, glancing around the stone chamber. There was a new note in her voice this time, an eagerness, a hunger. "Long Fist. I've waited a long time to see him again."

Kaden shook his head. "Escaped."

Pyrre's eyes narrowed. "We tracked you here. . . ."

"He leapt into the river just a quarter mile north."

The Skullsworn clucked her tongue in irritation. "A shame. I was looking forward to opening his throat."

Inside Kaden's mind, Meshkent coiled and uncoiled, his voice a silent, wordless growl.

"We have to go," Kaden said again, as much to blot out the god as to drive them into motion.

Pyrre pursed her lips, looked from Kaden to Triste, then back again. "I suppose we do."

"How?" Triste demanded, staring out the gap in the wall. The fire had died down, but the shouts and screams seemed to be coming from everywhere.

"I suppose it would be too much to hope," Pyrre said, "that one or both of you might have spent the past year studying something other than pottery or fellatio?" The assassin raised an eyebrow. "No?" She let out a long sigh. "I guess we'll stick with the same plan as last time, then."

"What *plan*?" Triste demanded.

"You run as fast as you can," Pyrre replied brightly, "while I kill people."

47

From the top of the watchtower halfway along Annur's old northern wall, Adare stared west. It was easier than looking north. There was nothing to the north now but burned-out wreckage, charred timbers crumbling under their own weight, backyard gardens buried beneath ash, the streets impassable, blocked by the crumbling hulks of shattered stores and stables, temples and taverns. The distinctions didn't matter now. Whoever had lived, loved, and prayed in those spaces just days earlier was gone. Safely evacuated, hopefully. Maybe just dead, hung in one of the dozens of squares, or crushed beneath the weight of the burned-down buildings and their own stupid stubbornness.

Atop the wall, at least, the situation was different. Terial's old fortification was a hive of activity: soldiers stacking crates of arrows and extra spears, masons laboring to repair cracks and rents, men dangling on ropes before and behind the wall, or standing on hastily erected scaffolding, or bent double in the middle of the walkway itself, slathering old stones with new mortar. Adare glanced up at the sky. According to the master mason in charge of the project, all the effort would come to nothing if the rain arrived before the mortar set, but there was nothing to be done. The Urghul wouldn't wait for the rain.

As Adare studied the ongoing work for her makeshift command post atop the tallest of the towers, Nira came puffing up the stairs, followed by Kegellen and Lehav.

"Near as any of those assholes with the numbers can figure, there's enough grain in the warehouses to last the city two weeks."

Adare looked up at the clouds, considered the figure.

"'Course, we'll have resupply," the old woman went on. "More rice than wheat, but food's food to a grumbling belly."

"Sixty percent of that food came from north of the Neck," Adare replied finally, "at least for Annur. Given what's in the warehouses and the trickle that'll keep coming up from the south, we can last three weeks."

"Longer," Lehav said. "A lot longer. Start the rations now."

Adare turned to him. "I just burned down the homes and neighborhoods of a hundred thousand Annurian citizens. I've told them to live in warehouses and whorehouses and any other kind of fucking houses with enough space on the floor for a curled-up body. It's astounding the city isn't rioting already."

"The Queen of the Streets has her thugs out," Nira said. "They're—"

"Encouraging calm," Kegellen interjected. Unlike nearly everyone else on the wall, Adare included, she didn't seem to be panting or sweating. The sky-blue silk of her robe fluttered lightly in the hot breeze. She patted her hair with a free hand, as though to check it had not fallen free of the elaborate pins and clips holding it up.

"And by *encouraging calm,* you mean killing people," Adare said, pressing a hand to her forehead.

Kegellen winced elaborately, as though the words themselves pained her.

Nira just shrugged. "Sometimes ya gotta kill people to save 'em."

"The grain . . . ," Lehav began again.

"The grain is fine," Adare said, shaking her head. "If we all survive long enough to starve, I'll count it a victory. The miserable fact is that this city is on the brink of extinction. We're one eloquent, heartbroken mother away. One firebrand of a soldier who saw his family home torn down with his aged father inside. If one of those bastards starts making speeches in the streets, *good* speeches, we'll have full-blown madness south of the wall, and even Kegellen can't keep putting knives in them all." She blew out a long breath. "We won't *need* Balendin and the Urghul to kill us. By the time they show up, there'll be nothing left of Annur but mud and blood."

For once Nira had no response. She was staring down at the burned-out houses, but Adare had a sense that instead of the recent violence, she was seeing the wreckage of her own wars, battles a thousand years dead and more.

"The people need hope," Lehav said finally.

Adare met his eyes. "So start handing it out with the grain," she growled. "Greatest city in the world must have a few warehouses just packed to the rafters with hope."

"A flip response," the soldier said. "One that ill becomes the prophet of Intarra."

"Intarra," Adare said, the word so bitter on her tongue it might have been a curse rather than a prayer. "Where's the goddess when you need her?"

Lehav's jaw tightened. "That you would ask such a question is the reason the people are losing hope."

"They're losing hope," Adare spat, "because I'm burning down their fucking homes and the Urghul are coming to finish the job."

To Adare's surprise, it was Nira rather than Lehav who replied. "He's right," she said. "Men don't need a goddess when the table's piled high and the bed is warm. They need her when the well runs dry. When the fire's all but burned out."

"I need her, too," Adare snarled. She could feel the heat seared into her skin at the Everburning Well, could trace the scar. But what good were heat and scar in defending a city? Where were the bolts of lightning stabbing down out of the sky to scatter their unnumbered foes? Where was the strength to melt rock and level armies? Adare's own glowing eyes were just that . . . glowing. They could barely illuminate a manuscript in a pitch-dark room, let alone save a whole city from destruction. "I need her, too," she said again, shaking her head.

"The goddess will guard us," Lehav said. "Think of the Everburning Well. It was only in your last, most dire moment, when you had committed yourself fully to the cause, that she showed herself."

Adare nodded. The memory was still vivid as a dream from which she had only just awoken—the spear in her hand, a scream sharp on her lips, lightning carving apart the sky, and that single command offered in a voice larger than the whole world: *Win*.

I'm trying, she'd argued back almost every day since. *I'm fucking trying.*

Nira spat onto the stones. "Far as I've seen, faith's about as much use as a piss bucket with a hole punched in the bottom. Ya need something people can *see*. When the faith wears out, people believe what they've *seen*. Sometimes, girl, ya gotta make your own miracles."

Lehav's face hardened at the old woman's outburst, but he knew better than to take the bait. Instead, he turned back to Adare.

"Another question remains. We have yet to determine the structure of command."

Adare glanced around the tower's top. The sad fact was that these were the only people in the city she came anywhere close to trusting. Lehav, Kegellen, and Nira. A religious zealot, the queen of all thieves, and an undying leach teetering on the verge of madness. It hardly made for a reassuring coalition, but then, even this unstable alliance was better than the council. When the council fled, Adare didn't even bother trying to stop them. At least the small group assembled on the tower's top was willing to *fight*. The problem was that they didn't trust each other.

"You have the command," Adare replied, nodding to Lehav. "You're the closest thing we have to a general, so you're in charge."

Kegellen pursed her lips. "While I appreciate this young man's fine . . ." She let her eyes rove over his legs and chest. ". . . qualities, I'm afraid that many of Annur's less savory characters might chafe if they are told to take their orders from him. It is a sad fact that many of the most dangerous men and women in this city, men and women whose help we will dearly want if the horsemen come to call—they are dissolute, anarchic, unaccustomed to true military discipline. If I ask them to salute, and march in step, I fear they will rebel."

Adare looked at the woman. Kegellen smiled blithely back.

"What do you want?" Adare asked, voice tight.

"Want?" Kegellen asked. She blinked once, as though shocked by the question.

"This is a negotiation. You know it, and so do I. So what do you want?"

Lehav stepped forward, addressing himself to Kegellen. "The prophet of Intarra does not negotiate, nor does the Emperor of Annur. I know the scum of Annur as well as you do, woman. I grew up on your streets." He turned to Adare. "We don't need thousands of killers and thieves playing havoc up here on the battlements. They're scavengers, not warriors. We're better off without them."

Kegellen raised her brows, but Adare cut in before she could respond.

"Yes," she said flatly. "We do need them. Look at this wall." She gestured to the stone walkway stretching away into the distance, the bustle of normal commerce to the south, a smoking, blackened wasteland to the north. "The Sons cannot hold it all. The Sons cannot hold one-tenth of it. Maybe you haven't been paying attention, but the Urghul broke past the *entire Army of the North*."

"Only after il Tornja left," Lehav pointed out. "The legions were compromised."

Adare stared at him. "And you don't think we're compromised?" She swept a hand over the smoking rubble. A quarter mile to the north, well out of bowshot, men and women were picking through the wreckage. Adare had given orders against it, but there was no time to enforce those orders, no men. If the scavengers got too close to the wall, the soldiers would take a shot. Otherwise, they were free to pore over the destruction, to search for something left in the wreckage.

"We are miserably compromised," she said again, more quietly. "We do not have il Tornja. The only fighters on these walls will be the fighters we put there, and I will not leave whole sections undefended because we were too squeamish to make use of Kegellen's people."

"Oh," the woman replied, pressing a palm on her broad chest. "They are not *my* people. I am just a fat, slow woman. . . ."

"Save it," Adare growled. "We know what you are. We need the bodies you can put on this wall. So *what do you want?*"

To Adare's surprise, Kegellen's smile, when it finally came, was almost sad.

"You're a smart woman, Your Radiance. But you're young. It would be well for you to remember that you don't understand the world as well as you think."

As Adare blinked, Nira stepped into the gap. "And just what the dolled-up fuck's that supposed ta mean?"

Kegellen kept her eyes on Adare. "It means I don't want anything. Not for myself. I only ask that the women and men I send to this wall operate in their own groups in their own ways. They are not accustomed to military structure, military discipline. It will get them killed, will keep them from killing."

"Impossible," Lehav said.

"No," Adare said, shaking her head. "It is not impossible. Here is what will happen. I've named you general, and so you will decide the deployment of Kegellen's people. You will give them their position and their orders, then you will leave them to carry out those orders in their own way."

Lehav shook his head. "You don't understand how an army

functions, Your Radiance. Units shift in battle, cover for one another, reinforce one another."

"And that would be wonderful," Adare said, "if Annur's cutthroats and thugs were organized into units. They are not. You might train them if we had three months, but we have three days. You will give them a clear task and you will let them fight in their own way."

The soldier's lips tightened, then he offered a stiff salute. "As you say, Your Radiance."

Adare turned to Kegellen, who was watching her between narrowed eyes. "Is that enough for you?"

The woman nodded slowly. "I will get all those who can carry a sword."

"Do better," Adare said. "Get me anyone who can still bite."

Before the woman could respond, a commotion erupted down below. Men were protesting on the wall to the west. Protesting, then shouting, angry, then afraid. Steel rang against stone. In all the madness of soldiers and masons coming and going, it took Adare a moment to find the cause of this new disturbance.

"There," Lehav said, leveling a finger at three figures in black advancing down the walkway at the wall's top. As he spoke, he dropped his hand to the sword at his belt. Even Kegellen had formed her lips into a pout, had slipped a fan from her jeweled belt and snapped it open. The black-clad figures were still a hundred paces distant, but the caution seemed more than warranted.

The leader was a woman Adare had never seen before—young, muscular beneath her blacks, red hair caught in the northern wind and streaming out behind her like flame. The Sons stationed on the walkway had moved to block her approach, barking orders and baring swords, squaring up across the path. The red-haired woman ignored them, if *ignored* was the right word.

One of the Sons stepped forward, leveling his sword at her chest. She swatted it aside with the flat of her hand, slammed the other into the soldier's throat, then stepped past him as he dropped. The motion didn't even seem violent. It seemed—sensible, efficient. She hadn't even bothered to draw her own weapons.

"Kettral," Lehav said grimly.

"Kettral indeed," Adare replied. "The question is, *whose*."

"Well, obviously they're not fucking *ours*," Nira snapped, "since we don't know them, and they're gutting our men."

Adare watched a moment longer. "Not gutting them," she said. "They're not even hurting them."

The red-haired woman looked up as though she'd heard the words, found Adare's eyes, and spread her hands. "Call off your dogs," she shouted. "We're here to talk."

Another man came at her, spear extended. She pivoted, grabbed the shaft, and tossed him half a dozen feet onto a flat-roofed building just south of the wall. She caught the next soldier's sword on the spear, kicked him in the crotch with a booted foot, knocked his blade away as he fell, and stepped past him. They were maybe forty paces off now. The woman didn't look frightened. She didn't even look winded. She looked pissed off.

"If they keep this shit up," she shouted, "we're going to have to hurt someone, and I don't like hurting Annurians."

"I will deal with this," Lehav said grimly.

"No," Adare growled. "Call back your men."

The commander glanced at her, face unreadable, then barked out the order. The Sons remaining between the Kettral and the tower—maybe a dozen all told—hesitated, then inched backward, blades still drawn. They might have ceased to exist for all the attention the red-haired woman paid them. From somewhere in the streets below, an arrow flashed up, but before Adare could shout, before she could even flinch, it glanced aside, as though striking an invisible wall. The leader of the Kettral didn't pay attention to that, either, but behind her another woman, not much more than a girl, really, drew her own bow and fired back, three times in quick succession. There were no more arrows from the street.

"Enough killing," Adare said.

"We're not killing anyone," the woman snapped. "Annick's shooting stunners, and I'm relying on my fucking palms." She held them up, as though to make the point.

"You are perpetrating violence against my men."

"Your men are idiots. I told them I needed to talk to you. They were unhelpful."

Kegellen chuckled merrily. "It is not often that people live up to their reputation, but I'll admit to being charmed by these Kettral."

The Sons of Flame had fallen back almost to the tower itself, and Adare studied the Kettral as they approached. It was possible that il Tornja had sent them; the man was the titular commander of *all* Annurian military orders, after all. On the other hand, it seemed a strange sort of assassination attempt that would take place here, in the full light of day, in the middle of a thousand soldiers.

"Leave your weapons with the soldiers at the tower's base," Adare said finally. "Come up, and we can talk."

The Kettral leader nodded, but Nira was grumbling at Adare's side. "Not sure if ya just saw that pale-skinned bitch slap her way through half your fucking army, but I don't think the not havin' of weapons is really gonna slow her down."

Adare glanced over at Lehav and Kegellen. "They're armed."

Kegellen spread her hands. "I am a slow old woman with a fan."

"This woman is fast," Lehav said, watching the Kettral intently as they approached and surrendered their weapons.

The three of them seemed to be carrying enough steel to arm an Annurian legion: twin blades and belt knives, throwing knives and bows and arrows. It all went into a glittering heap. If they were worried about disarming, it didn't show. The Sons, on the other hand, for all that they had the numbers and the weapons, looked ready to leap from the ramparts.

It was only when the red-haired woman finally stomped up the stairs that Adare was able to see how young she was. Despite the scars and the muscle knotting her frame, she looked younger than Adare herself, although the look in those eyes was anything but naïve.

"Your Radiance," she said, nodding so shallowly the motion barely qualified as a genuflection. "My name is Gwenna Sharpe. I knew your brother. Both of them, actually. Where's Kaden?"

Adare's heart thundered inside her. She kept her face still. "You were on Valyn's Wing."

"All three of us," the woman replied. She studied Adare boldly. "Not sure if you got the news, but he died. Up north in Andt-Kyl. Heard you were there, too."

Adare tensed, and Lehav, hearing something dangerous in the woman's voice, took half a step forward.

The woman glanced over at the soldier. "Nice sword. Get any closer to me, and I'll put it in your eye."

"Gwenna," said the man standing behind her. He was as dark-skinned as she was pale, as soft-spoken as Sharpe was brash.

"This is Talal," she said, nodding to him. "He thinks I need to have a better attitude. Walk more softly. Keep the blades sheathed. That sort of thing." As she spoke, her eyes never left Adare's. Her smile was almost feral. "Thing is, I've had pretty good luck with the blades so far. . . ."

48

"We missed," the Flea said grimly. "He's not dead."

"How do you know?" Valyn asked.

"I saw it. The explosion blew open the crown of the hill, but Balendin had moved off the crest a few minutes before. The blow hit him hard enough to knock him down. He was bleeding pretty bad, but he was alive. They carried him off while you were trying to fight the entire Urghul nation by yourself."

Valyn closed his eyes. It was cold inside the chamber at the heart of Mierten's Fort, cold in the darkness of his own mind. The savage joy that had borne him up all afternoon had vanished. His bones ached. His muscles felt strained beyond their limits. Dozens of shallow cuts burned on his skin. When he shifted, he could feel the scabs break open and the blood start weeping again.

And he was in better shape than some of the others. Of the six who had gathered just after the sun set to pound out the next day's strategy, none had escaped unscathed. Belton walked with an audible limp. Newt kept coughing over and over, blood rattling in his chest as he bandaged a wound to Sigrid's arm. The Flea and Huutsuu both smelled of blood, although Valyn had no way to gauge their injuries further. And they were, comparatively, the lucky ones. Outside of the old keep, sprawled out on the grass in the shelter of the crumbling wall, wounded legionaries were groaning, or cursing, or just dying silently.

"That leach bastard might be hurting," Belton spat, "but so are we. I lost twelve men today. Another dozen probably won't make it through the night, and I haven't even counted those busted up too bad to fight."

"Be glad," the Flea replied.

"*Glad?* Glad for what?"

"That you didn't lose them all."

"Not yet," Belton said. "The Urghul will come again tomorrow, leach or no. And now there's a hole in the 'Kent-kissing wall. My men are exhausted, and now they'll be up all night trying to plug that gap. What do you expect them to do in the morning?"

"I expect them to fight," the Flea said quietly. "Put your wounded on horses and send them south. Have them warn the farmers and townsfolk between here and Annur. The rest of us fight until we win or we die. Each day we hold buys time."

"*Win?* We can't *win*," the legionary exploded. "We're facing the entire Urghul nation."

"Then I guess we'll die," the Flea replied evenly.

"The horses," Huutsuu cut in, "are mine. I came here to kill the Kettral leach, not to give up my mounts to save a soft people from their own destruction."

The Flea shifted slightly. Sigrid smelled suddenly eager. The Urghul woman was fast and strong, but she was not Kettral.

"These people will kill you, Huutsuu," Valyn said. "If you do not give them the horses, they will kill you and the rest of your Urghul on this side of the wall."

Huutsuu hesitated. When she spoke, the scorn boiled in her voice. "So this is the Annurian way. You told me I must fight my own people in order for you to defeat the leach. I fought them, and you failed. *You* failed. And for that failure, you would betray our trust, kill my warriors, take my horses."

"You are welcome," the Flea said wearily, "to just give us the horses."

"You are lost to honor," the woman snarled. "All of you."

"Honor's a fine thing, but it's not much use in a fight."

The silence that followed was knife-sharp, poised to cut the first person who moved or spoke. Valyn listened to the heartbeats, half a dozen stubborn drums hammering out their cadences of wariness or rage, each one trapped inside its cage of bone. Breath sawed in and out between chapped, bloody lips. Breath and blood—that was all that separated them from the dead littering the ground outside. It didn't seem like much. Didn't seem like enough.

"How many times," Valyn asked finally, turning to Huutsuu, "have you called Ananshael the Coward's God?"

He waited. She refused to reply.

"Let's be clear about one thing," he went on finally. "I know the Flea. If he kills you, there won't be any pain. There won't be any glory. You will be alive, then you will be gone, off into death's endless softness. Balendin will be alive, and we will be fighting him, but you will have quit. Over a few horses."

Huutsuu ground her teeth. "This is not what we agreed."

"We agreed to kill the leach," the Flea pointed out.

"And you failed to kill him."

"When I am dead," the Wing leader replied, "then you can say I've failed."

Valyn could almost feel their gazes locked like horns, the Flea's eyes dark as mud, Huutsuu's sky blue and cruel.

"All right," she said finally. "You will have the horses you need. How do we kill the leach?"

Valyn exhaled slowly. "We go in now," he said. "Kill him while he's wounded, while his guard is down."

The Flea shook his head slowly. "It won't be down. It will be doubled. Remember your Hendran: *Wariness is the strongest armor.* Balendin has always been cautious. Now that he's wounded he will be more so. Worse, he knows he's facing Kettral. He's seen us."

Belton spat onto the broken ground. "Isn't this what you Kettral do? Sneak around? Kill people?"

"It is, and we've done a lot of it, so you'll have to trust me when I tell you this won't work. If we go after Balendin right now, there will be sneaking and killing. We will be the ones getting killed."

"There is no blade," Newt agreed, *"as keen as surprise."*

"I understand this," Huutsuu said. "A child of five understands there is a good time for a raid, and a foolish time. We do not have the choice. We cannot hold this wall forever."

"We will hold it as long as we can," the Flea replied. "Then we will fall back to the next position, then the next. We will purchase time for the men and women of Annur, and we will wait for the leach to make a mistake."

"Wait?" Huutsuu demanded. "That is how you plan to kill this leach? Wait? This is not the way of a warrior."

Outside the stone chamber someone screamed, a long, lost, awful cry, then fell viciously silent. Valyn's blood blazed at the sound, his hand dropped to his ax, but there was no attack, not yet. The soldier was battling his own agony, nothing more, nothing less.

"You call Ananshael the Coward's God," the Flea said finally.

Huutsuu stiffened. "He shields the weak from their pain."

"We have another name for the Lord of the Grave: the Patient God."

"Patience is no virtue for a warrior."

"I'm not a warrior," the Flea replied quietly. "I am a killer."

Late that same night, after the legionaries had finally plugged the breach in the wall with a jumble of hastily cut logs, after the Annurian dead were buried in shallow graves and the wounded given what comfort there was to give, after everyone on the south side of the wall had collapsed into a few hours of fitful sleep, Huutsuu found Valyn sitting atop one of the guard towers, staring blindly over the land to the north.

"How many are there?" he asked, not bothering to turn.

The woman smelled of blood-soaked leather and something else, a sharp, pungent scent. It took Valyn a moment to realize she was drinking some sort of strong spirit.

"I don't know. Our songs say the Urghul are numberless as the stars."

Valyn grunted. "Then we're fucked."

Huutsuu's earthenware bottle clinked as she set it on the stones next to him. "Drink."

Valyn took the rough bottle around the neck and lifted it. The liquor burned his split lip, burned all the way down his throat. "Where did you get this?"

"They were hidden in a back room of the fort. I don't know why."

"Smugglers," Valyn said. "Probably running the stuff up or down the Haag." It seemed strange that this place had been used for something so normal, strange that there were people beyond the scope of the battle, men and women inside the empire and beyond who knew nothing about the violence that had exploded there that day, whose thoughts were bent instead toward saving a few coppers on a jug of rotgut. Valyn shook his head, took another swig, then passed the bottle back.

Huutsuu drank long and deep, swirled the spirits inside the crock. The sound reminded Valyn of waves, of the sea around the Islands, of endless hours swimming or running the beaches. He had thought he was beyond sorrow, that the events of Andt-Kyl had hammered it out of him. Earlier in the day, he'd listened to thousands of men and women fighting for their lives, Urghul and Annurian alike, fighting and dying, and he'd felt nothing but a savage animal anticipation. That the sound of splashing should haul back all the old emotions—if only for a moment—baffled him. He took the jug from Huutsuu, threw back a slug, then another, and another, until the feeling subsided.

He could feel her eyes on him. "Tens of thousands," she said finally. "That is how many of my people came to your land.

There are more scattered through these miserable forests, but here, fighting us, maybe thirty thousand."

Valyn stared at her, then laughed. It seemed the only response. "Tens of thousands against less than a hundred. The Flea can talk all he wants about waiting to kill Balendin. If we survive one more day, I'll eat this 'Shael-spawned bottle."

Huutsuu hesitated. "I saw you fight today. . . ."

Valyn shook his head. "So?"

"You killed two dozen men. Alone."

The number sounded insane. Certainly, there were men and women among the Kettral who claimed to have killed scores of foes, but that was over the course of many missions, twenty or thirty years; not standing in front of a wall battling a whole army.

"Why didn't they shoot me?" he asked.

His memory of the battle was jagged and haphazard, as though he'd been viciously drunk, or only dreaming. There had been the wall behind him and the Urghul in front, the corpses of warriors and horses piled high on every side, a barricade of sorts, one he'd hewn from the flesh of his foes. It was an awful position, open to even the most amateur bowman, and the Urghul had never lacked for bows.

"They tried," Huutsuu replied. "The arrows . . . flew aside. It was as though they hit a wall of air. The leach, the Edish woman with no tongue, she stood on that wall. Her eyes were fixed on you until the sun fell."

"Sigrid," Valyn said slowly.

It made sense. According to the Flea, the woman was too exhausted to fight, too weary to work any significant kenning. Flicking a few dozen arrows wide, though—that might be something she could manage. Valyn found himself laughing again, the sound rough and ragged. "There you have it. I might have killed two dozen of your riders, but I was hiding behind a shield." He shook his head. "Some warrior."

"Shield or no shield," Huutsuu said, "I have seen many warriors fight. None like you."

She fell silent. Injured men and women, Annurian and Urghul
alike, cried out in their sleep, sharp sobs punched into the cold
northern wind. Already, the rot was settling into their wounds.
Valyn could smell it. Some would be dead by morning. Against
that backdrop of dismemberment and death, it seemed impossible that Valyn himself had walked away from the battle with
nothing more than a few scratches. He dragged a finger along
a rough scab running the length of his forearm. Huutsuu's knife
had cut deeper nearly every night than the lances and swords
of the Urghul army. The Kettral taught their cadets to face death
in battle, but in that long, bloody fight in front of the walls of
a crumbling fortress, Valyn had felt, for the first time in nearly
a year, fully, utterly alive. He shuddered at the memory.

"You can kill this leach," Huutsuu said to him. "I went into
the forests months ago searching for the wrong ghost. This Flea
of yours—he is strong, fast, but his way is all waiting and no
war." She put a hand on Valyn's chest, wrapped his leather jerkin
in her fist and pulled him close, so close he could taste the
eagerness on her breath. "You can do what he cannot."

Valyn knocked her hand away. "I'm fucking *blind*."

"Not when you fight. You have told me this yourself."

"I can't fight all the time."

He hadn't expected the words to emerge so heavy with regret.
There was something broken, something twisted about wanting
to live constantly in the midst of so much blood. Even the
Kettral, men and women who lived to fight, to kill, came back
to the Islands, they lounged on the beach, went fishing, stayed
up half the night swapping tales in shitty taverns over on Hook.
I would trade it all, Valyn realized, *talking, sleeping, eating,* all
*of it, just to stand in front of that wall burying my axes in the
necks of the Urghul.* A part of him recognized the desire as mad,
suicidal, but what was the point of living if that life was spent
plunged in darkness and regret?

"What am I supposed to do?" he demanded. "Blunder

through the Urghul camp with my hands stretched out in front of me calling out for Balendin?"

"I want you to learn," Huutsuu replied.

"Learn what?" Valyn demanded.

"To see."

As she whispered the last word, he felt the knife bite between his ribs, and again the sight came: Huutsuu leaning close, holding him by the shoulder with one hand, pulling him in even as her steel broke the skin. It was a ritual they'd played out a dozen times already, one ending in the same spasm of blood and sex, but this time Huutsuu made no move to lean close. Instead, she watched him, her blue eyes black, bright, shadow lips drawn back. He could feel her hot breath on his cheek, but unlike all those other nights, this time she smelled of determination rather than desire.

"You can see," she said.

As the knife's pressure eased, the vision faded.

Valyn shook his head grimly. "No, I can't."

Huutsuu pulled away. "You can."

"Only when I have to," Valyn said. "Only when I'm about to die."

Huutsuu turned her back on him, boots crunching over rough stone as she crossed the top of the small tower. When she reached the far side she paused, as though studying the wall below. She was still facing away from him when she spoke again.

"You are always about to die."

Then, with the sound of a distant wind picking up through the trees, she spun and threw. As her arm moved through the top of the arc, the world's form resolved from the darkness—Huutsuu's torso twisting with the throw, her fingers letting the knife fly free, the knife itself tumbling over and over, etching its own black path on the greater blackness. Just as it had on the battlefield below, Valyn could feel his body reacting before his mind, some part of him older and faster than thought making a dozen small adjustments, pivoting, throwing his hand up, closing his own fingers around the handle of the knife, snatching it clear of the air and then flicking it back at Huutsuu.

If she hadn't known it was coming, she would have died. Instead, even as she threw, she was expecting his impossible catch and diving aside. Even so, she was almost too slow. The knife clattered into the stone where she had stood a quarter heartbeat earlier. They both fell still. Valyn's darksight passed as quickly as the violence, leaving him with the sound of his own quickened breathing rasping in his ears.

"You think I won't kill you," he said quietly. "You think because we've fucked a dozen times and neither one of us has died that it won't happen." He shook his head. "You're wrong. One of these times, it will take over completely. . . ."

"It?" Huutsuu asked. He could hear her getting to her feet.

"This thing inside me. The thing that can see. That can kill."

"No, Malkeenian," she said. "It is not a thing inside you. It is you."

Valyn shook his head. "I'm not this fast. Not even close. Look . . ." He yanked one of the twin axes free of his belt, just to show her. It would have been a passable draw back on the Islands, but after the strange, impossible competence that came over him with the darksight, the motion felt clumsy, almost interminably slow.

Huutsuu shook her head, but made no move to approach. "A horse will not run at a fire," she said, "not when it is young. But fire—it is as much a part of war as blood. The creatures must be trained, and so we blind them, not with a blade, but with thick wool. I have done this many times. Blinded, the horse will ride toward a fire, will ride straight *through* a fire if you ask it to."

"I'm not one of your horses, Huutsuu."

"No. You are faster and more dangerous, but for you, as for them, there is a time for blindness, and a time to take the blindfold off."

"I don't know *how*," he snarled.

"You do. I have watched you all these days. Even when you say you cannot see, you see. You turn toward motion and light. When a branch looms before you, you dip your head."

"Do you have any idea how many branches I hit riding around that 'Kent-kissing forest?" Valyn demanded.

Huutsuu's laugh was sharp enough to cut. "Do you have any idea how many branches you missed?" She shook her head. "You are a fool, Malkeenian. You say you can only see when death looms close, but death is always close. Now, for instance . . ."

She lunged at him, her body resolving from the darkness. As she closed, she drew her sword, swinging it overhead in a vicious arc. Valyn stepped aside at the last moment, saw the dark sparks flash as it crashed against the stone. He kicked her in the back of the knee, and she fell, rolled away, came up in a crouch, the sword level before her, pointed at his chest.

"Can you see me?" she asked quietly.

"We've been over this," he growled. "When the fight is finished—"

"What if it is *never* finished, Malkeenian?"

He stared at her. She smiled.

"This is what Kwihna teaches. . . ."

"Kwihna's 'teachings,'" he spat, "are nothing more than blood."

"Your blindness is not a blindness of the eyes," Huutsuu replied. "It is a blindness of the soul. You think that you can draw a line in the dirt, that you can say, 'To this side of the line is fighting, to this side quiet. On this side war, and on this side, peace. On this side I can see, but here I am blind.'"

As Valyn stared, she hurled herself at him again. He let the blade go by his face, caught her wrist, and pulled her close.

"It is *all* struggle, Malkeenian," she whispered. "Life is suffering—*that* is what Kwihna teaches."

"Life is . . ."

"Suffering," she said again. "Pain is suffering because we

want to be free of it, and pleasure is suffering because we fear to lose it. Fools search for freedom, but there is no freedom. There is only the embrace. You say you are blind whenever you do not fight, but you are *always* fighting."

She shifted in his grip, hit him hard across the face with her free fist. The skin split open beneath the blow. Valyn's blood blazed. He bared his teeth, tightened his grip on her wrist, twisted until he thought her arm would break. She refused to wince.

"Life is *all* a fight," she hissed. "You deny this because you come from a weak people, and so you stumble around believing you are blind."

She spit in his face.

He wrenched the woman's sword around, forcing it back on her until the blade lay against her throat. He could feel the pulse hammering in her veins, see her pupils dilated in the moonlight.

"You think you're fighting me?" she whispered. "You are a fool, Valyn hui'Malkeenian. Look in yourself. See what you are fighting."

He stared, his own breath barbed and tangled in his chest. *Kill her,* something inside him whispered. *Cut her throat. Let the blood spill.*

"Even now, Malkeenian, you are fighting it."

A line of blood darkened the blade. Valyn pressed harder, wanting more.

"There is only one foe," she whispered. "Each woman has her own, and each man, his. Do you know its name?"

He realized, as the blood ran down the steel onto his hand, that he understood Balendin's joy, the bliss of standing among the dead and dying, of terrifying the terrified, of reaching out with strong hands to rip life from the living. The knowledge sickened him.

"You think I won't kill you?" he snarled. "You think I wouldn't enjoy it?"

He could feel her collarbone hard beneath the sword's blade, her hot breath in his face.

"Of course you would."

"You gambled," he told her, tightened his grip around her wrist. "And you lost."

She shrugged, indifferent to the blade's edge. "There is no sight without sacrifice. Name it before you give me to your Coward's God."

"Name *what*?"

Her smile was bloody, mocking. "The thing you fight. Your foe. Give it its proper name."

"There are dozens, hundreds—"

Huutsuu shook her head. "There is only one."

Kill her, something inside him whispered. *Open her throat and feel the life drain out.*

No. Not something inside of him. Him. The sick whisper was his own.

"Name your foe, Valyn hui'Malkeenian," the woman said again, "and then tell me if there will ever be a day, ever a moment, when you will not have to fight."

He would have killed her then, he realized, would have taken the head from her shoulders, would have bowed to the dark part of himself that prowled the corners of his mind. Only the horn stopped him, an Urghul horn that shattered the predawn calm, the long, angry note drawn out over a dozen heartbeats. It fell silent, then sounded again, and again.

"What is that?" he demanded

Huutsuu bared her lips. "My people. They do not wait for the dawn." She raised her free hand to the blade pressed against her neck, ran a finger along the steel. "Will you add me to the dead this day?"

Valyn stared, the shock of what he'd been about to do ringing in his head like the horn. He shoved her viciously away, staggered back. The blade fell from Huutsuu's numb fingers, clattering against the stone. Valyn's own hands shook as though diseased.

She watched him with narrowed eyes, then smiled.

"Life is war. Every heartbeat is war. This is Kwihna's truth."

Valyn turned away, sickened, from that truth, turned to face the coming charge—thousands of Urghul galloping toward the wall, dark figures on dark horses, the lines of their weapons and faces carved from the black wall of his blindness. They were still three hundred paces out, no threat to him at all, not yet, but he could see them, see them perfectly, see them all.

49

According to Pyrre, it was only twenty-five miles from Rassambur to the stone ruins by the river where she'd broken Kaden and Triste free. There were no straight lines in the mountains, however, and the miles had a way of multiplying. All night and all day they'd been fleeing il Tornja's soldiers, laboring up narrow defiles, racing across swaths of open slickrock, fording mountain streams, and then running again, cutting through the maze of canyon and cliff, all too aware of what would happen if they faltered or fell. For a long time, the Annurians trailed just a few hundred paces behind.

"The *ak'hanath*," Kaden managed, not slowing as he pointed back. "Tracking us."

He hadn't spotted the creatures—they were too quick, too nimble for that—but he had seen them move over stone back in the Bone Mountains, and had no illusions about his own ability to outrun them. He almost imagined he could hear, over the sound of his own breath and blood, the skittering of their hard claws on the rock, that high keening just at the edge of human hearing, the sound like a needle lodged inside the ear.

"We could kill them," Triste gasped as she struggled over the broken scree. "If they . . . come out . . ."

Kaden shook his head. "They won't. Il Tornja won't risk them. As long as they're alive, he can follow us anywhere."

Pyrre paused for a moment as Triste struggled to climb a

short ledge. The assassin looked every bit as exhausted as Kaden felt. Sweat matted her hair, her breathing was ragged, blood crusted her leather tunic and bare arms—some of it from the soldiers she had killed, the rest from her own cuts and gashes. Unlike Triste, however, she didn't seem concerned. In fact, even as she peered back down the canyon, shading her eyes with a hand, a smile tugged at the corner of her mouth.

"I am really starting to dislike those creatures," she said.

And then, just as she finished speaking, as if the soldiers and the spiders were not enough, the lightning came. The sky remained utterly cloudless, one great bowl of undivided blue, and then the lightning was there, massive actinic bolts stabbing down all around them, blasting cliffs and shattering stone. The closest struck a hundred paces distant, but violence stretched away on all sides for miles.

"The leach," Kaden said wearily.

Pyrre tsked her vexation. "It really does seem like cheating."

Another bolt fractured the cliff top a quarter mile ahead, the impact spraying smashed stone in all directions.

Kaden forced down the animal urge to flinch, to cower in some shadow until the unnatural attack was over. Instead, he stepped into the middle of the wide canyon, studied the pattern of bolts ripping through the sky. "It's random. They don't know where we are."

"He doesn't need to know," Triste shouted back. She'd fought her way up onto the ledge, and was waving them on impatiently. "He might be just guessing, but the lightning can still kill us."

"Indeed," Pyrre mused, gazing speculatively at the elemental savagery unfolding all around them. "Ananshael's will is unknowable."

"Do you want to stand here and test it?" Kaden asked, glancing over at the Skullsworn. He hadn't intended the question seriously, but found, even as he spoke the words, that there was a part of him that ached for just that—to stand and wait, to pass the weight of his own responsibility over to some other, greater power, to finally abdicate a fight he neither understood nor truly hoped to win. Meshkent raged inside him, wordless, slavering, furious, hurling himself against the walls Kaden maintained. It would be easy, effortless, to let those walls fall. To set the god free. To abandon the self once and for all . . .

Another bolt slammed into the stone canyon, where they had passed just a few moments before. The assassin didn't flinch, didn't even look at it. Instead she turned to study Kaden.

"You're not the skinny monk that I remember."

Kaden shook his head, hauling his thoughts away from sacrifice and surrender. "That monk wouldn't have survived."

"Survival." Pyrre frowned. "For just a little while there, I thought that might have finally stopped mattering to you. The god comes for us all."

"Then why are we running?"

Pyrre flashed him a smile. "Because if we run now, we get to fight later. And I like fighting."

By midday, the sky had fallen quiet. When they paused at a narrow stream to gulp a few mouthfuls of water, Kaden could no longer make out the angry clatter of pursuit. It was tempting to believe they had outdistanced the soldiers, but he had been battling against il Tornja's schemes too long to trust his own temptations. The *kenarang* was coming, whether Kaden could hear him or not; his goals were simple, even if his tactics were not. The question was, why had Pyrre and the other Skullsworn intervened?

"You could have let us die," Kaden said, straightening from the stream, savoring the cold water on his tongue, in his throat. "Il Tornja would have killed us. You cheated your god."

Pyrre shook her head. "Not cheated. Traded. Your two souls for those we left below."

Triste was staring at the assassin, her scarred face twisted with revulsion. "But why? Why bother?"

"It was an intriguing opportunity," Pyrre replied.

"To kill il Tornja?" Kaden asked.

The Skullsworn shook her head. "To take Long Fist." There was an unusual note in her voice when she said the name, something vicious and eager, utterly at odds with her habitual wry calm.

"Long Fist?" Triste demanded. *"Why?"*

Pyrre turned to her, then raised an eyebrow, as though debating inwardly whether or not to respond. "He is a priest of pain," she said finally. "A high priest of Meshkent. He would have made a fine offering to my god." She glanced over at Kaden, cocked her head to the side. "Speaking of which, where did he go?"

The words were deceptively mild.

Kaden shook his head. "Escaped. Jumped into the river."

Pyrre pursed her lips. "Then my god may have him after all."

"Maybe," Kaden agreed. Inside his mind, the ancient god raged. "So what happens to us now?"

"A good question," Pyrre said. "We will go to Rassambur, and then decide."

"What if we don't want to go?" Triste demanded. She was panting, doubled over with her hands on her knees, but her eyes were hard, defiant.

Pyrre offered her a broad smile, made an ostentatious little flourish with one hand, and was holding a knife. "The altars of my god are everywhere. Each patch of dirt"—she gestured with the blade—"that stone on which you stand. And my piety sometimes outstrips my patience."

"We'll go," Kaden said, holding up a hand, as though there were anything he could do to stop the assassin, then turning to Triste. "It's safer than staying here."

Pyrre chuckled. "Safe," she said, lingering on the word as though she could taste it. "Such a tricky term. Never seems to mean what people want it to mean." She shrugged. "But yes, I'd agree that Rassambur is safe."

Triste narrowed her eyes. "Meaning what?"

"Meaning I might kill you, but I promise not to hurt you first."

A fortress of dark iron and nightmare. A labyrinth reeking of carrion; long halls echoing with screams. A den of perversion, a home for men and women drinking blood from human skulls, offering their own infants as sacrifice on charred altars, slaughtering one another in twisted, blood-slick orgies. Halls of bones and altars of human flesh. Charnel pits brimming with the festering dead. Blasted caverns devoid of light, of hope, of all human comfort, given over to the veneration of the old and awful God of Death himself: Ananshael, unknitter of souls, savorer of rotting corpses.

Kaden had heard dozens of variations over the years of the tales told of Rassambur. Some, servants' stories whispered in the kitchens of the Dawn Palace; others, historians' accounts inked on expensive parchment and bound into codices for the shivering delectation of the rich. The fortress was a favorite subject of painters, too. Some, like Sianburi in his famous *Stages of Death,* used Rassambur as an excuse to explore human anatomy: a flayed arm here, an eyeball lolling from its socket there, perfectly drafted femurs and skulls stacked rafter-high in the background. The Ghannan ateliers, on the other hand, mostly ignored the corpses in their work, dwelling instead on Rassambur's infinite gradations of shadow and darkness. Kaden had read somewhere that Fiarzin Qaid, the greatest of the Ghannan painters, had labored for eight years, grinding and mixing two hundred different shades of black, before attempting his masterpiece, *The House of Death,* a horse-high canvas depicting Rassambur's most horrid hall.

Qaid never even saw the place, Kaden realized.

With Triste and Pyrre, he stood at a cliff's lip, staring across a gulf of empty air to a huge, sheer-sided sandstone butte and the fabled fortress of the Skullsworn that perched at its top. *Qaid didn't need* two *shades of black, let alone two hundred.*

In fact, the stronghold and the land around it were a study in light, air, and rich color: an azure sky nailed up above brilliant cliffs, dozens of shades of russet and rust and vermillion, and between them, the creamy white of Rassambur's small, graceful buildings. There were no defensive walls, no ramparts or towers, no murder holes or arrow loops. At the top of the sheer-sided butte, there was no need—the land itself was the fortification. The lair of the priests of death was not a lair at all, but a bright, white-walled, sun-drenched place of gardens, cloisters, and humble temples. Splashes of green dotted the grounds where the Skullsworn had cultivated the flowering desert plants. Even the shadows cast by the scattered loggia and trellises looked inviting, cool and quiet. It almost reminded Kaden of Ashk'lan—the clarity of it all, the cleanness—but where the Bone Mountains were viciously cold at least half the year, here, the hot sun warmed the stone even as the mountain breezes cut through the heat's worst bite.

A single bridge—a graceful arc of white stone with no railing or balustrade—spanned the chasm between Rassambur and the cliff where Kaden stood with Pyrre and Triste. It looked too slender to support its own weight, let alone that of anyone crossing. There was nowhere to hide on that bridge, nowhere to shelter. A single archer with enough arrows could hold it against an entire army for days. That was how it looked, at least. Kaden hoped it was true.

"We should get across," he said, gesturing, forcing his aching, trembling legs into motion once more. "Before il Tornja catches up."

"He won't," Pyrre replied.

Kaden shook his head. "You don't understand. He abandoned his post in the north, he risked letting the Urghul destroy Annur, all so that he could come here, after . . . us."

He glanced over at Triste as he pronounced that final word. She made no indication she had heard him. Instead, she stared fixedly at Rassambur, face bleak, as though she were peering into the freshly turned earth of her own grave.

Pyrre pursed her lips, studying the girl. "All this way for the two of you and an Urghul warlord. I so look forward to learning why."

"We can talk about why when we're on the other side," Kaden said.

He had no idea what he would say when that talk came, no idea what lies he might spin to save himself, save Triste, and the gods hidden inside them both. That could wait, though. First they needed to reach Rassambur's dubious safety.

"What I mean to say," Pyrre went on, gesturing to the mountains around them, "is that these cliffs are alive with my brothers and sisters, some hunting, some just standing guard. If il Tornja has read his history at all, he will know this, he will know better than to come within a mile of Rassambur."

Kaden squinted at the rocks through which they'd passed. He had seen nothing, no sign of guards or sentries. On the other hand, it had been all he could do to keep his feet as they stumbled over the rough stone, and he'd barely raised his eyes from the ground. He might have passed straight through the center of an army without noticing it. Still . . .

"He has a leach."

"Leaches die just like everyone else," Pyrre said with a shrug, "when you remember to put a knife in them."

There was no sign, when they finally stepped off the narrow bridge, that anyone from Rassambur had ever learned to put a knife in anything more dangerous than the cacti that they carved for the evening meal. Pyrre had learned to fight *somewhere,* that was obvious enough, but the devotees of Ananshael weren't training or fighting. All the Skullsworn that Kaden could see— men and women in white desert robes—were going about the quiet tasks of daily life: gardening, paring vegetables, drawing water from a central well, walking between the modest buildings or talking quietly in groups of two or three. The only weapons

Kaden could see weren't weapons at all, but small belt knives, the sheathed blades no longer than a finger, less dangerous than what he himself had carried back at Ashk'lan.

The place seemed more like a sanctuary than a den of death and violence, and though the Skullsworn fell silent as he passed, there was no malice mixed with their obvious curiosity. A few nodded to Pyrre, or murmured greetings. No one asked any questions. If they were concerned about the fates of those Skullsworn who had accompanied Pyrre, the men and women who had gone down to the ruined town and not returned, they didn't show it. No one seemed worried that the *kenarang* of the Annurian Empire had come to the Ancaz Mountains with a knot of soldiers—they didn't even seem *aware* of the fact.

"Should we . . . tell someone?" Kaden asked. "Prepare some sort of defense?"

Pyrre waved away the question. "The defense is there already."

"The sentries hidden in the rocks?"

"Among other measures. Rassambur has been guarded since before the first stones of the oldest buildings were set in place."

Kaden glanced at those buildings. Most were small, a single room or two, date trees espaliered against sandstone walls, small patios sheltered from the sun, flower and vegetable gardens in raised beds before or beside them.

Pyrre followed his gaze.

"Each priest keeps her own plot," she said. "It is a commandment of the god."

"Gardening?" Kaden asked. "Why?"

The assassin looked amused. "We need to eat. The hot blood of the slaughtered is delicious, obviously, but sometimes the body craves vegetables."

They passed a series of stone barns and pens filled with goats and sheep. The animals trotted toward the fence, evidently eager for a handout. Dozens of chickens scratched in the dry soil toward the outside of the enclosures. Just beyond one of the barns, a pair of priests, one old, one young, were butchering a goat. The older woman pointed to various ligaments and organs as she worked, pausing often to allow her student to inspect the carcass. It was the first blood Kaden had seen.

"Where are we going?" he asked.

"To see Gerra," Pyrre replied.

"Who is Gerra?" Triste asked warily.

"Gerra is the person," Pyrre said brightly, "who will decide whether we should help you, or offer you to the god."

When they finally tracked down Gerra the Bald, leader of the Skullsworn, he was asleep on his back, fingers neatly laced across his chest, lying atop a narrow wooden platform suspended over the cliff's edge, swaying lightly with the breeze above a sheer drop of hundreds of feet. The wooden platform was one of two, both part of a sort of strange scale, the type of apparatus a merchant might use to weigh grain or coin, but much larger, the whole thing built out over the abyss. The counterweight to Ananshael's chief priest, set on the platform across from him, was a sealed wooden barrel. The hole at its base was plugged tight with something that looked like a stone cork.

"What is that?" Triste asked, her voice tight.

"That," Pyrre replied, "is Ananshael's Scale. Today is Gerra's day."

"Not my day," the priest said without bothering to open his eyes or sit up. "It should have been Baird, but he has not yet returned from the west. Others wanted to take his place, but I was selfish." He smiled. "One of the few joys of leadership—the right to seize a day of peace and quiet when you can."

Pyrre shook her head in mock regret. "I didn't realize, when I spoke in your favor all those years ago, the true depth of your greed."

Gerra's smile widened. "The more fool you." He still hadn't opened his eyes.

"What is the scale for?" Kaden asked.

"It is a way of living close to the god," Pyrre replied. She gestured. "The barrel is filled with water. It's stoppered with a plug of rock salt. When the plug dissolves, the barrel empties, and the person on the platform goes to meet the god."

Triste took a step back, as though the apparatus might suddenly, violently snap.

"When?" she asked.

Pyrre shrugged. "It's impossible to predict. Some salt deposits are denser than others. On hot days, the water dissolves the plug faster than on cold days. Usually it takes a year or so, but not always."

"When I was young," Gerra mused, "there was a time the plug gave way in three days. Jes the Gray was sitting the scale that day. She must have been a hundred—bent nearly double, but still sharp in the head. We joked that Ananshael just got tired of waiting."

"And how long," Kaden asked, studying the barrel, "has this plug been in?"

Pyrre shook her head. "I can never keep track. Thirteen months, maybe?"

"Something like that," Gerra agreed. They might have been discussing the age of a particularly uninteresting sheep. "It went in last summer, after Torrel went to meet the god."

Triste was staring at the scale and the man lying upon it, her violet eyes wide, horrified. "That's awful," she whispered.

"Quite the contrary," Gerra declared. "It's the most peaceful place on the whole mesa. The only spot people won't bother me." He paused. "Usually. Who is that you've brought, my sister?"

"Acquaintances," Pyrre replied. "The almost-Emperor of all Annur and a somewhat threadbare prostitute. A nice enough young man and woman, but very serious."

"You think everyone is too serious. What about the Urghul, the pain priest?"

Pyrre grimaced. "Gone."

"To the god?"

"Perhaps. It's hard to say. He went into one of the rivers, but the Urghul are surprisingly durable."

"And your brothers and sisters?"

"Have made their last offering."

Even that revelation failed to jolt the priest from his rest. He remained so still for so long, in fact, that Kaden was starting to wonder if the man had fallen asleep. Pyrre seemed in no particular hurry, and so it was Triste, finally, who broke the silence.

"Are we prisoners?"

Gerra pursed his lips. "Most people are prisoners," he replied. "I can hear the fear in your voice. You live in it as though it were a cage. Did you come here to be free?"

"Free?" Kaden asked carefully.

"Free," Gerra agreed. "Liberated from the bonds of your fear. Do you wish to join our order?"

"Before you answer—" Pyrre began.

Triste cut her off. "No," she snarled. "*No*. We came here because we didn't have a *choice*. Not to become *murderers*."

"If what we've heard is true," Gerra replied mildly, "you have given more souls to Ananshael than almost any of our priests. I hear whispers that you slaughtered hundreds in the heart of the Annurian palace—truly a great offering."

Triste's face was frozen between horror and rage, her hands balled into fists at her sides. When she spoke again, her voice was barely louder than the wind. "I didn't want to. Didn't mean to. I'm not a killer."

"There are words," Gerra mused, "and there are deeds. Still, I will take you at your word. We all have something to offer to the god. If you do not wish to kill, then you can die."

"No," Kaden said, stepping toward the cliff's edge as Meshkent growled and hissed inside his mind. "Please. There is a larger story here."

"The story always feels large," Gerra replied without moving, without opening his eyes, "to those trapped inside of it.

Ananshael will cut you free. It is not so difficult as you think, dying. We will be at your side."

Fear flared inside Kaden. He crushed it out, tried to focus through his mind's smoke.

"There must be an arrangement we can make. My father paid once, for Pyrre to save my life. . . ."

"Which I did," the woman said. "That deal was done a year ago."

"So I will pay you again. The treasury in Annur . . ."

"Is irrelevant," Gerra concluded. "You came here, to Rassambur, which means you must serve the god in one way or another. Since you will not learn to offer sacrifice, you will *become* that sacrifice." He shrugged. "They are not so far apart."

"We'll join you, then," Kaden said. He just needed time, space to think, to plan. Escape could come later. "We'll become Skullsworn."

"No," Gerra said quietly, almost regretfully. "You have already spoken your truth. What you speak now is no true belief, but the desperate lie of a creature trying to flee. Tonight you will go to the god—there will be song to celebrate your sacrifice. Pyrre will help you to prepare."

The words sounded like a dismissal, and after a moment Pyrre put a steadying hand on Kaden's shoulder. He shrugged it off, glancing back the way they had come. It wasn't far to the bridge—maybe a quarter mile—but there would be no fleeing the flat space of the mesa, no escaping or fighting his way free. If he and Triste were going to survive, if the gods *inside* of them were going to live, he had to persuade this man, and he had to persuade him now, before the knives were sharpened and the fires lit. Kaden's mind scrambled for purchase. He forced it still, then slid into the *vaniate*.

Inside the trance, it was impossible to understand his urgency of moments earlier.

So we die, he thought. *And the gods are torn from this world.* It hardly seemed a tragedy. Kiel's warnings about the dangers of the *vaniate* echoed in the empty space. Kaden considered them, held them up to the light, then put them aside. He studied Gerra's reclining figure for a moment—the man still hadn't moved—then shifted his gaze to the mountains. What was the point in waiting for the Skullsworn knives? He could end it all with a few steps, could walk free of all the fear and pain, the running and the rage. It made sense, actually, what the priest had said: Ananshael's gift was freedom, freedom so perfect, so absolute, it could never be revoked. Triste's low sob broke into his thoughts, a human sob—regardless of the goddess locked inside her—the sob of someone utterly alone and almost broken. *And she, too, will be free,* Kaden thought. *Ananshael can save her.* Triste's life since arriving at Ashk'lan had been one of unbroken terror and flight, imprisonment and torture. How could death's annihilation be anything but welcome?

And then, as though Meshkent could hear his silent thoughts, the god began thrashing, growling: *No.*

The word rolled off the slick skin of the *vaniate.*

I have seen what you bring to this world, Kaden said silently, *and I have seen the clarity of the alternative.*

Pyrre was watching him warily. Kaden ignored her, took another step toward the cliff, then another, until he stood just at the verge. Hawks turned lazily in the hot air below. At the canyon's bottom, a narrow river gnawed at the stone. Someday, even the mesa would be worn to sand, that sand washed out to the sea. There would be no trace of the place where he stood. No trace of Rassambur or the priests. It was the way of all things.

"I will make my own offering," Kaden said quietly, looking down, imagining the wonderful weightlessness of falling, and that other, greater weightlessness of death. "I have no need of your knives."

"No."

The voice was barely more than a whisper. For a few heartbeats, Kaden couldn't be sure he had heard it at all, couldn't be sure that the words had any life outside his own mind. Then it came again.

"No."

Not Meshkent this time, but Triste, pleading.

"Don't, Kaden. Please don't."

It was the name that called him back. Strange, that. The Shin had spent years teaching him that the word was not the thing, that a name was just a set of sounds aiming at an ever-shifting truth, aiming and always falling short. The name *Kaden* was no more him than his breath. It was, like all words, an error, and yet, on Triste's lips, it called him back.

I can't save her, he said silently.

But you can be there when she dies.

Whose voice was that? Not Meshkent's, certainly. Not his own. It was something older than logic, old as his bones, something bred into his very flesh, one last human bond threaded through his thought even when all emotion was scrubbed away, something ineluctable, even inside the blankness of the *vaniate,* not a voice at all, but the wordless truth of what he was, of what he owed, and slowly, slowly, he let the trance go.

Fear came again, a fist clamped around his heart. Meshkent's ranting fury, so quiet from inside the space of the *vaniate,* echoed in his mind once more: *Free me. Submit and I will crush these worms. I will build a fire inside them that burns for a thousand days before I give them up to their Coward's God.*

Kaden pushed the words aside.

"Before I make this offering, however," he said, "I will pose one question."

The Skullsworn priest nodded thoughtfully.

Kaden glanced down once more, at the emptiness that waited, then raised his eyes.

"Do you want to kill me?" he asked quietly. "Or do you want to kill the Csestriim?"

For the first time, Gerra opened his eyes. They were a dark, vegetal green.

"If you kill us here," Kaden went on, "or let us go, Ananshael will claim us, and soon. We are human. We will bow to his will this year or the next. The Csestriim, however . . ."

He let the words hang as Gerra sat slowly, then turned to face him.

"The Csestriim are destroyed."

"Not all of them."

"Is this true?" Gerra asked, turning to Pyrre.

She shrugged. "There are stories. But there are always stories."

"They are not stories," Kaden said. "I can give you names. Names and a way to find them, fight them."

Gerra frowned. "Once already, you have tried to lie your way free of your debt to the god."

"And you heard that lie," Kaden said, matching the man's gaze. "Listen to me now. The Csestriim walk this world, undying, defying your god's justice." He cocked his head to the side. "If I am lying, say the word and I will go to meet your god."

For a long time, no one spoke. Wind honed its edge on the stone. Overhead, the sun hung hot and motionless in the blue. After what seemed like years, Gerra nodded.

"The god's ways are strange. I will think on this as I pray."

"And when your prayers are finished?" Kaden asked.

Gerra smiled. "Then I will know whether to give you to Ananshael, or whether to listen to your names."

From the ledge behind the low stone house, Kaden looked out over the mountains scraping the sky to the west. After so many days running, his legs throbbed. Blisters had burst across the soles of both feet, then bled, and then new blisters had formed beneath the ruin of the older skin. Those, too, had burst. He prodded gingerly at the cracked, livid flesh. In the days before Rassambur, there had been no time to consider the pain, no choice but to keep running. Now, with the luxury of stillness, of silence, that pain reasserted itself, aching and burning all at the same time, hurting all the way through to the bruised bone.

As if in response to the sensation, Meshkent uncoiled, pressed against the boundaries of his cage, testing, testing.

Free me.

The words were not words, but something old and alien moving in Kaden's mind, as though for just a moment he were seeing with someone else's eyes, or dreaming someone else's dream. Slowly, methodically, he went over the god's prison, shoring and securing it, finding the places where it had worn thin—the moments of doubt, the tiny cracks where weariness worked, patient as ice, to bring down the wall—and fixing them.

No, he replied silently.

A flash of purple rage.

These creatures will gut this body if they know you carry me inside.

Kaden shook his head, as though that made any difference.

They will not know.

You risk everything.

Risk and life are inextricable, Kaden said. Then, *How do I perform the* obviate?

For a long time, he waited for a reply, for Meshkent's awful weight against the walls. Instead, there was only silence, the god motionless as a stone inside his mind. He exhaled slowly, stretched his legs out before him, and began kneading the muscles of his lower back. Far out over the canyons, a pair of black birds he didn't recognize rode the thermals. It was almost like Ashk'lan, except for the fact that in Ashk'lan, even as a novice, he had never been a prisoner, not quite. He had never lived beneath the open threat of death.

Not that the Skullsworn had mistreated him or Triste. Quite the contrary, in fact. After the audience with Gerra, Pyrre had shown them to a modest stone house near the very edge of the mesa, a structure like those in which the Skullsworn seemed to live. Inside there were two rooms, two narrow beds, a hearth carved into the sandstone walls, and above it, hanging from hooks, a set of iron pots and pans.

"Whose home is this?" Triste had asked, eyeing the nondescript space warily.

"Most recently," Pyrre replied, "it belonged to two priests: Helten and Chem."

"Where are Helten and Chem?"

"They went to meet the god," the assassin said, her voice easy, matter of fact. "Yesterday, when we came for you, the Annurians killed them."

Kaden had paused inside the doorway, trying to read the woman's face.

"Why did they come?"

"I told them Long Fist was with you. I didn't realize he had escaped."

"Why do the Skullsworn care about Long Fist?" Kaden asked, shaking his head.

"They wanted to rescue him," Triste spat. She was glaring around the modest cottage as though it were the darkest dungeon of the Dead Heart. "Priests of death come to rescue the priest of pain so that together they can spread their sick worship over the whole world."

Pyrre's face hardened. "Obviously the brothel where you trained skimped on the theology."

"Murder is not theology," Triste snarled.

"On the contrary," Pyrre replied. "As you would know if the whores who raised you cared for anything but coin and pleasure. The Lord of the Grave, my god, is Meshkent's most ancient foe. In the face of the cat god's savagery, Ananshael's justice is our only mercy. We didn't come—my brothers and sisters and I—to save the Urghul shaman—we came to kill him before he could spread his sickness further."

"Sickness?" Triste hissed. "Justice? *Mercy?* You're a killer! You're all murderers. Assassins! Your god is a god of blood and bones, of death and destruction. What justice is that?"

"The only true justice," Pyrre replied simply. Her momentary anger seemed to have passed, replaced by an uncharacteristic solemnity. It had seemed to Kaden, since the moment Pyrre arrived at the monastery, that she cared for nothing, not even her own life. Faced with death and defiance, she simply laughed or shrugged. Only now, a year later, had they finally stepped, if inadvertently, on her sacred ground.

"Where is the justice," Triste demanded, "in murdering men in their sleep? Where is the justice in killing children? In cutting down the good along with the evil?"

"Precisely there—Ananshael spares no one. Emperor or orphan, slave or sovereign, priest or prostitute—he comes for us all. Your lady—Ciena—she doles out her pleasures according to her whims. Some live a life of unmitigated bliss while others struggle through their days in pain and agony. Ciena pities some, scorns others; only Ananshael offers up his justice to all. Ciena loves watching those she has spurned writhe in the claws of her love; only the Lord of the Grave can save a soul abandoned to Meshkent."

"They are in *league*," Triste protested. "In all the songs and stories—"

Pyrre cut her off. "The songs and stories are wrong. If Meshkent had his way, we would never die. He would hold us over his fires, flay the flesh from our bones, and we would live forever, screaming and bleeding, alert to every inch of his agony. He hates what my god does, hates the escape Ananshael offers, hates the release, the final peace."

And this is what I have caged inside me, Kaden thought. *This is the being whose survival depends upon my own.* For just a moment it seemed he should have stepped from the cliff after all, even if it meant leaving Triste to face the Skullsworn alone.

Triste, for her part, just stared at Pyrre, mouth agape, then finally mustered her anger once more.

"I don't believe it."

Pyrre's old smile crooked the corner of her mouth. "In this, too, Ananshael is just. He offers his boundless shelter even to the unbelievers."

And with that pronouncement, the assassin left them. There had been no admonitions, no threats about what would happen if they attempted to escape. Pyrre had taken a moment to point out the pile of wood outside, the vegetables ripening in the small raised beds, then left. Triste stood motionless a moment, wide-eyed and baffled, then cursed, stepped into the other room, and slammed the door behind her. Kaden had debated following, then discarded the idea. He was tired suddenly, viciously tired, but didn't think that he could sleep, and so he found his way onto the stony ledge behind the house, found himself sitting cross-legged in the way of the Shin, here, thousands of miles from those other, colder mountains where he had grown from a boy into a man. The peaks were different, but the sky was the same, the emptiness of it, the way it deepened as the sun set through azure and indigo to black.

Triste found him just after moonrise. At some point she had taken off her shoes, and her bare feet scuffed quietly over the stone. Kaden started to turn, then stopped himself. Whatever she'd said at the cliff's edge, Triste hated him, and with good reason. It was not Pyrre's priesthood that had betrayed her, but Kaden himself, first in the Dead Heart, and then again inside his own palace. If she was here, now, it was because she had nowhere else to go.

She sat a few paces away. For a long time, they remained silent as the moon climbed through the skein of stars. Behind them somewhere, the Skullsworn were singing in a haunting, polyphonic chorus. The Shin had had their music: low, droning chants, the few notes rough enough to grind away the self. This was entirely different. The twining melodies of the Skullsworn moved between dissonance and resolution, shifting from one register to the next. If the Shin chant had been a music of stone, this was human music, one that marked the passage of time, that anticipated with each aching cadence the inevitability of its own ending.

When Kaden finally glanced over at Triste, he realized she was crying silently, her tears bright in the moonlight. She didn't meet his eyes.

"It's not fair," she whispered. "It's not fucking fair."

Whether she meant their new imprisonment, or the god inside her, or Kaden's presence at her side, he couldn't say. Probably all of it. He searched for something to say, some explanation for everything he had done and not done. He found none.

"I'm sorry," he said instead. The words were weak as the night breeze, but of all the language in the world, that single phrase was the only one that seemed true.

Triste shook her head.

"Maybe we should let them do it," she said. "The Skullsworn. Let them kill us and just be done with it."

Kaden studied her face. "That's the first time I've heard you talk of giving up."

"What am I fighting for?" The words were bitter but quiet, the fire finally burned out. "For this?" She gestured to the stone and sky. "For this?" To her own scarred skin. "That heartless Skullsworn bitch is right about one thing, at least—when Meshkent gets you in his grip, he doesn't let go."

"You came a long way just to die."

"So did you," she replied. "We could have just stayed in the tent. Back at your monastery. Could have let Micijah Ut cut us apart with his broad blade."

"It would have saved a lot of running," Kaden agreed.

"It would have saved a lot of everything." Triste shook her head. "How many people died, do you think, because of what we did?"

"I don't know."

"And for what?"

"I don't know."

Triste glanced over at him at last.

"You never told me," she said finally, "why you went back to Annur in the first place."

Kaden turned from the sky's dark gulf to look at her. "I almost didn't go back. Valyn talked me into it, at least partly." He shook his head. "It seemed like the right thing to do."

"The right thing to do was to fight men you'd never met over a throne you had no skill to sit on?"

For a long time, Kaden didn't reply. In the starlight, he could make out little more than her eyes, two glinting points half hidden behind the tangle of black hair. Night hid the scars that the Ishien had carved into her skin, hid the drugged glaze of her eyes and the wary distance in that stare. Sitting a pace away from her in the darkness, it was easy to imagine he faced the same girl who had arrived in Ashk'lan a year earlier. Triste had been baffled then, even more terrified than Kaden himself, but she'd been . . . alive, afire with determination and, even more unlikely for a girl stolen from her mother and dragged across a continent to serve as an emperor's slave, hope.

Kaden remembered her facing down Pyrre Lakatur just after the assassin murdered Phirum Prumm. *Who are you?* Triste had demanded of the woman. *Who are you to decide which people get to live or die?* He remembered the way she had run through the mountains, keeping pace with the monks. She'd been pulling strength from the goddess inside her, of course, but the pain she'd suffered had been her own. Her goddess hadn't spared her the ache in her legs, hadn't spared her those bloody, shredded feet. And even beaten up like that, she'd played her part in the plan that saved them all, facing the traitorous Kettral and the leach who had stolen her from her home.

It was the Ishien who had hacked the hope out of her, but not just the Ishien. Triste had still had some fight, some hope, some fire when they returned to Annur. It was Kaden himself who had taken that from her, taken it when he told her the truth about her mother and father, and then again, when he gave her up to the dungeon inside Intarra's Spear. Whatever harm the Ishien had done he had more than matched. The girl had endured the violence of her enemies; it was the violence of her supposed friends that had shattered her spirit.

"Habit," he said finally, quoting the Shin, "is a chain to bind ten thousand men."

Triste broke a piece of stone from the ledge, rolled it in her hand a moment, then hurled it over the cliff. It fell into endless silence, as though the chasm before them had no bottom.

"You weren't in the *habit* of sitting on a throne," she said. "Not back then. When I first met you, you seemed . . ." She trailed off, shaking her head.

"There are habits of action and habits of thought. I never sat the throne, but I thought Annur needed an emperor. I thought the world needed Annur. For centuries the Malkeenians ruled, and I inherited that thought, too. The monks tried to teach me to set those habits of mind aside. I failed."

"I wish the monks had taught *me* that," Triste murmured. "I grew up believing my mother loved me." She had balled her hands into fists, clenched them to her chest as though she were holding something invisible and precious. Her body trembled.

"Maybe she did."

"She gave me to him," she hissed. "To Adiv. *She gave me away.*" The words dropped off, as though the thought of her betrayal had torn them from her. Then she exhaled, a long, shuddering breath. "Your monks were right. Our habits hurt us. They're like blades we hold willingly to our own breasts."

For the first time since fleeing the oasis, Kaden allowed himself to think about Rampuri Tan. All over again he watched as the old monk, the broken bones inside his body grating against one another, raised that gleaming *naczal* to strike the final blow. Tan, who had helped to save him from the Annurian ambush, who taught him the *vaniate*, who stayed behind in the Dead Heart so that Kaden could escape; Tan, who had trained in the vicious ways of the Ishien for so many years and yet still found his way free. Even Tan, with that hard, level gaze, that mind of stone, had, in his final days, seen the world askew.

A mind of stone. Kaden pondered the notion. It seemed apt. The mind, any mind, was like the land, the mesas and mountains, all that stone shaped moment by immeasurable moment, sculpted imperceptibly by the winds and rivers, the innumerable drops of rain, unable, in the end, to escape the logic of its own geology.

After a long silence, Kaden shook his head slowly. "The Shin were right about a lot of things, especially when it came to snuffing out, scrubbing clean, carving away." He turned from Triste to stare into the nothingness. "The monks told me a lot about what to destroy," he went on after a while. "The question they never answered, though, was this: when you scrub it all out, the fear and hope, the anger and despair, all the thousands of habits of thought—what's left?"

Triste didn't respond. The chorus behind them rose and fell, rose and fell like the wind. When he finally looked over at her, she was watching him. Her words, when she spoke, were thin as the wind. "Why does there need to be something left?"

It was the sort of answer Scial Nin would have given, a question for a question. For all the abbot's years and wisdom, however, he had never been forced to live the annihilation of all that he believed. Triste had.

Between one heartbeat and the next, Kaden made a decision.

"The god is inside me," he said simply.

Triste stared at him, eyes wide, lips parted. "Meshkent." She only whispered the word, but so fervently it sounded half a prayer, half a curse.

Kaden nodded. "It happened just before Long Fist died. I don't . . ." He tried to put into language what he had done to save the god, to chain him. "I don't know how it happened. Not exactly."

It should have seemed an outlandish claim, something utterly insane. It would have, probably, to anyone else, to anyone who had not lived with her own divinity locked inside her flesh.

"I'm sorry," Triste said. The words seemed pulled from her, torn from her throat with a hook.

"I suppose I deserve it. After everything."

"No one deserves it."

The Shin aphorism came unbidden to Kaden's lips. "There is only what is."

The Skullsworn chorus had fallen silent at last. Quiet crouched between Kaden and Triste like a dangerous beast.

"But that means . . . ," she said at last. "If you want him to survive. . . ."

Again, Kaden nodded. "The *obviate*."

Her face hardened. "I won't do it. I won't be shamed into it. I don't fucking *care* what you do. . . ."

"Triste," Kaden said. It felt like they were floating on a scrap of stone in a great void. She trailed off, as though the sound of her own name were a leach's kenning. Kaden spread his hands. "I don't know."

"Don't know what?" she asked warily.

The thought was almost too big to put into words. "The whole thing," he said finally. "The whole thing I've been fighting for. Defeating il Tornja. Saving these gods. Keeping our race alive . . . Why?"

She stared. His question was no more than an echo to her own, but there was something awful in hearing your own doubt and despair spoken back aloud. Maybe silence was the only answer, but Kaden felt drawn to force the rest into words, to speak it all at least this one time.

"I thought we should be saved, that humanity should be saved, that we were worth saving, but that was just a habit. Just a hope."

"Like everything else," Triste whispered.

Kaden nodded. "What if it's wrong?"

50

Chilten, whose missing top front tooth caused him to whistle when he spoke.

Jal, whose voice was high as a little girl's, but who took his ribbing from the other men and sang the songs of his hillside village anyway each evening before they slept.

Yemmer, who fought with two swords.

Sander, who could throw a head-sized chunk of rubble farther than any of the others.

Fent, who laughed in the middle of each day's battle, but sobbed all night in his sleep.

Dumb Tom, who could work any numbers in his head, who tallied up the dead each night, figured the odds, ran the betting books.

Ho Chan, who knew how to set traps in the crumbling fort for the rats that they roasted every night.

Belton, whose voice broke after two straight days of shouting orders.

Brynt, who pissed himself each morning at the first Urghul horns.

Ariq, who couldn't stop talking about the town where he grew up, the palms around the tiny lake, the way the moon looked closer there somehow.

Kel, who cut the ears from the Urghul dead, then threaded them on a leather thong that he wore around his neck.

Gruin the Brick, who was as wide as he was tall and knew three hundred Kreshkan poems by heart.

After four days fighting the Urghul from the top of Mierten's crumbling wall, these were the last of the legionaries left.

Four days. It seemed too little time to know a man, but Valyn found, as the sun's bloody rim dipped beneath the western hills, that he *did* know these twelve. Not all the little facts of their lives, obviously, but what use were those facts? Maybe somewhere else, hundreds of miles from any war, knowing a person might mean something different. Among other people—farmers, say, or merchants, or fishermen—all those tiny details accrued over a lifetime—the names of parents and pets, stories of drunken antics and earnest grief, tales of broken bones and broken hearts—they might actually matter. Not here atop the wall. Not with Ananshael sitting silently in the darkness beyond their fires, patient, inescapable.

The warrior had a different way of knowing. Death was always coming, always ready to obliterate the piles of facts that elsewhere in the world might constitute a life. What mattered wasn't a record of the days lived, but something more immediate and fleeting: the pitch of a scream, the shape of a bloody grin, the timbre of a prayer. It was as though, if you paid attention, if you looked at the person just right, you could see an entire life in the smallest detail, could find everything that mattered in a single act.

Had they been somewhere else, Valyn would have loathed some of the soldiers, liked others. Here, atop the wall, those words—*loathed, liked*—seemed stupid, pointless. Could you really hate a man who stood at your side, his face bathed in sweat, his spear bloody from having saved you over and over? Could you like him? The words just didn't apply. They were for another world, one where women and men could afford to choose their friends, where you could walk away because of something someone said or did. By the end of the fourth day on the wall, they were, all of them, beyond any walking away, beyond running or fleeing, beyond any judgment that was not uttered in blood.

It was amazing they had lived that long.

It was one thing to hear the Urghul army, to smell it on the northern wind, another thing entirely to see it flowing over the churned-up earth, thousands upon thousands of riders, lances stabbed up into the sky, hair flowing out behind them as they charged the wall again, and again, and again. All during that first day, Valyn expected his sight to fail, to go suddenly dark as it always had before. It remained; in fact, it sharpened, until he could see every scar on the faces of the charging horsemen. In the long months of his blindness, Valyn had forgotten what it was to see, how the world was full to bursting with shape and movement, packed from dirt to sky the long length of the horizon. It was dizzying watching the horsemen wheel and turn with each attack, all those riders shifting like the tide.

The Urghul would have finished the battle instantly but for one simple fact: Balendin was gone. After the botched attack on the hill, he had vanished utterly from the field of battle. When the leach remained absent for a second day, a few of the legionaries ventured to suggest that he might have been killed by the explosion after all, a notion the Flea flatly dismissed: *He's alive,* the Wing commander said, *and we'll have to fight him again. Just be glad the fight's even for now.*

Even wasn't the word Valyn would have chosen.

Leach or no leach, the Urghul numbered in the tens of thousands, *taabe* and *ksaabe,* the women every bit as hard, as vicious as the men, each with a bow and spear, each with a handful of remounts. They came against the wall from before dawn until after dusk every day, retiring only when the sky was so dark that any charge would risk the horses' legs. There was no nuance to the attacks, no scheming or subtlety. They galloped along the wall, stood on the backs of their mounts, and then leapt screaming onto the battlements where the legionaries scrambled to cut them down.

"It makes no sense," Valyn said to Huutsuu after the Urghul had retreated for the second day. "They could be building siege engines." He gestured to the forest. "There's enough trees to build a thousand catapults, trebuchets, ballistae. Instead of dying on the wall, they could be lounging a hundred paces away and pounding us into oblivion."

Huutsuu watched the retreating riders in silence. When she finally turned to face him, her eyes blazed with reflected starlight. When she spoke, every word was stitched with scorn.

"Whatever hardening you have had, you still think like an Annurian."

"If your people thought more like Annurians, they would have taken the wall already, and less of them would be dead."

"War is not a matter of the taking of walls."

"They've been trying hard enough to get on top of this one."

"What matters is the way it is claimed."

Valyn glanced over the edge of the wall at the carnage below. Some of the corpses—those that had fallen near the day's end—were almost undisturbed. There might be an arm missing, or a gash across the collar, but they still looked like people, men and women who, but for a rent in their flesh, might still stand up, stumble away. The other bodies, the older ones, were worse. Days of battle had ground them into the mud. Hundreds of hooves had shattered skulls, pulped flesh, annihilated almost all that had been human. Crows were at these older carcasses, finishing the work. Valyn shook his head. "You want to claim it's *good* to lose a thousand riders in the fight? Two thousand?"

"Better that," Huutsuu replied, "than to sit a hundred paces distant, to hide behind machines, to risk nothing while the enemy dies. This is not war; it is killing."

"As though the Urghul have respect for human life. I've been among your people, Huutsuu. I've seen what you do."

She raised her brows. Valyn studied her; he had not had the opportunity to watch a human face, to really *see* one for so long. "And what is it, Malkeenian, that you have seen?"

"The men and women you've murdered, torn apart. The blood."

"And you," she pressed, cocking her head to one side, "have not done this? You have not spilled blood?"

"Of course I have," he said. The memory of the day's fighting coursed through his mind, the perfect clarity of it, the life burning in his veins as he raised the ax and brought it down. "That doesn't make it right."

"There is a sacred way of war," Huutsuu said, "and a profane. I turned against my people, turned against the leach, because there is no struggle in the blood he spills. Like your generals with their engines, he risks nothing with his slaughter." She raised an eyebrow. "Is this not the way you were raised? The way you were trained?"

"It's what makes sense," Valyn ground out. "War's plenty dangerous even without the idiotic stunts."

The Urghul woman shook her head. "Your way of war is a pale, ugly thing. A perversion. You call yourselves civilized, and yet look at the things you fight for: borders, power, wealth . . ."

"As opposed to *what*?"

"As opposed to nothing. The war itself is worship."

"A sick sort of worship."

"Sicker than killing a woman because she stepped across an invisible line you have drawn across the dirt? Sicker than burning a man because he took some gem, some brick of gold, from another man?"

"Justice," Valyn said. The word felt brittle as a dead bird's bone. "The law . . ."

Huutsuu waved his objection away. "There is only the struggle. You know this, Malkeenian. You have seen it, lived it. Forget your justice and your law; what is real is the struggle between person and person. The struggle that takes place inside a bloody heart." Her smile was sharp as an ax's edge. "This is why you can see, Malkeenian. You may deny this truth, but you have understood its sanctity."

And so the Urghul did not scheme or build siege engines. For four days they came at the wall, bathed it in their screams and their blood, and for four days the wall held. The Flea's orders to Valyn, Newt, and Sigrid were simple: *Go where the shit's worst. When the men start to break, don't let them.*

It seemed like a ludicrous command, so reductive it was almost glib. As the battle raged on, however, as the Urghul threw themselves howling at the wall over and over and over, Valyn started to see the wisdom in it. The Kettral spent years studying tactics back on the Islands, poring over hundreds of battles from dozens of wars, learning the intricate dance of advance and retreat. Victory, those lessons seemed to say, was something hammered out in a general's head, a matter of maps and strategies.

Not here.

Atop the wall, any attempt at convoluted tactics could only obscure a series of simple, brutal truths: the wall was all that stood between the Urghul and the south. If the wall fell, the Urghul won. The wall could not fall.

"Go where the shit's worst," Valyn muttered to himself on the morning of the first day, chopped his way through two Urghul who had managed to get their feet beneath them. He buried an ax in the first, shoved the body into the second, then smashed them both back over the wall with his second ax.

Go where the shit's worst. When the men start to break, don't let them.

The first half of the orders were easy. The second, less so. All Valyn's training had been in small-team tactics, teams built of meticulously trained specialists. He had no doubt that the legionaries beside him on the wall were excellent at marching, at holding a formation, at stabbing with their spears and hacking over and over with their swords, but they were hardly Kettral. Valyn could smell the terror on them, ranker and thicker each time the Urghul came. Each time the riders attacked, a few more gained the walkway. Three or four, the men could throw back. More than that, and there would be panic.

All that first morning, Valyn searched in vain for something to say to the soldiers, a few words that might make a crucial difference. The history books were filled with noble exhortations from commanders, but Valyn had no exhortations. He'd told the truth when the legionaries first arrived: they were dead men, all of them—either that day, or the next, or the one following. There was no escaping the Urghul army, no way to hold the wall forever. Sooner or later, the riders would break through, and then Ananshael would wade among them, unmaking men and women alike, his fingers, terribly nimble, unbinding the tangled knots that were their lives.

The best that Valyn could do was to keep the men grounded in the fight. Rather than giving them time to think about what had to happen in an hour or a day, Valyn hurled the brute fact of the battle over and over again in their faces. Midway through the day, while the sun burned through the clouds overhead, Brynt took an arrow to the shoulder. It wasn't a killing wound, at least not right away, but it would have hurt, and the man collapsed to the battlements, pale face even more blanched with the pain.

Valyn had knelt beside the soldier for a moment, exploring the wound. Then he took the arrow in both hands, broke it off, slapped the man when he began to faint, then dragged the jagged shaft through the wound.

Brynt screamed. Blood flowed, hot and quick. The legionaries near them turned to stare, eyes wide, fear boiling off them. Brynt was a distraction, that was clear enough, and there was no room for a distraction. With a curse, Valyn hauled the man back to his feet, stabbed a finger at the mass of horsemen as they wheeled.

"There," Valyn bellowed, choosing one of the Urghul archers at random, a woman with fire-gold hair streaming out behind her. "Kill *her*. She's the one who shot you, so fucking *kill* her."

For a moment, he thought the young soldier was too lost in

his pain and panic to understand. Then Brynt pulled free of his
grip. He wobbled for a moment, leaning against the ramparts,
then steadied himself, raising his spear with his good arm. When
the woman galloped within range, he bellowed and let the shaft
fly. It lagged her slightly, burying itself in the horse's flank, but
that was good enough. The poor beast bellowed, buckled, and
went down, throwing the woman, then crushing her. Brynt didn't
have his spear anymore, but each wave of Urghul brought fresh
weapons, and more importantly, Brynt was standing again,
shouting, ignoring the blood on his shoulder, bellowing taunts
at the riders below. And just like that, the men around him,
soldiers close to buckling moments before, were yelling too.

They made it through the afternoon that way, and another
day, and another, Valyn choosing targets, the men focusing their
fear and rage on one particular face, fighting a single foe at a
time. Valyn lost himself so thoroughly in the battle, in the rhythm
of attack, hold, and regroup, that when twilight finally crept
into the sky on that fourth day, he almost didn't notice. One
moment the Urghul were hurling themselves at the wall, dying
by the dozen, and the next they were pulling back. The thunder
of hooves, the clash of steel against stone, the thousand-voiced
chorus of battle—it was gone, replaced by the whimpers and
sobs of the dying, the breathless, desperate gasps of those left
alive atop the wall.

Valyn glanced west to where the sun had set beneath the low
Nishan hills. Already, night was lowering over the old fort like
an iron bowl. The soldiers' pupils dilated in the growing gloom.
They moved over the bloody walkway atop the wall more hesitantly, uncertain of their fading footing.

"Sir?" someone asked.

Valyn turned to find Brynt facing him. The legionary's
shoulder wound was wrapped in a rough bandage. Somehow
he'd made it through four days of fighting with just one hand.

"What is it?" Valyn asked.

"The Urghul," Brynt replied, gesturing over the lip of the wall.

Valyn didn't bother to look. Today, as on every other day, there would be hundreds of Urghul dead, and among them, the wounded. The riders never made an effort to come for them. According to Huutsuu, this, too, was their way, their sacrifice to Kwihna. Even now, Valyn could hear the living crawling, limping, scrabbling across the churned-up no-man's-land between the wall and the Urghul camp. Those who managed to drag themselves back to the roaring fires would be honored with song and dance. Those who didn't . . . would not.

"The wounded . . . ," Brynt said, gesturing wordlessly over the wall.

Valyn turned back to the soldier. "What about them?"

The young man stared at him. "I don't know. It's just . . . shouldn't we *do* something? Put arrows in them . . . or send someone out with an ax. . . ."

Valyn shook his head. "Leave them. This is what they chose, and we have our own to care for."

Few enough, as it turned out—barely twenty, when you counted Huutsuu's surviving Urghul and the Flea's Kettral. There was a makeshift infirmary set up in the shadow of the wall, little more than a scrap of canvas to keep off the worst of the wind and cold. Each night, Valyn and the other Kettral labored by the shifting light of two lanterns to stitch the gashes that could be stitched, to scrub, then cauterize the wounds. They weren't trying to save anyone. That wasn't the point. The point was to find a way to keep each man who had survived the day's madness on the wall for another day, to keep the dying, for just a little longer, from joining the dead.

That night, when they were finished, the Flea beckoned to Valyn. The legionaries, exhausted from the vicious battle, had mostly collapsed at their posts atop the wall, each man falling into his own stunned sleep. Later, woken by hunger or pain, they would rise, cook the last of their remaining rations over low fires, stare silently into the blaze or exchange the day's grim tales. For now, however, they slept.

"Inside the fort," the Wing leader murmured, gesturing.

Valyn raised his brows.

"We need to talk about the next steps."

No one had bothered to light a lantern inside the stone chamber at the heart of Mierten's Fort; the wan starlight lancing through the crumbling roof was more than enough for Kettral eyes. Valyn glanced over his companions as he entered. None of them had escaped the battle unscathed. The Flea's right eye was almost swollen shut, Newt had acquired a limp, and an Urghul sword had taken off the two smallest fingers on Sigrid's left hand. The bandage seeped blood, but the woman ignored it. For the first time Valyn remembered, she didn't smell of delicate perfume. Her blacks were filthy and wrinkled. Like the rest of them, she reeked of blood.

"Just us?" Valyn asked, glancing over his shoulder toward the door.

"Just us," the Flea agreed. "Kettral business."

"I'm not sure I'm Kettral anymore."

"Neither am I," the Flea agreed, "but you might be important in what has to happen next." He looked around the room, studying each of them in turn. "We can't hold another day. We don't have the soldiers left. Tomorrow, probably well before noon, the Urghul will take the wall and the fight will be over."

Newt pursed his lips. "No man can stand against the tide. So what do you want to do?"

To Valyn's surprise, the Flea laughed. "What I *want* to do is to take off these 'Shael-spawned boots, dig up a barrel of ale, sit down somewhere with a view of the river, drink 'til I'm numb, then fall asleep for a week."

The admission seemed uncharacteristic, but Newt chortled, and even Sigrid's lips twitched incrementally upward. It was more spasm than smile, gone before it began.

"Wrong question," Newt agreed, still grinning. "What I meant was, 'What are we *going* to do?'"

"Ah," the Flea said, scrubbing his face with a hand. "That. That's less pleasant."

Sigrid licked her chapped lips, then hacked out a series of mangled syllables.

"My lovely and talented companion," the Aphorist began, "points out that this is as good as any other place to die."

The Flea shook his head slowly. "I disagree. For one thing, it's dark and cold and we're out of food. More importantly, we can still do some good if we survive."

Valyn stared. "You want to abandon them."

"As I said," the Wing leader replied, meeting his gaze, "what I want doesn't really come into it."

"When?" Newt asked.

"Tomorrow."

"Tonight is better," the Aphorist pointed out. He seemed to have no qualms about leaving behind the men beside whom they had fought so desperately and for so long. "A lot more hours to get out, get clear."

The Flea nodded. "I thought about that. I'm still hoping, though, that Balendin shows himself one final time. We stay until the last moment, and then we bolt."

Sigrid laughed, then shook her head.

"As the lady points out," Newt said, "we are well past our best running."

"We're not running," the Flea said. He nodded west, toward where the river's roar echoed between the banks. "We stay here, we fight, we hope for one more shot at Balendin. If we don't get it, we swim."

The Aphorist raised his bushy brows. "With that current? I believe the word you're searching for isn't *swim*. It is *drown*."

The Flea shrugged. "Maybe. I scouted it last night. I give us even odds." He turned to Valyn. "That's why you're here."

Valyn shook his head slowly. "I haven't swam in better than a year."

"Doesn't matter. You're half our age, almost uninjured, and stronger than anyone I've seen. I might ride out the current and get free. You definitely will."

Unbidden, the thought of Huutsuu filled Valyn's mind. She was probably asleep atop the wall somewhere, or curled up in the lee of the wall. *The Annurian way of war,* she would call it. Escaping just when the struggle peaked.

"I won't go," he said.

The Flea just watched him for a long time. "You think it's bravery to die here on this wall."

"I think we owe it to the men."

"What about them?" the Flea asked, jerking a thumb to the south.

Valyn narrowed his eyes. "Who?"

"Everyone else. The kids. The farmers in their fields. The grandfathers sitting on porches. What do you owe them?"

Valyn gritted his teeth.

"Dying is easy," the Flea said. The words were hard, but his voice was gentle. "When the time comes, we'll do it. It's just not time."

"It is for those poor bastards standing on the wall tomorrow."

The Flea nodded. "Yes. For those poor bastards, it is almost time."

Chilten, a sword.

Jal, an ax.

Yemmer, who fought with two swords, another sword.

Sander, a spear.

Fent, an arrow to the throat.

Dumb Tom, an arrow to the gut.

Ho Chan, who killed the rats, a spear in the eye.

Belton, four arrows before he dropped.

Brynt, a spear, and Ariq, a spear.

Kel, a fall from the wall's top, then hooves.

Gruin the Brick, who knew so many poems by heart, a slender Urghul knife.

These were the ways they would die the next day while Valyn and the others slipped silently away, making for the river while there was still time.

51

Adare had just risen to descend from the Unhewn Throne when the soldiers marched into the Hall of a Thousand Trees. There were dozens of them, then scores, then hundreds, so many that they forced back the assembled bureaucrats and courtiers, herding them into the empty space beside the throne through the sheer weight and volume of their presence. Their uniforms were clean but threadbare, ripped and restitched a dozen times over, their armor dented from blows no amount of polish could ever scrub away. Most carried spears; every twentieth man held the insignia of the Annurian legions on a long staff.

None of the men brandished their weapons. They entered in silence, assembled in neat ranks, and then just stood there, spear butts planted on the stone floor, all eyes fixed rigidly forward. There was no shouting. There were no threats. There was no violence or spilled blood. The whole display was so orderly that they might have come at Adare's own command. There was just one problem: she had issued no such command.

The last Adare had heard, the Army of the North was still in Aergad. That was the report from Ulli and Jia Chem. According to the messengers, the legions were supposed to be holed up in the old stone city, holding a ruined bridge while the Urghul rode south unopposed. To find them here, now, in Annur itself, should have been as much a relief as it was a shock.

More than anything, Adare needed bodies for the walls, experienced soldiers rather than Kegellen's loose knots of killers and thieves. An army of trained legions, veterans blooded in the furious northern battles, men who understood the Urghul and how to fight them—it was something close to the miracle for which she had prayed each night. And yet, when she stared out over those rigidly assembled ranks, she felt her heart go cold.

This is wrong, a small voice whispered. *Dangerous.*

She half reached up to pat the lacquered wooden pins holding up her hair—gifts from Kegellen—then forced her hand back down. The hairpins were poisoned, but Adare wasn't about to kill an entire Annurian legion with a pair of hairpins. Slowly, warily, she settled back into her seat atop the throne.

She'd been sitting atop the 'Kent-kissing thing all morning, trying to hold together the fundamental governance of the city while other people—Lehav, Nira, and Kegellen, mostly—made final preparations for the coming battle. It was amazing how even in the face of invasion the most basic functions of Annur still needed tending. There was trash to clear out and grain to distribute, docking disputes to resolve, and foreign emissaries to placate. Most of it was handled by an army of ministers, bureaucrats, and scribes, of course, but all of those men—and they were mostly men—turned to Adare to solve the difficult questions, and so, as the city readied for war, she had spent half the morning adjudicating idiotic disputes. It didn't feel heroic. It didn't even feel *useful,* but any one of the small crises, untended, could erupt into its own conflagration, and they already had plenty of conflagrations.

And this unexpected army, Adare wondered, studying the troops below. *Is it water to stop the burning, or another fire?*

At the base of the throne, the crowded ministers shifted nervously, then began to whisper. The fact that the legions had entered the palace unannounced, with no forewarning, suggested that they had marched straight into, then through the city. The fact that they had entered the palace at *all* meant that the guards on the gates had been sufficiently impressed or cowed to allow their passage. Meant that someone had cowed them.

"Who commands here?" Adare asked, heart thundering against her ribs. She ran her eyes along the line of soldiers, searching for the *kenarang*, for il Tornja, for the man who had taken her son. It was the only answer: he hadn't disappeared, he had been leading his legions south, sneaking past the Urghul, arriving in Annur just in time to reinforce the walls. "Where is il Tornja?" she demanded.

Instead of il Tornja, however, another soldier stepped forward. "The *kenarang* is fighting on another front, Your Radiance," he said. "The command is mine. I am General Van." He saluted. Saluted, but did not kneel.

Adare narrowed her eyes, studying this unknown commander. He was middle-aged and weather worn, tall, taller than her, though he seemed to slouch strangely to one side. *His leg,* she realized after a moment. Instead of a boot, instead of a foot, his right leg ended in a bright steel point. Whether he lost the foot in the northern campaign or much earlier, she had no way to tell. It seemed impossible he should have marched all the way from Aergad on that steel spike, but then, it seemed impossible that *any* of them could have made the trek on foot faster than the mounted Urghul.

"Where did you come from, General?" Adare asked carefully. "We were led to believe that the Army of the North had taken up the defense of Aergad."

He shook his head. "A ruse, Your Radiance. We were moving south almost as soon as we had crossed the Haag."

"Still, to cover so much ground so quickly . . ." She shook her head. "The legionary messengers arrived only days ago, and they were on horseback nearly the whole time."

"Horses need rest, Your Radiance. Ships do not. For months, the *kenarang* has been assembling a fleet near the headwaters of the Haag, as far north as the river remains navigable. We took those ships directly to the west coast of the Neck. From there, it is a short march overland."

Adare only half listened to the end of the account. Like fabric snagged on a nail, her mind was caught on those two words: *for months.* They meant that il Tornja had been assembling his fleet even when Adare herself was still in Aergad, assembling it without telling her, planning, once again, for contingencies she could neither understand nor foresee. Had he known, back at the winter's end, that he would need these soldiers in Annur two seasons later? When he looked at the madness of all the vast world, what pattern did he see?

"You say the *kenarang* is fighting on another front," Adare said. "Where?"

Van shook his head. "I don't know, Your Radiance, nor do I need to know. My own orders were clear."

Once again, Adare considered the assembled soldiers. Not a man had moved. If they were so much as breathing, she couldn't hear it. The whole thing could have been no more than a measure of martial respect, and yet, they could have paid their respects *outside* the Hall of a Thousand Trees. There was no need for them to have entered the throne room itself.

"And those orders," Adare asked slowly, "were what, exactly."

"To return to Annur," Van replied. "To fortify the walls . . ."

A breath of relief swept through the ministers and bureaucrats at the throne's foot. A few started cheering. For the first time in days, it seemed possible that they might all actually survive the coming month. Adare, however, kept her eyes fixed on the general. He had fallen silent in the face of the commotion, but she could see in his hard eyes that there was more.

"And?" she asked, when her own ministers had finally fallen silent.

"And to secure the Dawn Palace and the Spear."

It seemed so innocuous, an obvious part of the overall defense. And yet, the Dawn Palace had its own guards. Guards that Adare herself had reinforced with the Sons of Flame.

"I'm grateful for your arrival, General," Adare replied carefully. "By all accounts, the Urghul are not far off, and your presence here may well save this city." She shook her head. "But there is no need for legions in the Dawn Palace. They would be better deployed on the outer wall."

Van nodded. "Most of my force will be concentrated there, Your Radiance."

Most. It was the gentlest defiance, like a warm feather pillow held over a face in the dead of night.

"The Dawn Palace has its own complement of guards," Adare said. "I could not allow the city itself to go undefended only to strengthen my own fortress."

"We will secure the city, Your Radiance. You may be assured of it. We are speaking only of five hundred men here in the palace, five hundred men pulled from an army of thousands."

Dread's cold, dark well opened inside Adare. They were dancing around the issue, testing, probing, and yet, there should have been no need to dance. She was the Emperor, seated in her throne room atop her throne. The fact the conversation had gone on so long already was almost treason.

"Five hundred men could well turn the tide." She took a deep breath, straightened her spine. "Put them on the outer wall."

For several heartbeats, the general just watched her, his eyes unreadable beneath that weathered brow.

"It is with great regret, Your Radiance, that I must decline. I have my orders. . . ."

You are not declining, Adare wanted to scream at him. *An invitation to dinner is something one declines. One can decline an offer to spend the hot months at a summer estate. It is not* declining *when you refuse the clearly stated order of your emperor. It is a 'Shael-spawned* rebellion.

She wanted to hurl the words in the bastard's face, felt them aching inside her. Instead, she kept her mouth clamped shut.

History was filled with accounts of military coups. The greatest threat to any head of state was rarely another state. War was slow, expensive, exhausting work, a matter of endless logistics and marching, disease and lines of supply. Most emperors and kings were actually toppled from inside, by their own armies, by the very soldiers on whose strength they had relied.

Adare knew this well enough—it was a truism of history—but she had always imagined something different when she thought of a military coup: the army battering down its own walls, blood in the streets and gutters, crowns ripped from heads and those heads impaled, openmouthed, on pikes. It seemed only natural that the military overthrow of a nation should be loud, violent, obvious to all; the opposite, in fact, of what was unfolding before her eyes, on the flagstones of her own throne room.

Suddenly, Adare felt the weight of every sword inside the chamber, every spearhead, every piece of armor. The soldiers had not moved—they might have been carved from stone—but they didn't *need* to move. Everyone knew what they could do, what they were for. Against those silent ranks of men, her slippered ministers seemed soft and insubstantial; not men, but the ghosts of men.

"Of course," Van went on, "our only purpose is to serve, Your Radiance."

He kept his eyes on her as she slowly, agonizingly inclined her chin. There was nothing else to do. Any protest would only underscore her own impotence.

"You have my thanks," she managed, the words like tar on her tongue.

It was a good lesson, if she somehow survived to remember it: silence had its own violence; some reigns ended in blades and fire; some with the barest nod of a head.

52

No matter the training, no matter the book study and drills in the field, no matter the tactics and strategy, the missions completed, the years survived—sometimes you just had bad fucking luck.

True to his word, the Flea had waited until the last possible moment to pull his people off the wall. All morning, the Kettral stood shoulder to shoulder with those few Annurian soldiers who remained, beating back one more wave of riders, then another, then another. Only when it was obviously hopeless, when the Urghul were as thick atop Mierten's wall as the defenders themselves, did the Wing leader give the signal to retreat. The remaining legionaries—sweating, bleeding, locked in their own desperate struggles—didn't even notice.

They'll never know, Valyn realized as he turned for one last glance. The lines of battle had dissolved into madness. Fent was fighting with a broken sword, while Sander, who had no weapon at all, was punching his attackers, clawing at them, hugging them close enough to bite into their throats. Farther down the wall, Huutsuu and her Urghul were also losing ground, and though Valyn had fought beside her for the first part of the morning, she, too, was lost in her own struggle, oblivious to his betrayal. *They'll never know we left them to their deaths.*

He realized, as he backed away, that he'd been hoping someone would notice. He'd been waiting to see the fury in the eyes of those he was abandoning, readying himself for their rage. He'd been preparing to bear away, as long as he survived, their final curses. And then there were no curses to bear. No judgment. The ease of the whole thing made him sick. The Urghul swarmed over the wall, but that didn't matter, not to him, not anymore. The river was only a few hundred paces away. Even if he didn't run, even if he stopped to offer up a prayer before diving in, he was going to make it.

Then the bad luck hit.

There was no way to know, passing beneath the fort's southern gate, that the stonework had been weakened by the days of battle to the north. Or maybe it wasn't that at all. Maybe the weakness had nothing to do with the war. Maybe it was just a matter of rain and snow, hundreds of years of ice and wind gnawing at the mortar, eroding it a little at a time, chewing between the huge stone blocks until anything, even the softest footstep, could bring them down. Not that it mattered. What mattered was the way the stone shifted beneath Newt's feet, how the wall caved and the huge lintel came down upon his leg.

Anyone slower would have been killed. The stone was twice as high as Valyn and had to weigh two dozen times as much. Only the Aphorist's quick reflexes—he'd twisted his torso clear at the last moment—had saved his head. Not that it mattered. The leg was crushed below the knee, pinning him in place, and the Urghul were coming. Valyn couldn't see the northern wall beyond the fort's central structures, but he could hear what was happening there clearly enough—the sounds of fighting had drained away, replaced by the vicious ululation of victory.

By the time Valyn reached Newt, his face was twisted with pain, his eyes squeezed tightly shut. Shockingly, the man had refused to cry out, forcing the agony down inside him somewhere deep, silent, somewhere it wouldn't betray his Wingmates. Sigrid reached them a moment later, shoved Valyn roughly aside, then knelt next to the demolitions master. She made a quiet sound—half whistle, half croon—as she rested an open hand on his sweating brow. Valyn had never seen such a tender gesture from the leach.

Newt hacked out something that might have been a moan or a laugh.

"I understand the irony . . . ," he whispered.

The Flea had been lagging behind, covering their retreat. When he rounded the corner, however, he took the scene in at a glance and, barely breaking stride, threw his shoulder against the massive stone. For a moment, Valyn thought the man might actually move it.

The Islands had been filled with scenes of determination, hard men and women harnessing their will to perform nearly impossible tasks. Anyone who passed Hull's Trial had to be able to fight through exhaustion and despair, had to be able to keep moving, keep trying, long after the body was finished and the mind close to unraveling. Valyn had been there when Trea Bel dragged herself from the waves after seven days swimming laps around the Islands, smiling even as she collapsed because she knew she'd won her bet. He'd been there when Daveen Shaleel demonstrated to a whole class of cadets that a soldier could perform field surgery on herself, talking quietly between gritted teeth all while she stitched shut a shark bite that had taken out a portion of her thigh. It was easy, after a life spent training on the Islands, to think you had seen it all, but Valyn had never seen anything quite like the Flea as he threw his weight against that stone.

It wasn't the cords of muscle standing out in his neck, or the way the veins in his scalp throbbed with the blood beneath, or the sound of his teeth grinding—so loud it seemed his jaw would have to crack. Valyn had seen all that before, seen it dozens of times over in different variations. The thing he had never seen before was the sheer, granitic determination in the Flea's eyes. The Wing leader wasn't looking at Newt or the stone he had to move. He wasn't looking forward to the river or backward to the Urghul behind. He was looking at nothing, staring at the empty air a foot away from his face, his whole attention fixed so fully on that point he seemed to have forgotten his own body, which was bent to breaking beneath the load, forgotten the point of his awful labors, forgotten everything but that one goal, as though his entire life had been aiming at this single moment, this task beside which there was no other and after which nothing else mattered, this moving of the stone.

He failed.

He staggered, exhausted, reset his boots, tried to find new purchase. Newt shook his head.

"No good," he gasped. "One man can't . . . lift the world."

"Fuck that,'"the Flea growled as he threw his shoulder against the block.

Valyn was there in a single stride, hitting the rock from the same side, hitting it so hard he felt his shoulder lurch horribly in the socket. The stone didn't budge.

"Get out," the Aphorist said.

"When I die," the Flea replied, his voice level, quiet despite the strain, "then you can start giving the orders." He turned to the leach. "What can you do, Sig?"

She kept her hand on Newt's forehead, but closed her eyes. The plinth shuddered, raining down gravel from where it leaned against the doorframe above. It shifted a few degrees, then fell still. Sigrid made an awful broken sound, some hacked-apart kind of howl.

"She cannot raise the whole weight," Newt translated. "Not even . . . with my pain. All men must die, but this is . . . not your time. Get out."

The Flea let go of the stone, crossed to kneel beside Sigrid. "How much more?" he asked.

She looked up from the Aphorist. Tears stood in her blue eyes.

"No," Newt groaned.

The Flea ignored him. *"How much more?"*

At their backs, fifty paces away but obscured by the fort's crumbling buildings, the Urghul were howling. Valyn could hear the cracking of wood hauled aside, the crash of barricades thrown down. They were opening Balendin's gap in the wall, finishing the work they'd begun almost a week earlier. It wouldn't be long before the horses were able to pour through that gap, wouldn't be long before they'd come hunting for survivors.

"This . . . ," Newt began.

"Is not your choice," the Flea said. He kept his eyes on the leach. "Sig, I need you to tell me."

She made a strange, mute gesture, a sort of slice across her arm.

The Flea's face tightened. He nodded, slid his belt knife from the sheath, closed his eyes, then, in a decisive motion, scored the skin, notching a shallow V into the flesh. With the practiced motion of a cook in the kitchen, he flipped the knife, slid the steel beneath his own skin, then started peeling. Valyn stared. There had been a couple of classes on flaying back on the Islands. The accepted wisdom was that it wasn't much use as torture— it hurt too much. Instead of saying useful things, flayed soldiers passed out or went mad. According to the Kettral trainers, no one could take the pain.

Evidently, the phrase *no one* did not include the Flea.

He tore free the ribbon of bloody skin, yanked it off the way he might have pulled a recalcitrant peel from an apple, then went at it again, carving away another strip quickly, but carefully, refusing to let the knife bite so deep it might sever a tendon or artery. Valyn understood it all at once: Sigrid needed pain—that was her well—and the Flea was giving it to her without gutting his own ability to fight. He might die later from gangrene or wet rot, but not today, not until they had escaped. Blood washed his arm. Valyn could see the red cords of twisted muscle laid bare, the filaments of veins.

"Is that enough?" the Flea asked.

Sigrid took the mutilated limb in her hand, then closed her

eyes again. This time, when she put her free hand against the stone, it lurched. The leach groaned, a horrifying, broken sound deep in her chest. When she bared her teeth, they were bloody, as though she'd bitten open the inside of her cheek. The stone shifted up another inch, and Valyn lunged forward, seized the Aphorist beneath the armpits, pulling him from the wreckage.

"Clear," he said. "He's out."

Sigrid didn't seem to hear him. Her eyes were still closed, her pale face bathed with sweat. She might have been bearing the weight of that massive stone on her own body, letting it crush her slowly into the dirt.

The Flea pulled his arm from her grip, her eyes snapped open, the slab dropped, and the whole wall shuddered with the weight.

"Go," the Wing leader said, jerking his head toward the river as he hacked a length of cloth from the hem of his blacks, then began to bind the bloody arm. *"Go."*

Valyn heaved the Aphorist onto his back, ignored the man's stifled cry as his broken leg jolted, and began to move over the uneven ground, his eyes fixed on the spot a hundred paces distant where the grassy bank sloped down to the Haag. This far north, the river was barely fifty paces wide. There was a quiet eddy directly ahead, at the base of the bank, but beyond those calm shallows the current surged into a brown-white froth, churning through head-high standing waves and grinding over massive boulders.

The notion that any of them would be swimming that thing was ridiculous. The best that they could hope for was to stay afloat somehow, to keep from being sucked under, pinned beneath the river's weight, and killed. There was no way the legionaries they'd left behind could have survived it. The Kettral spent their whole lives swimming, and Valyn wasn't sure *he* could make it. Not that there was any choice.

He glanced over his shoulder. Sigrid stumbled forward as though in a daze. The Flea had her by an elbow, guiding her on, but he was losing blood despite his hastily bandaged arm, the rich dark skin of his face going gray, ashen.

"Problems for later," Valyn muttered to himself.

He hitched Newt higher on his shoulder, turned back toward the river, then staggered to a halt. Urghul riders were pouring out of another gap in the southern wall, massing up between the Kettral and the river. They'd found a way through Mierten's Fort, around it, over it—it didn't matter—they were *here,* half a dozen of them, then a dozen, and more coming, lances leveled, faces alight at the sight of their cornered quarry. Valyn slid an ax free of his belt, started to shift the Aphorist around to give himself more room.

"Down," Newt groaned. "Put me down. In a fight like this . . . a man needs all his arms."

Valyn hesitated, then lowered the demolitions master. As he was drawing his second ax, Newt forced himself to his knees, grimaced, almost passed out, steadied himself against the ground with a hand, straightened again, then slipped two knives from the belt at his waist. Knives against mounted riders with spears. It seemed almost pointless, but the worst of the soldier's pain seemed to have passed, and the Aphorist's eyes were sharp and bright as he watched the riders form up for their attack.

The Flea reached them a moment later. He was carrying Sigrid now, cradling the tall woman in his arms as though she were a child. Her lids were open, but her eyes lolled back inside her skull. Gently, patiently, despite the horsemen bearing down upon them, the Wing leader laid her on the dirt, then straightened with a wince.

"We get one chance at this," he said. "They'll come at us in a wave. There will be a moment when the wave breaks, then another when it is past. That's when we run for the river."

Before Valyn could reply, however, before he could even nod, before the Urghul could kick their horses to a full gallop, a new sound carved the noon sky, slicing through the river's roar and the cries of the horsemen, paring away the rumble of hooves and the hammering of Valyn's own heart in his ears, a dagger of scream opening the world's soft belly. Valyn stiffened, some animal panic older than all conscious thought striking through him, bellowing at him to run, to hide, to find some place where that bright, awful cry could never reach. It was the instinct of mouse and hare, of all small creatures naked beneath the sky, helpless and fleeing, the instinct of all prey when the predator finally arrives. And then, a heartbeat later, over that first instinct, a slower, greater thought: *Kettral.*

The Urghul horses pawed at the dirt, shifting unsteadily beneath their riders as the horsemen tried to bring them back under control. Valyn spun, axes in hand, scanning the horizon to the south, searching, searching, and then . . . there: screaming up the river valley, talons skimming just inches above the frothing water, wings almost wide enough to stretch from bank to bank, a bird, golden as the setting sun, black-eyed, wide-beaked, furious as vengeance itself.

This, too, the Flea took in stride.

"Change of plan. Ready for a smash and grab. Valyn, you're with Newt—use the corpse-carry. Signal we've got wounded, need to run the grab at half speed."

Valyn didn't move. The bird was still a mile off, but he could see the figures on the talons, tiny silhouettes against the gray sky behind. Even with his sight, he couldn't make out the faces, not at that distance, and so, for just a moment, he closed his eyes, found the darkness he had lived inside for so long, and listened. Behind the panicking horses and the cries of their riders, beneath the hiss of the wind and the river's roar, laid beneath all the sounds of the world, or over them, a voice:

". . . just ignore the fact that the whole fucking Urghul nation came out to play. We make the grab, and we're gone. . . ."

"Holy Hull," he breathed, eyes shattering open. "Holy fucking Hull. It's Gwenna."

"I told you," the Flea murmured, bending to lift Sigrid into his arms once more.

Valyn shook his head. "Told me what?"

"Back on the Islands, when you were still botching your barrel drops. I told you they'd make a good Wing."

The Urghul horses were trained for steel and fire, trained to charge a line of infantrymen with pikes, but no one had trained them to face Kettral. At the bird's deafening approach most reared up so violently that even the Urghul riders struggled to keep their seats.

"Now!" the Flea growled. "Get to the river. We make the grab there, where the horses can't follow."

Valyn slammed his axes back into his belt, hurled the Aphorist over his shoulder, and ran.

Only when he'd reached the water, wading out as far into the eddy as he dared go, only when he'd shifted Newt from his back into the corpse-carry position and checked the bird's angle of attack, did he realize that the Flea and Sigrid hadn't made it. The horror stuck like a bone in his throat as he spun to find them still halfway up the bank, pinned down, surrounded by riders who had wrestled their mounts back under control. The Flea's blade was a blur, hacking at the legs of the horses, chopping heads from the thicket of spears. Somehow, impossibly, he was holding the Urghul back, but he only had one hand, he was carrying a soldier who weighed as much as he did, and he was surrounded. Gwenna was coming, coming with the bird, but she was too late.

Quickly, gently, Valyn lowered the Aphorist into the current.

"What . . . ," Newt gasped. He had passed out during the run, come to only when the cold water reached his chest.

"I'm going back."

Even as Valyn started moving toward the bank, slowed by the water as though lost in the depth of nightmare, he knew that he was dead. There were too many Urghul between him and the other Kettral, too many lances and swords. Regardless of the slarn's strength running through his blood, regardless of his own uncanny speed, there was a weight of steel and horseflesh opposed to which no single soldier could ever hope to stand.

He felt no fear at the realization. No sorrow. There was only a bright bronze eagerness that tasted strangely like relief. After surviving Adare's knife and the fall from the tower in Andt-Kyl, he'd gone to the woods, partly because he could see no role for himself in the war, and partly because he was horrified; horrified of what he'd become, of what he'd learned to do, of what he'd done. His blindness had awoken something in the slarn's poison, something dark and vicious, and he felt certain that if he moved again among men and women he would commit some terrible, irreversible act for which there could be no forgiveness.

The most recent days with Huutsuu and the Flea had done nothing to diminish that feeling. Valyn could remember his hands wrapped around the Urghul woman's neck, their naked skin washed in their own blood. In those burning, freezing nights, he'd almost killed her half a dozen times. And then there were the people he *had* killed, the dozens and dozens of Urghul. That was what he'd trained for. That was war. It wasn't the killing that frightened him, but the fact that it felt so good.

It's time, he thought, breath afire in his throat as he struggled through the shallows. *Time to finish all this.*

Maybe he could save Sigrid and the Flea, make just enough of a distraction that Gwenna could lift them free. Maybe he couldn't. It didn't seem to matter either way. A roar erupted in his throat, a cry that had been surging up through all the fabric of his flesh since Ha Lin died, rising and growing until it seemed too large for the body that contained it, as though that body had dissolved beneath the pain and the rage, leaving behind a man that was not a man at all, but a scream in the shape of a man, a sob of fury dying to shake free its last mortal bond.

Then something yanked him back.

An arm wrapped around his chest, a little weaker than his

own but steadier, threaded through with some conviction he had long ago forgotten.

"Knock it off, you asshole."

Gwenna's voice at his ear, her whole body bent to the simple task of holding him back.

He strained against her weight, eyes fixed on Sigrid and the Flea. The Urghul were closing around them closer and closer. Of the golden bird, there was no sign. Valyn twisted in Gwenna's grip, tried to bring his axes to bear, but she just pulled him nearer, her arms so tight around his chest he could barely breathe. Valyn raged against the embrace, but could not break it.

She was hissing in his ear, snarling the same words over and over. ". . . another bird. There's another fucking bird coming, Valyn. Four of them. *They'll* save the Flea. We have to *go*."

Of the grab itself he remembered almost nothing, just one barren fact: that when they finally rose into the air, Gwenna's arm still wrapped around his shoulders, when the hammering of the bird's great golden wings lifted them up, away from the battle, away from all the danger, it didn't feel like flight. It felt like dying.

53

For a full week, the Skullsworn ignored them almost entirely. A young man or woman arrived each morning with a basket of food—vegetables and cheese, sometimes a piece of smoked meat—and every evening someone came to take the empty basket away. Aside from that, the legendarily vicious priests of Ananshael left Kaden and Triste alone.

No one had told them to stay in the house, and so, on the second day, after a long, exhausted sleep, Kaden had started limping around the mesa, tentatively at first, then more boldly, wandering the open spaces between the white buildings, exploring the bounds of his open-air prison. The only time anyone stopped him was when he approached the bridge, that one path leading back to the rest of the world. A young woman was on her hands and knees—rag in hand, bucket of soapy water beside her—scouring the stone. She stood up as he drew close, met his eyes, then shook her head.

"You can't go over."

"Why not?" He knew why, but wanted to hear what she would say.

"Too dangerous."

"I grew up in mountains like these."

"Not the mountains. The soldiers. Annurians just beyond our sentries. Dozens of them, and more coming."

Kaden looked past her to the rim of the far cliff, a wide ledge backed by a maze of red sandstone glowing with the morning light. He couldn't see anyone, assassin or soldier, but the crazed rock of the Ancaz, riven with cracks and fissures, offered a thousand places to hide. An entire army could be over there, a few men in this hollow, half a dozen behind the boulder. . . .

"Il Tornja's men are massing?"

The woman just shrugged, then knelt, returning to her work.

It didn't take long for Kaden to find Pyrre. The assassin was leaning against the open doorframe of a large stone barn, enjoying the shade as she watched something inside. As Kaden approached, he realized that there was a fight going on, or something like a fight. A man and a woman circled each other warily, feinting and darting, testing the empty space between them, gazes locked firmly as horns. Both were naked from the waist up, their skin slick with sweat. Neither one, however, seemed to be wielding a weapon. There were no axes, no swords. Their hands weren't even balled into fists.

"What are they doing?" Kaden asked quietly.

Pyrre glanced over at him. "Painting."

Kaden squinted in the gloom. As his eyes adjusted, he realized that the hands of the sparring Skullsworn weren't empty after all. Each seemed to be holding something delicately between the thumb and index finger. Sunlight pouring through the open windows flashed off steel. *Needles,* slender enough to draw thread through a torn hem.

"Painting?"

Pyrre nodded. "We're short on paper here, but there's plenty of skin." She smiled at his confusion, then flipped open the front of her own robe. Tattooed into the sun-dark skin between her breasts was a shape about the length of his thumb, the shading mottled, imperfect. It looked like someone had tried to build an image out of hundreds of tiny dots, then stopped short. Away from the ink's dense center, those dots splashed out haphazardly, as though the tattoo were dissolving across her skin. He couldn't quite make out the central shape, but something about the edges and angles tugged at his memory.

"A desert sparrow," Pyrre said, reading his confusion. "Similar to some of the birds I saw when I visited your monastery."

The words snapped the image into focus. It was a sparrow indeed, although the wings were more hinted at than fully inked.

"Why?" Kaden asked.

Pyrre shrugged her robe closed, then cinched the rope belt tighter around her waist. "Ananshael loves their song." She whistled a long, lilting call, a string of notes that reached toward music but never quite resolved into a tune. "We each have one." She gestured toward the sparring partners just as the woman feinted, then lunged, pricking the man's chest with exquisite delicacy. He fell still, smiled, nodded to his opponent. They both crossed to a stone bowl balanced on a window's sill, dipped their needles into dark ink, then returned to the center of the open floor. Another nod, and they were at it again, circling and testing, lunging and recovering. "It takes years," Pyrre went on, "to ink the full bird. Longer, for those who are quicker."

"And when it's finished?"

"We celebrate. There is music and food. At the end of the night, the one with the songbird goes to the god."

"You kill the loser?"

"There are no losers. There are only those who go earlier or later to the god's embrace."

Kaden shook his head. "If the god's embrace is so sweet, then why all this? Why go through the years of sparring at all?"

"It's a way of seeing who has the gift," Pyrre replied. "The slow or unskilled, those who have grown too old to fight—their priesthood quickly becomes personal."

"Meaning you kill them."

"Meaning they give willingly of their own lives."

"And those of you who are quicker?"

The assassin winked at him. "We're around longer. To spread the god's truth and his justice."

Kaden stared at the unfolding fight, but Pyrre had already turned away, stepping from the barn's cool darkness into the bright sun as though she'd lost all interest in the contest.

"Il Tornja knows we are here," Kaden said, following her.

"Of course he does."

"And he's coming."

Pyrre grinned her most wolfish grin. "Of course he is."

"He can't have more than a few dozen men with him. . . ."

"There are more coming. Many more. My brothers and sisters killed most of his messengers, but a couple got away." She stared eastward, as though she could make out those soldiers fleeing over the Dead Salts, toward Mo'ir and whatever reinforcements waited. "I'm looking forward to it, actually. Thousands of sweating young men camped out on the canyon rim just across the bridge. The Annurians aren't great soldiers, but there's no denying that all that marching and hauling and drilling—it makes a man fit. Just a shame that your empire won't allow women in the ranks. A woman's leg, well toned, is shapelier than a man's. Still, one makes do. . . ." She closed her eyes, savored some imagination of the besieging army, then hummed contentedly.

"Have you forgotten the leach?" Kaden asked. "The one who pulled lightning straight out of the sky? Il Tornja doesn't *need* his army. One powerful leach could level Rassambur without stepping foot on the bridge."

Pyrre shrugged. "If he has his well. And that's assuming your brilliant general . . ."

"He's not my general."

". . . is willing to risk bringing that leach close enough to mount a serious attack. He might be handy with lightning, but he'll die if someone puts an arrow in his eye. And we spend a lot of time here in Rassambur learning to put arrows in eyes."

Kaden exhaled slowly, trying to order his thoughts. "Even if that's true, we're trapped as long as we stay here, and the trap is only going to get tighter. If we're going to get out, we need to get out *now*. Have you talked to Gerra?"

"Gerra will decide what he decides in his own time," Pyrre said, then cocked her head to one side, studying him. "I don't remember you being so afraid, Kaden. The last time, back in those miserably frigid mountains of yours, there were moments when you seemed almost . . . calm. Where did that go?"

"Last time, there wasn't as much to be afraid of."

It was a weak response, and it did next to nothing to quench the question in the assassin's eyes. And yet, what else could he say? There was no explaining the god locked inside of him, raging and thrashing by day and night, no explaining the nihilistic temptations of the *vaniate,* no explaining that the trance had become more dangerous than the panic it replaced. Revealing any corner of the truth to Pyrre would see him dead—that much was clear. If she knew he bore the god she loathed inside his flesh, she'd cut him and the god to bloody shreds.

Maybe that would be best.

All over again he felt the doubt, a thick tide rising inside him. He turned away before the assassin could see it in his eyes.

It was night, and Meshkent was awake, raging in the back of Kaden's mind. More and more, he was learning to keep the god kenneled, to mute the endless demands for freedom and power, tamping them down until the voice was almost as incoherent as the wind over stone—constant and cold, but meaningless. Even when Kaden could ignore those words, however, he could feel the god there, a blight, a rabid creature that needed to be put down. All that fight, the clawing and the biting, it was the opposite of what il Tornja had described, and once again the *kenarang's* words drifted across Kaden's thoughts: *The beauty of a life lived free, unenslaved by brutish passions . . .*

"Can't sleep?"

Kaden turned to find Triste's slender shadow framed inside the door to the stone house. After a heartbeat's hesitation, she stepped out onto the ledge. Moonlight glinted off her eyes, off a belt knife she held before her, clutching it tentatively in one hand. For just a moment, he had the ridiculous notion that she had come outside to kill him, to plunge that meager weapon into his heart. The thought aroused more curiosity than fear.

All human life ends somehow, he thought.

As Triste crossed the stone to sit beside him, however, he realized she carried a lobe of sugar cactus in her other hand. The knife was a tool, not a weapon, and for a while the only sound was the wet slice of the steel through the vegetable's flesh.

"Here," she said finally, offering him a slice.

Give yourself to me, Meshkent hissed silently, something inside the god responding to another human voice, *and I will tear this hovel down.*

Be silent, Kaden replied. *You are a sickness. A plague. These priests have fattened you on lies. . . .*

BE SILENT!

The god went suddenly, utterly still. Kaden stared down into the pit he had built to pen in the divine, tried to keep his balance as he studied the mind inside his mind.

There was a knife-edge ridge back in the Bone Mountains, a mile-long razor of stone connecting two peaks. From time to time, the monks ordered their older acolytes to traverse the ridge—it was an exercise, among other things, about holding fear in check. There was no easy way to move over the rock; in most places it was almost impossible simply to walk along it. One gust of wind could tumble you into the abyss on either side. Kaden remembered it all in perfect frozen detail, holding the cold granite of the ridgetop, moving hand over hand as he searched for footholds in the steep walls. Sometimes the easiest passage was on the west side of the ridge, sometimes on the east. To get to the end, you had to keep switching, climbing back and forth over that jagged knife-edge, knowing that a slip on either side would mean the end.

Yes, it was an exercise about the controlling of fear, but Kaden had begun to suspect that, like most tasks the monks assigned their pupils, it was more than that. There was no safe place on that ridgeline. No flat ground where a boy could stop and rest. The only hope was in constant movement, constant change, climbing back and forth over that frigid stone, the fathoms of unforgiving air spread out below.

His own mind felt like that ridgeline now. If he stumbled too far to one side, Meshkent would seize him; if he slipped to the other, he would fall into the *vaniate*. The mind of the god and the emptiness of the Csestriim trance were each an abyss: enormous, endless, stretching to the very edge of thought. His self, on the other hand, the part of him that still felt like *him,* was no more than that narrow ridge, the stone rough in his hands, and crumbling.

Submit to me, Meshkent growled, his voice somehow impossibly distant and right inside the ear at the same time.

No.

Grimly, Kaden shifted across the ridgeline away from the god. The *vaniate* beckoned beneath his feet. It seemed impossible that he had ever not known how to enter that emptiness. It was as easy as falling.

"What does it feel like?"

Triste's words jerked him free of his mind's vertiginous ridge. Kaden turned to find her staring at him, eyes wide but hard in the darkness.

"The god?" he asked.

She nodded.

"It feels . . . ," he searched for the words, "like a great weight, a madness heavy as lead." He hesitated. "I can hear him."

Triste leaned forward slightly, as though Meshkent's commands might carry on the air, as though his words were something she might hear if she drew close enough. "What does it sound like?"

Kaden shook his head, trying to find the right language. Failing. After a while he shifted to face Triste—he couldn't say why—mirroring her cross-legged pose with his own. He felt carved out, hollowed by the running and the fighting and the lying. Suddenly, it was all he could do to sit upright.

"It sounds like Long Fist," he said at last. "Not the actual timbre of the voice . . . ," he struggled for the words, "but the force."

Tears slicked Triste's eyes, as though someone had smeared moonlight across her cheeks. "At least you can hear him. Talk to him."

Kaden shook his head. "He thought he would inhabit me the way he had that Urghul. He almost succeeded. . . ."

Triste watched him in silence for a long time.

"And . . . ," she prodded finally.

"And he couldn't. The Shin taught me just enough."

"Enough *what*?"

"Enough to control my mind. Divide it. Evacuate a space, seal it off."

"But I don't know any of that," Triste protested. "And Ciena's trapped inside me just the same way."

Kaden shook his head again. "I don't know, Triste. I don't understand it. I can barely articulate what's happening to me."

"Did he tell you . . . ," Triste asked tentatively. "The *obviate* . . . "

Kaden just shook his head.

For a while they sat in silence. Voices rose in the center of the mesa, laughing, then falling away. Kaden glanced over at the house, the cottage of two dead men that had become their prison. There was a time when he would have been thinking, scheming, trying to find some way out. He remembered that old, animal urgency. Remembered it—but couldn't feel it. For the first time, the old Shin expression made sense: *You live in your mind.* The two of them might be trapped inside Rassambur, but they would have no more freedom, no *true* freedom, even if they wandered alone through the most remote valleys of the Bone Mountains. The mind was the cage, and there was no escaping it. Not without dying.

"Why haven't you killed her?" he asked, looking over at Triste again.

The girl raised a hand to her chest, as though she felt something moving there, something she didn't recognize. The Skullsworn had provided them with desert robes not unlike those worn by the Shin, but Triste hadn't changed out of the simple pants and tunic she'd been wearing when he found her days earlier. He could see the scars running the length of her arm; they looked silver in the moonlight, almost beautiful. Her fingernails had grown back—the ones that Ekhard Matol had torn away—but they were ridged and ragged. Some things, once broken, could never be fully fixed.

Her face hardened at the question. "I won't . . ."

"I don't mean the *obviate*," Kaden said, raising a hand to forestall her. "That would save her, not hurt her. But if you don't go back to the Spear, if you don't perform the ritual, you can destroy Ciena, or damage her so badly she will never touch this world again."

"Only by killing myself."

Kaden shrugged. It seemed a trivial objection. "You're going to die anyway. We all are. If you hate the goddess so much, you can take her with you." He paused, turning the next proposition over in his mind before he made it. "We could kill them both."

Triste stared at him, lips parted. "What happened to saving everyone? To defeating the Csestriim and preserving humanity? That's why you kept me locked up in your Spear in the first place, right? That's why you came after me when I escaped. All you *cared* about was the *obviate*, to get your goddess out, let her free, to rescue her, and to Hull with the carcass you left behind. . . ."

She trailed off, breathless, chest heaving.

"Maybe I cared about the wrong thing," Kaden replied quietly. "I keep thinking about what we've seen—the Annurians slaughtering the monks back in Ashk'lan; the Ishien in the Dead Heart; Adiv and your mother; the conspirators that helped to overthrow the empire; Adare, who murdered Valyn, then lied to me about it. . . . Why would we want to preserve that? Why would we want to save *any* of it?"

"I don't," Triste said. "I'm not trying to save the goddess or your 'Kent-kissing empire. It can all *burn*. I'll set fire to it myself. . . ."

"We can do that," Kaden said.

Meshkent roared in the chasm of his mind. Kaden stared down into the bottomless emptiness of the *vaniate*. It would be so easy to fall. He gestured from Triste toward the real cliff's edge, the verge of Rassambur's sheer-walled mesa, just a dozen paces away. "We can end it right here."

When Triste finally replied, her voice was small, lost. "I don't want to die."

Kaden stared at her. She had come so close so many times already. "Why not?"

She shook her head helplessly. "I don't *know*."

"There is only more of this, Triste. More hiding, more hunger, more torture."

"We might get out. We might escape."

Kaden shook his head wearily. "It doesn't matter. Rassambur isn't the prison." He tapped a finger against the side of his skull. "*This* is."

Her lips twisted back. She looked as though she were getting ready to leap on him, to rip out his throat with her teeth, only she didn't move. The sound, when it came, wasn't a scream, but a hopeless sob. He watched her, watched her shoulders heave, studied her perfect, mutilated body as it convulsed with grief.

"This is what I mean," he said quietly.

She didn't reply. Just shielded her face with her hands.

"How can this," he gestured to her with one hand, "be right? Long Fist told me, before we came after you, that this is what we are for, but how can that be *true*?" He cocked his head to the side. "You are like a fish pulled from the water. This struggle, this suffering—you can't breathe it. None of us can."

Slowly Triste raised her head. Tangles of black hair fell across her face, but her eyes were fixed on him, steady, even as that unnamed grief continued to wrack her body. Meshkent shifted inside Kaden's mind as though he felt the girl's suffering, as though he were feeding off it.

"There is more," Triste said quietly, her voice like something torn apart. The tears still coursed down her cheeks, but she made no move to scrub them away.

"More what?"

"More to . . ." She gestured helplessly to him, to herself. "To this. To us. To life."

"That's the cruelest part of it," Kaden replied. "That belief. That hope. It's worse than all Meshkent's agonies. *That's* what keeps us here; it's what makes us accept our suffering. The young gods aren't just the children of Ciena and Meshkent; they are their generals, the keepers of their jails." He shook his head at the memory of Long Fist sitting across the fire from him in a hide tent in the Waist. "He said we were instruments. We are slaves."

He rose slowly to his feet, muscles and bones protesting. More of Meshkent's work there. He scrutinized that pain a moment, then set it aside. They lived in a world twisted by the god, but now the god himself was trapped. Kaden lifted Triste's belt knife from the stone. The blade was barely three inches long, and somewhat dull, but it would do. Bedisa wove the souls of living beings so weakly into their bodies. . . .

He placed the point against the inside of his arm, dragged the notched steel over his skin. Meshkent hissed and twisted. Kaden turned away from the god, studying the dark blood welling up behind the blade. Pain came with the blood, bright and hot.

That pain is there to stop me, he thought. *That, and the hope, and the fear.*

All his human feelings, just a fence, a wall built by the gods to keep their precious chattel penned.

Such a meager fence.

Meshkent was raging now, bellowing, his demands all tangled up with his defiance. It didn't matter, the god was on the far side of the ridge, caught deep in a chasm he could not escape. If Kaden dropped into the *vaniate* once more there would be no climbing free, not this time. Kiel had been warning him about that for months, but Kiel was wrong. How could the Csestriim understand how badly humanity was broken, how desperately in need of salvation?

The walking away. That was what the monks called that passage, the departure from the world of human need into a more perfect world of sky, and snow, and stone. They were wrong, too. The walking was secondary, unnecessary. All that was necessary was the letting go. Kaden considered the shape of his mind, that narrow knife of stone stretching on endlessly into the clouds. He felt his grip slipping. He smiled, and let go.

The *vaniate* closed around him, endless and unsullied. It seemed impossible, inside that emptiness, that he had ever considered the haphazard construction of flesh and blood his *self*. He looked at the knife, at where the blade's point opened the skin of his arm. He'd fought so hard to preserve his carcass, and for what? The Shin had thrown open the door to his cage, and he had slammed it closed again, had hung against the bars, refusing to be set free.

It's so easy. Easier than breathing.

Meshkent roared. The sound meant nothing.

Then Triste closed her hand over his wrist, pulling the knife away.

"What are you *doing*?"

Kaden turned to her, confused. "I'm leaving. . . ." He gestured to the slash along his skin.

"You can't," she snarled, face a rictus of fear and confusion.

"Triste," he said quietly. "You don't understand. Everything you're feeling now—you don't have to feel it. You're not *supposed* to. You're a sick woman insisting on the beauty of your sickness." He smiled at her. "We can be well. Whole."

He tried to go back to his work, but she had him by the wrist. Her fingers felt like steel.

"Let me go, Triste."

She shook her head. "No."

"Why not?"

"All of this, everything wrong in my fucking life, happened because of you, and you are *not leaving me here alone.*"

He smiled. "I won't leave you. We can both be done with this." With his free hand, he ran a finger along her neck. Her skin was smooth as cream. Something stirred inside him, some spasm of the beast he had been. He crushed it. "You're trapped," he said, tracing a line down to her heart. He could feel it slamming against her chest. "You don't have to be."

"Stop saying that."

Kaden shook his head. Blood slicked his arm, but it wasn't enough. He needed to cut deeper, further.

"Let me go, Triste."

"I already told you—you are *not* fucking *leaving me,* you *bastard.*"

She pivoted as she spoke, twisted his wrist so viciously that the knife fell free and then, he, too, was falling.

So strong, he thought vaguely. Even on that first night in Ashk'lan, when she was waiting for him naked in his bed, Triste had always been so strong.

He landed hard, the stone bruising his hip, then jarring his skull as it struck. For a few heartbeats, he reeled, dizzy, confused, the *vaniate* swaying around him. Pain blazed outside the trance, in his arm, in the back of his head, but he was free of the pain, if only . . .

"Stop it!" Triste screamed. She hit him across the face. "Don't you fucking retreat into your private trance. You're not *leaving* me here." She hit him again. "YOU ARE NOT LEAVING ME." Her breath was ripped and ragged. Her body shuddered with the terror and the strain. "I won't let you. I won't let you." Tears soaked her face, matting her hair to her brow and cheeks in scribbled tangles. She was a vision of suffering, of madness, of everything that was wrong with what they had become.

The Csestriim were right, Kaden thought.

And then she stopped shouting. Stopped moving entirely. He could feel her weight on top of him, suddenly still and steady. Only her chest rose and fell as her lungs struggled to drag in more air. When she spoke again, it was in a whisper, quiet, composed, but hard as carved stone.

"I won't let you leave me alone with this."

"Triste . . . ," he began again.

She shook her head. She was still crying, but her eyes were defiant, the way he remembered them. Strong. She leaned in, down, and pressed her lips to his.

It was harder than he expected to pull away. "You hate me, Triste."

"I do," she whispered.

"I betrayed you."

"You betrayed me, and you gave me away. And do you think that absolves you now? It doesn't. Just this one time, Kaden, this last time, I'm not begging you, I'm telling you, I'm demanding this of you: *don't.*"

Her eyes were wide as moons, bright, violent, violet, shifting with the light reflected from his own burning gaze. Her weight was like the whole warm night laid on top of him.

"Every choice that you have made was wrong," she whispered. "I am finished doing things your way."

The second kiss didn't pull him from the *vaniate,* not right away, but if the trance was a bottomless well into which he had been falling, Triste's touch was a hook lodged in his mind, arresting his fall, holding him spinning in the emptiness. And then, with a horrible, ineluctable slowness, pulling him up.

The monks had trained Kaden to be hit. They had trained him to sit in the snow for hours on end. They had trained him to haul stones until his hands bled, to starve, to suffer, and then to step outside that suffering. They had trained him for every manner of austerity to which the flesh could be subjected. They had not trained him for this.

He managed to pull away for a half a heartbeat.

"Triste . . ." The word scraped out. There were no others.

Her hands were cradling the back of his head, her chest pressed against his chest, her tongue running over his teeth. It was how she'd killed Ekhard Matol, pinning him against the *kenta* with her meager weight, then breaking him apart limb by limb. Only that hadn't been Triste. That had been Ciena.

When Kaden looked into the eyes of the woman who held him now, there was no sign of the goddess. There was only the woman, strong, furious, determined, pressing herself into him, tearing at his shirt, sliding her hands over his chest. He opened his arms, pulled her toward him, and woke from the *vaniate*.

The beast brain. That was what the monks called all the myriad impulses of the flesh: rage and hunger, fear and eagerness and lust. For all their warnings, Kaden had never really known its strength.

He slid his hands up Triste's back, over the ridges of her scarred skin, then pulled her light shirt up over her head. She twisted to help, hurled the shirt free, then was on him again, skin sliding over skin, firm and smooth.

Triste's breath came hot through her parted lips. "Suffering is not everything."

Kaden kissed her, then kissed her again. Then again.

"The monks were wrong," he whispered finally, his own words a revelation. "Il Tornja was wrong."

"Of course they were, you idiot. Of course they were fucking wrong."

They spent the night discovering just how wrong, clutching each other, whispering things they barely understood, finding something painful and perfect in the places where their skin touched, something old and undeniable, a truth that both had heard a hundred times but neither one had known, all while the desert moon slid down the sky, and the million stars, shivering and indifferent, burned their holes into the night.

54

Gwenna could still remember the day she'd fallen in love with Valyn. Or maybe *love* wasn't the right word—she was only twelve at the time—but whatever it was had hit her like a sack of bricks to the gut.

Every year there was a smallboat race around Qarsh. Vets went up against vets, and the cadets had their own division. Gwenna had never been much for sailing; the wind always seemed to be blowing the wrong way, and she'd been hit in the head by a swinging boom one too many times. Still, a race was a race, and she'd be shipped to 'Shael if she sat it out on the beach while the other cadets got all wet and beat up. There was a young soldier named Gelly. The girl wasn't much with a blade or a bow—she washed out long before the Trial—but she could handle a boat, and so Gwenna went looking for her a month before the race.

"We're a team," she said.

Gelly had looked at her, uncertainty painted across her face. "We . . ."

"The boat race," Gwenna snapped. "You want in?"

The girl nodded hesitantly.

"Good," Gwenna said gruffly. "And just so we're on the same page, I don't give a pickled shit if we win. I just want to beat Sami Yurl and that Malkeenian."

Gwenna had lumped them together, back then. Yurl and

Valyn were both rich, both nobility, and even the unending rigors
of Kettral training hadn't yet managed to wash the stink of
privilege off either of them. Everything about Valyn irritated
Gwenna—the way he spoke, the way he addressed himself to
the other cadets, even the way he sat in the mess hall, that royal
spine of his just a little too straight. Unfortunately, he was a
good sailor, better than Gwenna. Hence the need for Gelly.

The race was chaos before it even began. A summer storm
had blown up out of the south, and the swells were fifteen feet
high even when they were trying to coax the boats to the starting
line. By the time they rounded the West Bluffs the warm rain
came down like a wall, so heavy Gwenna couldn't see more than
a few feet in front of her. Gelly had managed the boat brilliantly
in the first stages of the storm, but as thunder smashed overhead,
Gwenna could see the girl starting to fray.

"We should go in!" Gelly shouted over the gale, pointing
vaguely south, toward where Qarsh was supposed to be.

"To Hull with that," Gwenna bellowed, hauling on the line,
trying to keep the sail from ripping free of her hands.

"We can't manage the boat," Gelly insisted. "Not in this."

"You just keep steering," Gwenna shouted. "I'll take care of
the sail."

In truth, however, Gelly was right. Two people could handle
the boat, even in brisk weather, but the storm had moved well
beyond brisk. They'd already buried the gunwale in the side of
a swell three times. If they didn't furl the sail, the boat was going
over, and they were headed into the drink. It was simple as that.

"Valyn and Yurl can't sail in this either," Gelly shouted.

Gwenna gritted her teeth, cursed the storm and her own
weakness, and prepared to pull the sail. Then, between one swell
and the next, another boat loomed up out of the rain. It was
canted over hard, the sail drum-taut, and on them before Gelly
could even swing the rudder. Ha Lin was hiked out over the
rail, hair plastered to her face, both hands wrapped around the
line as she tried to manage the sail. She noticed Gwenna half a

heartbeat later, tried to ease off the line, grimaced as she shouted something to Valyn. The prince ran his eyes over Gwenna's boat. He looked as beaten up as Gwenna felt, but there was no quitting in those dark eyes. He shouted something back to Ha Lin. Gwenna couldn't make out the exchange, but the other girl shook her head. Valyn nodded fiercely and kicked the rudder over.

Gwenna's first thought was that the Malkeenian bastard was trying to ram them. His boat slid down the south side of the swell, straight at her beam. Gwenna shifted, trying to get clear of the collision, but then, at the last minute, Valyn swung the rudder around again, running his boat tight in parallel with Gwenna's.

"Go," he shouted, handling the rudder with one hand while he stabbed his finger at Gwenna's boat with the other.

He wasn't talking to her. He was talking to Ha Lin.

The girl hesitated, glanced from Valyn to Gwenna, then back.

"Go," he shouted again. "I'll be fine."

Ha Lin gritted her teeth and jumped, caught the gunwale of Gwenna's boat and hauled herself in.

"Stubborn fucking bastard," she was muttering.

Without Ha Lin managing the sail, everything had gone straight to shit over on Valyn's boat. The boom swung crazily in the wind, and he looked likely to capsize as the vessel went dead in the water. Valyn, however, was grinning, waving them on even as he fought to keep the boat upright.

"Go win," he shouted as he faded back into the rain. "Go win!"

They did.

Valyn, on the other hand, didn't manage to coax his boat back into the harbor until late that night, when the worst of the storm had passed. When he finally climbed up onto the dock, Gwenna started to go to him, to throw her arms around him in a great celebratory hug. Ha Lin was there first. Gwenna, with nowhere to go, nothing to do with her arms, settled for a weak wave. "Thanks," she shouted. It wasn't clear if he heard her or not, but the damage was already done. She always remembered that smile, the way he'd waved them on even as his own boat foundered.

And now that boy is dead, Gwenna thought, staring at the grim specter of a man who sat across from her.

It had been a baffling shock to find Valyn at all. The last she'd seen of him had been in Long Fist's camp out on the Blood Steppe. Given what Talal had told her later, and what Kaden had said about Adare, she'd felt certain that one way or another Valyn had died up on that tower in Andt-Kyl. She'd carried the loss around inside her like an ache, and though it had faded over the intervening months, she'd expected that a part of her would mourn her whole life for Valyn and Laith both, good men who had died fighting, trying to do the right thing.

Except Valyn was alive. He had been alive all along, although what had happened to him, Gwenna had no idea. His eyes were ruined, destroyed by the same gash that someone had carved straight across his face. He was thinner than she remembered, strong but awfully gaunt, a spiderweb of scar cut into his skin. He was a long cry from the earnest, determined cadet Gwenna remembered, a long cry, even, from what he'd become as a Wing leader. It felt as though some creature had crawled into the body of the boy she'd loved all those years ago, crawled in and taken it over. A creature of hunger and darkness.

The rest of the Kettral were even more beaten up, just as surprising a discovery, but at least they were still recognizable. Something fucking awful had happened to the Flea's arm, which seemed to be flayed from the elbow to the wrist. Newt's lower leg was crushed all to Hull; he wouldn't be flying any more missions, that was clear enough, although the realization didn't seem to have dulled his strange spirit any. As Talal worked on his leg, the ugly demolitions master met Gwenna's eyes.

"The timely arrival of a friend is worth more than all the spice in the western islands," he said.

"Yeah," Gwenna replied. "I wouldn't rely on timely arrivals any more than you have to. We stumbled across you mostly by accident. We were scouting the Urghul army for the Emperor. Didn't expect to find a handful of busted-up Kettral trying to keep the fight all to themselves."

Quick Jak had put Allar'ra down on a gentle stretch of beach just northwest of the Neck, and the other Kettral, Gwenna's Kettral, had landed along with them. As the huge birds furled their wings, the newly blooded soldiers, abuzz with the recent action, checked their weapons and gear, talking excitedly the whole time. Gwenna didn't feel excited. She felt tired. Adare's orders had been to scout the Urghul and find il Tornja, which meant they'd managed one out of two. Maybe the Emperor wanted her to stay out in the field, but with the Urghul army hammering down on Annur, hunting around for a lone general didn't seem to make much sense. They needed to get back to the city, to help see to the coming defense. It had been tempting to fly directly there, but the Flea and his Wing needed medical care, and more than that, there were some questions that needed answers before Gwenna faced Adare again.

"So," she said, glancing over the small group. "Who wants to start?"

Valyn's scarred eyes were fixed on her. There was no way he could see through those, but he didn't move like a blind man. Gwenna studied him for a moment, then looked away.

"Where's Shaleel?" the Flea asked. "Who's in charge on the Islands?"

"Yeah," Gwenna said slowly. "Funny you should ask that."

It didn't take long to tell the story of the Eyrie's self-immolation, Jakob Rallen and his tyranny, the ultimate victory of the resistance. When she was done, everyone was silent for a long time, listening to waves lisp up onto the sand. Finally the

Flea looked over at the cluster of birds and the soldiers who were tending to them.

"They did well," he said simply. "You did well."

Gwenna felt herself coloring. "Well, if this was it, we could all sit back and drink ourselves warm, but there's a lot more doing to do."

"The Urghul . . . ," the Flea began.

"More than the Urghul," Gwenna said, realizing only once she'd done it that she had cut the older man off. "Sorry, sir."

The Flea waved aside her apology. "I'll shut up. You talk. We don't know a thing about the strategic picture. You do."

Gwenna took a deep breath. Valyn still hadn't spoken. He was stone-still, watching her with those awful blind eyes of his.

"The picture," she said, turning to face the Flea again, "is about as clear as a bucket of shit mixed with a liberal helping of mud.

"As I'm sure you've deduced from the Urghul fucking horde hammering down along the Haag, il Tornja left the northern front weeks back. The Emperor wants to know—"

Valyn spoke for the first time since landing, cutting her off. "The Emperor?"

His voice made Gwenna shiver. "Your sister. The one with the burning eyes—"

"Where is Kaden?"

"I don't know. We saw him before we went to the Islands— Talal, Annick, and I—he's the one who *sent* us to the Islands. He knew what had happened at the Eyrie and he needed birds. When we got back with the birds, though . . ." She shrugged. "Adare was here. Annur's an empire again. Sort of. She and the council patched up their rift somehow."

Valyn leaned forward, eager, hungry. "And just where," he asked, voice quiet as falling ash, "did my sister say that Kaden had gone?"

"*Elsewhere.*"

The Flea frowned. "Not much of an explanation."

"You didn't press her?" Valyn demanded.

Gwenna stared at him. "Last time I checked, we're soldiers. When the Emperor says, 'Go find the Urghul,' we go find the 'Kent-kissing Urghul."

"She is not the Emperor," he growled.

"Well, she's sitting on the throne," Gwenna snapped, "which is inside the Dawn Palace. She has burning eyes and everyone keeps calling her *Your Radiance,* so you could maybe forgive me for missing that particular point. In fact," she cocked her head to the side, "what is it *you've* been up to all these months, that you know so much about the internal workings of the empire?"

Valyn exhaled between gritted teeth. Gwenna tensed. She could smell his fury on the sea's salt wind. At her side, Talal leaned back, settling a casual hand on his belt knife, as though he, too, felt the danger. Then it passed.

"I've been recovering," Valyn said quietly, "from the time Adare planted a dagger between my ribs."

Waves rolled up the beach, crested, crashed, then fell away, dragged back into the great churning belly of the sea. For what seemed like a long time, no one spoke. Gwenna could think of nothing to say. She'd suspected something underhanded from Adare—Kaden had implied as much, and the Emperor herself had been evasive on the topic. Underhanded, however, was a long cry from murderous.

Finally, she shook her head. "Why?"

"She wanted to protect her general," Valyn said. "I tried to kill Ran il Tornja. She stopped me."

Gwenna whistled softly. "And now il Tornja's turned on her."

"Turned on her?" Valyn asked, head whipping around. "How?"

"Disappeared. Abandoned the front. Threatened to kill her son. Sounds like she should have let you kill him."

"Oh, I will," Valyn said. For the first time since landing, he smiled.

"That's gonna be tough," Gwenna pointed out, "given that he's disappeared."

"No, it won't. He'll come back to Annur sooner or later. In the meantime, I can pay back my beloved sister."

Gwenna frowned. "You mean stab her. To death."

Valyn nodded silently. She could smell the hunger on him again, as though he were some sort of starving beast.

"I'm sure you noticed," Gwenna began carefully, "that there's an Urghul army riding down on the heart of the empire even as we sit here. I've been to the capital. The place is a goat fuck. Adare's about the only one holding anything together down there. I'm not sure this is the perfect time to kill her."

Valyn coughed up a laugh. "And when," he demanded, "*is* the perfect time to murder one's sister?"

"After the war, for starters. I mean, the odds are decent the Urghul'll do your work for you. I had a good look at that army from up on the bird and it seemed to stretch north just about all the way to the mountains. Odds are, all our heads will be on pointy sticks by the end of the month anyway, but if we survive this, somehow, if we beat back those 'Kent-kissing bastards, then shit, by all means, stab your evil sister. For that matter, I'll *help* you take her down."

When she fell silent, Valyn didn't speak. He just stared at her with those ravaged eyes, stared *through* her, as though he wasn't seeing her face at all, but the wide gray sea stretching out behind.

The Flea shifted. "Gwenna is right. Whatever Adare's crimes, she is needed in Annur."

"We all need something," Valyn whispered.

"Yes," Gwenna said. "Well. Several *million* people need Adare's bony ass on that throne."

He shook his head. "I've heard this argument before. It's what Adare told me before Andt-Kyl. 'We need him, Valyn. We need il Tornja.' "

"And you went after him anyway. And that worked out about as well as having a sick goat shit in your soup."

To her shock, Valyn chuckled. For just a moment, a quarter heartbeat, he might have been the young man she remembered. Then it was gone. Gwenna blew out a weary breath.

"Just wait," she said quietly. "Wait until the war is over, and then, I swear, I'll help you do whatever needs to be done."

He watched her with those ruined eyes, then inclined his head.

"I'll wait."

55

The days Kaden spent with Triste in the small white house at the edge of Rassambur's sunbaked mesa waiting to learn if he would be murdered by the Skullsworn or set free were unlike any others in his life. His life, until then, had been split between luxury and struggle: a childhood sleeping in the feathered beds of the Dawn Palace, eating fresh fruit all winter, finding warm clothes delivered by a slave each morning. Then, an adolescence of stone and snow and suffering.

He had known siblings, friends, and mentors, periods of relative peace and even beauty. After eighteen years, he had seen the Bone Mountains and the Rift, Intarra's Spear and the cold cliff dwellings of Assare, the Csestriim fortress in the Dead Heart and the islands that served as the *kenta* hubs, scraps of green lost in a world of tossing sea. It seemed like a lot to pack into a single life, a short life. He had thought, when Meshkent retreated into his mind, when he realized what that meant, what had to happen, that he could die feeling that he'd seen the world, that he could let Ananshael unknit his soul knowing that he'd experienced the full range of what life had to offer.

And he had been wrong.

None of it, not the brotherly love of his childhood or the bawdy camaraderie he'd shared with Akiil, not his mother's kisses or his father's distant regard, had prepared him for what he shared with Triste during those warm, sunbright days at the mesa's edge.

The sex—tender and explosive, wrenching and soft and raw— was the least of it. It was all the rest, what happened when they stopped, when they were just lying on the rough blankets, the only light the one lantern the Skullsworn had given them, that Kaden realized how narrow the scope of his life had been. He felt like a child who had spent his years running through the chambers of a vast mansion over and over. He had seen every room, every corridor, every crawlspace and pantry. Then one day, someone opened a door, he stepped outside, and for the first time saw the sky.

"I didn't realize . . . ," he murmured one night, Triste tucked tight up against him, her body rising and falling with her breath.

"Didn't realize what?" she asked sleepily.

He shook his head. "Any of it."

She laughed at that. In all their time together, he'd never heard her laugh. Then she kissed him on the chest, moved on top of him, and he quit bothering with words. That part the Shin had right—the words were useless.

They made no effort to escape, partly because it was obviously impossible, partly because if they *did* somehow manage to get past the Skullsworn, they would only be delivering themselves into il Tornja's arms. They'd escaped him once, but he still had his *ak'hanath,* still had that crazed, ancient leach at his side, and though no one had seen the *kenarang* on the far rim of the canyon, he was there—Kaden was certain of it—laying his careful traps.

"What will we do?" Triste finally asked. They were lying in bed. It was late, and the stars had already scraped through most of their nightly course. Kaden didn't realize she had awoken until she spoke, then rose up on one elbow, tracing a finger along his ribs, down to his hip.

"I'm not sure we can do anything," Kaden replied. "Not until the Skullsworn decide if they're going to kill us or help us."

"We could tell them," she suggested hesitantly. "Tell them the truth."

Kaden shook his head. He'd been pondering that exact course since they first arrived; it seemed like madness. If they knew one thing for certain, it was that the priesthood of Ananshael loathed Meshkent and all his minions. The Skullsworn had already sacrificed a dozen of their number in a botched attempt to find Long Fist, and that was when they'd believed that he was merely an Urghul shaman, merely a minister of the god's misery. If Gerra knew he had the Lord of Pain himself in Rassambur, beneath his blade, they were as good as dead.

"They haven't killed us yet," Kaden said, "which is good."

Triste chuckled at the understatement.

"The Csestriim are an affront to everything the Skullsworn believe," Kaden went on. "Gerra seemed shocked to learn that they still walk the earth."

"And if Gerra helps us?"

Kaden closed his eyes, tried to remember the world beyond the mesa. "If we manage to get clear, free, we could start running again. Try to get to a *kenta,* go somewhere il Tornja can't go."

"There's nowhere he can't go," Triste replied quietly.

They fell silent. There was nothing to say. Half of Kaden's life had been given over to the stamping out of desire. It had almost worked. When Pyrre first brought them to Rassambur, he'd been ready to give up his life, to step outside himself once and for all. It would have been easy, then, to do what needed doing, and yet he'd seen no point in the *obviate* then. Now, finally, he understood what was at stake. The only way to understand it was to feel the love, and the pain that came with that love.

"I want to be with you," Triste said, pulling him close, so tight it was a struggle to breathe. "When we do it, I want to be right beside you."

It. She didn't say the word. She didn't need to.

Kaden nodded. For the first time since his childhood, he was crying.

In the small, quiet hour before dawn, Kaden woke to find Pyrre standing at the foot of the bed. He wrapped an arm tighter around Triste, who murmured something in her sleep, shifted beneath the blanket to press her body against his, but did not wake. How long the assassin had been standing there, Kaden had no idea. She was smiling—not the habitual wry smile that she usually wore, but something older, more honest.

"It is a truth most people refuse," she said quietly, "but there is peace in Ananshael's shadow." She nodded to Triste's sleeping form. "Joy."

Kaden started to object, but found he had no objection. The assassin was right. Rassambur, his imprisonment, the daily threat of death, had led to this: the long softness of the blue-black nights, shared warmth beneath old blankets, his breath and Triste's intermingled, even as they slept. Even Meshkent had fallen almost silent, as though the god himself understood the uselessness of all struggle here, in the heart of Ananshael's dominion.

"Has Gerra decided?" Kaden asked.

Pyrre nodded thoughtfully. "In a manner of speaking."

"Meaning?"

"You will see."

"I would have thought we were past the games."

The assassin's smile widened. "And I would have thought you understood by now that without the games, there is no life." She gestured toward Triste. "Wake her slowly, if you like, in your own way. . . ." She cocked her head at that, arched an eyebrow, ran her tongue over her teeth. "But be at Ananshael's Scale as the sun rises."

When they reached the rim of the mesa, Gerra was still on the scale, still lying down, much as he had been when they first arrived. The last of the stars spangled the western sky, but though Triste shivered at his side, Kaden could already feel the air warming behind them. He glanced over his shoulder, squinting against the watery glow. In moments, the hot rim of the sun would crest the eastern peaks, but for now, the air was a smear of pink light, something ripening, but not yet ripe.

"I have prayed," Gerra said without opening his eyes. "I vowed to the god that I would remain on his scale for a week after your arrival, and I have remained on it for the full week, fasting, praying."

Triste shook her head. "Why?"

Gerra sat up slowly, stretched his neck, rolled his shoulders forward, then back. "If the god gathered me to himself," he said finally, looking from Kaden to Triste, "it would have been a sign."

"A sign of what?" Kaden asked.

"Of the way forward. I opened my heart to Ananshael, showed the god my intention to offer you into his hands. If he didn't want my offering"—he jerked a thumb over his shoulder—"all he needed to do was drop me off the cliff." The priest glanced around himself, raised his brows as though just now noticing he was still alive. "This, he has not done."

Kaden's gut tightened.

"That's insane," Triste hissed. "You would be *dead*."

Gerra shrugged. "Sometimes it falls to others to interpret signs."

"And now?" Kaden asked carefully, studying the man's face.

Gerra stood, bent at the waist, exhaled his slow satisfaction as he stretched his back and legs, then straightened once more.

"The god has spoken in a way I did not expect." He waved the prisoners forward, waiting until Kaden and Triste stood at the verge of the cliff, then pointed to the barrel on the far platform. It was leaking, Kaden realized, the wood beneath the plug soaked with water. He glanced up at the crosspiece of the scale, which tilted slightly toward the priest. Soon, maybe in moments, the plug of rock salt would dissolve, the water would drain from the barrel, and the platform on which the priest stood would plummet to the canyon floor. Gerra seemed utterly unconcerned. "The week is done, and the god did not claim me, but this"—he gestured toward the leaking water—"it makes me think. I will not give you to the god myself. Instead, you will weight the scale, both of you, from the sun's rising until it sets—ample time, I should think, for Ananshael to do whatever it is he wants to do with you."

The first hour was the hardest. It was one thing to live beneath the vague threat of Skullsworn violence, another to sit on creaking boards hundreds of feet above the canyon floor, to wait while the wind tangled in the fraying ropes, water dripped from the barrel opposite, and slowly, horribly, by interminable degrees, the whole scale tipped toward the abyss. Kaden's body screamed at him to flee, but there was nowhere to go. Gerra and Pyrre sat a few dozen paces away, on the solid ground of the mesa. Neither had so much as drawn a knife, but Gerra had been clear: if either Kaden or Triste tried to escape the scale before sunset, it would mean death for both.

And so they sat, waited, watching the water draining slowly away.

It seemed important, at first, to remain at the platform's very center, to stay perfectly still, and for a long time they remained like that, like statuary, not speaking, barely daring to breathe. It wasn't until noon that Triste finally shook her head.

"To 'Shael with this," she said. Her voice was dry, dusty, angry.

Kaden raised his brow.

"We can't leave," he murmured. "We can't fight them."

"I know that. It doesn't mean we need to wait like terrified sheep."

"Is there another way to wait?"

"I don't *know*," she said, twisting away, "but if these are going to be our last moments, I'd like to live them."

To his surprise, Kaden found himself nodding.

"Look," Triste said, shifting her weight until she sat at the very edge of the wooden planks, legs dangling out over the void. "There are worse places to die."

Kaden joined her at the edge. It felt like sitting atop the Talon as the wind tugged at his robe, threatening to dash him from his perch. He'd spent so many days on cliffsides and the tops of spires. At the monastery, however, he had always been alone, sitting or laboring in solitude. He couldn't say why having a body beside him mattered so much. According to everything the Shin had told him, it shouldn't have. It shouldn't have, but it did. He wrapped an arm around Triste's waist, then glanced back over his shoulder.

"Can we have some rocks?"

Pyrre blinked. "Rocks? You are suddenly so eager to meet the god?"

"Not big rocks," Kaden said, gesturing to the gravel at the mesa's edge. "Just some of that."

When the assassin had deposited a large pile at the edge of the scale, Kaden turned back to Triste. "I used to do this as a novice," he said, hefting one of the stones in his hand, testing the weight. "We were supposed to be meditating, but I got bored of that. Throwing stones helped pass the time."

The platform lurched as he launched the stone out into space. He ignored the motion, watching the rock trace its slow arc down through the warm, empty air of the canyon. Triste stared at it, then pulled herself free of his embrace. "You think you can throw?" she asked, turning to take up a stone of her own. "Watch this."

All afternoon they hurled stones, traded taunts and jokes. All afternoon the barrel's water drained silently away. When the sun dropped behind the mountains to the west, when he stepped from the swaying scale to solid ground, Kaden almost felt regret.

Triste was right, it would have been a good place to die, better than whatever faced them.

Just as she joined him, stepping from the platform onto the rocky rim, a wooden *thwock* snapped the evening stillness, followed heartbeats later by a great shuddering. Kaden turned to find the barrel's plug gone, dissolved finally, the water, which had drained so slowly, gushing from the spout, the whole of Ananshael's Scale suddenly lurching out of balance. Then it collapsed. Triste wrapped an arm around his waist as the structure fell away, tumbling over and over, falling silently into the void. The crash, when it finally came, was so quiet it might have been nothing but the wind.

Triste laughed, a light, bright sound, and moments later Kaden found himself joining her.

When they turned, Gerra was studying them with open interest. "The ways of the god can be strange, hard to understand," he said. "Today is not one of those days. Clearly, Ananshael wants the names of these Csestriim. You will give them to me. What will we give you in return?"

The weight of what had to happen settled on Kaden like a stone, crushing the laughter.

"You will give us a path," he said finally, "a clear path, all the way from here, through il Tornja's gathering army, to the *kenta*."

Pyrre smiled, patted the knives at her belt. "Clearer of Paths. It sounds so much better than Assassin."

Skullsworn, Assassins, or Clearers of Paths, the priests of Ananshael tore into their vicious work with a strange, almost joyful veneration. Three dozen of Pyrre's brothers and sisters crossed the bridge first, drawing the Annurian soldiers from their hiding places between the stones. It seemed, at first, that the battle would be over before it truly began, but il Tornja had fortified his position. Instead of two dozen legionaries—the force that had first confronted Kaden in the canyons—there were hundreds, rank upon rank upon rank, so many that the dry dirt was slippery with their blood by the time Pyrre and Gerra herded Kaden and Triste through the swirling, screaming madness of the fight.

The two Skullsworn flanked them, Gerra's short, quick stride somehow matching Pyrre's lope. The man fought with a long spear, nicking throats and taking eyes as delicately as a gardener pruning back spring's most eager shoots. Pyrre wielded her customary knives, throwing them sometimes, sometimes lashing out to cut those who came too close. It seemed like she should run out—one woman could only carry so much steel—but she plucked the weapons from the falling bodies of the dead and when those flashed from her fingers, she dipped into her flowing robes for another blade, and another, and another.

It took them only moments to cross the narrow open ledge. Half a dozen Annurians, a rear guard of sorts, blocked the trail where it dropped out of sunlight into the maze of canyons beyond. They hefted their weapons. Their commander managed half of a bellowed exhortation, and then Pyrre and Gerra were on them, among them, moving delicately as dancers through the thicket of sword and spear, leaving only corpses in their wake.

Pyrre slipped behind the last of the living, caught him around the chest with one hand, slit his throat with the other. The soldier sagged against her as though suddenly weary, and she lowered his weight to the thirsty stone, gentle as any lover, brushed his forehead with a kiss, then straightened up.

"Did someone say to stop running?" she asked, cocking an eyebrow at Kaden. "Gerra and I are making this look easy, but I'm sure you noticed that there is still a small, angry army behind us, and just because we cleared a path through them doesn't mean they can't chase us."

Kaden glanced over his shoulder. The ledge was awash in blood and struggling bodies. Blinding sunlight shattered off steel. All human language was lost in a discordant chorus of screams.

Pyrre tapped the flat of her bloody knife against her thigh. "I understand. It's a gorgeous day to give men to the god, and a shame to be leaving. Still, I promised to take you to your secret gate. . . ."

Triste lurched into a run before the assassin could finish, and a moment later, Kaden followed, hurling himself from the sun's bronze hammer into the cool shadows of the canyon. For a long time, the four of them raced the rocky path in silence, scrambling over boulders, splashing through the gurgling streams, slipping down the more treacherous ledges, falling, gashing their knees and palms, getting up, fleeing again.

"Il Tornja," Kaden said, the first time they paused.

"He is one of those you named Csestriim," Gerra said. The Skullsworn priest was doubled over panting, hands on his knees, but his green eyes were bright, focused.

"He is," Kaden replied, "and he wasn't back there. Neither was his leach."

Gerra frowned. Pyrre just laughed.

"If it were easy to give these undying to the god," she said, "we would have given them long ago."

"At the *kenta*," Triste managed. She had dropped to her knees, was scooping water from a small pool between the rocks, dribbling it down her chin in her haste. "He'll be waiting at the *kenta*," she gasped, "like last time."

Kaden nodded. "That's what I'm afraid of."

Behind them, farther up the canyon, boots clattered over stone. Soldiers called out to one another, fierce, urgent shouts.

"Afraid?" Pyrre asked. "I put on my boots this morning just so I'd have the *chance* to face this undying general of yours. If he's not waiting somewhere between here and the hidden gate, I will be very, very put out."

"I am put out," Pyrre said, shaking her head as she eyed the pile of hastily thrown-up rubble.

Of il Tornja, there was still no sign. They had reached the ancient village—guided by Kaden's memory of the route—without encountering a single soldier. The flight had seemed easy, far too easy, and now he could see why.

"They blocked the gate," Triste said, staring at the huge stones where the *kenta* had been, some of which were almost as large as she was.

"A lot of work," Gerra observed. "Why didn't they just tear it down?"

"I don't think they *can* be torn down," Kaden said. "Not by any normal means, at least."

Pyrre ducked into one of the crumbling buildings, emerged a moment later shaking her head. "No leach. No invincible Csestriim warrior. Quite a disappointment."

Triste was turning in slow circles, as though trying to watch the whole town at the same time. "Where is he?" she whispered. "What's he doing?"

Kaden frowned. "I have no idea. I've never really known."

"Well," Gerra said, "it'd take the four of us all day to excavate your gate." He cupped a hand behind his ear, turned back toward the canyon from which they'd just emerged, "And I don't think we have all day."

Kaden could hear it, too, the racket of their pursuit. The way the sound echoed off the canyon walls, it was impossible to know how close the soldiers were. Maybe half a mile, maybe less. He turned back to study the heap of stone. It was almost twice as high as he was, thousands of pounds of rock, but haphazardly constructed. Clearly, the soldiers had dragged it together in a rush. Not that that mattered. Gerra was right; moving the whole thing, moving enough of it, even, for them to slip through the top of the *kenta,* would take the better part of the day. Maybe, though . . .

He stared at the pile a moment longer, then closed his eyes.

The stones were there, all of them, some the size of a man's chest, others not much larger than his head, some balanced on a single corner, others bedded so deeply a team of oxen would have struggled to pull them free. Still, there were gaps in the pile, some almost wide enough that Triste might fit inside. And suddenly, Rampuri Tan's words tolled in his mind, so strong it almost seemed the monk was still alive, standing just behind him, shaking his head: *You need to see what is* not *there.*

All at once, Kaden was back at Ashk'lan, a novice whose bowl had been replaced by a block of rock, licking soup off the unforgiving stone, listening to the laughter of Huy Heng, his first *umial,* as he learned the value of emptiness.

It's not the stones that matter, Kaden thought, staring at his private vision of that massive pile. *It's the space between them.*

And slowly, carefully, tracing the invisible lines of force and support, he shifted a single block, filling one empty hole, but leaving another in its place. The work was purely mental. He hadn't moved, hadn't even opened his eyes, but he found himself sweating with the effort, trying to hold that whole structure in his head, to see the entire thing at once, to find those hidden places that had been spared the weight, to parse the layers of emptiness, to find a way to move the stones that could be moved without disturbing the looming mass.

"Kaden?" Triste asked, her voice wary.

He shook his head, worked faster, shifting the rocks inside his mind, moving them back, stacking them, sliding them, searching for a way past, a way through, searching for the emptiness buried in all that unfathomable weight.

"There," he said finally, exhaling as he opened his eyes. He pointed. "We need to start with that block. Then move that . . ."

"Fascinated as I am by the mechanics of stonemasonry," Pyrre said, "I'm not sure this is the perfect venue."

"We can get through," Kaden said. "I can see it."

The assassin raised her brows, then gestured back up the canyon with her knife. The clatter of boots over stone was closer now, closing, undeniable.

"You're just in time to explain it to our friends."

"I just need time. Maybe a thousand heartbeats."

"We don't *have* time," Triste exploded, hauling him by the arm. "We need to get out of here, *now*."

Pyrre, however, was looking at Gerra, her eyes raised in a silent question. The priest ran a thumb along the point of his spear, as though testing the edge, then nodded.

"We'll give you your heartbeats," Pyrre said, turning away. "There is a place just around the bend, a narrowing of the canyon where the water drops off a small shelf. It is a good place."

Triste stared at her. "They'll kill you."

Pyrre smiled. "Why do you think we came?"

"No," Triste said, shaking her head. "No. There's another way. Around them or past them. A better way."

Pyrre's grin just widened. "Perhaps you are confusing us with another order of priests. I'm sure you would have preferred to go somewhere else, but you came to Rassambur, and this, you sweet, blood-shy children, the fighting and the dying—it *is* our way."

56

"We could kill him," Adare said quietly.

Kegellen took a long sip of wine, set the goblet on the table before her, leaned back in her chair, and pursed her lips. "I assume," she said finally, "that when you say *we,* you are not, in fact, imagining the three of us taking turns plunging knives into the poor man's heart."

"The *poor man*?" Adare demanded. "The son of a bitch has as good as seized the city. He's got men on the wall, men in the Dawn Palace, men in the Spear itself, and that's not all—there are patrols on all the major streets, barricades and checkpoints between neighborhoods. . . ."

Kegellen waved the objection away. "I am aware, of course, of General Van's . . . zeal when it comes to the defense of our city."

"He's so fucking zealous that I'm afraid to hold this meeting in my own 'Kent-kissing palace," Adare said. "It is because of his zeal that we are *here.*"

They were back in Kegellen's wine cellar. The same priceless, dusty bottles lay silently in their racks. The same marble gods fixed them with empty eyes. It wasn't lost upon Adare that the last time she'd been in the room had been with Triste, just before the leach escaped. It hardly seemed like an auspicious meeting place, but then, all the auspices had been pretty 'Kent-kissing bleak of late. At least Kegellen's manse wasn't overrun with the general's soldiers. At least inside the wine cellar the only person spying on them would be the Queen of the Streets herself, not that she had any need to spy, sitting as she was half a pace away, blandly sipping her wine.

Unlike Kegellen, Nira hadn't stopped moving since they closed the heavy wooden door. The narrow cellar didn't offer much room to prowl, but the old woman did her best, cane tapping against the stone floor as she stalked back and forth, muttering sometimes—mostly curses against il Tornja— sometimes silent. At first, Adare thought the constant motion might drive her insane, but she'd quickly come to find in it a strange sort of relief. At least one of the people in the room was as furious as she felt.

"I'm surprised that you're not angrier," Adare said, turning back to Kegellen, trying a different tack. "The soldiers are even more a threat to your power here than they are to mine."

"Anger," Kegellen said, closing her eyes, tipping her head back until it rested against the back of her chair. "It's so exhausting. Who has the energy for it?"

"Spare me the act," Adare spat. "I know your history. You've got more blood on your hands than I do. How many people did you kill to end up where you are? A hundred? More?"

"You can kill a man without being angry," Kegellen replied mildly. "You can kill a great many men without being angry." She took another sip of her wine, held it in her mouth a moment, swallowed, smiled. "I find it's better that way. Easier on the heart."

"Then kill Van. I don't give a pickled shit if you're angry when you do it, just make him *dead*."

"The one-footed general," Nira snapped, turning from the ranks of bottles, "is not the problem."

Adare raised her brows. "He's commanding the soldiers occupying the palace."

Nira snorted. "He's il Tornja's dog. You could kill the son of a bitch, and another son of a bitch would just take his place. That's the way an army works—chain a' command, and all."

"So we kill the next one," Adare said. "I'm sure Kegellen can manage more than one murder per month."

The Queen of the Streets opened her eyes. A smile tugged at the corner of her mouth. "Now it is just *me* doing this hypothetical killing? What happened to our happy triumvirate of high-minded murderers?"

"What do ya keep between those ears?" Nira demanded, raising her cane as though preparing to rap Adare on the skull. "A pair a' very small, very stupid worms? An army doesn't run outta commanders until ya kill the last man, and I don't think I need ta point out that you might *need* some a' those bastards on your walls when the Urghul arrive."

Adare blew out an angry breath. "They're not *all* part of il Tornja's plan. . . ."

"I wager shit against silver even Wobbly Van himself isn't part of il Tornja's plan. He has orders ta hold the palace, and so he's holdin' it. It's not him you have ta go after."

Kegellen nodded slowly. "Though your councillor and I don't always see eye to eye on matters, in this case, I have to agree." She tapped a finger against her generous chin. "Is there any word from that spirited young woman you sent north with all those birds?"

"Do you think," Adare asked, staring at the other woman, "that if the Kettral had returned, if they had word of il Tornja, that I would have forgotten to mention it?"

Kegellen heaved her shoulders into a shrug. "There is *so* much going on, and I find I grow more forgetful with each passing year."

"Well, I don't. The Kettral are still gone. Il Tornja is still missing. And Horonius Van still has his booted heel on the throat of this fucking city."

"Perhaps," Kegellen suggested, "you should let him leave it there. At least until after this . . . war." She frowned, as though that final word were unpleasant even to pronounce. "He will be weaker then and you might need him a little less."

That, in fact, was exactly what Adare would have preferred to do. Much as she loathed the military takeover of Annur, there was no way around the fact that Van would make a better commander for the coming battle than Adare herself, probably better than Lehav. Certainly, the addition of the Army of the North gave the entire city a fighting chance against the coming horde. The Urghul, however, were not the only foe; not even, if Kaden was to be believed, the greatest foe. Il Tornja's absence from the front was evidence enough that there was another struggle going on, a quiet war invisible to almost everyone, a battle that might decide far more than the fate of a couple of continents. Adare had no idea why il Tornja would want the Dawn Palace or the Spear, but the fact that he wanted them was reason enough to try to deny him those very things. Not that she could tell Kegellen that. Despite their alliance, she didn't trust the woman much more than she would a half-rabid dog.

"It ought to be possible—" Adare began again.

A sharp rap on the door cut her off.

Kegellen frowned. "I try to give the clearest instructions to my staff, and still they will disturb me when I have asked not to be disturbed." She shook her head as she set down her wine, then levered herself up from the chair. "If this is not a pair of naked young men—preferably beautiful but dumb, between the ages of twenty and twenty-five—I will be quite displeased."

Despite the woman's levity, Adare's stomach had knotted up suddenly, viciously at the sound of the knock. It had been a long time since unexpected tidings meant anything but death or disaster. All over again she saw her son's eyes, burning, terrified. She was clutching her wineglass, she realized, clutching it so tightly she was amazed it had not already shattered. Deliberately, she set it down as Kegellen swung open the door.

"What is it, Serise?" the woman asked.

Adare exhaled slowly. No stranger come calling after all. Just one of the household slaves.

"Apologies, my lady," a meek voice from beyond the door replied. "A note. It was delivered with some urgency."

"And did the bearer of this note speak the crucial words?" Kegellen asked.

"No, my lady, but—"

"Then it cannot be so urgent, can it?"

"Pardon, my lady, but the note is not for you."

Adare felt sick all over again.

"Ah," Kegellen said, extending her hand. "How interesting."

By the time the woman had closed the door, crossed the room, and passed the note across the table, Adare found she was trembling. There was no seal on the paper—it was folded over twice and tied with a length of rough twine. Hardly a terrifying epistle, and yet Adare eyed it as though it were a viper, and instead of reaching for the note, she raised her goblet, swirled the liquid around the glass, then drained it.

"And just what kinda lump-brained ritual is this?" Nira demanded finally. "Ya gonna look at the 'Kent-kissing thing or are we all gonna sit here guessin'?"

Adare ignored the woman, took up the paper, opened it. It didn't take long to read the hastily scrawled lines, and only a moment more to understand them. She looked up from the message, relief welling up inside her. There was no word of Sanlitun. It had nothing to do with her son. Which meant she could believe, if only for another day, that he was still alive.

Kegellen cocked her head to the side. "Good news?"

"Good news doesn't come creepin' in like a kicked dog," Nira said, watching Adare warily. "Out with it, woman."

Slowly, Adare dragged her eyes back to the text. Already, the relief was seeping away, replaced by something colder, more dangerous—some feeling balanced on the knife's edge between hope and horror.

"He has returned," she said.

Nira leaned forward, suddenly hungry, predatory. "Il Tornja?"

Adare shook her head. "Kaden. My brother. And he has Triste with him."

57

The Kettral returned to Annur a little after midnight, when the moon's blade had lodged itself in the dark horizon. Gwenna put the birds down in a quiet square just south of the city's northern wall. A couple of empty plinths flanked a fountain at the center of the open space. Someone had already toppled and hauled off whatever statuary had stood atop them, but the fountain still ran, water gushing up from the pipe's mouth, tracing a glittering arc through the night air, then splashing into the open sandstone bowl. The huge birds, free of their soldiers, gathered around the fountain, dipped their beaks into the water over and over. The motion was strange, almost mechanical, but delicate.

"Our staging area," Gwenna said. "Compliments of the Emperor." She gestured to a series of buildings fronting the square. "Barracks. Command. Livery. Infirmary. Supply. Our little slice of the Eyrie right here in Annur."

Valyn studied the silent structures. There were no lamps or candles in the windows. No smoke issued from the chimneys. He closed his eyes, listening for the rustle and murmur of sleeping men and women. Nothing.

"Where are the people?" he asked. "Who lived here?"

Gwenna shook her head. "Fuck if I know. I told your sister I needed a staging area, and she gave us this."

The Flea nodded. "A good spot. Close to the fight. Plenty of room for simultaneous landings."

"There's a bigger square a little to the west," Gwenna replied, "but this one's close to the Emperor's own command post." She pointed north toward a blocky tower rising above the wall a hundred paces away. "Figured it was worth trying to consolidate the command." She glanced over to where two soldiers were carrying Newt toward one of the buildings. "Enough bullshitting about the logistics. Your Wing needs medical care, better care than we could give you in the field."

"See to Newt and Sigrid," the Flea began. "I'm fine. . . ."

"Horseshit," Gwenna snapped. "You're bleeding through your bandages while we stand here."

"I know what this body can take, Gwenna. I've been fighting in it a long time."

"And I need you to *keep* fighting in it. We're not losing the best fucking soldier we've got to a case of his own stubbornness. You are going to the infirmary if I have to tie you up and kick you all the way there."

The Kettral close enough to hear the outburst turned, tried to watch the conflict unnoticed as they went about their work. They knew the Flea. Washouts or not, *everyone* knew the Flea, and this was not the way people talked to the Flea. Valyn himself took a step back. After a pause, however, the older man just chuckled.

"I won't say no to a bed and a few hours' rest. Just make sure you don't let me sleep through the war."

Gwenna grunted. "Don't you worry about that. When the war gets here, I'm planning to hide behind you the entire time." She turned to glare at Valyn. "You, *too*. The fuck's wrong with you people? *Get to the infirmary and put your heads on the 'Kent-kissing pillows.*"

Only when Valyn and the Flea had almost reached the building did Gwenna finally turn, barking orders at the Kettral who still remained in the square.

"Never should have put her in charge of Andt-Kyl," the Flea murmured, shaking his head with mock regret. "Now, anytime there's a city to defend, she acts like she runs the place."

Valyn just nodded.

Gwenna was a different woman from the headstrong cadet he remembered; there was no doubt about that. The old fire was still there, hot as ever, but she'd found a way to harness it. Back on the Islands she'd been almost out of control half the time, a danger to herself and everyone around her. Not anymore. She was still dangerous, *more* dangerous—that much was obvious just from the way she held herself, from the steel in her voice—but she'd found a way to hammer her anger into a blade, one that she could hold, wield, master.

It's what was supposed to happen to all of us, he realized.

When they fled the Islands, every member of his Wing had been raw, green, and unready. Battle and blood had changed them, changed Valyn himself most of all, but where Gwenna and Talal and Annick had grown into proper Kettral, disciplined, driven, allied in their shared mission, and bound, too, by a deeper, human bond, Valyn had become a solitary creature, a thing of the shadows, hungry for blood, violence, annihilation.

He glanced over his shoulder to where Gwenna was helping tend to the birds. She was arguing with Annick about something while the two of them rolled a huge barrel of feed away from the wall, then started prying off the top. The other Kettral had gathered around, trading barbs as they worked. Valyn hesitated, waited for the Flea to enter the infirmary before turning to stare at the scene. For a long time, he stood alone in the shadows, just watching, listening. It was nothing special, just a bunch of weary soldiers going about their work, but he felt, standing there in the starlight, as though he were gazing across an unbridgeable gulf into a different life, one he should have lived, *could* have lived, if only he had not made so many mistakes.

For a moment there, he almost stepped back into the square, almost walked back across the open space to join them. There was always work for another pair of hands, always another job to do. He could throw his shoulder behind a barrel or check over a bird's jesses. Learn the names of the new folks. Trade stories of the past year with Talal . . .

He shook his head. His own stories were all darkness and death. Now that he could see again, he saw the way people looked at him: warily, one hand always on a weapon when he came near. The Kettral were just a few dozen paces away. All that separated him from them were wide-open flagstones, empty air. Men and women had walked across that square every day for decades, centuries, going about the bright, boring business of their lives—buying bread, running errands, hauling water—things a child could do. For Valyn, though, there was no way across.

Talal glanced up, found him watching, but Valyn looked away, shifting his eyes from the square to the tower looming above. The Emperor's command post. Where Adare came every day to oversee her city's preparations. He'd said he would wait until the war was over, but then, he'd said a lot of things.

The Emperor's guard was heavier than Valyn had expected. They were in Annur, after all, in her own city, safe behind the walls, the Urghul still at least a day away. He'd expected a couple pairs of Aedolians, maybe six men total. Instead, a dozen soldiers armored in the steel and bronze of the Sons of Flame flanked her as she made her way down the street, riding, as Gwenna said she did each day, from the Dawn Palace to her tower on the wall.

Kill them, whispered a voice inside his head.

He could do it—twelve men, taken by surprise, their only training whatever drills their priestly commanders had cobbled together over the years—he could take them apart one limb at a time, leave the bodies scattered across the road. He started to lift an ax from his belt, then shook his head, settling it back in place. Though a part of him hungered to wade into the block of guardsmen, there was a chance Adare might escape in the chaos. Or worse, that she might die. Valyn had every intention of killing her, of course, but he needed to talk to her first, to learn what she'd done with Kaden, whether his brother was still alive, rotting in a cell somewhere, or already dead. Besides, now that he was back with the Kettral, there was another way, a more elegant way. He shifted his hand from the ax to the munitions he'd lifted from Gwenna's stores: one smoker, one flash bang— more than enough to kindle the necessary madness.

The whole thing took less than twenty heartbeats. He lit both charges at the same time, tossed them into the midst of the horses, waited a moment for the choking clouds of smoke to fill the narrow street, took a deep breath of clean air, then stepped into the swirling haze. All over again, he was blind. Even his preternatural sight was no good in the smoke, but that didn't matter. He'd learned, in his long year of darkness, to listen, to frame the world around him from the sounds it made. There, to his left, a pawing horse. To his right, the scrape of steel against leather. He ducked under one man's blind, stumbling attack, stepped past a panicking horse, and then he was there at the heart of the entourage. He could smell his sister, her soap and her choked-back fear. He could hear her lean heart pounding.

He gained the saddle with a single leap, landed behind her, yanked the black bag down over her head, then kneed the horse forward, out of the blind melee. Adare twisted, tried to scream, tried to slide a hand up beneath the bag, to pull it off. It snagged on her crossed hairpins, however, and a moment later he clamped a hand down over the fabric and her mouth beneath, slid a knife from his belt and held it against her side, at just the spot between the ribs where she'd stabbed him so many months earlier.

"Your choice," he whispered, leaning forward until his mouth was just beside her ear. "Silence, or death."

*

"Where is Kaden?"

Adare's only response was to twist awkwardly, tossing her head from side to side in a pointless effort to throw off the hood.

"Don't bother," Valyn said. "It won't come off. And don't bother screaming—we're in the storm drain two dozen paces below the streets."

That had been the trickiest part of the whole grab. The munitions were ready to hand, and the hood, but it had taken Valyn the better part of the preceding night to find a quick route from the street where he'd kidnapped his sister to someplace he could safely interrogate her. The narrow tunnel into which he'd brought her was barely high enough to stand up straight. A few inches of filthy water trickled over his boots, draining away toward one of the canals. Dark stains, the high-water marks of earlier storms, ran along the walls. It wasn't the perfect place—there was always the chance they'd stumble across a handful of vagrants, men and women desperate enough to make a home out of the drain during the dry season—but then, nothing was perfect. Most people he could frighten off, and anyone he couldn't frighten, he could kill. Besides, he didn't expect to need a lot of time.

"Who are you?" Adare demanded, her voice high, strident. "What do you want?"

"I want to know where Kaden is," he said again. "Did you kill him?"

Adare turned her head back and forth, more slowly this time, as though she could see anything in the darkness. The rank red scent of thorny panic poured off her, along with a confusion that reeked of rancid oil, both smells so thick it was a wonder she hadn't cracked already.

If only you'd been weak, he thought grimly.

"They'll be searching for me," she said. "People will be looking. . . ."

"They'll be following your horse. Which is at least a mile off by now."

"They'll double back. . . ."

He nodded. "In time to find you dead."

Adare went perfectly still, as though she were only now understanding the situation. Standing there in the murky water, bag over her head, wrists tied behind her back, she didn't look like an emperor. She looked like a frightened woman torn from her home, ripped out of the fabric of everything she found familiar.

"Who are you?" she whispered.

A part of him was tempted to draw it out, to make her guess, to breathe in her terror when she finally started to shake.

"I'm your brother," he said instead. "The one you tried to kill."

The running water carved a wet course through the silence. Adare's shallow, rapid breathing scratched against the close stone walls.

"Valyn," she whispered finally.

His name sounded like a curse.

"Hello, sister."

"How did you . . ."

"Live?"

"I stood at the end of the dock," she said, the words low, as though she were talking only to herself, as though he weren't there at all. "For half the day I watched them drag the lake. Every body they pulled free, I started shaking, thinking it might be yours."

"That's strange, considering you're the person who put that knife between my ribs in the first place."

She took a sharp breath, as though planning to object, then shook her head. Her fear, so sharp at first, had mostly faded, weariness washing in to replace the sick reek of terror.

"So you're here for your revenge."

"Among other things. First, I want to know what you did with Kaden."

Adare shook her head again. "I didn't do anything with him."

Valyn gritted his teeth. "I don't believe you. He was here, in Annur. Gwenna met with him. Then, when she came back, he had vanished, and no one seems to know where."

"He has come and gone more than once now," Adare said, anger's heat creeping back into her voice. "He uses those 'Kent-kissing gates—that's why no one sees him."

"How convenient," Valyn said.

"Not for me, it's not. I'm trying to hold this fucking city together, to get ready for the Urghul, to keep Annur from tearing itself to pieces, and meanwhile the First Speaker of the council has been coming and going according to his own whims, chasing his own monsters, showing up for a few hours, then haring off after that miserable bitch from the prison. . . ."

She trailed off, as though worried she had said too much. Valyn closed his eyes, breathed in her tangled scent: anger, blue-gray grief, confusion, and a deep, thick musk of sickening regret. But no deceit, not that he could smell. Gritting his teeth, he reached out, lifted the hood from her head. Most of her black hair remained pinned behind her head, but a few strands hung in her face. She tried to shake them away, then gave up, glaring at him through the mess of sweaty tangles. Her eyes burned more brightly than he'd remembered, so bright in the blackness of the storm drain it seemed her whole face might catch fire. When she opened her mouth, Valyn expected a blaze of defiance. Instead, her voice was quiet, even to his ears.

"I'm sorry."

He took a step back, as though the words themselves could burn.

"A little late to start begging. . . ."

"I'm not begging. From the moment I stabbed you I wanted to take it back." She shook her head, looking past him into the prison of her memory. "It all happened so fast. Fulton dead, and you going after il Tornja, even while the battle was still playing out. I had the knife in my hand, and I thought you were going to ruin it all, that you were going to destroy Annur, and I just . . . broke."

Valyn stared. Somewhere inside his chest his heart ground out its savage rhythm over and over, refusing to give up.

"Every day I wake up in the morning," Adare went on after a pause, "knowing I killed you. What's crazy is that most of the time I think that I was *right*. You'd gone utterly insane—you really *were* about to kill the only person who could hold the Urghul back." She shook her head. "Somehow, in the end, being right didn't matter."

Valyn dragged the next words up like shattered glass through his throat. "And you think I'll spare you for this belated sorrow?"

"I don't *care* if you spare me," she exploded. "I don't care what you think at all. You're even more insane now than you were then—that's obvious just from looking at you. I'm not saying this for *you*. I'm saying it because for all these months I couldn't say it, not to you, and now I can." She raised her chin, exposing her throat. "Go ahead. Kill me. Have your revenge. Then you figure out how to save this city, this whole fucking land that used to be an empire and now is something else . . . something different. You find a way to fix it, to put it right, to rescue all the millions of people about to be slaughtered on Meshkent's bloody altars, because I have no idea."

Tears were pouring down her face, glazing her cheeks, slick as molten glass with the light of her eyes. She shook her head wearily, angrily.

"Kaden is at Kegellen's manse. Go find him after you murder me, if you really give a shit. He needs you."

"Needs me for what?" Valyn asked. He was shaking, he realized. His hand ached. He looked down to find the bare knife in his hand, already drawn. He didn't remember pulling it from the sheath.

Finish it, the beast's voice hissed. *You've talked too long already.*

He stepped forward, put the knife against her neck.

She winced, but kept her eyes fixed on his.

"Go ahead."

Finish it.

All over again he could taste the bile of the night-black slarn egg pouring down his throat. He could feel Ha Lin limp in his arms, her heart still, her hair smelling of the sea. He could hear the hacking sounds of the legionary messenger he'd killed, feel the man's throat give as he ripped the knife through trachea and tendon. He could smell the smoke of the burning bodies of Andt-Kyl, taste his own blood hot in his mouth, and Huut-suu's as she screamed her awful pleasure. He could hear all over again the horror tattooed in the heartbeats of the men he'd killed atop Mierten's crumbling wall. He could feel the rotten softness of his axes sinking into human flesh, could taste his own eagerness as he pulled them free. Whatever he could have been, he was a beast, as much a monster as the slarn prowling the gullet of Hull's Hole, a creature of blood and darkness and death.

Finish it.

He could feel his sister shuddering beneath the blade, could taste her copper terror. It wasn't even about justice anymore, or revenge, or any other thing to which a man could put a word. There was only the urge in the blood, the need, that vicious, undeniable imperative.

FINISH IT.

It wasn't mercy that stopped his hand. His mercy was gone—chipped away, burned out, carved to the quick—along with whatever else had once made him a man. It wasn't justice. It wasn't love or even fellow human feeling. All that was gone. All that was left to balance the fury was a sort of dumb stubbornness, an animal unwillingness to simply submit, the same stubbornness that had kept him alive the whole northern winter, that made him check the traps and stuff raw meat into his mouth, the same stubbornness that kept his heart hammering stupidly away.

CUT OUT HER HEART.

Slowly, shaking, careful not to nick the skin, Valyn lowered the knife.

"No."

58

For a long time, Kaden just watched his brother, trying to decide if Valyn believed this story of gods and goddesses trapped in human flesh, of a Csestriim genius whose whole horrible purpose was to find those gods, to flush them out and hunt them down, to destroy them, of how close il Tornja had already come, of how little time remained.

Studying Valyn's face, it was hard to say. Those ruined eyes betrayed nothing. Kaden tried to find the brother he had known in the figure that stood before him now, prowling back and forth along the wall of Kegellen's wine cellar like some caged animal. The boy was gone, carved away by the long years of training and privation, and even the man Kaden remembered from their brief time together in the Bone Mountains, the Kettral Wing leader, seemed to have vanished. Kaden struggled to put a name to this lean, scarred, hungry creature that stood before him now.

Valyn had arrived barely an hour earlier, appearing with Adare just after the noon gong, escorted by Kegellen herself into the mansion's labyrinthine depths, where Kaden and Triste had been trying to figure a way around il Tornja's soldiers and into Intarra's Spear.

"How heartwarming," the Queen of the Streets had said as she threw open the door, then clasped her broad hands in front of her chest. "A reunion of siblings. Is there any love like the love of a brother or sister?"

Love was not the word Kaden would have used.

The tension in Valyn's shoulders and neck, the way his hands kept drifting to those vicious axes at his belt, the way he kept his broad back always to the wall as Kaden talked—it all spoke of loathing, wariness, distrust. Anything but love.

"And you have this god inside you now?" Valyn asked finally, his voice like rusted steel.

Kaden nodded. He could feel Meshkent pressing, testing against the boundaries of his prison.

"Why do you need to get into the Spear?" Valyn asked. "Why can't you perform this ceremony here?"

"That's not how it works," Kaden replied. "The Spear is some sort of . . . sacred place. A conduit between our world and the gods'. An altar."

Valyn grunted. "People die on altars."

"It's a risk," Kaden said quietly, leaving out the rest: *Death is necessary. Death is the* goal.

The trouble was, Kaden had no idea how that death was supposed to be accomplished. Meshkent had moved from fury to silence and back again a hundred times since Kaden had penned him inside his mind. The god had cursed, bellowed, cajoled, but refused to reveal the least detail of the *obviate*. According to Kiel, the Csestriim had found the human vessels of the gods dead at the tower's top all those thousands of years earlier, but *how* they had died, the historian had no idea. Was it enough simply to *go* to the tower's top, to stand there, to wait for the divine to unchain itself, for the human flesh to fail? Or were there words to speak, genuflections to make, paces of some arcane path to tread? Kaden had no idea.

In other circumstances, it might have made sense to wait, to try to pry the details of the ritual from the god's mind, but there was no more time for waiting. Il Tornja was too close, and his trap was drawing tight.

Triste shifted at Kaden's side, moving closer to him. She'd barely spoken a word since Valyn and Adare arrived, watching them warily, her shoulders tense, as though she were getting ready to fight or to flee.

"You can't get into the Spear," Adare said. "Il Tornja's men have it locked down."

Kaden shook his head. "We have to. There is no other way."

"I'll tell you another way," Valyn said grimly. "We find il Tornja and put an ax between his eyes. How's that?"

"Inadequate," Kaden replied. "Even if you manage to kill il Tornja, the gods are still trapped inside us. I'm battling Meshkent all the time, even when I sleep. I'm fighting against him now, fighting to keep control."

Adare studied his eyes, as though she could see the god behind his irises somehow. "Why not let him out? If he's really a god, he can save himself, right?"

"You don't understand," Kaden replied quietly. "This is the Lord of Pain I carry inside myself. He came here, to this world, to spread an empire of misery over the earth, to set up altars in every field and forest, to soak the earth with blood and make the air shake with screams. If I free him, if I give him this flesh, he will succeed or be destroyed. We can't allow either to happen. The fact that we are fighting against il Tornja does not make an ally of Meshkent. There is only one way to walk this path, and that is the *obviate*."

He realized, as he fell silent, that Valyn had stopped moving. He stood perfectly, preternaturally still at the far end of the narrow room, scarred eyes fixed on Kaden.

"Are you tempted?" he asked quietly.

Kaden studied his brother. "Tempted by what?"

"The other paths. The pain or the annihilation."

Triste wound an arm around Kaden's waist. Such a fragile link, binding him to the world.

He nodded in response to Valyn's question, remembering how it felt to stand on the mesa's edge at Rassambur, to feel the knife bite into his skin. "I was tempted once. Not anymore."

"Why not?" To his surprise, it wasn't Valyn asking this time, but Adare. Her eyes were flooded with flame, her hands balled into fists at her sides. "Where did you find the faith?"

"Is it faith?" Kaden asked. He searched inside himself, but in the thin ridge between Meshkent's fury and the emptiness of the *vaniate,* he found only memory and anticipation. Hope that with the Kettral's help they might reach the Spear's summit mingled with despair at the thought that il Tornja's soldiers might be already there. Joy at the fierce strength in Triste's touch, and sorrow at what had to happen next. In all of it, there was nothing he could identify as faith. "I don't think that's the word."

"His blades," Adare said quietly, angrily.

Kaden shook his head, confused.

"That's what he called us," she went on. "Our father. In his last letter. He said we were his last blades." She bared her teeth, as though the memory caused her physical pain. "It's a good thing, in a way, that he died before he realized just how broken we are."

To Kaden's surprise, Valyn laughed. It was an ugly, busted sound, but there was, Kaden realized, a rough sort of hope woven through it. Adare rounded on him.

"Annur's about to be destroyed. Kaden and Triste might kill themselves. Everything we *are* is hanging in the balance, and you're laughing?"

Valyn ignored her rage. "It's just funny, that word: *broken.* A better man than I'll ever be told me something recently: *Sometimes you need to break a thing to find out what's inside.*"

Kaden stared at his brother.

"And just what the fuck," Adare asked quietly, "do you think is inside us?"

"I have no idea," Valyn replied, "but I'll tell you this: whatever it is, it doesn't quit. It might be ugly, backstabbing, stubborn, but no one—not the Kettral or the Skullsworn, the Csestriim or the slarn or whole armies of Urghul—has been able to kill it yet."

Adare's mouth had just quirked into a ragged smile when the

door to the wine cellar slammed open. Kegellen stood in the doorway. Valyn's axes were out of his belt before Kaden could blink. He crossed the floor in two strides, to lay a sharp edge against the woman's neck. The Queen of the Streets' broad chest was heaving, but her eyes were hard.

"Don't waste your steel on me, soldier," she said.

"What's going on?" Adare demanded.

"The Army of the North is here."

"They've been here for days," Adare replied.

"I'm not talking about the city," Kegellen said. "They are here in this house. Now. And they are coming for you."

59

The basement of Kegellen's manse wasn't so much a basement as a labyrinth of intersecting corridors, stairwells, and storage chambers, stretching out beneath the streets above like the roots of some vast, ancient tree. Clearly, the walled estate visible from the street was only the barest fraction of a much larger, subterranean compound: part fortress, part storehouse, part hidden passage for all manner of illicit goods. Valyn caught glimpses, as the Queen of the Streets hustled them through the maze, of rooms piled high with unlabeled crates, bolts of cloth, huge clay amphorae standing patiently as soldiers in the gloom. Steel gates blocked the largest of the intersections, each one thick as a castle portcullis and guarded by a handful of men. Kegellen's toughs were an ugly lot—long on scars and short on teeth—but they seemed to know how to handle their steel, and they leapt into motion—uncoiling chains, hauling at the bars—the moment the huge woman swept into view.

"How did they know?" Triste asked, after yet another gate had clanged shut behind them. "How did the army know we were here?"

"I don't know," Kegellen replied tersely. Wrapped in a dress of exquisite red silk, her fingers flashing with rings, the flesh of her neck wobbling as she moved, the woman didn't look like a soldier. She would have been as out of place on the Islands as some doe-eyed priestess of Eira, and yet there was something about her voice, about the way she carried herself, something about her conviction and determination as she guided them through the narrow passages, that reminded Valyn of his Kettral trainers. She was dangerous, this one, despite all appearances. The only question was, dangerous to *whom*?

"You could have been followed," Kegellen continued.

Valyn shook his head curtly. "We weren't."

"Then you could have been spotted when you arrived. Even the back entrance is watched, although I'll admit I didn't realize the army had taken an interest in my humble home."

Adare glanced back the way they had come, as though she expected to find soldiers racing down the corridor after them. "Our faces were hidden," she said. "Both of them."

Kegellen shrugged and kept moving. "It matters less *how* they knew than what they will do next."

Valyn took a deep breath, sifting the scents of moldy stone and fine perfume, confusion and fear. He could smell the urgency on Kegellen, the bright tang of her haste, but there seemed to be no deceit. If she was lying, she knew how to hide it even from his senses, and besides, if the woman's goal was to hand them over to the Army of the North, she could have done so without warning them, without the whole charade of escaping through the corridors.

"Il Tornja," Kaden said. "He's here. This is his work."

Valyn turned to stare at his brother. The others were obviously frightened by the mention of the *kenarang,* but it seemed like a long time since he himself had felt frightened. Instead, he felt . . . eager. If Kaden was right, if Ran il Tornja was in the city somehow, it meant another chance, a final opportunity to put right what had gone wrong on that tower in Andt-Kyl all those months ago.

"That's impossible," Adare objected. "You said il Tornja was in the Ancaz . . . what? A week ago? A little more? Unless he used the—"

Kaden shook his head, cutting her off. "He didn't. The *kenta* are too risky for him. He can't bring his soldiers through the gates, which means he would have to travel alone, and it's too easy for the Ishien to guard the island hubs. Too easy for them to set an ambush."

"I thought the Ishien were dead," Adare protested. "That he killed them."

"Not all of them. It only takes one man with a flatbow to guard the whole island."

Kegellen reeked of curiosity, but she kept quiet, letting them talk as she swept along ahead.

"The leach," Triste suggested. "Maybe the leach helped him get back."

Valyn frowned, considering the map inside his mind. "No one saw him during the days you were at Rassambur."

Kaden shook his head. "It's possible he left for Annur the moment Pyrre rescued us."

"Why?" Triste demanded. "Why would he do that? How would he know?"

"The same way he's known everything else," Adare said bleakly. "The same way he knew the moment you escaped from the Spear. The same way he knew where to find you." She stared into the darkness as they moved down the corridor, as though waiting for the *kenarang* himself to step from the shadows. "He's been playing this game a long time, and he's better at it than we are."

"He knows where we have to go to perform the *obviate,*" Kaden said. "And he has the *ak'hanath.*"

Adare nodded. "The one thing brings him to Annur, the second to Kegellen's mansion."

As they spoke, Valyn traced the path on his mental map, calculating the various rates of travel. "He's only on foot from the Ancaz to Mo'ir. From there, all the travel is on river, lake, and canal. He can keep moving all day, all night, and the current's in his favor. He could be here by now. Him and the leach and those 'Kent-kissing *ak'hanath.*"

A grim silence settled over them as they walked. Valyn had lost all sense of direction in the twisting corridors, but Kegellen continued to forge ahead, choosing a path at every fork without pausing to think.

"They will have a difficult time following," she pointed out. "My basement is . . . complex, even without the gates and the guards."

"They're not following," Kaden replied. "Not all of them, at least." He pointed up at the vaulted ceiling of the stone corridor. "Most of them will be up there, on the streets, tracking us."

Kegellen raised an eyebrow. "That would be impressive. And inconvenient."

"Where will this let us out?" Adare asked.

"We've been moving east, toward your command center on the wall. The tunnels won't get anywhere close to all the way there, but they'll get us clear of whatever cordon the army set up around my home."

"We need to get to the Spear," Kaden said.

Adare shook her head. "No good. I already told you—it's packed with il Tornja's soldiers. Has been since they showed up in the city days ago."

"Kettral," Valyn said. "We get a bird to fly us to the top."

Kaden nodded. "Good."

"Where are the Kettral?" Kegellen asked.

"In a square just south of the wall," Valyn replied.

"That's unfortunate," the woman said. "You'll need to cover at least two miles in the streets above."

"So we'll cover two miles," Adare said. "We can stay ahead of these bastards for a couple miles."

The words were bold, but Valyn could smell the uncertainty on her.

"No," Kaden said. "The *ak'hanath* are tracking Triste. Maybe Triste and me both. That means that if we split up, Adare will have a chance to get to the Kettral while we're here, in Kegellen's cellar, undercover."

"All right," Adare said slowly. "And when I get the Kettral, what then?"

Valyn tried to figure the timing in his head. Two miles, through crowded streets. Adare was in sturdy boots, but she had nothing like the Kettral or Shin training. The whole thing ought to take about twenty minutes, but Adare was tougher than she seemed. The glare in her burning eyes said she could make the run faster, that she *would* make the run faster. "We count heartbeats," he said. "One thousand heartbeats from when Adare emerges. That's the timing. She gets to Gwenna, gives her our location. When we come out, if everything hasn't gone straight to shit, she should be overhead, ready for the grab."

Adare shook her head. "I thought things already *had* gone to shit. I thought that's why we were fleeing through this tunnel."

"I think you'll look back on this tunnel fondly as soon as you're aboveground," Valyn said.

"You go with her," Kaden said. "She'll need your protection up there."

Valyn shook his head. "Not a chance. Adare is expendable. You're not."

"We *need* her to get to the Kettral," Kaden insisted. "There's nothing you can do if the army catches up with us and we have no bird."

"Of course there is," Valyn replied. "I can kill them."

Gwenna had spent the better part of the morning trying to figure out just what in the fine fuck was going on. The Urghul were encamped beyond the desolation Adare had made of the northern third of Annur, and though they'd arrived only the day before, the horsemen were already busy trying to clear a path through the still-smoldering rubble. Of Balendin himself, there was no sign, which was more than worrisome, but instead of flying patrols north of the wall to scout the enemy position, she and the rest of the Kettral were trying to figure out what had happened to the 'Kent-kissing Emperor.

"Valyn." That was the Flea's assessment. "He has the ability to do it, and the reason."

Certainly, everything Gwenna had heard of the early-morning attack smacked of Kettral work: an ambush at a choke point, smokers and flashbangs, the Emperor gone without any of her guard spotting so much as a single soldier.... And, of course, Valyn himself was gone, missing since the night before. It all added up, except for one obvious question: If Valyn had gone rogue, slipping out of the compound to execute his sister, why wasn't she executed yet? Where was the body?

Gwenna had had all five of her Wings scouring the city near where Adare disappeared, both on foot and in the air. So far they'd found nothing.

No, she reminded herself, staring grimly at the map that she'd unfolded across the table of her command post just inside the courtyard. *Not nothing.* She studied the series of black *ko* stones that she'd been adding to the map all morning. Each one represented a sighting by her people of Annurian soldiers, men under the command of General Van, men who should, given the Urghul threat just north of the wall, have been *on* that fucking wall getting ready to defend the city. The stones showed an obvious cordon, as though the legions, too, were searching for Adare. That search, however, was proceeding more methodically than Gwenna's own, as though Van's soldiers were privy to information that she lacked.

"What are we missing?" she muttered, staring at the map.

The Flea shook his head. Over Gwenna's strong objections, he and Sigrid had both dragged themselves out of the infirmary. The new cloth wrapping the Wing leader's arm was still spotted with blood, but his face didn't look as ashen as it had the night before. The leach, too, looked better than Gwenna would have expected. Once again, her blacks were immaculately clean, her long blond hair perfectly coiffed, as though she'd been at it all morning with a fine Rabin comb.

"You use a kenning for that, don't you?" Gwenna had demanded, squinting at the woman when she first emerged from the infirmary.

"We all have our own personal acts of discipline," the Flea replied quietly.

Gwenna would have been a good deal happier if Sigrid had used her power to find the 'Kent-kissing Emperor instead of fixing her hair, but then, as Talal was always telling her, leaches couldn't do everything. As the sun rose over the towers of the Dawn Palace, climbing past Intarra's Spear itself, reaching its zenith, then dipping down toward the west, Adare was still missing, the Army of the North was still scattered over half the fucking city, and the Urghul were still massing to the north, preparing for their inevitable attack.

Gwenna glanced at the map again. "To Hull with it. The next time the birds report in, I'm sending them north. You don't need an emperor to have a war."

The Flea studied the deployment of the stones. "It's hard to win a war, if you don't know what's going on on your side of the wall. Delka said she'd heard people whispering that il Tornja has returned to the city."

"You'd think, if that were true, that the bastard would pay a little more attention to the horde of barbarians. He is the *kenarang,* after all, and defending Annur from the threat of annihilation is a fairly substantial part of his job. At the very least—"

She broke off at the sound of cries from the edge of the courtyard, searching for the source of the commotion.

"Well," the Flea said a moment later. "That's one question answered."

Adare. The Emperor. She was running across the flagstones of the open square, flanked by a small knot of men who looked as ruthless as they were unkempt. Gwenna's first thought was that they had seized her somehow, but no . . . they were moving in something like a guard formation, protecting her.

Gwenna left the table, broke into a jog, the Flea and Sigrid at her side. She met the other woman halfway across the square.

"Kaden," Adare gasped. Sweat poured down her face and soaked her robe. She was desperately out of breath, hunched over and panting, but she managed to choke out the message all the same. "Triste and Valyn. Just at the corner . . . of the Wool District and the Flowers . . . where Anlatun's old market spills over. They need . . . a bird. . . ."

It was tempting to ask why, but Adare hadn't run herself half to death in order to play questions and guesses.

"Get her inside," Gwenna said, turning to the Flea. "Make sure she's all right. When the other birds come in, send them north, high, scouting the Urghul—we need to start getting ready for that fight. *Jak*," she shouted, breaking away from Adare, racing across the courtyard to where Allar'ra waited in the shadow of the wall. "Get us in the air."

Talal and Annick had been on top of Adare's tower, watching the Urghul deploy. They had a clear line of sight, however, from there back into the courtyard, and by the time Gwenna reached Jak and the bird, they were already running across the cobblestones at a full sprint, the sniper with her bow in one hand. It couldn't have taken more than a hundred heartbeats from the moment Adare arrived until they were flying, but all the time Gwenna felt her stomach twisting.

Too slow, she thought, shaking her head as they climbed above the slate and copper rooftops, remembering Adare's exhaustion, her desperation. *What if we're too slow?*

It was only a matter of moments to reach the corner of the Wool District. The miles Adare had covered on foot melted away beneath the great bird's wings.

"What are we looking for?" Talal shouted, scanning the streets below as they approached.

"Probably something ugly. Kaden and Valyn. Triste. Maybe

a fight." She shook her head, silently urging the bird to go faster. "I don't know." Over on the far talon, Annick just leaned out in her harness, an arrow nocked to her bow, face calm, composed, even serene, as though they'd taken to the air simply to enjoy the breeze. Gwenna felt ready to jump off the talon and start running.

As they drew closer to the target, she ran her eyes over the streets below. There was a logic to the city, to the movement of people within it, a pattern that emerged from the thousands of random interactions, a pattern, she realized after a moment, that was being disrupted. At first she thought it was just one street, one inexplicable knot. Then she noticed another, and another: groups of soldiers, Annurians, forcing their way through the avenues and alleyways below.

"They're not converging on the Wool District," Talal said, pointing.

Gwenna followed his finger, gritted her teeth, then cursed.

"They're not searching for someone," she said. "They're chasing them."

They banked slightly, as though Jak were preparing for a slow, high circle. Gwenna yanked on the straps instead, a series of vicious tugs. A moment later, the bird tucked his wings in closer, and they began to drop.

"You have them?" Talal asked.

Gwenna pointed to a low stone building half a mile off. She couldn't articulate what she was seeing, the precise nature of the pattern, the convergence of dozens of factors, but that didn't mean she couldn't see it. "They're there. Kaden and the rest of them. That's where the soldiers are headed."

"How do you want to make the grab?"

Gwenna grimaced. "We're going to have put the bird down. You get the girl. I'll take care of Kaden. Valyn can load his own ass up, while Annick shoots whoever needs shooting. We get 'em on the bird, get 'em up, and then we can figure out what the fuck's going on."

She was signaling to Quick Jak even as she spoke. Allar'ra dipped his head, and they were descending, coasting down the air's invisible slope, then leveling off just above the tallest rooftops. It was easy to forget, when you were five thousand feet off the deck, just how fast the kettral really were. Ten feet above the rooftops, however, that speed was suddenly, gut-wrenchingly obvious. Tiles, chimneys, and shingles smeared to a blur beneath their feet. Gwenna fixed her eyes on the blocky skyline, waiting to make the turn.

She caught just a glimpse of them: Kaden and Triste running side by side, Valyn a few paces ahead, his axes naked and bloody in his hands, and then, while the bird was still forty feet up, something hard and viciously strong slammed into its side.

Gwenna's world went upside down, turned right side up, and then she was hanging in her harness, twisting as the wind tore at her. The bird was screaming, Talal was tangled in his straps, while over on the far talon, Annick was trying to drag herself back into something resembling proper position.

"Another bird," Gwenna shouted, as she got her feet under her, craning her head in an effort to see past Allar'ra's wing. "Someone's got another fucking bird."

It only made sense, but when she scanned the sky for a second kettral, she found only a few high clouds, smoke drifting from the chimneys, and the wide, unblemished blue. Then, even as she searched, something smashed into the bird again.

"There's no second kettral," Talal shouted. "A kenning." He was stabbing his finger down, not up. "It's a *kenning*."

Gwenna took half a heartbeat to absorb the information.

"New plan," she said. "We drop—"

Another vicious blow hammered into Allar'ra, smashing him so hard that his right wing grazed the wall of a long stone building, and then they were peeling away to the east.

"Jak, you son of a bitch," Gwenna cursed.

"He's right," Talal shouted, shaking his head. "We're too easy a target up here."

"I understand that," Gwenna spat. "Which is why I need him to put the fucking bird down. We'll do this on foot."

She reached for the leather strap, but at some point in the violence it had torn free. Whatever plan she had, there was no way to communicate it to Jak, no way to do anything but hang in the harness and hope that Valyn could get the other two clear of the army somehow, hope that Gwenna's own bird wouldn't be slammed straight out of the air, shattered on the streets below. As she twisted in her straps, another blow hit the bird. Allar'ra opened his beak to scream, and then Quick Jak was nudging the creature lower, so low they were skimming along one of the wider city streets, windows and balconies whipping by to either side.

The moments that followed comprised the most terrifying flying of Gwenna's life. She had no idea where the attacks against Allar'ra were coming from, no idea if they could be blocked or turned aside, no idea of *anything,* really, except that some leach they couldn't even see was kicking the living shit out of them. She couldn't communicate with Jak, but that hardly mattered now. He was doing the only thing he could—getting them low enough to hide, to stay alive.

An adult kettral had a wingspan of at least seventy feet, which didn't leave much room for flying, even in Annur's largest streets. Gwenna could feel the creature straining under its own weight, trying to rise above the buildings without fully spreading its wings. And then, when they were just clear of the highest roofs, the leach hit them again, knocking the bird a few paces sideways in the air.

'Ra screamed his rage and frustration. Gwenna had no way of knowing how badly the bird was hurt. That they were still in the air at all seemed like a 'Kent-kissing miracle, one that only an idiot would trust any longer than necessary. Jak seemed to agree. He gave the bird its head, letting it climb for seven or eight powerful wingbeats, and then they fell into another steep glide, 'Ra's wings tucked halfway back against his sides, the city's streets rushing up at them all over again. It was desperate flying, getting high enough to keep air speed, then dropping down to hide below the rooflines, soaring through streets so tight that any error meant all of them were going to end up as stains against the side of some tenement or temple. It was madness and genius all at the same time, and it kept them alive.

When they finally burst out of the final street into the wide-open space of Annur's lower harbor, nothing hit them. Quick Jak guided the bird cautiously higher, then higher still. Nothing.

Gwenna glanced over at Talal. "We safe here?"

The leach spread his hands helplessly. "No idea. I couldn't do something like that even if the whole world turned to steel."

Great, Gwenna thought as Jak banked the bird north and west, back toward their improvised command center. *An unknown leach of incalculable power who is not on our side.*

Adare felt like a condemned woman climbing to her death as she mounted the stone stairs of the tower. There was no gibbet at the top, of course—just the bare stone with a clear view out to the north, but that view, in its way, was worse than any hangman's noose. A noose might mean death for a single woman, but the Urghul army that waited—that might spell the doom of all Annur. And that was forgetting all about the disaster she'd left behind, the two brothers she'd abandoned in Kegellen's tunnels.

She was still winded from the sprint through the city, a mad rush in which she'd barely managed to stay on her feet. The gamble had worked, at least for her. Whatever method il Tornja's soldiers were using to track her through the underground labyrinth, it stopped working as soon as she split off from the rest of the party. Kegellen had dispatched a dozen men alongside Adare, but there had been nothing for them to do besides run and look menacing. She would have found more relief in the escape if the implications hadn't been so obvious: the army wasn't searching for her. As Kaden had suggested, the men were looking for him and Triste.

As she climbed the stairs, Adare stared south, where the huge, golden-winged kettral had disappeared. Gwenna and the three soldiers with her had proven themselves more than competent. If anyone had a chance to snatch Kaden and Triste out of the clutches of il Tornja's army, it was a Kettral Wing with a bird. The plan was working, they had made the *right* call, and yet something inside Adare felt sick, soiled, cowardly. She'd run as fast as she could as long as she could in an effort to get to the Kettral quickly, to save the people she'd left behind, but that didn't change the basic fact: she had run.

And there's nothing you can do about it now, she told herself viciously. Whatever triumph or tragedy was playing out to the south, a contest compared to which the war with the Urghul was some pedant's marginalia, she could do nothing to affect it. Either Gwenna would get to Kaden and Triste in time, would carry them to the Spear in time to perform the *obviate,* or she would not. Adare's job now was making sure that if the others succeeded, if il Tornja didn't manage to annihilate the very gods, that those humans who remained might inherit something other than the Urghul's savage kingdom of agony and ash.

As she reached the tower's top, Nira's voice jerked her from her thoughts.

"If ya were pickin' times to fuck off and disappear," the old woman said, "this was a pretty shit pick."

The old woman stood alone at the tower's top, wind tearing at her tangled gray hair. Even as she turned to face Adare, she leaned heavily on her cane, as though the weight of her hundreds of years had settled down on her all at once. Her eyes were still bright, but sunken deep in their sockets. When her gaze settled on Adare, it felt like the gaze of someone in a portrait, someone once strong, determined, resilient, but long since dead.

"What's going on?" Adare asked.

"Aside from an army a' Urghul gettin' ready to turn your nice shiny city into a stable?"

Adare took the final stairs two at a time, then stopped, staring north over the devastation she had visited on her city to the Urghul army beyond. For the better part of the year she'd been near the front, just a few dozen miles from the most brutal fighting, but not since Andt-Kyl had she actually *seen* more than a few of the horsemen at a time. The sight filled her with both dread and fascination. They poured over the low hills, more and more and more, until it seemed they would fill all the fields north of the burned barricade she had created.

"How many are there?" she asked.

"Enough," Nira grunted, as though there were nothing more to say about the matter. "Was it him?"

Adare shook her head in confusion. "Him?"

"Il Tornja," Nira replied. "Was he the one that grabbed ya?"

She was staring south rather than north, not at the Urghul, but over the innumerable walls and rooftops of Annur. Adare's stomach went cold inside her.

"We thought he might have returned. Is it true?"

Nira nodded slowly, wearily. "And my brother with him."

"How do you know?"

"I can feel him, for one thing," Nira replied quietly. "Oshi. I never told ya this, but he's my well. I can feel him moving through the city, somewhere to the south."

Adare followed the older woman's gaze. "If Oshi is here, then so is il Tornja."

"Ya don't need me ta tell you that," Nira said, rummaging in the folds of her dress for a moment, then extending a gnarled hand. "He sent ya a love letter."

Adare stared at the folded parchment. The letters she had received of late had brimmed with disaster. "You opened it," she said.

Nira nodded. "'Course I opened it. Thought ya might be dead."

"And what does it say?"

Even as she asked the question, Adare could feel the dread coiling around her heart, squeezing tighter and tighter, until her own pulse hammered in her ears, drowning out the awful noise of the horsemen to the north. War and worse than war had come to Annur, and yet that single sheet of parchment terrified her more than all the Urghul nation, more than whatever fight was unfolding in the streets below.

"What does it say?" she asked again, the words dry as sand inside her mouth.

Nira grimaced. "It says he has your son."

It felt as though someone had closed a fist around her lungs. For a moment all she could do was gape, staring at Nira like some dumb fish hauled up from the depths to flop itself to death atop the tower. Finally, she managed one more word. "And?"

"Focus on the Urghul," Nira said. "Leave what's happening inside the city alone, and your boy'll be fine."

Adare exhaled slowly, the breath rattling out of her.

Just focus on the Urghul. That was what she'd climbed the tower to do, and yet, she'd already sent Gwenna south. Il Tornja couldn't miss that golden bird knifing through the air. Would he see Adare's hand behind it? Was it already too late?

Trembling, she placed her hands on the stone ramparts, trying to find some strength in the ancient masonry. Down the wall to the west, she could see Lehav readying the Sons of Flame. She suddenly wished Fulton were there, the longing for his stern, steady presence an ache so vicious that it momentarily stole her speech.

"So," Nira said, the syllable simple and unforgiving as an anvil.

"So," Adare replied, trying to keep the scream inside her from ripping free.

"What are you going to do?"

"What I came here to do. Hold back the Urghul while the Kettral finish what needs doing in the city."

Nira narrowed her eyes. "And what is it, exactly, that needs doing? What is it everyone's so worked up about that the whole 'Kent-kissing army seems ta have not noticed the arrival of the entire Urghul nation?"

Adare shook her head, unsure how to tell the story, unsure what words would suffice. "Trying to save us," she said finally.

After studying her a moment, Nira nodded. "And if it comes ta your brothers or your son, who'll ya choose?"

"It's not going to come to that."

"Sayin' a thing don't make it so. . . ."

"It's not . . ." The words died in Adare's mouth.

She stared north. While she'd been standing on the tower's top, the Urghul had divided into two groups, separated by a wide lane. She hadn't been paying any attention to the maneuver—they were still days from being able to attack. Or so she'd thought.

Without shifting her gaze from the Urghul, she groped at her side, found the long lens, and raised it to her eye. A figure leapt into view, riding down the center of that lane, a man she'd heard discussed a thousand times, but never actually seen. He was decked out in the Urghul style, all leather and fur, though his skin and hair were far too dark for any Urghul. Despair's gray, sickly flower unfolded in Adare's mind. Through the long lens, she could see the grim smile on the man's face, the leashes trailing from his saddle, and collared at the end of those leashes, naked, terrified, and bleeding from some recent lash, a dozen prisoners, men and women, all Annurian.

"Balendin," Adare said quietly.

That got Nira's attention finally. The old woman turned, took up a long lens of her own, and studied him silently.

"He's the leach, eh?" She shook her head. "Emotion. It's a strong well. One a' the strongest."

"What can he do?" Adare asked. The story from Andt-Kyl was that he had used his foul power to hold up an entire bridge while the Urghul rode across. Adare wasn't sure whether to believe it or not—the bridge had been destroyed by the time that she arrived, Balendin gone.

Nira frowned. "A lot. He's not just leaching off those poor doomed fucks." She gestured down the wall with her cane. "There must be five thousand men on these walls. They've heard a' him. Everyone in the 'Kent-kissing city's heard a' him. Once they know he's here, once he can feel all that hate, and rage, and fear"—she shook her head again—"even the Army of the North might not make a difference."

When Quick Jak finally put Allar'ra down inside the improvised Kettral compound, the entire place was on the verge of madness. The other Wings were all there, back from their own scouting missions. No one had found Kaden, obviously, but everyone had seen the same thing north of the wall: the Urghul army parting down the center to make room for Balendin and his string of blood victims. Sigrid and the Flea had managed to impose some sort of order, but Adare was up on top of her tower, stabbing a finger to the north, and a string of terrified messengers were waiting on the cobblestones, all bearing the same message: kill the leach.

"Son of a bitch," Gwenna cursed, dropping off the talon, "how long has he been there?"

"Not long," the Flea replied. "Just getting ready, from the sound of it." He nodded to the south. "What happened to you?"

Gwenna shook her head, unsure how to cram it all into a few words. "Nothing good. Valyn's with Kaden and Triste. According to Adare, they all need to get to the Spear. I have no idea why, but everyone seems to think it's pretty fucking important. Including the Army of the North, who is hunting them."

"You couldn't manage an extract?"

"The bastards have a leach. Almost knocked us clear out of the air, and we never even saw him."

"A leach?" the Flea asked. He glanced over at Sigrid. The blond woman just shook her head, made an angry growl in the back of her throat. "That's two of them," the Flea said grimly. "Whoever this is south of the wall, and Balendin to the north. Sig thinks that after half an afternoon of cutting out hearts he'll be strong enough to clear a path through all Adare's hard-earned wreckage, maybe strong enough to punch straight through the wall."

"Well that's unpleasant," Gwenna said, scrambling for anything resembling a plan, something that would save Kaden and Triste and Annur at the same time.

"Valyn and Kaden," the Flea said, slicing through her thoughts. "What was their last location?"

"West of the Wool District, heading farther west."

The Wing leader's brow furrowed. "Thought you said they wanted to get to the Spear."

"Yeah. Well. Looks like wanting not to get killed counted a little higher than wanting to get to the Spear. Valyn's leading them west, which, given the way the army's arranged, seems like a pretty good idea."

The Flea glanced over at Sigrid. The blond woman met his gaze, then nodded.

"We'll get them," he said, turning back to Gwenna. "We don't have a bird anyway, and this is a job for a foot team. You take care of Balendin."

Gwenna stared. "Take *care* of him? You have any ideas how to do that?"

"Nope. That's why it's your job." The Flea gestured toward the birds. "You've got five Wings here. Use 'em."

For a moment, Gwenna couldn't move. The thought was too large, the responsibility too daunting. Then the Flea stepped forward, set a solid hand on her shoulder. "You're a good soldier, Gwenna."

She met his eyes, but could find no words.

"This is what you trained to do," the Flea went on, his voice quiet, low, steady as the waves on the shore. "No one ever thinks they're ready for something like this, but I'm telling you now, and I'm only going to say it once, so listen good. . . ." He paused, smiled that crooked smile of his. "You're ready."

Then, before Gwenna could respond, he and Sigrid were gone, racing south toward Valyn, toward the Army of the North, toward a viciously powerful leach, and in all likelihood, toward an immortal Csestriim general against whom every human attack had failed.

"Well, shit," Gwenna muttered.

"I agree," Talal replied. He was standing just a pace distant, Annick at his side.

"We could go with him," Gwenna said. "Provide air cover."

"That didn't work so well last time," the leach pointed out, "and besides. Balendin's here. We can't fight all the fights."

Gwenna nodded, looked past him to where Quick Jak was going over Allar'ra's wings, sliding his hands beneath the feathers looking for damage.

"Can he fly?" Gwenna shouted.

The flier hesitated. "He can fly, but I need more time to assess the damage. . . ."

"We don't have more time. We have to hit Balendin now. Once he knocks down half the wall, there won't be much point." She gestured to the other Kettral, most of whom had dismounted to check over weapons and birds. "Fliers and Wing commanders on me."

The plan was as shitty as it was simple. They had five birds. Balendin couldn't look five directions at once. Four Wings would come in from the cardinal directions, and one would stoop from almost directly above.

"Balendin shields himself," Talal pointed out. "He did at Andt-Kyl, anyway. If the leach attacking us to the south was using a hammer, Balendin's kenning will be like an invisible wall."

Gwenna nodded, wondering if she had it all wrong. "He

shields himself against arrows, flatbow bolts, spears. You think he can hold out against eight tons of bird coming at him faster than a galloping horse?"

Talal hesitated. "I don't know. Maybe. Maybe not."

The other Kettral looked nervous. Quick Jak, for all his slick flying just moments earlier, seemed close to panic. He had picked at the cuticle of his thumb so viciously that the nail was awash in blood, but he just kept at it, not seeming to notice.

"Look," Gwenna said, stepping forward. "Balendin's only going to get stronger. The more people in this city learn that he's here, learn who he is and what he does, the harder it's going to be to kill him. I can't say that my plan will work. Maybe we get lucky, maybe someone gets through, and maybe we all die.

"I will tell you this, though. You are Kettral, every 'Kent-kissing one of you. We called you washouts, but you're not, not anymore. You went down in the Hole, you fought the slarn, you drank the egg, and you came back out. That makes you Kettral, you crazy sons of bitches, and let me tell you something about being Kettral. We don't get the easy jobs. We don't pull wall duty or guarding the baggage chain. In return for getting to fly around on these enormous, manslaughtering hawks, we actually have to go do the dangerous shit, the shit that gets men and women killed, and so if this isn't what you signed up for, you tell me now." She paused, shifting her eyes from one soldier to the next. "Which one of you isn't Kettral? Who wants to wash out all over again?"

No one stepped forward. No one spoke.

Finally, Gwenna allowed herself to smile. "Good. Mount up."

Their hastily constructed plan failed almost the moment they stepped from the shelter of Kegellen's street-level warehouse and into the street beyond. They needed to go outside in order for the bird to find them, of course, but when they stepped, blinking, into the afternoon heat and sunlight, there was no kettral in the sky. Kaden stood with Valyn and Triste in a wide, treelined avenue, one of Annur's larger thoroughfares. Shops occupied the bottom floors of the buildings to either side— leatherworkers, mostly, judging from the wares on display—and the street itself was busy with men and women haggling or selling, pushing handcarts loaded with stock, making purchases or deliveries. It almost might have been a normal city street on an everyday afternoon, except for the Annurian soldiers, at least a dozen of them, jogging up the center of the road from the south. They hadn't spotted their quarry yet, but they weren't bothering to stop, not even pausing to search inside the shops. They moved with the certainty of hunters who knew exactly where to find the beast they sought.

Valyn glanced at the soldiers, then gestured to Kaden and Triste. "North. Walk fast until they see us, then run."

"Where's the kettral?" Triste hissed.

"No idea."

"We could retreat," Kaden said, nodding toward Kegellen's warehouse. The Queen of the Streets had remained behind, inside, along with a knot of her guards.

"No," Valyn growled, dragging him into the foot traffic. "We can't. You can't hide, not as long as il Tornja has those 'Shael-spawned spiders. You go back in those tunnels, and you'll die there. He's got the whole Army of the North to pin you down, smoke you out."

Even as he spoke, Valyn's eyes roamed over the street ahead. He hadn't drawn the axes from the belt, but that ruined gaze was enough to make anyone who met it jerk back, turn hastily aside, find somewhere else to look, somewhere else to be.

"The bird's our best shot at getting to the top of the Spear."

"And if the bird doesn't show up?" Kaden asked.

"Then we do it the hard way."

"What does that mean?" Triste demanded.

"We go on foot," Valyn said. "Fight our way in, up. There's no choice now—we have to keep moving."

Triste stopped walking, turned to stare at Valyn. *"Fight our way in?"*

"There are three of us," Kaden said quietly, taking Triste by the elbow as he spoke, urging her into motion once more. "Three of us against il Tornja's entire army."

Valyn's smile was like something carved across his face with a knife. "I'm not sure you understand."

"Not sure I understand what?"

"Everything that's happened this past year," Valyn replied, then trailed off, shaking his head. "I'm not the brother you remember, Kaden. I'm something . . . different. When you tally up the good people in this fight, the noble ones, the ones who've been doing the right thing: I'm not on that list. Not anymore. I don't think I've been on that list for a very long time."

The words were lost, haunted, as though someone had hollowed out this warrior who stalked down the street, his scarred hand on the head of his ax.

"That doesn't matter," Kaden said. "Not right now."

"Yes, it does."

Behind them, a sudden cry cut through the everyday babble of the avenue. The soldiers were shouting, bellowing questions and orders. Kaden risked a glance over his shoulder. The men weren't jogging, they were running, fingers leveled directly at Kaden himself. When he turned back to the north, he found the far end of the street blocked by a hastily assembled cordon of armed men. Valyn was still smiling.

"The thing you don't understand, my calm, quiet brother, is that sometimes goodness and nobility aren't enough. Sometimes, when the monsters come, you need a dark, monstrous thing to pit against them." He slid one ax from the loop at his belt, then the other. People cried out in alarm, lurched away. Valyn ignored them. "I am that thing, Kaden. The human part of me . . . the part that should feel camaraderie, friendship, love . . ." He shook his head. "It's gone. There is only darkness. I'm not a brother, not really. Not a friend. Not an ally or son. I don't know how to be those things. All I know is blood and struggle. It is all I am. This fight, right now, is what I am for."

And then it began.

Kaden had spent years as an acolyte in the Bone Mountains, unseen atop the granite spire of the Talon, watching crag cats hunt. They had struck him as perfect predators, flowing over the stone like winter shadows, silently pacing their prey, moving from ledge to boulder so smoothly they seemed otherworldly, like creatures culled from a dream of hunting. He'd watched them stand utterly still for an hour, then uncoil all at once, leaping a dozen paces in a single, unerring strike. Death, Kaden thought, must be like that: perfect, patient, waiting one moment, striking the next, unstringing tendons so quickly, so precisely, that the dying thing—a bear, a mountain goat—was gone before the carcass struck the stone. Those crag cats, however, for all their perfection, all their silent, predatory grace, seemed clumsy, slow, almost comically awkward when Kaden compared them to the creature Valyn had become.

Valyn didn't attack the soldiers blocking the street to the north; *attack* wasn't the right word. An *attack* implied a fight, implied some defense—if only feeble, notional—on the part of those attacked. The Annurian soldiers had no defense. They might as well have stood at the ocean's verge, trying to hold back the steel-gray sea with their feeble spears. When Valyn was still twenty paces distant, he hurled his axes, one then the other. Kaden could barely follow the flashing blur of the vicious wedges tumbling end over end, but in the moment it took for both to find their marks, Valyn had already slipped knives from inside his blacks and hurled those, too, at the line of men. The sound reached Kaden a moment later—four sick wet *thwacks,* steel hacking into unready flesh.

The line of soldiers shuddered as the four men at the center collapsed into their own agony. Valyn didn't break stride.

Between him and the Annurians, an ironmonger's wagon laden with pots and heavy pans had skewed across the street.

The mules, panicked by the scent of blood, were bellowing, stamping, hauling their groaning load in different directions. The bearded ironmonger hesitated a moment, torn between the need to protect his goods and the awful realization that there could be no protecting them, not against the madness coursing through the street. As the baffled merchant hurled himself to the dirt, Valyn leapt over the wagon, stripping two heavy iron pans from the load as he passed, hit the ground with a shoulder, rolled to his feet, knocked aside the arrows flying at his face, and then he was among the legionaries, caving in faces and shattering arms, bellowing at Kaden and Triste to follow.

It was only a few dozen paces, but by the time they caught up, the legionaries were dead, blood chugging out onto the earth through ragged, ugly wounds, and Valyn was holding his axes once again.

"Let's go," he growled. "And this time, try to keep up."

There was a moment early on in all the blood-slick madness when Kaden caught a glimpse of a golden-winged bird. The creature screamed, careened through the sky as though it were a huge puppet yanked by vicious, invisible strings, and then it was gone, vanished behind the rooftops. He ran on, waiting for the kettral to reappear even as dozens of men wielding spears and swords flooded into the street behind them.

"Where is it?" he shouted.

"Gone," Valyn said. "Can't make the grab."

Even as he spoke, another knot of armored men erupted from a side alley a dozen paces ahead. Valyn, already charging, charged harder. Kaden had never seen any human being move so fast, had never seen *anything* move that fast. Valyn wielded the axes as though they were part of his own flesh, as though he'd been born holding them, and the Annurians could find no defense that availed against that brutal steel. Valyn went over their guard or under, found holes in whatever feeble attacks were thrown up, sometimes just slammed straight through a raised blade, shattering it or knocking it aside as though three feet of sharpened sword were no more than a reed.

"Come on," he growled, gesturing through the hole he'd carved. Blood spattered his face.

The flight that followed was madness. Not since the Aedolians had come to Ashk'lan to kill him had Kaden run so hard. This time, too, the Annurian soldiers were his foes. This time, too, Triste ran at his side, her breathing ragged, but steady. This time, too, he understood the stakes, how it would only take a single misstep, a twisted ankle, and the race would be over. It was all the same, and yet it was not the same at all.

There had been a hope of escaping the Aedolians back in the Bone Mountains where the terrain favored the monks. Kaden enjoyed no such advantage on the streets of Annur. Worse, il Tornja's soldiers weren't trailing along somewhere behind, they were *everywhere,* lunging out of doorways and alleys, appearing at intersections, calling out to one another in ear-shivering blasts on their horns. Were it not for Valyn, the Annurians would have killed both Kaden and Triste a dozen times over, but Valyn, somehow, was everywhere.

When Annurians came on horseback, he killed the horses. When they came with spears, he rolled beneath the shafts and cut the arms from the attackers. Once, when Kaden rounded a corner to find two legionaries leveling flatbows at his chest, Valyn lunged in front. An ax flew end over end into the face of one of the bowmen. Kaden couldn't see what happened next. Or he saw it, but his mind couldn't work through the fact. There was an arrow. A flying arrow. Then there was not. It looked as though Valyn had snatched it from the air, but that was impossible. There was no time to dwell on it. Valyn had reached the other bowman, caved in his throat, retrieved the first thrown ax, and was waving them on again.

His look brought Kaden up short. Despite the blood bathing his arms, soaking the tattered cloth of his clothes, Valyn didn't look like a man fighting for his life. He looked . . . glad.

No, Kaden thought. *Not glad. Something else.*

There was no time to ponder words. Even as he paused, the Annurians were closing.

"Come on, Kaden," Triste said, dragging him forward by the wrist. "Come *on.*"

Kaden met her eyes, saw the fear and determination there, and he ran.

The red walls of the Dawn Palace nearly proved their undoing. They'd come at the fortress from the west and south, working their way through the streets until they burst from one final crowded lane into the open space before the walls and the short bridge leading to the Water Gate.

The Water Gate was nothing compared to the towering Godsgate that opened west onto Annur's main thoroughfare. It was an entrance for minor ministers, deliveries of food and wine, workers come to repair roofs or walls. It was a small gate, but it was blocked by a steel portcullis, and for all Valyn's ability to hack his way through human flesh, his axes would do nothing to get them past that grille.

"West," Valyn said, checking his momentum before he reached the short bridge over the moat. "We'll go in the Great Gate."

Even as the words left his lips, however, a knot of twenty or thirty soldiers, half bearing loaded flatbows, marched out from a side street at the double to block the way west.

"East," Kaden gasped. "The harbor."

But there were men to the east, too, spreading out in a tight cordon across the street.

Valyn hefted his axes, as though testing their weight. "We'll go through them."

"That's insane," Triste hissed.

"She's right," Kaden said. "I don't care how good you are, we're not going to survive, not through that."

"So we don't survive," Valyn said. "So we die."

His voice sent a shiver up Kaden's spine.

"The canal," Kaden said, gesturing to the filthy water swirling along the base of the wall.

One twitchy bowman loosed his bolt. It landed twenty paces distant, steel head striking sparks as it skittered across the stone.

"We didn't make it," Triste whispered. "We didn't make it."

Then, before Kaden could reply, madness erupted in the western rank of soldiers. Men cried out in pain and surprise, turned, tried to bring swords and bows to bear on some new, unseen foe, calling out conflicting orders even as their companions fell. The line of men, so strict and disciplined just moments earlier, flexed, then caved inward, like a river's high bank before the rising waters of a flood, calving off at first, then collapsing. Kaden could just make out, at the center of the violence, two figures, little more than shadows, really, in all the kicked-up dust, fighting back to back, hacking their way through the stunned ranks of Annurians.

"It's another army . . . ," Kaden began, then trailed off as a gust of wind shoveled away the dust.

There was no army. There were no rows of newly arrived soldiers to rank against those other deadly rows. There were just the two shadows, neither of them as fast as Valyn, but fast enough, twin blades naked in their hands as they forced their way forward step by bloody step, leaving a screaming, twisted human wreckage in their wake. Then, a moment later, they were free, bursting from the front rank of the legion, charging full tilt at the bridge. Both wore Kettral blacks, but their similarity ended there. The man was short, pockmarked, coal black, shaved-headed. The woman was tall, beautiful but freakishly pale, her yellow hair streaming out behind her.

"Well, Holy Hull," Valyn said, taken aback for the first time since their desperate flight began.

"Not Hull," the man said as they reached them. "Just a couple beat-up soldiers." If Valyn was some preternatural hunter stalking the streets of Annur, these two looked half dead. Both were drenched in blood; a vicious blaze had singed the hair from half the woman's head. The man's blades were notched in half a dozen places. Somehow, though, they'd come across the city, cutting their own way through the Army of the North, and when the man spoke again, his voice was hard, level, focused. "What now?"

Valyn pointed. "We need in, past the gate."

Neither of the Kettral asked why. The blond woman just threw up a hand, a casual gesture, as though she were flicking water free of her fingers. Behind Kaden there was a groan like the earth itself were breaking apart, then a deafening crash. He turned to find the steel portcullis crushed, crumbled, shoved aside.

"Go," Valyn said, seizing him by the shoulder, hauling him onto the bridge even as the bolts and arrows started falling once more. *"Go."*

"Triste," Kaden said, but the short man had her by the arm, was dragging her with him as he ran.

They were Kettral—that much was clear enough—although beyond that Kaden had no theories. It didn't matter. There was only one thing left that mattered.

"The Spear," he gasped, pointing up at the impossible glass tower looming above. "We have to get to the Spear."

Adare watched from the wall as the Kettral attacked.

Balendin stood atop a small, charred knoll, the site, until days earlier, of some temple, the ruined walls and buttresses of which still stood, protecting him from anyone approaching from behind. He'd been plying his stomach-churning violence there for half the day, unseaming men and women as though they were dolls, opening the skin, holding up the dark, pulsing organs to the light, bathing in the cries of the surrounding Urghul and, presumably, the horror of the soldiers atop the wall.

He had just torn the tongue from another helpless prisoner when the five birds came at him, one from every point of the compass and one stabbing down from above. It seemed an impossible attack to stop. Each of those birds was the size of a large canalboat, all wing, and beak, and claw. Through the long lens, Adare could see the Kettral on the talons beneath, armed to the ears with blades and bows. They started loosing arrows early, and kept shooting as the birds closed.

"They're going to do it," Adare breathed quietly. "They're going to kill that fucking bastard."

Nira was silent at her side a moment, studying the battle through her own long lens. Then she shook her head.

"No," she replied grimly, lowering the lens. "They're not."

The first kettral exploded into flames when it was still a hundred paces from the leach, the second a heartbeat after that. One moment the birds were flying, screaming their defiance, the next they were charred, already dead, tumbling from the air, the burning Kettral struggling to cut themselves free of their harnesses. Struggling and failing.

"Sweet Intarra's light," Adare breathed.

"They could use a little a' that right now," Nira agreed.

Whether the leach had used too much strength too quickly, or he just didn't see the full scope of the attack early enough, the other three birds got closer. Closer, but not close enough. Balendin raised his hand, dropped it down, and the nearest kettral, already coming in low for its attack, slammed into the earth, scattering horses and riders, plowing up the soft ground. The mounted Urghul surrounded it, screaming, swarming over the broken creature and the soldiers beneath like so many ants on a rotting carcass.

The fourth bird careened off some invisible wall, and though it managed to stay airborne, even Adare could tell from the stuttering wingbeat that the creature was injured, and badly. This one, however, managed to limp off toward the north, and though a group of the horsemen gave chase, it seemed at least possible that the soldiers strapped to the talons beneath would survive, escape.

That left the fifth bird, the one dropping straight down out of the clouds.

That one's Gwenna, she realized, staring through the lens. *The largest bird, the golden one, is hers.*

Adare allowed herself the smallest spark of hope. It was possible Balendin hadn't noticed, that he'd been too busy knocking back the first four attacks to notice the fifth. He couldn't see everything at once; he had to miss something eventually. The long lens was shaking so badly in Adare's hand that she couldn't see the leach's face. She leaned it against the top of the stone wall, took a moment to find the range again, and then her stomach recoiled inside her. Balendin was staring straight up. Staring straight up, and smiling.

Adare clenched her teeth, waiting for the inevitable, for this bird, too, the last of a shattered hope, to burst into flame or be smashed into the dirt. At the last moment, however, the enormous creature sheered off, peeling away toward the east, abandoning the attack. Not that it mattered. Another blow, just as vicious as the one that crippled the other four kettral, hammered into the huge golden bird from the side. It tumbled sideways, screamed, managed to right itself, then disappeared behind the rooftops, flying toward the Broken Bay.

For a moment, it was all Adare could do to stay on her feet.

"They didn't even get close," she breathed quietly. "Five Wings of Kettral attacking simultaneously, and they didn't even get close."

"It's worse than that," Nira said. "That victory just dug his well deeper, filled it higher."

Adare turned to the older woman.

"Think of your awe," Nira continued quietly. She gestured to the Urghul, to the Annurians manning the walls. "Now multiply that by a hundred thousand."

Gwenna was still cursing when Quick Jak put the bird down south of the wall, in the open square that served as the Kettral command and control. Only there were no Kettral left, none but her own Wing.

"The 'Shael-spawned son of a fucking whore," Gwenna snarled. "That bastard. That son of a *bitch*."

The curses weren't directed at anyone, they weren't even coherent, but they kept her from sobbing.

She'd known it was a risk. They all had. She'd known, when she gave the order to attack, that people wouldn't be coming back, that Balendin would put up some kind of fight and that people would die. She'd known there was a possibility that the leach was just too strong, and she'd made the choice to go after him anyway, before he got even stronger. She'd known all of it, and yet seeing the birds burst into flame, seeing the men and women she'd so hastily trained burning, falling, dying . . . she hadn't known how much that would hurt.

The fact that her own Wing had survived only made it worse, and when Quick Jak dropped off Allar'ra's back, Gwenna went at him with a fury, seizing him by the throat and throwing him to the ground. The fact that she could see the fear in his eyes, that she could smell the stink of panic on him, made her want to kill him right there and be done with it.

"Why did you peel off?" she demanded.

"Gwenna," Talal said quietly.

"Stay out of this, Talal." She didn't take her eyes off the flier. *"Why did you peel off?"*

Jak managed to shake his head slightly. "He . . . had us. You saw. . . ."

"You don't know that," Gwenna shouted. "You don't *know* that, you worthless piece of shit. The plan, the fucking *plan,* was to go in hard and *keep going*. That's what the other Wings did, or maybe you were too busy shitting your pants to notice."

Jak's face was purpling, but he made no move to fight back or try to pull free.

"Other Wings . . . ," he managed, "died."

"Sometimes that happens," Gwenna screamed. "Sometimes

when you're fighting, people fucking *die*. It doesn't mean you stop fighting. The only reason you stop fighting is you're too frightened, because you're a coward, because something's fucking *broken* inside you."

The flier opened his mouth, then closed it, shut his eyes.

"Gwenna," Talal said again, taking her by the shoulders this time, pulling her back. "Get off of him. We're alive because he saved us."

Gwenna slammed the flier's head against the ground once, then straightened up to shove a finger in Talal's face.

"He saved us," she hissed, "by *running away*. I ordered those other Wings into the fight. I told them we were all going, that we were making a concerted attack, *together,* and then I ran away."

"Would it be better if we were dead?"

"Yes!" she said, shocked at her own conviction. *"Yes."*

Talal shook his head slowly. "No."

Behind them, Quick Jak was getting unsteadily to his feet. Gwenna took a long, shuddering breath, held it for a few heartbeats, then let it out. Then she did it again, and again. *When you fight,* Hendran wrote, *people die. It's only human to care, but you need to cut out that human thing. If you care too much, you lose.*

When she thought she could speak without screaming, she turned to face her Wing.

"Stay with the bird," she said, then gestured toward the wall and the tower punctuating it. "I'm going to tell the Emperor we failed."

Adare had just sent out a dozen runners east and west along the wall. The fight with the Kettral had been pretty hard to miss, but all the same, she wanted to make sure the Sons of Flame understood what was coming.

The leach is going to hit us today, she told the messenger. *And we think he's going to hit us here, at this tower.*

That, at least, was what Nira believed, for reasons Adare didn't fully understand. Maybe the old woman was right, and maybe she was just finally going insane, but after seeing the Kettral scrubbed from the sky, Adare needed to do something, and sending out a warning was something. She was searching for another task when Gwenna stepped up through the trapdoor and onto the tower's top.

"Your Radiance," she said, bowing her head. The genuflection was uncharacteristic. "The attack failed."

Adare bit back the first sharp retort that came to mind. "I saw," she said instead. "I'm sorry for your soldiers."

The words sounded stiff, useless, formulaic, but what else was there to say? The leach had just shattered the best weapon that Adare could bring against him, shattered it without even the slightest hint of effort.

"Thank you, Your Radiance. We can mourn the fallen later. We have one bird left. What are your orders?"

Adare was still trying to formulate an answer when a runner stumbled up through the trapdoor, sweating and out of breath.

"The *kenarang,*" he managed after a moment. "Your Radiance, I've come from the palace. Kiel sent me. He says he had eyes on the *kenarang.* . . . "

Nira stiffened at Adare's side. "Where?" she demanded.

"Inside . . . the Spear," the man gasped. "He had a hundred soldiers, and he went into the Spear."

Adare stared. She could feel the warning from il Tornja, the single slip of paper folded inside her pocket.

"That's where Kaden's going," she murmured. "That bastard. He's always a step ahead."

Gwenna studied her. "I don't know why in Hull's name Kaden would want to get inside the Spear, but he's not headed that way. We caught a glimpse of him. Valyn was taking him west. *Away* from the palace. Which is just as well, since the whole 'Kent-kissing Army of the North was in his way if he tried to go east."

"West," Adare murmured. "They changed the plan?"

Nira snorted. "Faced with a whole army. Wouldn't you?"

Adare took a deep breath. She could feel a sudden spark of hope inside her, hot, bright, horrible. *Do not interfere,* il Tornja had warned her, *with anything south of the wall. I have your son.*

Adare shuddered, replied silently, *But I have you. Now. For the first time. I have you trapped.*

"When?" she demanded, rounding on the messenger. "When did he go in?"

"Long time ago," the man replied. "It took . . . time to cross the city." He shook his head wearily. "I'm sorry, Your Radiance."

"A long time ago," Adare said, hope's spark kindling to a fire. "And he hasn't left?"

The man shook his head. "Not that I know, Your Radiance."

"Good," Adare said, nodding slowly. "Good."

"'Fuck's good about the *kenarang* takin' control of your palace?" Nira demanded.

"He's not in the palace," Adare replied, smiling. "He's in the Spear. It's time for Intarra to pull her weight."

"Meanin' what?"

"It's time for a miracle."

Nira studied Adare from beneath hooded lids. "And if the goddess don't comply?"

"Oh, I'm through waiting for the fucking goddess."

"Meanin' what?" Nira asked again, even more quietly this time.

"Meaning I'm going to set her Spear on fire."

We're killing good men, Valyn thought as the palace guardsman crumpled beneath his ax. He'd hit the man with the blunt back of the metal head, trusting to the soldier's helmet to cushion the blow. He'd probably survive. With any luck, *most* of them would survive. The Flea was fighting mostly with the flats of his blades, and Sigrid, too, but sometimes the only way past a man was through him, and Valyn would be shipped to 'Shael if he failed in this last, mad dash because he was too delicate to spill the necessary blood.

After Sigrid smashed through the Water Gate, the Dawn Palace had erupted into utter madness. The normal guardsmen, baffled by what seemed an unprovoked attack, were coming at them from every direction, spears waving stupidly in the air. If there had been more time, Kaden might have talked to them— he had the eyes, they would accept him in his own palace—but there was no time. Il Tornja's soldiers were inside the red walls, too, just behind them, fighting their own way forward, and if that weren't enough, the Aedolians, drawn to the sound of violence, kept attacking in knots of two or four.

At least Kaden and Triste had managed not to panic. They moved forward in the center of the rough triangle of Kettral, Kaden trying to shield Triste with his body. *Trying to shield her,* Valyn thought, *or the goddess inside her.* His brother's claim still sounded outlandish, insane, but there was no time to dwell on it. They were ducks moving through the various avenues and courtyards of the palace. Whatever had to happen inside the Spear didn't matter, not in the instant; getting there was a simple, tactical imperative. The staircase above the lower floors was almost perfectly defensible. With high ground and a vertical choke point, the three Kettral should be able to hold against whatever soldiers il Tornja threw at them. They just needed to get inside.

The Jasmine Court was the last open space before the Spear, and they hit it at a full run. The Flea had snatched up a bow somewhere in the fight. Halfway across the courtyard, he dropped to a knee, loosed half a dozen shafts at the cordon of men lined up in front of the entrance to the tower.

Not palace guards, Valyn realized grimly. *Il Tornja's soldiers.*

"Army," the Flea shouted, noticing the same thing, dropping the bow, and drawing his blades once more.

"Stay behind me," Valyn bellowed back to Kaden. "Stay low."

There were seven or eight men remaining, three with flatbows. He could see the terror painted across their faces, could hear the panic in their smashing hearts. They were legionaries, like the ones he'd been killing in the street beyond, but that didn't mean they were evil. They were following orders, obeying the general who for the past year had saved Annur over and over. Maybe they were good men and maybe they weren't, but they hardly deserved to die for their loyalty. It had been a long time since he'd lived in a world where anyone got what they deserved.

Without breaking stride, Valyn threw one ax, then another. Two soldiers crumpled. The third managed to get off a shot without even aiming. It flew preposterously wide, and then the Flea and Sigrid were on them, moving like dancers, all steel and fists as they slashed knees, broke faces, opened the bodies for Ananshael to do his final, quiet work.

Only when they were inside the tower did the violence die off. It was like racing from the chaos of a stampede into a quiet chapel, all polished wood and bronze, robed men with soft flesh and quiet slippers going wide-eyed at their approach, then jerking back to the sides of the staircase, standing still, silent, frozen as deer, waiting for death to pass them by.

"We made it," Triste groaned.

"Not yet," Kaden replied. "We need to reach the top."

The Flea grunted, kept his blades out. "Lot of stairs between here and there. Keep the feet moving."

And so they moved, climbing first through the human floors built into the ancient structure, then clear of that mortal work, into the enormous column of light and empty air. Valyn paused, his chest heaving inside him. It had been almost ten years since he was last inside Intarra's Spear, ten years since he and Kaden had climbed these same stairs together, pausing on the landings to spit over the edge, ignoring the admonitions of their Aedolians as they watched the spit fall away, break apart, disappear long before it struck the roof below. The memory twisted inside him like a knife. That child was a stranger, one more Annurian murdered in the war, vanished without even leaving a corpse.

He glanced over at his brother. Kaden's eyes burned. *Hotter than I remembered,* Valyn thought. *Brighter.* He was still calm, preternaturally so for someone who had just fled for his life through the streets of Annur, who had just watched dozens of men cut into meat, who carried in his breath and bones the Lord of Pain himself. That glacial indifference Valyn had smelled on him back in the Bone Mountains, however, was gone. There was no monastic self-abnegation in the arm he had wrapped around Triste's slender shoulders. Kaden cared what happened here. Valyn could smell the sorrow on him, the wet-rain scent of coming loss.

"More movement," the Flea called out. He and Sigrid had taken up a position just behind them. "Il Tornja's friends can climb stairs the same as we can."

The warning was hardly necessary. Valyn could hear the heavy clomp of boots. Ten floors down, maybe twelve, but coming. He turned back to Kaden.

"Where?" he demanded.

Kaden raised a single finger. "Up," he said again. "We need to reach the top."

Valyn nodded. "Get to the prison level. Sigrid, the Flea, and I can hold them there. How long does this ceremony take?"

Kaden shook his head slowly. "I don't know." He seemed, suddenly, to be struggling with something, some unexpected pain welling up inside him. His face twitched, then went still. "Just get us up there."

He held Valyn's gaze a moment, then turned back to Triste. She was crying, tears standing in her violet eyes, obviously exhausted. Despite it all, she nodded. Then they were moving once again.

The fierce, vicious bliss that had buoyed Valyn up during the whole race through Annur had faded the moment the violence lapsed. His legs were a leaden blaze as he labored up the stairs.

Breath burned his chest. From the sound of it, the others were struggling, too, and yet it was working. Once they reached the prison level they could throw shut the steel doors. The soldiers below wouldn't be able to touch them.

He glanced over at Kaden.

"We're going to make it," he said.

Then he smelled the smoke. There was just a hint of it at first, faint and acrid, then stronger and stronger. He paused, holding the railing to keep from falling over, closed his eyes, and listened. His stomach twisted when he realized what he was hearing: below the rumble of boots on the stairs, below the desperate breathing of the people around him, below his own blood pounding in his ears, a quieter, more dangerous sound: the hiss and roar of fire, fire inside the Spear itself, gnawing through the floors below, quiet, but getting louder.

Quick Jak was going over Allar'ra's tail feathers when Gwenna returned to the Wing. Annick and Talal were talking quietly a few paces from the flier—Gwenna couldn't quite make out the words. She hesitated at the edge of the large square, stayed in the wall's cool shadow for a moment. It was easier than facing them all again, easier than seeing her failure reflected in their eyes. She started to lean against the stones, then shoved herself upright.

"Knock it off, you bitch," she muttered to herself.

She straightened her shoulders, checked her blades, then strode from the shadows into the open space.

"We failed," she said. The three turned to watch her approach. Talal looked concerned; Quick Jak, wary, then scared. Gwenna shoved down her own fury. "We failed," she said again, "but we are not done fighting. Right now, I need to hear it, all your best ideas on how we can get at Balendin before he blows the doors right off this 'Kent-kissing city."

"Go in on foot," Annick said after a pause. "He's seen the

birds. He knows we escaped, so he'll be prepared for another air attack. If we can infiltrate that group of prisoners, get close to him . . ."

"We'll just be easier to kill," Talal said quietly. He shook his head. "He's too strong. He has the awe of the whole Urghul nation to draw on, and the growing terror of every citizen in Annur. Right now, he might be the most powerful leach since the Atmani, and that power's not going away unless a million people suddenly forget all about him." He shook his head again. "I'll go with you. I'll try it the way Annick says. I just don't see how we can win."

Jak hadn't spoken, hadn't met Gwenna's eyes since she returned.

"What about you?" she asked, more harshly than she'd intended.

For a long time, he didn't reply. Then, instead of turning to her, he leveled an unsteady finger over her shoulder, southeast, toward Intarra's Spear. "What," he asked quietly, "is happening?"

Gwenna knew what was coming, and still she couldn't help but stare. The base of the huge tower had begun to glow. It might have been a trick of reflected light, the sun's low rays glancing off the unbreakable glass. That light moved, however, writhed inside the column, growing brighter and brighter until the whole tower seemed ablaze with it.

"The Emperor," Gwenna replied grimly. "She heard il Tornja went inside, so she lit the fucking thing on fire."

It had seemed like an insane plan, reckless and desperate, but then, Gwenna's own plans hadn't worked out so well, and so she'd kept her mouth shut when Adare sent the orders. She was the Emperor, after all. She could set fire to her own tower if she wanted to.

The blaze, however, was like no ordinary fire. The glass walls soaked in the light, and though the glow had started in the lower floors, the whole Spear was red-gold with it now, like a lance of flame stabbed into the cloud. Quick Jak's jaw had dropped wide open, and even Annick looked impressed. Adare had wanted a miracle, and she had one, a raging, golden column high as the sky. Gwenna could hear the amazement up on the walls, soldiers gasping, turning, pointing at the pillar of fire in the center of their city, forgetting, if only for a moment, the army to their north.

And then she saw it.

"The bird," Gwenna growled. The urgency was so sharp it hurt. She shoved Jak with one hand, dragged Talal with the other. "Get on the fucking bird, this is our *chance*."

The Kettral stared at her as though she'd gone mad.

"They're all looking at the Spear!" she shouted. "The Urghul, the Annurians, *everyone*."

No one moved for moment, then Talal nodded. "Holy Hull," he whispered. "No one's thinking about Balendin."

It was the ugliest liftoff since Gwenna's first year as a cadet—all tangled straps and shouting, unbuckled harnesses slapping in the wind—but Jak got them in the air less than twenty heartbeats after they started running.

It has to be enough, Gwenna thought as they soared clear of Annur's wall. *Please, Hull, let it be fast enough.*

Behind them, the Spear was still burning; not the glass walls, of course, but the wooden floors built into the tower's base, illuminating the entire shaft. For a moment, Gwenna could only stare. It was as though Intarra herself had come down at last to plant her pennon in the center of Annur, to claim the ancient structure for her own. The streets were filled with people, every house, temple, tavern emptied out, the princes and paupers of Annur speechless, staring, rapt.

Gwenna wrenched her gaze away, north, toward the Urghul. She could see the low hill clearly enough, the burned-out temple, and Balendin surrounded by his victims at the center. They, too, were staring south, at the impossible pillar of flame. Jak banked the bird, fixing on the target, coming in low and fast.

"Is this going to work?" Gwenna bellowed to Talal.

The leach had his eyes trained on the ground below. "I don't know. The Spear will be stealing a lot of his power, but not all of it. Those poor people dying in the mud around him might not even notice the light. Even if they do, it won't wipe out their terror. He's weaker, far, far weaker than he was, but weaker doesn't mean weak."

"Sweet 'Shael on a stick, Talal, can you just tell me it's going to work?"

The leach smiled at her, a grim, quick smile. "It's going to work."

It seemed like she should say something else, something more, but then, suddenly, she was wrenched sideways, almost yanked down off the bird's talons as Jak pulled Allar'ra into a vicious climb. Gwenna regained her footing, then stared in horror as the ground fell away below; the ground, and Balendin with it. She seized the hastily mended leather strap, hauled on it furiously, the same simple code over and over: *Attack. Attack. Attack.*

Quick Jak did not attack. Instead, they continued to climb, each beat of the bird's wings carrying them farther from the target.

"That son of a bitch," Gwenna bellowed. "We have one chance at this. *One fucking chance,* and he's running away."

Talal's face was grim, his jaw tight. Over on the other talon, Annick was shaking her head in disbelief.

"I'm going to cut his fucking heart out and feed it to him," Gwenna snarled. It didn't matter. It was a stupid threat. Jak was on the bird's back, and she was below, with no way to get at him, no way to reverse the disastrous climb, no way to force the bird back down. Even if she killed the flier a dozen times over when they finally landed, it wouldn't matter. The window for the attack was tiny, and already she could feel it closing.

Allar'ra's wings kept beating even as they rose above the clouds. The climb grew steeper and steeper, as though Jak were trying in his mindless panic to force the bird all the way into the stars. Gwenna could feel the air thin in her lungs, frigid on

her skin. The bird's angle of ascent had grown so severe she
had to strain to stay on the talon.

"No," Talal said, the syllable almost lost in the wind.

Gwenna turned to him, her heart like stone inside her chest.
"He can't hear us. It doesn't matter."

"No," Talal said again, staring at her, head cocked to the side
as though he were listening to some impossibly distant tune.
"He's not running away." The words were slow, quiet, but filled
with grim triumph.

Gwenna stared. "What the fuck are you talking about?"

"He's not running away," Talal said again. "He's getting more
height."

The bird had gone absolutely vertical, beak stabbed through
the center of the sky. And then, suddenly, Gwenna was weightless.

As a child, before she left for the Islands, one of her jobs
had been splitting wood for the family farm. She'd spent whole
weeks of the late spring at the work, and she could still remember
the feel of the maul in her hands, the way she had to strain to
swing it up, and then that wonderful moment of weightlessness
as the steel head moved through the top of the arc, poised for
a fraction of a heartbeat against the blue sky. . . .

"We're the axhead," Gwenna whispered.

There was a moment of stillness, silence. She could just hear
Quick Jak's voice, trembling but determined, the same mantra
repeated over and over:

"I am Kettral. I am Kettral. I am Kettral."

Then the bird screamed once, the sound bright as the sun,
and they were twisting, tumbling over, falling backward, wings
tucked tight against Allar'ra's side as they plunged toward the
cloud, toward the earth beneath it, toward Balendin.

The leach had time for one desperate blow. Gwenna saw the
surprise and fear in his wide, dark eyes, saw him throw up a
hand, felt the air around them stiffen, then shatter, as though
they'd smashed through a pane of ice. She drew her blades,

ready to jump, certain she couldn't survive a landing at that speed. And then, like spring's first green shoot, invisible beneath the warm dirt, then suddenly, inexplicably *there,* the arrow sprouted from Balendin's eye. He raised a baffled hand, touched it, turned in a slow half circle, as though surveying the carnage, looking over the broken bodies piled around him. Then he fell. It seemed like there should have been more. More rage, more fight, more uncertainty and violence, but humans, at the bottom of it all, were weak creatures, souls bound so lightly to their bodies that a single arrow, a little metal grafted to a shaft of wood, could end them. The thing that had been Balendin, that had wrought so much pain and horror, was gone between one heartbeat and the next.

As Quick Jak hauled the bird out of the stoop, Gwenna looked over. Annick stood on the far talon, her bowstring singing like a harp in the wind, tears streaming from her cheeks.

It happened almost too fast for Adare to understand. One moment the bird had seemed ready to attack, the next, it disappeared abruptly into the cloud above. Adare had almost turned back to stare at the blazing immensity of the Spear once more when Nira hauled her around.

"There," was the only syllable the old woman managed before the bird, which had plunged back through the cloud, leveled out over the Urghul horsemen, wheeling around to the east. When Adare raised the long lens to her eye, it took her a long time to find the corpse of the leach sprawled out across the mud. His prisoners, some mutilated, some dying, were already swarming over him, tearing him apart. Adare couldn't hear their cries, but their faces weren't human. They were the faces of beasts.

"They killed him," Adare breathed, setting the long lens down.

Nira nodded. "It was the Spear. Everyone was looking at it. Gutted that bastard's well."

Adare blew out a long, unsteady breath, understanding it at last, then raised the long lens again, studying the land to the north. "Now what?"

The Urghul were milling around, some riding away from the site of the recent violence, others forcing their horses toward it. One thing was clear—without the leach, they had no way to shove past the wreckage of Annur's northern quarters, no way that didn't involve days of hauling timber and clearing a path.

"Now we wait for your general and my brother to die," Nira replied quietly. She was staring at the Spear, eyes distant, hard.

Adare turned. "They're dead already, Nira." She laid a hand on the old woman's shoulder. "I'm sorry, but nothing can survive that."

"Roshin isn't dead," Nira replied. "I can feel him. Feel my well. This close, I would know if he had died. I would feel him . . . gone." She gestured toward the Spear with her cane. "The bottom floors are burning, but the fire doesn't reach the top. That's just the light in the walls."

Adare nodded slowly, then gritted her teeth. "If Oshi's still alive . . ."

"Then il Tornja is, too."

Adare closed her eyes, studied the afterimage of flame scrawled across her lids for a long time, then finally opened them. "Can you kill him?"

"Il Tornja? Or my brother?"

"Both," Adare said.

Nira sucked a long, unsteady breath between her yellowed teeth. She might have been watching her thousand years slide past, a thousand years watching Oshi, the last of the mad Atmani, guarding him, loving him, always searching for a cure.

"I can kill them," she said, "if I get close enough. My brother is strong, but his power is mine." She shook her head. Her sudden, unexpected laugher was sharp as something breaking apart. "And he's fucking crazy."

"The bird," Adare said, stomach lurching inside her as she

spoke the words. The huge kettral soared back over the city wall and settled in the courtyard below. Gwenna and the others had just dismounted from the talons. "The bird can take us to the top of the Spear."

"There's no *us,*" Nira growled. "Your place is here, on the walls defending the city. Did you forget il Tornja's warning?"

"No," Adare said quietly. "I did not forget it."

Nira locked gazes with her. "He does not play games, girl. He will kill your boy if you defy him."

Adare watched the woman helplessly. "He might have killed him already. He might kill him even if I do exactly what he says." She felt as though someone had opened her up, stitched her organs together, yanked the thread too tight, then tied it off. Every moment hurt. Breathing hurt. Thinking about Sanlitun, about his grasping hands, his bright, baffled eyes—it all hurt. "My son is not the only child in this city," she forced herself to say. The words were like blades. "Maybe I could save Sanlitun, maybe not. Il Tornja is the foe of everything we are. How could I look at my son, how could I look at anyone, knowing that I let him go."

"You're not letting him go," Nira growled. "You're sending me."

"We are both going," Adare said, surprised by the iron in her own voice. "The creature who murdered my father, blinded my brother, and stole my son is inside that tower. *I am going.*"

Nira spat. "There's nothing you can do."

"I can see him die."

"Or die yourself."

Adare nodded. When she spoke again, the words felt right. "Or die myself."

The steel of the prison blocked the fire. Blocked it, at least, for a brief time. As the prisoners screamed in their cages, Valyn slammed shut the huge metal doors, wrapped them with chain, trapping il Tornja's soldiers in the horrible furnace below. Strangely, of the prison guards there was no sign, as though they had abandoned their post long before the fire came to the Spear. Kaden could think of no reason why, but there was no time to ponder the question. Even as they climbed, he could hear the protestations of the wooden beams and metal plates supporting the floor, screeching, snapping, warped by the vicious heat. Finally, the whole thing twisted, screamed, cracked, and then collapsed.

Kaden seized the railing of the stairwell as it bucked and shuddered, waiting to be dragged down with the rest of the structure into the inferno boiling below. The wave of heat hit him a moment later, knocking him back into the shadow of the stairs. It was like standing inside the huge stone hearth back in Ashk'lan, and though the flames were too far below to reach them, the air seared his throat, scalded his lungs. He squeezed shut his eyes against the heat blasting up from beneath. Triste wrapped her arms around him, seeking solace and giving it in the same gesture.

The Kettral were talking in low, urgent tones. There was no fear in their voices, only weariness mixed with determination. A few moments later, the staircase stopped shuddering. Valyn leaned out over the edge, stared down for a moment, then pulled back.

"It's gone. Broke off about five hundred feet below us. Takes care of the soldiers."

"Beats having to fight them," the Flea said.

Triste stared up at the stairs twisting away out of sight. "Why haven't *we* fallen?"

"Cables," Valyn said, gesturing up without looking. "The lower stairs were built from the ground up, the next section hung from the prison level. Both of those are gone. We're on the last part. It's suspended from the ceiling, not built up from the floor, but we need to keep climbing, get clear of this heat."

The climb was an agony of burning lungs and legs pushed

past all exhaustion. Kaden counted a hundred stairs, then a thousand, but instead of flagging, the fire below burned higher, brighter, gnawing through the wreckage, rendering all human instruments inside the Spear to ash and char, as though the goddess herself had come down to purify the monument, to consecrate what was divine in a bath of perfect flame. It seemed, for a while, that the fire would overtake them, claim them, too, but there was nothing to do but climb, and so, soaked with sweat and blood, the stairs swaying ominously beneath them, they climbed.

Finally, after another thousand stairs, the air began to cool. Kaden dragged a breath into his lungs, savored the relief, then another, then another, pausing to haul in great deep gulps of it. He tried calling out to Valyn, who was plunging up the steps above, blood burned onto both axes. His voice came out a desiccated husk. He licked his lips, swallowed, then tried again.

"We have to stop," he managed. "We have to stop."

Valyn paused, turned. He looked lost, as though he'd forgotten where they were or why they had come. Those ravaged eyes roamed across Kaden's face for what seemed a long time. Finally he nodded.

"Good a place as any."

Triste leaned against the railing, groaned, then slid down until she was half sitting, half slumped. She vomited noisily onto the platform, over and over, long after her stomach was empty. The Flea and Sigrid took up opposite positions, one a dozen steps above the landing, one below. What foe they expected to fight, Kaden had no idea. Neither soldier had asked why they were here inside the Spear or what they had come to do. Their presence should have been a comfort; without them, il Tornja would have won the fight already. And yet, there was something terrible about warriors willing to kill in the total absence of question or explanation. What they felt about the trail of corpses they'd left littered across the city, Kaden couldn't say. Maybe nothing at all. Maybe that was part of what it was to be Kettral. Maybe, like the Shin, they trained the feeling out of you.

"What now?" Valyn asked.

Kaden glanced at his brother, then looked over at Triste. She had stopped throwing up, mopped the vomit from her chin, then closed her eyes and nodded.

"The *obviate*," Kaden said slowly, trying to frame a truth larger than the human world with a few words. "It is almost time to free . . . what we carry inside us."

The Flea didn't turn. Neither did Sigrid. Just soldiers doing a soldier's work. Suddenly, Kaden envied them that simplicity. Kill. Run. Guard. Already they'd faced down dangers by the thousands, and yet those were human dangers—swords, arrows, fire, threats such as men and women were built to face. They might die in a fight, but no one would ask them to grind out their own lives.

"This tower," Kaden went on after a pause, "is a link. A bridge. Between this world and another."

"Whatever that means," Valyn growled.

"I don't understand it any more than you. The only thing I know is that this is the only place from which the gods can ascend."

Valyn looked like he was going to object, question the notion further. Then he just shook his head. "Great. We're here. We'll get you to the top. What happens then?"

Triste let out a small noise. It might have been a whimper or a twisted little laugh.

Kaden put a hand on her shoulder, but turned inward, to the mind locked inside the depths of his own mind.

We are close, he said to the god. *It is time. Explain the* obviate. *Tell me how I can set you free.*

For a long time, he thought Meshkent would not respond. Hundreds of feet below, flame chewed eagerly through tons of flesh and wood, roaring as it feasted. Each breath was ash and hot iron. Kaden's legs quaked beneath him. Triste's sweat-drenched skin was molten beneath his touch.

Tell me, Kaden said, *or you will die here.*

Inside, silence. The world beyond, fire. Then, at last, the god spoke.

Submit, and I will burn these foes to ash.

Kaden shook his head grimly, released Triste, then stepped to the edge of the railing.

Explain the obviate, *or I will end you myself.*

Meshkent's snarl was a notched blade twisted in the brain.

You would pit yourself against your god?

Kaden gazed down into the conflagration. *I trained at the feet of an older god than you.*

I will flay you with a blade of screams.

Kaden shook his head. *You cannot flay what is not there.*

Then, with a motion of thought, he brought the honed blade of his own emptiness to bear against the god's throat, a promise, a threat. *I carried you this far. Do not test me further.*

Meshkent, the Lord of all Pain, shuddered, raged, and then went slack. His voice, when he finally gave up the truth of the *obviate,* echoed in Kaden's mind like a child's voice lost in a vast cavern.

"What happens when we get to the top?" Valyn demanded at last. "The gods just . . . float away?"

"Not quite," Kaden said quietly, the truth heavy and simple inside him.

"What does that mean?"

"There is a ceremony to perform. Words to speak." Kaden paused, forced himself to meet his brother's eyes as he said the rest. "And then we have to die."

For a moment, no one spoke. Valyn's face twisted with something that might have been rage or confusion. As though something human were trying to tear itself free of the bestial fury in which he had fought his way across the city. For a fraction of a second, there was confusion there, confusion and grief and anger. Then it was all gone, the emotion wiped away like so much blood—something messy, unnecessary once it had been spilled.

"What's the other way?" Valyn asked.

Kaden shook his head. He hadn't explained this part back in Kegellen's manse. There had been no reason, and he could find no words. "There is no other way. Humanity depends on Ciena and Meshkent. No one will be safe until they are free, and they can't be free while we are still alive."

"How in Hull's name did the bastard get inside *you*?" Valyn growled.

"I told you already. I let him in."

"So let him out."

"This is the only way."

"Well, we'll find *another* way," Valyn growled. "We're safe here. We've got time. We—"

He broke off mid-sentence, cocked his head to the side, then closed his eyes as though listening to something. Kaden watched his jaw tighten. Valyn half raised one of the axes, as though he were about to attack Kaden himself.

"No," he said, dragging the word out in a long, quiet growl. Then again, "No."

"What is it?" Kaden asked, though he could already see the bleak contours of the answer.

Valyn's eyes opened. His face was blank, awful.

"They're above us."

Triste stumbled to her feet. "Who is?"

"Ran il Tornja."

"Alone?" the Flea asked. He didn't look down, didn't raise his blades, didn't move at all. It was as though he were getting ready, wringing out every last moment of rest, savoring a final stillness, preparing for whatever had to come next.

"No," Valyn replied grimly. "There are at least fifty men with him."

"How do you know?" Kaden demanded.

"I can smell him. Them."

Fear surged like a fire inside Kaden. He wrapped it in a fist, crushed it out. There was no time for fear. He leaned out over the railing of the stairs, craned his neck to look up.

"We're maybe three hundred feet from the top."

Valyn nodded. "They're coming down."

"Can you hold them?"

The Flea shook his head. "Not for long. They have the high ground."

"And a leach," Valyn said.

Sigrid's head snapped around at that. Valyn nodded.

"He almost knocked Gwenna's bird out of the air. I thought he was down in the streets somewhere. I was wrong."

Sigrid bared her teeth, made a vicious sound somewhere deep in her throat, and abandoned her post below them, climbing the stairs until she stood shoulder to shoulder with the Flea. Her blacks were a spray-spatter of gore: blood, and brain, and chips of bone. Sweat-streaked char smudged her face. She closed her eyes, put a hand on the Flea's shoulder, and then, as Kaden stared, the grime lifted away from her clothes, her face, her arms, rising clear of her, then sliding aside, hanging in the air a moment like a shadow, then collapsing, blown away on the hot wind. The woman was immaculate, radiant, as though she'd just stepped from a day in the baths. Even her hair fell in graceful waves around her face. Her eyes, however, might have been chips of ice.

The Flea looked over at her, then chuckled. "You always did say you wanted to die looking good. Well, I'll tell you, Sig, you're stunning."

Triste ignored the woman. She was pacing around the narrow landing like a trapped animal. "We'll do it here," she said finally. "We'll do it here." She turned to the Kettral. "If you keep them back, we'll do it here. The *obviate*." Then she faced Kaden. "You know how, don't you. He told you."

Before he could respond, she crossed to him, took his hand in her own, then squeezed it gently.

Kaden met her eyes, held them, then nodded.

"Are we high enough?" Valyn asked roughly. "You said the *top* of the Spear."

"I don't know," Kaden replied quietly. "But we're as high as we're likely to get."

"I hear them now," the Flea said. The Kettral commander turned to Sigrid. His voice was soft, but Kaden could hear it clearly enough. "What do you need from me?"

The woman met his eyes, then reached out to take both of his shoulders in her hands. She made no effort to speak.

"Do it," the Flea said.

She didn't move.

"Do it," he said again. "I'm ready."

She didn't move.

"I've been ready since he died, Sig." His voice was quiet, gentle. "Do it."

Then, the movement so fast that Kaden almost couldn't follow it, the woman slid a knife from her belt and slammed it into the man's side. He stiffened with the blow, almost fell, then steadied himself.

"What . . . ," Triste said, lunging forward despite herself.

Kaden held her back, his arm wrapped tight around her shoulders. He could feel her heart slamming in her chest.

"Her well," Valyn said grimly. "It's pain. He's giving her the strength to fight il Tornja's leach." He exhaled slowly. "And I'll do the same."

"No," the Flea ground out, his voice on the verge of snapping. "You need to fight . . . shield her while . . . she works."

Valyn gritted his teeth, but even Kaden could hear the footsteps now, dozens of boots pounding down the stairs from above.

Sigrid drew another knife from her belt, more slowly this time, then drove this one, too, into the Flea's flesh. He dropped to his knees. *Dead,* Kaden thought, then paused, made himself really *look* at the wounds, at the angle of the steel where it entered the skin. They were savage, cruel, almost too painful to contemplate, but they weren't fatal. And slowly the Flea rose, met the leach's eyes, and made an animal noise. *No,* Kaden thought. Not a noise. It was a word: *Another.*

And so a third time the blond woman buried a blade in her commander's flesh, a third time he dropped, and a third time he rose slowly to his feet.

"Is it enough?" he whispered.

Sigrid watched him a moment, then took him by the shoulders, leaning over to kiss his blood-smeared forehead with those perfect lips. She nodded, and they both turned toward the stairs, to hold at bay whatever was descending from above.

"We have to do it, Kaden," Triste said finally, roughly, breaking him free of what felt like an awful dream. "We have to do it now."

Kaden nodded. It seemed impossible that after all the running, all the fighting and climbing, all the fire and dying, it should come down to this. A whole life, whittled to a few final instants. Slowly, his legs trembling with the strain, he knelt on the narrow landing. Triste knelt beside him.

"How do we . . . ?" she asked.

"Close your eyes," he replied. Men were shouting above them, pounding down the stairs. Kaden ignored the sound.

"Wait!" Triste said, clutching his face in her hands.

Kaden shook his head. "There's no time, Triste. If we had a year or ten years, there wouldn't be time." He reached out to touch her cheek. "It doesn't matter. You don't need to say it."

Tears poured down her face. All over again, he saw her as he'd seen her that first night in Ashk'lan, the same violet eyes, the same perfect face, the same fear. . . .

No, he thought, gazing at her. *Not the same at all.* Her face was scarred now, and her eyes . . . there was fear in her eyes, but this time, it wasn't a fear of him. This time, when she reached out to touch him, there was none of the frenzied desperation he remembered from that night in his tent, none of the mad, animal haste.

All my life, Kaden thought. *I'll remember her all my life.* It was an inane thought, given they were both about to die, but somehow that didn't matter. Everyone was always about to die, always a breath away, a dozen breaths, ten thousand—that was the lesson of the Skullsworn, the surprisingly gentle tutelage of Ananshael.

"I'll remember you all my life," Kaden said. For some reason, he wanted to speak the words aloud.

The Shin had been wrong about so many things, but the old aphorism came back to him all the same, spoken, for some reason, in Tan's gravelly voice: *Live now. The future is a dream.*

Triste smiled at him, smiled through her tears, leaned forward, kissed him once, then settled back and closed her eyes.

In the stairwell above, steel smashed against steel. There was a savage, animal howl, half defiance, half hunger. *Valyn,* Kaden realized. Valyn, standing alone against il Tornja and his army while Sigrid drew from the Flea's agony to hold back the leach. Kaden listened for a moment to the discordant music of his brother—the screaming, the ringing of blades—all of it, too, beautiful in its own way. There was a time when he might have wished something for his brother—luck, maybe, or strength—but they were, all of them, well beyond wishing. Kaden closed his mind to the carnage, focused only on what was inside of him.

"When the goddess entered you," he said, repeating what Meshkent had told him, "she built a doorway. All you need to do is open it."

He could hear Triste panting just a few inches away. "A doorway? What kind of doorway?"

"Like the *kenta*," Kaden said. "But in your mind."

"How do I find it? How do I open it?"

"The phrase isn't in our language," Kaden replied. "Not anymore." He closed his own eyes. *"Ac lanza, ta diamen. Tel allaen ta vanian sa sia pella."*

He felt something shudder inside his mind, as though the language were a pry bar, as though some deep-buried stone foundational to his very being had shifted.

"I am a gateway for the god," Triste translated, voice terrified, awed. "I will unmake my mind so that she might pass."

Kaden nodded, and then, this time together, they spoke the awful words.

Above them, men were bellowing, screaming, falling from the staircase. The air shuddered with fire. None of it mattered. Only the words mattered, words growing, spreading, until they were huge as the world itself.

"I am a gateway for the god. I will unmake my mind so that she might pass."

The staircase trembled, as though it were about to plunge into the abyss.

"I am a gateway for the god. I will unmake my mind so that she might pass."

Il Tornja was shouting something, voice hard, confident.

"I am a gateway for the god. I will unmake my mind so that she might pass."

Triste was sobbing through the words, her hands clenched around Kaden's own. He held them, as though through that holding he could keep her from some unfathomable abyss, as though she, in her turn, might bear him up even as the world itself collapsed.

"I am a gateway for the god. I will unmake my mind so that she might pass."

Each time they said the phrase, Kaden could feel the gateway opening inside him. At first it was uncomfortable. Then the pain came, a bright, invisible knife carving a hole out of his mind. He shuddered. It was bright beyond any human light. Too bright.

"I am a gateway for the god. I will unmake my mind so that she might pass."

Inside his mind, Meshkent was bellowing. *No. NO! Not here! THIS IS NOT THE PLACE!*

Too late, Kaden thought, the doorway opening on its own now, prying him apart, destroying him. He held tight to Triste's hands. They were the only thing left. *It's too late.*

Hanging in the harness from the kettral's talons as the bird rose up above the city was the most terrifying and exhilarating thing Adare had ever experienced. She stared, heart in her throat, as Annur fell away beneath her, the streets, and squares, and avenues, everything she'd been trying so hard to protect suddenly small, then tiny, then miniscule. There was the Temple of Intarra, small as a gem and flashing in the sun. There was the wide avenue of the Godsway plunging through the city's heart, the statues of the gods smaller than bugs. There were the green-brown canals, winding from the Basin out to the sea, and the boats bobbing at anchor in that Basin. There were the crooked alleys of the Perfumed Quarter, and the long docks lined up along the harborside. There were the red walls of the palace, the leafy, flowering pavilions. Her city, so slight at this altitude it seemed impossible it could be the home to a million souls, so fragile that a single blow might break it. Adare would have stared at it forever, had Gwenna not pulled her around, a rough hand on her arm.

"They've taken the top of the Spear," she shouted, pointing.

Adare squinted. The bird had climbed so high so fast that even the top of Intarra's Spear was below them, flashing with trapped fire. She could barely make out anything at that distance—how Gwenna could see, she had no idea—but as the kettral drew closer, she saw them, dozens of tiny figures spread out on the tower's top. One of them had to be il Tornja. Even with the fire, he'd escaped somehow, escaped again. *Not anymore,* she swore silently, turning her attention back to Gwenna.

"Can you . . ."

"Kill them?" she asked.

Adare nodded.

The Kettral woman's smile was feral. "What the fuck do you think they teach us to do on the Islands? Write love letters?"

"What should I . . ."

"You stay out of the way, right here on the bird. You and the old woman. We'll drop on the first pass, Jak'll circle, then bring you in when we've cleared the space."

Adare wanted to protest, to object, to insist on joining the others, but that was just pride and idiocy. Besides, there was no time. The bird had dropped a thousand feet, level with the tower's top. Adare stared as the Spear approached. Now that she had a way to gauge the speed, it seemed like madness. They were going to die, all of them, dashed against the tower's top. No one could survive that approach. Then, as they swept overhead, just a pace above the tower's top, Gwenna was gone, and the sniper, and the leach, the three of them leaping from the talon into the mass of men. There was a flash of steel, a sudden chorus of shouts and screams, and the bird was past the tower's top, dropping down the other side.

Stomach lodged in her chest, Adare looked over at Nira.

"Did you see Oshi?"

The old woman's face was grim. She held on to the strap above her head with one clawlike hand, but unlike Adare, she didn't seem frightened by the flight. "No. Not him or the Csestriim."

"They must be below," Adare said. "In the Spear itself."

"Those three idiots we just dropped on the roof better hope they stay there. I don't care how handy they are with those blades. Oshi'll leave them splattered across the wall."

When the bird came back for the second pass, however, the Kettral were most definitely not spattered. They stood in a rough triangle near the center of the tower, blades bare and dripping blood. The soldiers around them were dead—dead or dying—frozen in the awful postures of their slaughter. Annick and Talal began stalking the platform, cutting throats, working with all the bleak efficiency of laborers in the field, trying to get the last of the grain in before the rain.

"Sweet Intarra's light," Adare whispered.

"That glittery bitch of a goddess already did her work," Nira snapped, gesturing to the glowing Spear below them. "It's our turn now."

This time, the flier put the bird down right on the roof, ignoring the corpses altogether. The whole space stank of blood and urine. When Adare tried to walk, to cross the empty tower's top, she slipped in the spilled viscera.

"They're down there," Gwenna said, stabbing a finger at the door leading into the Spear. "And there's 'Shael's own fucking fight going on, by the sound of it."

Adare took a slow breath through her nose, tried not to vomit. They were doing what they'd come to do, kill il Tornja's men, find the *kenarang* himself, and yet she found her eyes drifting away from the dead. Grimly, she forced herself to look at the bodies, to witness, even if for just a moment, the carnage she herself had ordered. The Kettral might have held the blades, but Adare had helped to make these men dead. And they weren't finished yet. She glanced at the trapdoor, the woman's words registering for the first time.

"Fighting?" Adare asked. "Il Tornja's supposed to be in here alone. Who is he fighting?"

"How the fuck do I know?" Gwenna spat. "You want to stand up here with our thumbs up our cunts while we talk about it?"

Adare found herself grinning viciously in response. "No," she said. "I don't. I want to go down there."

Her grin vanished as soon as she stepped into the tower. The wind outside was cool, sharp. Inside, there was nothing but flame and screaming and heat like a brick to the face. Most worshippers thought of Intarra as the Lady of Light, but there was another truth to the goddess, a harder truth, one Uinian had learned as he burned inside his own temple, one Adare herself had had seared into her flesh at the Everburning Well: Intarra was a goddess of heat as well as light, the awful mistress of all conflagration and the annihilation it brought.

"He's here," Nira said, following the Kettral down the winding staircase, breaking into Adare's thoughts. "Oshi. He's close."

"Can he feel you the same way?" Adare demanded, pulling up short.

Nira shook her head. "He's my well. I'm not his."

When they reached the first landing, the old woman shouldered her way past the Kettral, then paused, gazing down the stairs into the inferno.

"This is my fight now," she said. The words were quiet, as though meant for no human ears.

"Hold on . . . ," Gwenna began.

"No," Nira said, rounding on the younger woman. "I will not. I am going down there to kill my brother, and then to kill the creature who made us what we are, and I am going alone." Her voice softened. "You're a vicious, feisty bitch, kid. I like that. But believe me when I tell you there's nothing you can do down there but die."

Gwenna opened her mouth to reply—to argue, no doubt—but Adare laid a hand on her arm.

"Let her go," she said. "There's more to this than you know."

Gwenna gritted her teeth, then nodded. "You have two hundred heartbeats," she said, "and then we're coming down."

Adare searched for the words. It seemed a lifetime ago that Nira had pulled her out of the crowd on the Godsway, seeing a truth that no one else had seen. After all the months fighting and marching, what Adare remembered was the woman's swearing, her mockery and recriminations. A hundred times she'd thought of sending Nira away, of being free of her constant abrasion. *But she wouldn't have gone,* Adare realized, staring at the old woman's seamed face. *She never left Oshi, and she didn't leave me.*

"Thank you," she said.

"Oh, fuck off with your thanks . . . ," Nira began. Then she broke off, shook her head abruptly, closed her eyes, straightened her back. When she opened them again, that gray gaze was level, regal. When she spoke, there was nothing of the gutter slang, no hint of the profanity that had marked her every utterance since they first met. She was a queen, once a leader of millions, and the weight of her years was in her words.

"You are a fine emperor, Adare hui'Malkeenian," she said. "A truer sovereign than I ever was, and mark this well, because these are the last words I will speak to you: if you survive this day, you will be a light to your people. Whatever you believe of your goddess, it is your own fire that blazes in your eyes."

She held Adare's gaze for a moment, then nodded once, as though that were something done, done well and finished forever. Then she smiled, tossed her cane aside, and turned away, descending the stairs toward the screaming, and the dying, and the fire.

Gwenna took a long breath, held it for a moment, then blew it out.

"Where the fuck did you find her?"

Adare just shook her head, counting off the heartbeats in her mind, each one final as the great bronze bell that had tolled her father's passage. The stairwell shuddered, steel screamed, as though wrenched awry by some vicious hand. Adare stumbled, seized the railing to keep her balance. There was a great thunderclap, then another, and another; fires of unnatural color leapt up around them, then fizzled out in the hot air. By the time Gwenna waved them forward, the sounds from below had subsided.

"Let's see who's dead," the Kettral woman said grimly. "And who's left to kill."

They found Nira and Oshi first, two hundred feet below, seated, leaning against the low railing with their arms wrapped around each other. At first, Adare thought they were still alive. Then she saw the blood soaking Oshi's clothes, pooling beneath him, and the vicious wound that had caved in the side of Nira's head.

They look so ordinary, she thought.

The palace was filled with paintings of the Atmani, storm-eyed, muscle-bound figures striding an earth that cracked and groaned beneath their very feet. Nira and Oshi, by contrast, looked small and gray, slight, like someone's grandparents, just people like any of the people living in the city below; not rulers, just a brother and sister who had lived out a normal life. And, of course, they had. Not just one life, but dozens, all those centuries side by side, posing as peddlers and farmers, haber-dashers and fisherfolk, dozens of names and disguises, one after the next. Despite the violence of their end, their eyes were closed. They may have died fighting, but Nira's arms were wrapped around her brother, holding him as she had held him so many times before, cradling him finally to sleep.

Gwenna scanned the corpses.

"That the leach?" she asked.

Adare nodded mutely.

The woman stepped over the bodies as though they were so much stacked wood. "Il Tornja's further down."

Slowly, Adare let go of the railing. She was sweating, her heart beating so hard she thought she might die. "Then let's go kill him."

Together, the four of them descended the trembling steps.

Another twenty feet below, on a narrow landing, they came to the battle—what was left of it, at least. There were bodies, dozens of them, scores, hacked apart, strewn across the platform, the blood so thick it poured over the edge of the landing into the fiery abyss beneath. *Annurians,* Adare thought dully. They all wore the uniform of the Army of the North.

Amidst the carnage, there were only two men standing, one holding a slender, elegant blade, the other wielding dripping axes: Valyn and il Tornja, facing off again, just as they had that awful day on the tower in Andt-Kyl. Despite the slaughter, the *kenarang* looked calm, even urbane, endlessly patient. Valyn, on the other hand, might have been a monster out of nightmare, a horrifying figure in filthy wool and leather, hair plastered to his face, scarred eyes empty as the winter night. Unlike il Tornja, who stood perfectly still, poised, Valyn shifted back and forth, moving his weight from one foot to the other as though there were some violence inside him kept just barely in check.

Then, even as Adare watched, he loosed it.

She could barely follow what happened next. Despite a year of marching with her armies, despite witnessing one of the most important battles in Annurian history, Adare knew almost nothing about fighting, dueling, or swordplay. It didn't matter. Even to her untrained eye, even in the whirlwind of all that mad, dizzying steel, the difference between the two warriors was obvious.

Valyn was faster. His axes were everywhere at once, high and low, striking in concert sometimes, sometimes in counterpoint, shattering in a steel hail against il Tornja's guard. And yet, somehow, that guard held. The long, elegant sword was always there to deflect the blood-smeared wedges. Valyn roared and snarled his rage, but il Tornja moved in an eddy of calm. He was slower than his opponent, far slower, but was always where he needed to be, always sliding into that slender empty space where Valyn's axes were not, as though he'd seen the whole fight in advance, had studied it for years, had rehearsed every step of this savage dance.

But there's a gash along his arm, Adare realized as Valyn broke off his attack. Valyn's chest was heaving, but his bloody teeth showed in something that might have been a smile.

"Hello, Adare," il Tornja said, speaking into the momentary stillness without taking his eyes from her brother.

"Kill him, Annick," Gwenna said.

To Adare's shock, the *kenarang* dropped his blade and turned, hands raised. "I give myself up." He met her eyes and smiled, that same smile she'd seen so many times before. There was no hint of concern in his voice. "My work here is finished, and there are Urghul to fight." He raised an eyebrow. "I don't need to remind you I have your son."

Valyn took a predatory step forward, but Adare threw up a hand. "Don't kill him."

She half turned to find the sniper holding that strange bow of kettral bone, the string drawn back to her ear, sighting down the arrow's shaft at il Tornja. Annick's eyes didn't waver from the target, but she held the string.

"Oh, for 'Shael's sake," Gwenna spat.

"Don't kill him," Adare said again, louder this time, more forcefully.

Valyn shifted forward, his axes light in his hands. Like Annick, he kept his scarred eyes on il Tornja even as he spoke to Adare. "We have been here before, sister."

"Indeed we have," the Csestriim agreed cheerfully. "You might recall that the last time, in Andt-Kyl, I urged you to put down your blades. As I told you then, there's a lot that you don't understand." He spread his hands as though welcoming the group. "A lot that *all* of you don't understand."

"That was a long time ago," Valyn said, testing the weight of his ax. "We've been learning."

Then, before Adare could object, before she could even *think,* he spun. The movement was too fast to follow, as was the single ax hurtling toward il Tornja. Somehow—she could not begin to fathom how—the Csestriim had seen it coming, had managed to slide aside as the steel parted the air inches from his head. He turned, unconcerned, to watch it fly into the void, smiling as it disappeared into the roaring fire far below.

"That's not what I had in mind," he said finally, turning back to Valyn, "when I asked you to put down your blades."

Valyn's lips curled back, showing his teeth. "I am going to kill you," he said. "I am going to cut you apart."

"No," Adare insisted, stepping forward.

"Get out of the way," Valyn said.

She pressed ahead despite the death in his voice. "I won't."

"What's wrong?" Valyn demanded. "You still want him to fight your wars? You still think you need him? You still willing, after all this, to play your fucking politics?"

"No," Adare said, meeting her brother's ravaged gaze as she slipped the polished poisoned hair stick—Kegellen's gift—from the coils of her hair, then turned, slamming it into the *kenarang's* gut, screaming as she shoved it deeper and deeper still, pulling it out, then stabbing him again. The Csestriim half lifted a hand as though to protest, then let it fall. Adare stared at the wound, the blood soaking the cloth, then raised her eyes to il Tornja. "You can't kill him," she said quietly, "because I'm going to do it." She held the poisoned stick in her trembling hand, then buried it between his ribs once more.

Il Tornja's eyes went empty as a starless sky. The jocularity was gone, the wry act he'd worn for so long replaced by his true face, that unreadable, unknowable alien gaze. Even now it made something in Adare quail.

"But I had your son," he murmured.

"What did you *do* to him?" Adare hissed, seizing her *kenarang* by the lapels of his coat. *"What did you do to him?"*

The Csestriim shook his head. "Nothing. He is safe."

Adare stared, scouring that inhuman gaze for the truth. "I don't believe you," she whispered. "Why? After everyone you've murdered, why would you spare one infant?"

Il Tornja stared past her, past the landing and the stairs, into the bright, empty air of the Spear. "One grows tired," he said finally, voice slender, "of killing one's own children."

Adare's sob was like some jagged, broken thing torn bloody from her throat. The tears sheeted down her face. Il Tornja cocked his head to the side, studying her the way a botanist might scrutinize some strange, inexplicable flower.

"So broken," he murmured, slumping to the floor. "All these years I tried to fix you, but you are still so broken."

Strong hands gentle as air under his arms and legs, lifting, carrying.

Kaden tried to cry out, but there was nothing left inside him that could still cry. Where his mind had been, there was only a gaping hole, a passage to nothingness, oblivion. Meshkent was bellowing his fury, clinging with long claws to the remnants of Kaden, but Kaden himself was failing, unraveling. There was no way to undo what he had done. A few more heartbeats now, just a little more time, and it would be over.

We failed.

The words were vague, more sounds than words. He struggled to put a meaning to them, then gave up.

". . . up. To the roof. Both of them . . ."

A brother's voice, fierce and urgent, so tightly tethered to the world.

". . . breathing's weak. Can't find a heartbeat. Wait . . ."

The voice went with a woman with hair like fire.

". . . go. Go. *Go* . . . "

He was floating. The furious violence was gone, and he was floating up, light as smoke into the light.

We failed.

Meshkent raged desperately inside him.

Kaden could feel, with the little life that he had left, a sharp knife of regret, but even that was fading.

". . . there. Open it. Open it! Through the door . . ."

"Kaden." A sister's voice. "Kaden!"

He tried to open his eyes. Failed. The hands were lowering him onto something hard and impossibly far away.

Meshkent—instantly, awfully silent.

We failed.

Then the god's voice, composed this time, free, huge as the whole world, brutal and triumphant: *NO*.

The hole in Kaden's mind, so dark a moment earlier, filled with light, so much light, *too* much. Kaden opened his eyes to escape it, and there, lying against the ironglass a pace away—Triste, her violet eyes fixed on his.

She smiled.

Something that had been Kaden remembered falling, a cold place full of stone and snow. A memory of falling like this falling. He waited to strike the ground, but this time, there was no ground. The whole world was those eyes, that face. Her name was gone, but the name didn't matter, had never mattered. There was only the falling, endless, effortless, only a death that felt somehow as wide and strong and bright as any love.

60

Morning's blue ax split the Valley of Eternal Repose. At the land's crease, white-gray and lazy, the thin, indifferent river traced its ancient course. Years earlier, Adare had labored through a treatise on hydraulics. Mostly it focused on the building of canals, but there was an entire section on the natural history of rivers, on the way that even a small stream could carve a canyon through the land, given enough time. She tried to imagine the valley before it was a valley, before the current had cut down through the topsoil, exposing the low limestone walls that would serve as tombs to her people. How long had the water toiled through that stretch of ground? Tens of millennia? Hundreds?

And it's not finished.

Even now, while the Annurians who had gathered in the valley stood still, silent, waiting for her to speak, the current was moving, going about its patient work, chiseling away at its bed, digging deeper, deeper. One day, the stone tombs along the valley's walls would be too high to reach. Some traveler would stand at the bottom of the gorge and stare up, baffled, at the monuments of Malkeenian emperors—the weathered lumps that had been Alial the Great's stone lions, Olanon's martial bas-relief, the rising sun carved around her own father's tomb—and wonder who had built so far up the wall of the cliff, and why, and where they had gone.

They might not notice Kaden's grave at all. The huge cedar doors would have rotted away by then, leaving a simple aperture into the cliff's darkness. Even if that future traveler climbed the limestone cliff to look inside, the body would be gone, ground to dust beneath time's silent hammer. Even if people remembered, so many millennia hence, names like *Annur* or *Malkeenian,* there would be no proof left of the lie Adare was about to tell, no corpse to gaze upon, no evidence to suggest that the Malkeenian laid in that last tomb was no Malkeenian at all.

She had burned Kaden's body ten days earlier, the night after the fire inside Intarra's Spear. She could have asked Gwenna to carry the corpse down. The Kettral had already made two trips—the first, to lift the Flea and Sigrid to the palace infirmary; the second, to bring the bodies of Nira, and Oshi, and Ran il Tornja.

"I'll get your brother next," Gwenna announced gruffly. "Him and Triste."

Adare shook her head. "We will burn them here."

Below her, the tower glowed with still-smoldering fire. Overhead, the smoke-smudged stars carved their slow arcs through the dark. Valyn was watching her with his scarred eyes.

"Here?" Gwenna asked.

Adare nodded. "Here." Her own conviction surprised her. "This is the place they fought so hard to reach. It is the place they made their stand. It is here that they won our war. Why take them down? Why cover them with dirt?"

And so she had labored half the night alongside Gwenna, and Annick, and Talal, and Valyn to build a rough pyre from the wreckage of the staircase below. When they were finally finished, her hands bled. Her back screamed.

"You're limping," Gwenna pointed out quietly. As though that were worth worrying about, as though, compared to everything else that had happened that day, it constituted some kind of sacrifice.

"I'll survive."

They laid the two bodies atop the pyre just before dawn. The leach kindled a spark. It wavered, then caught. The flame's blades made smoke of the dead. The Kettral stood their vigil silently. Even Valyn just stared into the flame as though hoping to go blind. Adare opened her mouth, then shut it. What did she know of Kaden or Triste? Anything she said might be a lie. Silence was the truest eulogy, and it was a relief to remain silent. There would be time in the weeks to come, too much time, for speeches, ample need for noble-sounding lies.

And now, she thought, gazing out over the throng assembled in the valley, *that time has come.*

She took a deep breath, steadied herself, and then began.

"Some of you who have gathered here will see the splendor of this funeral and whisper, *'Waste.'*"

She gestured to the columns of soldiers—bull-thick Aedolians, legionaries, Sons of Flame in their flashing bronze—that had marched all the way from Annur, through the wreckage north of the wall, over the low hills, then into the long, winding valley, halting, finally, before her to stand motionless as stone men. The steel heads of a thousand spears blazed like torches in the morning light.

"You will look at these warriors and you will see men who could be laboring, even now, in the service of the living rather than standing pointless vigil for the dead.

"You will look at the horns of these oxen, gilded with gold, and you will think, *What need have the dead for gold?*"

The oxen—eight huge black beasts, their coats oiled and groomed to a glistening sheen—had drawn the bier all the way from the Dawn Palace. They stared west now, motionless in their harnesses, round, dark eyes inscrutable as stones. Soon, the Aedolians would take up that slab of sweet-smelling cedar, bear the silk-wrapped corpse into that chilly passage carved into the cliff, set it gently down on the stone plinth, file out, put their shoulders to the massive doors that would block up all access to the tomb, and it would be done. After so long, it would finally be done.

Adare would have come sooner, but in the days after the Spear burned, it was impossible to reach the Valley of Eternal Repose—the Urghul were still north of the wall in all their thousands. Without Long Fist or Balendin to cleave a path through the wreckage, the horsemen had no viable way to attack, no path by which to bring their horses to bear, and yet they came on, day after day, hurling themselves through the burned-out ruin of Annur's northern quarter, screaming in their strange tongue, brandishing spears from the improvised barricades even as Annurian archers cut them down.

Adare had watched most of the carnage from her tower atop the northern wall. "It's madness," she muttered halfway through the second day.

Valyn stood a pace away, his scarred eyes fixed on the slaughter. After a long time, he shook his head. "Not madness. Sacrifice."

"Dying in an insane attack that can't possibly succeed?"

"Not the dying, the fighting. The Hardening."

Adare watched as a sun-haired warrior, chest stitched with arrow shafts, began singing in the street below. More arrows. The song turned to blood in his mouth.

Only after a full week, when the ruined streets north of the wall were choked with Urghul bodies, did the horsemen finally stop. It was hard to say why they broke off their attack. Through the long lens, Adare had spotted a woman—blond and scarred as the rest of them, middle-aged but hard as carved wood—standing barefoot on her horse's back, arms spread as though inviting a spear to the chest, bellowing some inexplicable exhortation.

"Huutsuu," Valyn said. An unreadable expression tugged like a hook at the corner of his mouth.

Adare stared at him. "Is that a name?"

He nodded slowly.

"You know her?"

Another nod.

"What in 'Shael's name is she *doing*?"

He cocked his head, as though he could hear the words from almost a mile away. "She is telling them to go home."

Adare studied the woman, studied the thousands of howling horsemen circling her like wolves. "They're going to kill her."

"It is possible. I do not think so."

Then, to Adare's shock, Valyn stepped up onto the low tower wall.

"What are you doing?"

He gestured north. "Going."

"Going *where*?"

"Huutsuu helped me once. I will help her now, if I can."

"The Urghul will fucking *murder* you, Valyn."

He stared at her, through her, considering the possibility. It seemed impossible that this stranger, this creature of sinew, scar, and darkness, could somehow be her brother.

"Maybe."

Then, before Adare could respond, he jumped. It was thirty-five feet to the street below, but Valyn landed like a cat, rose to his feet, dreadful as any unkillable thing from nightmare, then disappeared into the wreckage. Somehow Adare had understood, even then, that he would not be coming back.

She could have skipped the funeral. No one in Annur aside from Gwenna and her Kettral knew how Kaden had died. Besides, Kaden had, by his own choice, abdicated the Unhewn Throne. Funerals, however, were not for the dead, and after the Urghul disappeared over the northern horizon, riding back to their steppe, Annur needed something—a ceremony, a shared moment—to mark a turning point.

The tomb was there already. Stonemasons had hollowed the hole from the cliff the day after her father was laid to rest. There were no carvings, however, no statuary or reliefs to decorate the stone face. Those were chosen, traditionally, by the Emperor before his death, but Kaden had given no instructions, and all those who truly knew him—Rampuri Tan, Triste, the Shin monks among whom he had lived so long—were dead. Perhaps it didn't matter—he was already so much ash and bone—but the people would expect carvings, and so Adare went to Kiel, the Csestriim.

"What would he want? Have wanted?"

Death's grammar was slippery.

The historian looked at her with unreadable eyes.

"Are you speaking of your brother? Or of the one who will take his place in the tomb?"

Adare blinked. She had told no one but Valyn and Gwenna, had wrapped the body herself, winding the water-smooth cloth around the naked figure, circling the feet first, then the legs, all the way up to the face, pausing for a long moment before winding it tight around those open eyes. The lie was easy: *His wounds were too gruesome. The people should not see a Malkeenian so defiled.*

"How . . ."

"Rest easy, Your Radiance," the Csestriim said. "I have been studying this world a long time. No one else is likely to notice." He moved the planes of his face into a smile. "Your brother needs no stone for his monument. But then, you know this. Kaden's monument, and Triste's, is carved into the minds of all your kind."

Adare hesitated, then gestured to the silk-wrapped figure. "And for him?"

The historian closed his eyes, cocked his head, as though listening to some music she could not hear.

"We do not want. Not in any way that you could understand."

"I have to do *something*."

"No, you do not. The tomb's emptiness is all."

And so Adare found herself standing before a doorway unadorned by any carving, a perfect rectangle cut into the cliff. She would have preferred to remain silent, as she had been silent while Kaden burned atop the Spear, but the time for silence was over, and there was no one else to speak.

"Perhaps you will look at me," she continued, raising her voice above the breeze, "and wonder, *Why is she here? If she would rule Annur, let her rule. Let her see to the millions left alive. The dead have no need of her ministrations.*"

She nodded.

"And it is true. The dead are dust."

The crowd stirred at that, as though all those thousands of bodies formed one creature and the creature had grown uneasy. The men and women might have made the long walk from Annur for any of a dozen reasons, but after the madness of the past year, after the unreasoning fury of the weeklong Urghul assault and the blood-drenched fact of the final Urghul collapse, most would be looking for reassurance, certitude, a trotting out of the old phrases, all of them docile as sheep: *died a hero . . . for the glory of Annur . . . in our memories forever.*

They expected an emperor who would stand before the tombs of her fathers and conjure up the old imperial theater. They wanted a prophet to open her mouth, and to see, instead of words, Intarra's light sluicing forth, scouring away the darkness lodged inside their hearts.

But I'm not a prophet, Adare thought.

The miracle of Intarra's Spear was not a miracle at all, but an act of calculated arson. The Malkeenian fire burned in her eyes, but the script of scar laid into her skin remained illegible. She remembered the lightning strike at the Everburning Well. That single syllable—*Win*—remained carved into her mind, but whether it had been a voice of the divine or something else, something less, Adare had no idea. Of the will of the goddess, she understood no more than the blank-eyed oxen standing on the churned-up dirt.

For a moment she imagined telling everything: *"I am no prophet. The goddess does not speak, either through me or to me. My scars are only scars. My blessings were lies."*

And then? The righteous would rise up to kill her. Others would kill the killers, declare her a martyr. It was an old story, told over and over in the histories: bodies dragged from homes, butchered in the streets, burned alive, faith pitted against faith, belief against belief. The only way out was to stay alive, to keep wearing her bright mantle of lies. She had a lifetime to find a way to abdicate, to dismantle the broken apparatus of empire, to find a way to avoid passing the horror of her position on to her only son, that tiny child who was, even now, being carried down to her from the chilly fortress in Aergad.

"The dead are dust," she said again, "but you know this already. You have seen it."

She gestured to the bier.

"My brother, Kaden hui'Malkeenian, died to save our city, to defeat a traitor at its very heart—but he is gone. Gone beyond all human reach, gone certainly beyond any meager language I might muster.

"So are the loggers of the Thousand Lakes hacked apart by the Urghul. So are the soldiers sacrificed on bloody altars across the north. So are the Channarians who starved during Dombâng's blockade, the warriors of the Waist who rose up to be slaughtered by our legions, and the legionaries slaughtered in their turn. So are the unnumbered Urghul buried, nameless, in their twin mounds north of Annur itself.

"My brother lies right here, at my feet"—the lie was easier this time—"but he will not hear the words I speak today, nor will the rest of the dead spread across Vash and Eridroa, whom we will never fully tally."

Nira, laid to rest beside her brother in a tiny cemetery by the sea . . .

The fallen Kettral, whom Gwenna had carried back to the Islands in the claws of a giant bird . . .

Fulton, buried with pomp in the northern forests; Mailly, dragged from her hanging cell and burned without remark . . .

"The dead are beyond all speech and hearing, so why speak at all? Why have we come here today?

"I will tell you. Forget the dead. A funeral is the time for the living to speak with the living."

She thought again of Valyn walking away, of the Urghul finally riding north, disappearing like a storm over the horizon.

"And what should we say, those of us who have survived? Should we drag out the old platitudes?

"The dead will never be forgotten. . . .

"They fell that we might live. . . .

"The living will rebuild. . . ."

She shook her head.

"No.

"Each death is a smashed glass, a burned pyre, a broken bow. Nothing can be put back."

Two dozen paces off, silent in his tomb, her father lay. In front of Adare, almost at her feet, wrapped in Liran silk, waited the corpse of the creature who had killed him.

He will be the last, Adare decided. She gazed the length of the valley, the final resting place of so many Malkeenians. *It was his, anyway, this empire we called Annur. He made it, and he is dead.*

She raised her chin.

The sun was cold on her face.

When she spoke, her words sounded like something written down long ago, as though she were listening to herself from some inexplicable distance.

"What remains is the oldest work, the only labor, that endless task from which the dead have been absolved at last: to go into this smoldering, splintered world, and to make from the wreckage something strange and new, something unknown to us until now."

EPILOGUE

A woman with eyes that burn like fire walks to the center of a bridge over deep, fast water. The woman has a name, as does the river, as does the bridge—Adare hui'Malkeenian, the White River, the Span of Peace—but the name is not the thing. This is the first of many challenges facing the Historian.

All record is translation. There is no way to press that woman between the pages of a codex, no way to preserve the scarred man who approaches her but in words. All approaches are imperfect:

Valyn hui'Malkeenian, the first son of Sanlitun hui'Malkeenian, first of that name . . .

A badly scarred young man, his dark flesh twisted with muscle, stalking across the span . . .

Chosen by Hull in the caverns beneath Irsk, a warrior-prophet faster and stronger than all other men . . .

The Kettral commander who defected from Annur to join the Urghul north of the White River . . .

Murderer of hundreds, traitor to his own people . . .

Loyal brother . . .

Beast . . .

The characters shift with the focus, like the clouds scraping across the bowl of the sky, like the never-still shapes of the river surging between the piers below. Like waves, men and women exist only in motion, in change. Put them on the page, and you have already failed.

And then there are *their* words:

"This bridge," says the Emperor, the sister, the mother, the prophet, gesturing to the stones beneath her feet, "this edifice, is a monument to the newfound peace between Annurians and Urghul."

This is a lie. The bridge will be different things to different people over the long years. To Adare, now, it is the price she has paid to make the Urghul stay out of Annur. Her brother does something like a smile with his face. How to describe it?

"A link," he agrees, "between two great lands."

This, too, a lie. To Valyn, the bridge is the knife he holds against his sister's throat. He is not the chieftain of the Urghul; they fractured into a hundred rival tribes when the Kettral killed the leach who led them, their assault on the city suddenly inchoate, hopeless. He is not their chieftain, but as the only Annurian who rides among them, he speaks here for all the pale riders. He translates their Urghul words into Annurian, then translates the plain truth once more into this lie he sets before his sister.

"It will bring us closer."

The bridge was his idea. The paved span took half a year to build. It is wide enough for twenty Urghul to ride abreast, which they will do, if the Emperor closes her fist too tightly around her empire. If it is even still an empire.

The word that the historian might use for the bridge is *bond*—the bridge binds as surely as any chain—but it is not a historian's place to use his own words. When he pens this moment, he will record the words as they were spoken: *Monument to peace. A link between lands.*

What else will he record? The detail is infinite. A full description of the scene, of each of the tens of thousands of horses gathered on the northern bank, of every ranked legionary at the Emperor's back, would be impossible. There is a universe of truth in the green-gold dragonfly that buzzes between these two Malkeenians, in the patterns of its fine-veined wings, in the refractions of its multiform eyes. A diligent historian could reflect for a lifetime on a single, swaying nuns-blossom, on the tessellation of the flower's white petals. . . .

For millennia, this was the way of the Csestriim: accounts of glaciation, records of water levels in flood and drought, examinations of the courses of the stars, investigations into heredity, numerical pattern, river formation, each with its columns and tallies, charts, maps, graphs.

They had no stories—irrational to labor in the creation of the unreal. Their histories, before the humans came, were lists of dates, of deeds. Even after, the Historian cleaved to this approach, cleaved to it until it failed him.

The brother and sister have locked eyes: his black, scarred; hers on fire. The thousands watching from either bank will try to read the future in this moment, but they will fail. The Historian has been at his task long enough to understand that the future is beyond him. Even this present is unreachable. There is too much of it, even for him. It is too bright; there are too many layers. The past, the present, the future—it is all beyond his grasp, the translation of a translation of a translation. Even the spoken words as they reach his ears are late, caught in the air's clear amber.

If the work cannot be done, what will he do?

The Historian smiles. It took him centuries to learn to smile.

The world is the world; his history is something else. What will he do? He will make the story up.

GODS AND RACES, AS UNDERSTOOD BY THE CITIZENS OF ANNUR

RACES

Nevariim—Immortal, beautiful, bucolic. Foes of the Csestriim. Extinct thousands of years before the appearance of humans. Likely apocryphal.

Csestriim—Immortal, vicious, emotionless. Responsible for the creation of civilization and the study of science and medicine. Destroyed by humans. Extinct thousands of years.

Human—Identical in appearance to the Csestriim, but mortal, subject to emotion.

THE OLD GODS, IN ORDER OF ANTIQUITY

Blank God, the—The oldest, predating creation. Venerated by the Shin monks.

Ae—Consort to the Blank God, the Goddess of Creation, responsible for all that is.

Astar'ren—Goddess of Law, Mother of Order and Structure. Called the Spider by some, although the adherents of Kaveraa also claim that title for their own goddess.

Pta—Lord of Chaos, disorder, and randomness. Believed by

some to be a simple trickster, by others, a destructive and indifferent force.

Intarra—Lady of Light, Goddess of Fire, starlight, and the sun. Also the patron of the Malkeenian Emperors of Annur, who claim her as a distant ancestor.

Hull—The Owl King, the Bat, Lord of the Darkness, Lord of the Night, aegis of the Kettral, patron of thieves.

Bedisa—Goddess of Birth, she who weaves the souls of all living creatures.

Ananshael—God of Death, the Lord of Bones, who unknits the weaving of his consort, Bedisa, consigning all living creatures to oblivion. Worshipped by the Skullsworn in Rassambur.

Ciena—Goddess of Pleasure, believed by some to be the mother of the young gods.

Meshkent—The Cat, the Lord of Pain and Cries, consort of Ciena, believed by some to be the father of the young gods. Worshipped by the Urghul, some Manjari, and the jungle tribes.

THE YOUNG GODS, ALL COEVAL WITH HUMANITY

Eira—Goddess of Love and mercy.
Maat—Lord of Rage and hate.
Kaveraa—Lady of Terror, Mistress of Fear.
Heqet—God of Courage and battle.
Orella—Goddess of Hope.
Orilon—God of Despair.